THE

ifornia

LD RUSH

NCE COLLECTION

9 Stories of Finding Treasures Worth More Than Gold

THE
California
GOLD RUSH
ROMANCE COLLECTION

Dianne Christner, Cynthia Hickey,
Amanda Barratt, Angela Bell, Anne Greene,
Linda Farmer Harris, Pam Hillman,
Jennifer Rogers Spinola, Jaime Jo Wright

BARBOUR BOOKS
An Imprint of Barbour Publishing, Inc.

Print ISBN 978-1-63409-821-2

eBook Editions:
Adobe Digital Edition (.epub) 978-1-63409-911-0
Kindle and MobiPocket Edition (.prc) 978-1-63409-912-7

Published by Barbour Books, an imprint of Barbour Publishing, Inc., P.O. Box 719, Uhrichsville, Ohio 44683, www.barbourbooks.com

Our mission is to publish and distribute inspirational products offering exceptional value and biblical encouragement to the masses.

Member of the
Evangelical Christian
Publishers Association

Printed in Canada.

Contents

The Price of Love by Amanda Barratt 7

The Best Man in Brookside by Angela Bell 51

Civilizing Clementine by Dianne Christner 97

The Marriage Broker and the Mortician by Anne Greene 153

The Lye Water Bride by Linda Farmer Harris 197

A Sketch of Gold by Cynthia Hickey 249

Love Is a Puzzle by Pam Hillman 293

The Golden Cross by Jennifer Rogers Spinola 345

Gold Haven Heiress by Jaime Jo Wright 397

The Price of Love

by Amanda Barratt

Dedication

To my dad. Thank you for your support, for reading my books despite their lack of airplanes and action, and most of all, for your love.

And for the glory of my Lord and Savior.
Always.

Chapter One

My office. 10:30 sharp. New assignment.

Arnold Payne wasn't exactly known for detailed memorandums. Or readable penmanship.

Lorena Quinn studied the scrawl-covered stationery, wishing she could decipher the man who wrote it as quickly as she did the scribbled handwriting. She'd never held much fondness for waiting. Especially when the one who dangled her future was her unpredictable and capricious senior editor.

Her gaze swung to the wall clock. Only fifteen minutes left. Fifteen minutes before she must leave the safety of her little office, cross the hall. . .

Enter the grizzly's den.

Perhaps she was being a bit melodramatic. A fault of hers, one Payne made abundantly clear every time he covered her painstakingly written pieces with editorial marks and ink blots.

She stood, smoothing the folds of her gray silk dress with shaking hands. Though a bolder color would have boosted her confidence—mauve perhaps, or daring red—as the only female editor employed by the *Weekly Observer*, she did her best to appear matronly.

A glance in the mirror confirmed her failings. With a face full of freckles and rebellious curls too red to be called anything but, she was still little Lorena Quinn. Teased and tormented by every girl in Miss Harden's Grammar School.

Tomato head. Tomato head. Red, red tomato head.

Lorena pressed chilled fingertips to her eyes, willing the memories to return to the recesses of her mind and stay secreted away for good. It didn't matter what they called her. She wasn't that girl any longer. She was successful, talented, and had a nose for news rivaling that of any male competitor.

"Quinn!"

Payne's cavernous voice made her whirl. She squared her shoulders, straightened the cameo at her throat, and strode out of her rabbit hutch of an office.

Well, as much as a lady *could* stride wearing a crinoline and several starched petticoats.

As always, when she entered the senior editor's office, a sneeze tickled her nose. Arnold Payne sat, bulky frame ensconced behind a huge oak desk, clouds of cigar smoke wafting up like a chimney at full blast.

"I'm not late, am I?" She moved forward until only the desk stood between them.

Payne opened his watch with a click. "A full ten minutes. I suppose it's too much to expect punctuality from the feminine persuasion."

"You said ten thirty, did you not?" She drew in a breath of smoke-laden air, the whalebone of her corset pinching.

"Ten twenty."

"Forgive me for my inability to read your chicken scratch. Shall I sit down?" As with every other available surface, stacks of papers and dozens of cigar butts cluttered the leather chair. Honestly, with the thousands he made, couldn't the man afford a simple ashtray?

"I doubt it would be worth the time it would take to move everything." Payne leaned back in his seat, surveying her with heavy-lidded eyes. "In short, Quinn, you'll be leaving on the next ship out to San Francisco. Gold fever is on everyone's lips, drummed into everyone's brain, and dreamed about on everyone's pillow. Thus, it seems only fitting that the *Observer* should join the fray with a series of firsthand accounts of the neck-or-nothing excitement of striking it rich. It was a tough debate deciding whether to send you or Galsworth, but I've made my choice. You'll set sail and enjoy shipboard luxury, if you can call it that, for a couple of months, dock in San Francisco, then get busy on detailed accounts of the money to be made simply by dipping a pan into a creek." He leaned forward, his half-smoked cigar between stubby, ink-stained fingers. "Understood?"

Her mind spun like an out-of-control top. Leave New York? Her comfortable room at a downtown boardinghouse? Her reading club and literary society? And for what? To spend months aboard a ship, and even more months amongst uncivilized miners? Despite the tales of easy cash and gold for the picking, Lorena had her suspicions that very few had actually become rich. Hundreds upon hundreds had left the East and headed for these uncharted places. There couldn't possibly be enough gold for all.

Besides, she wasn't that kind of writer. Nor was the *Weekly Observer* that sort of magazine. Her specialty involved attending various social events and reporting on gossip and Mrs. Astor's latest Parisian ball gowns. And honestly, she was content with the way of things.

"No. That is not understood. This is not just some pleasure jaunt across New York State. It will involve months of travel. How can I possibly undertake such a trip?"

He drummed his fingers on the desk. "Shall I tell Galsworth I've changed my mind? That our *lady* employee has objections to a bit of discomfort?" His eyes gleamed with a knowing look.

She swallowed hard. There *were* moments when she longed for a real story, something of substance and value. Something that would shake the world, or at least New York City.

Perhaps. . .this was her chance. If it involved a bit of discomfort while traveling, so be it. She could manage. She wasn't like the society misses who were featured in her columns, all prim and proper, furbelows and finery. No, she had pluck. Spirit, some called it. A spirit that could never be content knitting by the fire, while a husband conquered the world and kept her sheltered in a golden cage.

"How soon should I start packing?" She lifted her chin.

"You'll leave a week from today. That should give you plenty of time to sort through your female arsenal and decide which weapons of dress and decorum to take along for the benefit of those lonely miners. I'll say good-bye, Miss Quinn. It's a sorry day when the most dedicated member of my staff leaves my employ, but so be it. I expect a thank-you note from the man who claims you."

Confusion tumbled in her mind. "Leave your employ? You don't expect me to return?" Was the Wild West really so dangerous that Mr. Payne feared for her life?

"Oh, I expect you to return all right." He chuckled, the sound sending a shiver down her spine, like a spider crawling under her chemise. "But the little gold band on your finger will certainly prevent you from working for me."

"Little gold band?" A gasp broke loose—and not because of the smoke.

"Why, of course. Don't you realize that there are literally thousands of men out there and not a woman in sight? Even with your...um...unusual appearance, you're sure to find someone. Those men are desperate."

Her hands balled into fists. Oh, if she were a man and Payne were not her employer. She'd demand satisfaction and knock some sense into his melon-shaped head with a few well-placed blows. Unfortunately, she was a lady and Payne was the man who paid her salary. Still...

"Mr. Payne! Are you suggesting that I travel to the gold fields in search of a husband? Those men may be desperate, but I certainly am not. Even with my 'unusual appearance,' as you so tactfully put it, I could find a man to marry in New York quite easily if I so desired. But I do not, and I have every intention of returning to New York City, and to this office, single, unattached." She lowered her voice, making every syllable count. "And without a husband."

"Humph!" Payne snorted. "My dear lady, the likelihood of such a happy event failing to take place is about as probable as pigs flying."

She ground her teeth. "As I said before, Mr. Payne, I shall return, not only unmarried, but with my heart unswayed by the cadre of 'lonely miners,' no matter how many ask for my hand."

He hefted his substantial bulk out of the chair. "Care to place a little wager on it?"

"I'd be delighted."

"Well, if...*if* you return without accepting a single proposal of marriage, I might...no, I *will* be inclined to offer you that oh-so-coveted position of assistant editor that should become available as soon as dear old Grimsby hands in his notice of retirement. Are we agreed?"

The opportunity danced before her, as golden as the nuggets residing in California's streams. Assistant editor! Never in all her born days had she imagined holding such a desirable title. Her breath caught. Just think what it would mean for women. If she gained the position and did well, it could open up opportunities for women everywhere, showing men that not all ladies were content with only marriage and babies. And she would do well. More than well.

"Agreed." She held out her hand, ink-smudged fingers clasping ink-smudged fingers. What traitors her emotions were. Moments ago she'd wanted to throttle the man. Now she wanted to hug him. Her nose wrinkled again at the odor of stale cigars.

Maybe not.

"Now, get out of my office. I've got a load of work to do, and you have a trip to pack for." He resumed his seat.

She nodded and let herself out, a smile finding its way to her lips. A trip to pack for. A voyage to undertake.

And when she returned, a destiny to fulfill.

◆　◆　◆

San Francisco, California

Caleb Maddox had boxed sixteen rounds with life. The result? Beaten, soundly beaten.

Bloody.

Brutal.

Annihilated.

Now, all he wanted to do was close his eyes and let life go on around him. Or stop. He didn't much care either way.

He stood, stretched some of the tension from his shoulders, and crossed the room. A cup of lukewarm coffee and a square of cornbread sat on a table near the window. He took a sip and barely suppressed a groan. As usual, his coffee-making abilities had not improved. But then, what had?

Across the street, whoops and hollers pierced the air as the saloon doors swung open and three grizzle-bearded miners stumbled out, clutching small sacks in their fists. Undoubtedly they'd just returned from the fields, ripe with their findings, with hopes of doubling their riches at the roulette wheels and card tables within. Surprising that the fellows had anything left in their hands. Most played until the greedy saloon owners had taken all but the shirts on their backs. Then the men would go back to work long enough to conjure up more dust, so they could return to town and repeat the entire blasted process all over again.

Caleb turned away from the window. He had no right to judge them. Less than a year ago, he'd been like the rest. Eager. Rash. And like the rest, he'd ended up broke. No gold. His savings spent. Thankfully, he'd been able to take out a loan and start up a printing press and newspaper office in San Francisco. As for the gold fields, he'd said good-bye for good.

Contrary to what children's stories and Eastern newspapers said, there was no pot of gold waiting at the end of a rainbow, or the bottom of a stream. Only frostbitten feet, aching joints. . .

Dark disillusionment.

He returned to his desk and, after perusing the article he'd just written about the price of vegetables, flipped through the stack of mail. If one could call two letters a stack, though by California standards, it probably was. Mail of any kind was about as scarce in these parts as a proper, Eastern woman.

The handwriting on the first envelope made a sheen of perspiration break out on his forehead. He'd know it anywhere. Chicken scratch, plenty of ink blots.

Heedless of the fact that paper was scarce and the envelope could have been reused, he ripped it open, unfolded the single sheet atop his desk, and read.

Maddox,

To use a cliché, I'll cut right to the chase. How long are you going to slave and sweat in the middle of heaven knows where? I heard from a friend that you've given up panning for the shiny stuff and are running a newspaper office instead. The idea is preposterous. Why don't you return to New York where you belong? Your old job is about to come up for grabs, and I'll let you have it back. We'll let bygones be bygones and say no more about the events surrounding your departure.

But first, I have an assignment for you. I'm sending out one of my reporters to do some stories on the riches to be found in your lovely little part of the state. I want you to look after her and help her retrieve material for the articles. Not only that, I want you to lay on the charm heavy as iron ore, convince the miss to fall head over slippered heels in love with you, and return to New York with her in tow. Once this is accomplished, you'll find your old office all shined up and ready for use. Only if you succeed, however.

The lady's name is Miss Lorena Quinn. She should be arriving by ship in San Francisco right around the time you receive this letter. I expect you to be at the dock waiting to pick her up.

So long for now. Remember—enjoy yourselves.

A. Payne

Caleb scrubbed a hand over his jaw, the words taking root in his mind. What kind of a crazy scheme was this? Convince some lady reporter to fall madly in love with him? Some New York lady reporter. And as a reward for his success, he'd gain his old job. How many times since arriving in California had he dreamed of the days spent in his office at the *Weekly Observer*? How many moments had he mentally kicked himself for leaving that life in the first place? He'd never thought to have such an opportunity again, yet here one was, put right under his nose, dished up on a silver. . .no, make that golden, platter.

Never again, he'd promised himself. Never again would he let himself flirt, allow himself to be close to a woman of high society. He'd done it only once before.

And once had been more than enough.

Chapter Two

Never in all her born days had she imagined such a quantity of mud could exist i[n] any place on the Lord's green earth.

Exist it did. With an extra-large portion finding residence on the hem of he[r] skirt and the tops of her boots.

So this was San Francisco. The place where fortunes were made, gold changed int[o] coin.

It didn't look like much. Ramshackle buildings with rough wood exteriors, lik[e] patchwork quilts pieced together by a child's clumsy fingers. Huge tents mingled with [a] few brick buildings that stuck out like kings amid a field of peasants.

Lorena glanced behind, hoping to glimpse the reassuring sight of Brock and Melani[e] Jordan. Acquaintances of Mr. Payne, they'd been her traveling companions on the two[-]month voyage from New York to San Francisco. They seemed to have vanished, luggag[e] and all. No doubt to act upon their visions of nuggets and dust. Visions they'd share[d] with her on the journey more times than she cared to remember.

Deciding there was nothing she could do except forge ahead, she lifted the sodde[n] skirt of her traveling gown with one hand and her valise with the other. Her trunk[s] would have to wait. Perhaps she could hire a wagon to transport them once she procure[d] suitable lodging.

Hopefully her cases would still be there when she sent for them. No knowing ho[w] many thieves and vagabonds preyed upon this very street.

With one final glance toward the wharf and the pitiful sight of her two trunks, pur[-]chased especially for the voyage, she took a soggy step, keeping her gaze on the state o[f] her dress.

"Well, I'll be ding-danged if this ain't a sight for sore eyes. Lookie here, Jimmy. [A] gen-u-ine woman."

Lorena glanced up. A beast…no, a man stood a few feet away, staring at her as if sh[e] were the mother lode incarnate. A scraggly beard obscured most of his facial features an[d] the front of his blue flannel shirt. Behind him, a younger, cleaner-shaven fellow gape[d] with equal awe.

"Don't you realize that there are literally thousands of men and not a woman in sight? Eve[n] with your. . um. . .unusual appearance, you're sure to find someone. Those men are desperate."

Payne's words clanged in her mind like a gong. She sucked in a breath of fog-lade[n] air. Surely these uncivilized miners wouldn't have the audacity to propose marriage o[n] the spot.

Would they?

"I ain't seen one of them for a month of Sundays." The man called Jimmy took a step closer, his boots making sucking sounds in the muck. Not that the dirt seemed to daunt him any, for in the next second he was down on one knee, staring up at her.

"She's real pretty, ain't she?" He glanced at his bearded friend. Then back at her. "Little lady, will you marry me?"

"Aw, come on, Jim. I saw her first." The other man approached with giant steps and, before she could protest, swallowed her hand in his gnarled paw. "Don't you listen to Jimmy none, you pretty little thing. You come on and marry ole Abner Hopkins, and you'll be as happy as a cow in a patch of clover."

Good heavens, it was even worse than she expected. She yanked her gloved hand from the man's grip and took a step back. A crowd had gathered, and their whistles and hollered proposals mingled with the banjo and piano music spilling from a nearby saloon.

She lifted her chin, wishing she possessed more than her five feet, four inches in height.

Lord, if it wouldn't be too much trouble, I'd appreciate some help right about now.

"Mr. Hopkins! Much as I am gratified by the honor of your proposal, I cannot accept. And that goes for every last one of you." She scanned the motley group, comprised of rough-looking miners and dark-skinned foreigners attired in flamboyant sombreros. Even a few men with long black pigtails, who surely hailed from China.

"You don't mean that, missy. Give us a chance," came the calls from the crowd as they moved closer, circling her like hunters around a fox.

"I most certainly do!" Using her valise as a battering ram of sorts, she shoved through the fray, crinoline swinging. Her bonnet tipped off her upswept hair and dropped in the mud, only to be trampled by booted feet as the men surged around her.

Free from the confines of the crowd, she barreled forward, intent on moving as fast as she could from these much too eager, so-called gentlemen. All of a sudden her foot slammed into something hard. Strong arms wrapped around her, steadying her. Her breath stopped mid-inhale. The valise landed in the mud.

"What the deuce!" muttered the something. Another man. One with no beard, broad shoulders, and a rather pleasant-smelling brown flannel shirt. The cloth actually smelled clean. Like soap and the faintest hint of spice.

Lorena struggled to extricate herself from his grip, pressing both palms flat against his chest. His arms held her like an iron band.

"Let go of me." She whispered the words through gritted teeth, indignation soaring. He had no right, no right at all, to manhandle her. Did no one in this golden city possess any sense of propriety?

The man stepped back. Gracious, he was tall. Hair a cross between brown and blond brushed his shirt collar, and as his caramel-colored eyes found hers, amusement sparked in their depths.

"My apologies, miss." He tipped his broad-brimmed felt hat. "I didn't know quite how to respond when you slammed into me like that." He rubbed his ribs, wincing slightly.

Heat blazed in her cheeks until her face surely matched her hair.

"No offense taken."

"Good. Because I'd hate to infuriate the only genuine lady in the city of San Francisco."

Her fingers fumbled to secure her unkempt hair as she swung her gaze behind. The crowd had silenced some, but still watched them. She cut her voice low. "You cannot possibly mean I am the only respectable lady in this. . .city?" Though she didn't know this man, at least he was well kempt, a virtue in itself in such a dirty place.

A breeze scoured the air, sending the scent of soap and spice wafting over her again. "Perhaps not the *only* lady, but there aren't many of you, Miss Quinn."

She bent and picked up her bags. "How do you know my name?"

A grin softened the angles of his jaw. "Forgive me for not introducing myself sooner." He stuck out his hand. Her reporter's eye instantly noted the ink stains on his fingers. "Caleb Maddox from the *San Francisco Herald*, at your service."

"Lorena Quinn, the *Weekly Observer*," she said on instinct.

"I know." Another smile. "I just received Mr. Payne's letter. I've been expecting you."

Her grip tightened on her valise. "You know Arnold Payne?" This had to be some sort of joke. Someone who dwelt in these. . .wilds couldn't possibly know the editor of a New York magazine. No matter how fine such a person smelled.

Caleb Maddox nodded. "He told me he was sending one of his reporters out and asked if I might help with some of your research. I used to work for Mr. Payne back in New York, before I came out here."

"He told me nothing of the sort." She jolted as Mr. Maddox pulled her out of the path of a group of swerving men exiting one of the buildings, bottles held aloft, obscenities spewing from their mouths.

"Then I guess you'll just have to trust me, won't you, Miss Quinn?" He released his hold on her.

Trust him? She'd only just met the man. Every lesson learned amongst high society came flooding back. A single woman never put her trust in an unknown man. No matter his behavior, his attire, or how charmingly he might grin.

But a single woman also didn't travel alone to a town populated by characters such as she'd seen in the past half hour. A single woman didn't seek a high position, adventure, or anything other than a wealthy husband.

She sighed. Though she knew them like the steps of a quadrille, she'd never been one to follow the rules of propriety laid out for a single woman.

◆　◆　◆

The lady studied him as if he were no better than a bucket full of mud. Clad in a pretty dress, the likes of which he hadn't seen since arriving in California, she stood tall, though he dwarfed her by half a foot.

Blast it all, did she ever have a face full of freckles. They dusted her forehead, covered her nose, and sprinkled across her cheeks like tiny flecks of cinnamon on an otherwise creamy white canvas. And her hair. . . It hung in disarray; long, wavy, and very red.

"I guess I will." Her syllables were clipped, her nose lifted high. By George, she emitted society the way these men emitted stench. Clear. Unmistakable. No apologies.

And Payne had instructed him to capture her heart? What a laugh his former boss must be having at his expense. Knowing how cucumber-cool Miss Quinn was, Arnold Payne was undoubtedly sitting at his desk this very minute, jowls jiggling and stomach heaving with giant bursts of laughter.

If he'd been a sane man, Caleb would've turned on his heel and let Miss New York fend for herself. A couple of days alone in this city of vice would knock her down a peg or two.

Yet nearly a year in this town, this place of broken dreams and easy bloodshed, had rendered him anything but sane.

Lord, I know I'm not in the habit of conversing with You as much as I used to, but if ever I needed Your help, it's now.

"Did you bring any luggage?" He glanced at the fancy valise clutched in her gloved hand. Surely she'd brought more than this, what with all the Eastern gewgaws she was wearing now. Women of her ilk never traveled with less than half a dozen luggage cases.

"Two trunks. They're at the wharf. As soon as the sailors docked, the crew vanished. Thankfully, one of them was kind enough to bring my luggage ashore."

"I'll have them sent for. There isn't much in the way of respectable rooming houses, but I do know of a place. You don't mind a bit of a walk, do you?"

For a second, her shoulders wilted, the skirt of her dress following suit. Apparently she'd concluded it was fruitless to try to protect her garments from the mud any longer. Yet a glint of determination lit her emerald eyes and she nodded. "I don't mind."

He moved to carry her bag, but she clutched it tight, despite the trail of mud it left on her skirt. "I can manage on my own, thank you very much."

He shrugged. "Suit yourself."

Years spent among New York City's gentry made him hold out his arm for her to take. She gave it the sort of glance one might a poisonous spider, before sashaying ahead. That is, as much as a lady could sashay wearing a skirt weighted down with a whole lot of mud.

Right, then. So fancy Miss New York didn't want chivalry. Fine by him. He stood for a moment, watching as she stormed ahead.

"Do you have any idea where you're headed?" he called. "Because I do. Straight toward the center of San Francisco's saloon district. 'Course it matters little to me whether or not you've a taste for the gaming tables. And if it's cards you're interested in, I can recommend a few places that offer a decent hand of poker."

The words brought her around. Something akin to a flush enveloped her freckled cheeks. He noted it with satisfaction. Valise swinging, she returned to where he stood.

"Very well, Mr. Maddox." She held out the bag with the tips of her blue-gloved fingers. "I shall trust myself entirely to your estimable sense of direction. As long as you actually know where you're going."

For a moment, he considered taking her luggage case and chucking it in the mud. It would serve the lady right, her with all her airs and graces and superior attitude.

Just think about that office. If he thought of that, he'd make it through somehow. Those fine leather chairs, the smell of ink, his elegant letterhead. The tidy brownstone he'd called home. Evenings at the theater, lunch with his colleagues. A month or two of charm would be well worth it, when at last he returned to his life.

So with a smile and a wink, he took Miss Quinn's valise from her finally willing hands.

Score one for Maddox.

Chapter Three

The longer she traversed this golden city, the more convinced she became of its utter lack of moral principle. Prostitutes hung out brothel windows, brazenly advertising themselves to the passing men. Gunshots erupted at the slightest provocation, and she'd already witnessed one fistfight.

Lord, this must have been the state Sodom and Gomorrah was in. And honestly, I don't blame You in the least for wanting to destroy it.

The room Mr. Maddox had procured was little more than a canvas-partitioned closet on the top floor of a restaurant. At least the lady who ran the place seemed respectable. Kind even. Though with her graying hair and substantial middle, Mrs. Dougall probably didn't experience the constant ogling.

Lorena studied her reflection in the mirror. The pitcher and basin on her bedside table had been a godsend, and she'd managed to wash most of the dirt from her face and hands, though unfortunately not the hem of her skirt. With damp fingers, she smoothed back her hair, repinning it into a knot at the nape of her neck.

She turned and bit back a cry as the corner of her trunk connected with her shin. An obliging man had hauled both trunks up the narrow stairs, and they now occupied most of her floor space.

A sigh lifted her chest. After lending her the help of his muscles, the man had proceeded to offer her his hand, heart, and home in the bargain.

I hate to admit it, Arnold Payne, but you're right. These fellows are nothing if not desperate.

Thus, it would be a more tedious task than she'd first envisioned to keep refusing them all. But she would manage. She hadn't become a reporter based on her looks, that's for certain. She had mettle and wouldn't be daunted.

"Miss Quinn?"

She spun around, bumping her shin again. Sparks of pain shot up her already bruised leg, and she thrust back the canvas.

Caleb Maddox stood outside, hair neatly combed, a bouquet of flowers in his hand.

Oh good heavens. This civilized man wasn't about to join her troop of admirers.

"Yes?" She smoothed a hand down the front of her skirt and discreetly rubbed her leg.

He held out the flowers. She had to admit, they were some of the loveliest she'd ever seen. Blue and pink, with a fresh, wild scent. The first bit of anything resembling nature she'd seen since leaving New York. Yet she couldn't take them. For to do so would imply mutual interest. Something she could not afford. Especially when the man offering was tall, reasonably good-looking, and smelled almost as good as the wildflowers.

"These are for you." He shifted a bit. "I also would like to extend an invitation to dine.

Mrs. Dougall makes a fine vegetable stew, and her biscuits are lighter than any this side of the Sacramento River."

At the mere mention of biscuits, her mouth watered. The food on the ship had been edible at best, weevil-ridden at worst. Yet it was out of the question to even consider accepting his invitation. She straightened her shoulders and put on her best society tone. "How kind of you, Mr. Maddox. Regretfully though, I must decline. I am rather tired from my journey and would prefer to dine in my room."

He took a sudden step back, as if startled. Though why should he be? It wasn't as if the ratios were reversed and he the only man amid dozens of single women. Why, she could have her pick of a hundred men to sup with, if she chose.

If the people she'd seen so far were any indication of the type of dinner companions she could choose from, it would be more agreeable to eat in the barn.

"Very well. I'm sure your journey was most fatiguing. But you must at least take the flowers." He held them out again.

She shook her head. "I'd prefer not to." Then she pushed the canvas closed, leaving him standing outside. Whether he left or continued to stand there, she couldn't care less.

Hitching up her skirts, she sank onto the lumpy cot, pressing her fingers against her eyes. How ironic that she, who had been rejected her entire life, was now the one rejecting. A tiny stab of guilt pierced her conscience. She just as quickly shoved it aside. It wasn't as if she wanted to break men's hearts. This whole affair had been Payne's idea. Not hers. She only wanted the position of assistant editor. The security it provided. The success of proving to the world, or at least a small part of it, that women were not mere playthings. That they could do more than wait upon the whims of conceited men like those she'd encountered all her life.

Determination brought her to her feet. She would succeed. No matter how many marriage proposals, dinner invitations, and flower bouquets she must refuse.

◆　◆　◆

So this was where kindness got him. Caleb had purchased some flowers from a street vendor, donned a clean shirt, and prepared to take Lorena Quinn to dinner.

Only to have her refuse and shut the door—canvas, rather—in his face.

He'd skipped dinner himself, any appetite forgotten, and now sat in his room at the back of the newspaper office.

It had been just the same with Emily. Only she had begun by giving him smiles, showing him attention. He'd fallen for her hard, spent what he'd been saving for an encyclopedia set on a ring, and laid his heart out for the taking. Oh, she'd taken it all right. Stomped on it with her silk-slippered foot. Crushed it with her lily-white hands.

That moment—branded into his memory—had been enough to obliterate any thoughts of marriage and love. With anyone. For though all women might not behave as Emily did, they were all the same deep down at their core. They didn't care. To them, men's affections were laughable. Replaceable. They didn't realize the sacred gift a man bestowed on them when he offered them his heart, overcoming months of hesitation to get up the courage to ask. They couldn't care less.

Which was why he had no qualms about leading Miss Quinn on and making her fall in love with him.

A knock sounded on the front door. He stood, grabbing his shirt from where it hung on the back of a chair. Who in tarnation could be knocking at this hour? Of course, San Francisco rarely slept, much less silenced. The bars and brothels were never closed, always ready to snatch the sprinklings of gold dust in exchange for a temporary antidote to the loneliness all men experienced.

With one hand on the pistol at his waist, Caleb opened the door a crack. He grinned at the sight of his friend Mitch Laramee.

"Come in, come in. Haven't seen you in a while." He held open the door, and Mitch entered.

"That's why I decided to pay you a visit." Mitch crossed the room and took a seat in front of the small fireplace. Caleb followed suit. "I thought to myself, I wonder what good old Caleb Maddox is doing tonight. So I decided to wander on over here and sit a spell."

"I'm glad you did." Caleb took the pot of coffee from where it simmered over the fire and proceeded to pour a cup for Mitch and one for himself. "How's the business of getting rich?"

Mitch downed the cup in a thirsty gulp, obviously not caring how bad it tasted. "Glad you asked. That's what I like about you, Maddox. You don't beat about the bush like some fellers do. Truth is, my friend, things aren't as good as they used to be. My last claim turned out to be nothing but dirt, and I came into town tonight with my last few ounces of dust, hoping to double them enough to buy a decent meal at a restaurant. A man can only eat salt pork and beans for just so long, you know. But luck wasn't in the cards for me tonight, and I lost everything. Not only that, I lost my grandfather's watch and that fancy pair of woolen socks Susan knitted for me just before I left." He let loose a doleful sigh, rubbing bony fingers through his scruff of a beard.

Caleb wanted to echo the sigh with one of his own. Simply because he no longer panned for gold like the rest of them, men assumed he had a constant supply of ready cash for the loaning. He wasn't above helping those in need, but this wasn't the first time Mitch had asked.

"How much do you need?" He wrapped his hands around the cup of coffee.

"Not much. Just enough for some grub and a few supplies."

"Mitch, in San Francisco, 'some grub and a few supplies' can cost ten times more than they do back East." Not that Caleb didn't have the money. But he'd been saving for some time, and if things went the way he intended, he'd soon need every cent to pay for passage back to New York City.

"I know, old friend. But it's just a loan, mind. I'll pay you back. I've got my sights on a new claim, and I've an inkling this will be the one. I feel it in my very bones, I do." Mitch leaned forward, anticipation in his eyes. Eyes that were becoming more sunken and bloodshot as the weeks wore on.

"Tell you what." Caleb set his cup down and placed both hands on his knees. "I'm of a mind to be out of this place in a couple of months, and I'll arrange for your passage in lieu of a job with the crew. You can return to Pennsylvania. Take up your life with Susan and the children again. Until then, I'll see you have enough to eat and a place to stay."

Mitch shook his head slowly. "No. Sorry, old friend, but I ain't leaving. I'd be a fool to give up my chance at getting rich. There's gold in these parts, and I'm aiming to find it.

Every day someone gets a lucky strike, and if I leave now, I'll miss my chance."

Caleb loosed the sigh building in his chest. "I panned for gold for six months and in all that time, I saw two men find enough gold to make them rich. Two. I thank the Lord I realized my odds and came to my senses when I did. You can do the same. I've got enough put by to return home and intend to do so once the promise of my former job is assured. It isn't too late, Mitch. You have a wife and young ones back home who need a father and provider. You may not be up to your ears in gold dust there, but at least you have a life."

Mitch stood, jamming his hat down over his ears. If ever gold fever wrote itself upon a man's face, it was written upon Mitch Laramee's. "I hate to disagree with friends, but disagree I do. You're wrong, Maddox. There's gold out there. And I won't rest until I find it."

Chapter Four

Rubbing the last traces of sleep from her eyes, Lorena made her way into the warm sunshine of a San Francisco morning. She lifted the skirt of her green delaine walking dress with one hand, stifling a yawn with the other. The sound of gunshots had bolted her out of bed half an hour ago, far too early for her travel-weary body. At least she would be free to explore at leisure.

Some of the mud had begun to dry, but she still took care, making her way down the street. If one could call it such. With half of the buildings constructed of canvas and the other half rough, unfinished wood, San Francisco's architecture was a far cry from the elegant brownstones and brick homes she'd grown up around.

Few paid her any mind this morning—thank goodness—and she passed only a handful of people on the streets, mostly shopkeepers preparing for business.

Thankfully, none of them took it into their heads to propose.

She drew in deep breaths of the surprisingly fresh air, letting the faint breeze stir the matching green ribbon on her bonnet. Though it was perhaps at odds with her professional aspirations, she did love fashion. Bright colors. Rich silks. Fanciful trim.

Lorena turned down another, narrower street, passing a large wood building bedecked with an ornate front door and lavishly carved sign.

THE MANSION, it read.

A shiver wrapped chill fingers around her spine. "Those" sort of women worked there, catering to the base needs of disreputable men. Revolting. How could any woman subject herself to such a thing? Why did they not seek decent work? Surely in a town of this size they could take in laundry, run a restaurant, or—

A faint cry. The sound halted her thoughts, sending her gaze upward, toward the curtained windows at the top of the building. It came again, low and mewling. Hefting up her skirts, she followed the sound behind the building. The cloying scent of rotting garbage assailed her nose, and she swallowed back the bile rising in her throat.

Her breath caught. Atop the pile of rubbish lay a squirming, swaddled bundle.

A baby.

Heedless of the mess, she gathered the bundle in her arms as the cry came again.

"Why, hello there, sweet one. Whatever are you doing here?" She bounced the infant in her arms, soothing the babe's fussing. Wide blue eyes gazed back at her, drool leaking from the tiny pink mouth.

Dear Lord, who would leave such a precious child in a garbage heap?

Kneeling down, she unwrapped the tattered gray shawl. Beneath the woolen covering, the baby girl wore nothing at all. Bereft of her clothing, the infant began to wail afresh and Lorena rewrapped the blanket.

What now? She couldn't very well leave the baby here. Yet she also couldn't take the child to her hotel room. . .could she?

Why not? It was her room after all. She'd find the little one and herself something to eat and then go in search of the baby's mother. Though the thought of where she'd have to begin her quest made her skin crawl.

She glanced from the baby in her arms to the hem of her dress. A sigh found its way to her lips. She couldn't very well protect her skirt and carry the child.

"Wretched mud," she said aloud to no one in particular.

In a quarter of an hour, she stood outside the hotel, considering how to open the door while carrying an infant. The child had fallen asleep, lulled perhaps by the warmth of the sun and the shelter of her arms. Lorena gazed downward, throat tightening.

What desperate circumstances had some poor soul found herself in to abandon her precious baby?

"Don't tell me that was in your trunks."

She started forward, stopping herself from running into Mr. Maddox just in time. Seemed to be a habit of hers, darting forward and smacking into this man. "*That* is a baby."

"I know what it is, but why are you holding it?" He put his hands in his pockets, looking genuinely befuddled.

Lorena raised her eyes to his, surprised by the tears that threatened to spill forth. "I was taking a walk and found her. She was in a trash heap. A trash heap! Can you imagine that? An innocent baby abandoned." Her arms tightened around the bundle as if, by the shelter of her arms, she could resurrect the story of this child's past.

Concern flecked his eyes, and he rested his hand atop the baby's head. "I can, actually. I've seen things during my stay here. . ."

For a moment, they simply stood. The warmth and weight of this tiny person sent a sudden spark of longing through her heart. Once, she'd been just as abandoned as this little girl. Not in a rubbish heap, of course, but the memories returned with painful clarity. The darkness and isolation of her bed at the orphanage. The ache every time another child was adopted by a family. The tears she muffled night after night, the anticipation and anxiety when a couple decided to take her on. She'd dreamed, prayed that Mr. and Mrs. Ramsay would prove to be the loving parents her heart longed for.

It hadn't worked out as she had dreamed. She'd gotten parents. But they hadn't been loving. And as time went on, it had become apparent that they viewed taking her on as a mistake more than anything else.

"What are you going to do?" Mr. Maddox's voice brought her back to reality. As did the touch of his hand on her shoulder.

"Find her something to eat first. Then search for her mother. She's got to be out there somewhere. There aren't that many women. . .even improper ones. Someone should know."

His hand lingered on her shoulder, the sensation foreign. In New York, respectable men didn't take such liberties with a single woman. No matter how badly comfort might be needed, no matter how much one might want the connection that came with another's hand against theirs. "You intend to do this all by yourself? Go into these establishments, rub shoulders with the patrons? You're not from these parts. Around here, if a decent lady set foot in places like those, she'd be, well, the only way I can say it is. . .eaten alive."

"How else do you expect me to find her mother?"

He cocked his head, as if in thought. "This child's mother wouldn't have abandoned her if she had any way to keep her. What would be a more logical thing to do is to pay a visit to Reverend Howell. He runs the largest church, well, the only church, in town and might know of a God-fearing couple willing to give this child the home and the love she deserves."

Lorena hesitated. They had told her Mr. and Mrs. Ramsay would give her love, provide her a home. They'd done the latter, at least.

Still, if she interviewed the couple and found someone with a tender heart. Someone who could provide more than what this child's mother could possibly offer. And Mr. Maddox had agreed to help her. Not that she'd ever relied on help from anyone of any kind. Though it would be of use to have someone with her who had been in the town longer than she.

"Very well, Mr. Maddox. But first we'll need to find some milk."

He raised a brow. "A cow might be the only thing scarcer than Eastern ladies around these parts. Lucky for you, I have connections." He tossed her a smile, one that crinkled the corners of his eyes, making butterflies take flight in her stomach. Caleb led the way down the street. She followed.

Oh yes. Lucky for her.

◆　◆　◆

So Miss Friendlier-Than-a-Rattlesnake had a woman's heart beneath those layers of petticoats and propriety. He had to admit that when she'd stood there, the slightest trace of tears in her eyes, something inside his heart had twisted.

She clutched the child close against that pretty green dress she wore, a strand of hair falling from its pins and fluttering in the breeze. He had to force his fingers into a fist to refrain from reaching out, brushing it aside.

They reached the half-canvas, half-wood structure that served as Reverend Howell's church and living quarters. Motioning for Miss Quinn to wait outside, Caleb stuck his head in the opening that, in civilized New York, would have been called a door.

"Hey, Reverend Howell. You in there?"

The middle-age man emerged from his living quarters in the back. Ascertaining he was decently attired for visitors, Caleb turned and called outside.

"You can come in now, Miss Quinn."

She stepped inside, the baby in her arms. At the sight of a well-dressed, genteel-looking lady, Reverend Howell ran his hands down the front of his suit coat and advanced, hand outstretched.

"How do you do, Mrs. Maddox? I'm Reverend Howell. Though I'm surprised that Caleb here hasn't mentioned you, I'm glad to finally make your acquaintance."

Beneath the freckles, Miss Quinn's cheeks turned a dozen shades of red. Heat crept up Caleb's shirt collar.

"She isn't—"

"I'm not—"

"We're not married," they said almost at the same time.

Reverend Howell shook his head. "That is indeed a surprise. And a disappointment. I expected better of you as a man of God, Caleb. Of course, sin can be forgiven and we can remedy the situation with a marriage license posthaste."

Caleb cleared his throat, the confines of the tent and the intensity of Reverend Howell's stare making him shift from foot to foot. "You've got this all wrong, Reverend. This lady here. . .Miss Quinn, we're not romantically entangled. She's a magazine columnist from back East. I only just met her yesterday."

"Well now, that puts things in a different light." Reverend Howell's face broke into a relieved smile. "My apologies for the mistake, Caleb, Miss Quinn."

"No offense taken." Miss Quinn's answering smile rivaled the glitter of gold.

"We came to see you about a different matter entirely. Miss Quinn found this child abandoned in a rubbish heap, and we were wondering if you might know of a Christian family who would be willing to consider caring for and possibly adopting the little girl."

Miss Quinn stepped to his side, her petite frame barely reaching his shoulder. That wayward strand of hair brushed her face, and he once again resisted capturing it.

No doubt last night's lack of sleep had started to turn him into a dad-gummed fool.

"Whereabouts did you find the child?" Reverend Howell leaned forward, peering down at the baby.

"Behind the Mansion, abandoned in their trash heap." Another flush stole over Miss Quinn's face.

Caleb sucked in a breath. She hadn't told him *that*. What had the lady been thinking, taking a walk near San Francisco's most notorious brothel? Had the California sun scrambled her brain? She could have been accosted. . .or worse.

Reverend Howell heaved a weighty sigh. "That doesn't surprise me. I'd like to help you, Miss Quinn. My heart goes out to cases like this, truly it does, but with prices so high and gold harder to find by the day, I can't think of a single family around these parts with the financial means to take on a child. There are prosperous farmers, to be sure, but I'm not personally acquainted with them. You could make inquiries on your own, of course, and that might be your best course of action."

"I understand." Caleb nodded. With spiritual need as rampant as gold fever, the reverend could only do so much. "I can spend some time asking around, after I finish my work for the day. But in the meantime, where will the baby stay?"

"With me." Miss Quinn's voice rang loud and clear. "That is. . .I'll take care of the child until other arrangements can be made."

"Haven't you forgotten?" Caleb spoke with exaggerated slowness. "You're supposed to be working on your articles while you're out here." Not taking care of an infant who would keep her up at all hours of the night with crying and carrying on. How well he remembered the squalls of his baby sister, how they kept the whole family up night after night. And Miss Quinn had a job to do, places to go that wouldn't suit a baby at all. Nor a lady for that matter.

But Miss Quinn simply looked at him as if he'd gone plumb crazy. No doubt, he matched her gaze with much of the same. "I *know* that. And I can easily write while caring for a child. I can even take her on my expeditions. I'll just need one of those knap-sack things the Indians use to carry around their babies."

The reverend spoke first. "That sounds like a reasonable plan. No doubt, you'll find things rather rustic out here, Miss Quinn, but I do hope you'll join us for Sunday services."

Caleb barely resisted the urge to shake his head. The reverend stared at Miss Quinn just as the other men had—as if she were an oasis in the hottest, driest desert ever to be found. Of course, who could blame him? Even Caleb had to admit it got mighty lonely without civilized womenfolk about. Their very presence added a certain some-thing. Respectability, perhaps. A touch of gentility. A tender warmth to temper the rough edges of masculinity.

"I'd be delighted." Shifting the baby, Miss Quinn offered her hand. The reverend took it and, for a second, Caleb expected the man to kiss her fingers. Yet Miss Quinn had the good sense to draw away first and turned toward the door with perfect grace. "Until later, Reverend Howell."

"Thank you for your time." Caleb didn't once look back, not wanting to see the rev-erend's gaze following Miss Quinn's every move. With a roll of his eyes, Caleb closed the canvas with more force than necessary.

"Well, he seemed like a very nice man." Miss Quinn bounced the baby.

Caleb had always thought so, too. Yet after watching the reverend's near drooling over the pretty Easterner, he wasn't so sure. After all, it was Caleb who had the task of winning the heart of Lorena Quinn. From the looks of things, there wasn't much time to waste.

"Come on." He guided her along the street. "I'll walk you home."

Chapter Five

S he'd never been fond of dolls and kittens. Or babies. Or anything small and helpless that she might possibly drop.

Since finding this little girl, something within had shifted. Changed course. Awakened the sudden, sweet desire to love, care for, and protect.

After begging a basin of water from Mrs. Dougall, Lorena had clumsily proceeded to give her new charge a bath. Now the infant slept in one of her trunks, which she'd lined with a blanket, while Lorena took apart a night dress for baby clothes and a pair of drawers to make diapers. Reminding her again why she'd always despised sewing.

Shadows flickered across the room, sending her eyes in a squint to better see the tiny stitches. The reverend's suggestion had been sound, and Caleb had agreed to assist her in finding a family. Yet what would happen when the little girl grew up? When she began to wonder, ask questions. What story would her new parents give? The truth would leave a wound too deep.

Though lies would be no better.

What if. . .she made inquiries on her own? Visited the Mansion and searched for answers? She might come up empty-handed, but at least she would've tried. And perhaps. . .perhaps she would find truth. The story behind the baby's birth. Something to offer when the infant became a young woman and wanted to know.

Her own story had been unremarkable. Her parents had owned a farm in New York. Father had died in an accident while Mama had been pregnant with her. The doctors had cited childbirth complications as the reason for Mama's death, but Lorena knew better. Love had created her, and when love left Mama's life, so did the will to live.

Perhaps this child would never know her past. She most certainly wouldn't if Lorena stood by and did nothing.

Never one for wasting time, she made her way downstairs and asked Mrs. Dougall if she might leave the baby in her care for a few hours. The kind woman readily agreed.

Steeling herself, Lorena donned her plainest brown dress and pulled her hair into a severe knot. She let herself out of the hotel and made her way toward the Mansion.

At this hour, the place overflowed with customers. Most of the men were young, though veiled despair carved lines onto their faces. Tinny piano music grated on her ears, and for a moment she doubted her own sanity.

Almighty God, protect me.

A measure of peace swathed her and she climbed the steps, slipping inside undetected.

Her breath hitched. The grandeur of the interior clashed with the simple outer front. Gilded mirrors hung from red damask walls. Card tables overflowed with customers, women in lavish, low-cut evening gowns dealing the decks. A roulette wheel spun as a group watched in breathless silence. Whether they stared at the woman's barely concealed figure or the number they'd bet on, Lorena couldn't be sure.

A man in a black suit served drinks at the mahogany bar, collecting bags of dust in exchange for small glasses of amber liquid.

The music died.

The man behind the bar left his customers and crossed the room. Lorena's mouth went dry. So far, she'd remained ubiquitous. Apparently, that was about to end.

The man looked her up and down, sending a rush of heat across her cheeks. Though the dress she wore was perfectly modest, his roving eyes made her feel clad in nothing at all.

"I'm going to have to ask you to leave, miss." He smirked.

Her temper found tinder and caught fire. "I'm going to have to refuse."

"You looking for a job?"

Everyone at the tables sat stark-still and dead silent. Apparently, just by walking into the room, she had become the evening's entertainment.

"No, merely some information." She inflected her tone with all the society she could muster.

"Too bad," one of the men at the tables called out. "I would've paid all this week's findings to have a piece of her for a half hour or two."

She'd never had any trouble standing up for herself. Not with her adoptive parents, nor with Mr. Payne. She gave back as good as she got and generally won the argument. Still, she'd never before been faced with this.

"You men have been in the gold fields much too long, or you would've recognized a respectable woman upon seeing one. As it happens, I'm not in the market for a job. I simply wish to speak to a few of these. . .ladies."

"What about?" The man eyed her with an equal mixture of innuendo and suspicion.

"This morning, I found a child in your rubbish heap. A little girl. I was just wondering if any of the women had any notion of who this child's mother might be."

"We don't have time for you crusader types. My girls have work to do. Now get out of here, or I'll have you thrown out. Be assured, these fellers won't play nice about it." He leered.

Drawing in a gulp of air, she squared her shoulders and looked the man dead in the face. "You, sir, are a revolting pig of a man, a weasel of the lowest order, and a snake unlike any I have ever had the misfortune to meet." She spun on her heel and whirled around, crinoline flying.

She had barely gained the door when rough hands hauled her back. The black-suited man hefted her over his shoulder as if she weighed no more than a bag of meal. Panic gripped her with icy claws. *Lord, send someone to my defense. Stir the conscience of one of these men. . .before it's too late.*

"Nobody talks to me like that without the devil to pay for it." Expletives spewed from the man's mouth as she pounded on his back with all her might, kicking and writhing.

"Put the lady down." The words rent the air, firm and calculating.

Lorena struggled to crane her neck to see who had uttered them.

"Says who?" The vile man still retained his grip on her.

"Says a man who in about two seconds is gonna pull this trigger and blast your brains to kingdom come."

The man dropped her like a hot coal. She crumpled to the ground, pain stabbing her backside. Her gaze swung up into the face of Caleb Maddox. He still held the pistol, aim steady.

Stifling a moan, she scrambled to her feet and hurried to his side. Never before had a face been so welcome.

"We'll be taking our leave now." Caleb grabbed her by the arm none too gently and set off at a breakneck pace out the door and down the steps. He didn't stop until they'd reached the hotel door.

She bent down, gasping for breath.

"What in tarnation do you think you were doing, going into a place like that? I thought you were crazy before. Now I'm going with downright insane. Do you realize what could have happened to you had I not come in? You have got to be the most dad-blamed, stupidest female ever to set foot on this side of the Sacramento River!" Caleb paced in front of the door, arms swinging.

She kept her gaze downward. It wasn't like her to listen in silence, but perhaps she deserved his rebuke.

"Are you truly aware of the danger you were in?"

She chanced a glance upward. He was breathing heavily, yet no anger filled his eyes. Only. . .could it be concern?

"I was only going to look for the baby's real mother. I didn't think anything would happen. . . I didn't. . ." No matter how hard she tried, she couldn't stop the flood of tears that followed. Covering her face with her hands, she allowed sobs to rack her frame, tears to drip down her face and trickle over her fingers, until she thought she would never stop crying. She tried in vain to calm herself, tried in vain to stop her sobbing, but the overflow of relief after those moments of terror proved too much for even her self-control.

She didn't know how or why it happened, but the next instant she found herself enveloped in Mr. Maddox's arms. Powerless to do anything but let the tears flow, she allowed him to hold her, taking comfort in his strong embrace. She inhaled the faint scent of soap and spice that lingered on his flannel shirt and her pounding heart quieted. The warmth of him, the sensation of being held, cherished, wrapped around her like a handmade quilt and she let herself breathe it in. . .

Had she gone mad, embracing a man in a public place? She yanked away.

"P–please go," she stammered. His gaze rested on her a moment longer, before he turned and went down the sidewalk, his footfalls echoing behind him.

◆　◆　◆

After a week of baby smiles, bath times, and midnight bottle feedings, donning the mantle of magazine columnist felt a bit like putting on one's winter coat after a carefree summer.

Lorena pressed her cheek against baby Hope's. "It'll only be for a few days, Sunshine. Then I'll be back in San Francisco."

That is, if I make it back in one piece.

She handed the baby to Mrs. Dougall, and the older woman cooed and clucked, enamored with the little one. A baby was even rarer in these parts than womenfolk, and though she'd hardly have thought it possible, Lorena attracted even more of a crowd whenever she and Hope—such a lovely name she'd chosen—ventured out.

Mr. Maddox had been firm. There was no way in Sam Hill he would travel with a woman *and* a baby. So Hope stayed behind.

Adjusting the angle of her bonnet, Lorena grabbed two bags of luggage and her sun parasol then exited her tiny bedroom.

Downstairs, she found Mr. Maddox pacing the hall like a leashed animal. His felt hat sat at an odd angle on his head and he wore two holsters, one on each of his thighs.

"You're late," was his clipped greeting.

"Hello to you, too." Though Caleb wasn't half as gruff as Mr. Payne, he could glower with the best of them. And glower he did when he saw the bags she carried.

"Everything we need has already been packed. You get one bag."

She set the bags on the floor and placed her hands on her hips. "I need both."

His chiseled jaw hardened. "You can only have one."

"How do you expect me to survive? I've packed only necessities." She had, truly, even forcing herself to leave many things behind.

"You call dresses, perfume, and a lace parasol necessities?"

"They are to me." Just how did he know what she'd packed? Was he some kind of mind reader? Deciding not to press the issue, she bent down and riffled through her things. It would be difficult, but she could live without an extra nightdress, hand lotion, and a sewing kit.

A few minutes later she stood, dusting off her blue traveling skirt. "There. Satisfied?" She thrust the single bag under his nose.

He grinned lazily. "Immensely."

Within a couple of hours, they were gliding along in the small sailboat that would carry them to Sacramento. Lorena settled back in her seat, opening her parasol to shield her face from the bright rays. She drew in a breath of the warm air, reveling in the gentle rocking of the boat and the vista of scenery they passed. California certainly had natural beauty aplenty, with hundred-year-old trees, lush green grass, and rolling hills. No wonder people wanted to settle here.

"Pardon me, miss?"

Her gaze swung up. Three men stood gathered around her bench. Blast! Couldn't the male populace of California leave her in peace for a few hours?

"Yes?"

"My name's Sam and this here's Clem and Andy." The men looked to be between the ages of twenty and thirty. All wore felt hats and flannel shirts. All gazed at her like she was Queen Victoria herself.

Lorena inclined her head slightly.

"We've come to make you a proposition, miss. You headed for the gold fields?"

She made a brief nod.

"We are, too. None of us are married, see. But you have got to be the prettiest little gal we've ever clapped eyes on. So we've been thinkin' and decided amongst ourselves that the first of us to find gold would be the one to have your hand."

It might have been almost comical, had the men not been perfectly serious. Lorena stifled a groan. What she wouldn't give for the streets of New York, where she could go through her day without showers of male adoration.

To make matters worse, Mr. Maddox—her self-appointed bodyguard—had gone below to stow their luggage.

"What an interesting idea." She forced her lips to curve upward.

"We thought so, too." Clem—or was it Andy?—piped up.

"Unfortunately, gentlemen, I'm afraid I'll have to refuse. I'm a magazine columnist and not in the market for marriage." Out of the corner of her eye, she glimpsed Mr. Maddox heading her way.

"You're just joshin', aren't you? I've never met a lady not interested in getting hitched." If they found a gold nugget as large as their widened eyes, the men would be happy indeed.

"Well, now you have." She smiled. "Good day, gentlemen."

They didn't look in the mood to refuse, but when Mr. Maddox shoved through their midst and claimed the seat beside her, they scattered like a flock of chickens, taking seats on the opposite side of the boat. She drew in a breath of relief. Never before had she realized how reassuring it could be to play damsel in distress, when one had a knight in shining armor. Or in her case, knight with deadly pistols.

"They bothering you?" Mr. Maddox removed his hat and swiped a hand through his hair. She tried not to notice how it sifted through his fingers, the ends curling just above his shirt collar.

"Not really. I told them I wasn't in the market for marriage."

"Is that true?" His eyes met hers, their depths a shade between coffee and caramel.

She swallowed. "I'm not sure."

He leaned closer, capturing her senses in a swirl of soap and spice. This close, his vitality, his strength. . .the power of it all but stole her breath. "Have you ever been in love, Lorena Quinn?"

She glanced downward, to her gloved hands. For a moment, rationality bid her pause. They shouldn't be having this conversation. Shouldn't be leaving the shallow waters of banter and business talk to traverse deeper depths.

It was a rare sensation to do so. Rare that someone took the time to ask hard questions. Sought to go beyond the facade she kept firmly in place. A successful woman in need of no one. A proper lady who kept men at arm's length.

"Once. Perhaps it wasn't love, just girlish infatuation."

His gaze still held hers and she found herself unwilling to be released. "Who was he?"

"The head editor at my first job."

"Not Payne?" Incredulity lit his eyes.

A small smile found its way to her lips. "No. It was another magazine. I was just twenty years old and on fire with enthusiasm. He was brilliant. When I read his work, his words made me dream. He was also. . ." Now her cheeks blazed and she turned her face from his. She'd never told this to another person, save the reverend at the church she'd attended. As she opened her mouth to say the next word, she knew shame would bathe her. "Married."

He would turn away now. The look of compassion would abdicate his gaze, censure in its place. Perhaps he would even refuse to travel farther with her, leave her stranded at the first town.

He did neither. Only reached across the space between them and took her hand, cradling it between both of his, his touch more comfort than caress.

"Thinking back on it, I can see it was his words, his talent I was in love with, not the man. One evening I went into his office. He'd fallen asleep after a hard day. I was overcome and I. . .I kissed him. He awoke and dismissed me on the spot. Since that day, I've avoided mixing my job with my personal life. And to be quite honest, I've poured every bit of effort into the former. Having a personal life got me nothing but trouble."

Caleb still hadn't released her hand, and she didn't pull away. "God forgives, Lorena. You don't have to live with shame eating you up and stealing your joy. You don't have to carry the past around with you like a bag of rocks. You don't have to live like me." He stood abruptly, knocking over her parasol, and moved across the deck to stand by the railing.

Leaving her mind aswirl with questions.

Chapter Six

Hours later, the memory of Lorena at his side, confiding her past, dug deep into his heart, not letting go. Making him feel worse than a cad for what he had agreed to do. Travel with her back to New York and deposit her with Payne like some sort of trophy. Parading her before his former employer as if she carried a placard—*heart won and broken.*

How could he, a man of honor, do this thing?

He had to. She was his means of claiming his old job. Payne had agreed to take him on, but only if he played the escort, won her affections.

What if. . .he didn't win her heart? What if he simply treated her as a colleague and then traveled with her back East? What if he asked her to play along and begged even, for Payne's benefit. Surely she would agree to help him, pretend to have fallen for him. Then he would have one less regret to carry around, one less stone to add to his bag of rocks.

By late afternoon, they'd reached Sacramento and, after procuring some mules, made their way down to the mining camp. Though not as large as San Francisco, the town still bustled and boomed. Raw excitement lived in every face. At least, those whose visages weren't already marked with disillusionment.

For a city girl, Lorena rode a mule remarkably well, skirts spread out around her, gentle on the reins. Since their conversation that morning, she'd said little. More than once, he'd opened his mouth to reassure her that nothing she'd said had changed his good opinion of her as a lady, but he just as quickly choked back the words.

She was his colleague. He, her assistant and tour guide. Plenty of space between them. No personal conversation. And definitely no reflection on how warm her hand had felt, how pleasure had made his breath halt when she wrapped her fingers tighter around his.

"Are we almost there?" Lorena's voice woke him from his thoughts.

"Up ahead a little ways." Already the camp had come into view. Canvas tents and smoking fires. Men cooking, sleeping, talking. All centered around the Sacramento River. All living with three goals. To find gold in the rippling depths. To strike it rich. To establish their destiny.

Caleb knew all too well that destiny was the last thing they would find in California's hills and streams. Pain, yes. Rampant greed, yes. Not destiny.

"So the men here have already established claims?" Lorena glanced at him.

"There are no actual claims on this river. Anyone with equipment can pan. Though as more and more men find their way here, good claims on any river become harder and fewer to come by." Caleb located an empty stretch of grass. They would make camp here.

He dismounted and waited for Lorena to do the same. She struggled to manage her skirts without losing her balance. He probably should have helped her. Yet putting his arms around that willow-thin waist, feeling the fabric of her dress under his fingers, well, that wasn't in his job description as a colleague.

"I hope you're good at cooking beans, 'cause that's what I brought." He rummaged through his pack until he found the tin of beans and the bag of cornmeal.

Alarm lit a fire in her eyes. She took the bags from him but made no move to go about starting a fire. He'd bought enough wood for one night; the next day they'd have to scavenge for more.

"Aren't you hungry?" He unrolled the tent and began to set up camp.

She said nothing. The ride had pulled her hair from its pins and her bonnet off her head. It hung around her neck with velvet ribbons. Velvet ribbons that bespoke a life free from domestic chores.

"Right. You can't cook." He dropped the tent and crossed to her side. "You know, Lorena, there's no shame in admitting you can't do something."

Even in the semidarkness, he saw her blush and scrunch her freckled nose slightly. "My adoptive parents had a cook and maid. Once I moved out on my own, I lived in boardinghouses. Left to my own accord, I would most likely starve."

He took the bags and shifted them in his hands. "Somehow I doubt that, but for tonight, I'll do the honors. And I can make the best beans and cornbread you've ever had the privilege of tasting."

She exhaled, relief evident. "I'm very glad to hear it, because, quite frankly, I'm hungry enough to eat the hind end of a horse."

He laughed, a full-out belly laugh like he hadn't done in. . .he couldn't remember when. She joined in, head tilted back, lips parted, giggles spilling from her mouth like sweet music, auburn hair falling down her back.

Why in tarnation did she have to be so beautiful?

Colleagues. Think colleagues.

"All righty." He grabbed the firewood off the back of his mule. "One hind end of a horse coming right up."

◆　◆　◆

So this was how one got rich. Knee-deep in water, back bent low, swishing a tin pan round and round.

Lorena drew closer, notebook in hand, Caleb at her side.

"Isn't that water cold?"

He nodded. "Freezing. The men stand in it for hours a day. Some end up with rheumatism; others lose feeling in their feet."

"How do they stand it?"

"Well, as the saying goes, 'You can accustom yourself to anything, even getting hung.'"

She smiled. "Give me a few more nights of sleeping on that hard ground, and I might start to believe you." She rubbed a hand over her sore shoulder. What she wouldn't give for a hot bath. Steam rising up, rose-scented soap. Ah, bliss.

But for now, she was a reporter, with information to gather and pieces to write.

The sight of a lady had attracted no small interest amongst the group of men, yet none of them paused for more than a minute from their work. Obviously the lure of gold outweighed the allure of a petticoat. At least at present.

"What exactly are they doing with that pan thing?" Grateful for Caleb's steadying hand to guide her along the uneven bank, she took a few steps closer.

"Scraping gravel from the riverbed. That's where the gold is. Once they've got a pan full, they swirl water around to rinse away the sand and gravel. The gold flakes will be left behind. It's quite simple, really. Just exhausting. After a few hours, your feet start to feel like chunks of ice, and every muscle in your body begs for a break."

"I can imagine." She made a few notes with pencil and tablet.

One of the men left his work and climbed the embankment, his booted feet squishing against the grass. At his side, two lethal-looking pistols hung, his hand resting against one.

"Can I help you folks?" He narrowed his eyes.

Rather than allowing herself to be daunted, Lorena held out her hand. "I'm Lorena Quinn from the *Weekly Observer*."

"The Weekly what?" With his other hand, the man scratched his scraggle-bearded chin.

"The *Weekly Observer*. It's a magazine. In New York."

"Then what in Sam Hill are you doin' here? You ain't after gold, are you?" His hand closed around the pistol.

Caleb placed fingertips on her shoulder, as if to draw her behind him, but she shrugged him off. This man wouldn't shoot a lady. Not when they were so scarce and she posed no threat.

"Merely the gold of knowledge. I'm looking to interview a few prospectors. Would you mind if I asked you some questions?" She added her sweetest smile. "Please."

The man melted like honey on hot cornbread. "I'd be honored to assist you in any way I can, ma'am." If he wore a hat, Lorena would bet he'd have tipped it.

"Thank you." She flipped to a fresh sheet of tablet paper. "How long have you been in California, Mr. . . . ?"

"Walton, ma'am. Joe Walton. About six months. I came from a farm in Tennessee."

"What made you decide to leave home?"

"Well, it was the article I read in the newspaper while I was a-sittin' a spell at the dry goods store. I like to do that now and again, sit a spell while my missus does her shopping. When I heard about those nuggets people were finding, that was it. I caught the fever, and I ain't recovered since."

"And have you struck it rich?"

"Nope." The man pulled a plug of chewing tobacco from his pocket and popped it in his mouth. "But I did make quite a pile last month. Found a nugget this big." He pressed his thumb and forefinger together to form an o.

"Impressive. I have just one more question." Her gaze turned to Caleb. He stared down at the river, watching the men at work. She hesitated. Did his own heart stir for riches? What had made him choose ink and newsprint over the potential for fortune and glory? Did he see the futility of it, or was there something more? "If you could give a piece of advice to fellow adventurers, what would it be?"

Walton spat a brownish stream of saliva out the side of his mouth then wiped his lips with the back of his hand. "Don't work in the rain."

"The rain?"

"Yes, ma'am. Standing in the freezing water while it's raining dogs and polecats is liable to kill a body."

"I see." She made a few more notes. "Thank you for your time, Mr. Walton."

"You're mighty welcome, ma'am." The miner made a jerky bow, spat the brownish lump of tobacco into the grass, and then turned away, whistling "Old Dan Tucker" as he waded through the water.

By nightfall the following day, her notebook was brimful with notes, interviews, and ideas. After conducting one last interview for the evening, she settled beside the campfire, pencil scratching. . .

The Miner's Ten Commandments

I. Thou shalt have no other claim than one.

II. Thou shalt not make unto thyself any false claim, nor any likeness to a mean man by jumping one.

The idea had come to her as she gathered advice from miner after miner. Payne would love it. It would be near the front of the magazine, surrounded by sketches. . . .

VI. Thou shalt not kill; neither thy body by working in the rain, even though thou shalt make enough to buy physic and attendance with; nor thy neighbor's body in a duel. . .

On and on she scribbled, crossing out, changing, and rewriting. Until she came to the final commandment.

X. Thou shalt not commit unsuitable matrimony, nor covet "single blessedness"; nor forget absent maidens; nor neglect thy "first love";—but thou shalt consider how faithfully and patiently she awaiteth thy return; yea and covereth each epistle that thou sendest with kisses of kindly welcome—until she hath thyself.

A new Commandment give I unto thee—if thou has a wife and little ones, that thou lovest dearer than life—that thou keep them continually before thee, to cheer and urge thee onward, until thou canst say, "I have enough—God bless them—I will return." Then from thy much-loved home, with open arms shall thy come forth to welcome thee, with weeping tears of unutterable joy that thou art come; then in the fullness of thy heart's gratitude, thou shalt kneel together before thy heavenly Father, to thank Him for thy safe return.

Chapter Seven

Three months later

He should have become accustomed to these outings by now. Visiting saloons while Lorena dug for answers with the avidity of a prospector on his first day. So far, they'd found none. Apparently, no one in San Francisco knew of a child being born or a mother desperate enough to leave her baby in a rubbish heap.

He had to hand it to Lorena. She had spark. Enough to barge into dens of ill repute, demand audiences, stare down hardened barkeeps with the mettle of a compatriot.

Tonight was their final chance. For in a week, a mere seven days, Lorena Quinn would board a ship and leave San Francisco behind for good.

He hadn't yet broached the subject of going with her. Didn't want to ask her to play along with Arnold Payne's ridiculous scheme. But he must. Soon.

She stood within his line of vision, head bent low, hand resting on the arm of a heavily painted young woman, who wore a dress that could hardly be called a dress at all. Most society women would've turned up their noses at a dance hall girl. Not Lorena. To her, people were people, despite the snobbish veneer she slapped on for bravado. Regardless of their class, profession, or circumstances. This quality was what made her writing so brilliant. Far better than his could ever be.

After her first piece on the Miner's Ten Commandments, she'd penned four more. Each had been vivid and brutally honest. An antidote to the "streets paved in gold" myth that had drawn Caleb out to California in the first place.

He leaned one hand on the polished bar, keeping an eye on her. She met his gaze, motioned him to her side with a tilt of her head.

"We've got something here, Caleb." The sparkle in her gaze far outshone any nugget of gold. "Tell him, Ruby."

The girl couldn't have been more than seventeen, yet her eyes lacked the luster Lorena's carried. Underneath the layers of rouge and kohl, she might've been pretty, had the hard realities of her life not sapped all particles of vitality. She crossed her arms over her chest and spoke, head bent low.

"Mattie came here a few months ago and then left all of a sudden. I think she birthed a child during her time here and was managing to keep it a secret. Then Roy found out and gave her the sack. I don't know what happened to her after that."

"Did she ever speak of a family?" Lorena asked, raising her voice above the din of fiddle and piano music.

"No. Her last name was Sutherfield, if that helps you any."

"Can you be sure she actually had a child?" Caleb tried to keep his tone quiet so as not to alarm the girl.

"No, sir. But she took sick for a couple of weeks and didn't work. Sometimes I heard crying in the night. I guess I just thought it was one of the girls, but it sounded too little for that. Roy liked her. That's probably why he never investigated the matter. But one day they had a big fight... I've got to go now."

She made a move to turn, but Lorena stayed her. "Thank you for your time, Ruby." She pressed something into the girl's hand.

Ruby smiled slightly then brushed past them and hurried up the stairs.

"We can go now, Caleb." Lorena placed her hand on his arm. He had to admit, he'd gotten used to the feeling of her fingers on his sleeve, the rustle of her skirts at his side. When they parted ways, he would miss it. A whole lot more than he'd ever expected.

He led her past the card tables and out the swinging doors, past the gazes of a dozen admiring men. Outside, steady rain pelted the ground, thunder growling overhead. Already a river of mud coated the street.

"Do you want to wait till it stops?" He glanced at her.

She shook her head. "Not in there, I don't. Let's make a dash for it." Without an ounce of hesitancy, she laced her fingers within his and started off at a run. He had no choice but to move alongside, dashing past dark and deserted storefronts, brightly lit saloons, and gaming houses.

Rain drenched his shirt, soaking it to his skin, trickling over his hair. Despite her dress and crinoline, Lorena had little trouble keeping pace with his stride, though he lessened it to accommodate her smaller steps.

There was something about rain. The drops cleansed not only the earth, but the soul as well. Loosening the layers of tension and restraint, making one want to stop and gaze upward, let the life-giving drops trickle onto the tongue.

Releasing his hand, Lorena Quinn did just that. In the middle of a deserted San Francisco street, she pulled off her bonnet and tipped her head back, laughing with the joyous abandon of a child.

Caleb leaned against a post of one of the buildings, gaze riveted. What would it be like to live as this woman did? She cared little for others' opinions, pursuing a place in a world dominated by men. And though she was as graceful as any debutante, she emitted a grace far deeper. Grace of heart. Of spirit.

She faced him, hair in tangles around her shoulders, water soaking her bodice, plastering it to her waist. Her hand captured his, and she drew him forward, leading him in an impromptu waltz, singing softly.

> Molly do you love me?
> Can the morning beam
> Love a lowly flowret
> Living in its gleam?
> Let one gentle whisper
> All my doubts destroy
> Let my dreamy rapture
> Turn to waking joy.

It had been too long. Far too long since he'd lost himself in such a simple pleasure.

Her fingers rested lightly on his shoulder, and the lilac scent of her perfume filled his senses. Twin ringlets fell across either side of her cheeks, damp and dislodged, and he longed to brush them back, tangling his fingers into the softness of her hair. Instead he drew her closer and intertwined her fingers more firmly within his.

She looked up, directly meeting his gaze. The endless depths of her eyes, as dark and vibrant as emeralds, were enough to make any man lose track of his very senses and have no wish to find them again.

He was no exception.

◆　◆　◆

No one occupied the hotel common room. So Lorena led Caleb inside. After all, she couldn't let him walk to his newspaper office soaked to the skin and with rain still pouring down.

"I'll fetch some towels." Slipping off her muddy boots, she crossed the hall to the kitchen. She gathered an armful of towels and returned to the common room. Light glimmered from a pair of candles, though Caleb hadn't lit a fire. She passed him some towels, grateful for the semidarkness as she dried her own face and hair.

"It hasn't let up." Caleb peered out the window, raindrops pebbling the glass. He turned back to her. "You should get into some dry clothes."

She shivered. "What about you?"

A slow grin angled his lips. "I'm a reformed miner, remember? Used to being wet, cold, and miserable."

"Whereas I am a lady of gentility. Accustomed to plush carpets, fires in every room, and tea and toast before bed."

His grin deepened. "That's about the size of it."

It would be far too easy to lose herself in his smile. In the way his eyes crinkled around the edges, the barest hint of a dimple appearing in his chin. Lose not only herself, but her common sense, her mind, and most dangerous of all, her heart.

"I'll be right back." Taking a candle from the mantel, she hurried to her room. Mrs. Dougall sat in a chair, nodding off, baby Hope in a cradle at her feet. As she brushed her fingers across Hope's petal-soft cheek, a sigh whispered from Lorena's lips. In such a few short days, she would part with this precious child. Reverend Howell had found a respectable farming family willing to take on a baby.

And Lorena would return East. To her job, her life. Without the warmth of an infant snuggled in her arms, instilling within her a sense of purpose, a new meaning to the giving and receiving of love.

She'd often wondered how women could consign themselves to a life spent raising children. Now she sensed it was more than that. There was a nurturing, a life-giving, and it wrapped around one's heart with binding ropes, cords that could not be severed without bleeding inwardly.

She changed out of her wet clothes and into a simple skirt and shirtwaist, pulling a pair of thick wool socks over her chilled toes. She crept back downstairs and stood in the doorway.

Caleb had lit a fire and he sat beside it, head in his hands, fingers tunneled through his damp hair. Though he exuded confidence with every turn, at this moment he seemed nothing but a lost little boy, the weight of the world resting on his shoulders.

Lorena stepped inside. He lifted his head, gaze seeking hers. The glimmer of firelight caught the angles of his face, the shadow of stubble dusting his jaw. Something lived in his eyes, wild and untamed. Danger, perhaps. Or sorrow.

Swallowing hard, she seated herself in the chair opposite, working the knots from her hair with shaking fingers.

"You don't have to live like me." Caleb's words filled her mind. What had he meant? What regrets chained him to the past? She drew in a breath. If she asked, would he lash out like a wounded animal? Turn his back on her and shun speech? Could she risk the ache in her heart that would well at his coldness?

"What do you regret?" Rare was the day when she sounded so hesitant.

"You read my thoughts too well." A crooked smile found his lips. "Are you always so adept at perusing the mind of another, Lorena Quinn?"

"Not usually." She leaned forward, letting silence salve his wounds, hoping her encouragement would be enough for him to speak.

"I sought fame and fortune and found neither. A few months ago, a friend came to me asking for money. I'd helped him before but couldn't bring myself to fund his efforts this time. What I saw in his eyes could have been me looking into a mirror last year." A muscle jerked in his throat. "I'm so ashamed, Lorena. I let my family down, forsook a steady job. For what? The promise of riches that never came! I've been vain and foolish, and I want so much to change. But how do I know anyone will give me a second chance?"

"God forgives, Caleb. You said so yourself. The prodigal son returned home—why shouldn't you? You are a man of honor, all the more so because of your willingness to admit your wrongs. No one should hold that against you. We all make mistakes. You just need to forgive yourself." Hairpins had ensnared themselves in her curls, and she winced as she tugged on a particularly tangled strand, shaken by all she had just said.

He stood and crossed the room. Would he rage at her for all she had said? No. His eyes were not angry but. . .

"Allow me." His words were summer-wind soft, spoken near her ear.

"Allow you to what?" Her heart pounded in her ears.

He didn't answer, simply removed her hands from where they struggled in her hair and placed them in her lap. Then tangled his fingers among the strands, his movements gentle, his touch soothing.

She leaned into his touch with a sigh as he removed the last pin, then combed his hands through each section, the even motion lulling her, making her eyelids drift shut.

Always, she'd longed for someone to brush her hair.

Always, she'd struggled alone, as a child at the orphanage, growing up with her adoptive parents, as a young woman at boardinghouses.

Tears gathered in her eyes and she opened them, blinking the moisture back. Her hair fell like a sheet of silk to her waist and his hands suddenly stilled. He knelt down in front of her, cupping her face in his hands, wiping the drops from her cheeks.

"Did I hurt you?" The hesitancy in his tone nearly undid her afresh.

She shook her head.

The how or why of it she couldn't comprehend, but in the next moment, his lips were against hers, firm and gentle all at once. He tasted of peppermint, smelled of spice, and in that moment she truly did lose herself, running her fingers through his hair, against his stubbled jaw.

Not lost, perhaps, but found.

Surrendered.

He broke away, breathing ragged. Ran a hand through his hair, then found her eyes again.

"Heaven help me, Lorena Quinn. I think. . .I think I've fallen in love with you."

Chapter Eight

Heaven help me, Lorena Quinn. I think. . .I think I've fallen in love with you."

Hours later, the words still rang in her ears. The moment they'd left his mouth, ice-cold reality had pelted them with more fury than the rain. He'd stood to his feet, stammering a good-bye, leaving her to crawl beneath her covers and stare at the ceiling, each minute dragging by like an hour.

The touch of his kiss still burned her lips, the feel of his hands burrowed in her hair. Life had overflowed in her veins in those moments, leaving her dry and empty when he'd pulled away.

Lord, give me wisdom. Because. . . Because against my better judgment and against all my ideals and dreams, I think I've fallen in love with him, too.

She needed to see him again. With the broad light of day between them, they must discuss what had happened like sensible, grown-up people. Though first, she might just kiss him again. Reassure herself that he really had held her, loved her with his touch.

She picked up Hope, letting her fancy take flight. Together they could make a home, raise this child. Though she would have to give up her dreams of becoming assistant editor, she could still write. And if Caleb continued to look at her as he had last night, lack of promotion would be a small price to pay.

"Lorena, you awake?" It was Mrs. Dougall.

"Yes." She laid Hope in her makeshift cradle and pulled back the canvas.

"Mail delivery came early this morning. I've got a letter for you." The woman pulled an envelope from her apron and held it out with a flour-smudged hand.

"Thank you." Lorena smiled at the woman and closed the canvas. She recognized the chicken scratch immediately. Her heart thrummed as she tore open the envelope. Had Mr. Payne received her articles? Was he pleased with her work? Perhaps some of the pieces had been a bit blunt, but he'd always told her to tell the truth.

Quinn,

Bravo, girl. Just as I expected, you're a fine writer. Your pieces were brilliant, and after I toned down some of your descriptive flummery, I got them all set to go. They should appear in next week's edition.

Having fun in California? I suppose you're enjoying the company of Charmer Maddox. Seriously, Quinn, matchmaking with you two was just a joke. Maddox probably didn't tell you, but he used to have that assistant editor position, and I offered it to him in exchange for claiming your heart. Of course, this was only to ensure that none of the other saps would have a chance, and you would return to

New York without a ring on your finger. I couldn't bear to lose my best writer, after all. Don't be too hard on Maddox. He's just desperate to redeem himself after the whopper of a fight we had before he left in '49. Don't worry. Once you both come home, I'll conduct proper interviews and give you each a fair shot. Since you've both been pieces in my little game, I figured you each deserve that.

Payne

The letter fluttered to the floor like a wounded bird, and Lorena curled herself into a ball and let the sobs drown her.

◆　◆　◆

He didn't belong in California. Or in New York.

He belonged in Lorena's arms, her untried kisses on his lips, her heart in every touch. She cared for him, and he would make that caring into love. Court her until her defenses crumbled like sunbaked sand. They could return to New York together, work together at Arnold Payne's office.

He'd even let her be assistant editor. She'd earned the job, with her stirring pieces and meticulous research. As long as Mr. Payne would give him some type of employment, he wouldn't care if she became his superior.

Ink splotched his hands as he set the type for this week's edition. He could sell the building and it would fetch a high price. Who cared whether or not it stayed a newspaper office? Few in San Francisco cared for literacy anyway.

The door bludgeoned open. Lorena burst inside, her hair wild around her face, skirts hiked high.

She ran at him, and at first he opened his arms to receive her.

The fury in her eyes made it clear. She didn't have romance on her mind.

"How could you! You fraud. . .you womanizing, low-down cad of a man." She pounded on his chest, her hair flying as she delivered blow after blow. For a moment, he just stood there, stunned, immune to the pain.

Grabbing both of her hands, he held her back. "What in the Sam Hill is going on?"

She yanked her hands away and fisted them at her sides. With trembling fingers, she reached into the pocket of her skirt and held out a piece of paper. He took it and scanned the words. Each drove a knife into his gut; each branded him the blackguard he was.

"Well?" Her words rasped low and harsh. "Is it true?"

He said nothing.

"Is it true that you made me fall in love with you for a stupid job? Is it true that you kissed me on orders from your former employer? It was all probably a terrific game for you, winning my heart like one might claim a sporting trophy. I thought you were a man of honor. A God-fearing gentleman. I trusted you! Trusted. You." She stopped, the words leaving a trail of venom in their wake.

"I didn't make you fall in love with me. Not for Payne's benefit." He couldn't meet her gaze, couldn't bring himself to see the censure in her eyes. The truth.

"So why would he write such a letter?"

"When I first met you, yes, it was my intention to go along with Payne's plan. But once I got to know you, I realized I couldn't do such a thing. I figured maybe I could convince you to play along once we arrived in New York, so Payne would still be satisfied."

"Satisfied! With you, and no one else. And what makes you think I'll believe you now when all I have to stand on is a basis of lies?" Her words sliced the air like daggers, each hitting their mark.

The enormity of his sin sluiced out in a sigh. "I don't think anything. I have no right."

She shook her head slowly. "No. You have no right at all." She turned on her heel and shoved open the door, slamming it behind her.

He sank onto the floor, covering his face with his hands, buckling under the waves of regret crashing over him. He'd failed so much. Disappointed his parents and employer when he chose dreams of wealth over them. Failed to find so much as a single nugget. Squandered the inheritance left him by his grandfather until all that remained was enough to buy this office.

He had tried to follow God. Read his Bible as often as he could, sat in church week after week, prayed before meals and for help in time of need.

Had he ever truly listened? Ever bared the ugly scars on his soul and held them up for healing? Ever allowed God to light the darkness of his path, show him which way to walk?

No. He'd relied on himself. Caleb Maddox. A man who could get himself out of any fix, build something out of nothing.

A cry welled from deep within.

Caleb Maddox by himself was worth no more than ashes. Caleb Maddox in his own strength could do nothing well, leave no legacy behind that truly mattered.

He stumbled across the room to his desk and found the small, worn Bible. Pressing it against his chest, he resumed his seat on the floor.

Give me something, Lord. I need a light to navigate this darkness. . .such pain. . .

Desperate tears streamed down his face as he opened to where the ribbon bookmark lay in Second Corinthians.

"For God, who commanded the light to shine out of darkness, hath shined in our hearts, to give the light of the knowledge of the glory of God in the face of Jesus Christ. But we have this treasure in earthen vessels, that the excellency of the power may be of God, and not of us. We are troubled on every side, yet not distressed; we are perplexed, but not in despair; persecuted, but not forsaken; cast down, but not destroyed."

The words found soft soil in his heart, a gift from a God who still cared enough to redeem the broken. Still loved enough to make the shattered pieces whole.

But it couldn't happen in his own strength. No, he, Caleb Maddox, must become powerless. . .powerless before an all-powerful God. God could fight every battle, douse the shadows on each path. All he had to do was invite His presence. Let Him into the weary mess of mistakes, human failings, and daily struggle that was life. God wouldn't fail or leave him.

Even if the woman he still loved, Lorena Quinn, did just that.

Chapter Nine

Giving Caleb Maddox a piece of her mind should've made her feel better.

All it had done was leave a dull ache in the center of her chest, right where her heart should have been. Never before had she considered herself a weeping sort of female. But since returning from the newspaper office, she'd done nothing but cry, using up a pile of hankies and the last of her strength.

How could she have been so blind, falling for the handsome physique and honeyed flirtations of a man anything but trustworthy? None of them were. All out for themselves, using women as a means to an end. It was why she longed for change, dreamed of the day when women would take their rightful place in society, not as helpless subordinates but rational equals with opinions and a voice.

Lord, give me the strength to forget Caleb Maddox. I want to give my heart completely to You and let You lead my life. So often I seek my own way of doing things, instead of Yours. Help that to change. Why does it always take reaching the end of our rope before we realize we're drowning? Be near me, please. . .

At least she had peace about one thing. She would take Hope with her back to New York and raise her as a daughter. The child would have a good life, the best education, friends. Together, they would be a family. The first true family for either of them.

Drying her tears and squaring her shoulders, Lorena carefully packed each item. She saved out her prettiest bonnet as a gift for Mrs. Dougall. One thing she'd learned during her time in San Francisco—fashion did not make a woman. Courage and faith did. Not clothing. As the days passed, she'd even forsaken her bulky crinoline, wearing simple petticoats under her dresses. Though when she returned to New York, she'd have to go back to the old ways or it would create a scandal.

Some old ways, like her self-reliance, would never be resurrected.

"Miss Quinn?" She recognized the voice instantly. Caleb. If she saw his face never again, it would be too soon.

"I'm busy." Lorena bent and picked up Hope from where she lay on the bed. "You're through with your obligations as my guide. I'm leaving as soon as I can."

"Please." Although a swath of canvas separated them, she could sense the urgency of his tone. "It's about Hope."

"If this is another one of your underhand schemes, I'm not interested. I've been your plaything long enough." She didn't try to keep the bite from her tone.

"It's not. Lorena, I found Hope's mother."

His words brought her up short, sending her heart to racing. After a dozen saloon visits and countless inquiries, could it be possible they'd found the woman who had abandoned this child?

"How can you be sure?" Though her fingers reached forward, she didn't pull back the canvas.

"Ruby came to my office. She said Mattie Sutherfield is in her room this very moment. We don't have much time, Lorena. Mattie is dying."

She pushed back the curtain. Desperation, and something else she couldn't place, lined Caleb's expression. He looked like a man who hadn't slept, taken food, or breathed since their argument. He looked like a man in anguish over what he'd done.

"Then we'd better not waste any time." Clutching Hope closer, she followed him down the stairs without another word. Once in the street, he led the way, past wagons, storefronts, and the hordes of men and boys who jostled through the streets intent on their universal mission.

They reached the saloon and Caleb preceded her inside. Since it was only afternoon, few patrons inhabited the green baize tables, only a handful nursed drinks at the bar. After speaking with the barkeep and handing over of a few ounces of gold dust, Caleb motioned Lorena up the stairs, following at her heels.

Ruby met her in the hallway. Her eyes were red and smudges of kohl streaked like soot across her face, as if she'd been crying and spoiled her cosmetics.

"She's in here."

"When did she arrive?"

Ruby sighed, the bodice of her scanty dress heaving. "Late last night. She about near collapsed on the outside steps. It took me and another of the girls to bring her up here. She's in a bad way, miss. I don't expect she'll last much longer. I told her you was coming with the baby, and I think she's been holding on for that."

Lorena spared not a moment, brushing past Ruby and opening the door.

Death hovered on the edges of the room, its presence so palpable that she caught her breath. On the quilt-covered bed lay a slight frame.

"Did you bring the baby?" rasped the young woman.

"Yes, I brought your daughter." Lorena knelt beside the bed and held up Hope for the woman to see. A look of joy filled her sunken eyes, flitted over her chalk-white cheeks. Once, this pitiful creature had been young and vibrant, her still-evident beauty captivating men. Perhaps she'd even dreamt of love in that wistful way employed by all young women, no matter their outward show of propriety.

Hope's mother reached bony fingers upward toward the bundle. "She looks just like I always pictured. So clean and happy. It was the good Lord who brought you to my baby's rescue, and I am grateful. To you and to Him. He's done saved me, He has. The reverend prayed with me, told me how the good Lord has a mansion waitin' just for me. I've never had a place of my own before. It will be grander than—" A racking cough cut off her words, and Ruby hurried to hold a basin under Mattie's mouth. The spasm subsided, and she collapsed against the mattress.

A knot formed in Lorena's throat and she forced the tears from her eyes. "You don't have to worry about a thing, Mattie. I'll take care of your baby. She'll have a beautiful house in New York, a fine education, and lots of friends."

A smile edged Mattie's pale, cracked lips. "I don't much care if my little girl lives in a fancy house or learns readin' and writin', though it would be grand if she did. All I want for my baby is for her to know love. That's all. . .that matters to me."

"She will." Caleb's voice came from behind. Lorena turned and met his eyes. He smiled slightly. "She will know love. I promise you that, Miss Sutherfield."

"Thank you." Mattie's shrunken frame seemed to dissolve against the pillows. "I do apologize for all this. For leavin' this world without having known. . ." The scarcely audible words trailed away, Mattie's breath fading and then stopping altogether. Lorena fought back a sob. She gazed down into the baby—her baby's face. Hers for always now.

Ruby rounded the bed, gently closed the girl's eyes, and folded her hands over her chest. When she looked up, tears streaked her face. "She's with the angels now, miss. In a far better place than this dreary world."

Lorena nodded.

"You and your young man had better go now. I'll see to everything here."

Heart heavy, Lorena stood and took Caleb's offered arm. At the door, she paused, turning for the last time to fix her eyes on the shell of a woman lying in the bed. "Rest in peace, Mattie Sutherfield. With God's help, I promise to take care of your daughter."

◆　◆　◆

Death could teach you about a lot of things. How to live, the things that really mattered.

Second chances only came around so often. When they did, you had to reach out, grab hold, and hang on with the tenacity of a drowning man clinging to a rope.

He couldn't let Lorena get on that boat. Couldn't let her walk out of his life, so much still unsaid between them.

His watch read eleven twenty. The boat left in less than an hour. Could he make it to the wharf in time?

Caleb pushed open the door of his office and let himself outside. A horse stood, tied to a hitching post at the building next door. A felt-hatted man patted the animal's rump and ambled down the street, whistling "Oh, California."

"Mister! Mister!" Caleb waved his arm.

The man turned, giving Caleb a bemused look.

"Can I borrow your horse for an hour or two?" He clapped his hand to his hat to keep it from blowing away in the wind.

"Nothing doing. I paid half my life savings for that animal, and I need him to get to Sacramento. I'm gonna make my fortune, you see."

"Mister, I need that horse. I'm going after the girl I love. Please." Caleb reached inside his pants pocket and pulled out a one-hundred-dollar bill. Only one more remained, all he had left after selling the newspaper office that morning. "I'll give you this as surety. If I don't come back, it should be enough to buy you a new horse. If I return, you'll give me back the money."

It was taking a risk, a big one. The man could easily hightail it out of San Francisco with the remains of Caleb's life savings. But sometimes, when the future dangled on a pendulum, one had to take risks.

The price of love was far too great.

The man eyed the bill with a hungry look. "Well." He scratched his head. "All right."

Caleb handed the man the money, untied the horse, swung his leg over the saddle, and took off down the street. He reached the wharf in record time. Around him, hundreds and hundreds of abandoned ships sat, empty shells in the aqua water.

How did he expect to find Lorena in this mess?

Leading the horse with one hand, he squished through the muck, gaze searching for a petite redhead in petticoats. Muddy petticoats, more than likely. Yet the longer he searched, the further his hopes plummeted.

Lord, if I'm not meant to find her, help me trust in Your plan.

Wind licked the air. A flock of birds circled the clouds overhead. People talked and laughed, strolling past. The world went round and round, while his stood still. Waiting, breathless.

Across the mass of people, he glimpsed a splash of green that could only be her bonnet.

"Lorena!" he shouted. Would his words carry across the crowd?

She turned. Their gazes locked. For a moment, she seemed ready to turn away.

Then she pushed through the crowd and walked toward him—muddy petticoats, red hair, outrageous freckles—all the things that made her the woman he'd grown to care so much for. He wanted to swallow her up in his arms, baby and all. Wanted to press his lips to hers and tell her with his touch what he struggled to do in words.

I'm sorry. I love you and can't seem to stop.

"Why are you here, and why do you have such an ugly horse, Caleb Maddox?" He expected her to glare at him, but the faintest of smiles touched her lips.

He drew in a deep breath. "Because when a man has found gold, he won't rest until he draws it to himself. He'll fight for it, protect it, and cherish it all the rest of his days. You are my gold, Lorena Quinn. My treasure. And I *will* fight for you. I will do everything, even beg, if you'll let me apologize for the wrong I have done. Just give me one more chance."

She drew in a long breath.

He waited, his world hanging on her answer.

God, please. Yet not my will, but Yours be done.

Her smile widened. "I'll let you apologize. But first. . .please kiss me."

He needed no further invitation. Just pulled her against him, the baby between them, pressing his lips against hers, breathing her in. She smelled so good, felt so right, and he let the kiss linger.

She drew back, a bit breathless. "You apologize very well, if I do say so."

"You accept apologies equally so." He gave her a heated look, just to make that endearing blush flame her adorably freckled cheeks. "There's no way this boat might wait a couple of hours, is there?"

She shook her head. "But I can stay. I don't need to leave today."

"Oh, yes you do. Don't worry. I'll be there as soon as I finish up a few things. Probably catch the next boat heading back East."

"To New York?" Her eyes widened.

He nodded. "That's right. New York. Me. You. This baby. We're going to make a life, my society girl reporter. And do a whole lot of living and loving. First, I'm going to win your heart. Without Mr. Payne's prodding."

She glanced at the group of passengers preparing to board, before launching herself into his arms. "I would like nothing more, Caleb Maddox," she whispered against his cheek.

He held her for the longest time, storing up this memory for the weeks they would be apart. He would miss her dearly, but it would only make their reunion all the sweeter.

Kissing her softly, he spoke words meant for her alone. "I've been thinking about those Miner's Ten Commandments."

"Any one in particular?" She pulled away enough to meet his gaze. "Do not kill thy neighbor in a duel?"

He grinned. "Nope. The last one. 'Do not neglect thy first love.'"

"And?"

He gave her one more lingering kiss—the last for a while, but the first of hundreds to come. "You, sweet Lorena. Only you."

Author's Note – The Miner's Ten Commandments were written by James Hutchings and first printed in the *Placerville Herald* in June of 1853. When I discovered them during the course of my research, I knew I had to include them as one of Lorena's articles. They rang so true of the attitude many had as the Gold Rush continued—that though everyone longed to find riches, the greatest wealth of life was in faith, family, and the Lord.

May it be so today!

Blessings!
Amanda

Amanda Barratt has won several awards for her work and enjoys writing about eras such as Regency and Victorian England and the Gilded Age. A member of American Christian Fiction Writers, she lives in northern Michigan with her family, where she reads way too many old books, watches period dramas to come up with new plotlines, and dreams of taking a trip to England. Amanda loves hearing from her readers on Facebook and through her website, amandabarratt.net.

The Best Man in Brookside

by Angela Bell

Dedication

In loving memory of my granny, Norma Jean,
who always believed in this dream and told me never to give up.

Acknowledgments

Deepest gratitude to my supportive family, especially my dear parents.
And special thanks to my "horse whisperer" sister, Tabitha,
whose experience and equine knowledge were vital to the writing of this story.
I couldn't have done it without you!

Chapter One

Donovan shoved the worn tarp that served as a tent into his pack and glared at the river, which for the past three weeks had broken California's promise of boundless gold. Like a rebuke from heaven, the July sun's rays penetrated the cluster of giant redwoods and smothered him with wave after wave of searing heat. No, t'was unfair to blame the land. That's what Da had said whilst the great famine ravaged their farm. The soil couldn't provide what it did not possess. But him? Aye, he was the true promise breaker. A thief. A failure who had to place Kelly, his own sister, in the care of others.

No matter how he tried, God would never reward the efforts of a man like him.

Yet he must keep going. Keep trying to honor his promise to Ma and Da so their memory never dimmed. Donovan knelt and continued to break camp, packing his dwindling food supplies along with his pick and pan. One more stretch of unpanned river remained in the land to which he'd staked a claim, and he refused to stop till he'd searched every last piece of gravel. He couldn't return to England empty-handed, not with Kelly counting on him to reverse their dire lot in life. Again.

This time around he had to get things right.

Shouldering his heavy pack, Donovan strode along the river, its clear waters rippling over blue and gray stones. *Kelly, dear lass.* How she loved to skip stones. What might she be doing today? Helping Mrs. Tooley with her seamstress trade, no doubt. Mending dresses, darning socks, and the like. Hopefully the mischievous sprite wasn't laboring too hard or walking through town without her crutch. A hollow ache burrowed in his chest. He quickened to a march.

In a few days' time he must hazard a trip into town, amongst the rough crowds of ungoverned forty-niners and greedy shopkeepers out to leech the prospectors dry, and send Kelly another packet of money. Despite Mrs. Tooley's kind offers, he couldn't allow himself to be beholden to any soul, especially not one residing in Brookside. Doing so could only fuel the false accusation of theft made against him by. . .that woman.

The one who had forced him to leave Kelly behind, flee Brookside in disgrace.

The one who had stolen his reputation in the town, his respected position as valet to Baronet Heyer, everything he'd labored for after immigrating to England during the famine. Donovan's feet pounded the earth faster and faster as if to escape the past and the infuriating smile that still haunted him. The smile of Miss Sophia Heyer. *"Only confess, tell the truth as a witness of good character, and I shall be sure to give you a fine reference."*

"A confession from me would not be truth. I've done nothing wrong!"

Out of breath, Donovan halted and braced himself against a tree. Coarse bark pressed into his face, and the scent of pine sap battered him, all whilst memory of his defiance rang in his ears. He had done nothing wrong. That day. Yet what member of the privileged English gentry would believe the word of an Irishman with a past conviction? Not one. If he wanted to create a better life for Kelly, he must accept that and move onward.

Besides, he had no way or hope of ever gaining vindication.

Miss Heyer had won, by means of superior position and wealth.

Wiping sticky sap from his cheek, Donovan adjusted his pack and marched on an hour or so to his previously scouted new work site. After setting camp and having a quick meal, he snatched up the pan and lumbered to the river. He'd probably find nothing, but he wouldn't waste a moment's daylight to idleness. Once he had waded into the cool water, he knelt in the refreshing flow. He dipped the pan in the current with both hands, scooping gravel from the river bed, lifted it out, and shook. As the water seeped away, something gleaming settled in the pan.

Donovan stared, blinked. *Gold.* Two nuggets, each about the size of a small potato. At sixteen American dollars apiece, these were worth several months' wages. Might there be more? He tucked the nuggets in a shirt pocket for safekeeping and panned again. Three larger nuggets emerged. A third scoop produced five more shining lumps the dark yellow of crystallized honey. With his pockets now bulging, he ran to the shore and dumped out his pack. He gently placed the gold nuggets inside and then hastened back to the river.

By the time the sun had retreated behind the snowcapped mountains, his pack overflowed with gold. Donovan stared at it glinting in the campfire's light, just stared. Sweat and water drenched every part of him, but he didn't care. With one hand, he picked up a single nugget. He'd done it. He had found enough to start life over again, purchase a cottage, care for Kelly under his own roof. Mayhap, after they had settled, he might even buy a horse. Something he'd not owned since their days in Ireland.

A laugh shook his chest. Forget a cottage and single horse. He could purchase ten horses, if he chose, and a manor with acres of land. Donovan turned the gold over and over in his fingers. He was rich. As rich as Baronet Heyer. His fingers stilled. Miss Heyer no longer had the advantage of wealth. The gold now in his possession made them equal in fortune, and if he used it wisely, they might soon be equal in stature. He slowly clenched his fist round the nugget. Now he could win the vindication he deserved. Now he could beat Miss Heyer at her own game and exact justice. After what she'd done—accusing him without cause and firing him without reference after years of faithful service—she deserved to pay.

And he would ensure she paid in full.

Donovan could never be as good a man as Da anyway, so what did he have to lose?

◆　◆　◆

Sophia clutched Papa's feeble arm as they took a turn about the garden, allowing him to bear weight upon her shoulder in lieu of a cane, which would no doubt alarm her sisters, as they always expected her to stumble. Thank God husbands and the lures of high society corralled their critical gazes in London. Now if only the post would have the decency to lose their snide letters, she'd have no cause for worry. Except, of course, the upcoming summer fair.

Inhaling the sweetness violets whispered into the breeze, Sophia placed her free hand on Papa's arm for added stability and rubbed her thumb along the sleeve of his dear woolen coat, his final present from Mamma. Bother, how she'd muddled things. Instead of maintaining Mamma's shining legacy, she had faltered under the burden of organizing the fair until its previous glory had all but been forgotten. This year she must turn things around. She couldn't let Mamma down with another miserable failure. Nor could she afford one. Soon the townspeople might run out of patience, or worse, her sisters might cease pretending to possess the virtue.

Perhaps reminiscing about Mamma would spark a much-needed plan. "Papa, can you recall Mamma's original purpose for establishing an annual fair in Brookside?"

Papa's chestnut-hued eyes stayed fixed on the task of watching his step. "It wasn't so much a purpose." His silver brows drew together, accentuating the dignified wrinkles on his forehead. "More like a heart-stirring passion. Despite having traveled extensively, Caroline loved her hometown better than anyplace in the world and desired to create a day when it should be celebrated. When people from across the county and beyond could gather in Brookside to admire its rich land and skilled craftsmen."

She need not travel to know the world held no finer place than Brookside. Without stepping beyond the garden's manicured hedges, she could envision every proof of this fact. The rolling hills of plush grass below, the azure sky incapable of producing a gray cloud above, and between, the cobblestone bridge that carried one over the brook and into the town of timber-framed shops and homes. Every stone, board, and blade of grass was branded on her heart. How could her sisters prefer the smoggy streets of London to this quaint paradise?

Sophia gnawed her bottom lip. She should not trouble herself attempting to understand them. For they had never bothered to understand silly little Sophia.

Gypsy's distinctive whinny awakened Sophia from her daydreaming and drew her gaze past the hedges to the stables. Poor Gypsy was growing more restless as her pregnancy progressed. Later she ought to take Gypsy out for some air on a tethered stroll, give the energetic mare a chance to unwind. As she and Papa made their turn, the view shifted from the stables to the attached carriage house. Mamma's voice tiptoed through her mind. *"Phaetons are for bachelors and coxcombs, and you, my dear, are neither."*

A smile erased the tension in Sophia's jaw. How distraught Papa had been when Mamma requested he sell his sporting phaeton, unconvinced of its *dangerous risk* to his health. Until the accident that ruined his knee. Now the only thing stored in the carriage house was the family's sensible coach and. . .the carousel! She paused midstep, halting Papa at her side. Of course, why had she not remembered it before?

"Something wrong, my dear? Am I too sprightly for you to keep pace?" Papa offered a crooked grin.

"Indeed, sir, your record cantor across the garden has left me winded. I beg mercy for the remainder of our walk lest I faint from weariness." *Or lose hold of the idea beginning to unfurl*. With a wink, Sophia helped Papa make the final turn and directed him toward the house. "That carousel Mamma commissioned for me ages ago, is it not still in working order?"

"I believe so. Although, probably in dire need of a coat of paint. Whatever are you thinking, Sophy? You've the same starry look from when you were a girl of six, begging to ride my stallion."

"I'm thinking Mamma's forgotten carousel may be just the thing to revive the summer fair. We can make the carousel a showcase for our craftsmen's skill by renovating it into something truly unique and grand. Perhaps we could even modernize it with the latest technology. Only recently I've read an article in the paper about farmers replacing their horse-drawn plows with machines powered by steam engine. If our fair could display the world's first steam-powered carousel, such a fantastic sight would be sure to draw visitors and return commerce to Brookside."

Papa squeezed her arm gently. "You always were my dreamer."

Odd how that word possessed such a different meaning coming from Papa than from her sisters, especially Gertrude. From her prim mouth, there was no higher insult.

When they reached the house, Sophia led Papa through the pane-windowed doors and into the parlor. Papa claimed his favorite chair beside the fire, and she aided in elevating his feet upon the velvet tuffet. As she straightened, Rowland entered with the day's mail on a silver tray. Sophia smiled away a cringe. *Please no letters from Gertrude, please, not today.*

Refusing to hazard a glance, Sophia took hold of the tray's contents—a single correspondence—with a nod and expression of gratitude she did not feel. His task completed, Rowland exited in silence. Sophia simply held the letter for a moment. Not wanting to look down lest she find Gertrude's crimson wax seal. However, look she eventually must. One cannot evade the howl of a thunderstorm, not even in the presumed safety of one's home. She inhaled and forced her gaze downward. The familiar fleur-de-lis imprinted in blazing red seemed to set her cheeks afire. *Ragwort.*

Sophia trudged to her writing desk nestled in the corner and sank to her chair, head downcast as if Gertrude's letter were the wag of a scolding finger and she a mere child sent to the corner for punishment. She sighed, stomach roiling. *Might as well get it over and done.* Seizing her letter opener, she broke the note's seal and studied the austere, flawless handwriting she'd always admired.

March 11, 1850

> *Dearest Sophia,*
> *I would remind you to keep Papa firmly bundled on his afternoon walks, however, I'm now convinced bestowing such sage counsel on you is a futile effort. In fact, our sisters and I tire of fighting your stubborn nature.*

Just as she tired of their never-ending stampede of condescension. She might be the youngest of the six sisters, but at five and twenty, she was no infant in pram. Sophia dragged in an exaggerated breath to cool the increasing heat in her cheeks. *Brave face now.* She had endured countless such letters of censure in the four years since Mamma's passing. She could bear through one more. Certainly she could. Holding her shoulders rigid, Sophia read further.

> *Therefore, I've devised a proposition, a wager of sorts, which I hope will put our disagreements to an end.*

A wager? Whatever did Gertrude have up her sleeve?

> *Here are the conditions. If you can manage to make a success of this year's fair, myself and our sisters promise to henceforth cease from recommending our services and acquired wisdom in your affairs.*

Sophia's breath stalled. No more meddling or interfering? Forever? What was the catch?

> *However, if the fair once more proves to be beyond your capabilities, you must agree to do as we have advised since dearest Mamma's passing: convince Papa to sell the estate in Brookside and join us in London.*

In other words, admit defeat and let them assume control. Sophia exhaled, elbows sinking onto the desk. That was quite a catch. Leaving Brookside. Where she had been born and raised. Where memories of Mamma remained vibrant in each stairway banister, rolling hill, and summer fair.

"If the fair once more proves to be beyond your capabilities. . ."

Sophia shut her eyes. Memories dragged her back in time to Mamma's funeral where all five sisters had ambushed her with a similar proposition. Similar insults. Gertrude's voice reemerged, grave as her mourning dress. *"You might know about horses, little Sophia, but you know absolutely nothing about keeping house, nursing a cripple, or organizing the needs of Brookside. You simply aren't fit for the task."*

Sophia's eyes opened to avoid the verbal barrage only to receive a written slap.

> *My husband has kindly offered Papa our home wherein he can receive the sufficient care he lacks, and Prudence's invitation to take you on as our niece's chaperone during her debut season next spring still graciously stands. While it's unlikely to happen at your age, remember there is always the hope of you procuring a husband thus employed.*

How they loved to point out she was the only sister unwed.

> *This wager can of course be forgotten, if you wish to come to London now. Consider your options wisely before you answer, little sister.*

> *Ever at your service,*
> *Gertrude*

Folding the letter in half, Sophia buried it within her desk drawer. Yet Gertrude's words seeped from the woodwork like a foul poison. *"Beyond your capabilities. Care Papa lacks."*

"You simply aren't fit for the task."

Sophia's lip gave way to a tremor, her posture withering further. She was tired of being the inferior sister. Tired of Gertrude's words always being proven right. Over her shoulder, Papa comfortably read the day's paper. Whatever Gertrude said, he would not thrive in London, taken away from his routine, his familiar house, and memories of Mamma. And neither would she. They belonged in Brookside, and it was time to prove, once and for all, that she was capable of keeping them here.

Straightening her shoulders and lifting her head, Sophia reached for a pen.

Chapter Two

April 1850

Mr. Donovan Gallagher, master of Wilmore Manor.

That had a fine ring. On the far side of the Brookside bridge, leaning against the gray cobbles, Donovan admired the deed to his new home, paid for in full and acquired under his name. He ran a thumb over the fine parchment. No more impatient landlords barking for rent or threatening eviction. No more living under another man's roof without even a bed to call his own. No more masters, livery, or life in service.

Now he was the master. Now he could finally care for Kelly.

Donovan rolled the deed and, tucking it in the pocket of his new overcoat, strode across the bridge into the heart of town. On either side of the cobbled street, timber-frame homes and shops clustered together like rows of spring barley. Unique signs still hung over each shop, creaking as they swayed on their chains. A black mallet speckled with rust dangled above the smithy whilst the familiar clang of iron striking iron resounded within. Not a stone or board had changed in Brookside.

T'was likely local opinion about him hadn't changed either. Not with that woman influencing people with her unfair judgments.

But once tell of his golden fortune got round, it should repair some of the damage done to his name. Wealth had a way of changing folks' minds about a person. He patted the house title in his pocket. He could just imagine Kelly's expression when he showed her the deed. Sparks of joy would illuminate her green eyes as a smile lifted her cheeks. Her crutches would fall, clattering forgotten to the floor, and he'd scoop up the wee lass and give her a twirl.

As he passed under the carpentry shop's timber hammer, the scent of sawdust overwhelmed and then dissipated. Kelly could have her way with the house. New furnishings, whatever her heart desired. Mayhap it'd be wise to construct a gazebo, so Kelly might enjoy the beautiful gardens from the shade. They could oversee the gardens together, if she liked. Most of his time would be spent aiding the tenant farmers in revitalizing the crops, which he'd been warned were in sore shape, especially compared to the neighboring Heyer estate.

Donovan took a left, just after the clock maker's shop with its suspended bronze watch hands. A chorus of *tick-tick-tock* followed him a ways. Mayhap choosing the manor adjacent to Heyer Hall had been unwise. Rash, even. He studied the cobblestones underfoot. In California, seeking retribution from Miss Heyer had seemed so alluring. A worthwhile perusal of justice. Yet now with the prospect of cultivating land and caring for Kelly under his own roof, did he really want to risk such an endeavor?

He raised his head and spied the spool-shaped sign for Mrs. Tooley's shop. *Kelly.*

Donovan covered the remaining distance in a few bounding strides. His heart pattered fast and frenzied like drops of the first hard rain after an extended drought. *Now to make up for time lost.* Straightening his silk-lined waistcoat, he knocked.

Mrs. Tooley answered, a filled pincushion sewn on the top of her bonnet, just like the day he left. "Donovan Gallagher, why I never. Back from the continent. And in one piece?"

"Aye, I've come to collect a sprite I heard lives hereabouts." Donovan entered the shop, empty of customers, with its shelves of fabric and garments. Where had that sprite got to? Striding to the back, he halted at the bottom of the staircase to Mrs. Tooley's second-floor apartment. "Kelly!"

He waited, gaze planted on the stairs.

Mrs. Tooley tugged his sleeve. "Kelly's not—"

"Out o' bed? The wee rascal." Donovan chuckled and slapped the banister. "Greet the day, sprite."

Creaking responded to his call, but it wasn't the groan of a loose stair plank. Nay, t'was more akin to the sound of a carriage wheel. And it wasn't coming from upstairs. Donovan eyed the door to the shop's back room as it swung open.

Kelly held the door ajar with one hand and, with the other, wheeled herself into the shop. Donovan's breath caught. Wheeled? Not walked, not hobbled on crutches. His sister—who once danced jigs in the kitchen whilst Ma and Da clapped time—rolled toward him on a chair fitted with two wheels. An invalid chair. His heart slowed to an irregular pitter. *God, no.*

"Donovan, am I ever glad to see you." Kelly's bright tone drew his attention to her smiling face, eyes sparkling like he'd imagined. The only thing that had turned out as he'd imagined. How she'd changed. He'd left a gangly-armed girl and returned to find a little woman. In an invalid chair. Would any man look beyond those wheels to Kelly's beauty? Was she to be denied the happy life she deserved—because of *his* transgressions?

Kelly grabbed his hand. "I wrote months ago so t'would not be a shock. . .but I see my letter didn't reach you. Don't look grim, Donovan. You've returned home—this is a happy day."

Brookside was not home, and he was beginning to doubt he'd ever experience another happy day. Donovan knelt beside the invalid chair, squeezing Kelly's hand. He fought to keep his voice from breaking. "Did you take a fall?"

"Nay. I just. . .couldn't hold myself up with the crutches anymore. My legs couldn't bear the weight o' me. The doctor called it a 'natural progression' o' my condition."

Natural? There was nothing natural about a woman of twenty withering away to lameness, unable to walk or even stand. "Isn't there anything can be done?" Donovan turned to Mrs. Tooley. "If it's a matter o' payment—"

"No. Nothing like that, Mr. Gallagher." Pity saturated Mrs. Tooley's round face, pincushion bobbing atop the bonnet as she shook her head. "I promise Kelly's had the best care possible. The doctor has done all he can, all anyone can."

Donovan's jaw trembled, clenched. Why must God be discontent punishing him alone for his sins? Must He punish Kelly, too?

Kelly sweetened her tone, trying to cheer him. "Let's not talk about what we can't change. You're returned to me, and we've much to look forward to now. Church on Sundays. . .and the summer fair's in a few months. T'was small last year, but I didn't mind. I always enjoy the fair so, even more than Christmas. And havin' you there this year will make it all the better."

Much good having him round now would do. He should have been here months ago.

"And you must tell me of your travels. Was California beautiful? Was the gold rush as fantastic as the newspapers tell? Did you feel like a pirate searchin' for buried treasure?" Her voice lowered to a whisper. "Was there much gold left?"

A heavy smile attempted to lift Donovan's mouth. At least he'd done one thing right by Kelly. He removed the deed from his coat. "Enough."

Kelly unrolled the fine paper and gasped. "Wilmore Manor? It's ours?"

"Ours."

"Why I never." Mrs. Tooley clapped a hand over her mouth.

An airy smile floated onto Kelly's lips. "Let's go see it. I'll fetch my shawl." With the deed on her lap, she rolled into the back room.

Donovan faced Mrs. Tooley. "Were the parcels o' money I sent enough to cover everything, including the wheelchair?"

"Money?" Brow furrowing, Mrs. Tooley tilted her head and lost a few needles off the pincushion. "Mr. Gallagher. . .I never received any parcels."

Donovan's jaw slacked. *No.* All that money. . .lost. How could so much go wrong? Kelly in a wheelchair, and he'd failed to provide for her needs. Failed to protect her. Failed to be there when she needed him most. All because of that woman.

"Don't fret, Mr. Gallagher. I—"

"No." Donovan reached into his coat and withdrew a wallet. "A good man cares for his family, pays his debts. I may not be capable of the former, but I shan't fail to do the latter. Write an honest account o' Kelly's incurred costs. I'll pay in full." But he wouldn't be the only one.

Mrs. Tooley reached behind the sales counter, pulled out an account ledger, and on a clean sheet of paper, started a tally. Her gaze blew from ledger, to paper, to him. Clearing her throat, she spoke as if to make the situation less discomfited. "Now that you're no longer in service, you're eligible to attend town council meetings. Miss Heyer has scheduled the next for tomorrow afternoon. They'll be discussing the upcoming fair, I believe. Think you'll attend?"

The seed of an idea dropped into Donovan's mind. "Aye, I will that." He had business to tend to with Miss Sophia Heyer.

◆　◆　◆

Nothing must go wrong today. Sophia examined the town hall for any infractions against orderliness—wooden floor freshly swept, chairs aligned in straight rows of even number, all facing the dais situated in the very center of the farthest wall—nothing out of place. Good. With Papa's life in Brookside on the line, she couldn't afford anything other than perfection. For that was exactly what Gertrude would expect.

Sophia faced the closed double doors that kept the waiting townspeople back like racehorses at a starting barrier. She inhaled, released it slowly. *Brave face.* She reined in a smile and swung the doors open. "Good afternoon, do come in."

A stream of people entered, returning her greetings while she attended the door. Mrs. Tooley, pincushion stuffed with needles like so many hat pins. Mr. Stroud, hands scrubbed clean but still reeking of smoke from his forge. Mr. Brown of Hillside farm on the waning Wilmore estate. Each received a smile and cordial "How are you?" as they took their seats. Sophia surveyed the group. Everyone accounted for and punctual. Perhaps a sign from God that all would go well this time?

"Miss Heyer, how is your sister?" The deceptively charming, melodious voice tangled Sophia's stomach. Perhaps not.

Sophia rescued her countenance from the brink of a wince. "Gertrude and her family are well, Mrs. Corbyn, thank you for inquiring." Even though it was completely unnecessary as she corresponded with Gertrude almost daily. Like a French spy reporting to Napoleon.

"What a fine turnout." Mrs. Corbyn fluttered a fan before her perfect skin, irritatingly free of blemish or freckle. "Pity we cannot expect more than this number at the fair."

Every freckle on Sophia's face and arms burned. Why must people keep reminding her of her previous failures? As if they did not weigh on her every day? "I'm aware last year's attendance was low, but—"

"Low?" A cruel mixture of scoff and giggle erupted from Mrs. Corbyn's dainty frame. "If you subtracted Brookside residents, a child could count those in attendance on their tiny hands."

"That's a bit of an exaggera—"

"And when I think how grand the fair once was, I could almost weep. If your sweet mamma had peered from heaven last year, I'm certain she would have wept. Perhaps that explains the rain which soaked the few brave faces who remained past noon."

The words hit Sophia with the force of a hoofed kick. "I should start the meeting." Before she began to weep or surrendered to the temptation to slap Mrs. Corbyn's flawless face. She stepped away from the door.

"Then I should take my seat." Mrs. Corbyn brushed against Sophia's shoulder with a delicately concealed, oh-so-accidental shove. She glanced behind, all sweetness. "And Sophia, if you manage to be elected chairman of the fair again, know that you'll have my full support."

Demonstrated by a kindhearted shove in front of a raging stallion, no doubt. Sophia emphasized her unfortunately masculine height by straightening her spine to the utmost. "I intend to do my best to be worthy of Brookside's support, as Mamma was before me. Your support, however, is neither required nor wanted. Therefore, unless you can manage to sit through the meeting's duration without a single incident of backbiting, gossiping, or superfluous fan fluttering, I suggest you return home. Perhaps write Gertrude a letter."

Mrs. Corbyn gasped, and fan flitting as if taking flight, she sauntered homeward.

Sophia closed the doors and walked toward the dais. *Good riddance.* She might have lost one vote, but it was not as though she had competition. Brookside had awarded her fair chairman ever since Mamma's death, conducting the election purely out of ceremonious tradition. There was no reason that should change now. Despite their lack of confidence in her abilities.

At the dais, she faced the gathering. "Thank you for coming to today's election for fair chairman, a position which holds the responsibility of—"

A squeaking hinge turned heads as a tall gentleman entered. Who could this be, late no less? Mrs. Tooley stood to greet the stranger while half the gathering shot him disapproving looks and the rest offered smiles of recognition. He did look a trifle familiar, but she couldn't place his face or retrieve the name. The stranger sat beside Mrs. Tooley and waved for her to continue.

Impertinent man. "As I was saying, the chairman is responsible for planning Brookside's annual summer fair. I will now open the floor to nominations."

Mr. Stroud rose. "I nominate Miss Heyer."

Sophia smiled. Mr. Stroud must've approved of her note about the carousel renovations. Having his assistance would ease the process. She allowed a few moments of ceremonious silence to tick by. "As there are no more nominations, we—"

"I nominate the lord of Wilmore Manor." Having shot to his feet, the stranger now stood amid the gathering's mixture of amused grins and muttered outrage.

This man's interruptions were becoming increasingly irritating. "Wilmore Manor has no master. The estate has been for sale since Lord Wilmore fell upon hard times." Brought on by his insatiable gambling addiction. She'd been grateful to lose such a neighbor.

The stranger tucked a thumb under his overcoat's collar, a smug air puffing his chest. "It was for sale. I purchased it yesterday."

Purchased? Then this cheeky, brazen man was to be her neighbor? "You are the new master of Wilmore? Then am I to understand that you are nominating. . .yourself?"

"I am."

The nerve. Of all the prideful, arrogant, conceited. . . How dare he presume to waltz into town, into her meeting, disregarding every semblance of order and ceremony and punctuality. A smirk formed on the stranger's face as everyone in the town hall stared at her, awaiting a ruling. Yet what could she do but approve his nomination? There were no rules against nominating oneself. No polite way to refuse. Sophia ground her teeth. Fine, she would entertain his pompous ideas of grandeur. It mattered not. She would surely be voted chairman over an outsider.

Sophia gave a nod of defeat. "Any further nominations?" All remained silent. "Very well. Please locate the ballots which were placed atop your chairs, write your vote, and bring it to the dais for counting."

Silence prevailed except for the *scritch-scratch* of pencils on paper. After a few moments, all the votes had been submitted. Sophia invited the reverend to count the votes as per tradition. When he had finished, he stood to make the announcement.

The reverend cleared his throat. "The results are as follows: ten votes Miss Heyer and ten Mr. Gallagher. For the first time in the history of Brookside's summer fair, we have a tie and co-chairmen."

A tie? Sophia's stomach plummeted. Half the town chose a stranger over her, someone they had known for all her life? Did they truly doubt her so much? A quiver unsettled her jaw. If that was how the town felt, she'd respect their decision. "The votes have it. Meeting dismissed."

Sophia rotated away from everyone to gather her things in her reticule. She had too much riding on this fair to let a usurping stranger upset her. However much she disliked the circumstances, she must make the best of things. For Papa's sake. She waited while the stranger finished a conversation with his new tenant, Mr. Brown, who must have provided one of the votes in his employer's favor. Once Mr. Brown headed for the doors, she walked across the hall. *Brave face now.* She extended a gloved hand to her co-chair. "Congratulations. I look forward to working with you, Mr. . . . ?"

The stranger glanced at her hand but refused to accept the gesture. "It's Gallagher, Mr. Donovan Gallagher."

Donovan. Sophia's breath stalled within her throat and solidified. It couldn't be. He was in California. The stranger's green eyes hardened, boring straight into her own with a disturbing intensity—an anger—she knew all too well.

Sophia's hand withered as it dropped to her skirt. The man before her was in fact Donovan Gallagher, Papa's former valet whom she'd fired for stealing a gold pocket watch. The gold pocket watch she'd found too late. . .in her lady's maid's possession. How could she make the fair a success while working alongside her biggest mistake?

Chapter Three

*S*wear *not ta do a thing an' it's good as done.*" How had Da always known the truth about everything? Donovan strode up the neatly graveled path, framed with rows of spherically trimmed hedges, toward the home of his former employer. He tugged at his tight cravat. Aye, he'd sworn to never again step foot in Heyer Hall, but that oath had been made by a valet who tended the baronet's wardrobe and entered through the servants' back door. That Donovan would be keeping his oath.

It was Mr. Donovan Gallagher, master of Wilmore Manor and co-chairman of Brookside's summer fair, who aimed to keep his appointment for tea with Miss Heyer. And do so by means of the front door. After all, how could he refuse the honor of such an invitation? Or the prime opportunity it offered to discreetly find means of Miss Heyer's downfall.

As Donovan reached the imposing white columns, standing sentry at the entrance in their green livery of climbing rose vines, the door opened. Mr. Rowland held the knob, wrinkled skin ready to slip off his face as it sagged from baggy eyes, to deflated cheeks, to wobbly jowls. His voice tolled deep and melancholy as mourning bells. "Welcome, Mr. Gallagher. I'm to escort you to the parlor."

Ah, ever the cheerful soul. Donovan stepped into the foyer. "I'm happy to see ya, too."

Mr. Rowland gave Donovan a frigid glare before heading toward the parlor. Donovan followed down the long hallway sown with portraits of the Heyer family. Clearly he was still naught but a thief in Rowland's eyes, as he was to half of Brookside. Wealth might've swayed those now in his employ, along with shopkeepers who wanted the business of refurbishing Wilmore, but his good name was by no means restored.

A concealed servant door opened, severing Donovan's view of Mr. Rowland with a barrier of oak. He halted. In the doorway, the two footmen of the house waved whilst a few maids attempted to peek over their shoulders.

"Is it true you found gold, Donny?" Young Henry's eyes beamed with curiosity.

The elder footman Nigel slapped Henry's shoulder. " 'Course he did, half-wit. Just look at his clothes. And why else would he be having tea with Miss Heyer, I wonder? Our Donny's a gentleman now with a gentleman's fortune." He quieted to a whisper, lifting an eyebrow. "Speakin' of, could I borrow a few shillings? My girl's got her eye on a bonnet from Tooley's."

"Rascal." Donovan laughed. "Best keep things quiet and proper or Mr. Row—"

"What's this?" Mr. Rowland appeared round the door, resulting in gasps from the maids. His jowls wobbled. "I don't recall the Queen making this a national holiday. Back to work."

The rustle of skirts and click of heels announced the maids' escape downstairs. Henry flashed a sheepish grin and Nigel a playful wink as they trailed behind. Mr. Rowland shut the door with a firm thud. "Come, Donovan, we don't want to keep Miss Heyer waiting."

Actually, having to wait for once in her life might do the princess a world of good. With Mr. Rowland in the lead, Donovan trekked farther down the corridor and entered the parlor. Warm sunshine fell through two french doors onto a sofa flanked by side chairs, opposite a barren fireplace. Between the sofa and nearest chair sat a three-tiered rolling table. A steaming teapot and pair of cups occupied the first tier whilst an array of tiny food had been arranged on the bottom tiers. His hostess, however, was nowhere to be seen.

Mr. Rowland's wrinkles gathered in exaggerated trenches. "Mind your tongue this time." With that, he left Donovan alone in the parlor.

Donovan huffed. If he chose to watch his mouth, it'd be only to prevent Miss Heyer from suspecting his true motivation for accepting her invitation. Justice. His gaze roved about the room, panning, searching, and every now and again, glancing at the door. Where would the princess hide her secrets? A small writing table with numerous drawers occupied the far corner. Mayhap he could again strike gold. He hurried round the sofa and gripped a drawer knob.

A latch clicked.

Donovan whirled about as Miss Heyer opened the door.

Miss Heyer nodded in greeting. "Pardon the unseemly delay, Mr. Gallagher. Papa is accustomed to taking tea in the parlor with my company, and persuading him to alter routine, even for one afternoon, took more convincing than I anticipated. You know how habitual Papa can be." She granted a faint smile as if they shared a confidence.

Was that the only acknowledgment of his past employment she meant to offer?

Leaving the parlor door open—no doubt to protect her glistening reputation—Miss Heyer sat beside the tea table and proceeded to pour them each a cup. Like they were at some ridiculous society tea party. Like nothing had ever happened between them. Like she'd never forced him away from Kelly. Donovan's teeth grated. Miss Heyer's privileged life had cultivated a fine actress.

With a wave of her hand, Miss Heyer motioned toward the sofa. "I am quite keen to discuss plans for the fair, but before we begin, I wish to say how delighted I am to have your aid in the process as my co-chairman."

Donovan swallowed a snort. Oh, she'd made her *delight* clear when she'd failed to recognize him at yesterday's meeting. Failed to acknowledge her mistake and apologize like a decent person. He took the offered seat but refused to dignify her sugarcoated lie with a response.

Using a pair of silver tongs, Miss Heyer arranged selections of the dainty foods on the two plates. "It is very important to me that the fair should be a success."

Now that he would respond to. Donovan accepted his cup and relaxed into the sofa, crossing one knee over the other. He kept his voice casual. "Understandable. Seein' as the last few fairs were such stark disappointments."

Miss Heyer's fingers fumbled, dropping the tongs onto the cart with a less than graceful clatter. Her fake smile managed to remain intact as if held together by the freckles dusting her lightly bronzed face. But it now appeared taut. Fragile.

Aye, let the princess squirm. "I heard tell attendance at the last fair was so minimal, stall keepers had to close four hours early." Donovan sipped some tea and then glared at Miss Heyer over the cup's rim. "This year we don't want to be repeating mistakes."

Miss Heyer's smile fractured. "I. . .am sure we have learned from those past mistake. . .and are quite sorry for them."

Lifting an eyebrow, Donovan allowed a grain of contempt to sprout in his words. "Are ya really now?"

"Pardon my intrusion, ma'am." Mr. Rowland stood in the entry, addressing Miss Heyer. "Your father is complaining of an unusual draft in the study. He requested that I bring him the afghan from his usual spot."

"Oh dear." Sighing, Miss Heyer stood and fetched a blanket off the chair on the opposite end of the sofa. "I shall accompany you, Rowland. Perhaps I can shoo this silly notion of drafts from his mind. The study is quite well insulated. Excuse me, Mr. Gallagher."

Donovan nodded as Miss Heyer left with Mr. Rowland, thankfully shutting the door behind. Now was his chance. Donovan rushed to the writing desk and quietly began opening drawers. Scissors, wax seal, bottle of ink. Nothing useful. He glanced over his shoulder before opening the larger drawer. A stack of papers, no, letters. Now these held promise.

Donovan opened a red-sealed letter, taking in the words quickly. It appeared to be from one of the other Heyer sisters.

> *I've devised a proposition, a wager of sorts, which I hope will put our disagreements to an end.*

A wager? He absorbed the words faster.

> *. . .if the fair once more proves to be beyond your capabilities, you must agree to do as we have advised since dearest Mamma's passing: convince Papa to sell the estate in Brookside and join us in London.*

Donovan folded the letter and glanced at the door again. This was too perfect. The exact opportunity he needed for Miss Heyer to meet justice. But had Miss Heyer accepted the wager? He returned the letter to the drawer as he'd found it and located another with the same red seal.

> *I admit to hoping that you would have better judgment than to accept my wager, but now it is done, I hope it will result in what is best for us all.*

What was best for them all was for Miss Heyer to be driven from Brookside in disgrace. Justice achieved in poetic style. And all he had to do was sabotage the summer fair.

"I always enjoy the fair so, even more than Christmas."

Ack, Kelly. Donovan put the note in the drawer with a thunk. Mayhap this wasn't so perfect. If he ruined the fair, Kelly would be disappointed. And if his sabotage were discovered, it could ruin her new life in Brookside. He trudged back to his place on the sofa. *"And havin' you there this year will make it all the better."* He scratched at the disgusting pomade he'd used to tame his hair. Mayhap he needed to find another way? Were his actions even right?

Donovan gripped his chin, staring at the untouched plates. When he'd first been taken on at Heyer Hall as a lowly footman, he'd have been the one to serve tea under the watchful supervision of Mr. Rowland. Years and years he'd worked to train, gain respect, and earn the promotion to valet. Years of labor, wasted. All because Miss Heyer refused to look beyond her prejudices and see the truth.

He scoffed. *Right and wrong.* Since when had right or wrong mattered to the people of Brookside? Not then. No one had questioned his unfair dismissal or defended his honor. No one had cared, so why should it matter now? If Miss Heyer chose to deal bad hands, then she deserved to get one. And he needn't worry about being found out, because this time he'd not fail. His plan would succeed. And one day, Kelly would understand the poetic justice of it. As for her disappointment, it would be temporary. There'd be other summer fairs. Better fairs.

Without Miss Sophia Heyer.

Chapter Four

One hour and fifteen minutes late.

If Mr. Gallagher were still in her employ, Sophia might fire him all over again.

Pacing outside the entrance to the stables, her gaze alternated between the pathway flanked in the distance by two horizontal walls of trimmed hedges and the small watch dangling upside down from a brooch on her bodice. How unfortunate that one couldn't fire an elected co-chairman. More unfortunate still when one's co-chairman was bent on dragging his feet like a stubborn plow horse. Since her invitation to tea the week prior —a disastrous attempt on her part to make peace—Mr. Gallagher had canceled one scheduled meeting, *forgotten* another for which he had volunteered the date and time, and otherwise been a complete nuisance.

Sophia's posture failed. She did not know which was worse—Mr. Gallagher's obvious disdain or the fact that she rightfully deserved every biting word, glower, and minute of purgatorial delay. *"I've done nothing wrong!"* She could not escape those words, nor the truth she had failed to see. She blinked, and for a moment there was Fanny, the lady's maid she had personally interviewed and selected, attempting to return the pocket watch to its rightful place undiscovered. *"I just wanted one pretty thing in life to call my own, Miss Heyer. A new dress or bonnet, like in* Godey's *magazine. I never thought you'd fire him."*

But she had fired him.

Unjustly she had ruined Mr. Gallagher's reputation. Failed to make things right despite previous attempts. Indeed, she shared his disdain of Miss Sophia Heyer. Her stomach churned with anxiety she couldn't bridle. Whatever would she do if he exposed her mistake to the servants, the town, or worse, to Gertrude?

Brave face, Sophia. She could not permit worry or Mr. Gallagher's sourness to impede preparations for the fair. Somehow she must get his approval for the carousel renovations, and quickly. With only two months until fair day, further postponement might prevent the carousel from being ready on time. Hopefully, the cheery promise of May Day found Mr. Gallagher in a more agreeable mood. Assuming he decided to remember today's meeting.

Her pacing slowed. Perhaps she should walk to Wilmore? He could not refuse her entry, not without creating for himself further scandal. Perhaps being surrounded by his new wealth would set his ego at ease and allow them to get down to business. Actually... an appearance at Wilmore might also provide another chance to right her wrong. If she, the baronet's own daughter, made a point of being seen in Mr. Gallagher's company, it should mend his reputation by bringing around those in Brookside who still eyed him warily. Then, perhaps, she might finally earn his forgiveness?

Sophia strode up the path, turned left at the hedges, and collided with someone skull to skull. Pain burst through her head. *Ragwort*. Lowering her face and shutting her eyes, Sophia gingerly touched her brow. No abrasion, though fresh pain throbbed to life with every pulse of blood through her veins. She stifled a groan. Who would be so careless as to not watch where they were going?

She opened her eyes. A gentleman's hat lay in the gravel at her feet. *Oh no.* She lifted her head slowly. *Please don't be. . .*

Mr. Gallagher stood, glowering. A strand of black hair, freed from a thick application of pomade by the force of the blow, hung over one eye. Some emotion ranging in the area of irritation or anger strained his words. "You all right, Miss Heyer?"

No. She was tired, frustrated, pressured on all sides, and now, plagued by a pain who had neither the decency to leave her be nor to arrive on time. A pain she must convince to work in her favor. "Quite all right, Mr. Gallagher. Nothing a cold compress won't cure. Shall I have two prepared while we begin our meeting?"

"I'd have no need of a compress if ya hadn't assaulted me."

"You wouldn't have suffered an assault if you had the courtesy to be punctual." She bit her cheek as if she might snatch the words back. That remark wouldn't win him over.

Mr. Gallagher rescued his hat. "Anyone ever told ya that you've quite a hard head for a woman?"

Her sisters, every day of her life. Like them, Mr. Gallagher seemed determined to show her no kindness or favor. Tacking on a demure smile, Sophia closed the distance between them with one step and met Mr. Gallagher eye to eye. "Has anyone ever informed you that you possess the obstinate charm of a mule?"

He didn't bat an eye, simply smirked. "Worried my company might dirty your pure-bred reputation?"

Sophia swallowed a retort as her stomach again roiled. Was that a threat? Might he truly expose her mistake to the whole of Brookside? She must guard her hasty tongue, turn this around. "What concerns me, Mr. Gallagher, is that our inability to cooperate with one another could adversely impact the people of Brookside. There are some whose very livelihoods and well-being hinge upon the success of the fair we've been charged to plan. Can we not work together, for their sakes?"

Mr. Gallagher nodded in concession. "I won't be tardy again. You're not alone in wishin' to make this summer fair memorable." Sweeping a hand over his head, he fixed the damage done to his hair. "Now, what were you wanting to show me?"

Sophia walked back to the stable, with Mr. Gallagher on her heels, and threw the doors wide open. The warm, earthy aroma of hay combined with manure welcomed their entry. Her boots clacked on the floorboards as she guided Mr. Gallagher through the stables, lined on left and right with rows of stalls painted crisp white. Velveteen noses presented themselves over stall doors and tall ears faced forward in inquiry of their guest. Sophia paused to give each a scratch under the chin in silent hello and assurance that Mr. Gallagher meant them no harm.

A thunderous snort resounded from Gypsy's stall. Was it the mare's time?

Hoisting her skirts, Sophia hastened to the back of the stables. Inside the large stall

Gypsy had a young groom cornered, hands in the air as if he were being robbed by a bandit. In this case, one with a ravenous sweet tooth. She sighed. "Billy?"

A young male voice cracked. "Yes, m'lady."

"Do you have sugar chunks in your pocket?"

"Yes, m'lady."

Dear, foolish boy. "Keep calm and remain still for me, Billy." Sophia grabbed a lead rope from a nearby hook. Having done so, she entered the stall at a pace of leisure while clicking her tongue on the roof of her mouth and leaving the gate open for Billy's escape. "There, there. Gypsy Queen, let's not be a bully."

Gypsy's black ears turned toward her.

Clicking her tongue some more, Sophia ran a hand along Gypsy's back and then looped the rope over the mare's neck. "Come, your highness. Walk off." She gave the rope a gentle tug and made a kissing sound.

Gypsy followed the rope's lead to the other side of the stall. Sophia met Billy's gaze and nodded toward the open door. Eyes round as carriage wheels, Billy fled. Once he had done so, Sophia removed the rope and kissed Gypsy on her shaggy jowl. At least she had solved one problem today.

Exiting the stall, she latched the gate. "Are you well, Billy?"

Billy nodded and took up studying the floor.

"Good." Sophia exhaled. She hated giving reprimands, especially after what had happened before, but sometimes it had to be done. "Until you've had more training, Billy, I prefer that you not enter a stall without supervision. Please tell this to chief groomsman Gregory and also relay that Gypsy is only to be tended by him and myself from now on."

"Yes, Miss Heyer." The floor retained Billy's gaze.

Sophia ruffled Billy's hair. "Run along. I shan't tattle to your mother, this time."

A sigh whooshed from Billy's lips and created a grin as he ran out the back door to follow his instructions. She chuckled. *Silly lad.*

The clearing of a throat startled Sophia. *Oh yes, Mr. Gallagher.* He was now the one waiting and gawking at her in impatience—or was that interest?

"Pardon the delay." Sophia led Mr. Gallagher through the door at the end of the stables, which opened into a narrow hallway that contained a staircase to the groomers' rooms on the second level and another door across the way. Proceeding through that door, she entered the attached carriage house with its vaulted ceiling and exposed beams. She skirted their carriage and with one hand indicated the large mound beside it covered with a tarp.

"Behold, Mr. Gallagher." With both hands she yanked down the tarp in a flurry of dust to reveal Mamma's old carousel, paint chipped and flecked and peeling. "The centerpiece of Brookside's summer fair."

Mr. Gallagher raised an eyebrow.

"Hear me out." After the literal headache to get him here, he must at least listen. "I've read recently about steam-powered machines replacing farm horses. With said technology and the skill of local artisans, I believe our fair can boast the first steam-powered carousel. An attraction sure to draw people to Brookside. Smithy Stroud and our local clock maker, Mr. Dickerson—who has a notion to mechanize the horses themselves with a series of gears and pulleys—have drawn plans and await our approval to purchase the needed parts and begin the renovation." She withdrew the plans from her pocket and handed them to him. "What do you think?"

Mr. Gallagher examined the papers for a while before lifting his gaze to where hers waited. "I think that blow rattled your brain from its perch. What made ya think such a mad notion could work?"

Sophia's cheeks ignited with searing heat. Why had she imagined she could work with this odious man? Why must God side with her sisters by setting her up to fail? "Whatever made you think you could pass for a gentleman? The pomade fools no one. You lack every required virtue: chivalry, decorum, polite manner, k—"

"Ack! You're blind, woman, if you think any o' those things exist in the gentry. Let alone matter to them. To be called a gentleman or lady, ya just need a full purse and a pretty smile. And only the money need be real."

Another retort whipped into Sophia's mouth, ready to fling at Mr. Gallagher's insipid face, but she clamped her mouth shut. Argument was futile. She must alter the course of conversation. Change Mr. Gallagher's mind. For Papa's sake. She had agreed to Gertrude's wager in writing, and there could be no backing out now. She softened her tone. "Earlier we agreed to work for the sake of Brookside. This carousel is the only way I know to help them and save the fair. Unless you've a better idea to offer, please approve the design and let us move forward."

Mr. Gallagher examined the carousel plans once more, page by page, brows knit in thought. "I suppose it could serve our purposes." He shoved the plans in her direction. "If it fails to work, on your head be it."

She snatched the papers away. "Of course it will work."

It had to.

Chapter Five

Only a fortnight into their labor and already Sophia could tell the carousel would be a wonder, the sight of which would render her sisters utterly gobsmacked. And with any luck, their sudden muteness would be a permanent condition.

A grin played about Sophia's mouth as she oversaw the renovations in the carriage house. Mr. Stroud and Mr. Dickerson, shirtsleeves rolled to the elbows, worked installing the gear and pulley system that would enable the wooden horses to trot. Additional volunteers, including Brookside's carpenter, sanded the wooden surfaces in preparation for fresh paint. She couldn't wait to revive color to the poor, faded horses.

Restore the shine to dear Mamma's legacy.

An ache settled upon her chest, heavy and all too familiar. Tears shrouded her vision, threatening to make themselves known to present company. Sophia turned from the laboring men, toward the open doors, blinking away the mist until it was no more and only the ache remained. The ache, and Brookside's sky of brilliant cerulean. The bitter and the sweet. It seemed for her they would be forever intertwined. Unfortunately, she was inept at caring for the remaining sweetness in her life. A strong breeze lathered the clouds across the sky thick and foamy. *God, let them prevent Mamma from seeing the state of things. Let her still be proud.*

A shout drew Sophia's attention back to earth. Muffled voices and grunts grew louder as if drawing near the carriage house. Whatever could that be? Two footmen and four grooms shuffled inside, carrying a large crate, their knees bent and faces etched with strain. Had the steam engine arrived early? Sophia vacated their path and motioned them to set the crate beside the paint cans. "Is it the engine?"

The men nodded and lowered the crate with a collective moan.

As they dispersed to previous tasks, Sophia bit back a childish giggle. Heartbeat galloping, she rushed to the crate and ran her fingers across the shipping label from London. Now they were back on schedule. Perhaps the worst of her troubles had passed.

"Charmin' mule at your service. And I've a surprise."

Ragwort. She spun and looked trouble square in the face. "I'm not a fan of surprises, Mr. Gallagher." Especially not ones concerning him.

"You'll like this one. 'Tis going to make the fair a smash."

Heaven help her. "I am willing to consider any idea you supply and, if we come to a mutual agreement, assist you in implementing it."

"That's the surprise of it. 'Tis already done." Slipping a thumb under his lapel, Mr. Gallagher's face lit with an unsettling satisfaction. "I contacted a London reporter, and he's agreed to advertise the fair and write a follow-up story—'Triumph of Innovation:

Steam-Powered Carousel Amazes Fairgoers.' Assuming, o' course, the carousel works."
A dry chuckle emerged from his throat, one that seemed to expect her accompanied
amusement.

But she could not laugh.

One must breathe to laugh, and right now her lungs seemed paralyzed. *"Assuming, o'*
course, the carousel works." What if it didn't work? What if it failed before the fairgoers and
the note-taking London journalist? Then not only Gertrude but the whole of London
would know she *wasn't fit for the task.* She'd be publicly humiliated before a few at home,
and then as a consequence of the wager be forced to move to the city for a magnified
humiliation. *Silly little Sophia,* to all, forevermore.

"Aren't you goin' to thank me, Miss Heyer?"

Thank him? Sophia's fingers curled into fists. If she thanked him, it would come in
the form of a good throttling. Ear-ringing silence permeated the carriage house. Smithy
Stroud and the other volunteers watched her and Mr. Gallagher sideways, trying to
appear like concentrated workers instead of attentive eavesdroppers. Their acting talents
left much to be desired. She kept a firm rein on her tone. "Gentlemen, give us a moment,
please. Refreshments are in the house."

The entire group exited the carriage house, leaving her quite alone with Mr. Gallagher, which was convenient as she preferred not to have witnesses who might spread
rumors in town. Or testify against her in a court of law. After all, she was trying to repair
Mr. Gallagher's reputation with her influence. A task he was not making easy. Sophia
slackened the rein on her mouth, fists still clenched. "What ought I to thank you for, Mr.
Gallagher? Shall I thank you for blatantly ignoring my position as your co-chairman? For
proceeding without my vote of approval? For placing an advertisement and inviting the
press, behind my back—without a single thought of consideration or word of warning?
Oh, yes, thank you very much indeed, Mr. Gallagher. Did I cover everything or have you
implemented more schemes to ruin the fair?"

Mr. Gallagher glowered so intensely the expression seeped into his voice. "Anything
I've done has been for Brookside's benefit."

"And I'm a prancing pony. If you truly cared for Brookside, you would have taken
more care instead of acting in such selfish haste."

"Selfish? You're the only one thinkin' of self."

Sophia stepped forward, losing hold of the reins entirely. "Do not dare be so pre-
sumptuous, sir. You know nothing of my character or my life."

"'Course I don't." Mr. Gallagher matched her step with a single deliberate stride.
"That's what makes presumptions so frustratin' and damagin'." His green eyes darkened.
"But at least I'll be courteous enough to admit my mistake and apologize."

"I've done nothing wrong!" Sophia retreated two steps, three, her gaze seeking refuge
between the floorboards where those penetrating eyes could not find her out. Illuminate
her mistakes. Failures she could not admit unless, somehow, she managed to set them
right. Fix what she'd broken. If only Mr. Gallagher could understand that she could
not acknowledge her sins aloud until she had earned the forgiveness she so desperately
desired.

But she could never make Mr. Gallagher understand. All she could do was shut the gate on *then* in order to get through *now*. For Papa and Brookside. Sophia made herself look into Mr. Gallagher's eyes and speak softly. "You've placed Brookside in a vulnerable position. Having a journalist here will only cause trouble."

Mr. Gallagher stepped closer, pushing the boundaries of personal space and propriety. "What are ya afraid they'll see?"

A tremor unsettled Sophia's stomach. *Silly little Sophia.* The pitiful foal, fumbling and struggling behind a paddock door to stay upright on her wobbly hooves. She bit her lip before it could divulge evidence of the quaking inside. She had tripped before watchful eyes many a time. Grown accustomed to the risk, the low expectations. Yet how could she open the door now, knowing someone would be there to not only observe but document her fall?

Behind Mr. Gallagher's form, the wind continued to swirl the clouds into a white froth that hazed Brookside's signature blue. Good, she'd hate for Mamma to see her today.

An equine scream resounded in the neighboring stables followed by the banging of hooves against wood and a human cry.

Gypsy. Sophia turned in the direction of the stables as chief groom Gregory ran around the carriage. A bruise blackened his left eye. "Gypsy's time has come, and she's spinning about the stall berserk-like, biting herself. I can't calm her. She's going to injure herself or—"

"The foal." Sophia hiked her skirts and raced toward the stables. Forget uncontrollable Mr. Gallagher with his meddling reporter. This she could handle.

◆　◆　◆

What was Miss Heyer going to do—calm the mare with a proper cup of tea?

Donovan shed his overcoat, tossing it on a carriage wheel, and began to unbutton and roll his sleeves. Why had the stable master called for her anyway? Just because she'd righted that sugar incident didn't mean Miss Heyer could handle the bloody business of delivering a foal. Another high-pitched horse scream penetrated the walls and rattled his chest. He sprinted toward the stables. If the mare and her foal were to have any chance of surviving, they needed a skilled farmhand in charge. Not a porcelain doll afraid to get her dress mussed.

Donovan arrived at the mare's stall and careened to a stop. Blinked.

Blinked again. Had the world just tipped over?

Miss Heyer stood behind the mare, one hand placed on its hindquarter and the other inside—inside—the birth canal. Brown fluid dripped onto her fine boots and smeared across her dress, but she didn't pay it mind. Didn't seem to care. Her brow furrowed, connecting her freckles with tiny lines as she stroked the mare with her free hand. Either God had knocked the world on its side or. . .Miss Heyer wasn't the stuck-up aristocrat he'd taken her for. Donovan shook his head. That changed nothing.

His plan was formed, and he'd see it through.

Miss Heyer met his gaze, irritation flashing across her blue eyes. "If you're not going to help, Mr. Gallagher, leave the premises."

Right. "I mean to help. Is the foal rotated backwards?"

"No, it's not as bad as that." The mare groaned and shifted, knocking Miss Heyer off balance, but she held on and pushed against the horse in a show of strength, managing to keep her footing. Strain pinched her face and voice. "Although Gypsy would seem to disagree. The foal is in the proper face-first position, but only one hoof was emerging; the other got lodged somewhere. I've returned the emerged hoof to the birth canal and am trying to locate the trapped one in order to guide them out together."

Donovan's jaw slackened. Not only was Miss Heyer unafraid of getting dirty, but she actually knew what she was doing.

The mare grunted and took several steps in reverse, pushing Miss Heyer—who refused to let go—toward the back of the stall.

Not good. Heart battering against his ribs, Donovan approached at a slow pace and stroked the mare's neck and white mane. "Whoa, lass. Shhh, it'll be fine."

The mare lunged and nipped at his face. He dodged the teeth. How did Miss Heyer stay so calm? The mare took another step back, away from him. Toward Miss Heyer. Threatening to crush her against the wall. Tension rooted in his shoulders. "What can I do?"

"Rub your first two fingers in a circle between Gypsy's eyes."

Was she trying to get him bit? The woman was mad.

"Hush-a-loo, hush-a-by, my darling so dear."

Singing? Aye, the woman was definitely mad.

The mare unleashed a mournful, deep whinny.

"Hush-a-loo, hush-a-by, Mr. Gallagher rub between Gypsy's eyes." An edge sharpened Miss Heyer's tune. "Now."

The horse stomped, bit her side, black eyes flitting in search of escape from her pain, escape she couldn't find.

He could not wait. He had to obey the mad woman's instructions. *God, help me.* Hand outstretched, Donovan shuffled toward the mare slow-like, till his fingers met the soft coat betwixt her eyes. *Rub in a circle. There.*

"Good, Mr. Gallagher. Hush-a-loo, hush-a-by, my darling so dear. Hush-a-loo, hush-a-by, you've no cause for fear."

The crazed look in the mare's eyes dimmed.

"God catches each tear in a bottle of glass. Hush-a-loo, hush-a-by, this too shall pass."

As Miss Heyer started the song again, the mare's muscles relaxed, body stilled, gaze mellowed and stopped its search. Donovan drew closer, stroked her mane with his other hand. The tension disappeared from his shoulders. Miss Heyer's song was like faerie magic.

"I'm. . .almost. . .there."

Donovan craned his neck. A pair of tiny hooves reached out to the world bathed in the mixture of lantern glow and sunlight. Miss Heyer stepped away from Gypsy's hind end, black horse hair matted to her dress and cheeks, gold locks hanging loose from their former coiffure. And yet she smiled, nay beamed. "Queen Gypsy can take it from here."

Unusual warmth crackled inside him, like a field bursting with fireflies. He joined Miss Heyer as Gypsy sank in the hay and rocked onto her side. Gypsy pushed, panting. The foal's wee head followed the hooves into the light, coated in a milky bubble.

More pushing, waiting, pushing, groaning.

In a rush of bloody fluid, the foal slipped to the hay-covered floor.

The mare turned to inspect her foal. Slowly she got to work freeing the foal from the bubble, cleaning its little muzzle.

"Isn't it the most beautiful thing you've ever witnessed?" Something lilted Miss Heyer's voice in a way he'd not heard from her lips, a freshness that drew his gaze. Could it be sincerity? For a moment Miss Heyer met his stare and somehow managed to add brilliance to her smile. Mayhap t'was the hay strewn in her hair.

The fireflies buzzed warmth all the way to his cheeks. Donovan's jaw relaxed, but he refused to smile back. However, he might be tempted. "Where'd you learn that song?"

A shadow wisped over her blue eyes. "Mamma sang it at my bedside after a nightmare or here in the stables."

"The stables?"

A spark of amusement cast aside the shadow. "As a little girl, I was terrified of horses."

Donovan tried to swallow a chuckle, but it came out a snort.

"Pitiful, I know. That is actually why Mamma commissioned the carousel on my fifth birthday, to rid me of my fear."

"By that age, I was raisin' a horse on our farm in Ireland. Thunder, his name was, because he came during a storm. Don't think I could find a better beast, though this wee foal's a strappin'. . .thing." He bit his lips. *Shut up, man.* She'd no need to know so much. No right.

"What happened to Thunder?"

They'd sold him to survive another day, come to England. The fireflies winged away, taking with them their warmth. With the famine raging, people starving, he'd rather not know what became of Thunder. "Doesn't matter. Some things can't be undone."

Miss Heyer's smile faded, the shadow descending over every feature. "I t–tried." A tremor sliced her voice. "After you left. . .I t–tried to find you. I tried to make things right."

Tried? Donovan's jaw seized. Another attempt at apology weak as her penance tea. Another blatant failure to just come right out and admit her wrongdoing.

Donovan turned his back on Miss Heyer and marched toward Wilmore Manor. He'd be the one to set things right—when he sabotaged the carousel's engine on the eve of the fair, putting Miss Heyer on a train out of Brookside and his life, forever.

Chapter Six

*N*ow God had turned even the wind against her, fantastic.

The blustering June breeze pushed Sophia's back as if to hurry her along to Wilmore. She shuffled her boots across the hedged path in front of her house. Like a horse being led by reins to where it did not wish to go. Why couldn't the wind entice a storm into Brookside so she would have a legitimate reason to stay home and ignore Mr. Gallagher's week–long avoidance of her?

She kicked a piece of gravel, sending it skittering down the lane. Alas, she had no such excuse. With the steam engine installed in the base and the gear-driven pulley system in the horses, the carousel was ready for its first trial run. A trial she was obligated to inform her co-chairman about. Even though the odious man had shown her no such civility. Even though he refused to accept her olive branch of an apology. How could she mend Mr. Gallagher's reputation when he spurned her efforts by declining her social invitations?

"Some things can't be undone." The wind snatched at her pinned hair, loosening strands and whipping them across her eyes. He was right. She ought to stop trying. Since she obviously couldn't do anything right outside the stables.

As she neared the path's end, voices mingled in laughter on the other side of the hedges. Some merry party must be heading into town. Sophia took the corner and halted. The merry party was in fact a duo. Young Kelly Gallagher beamed from her wheelchair as it rolled down the lane, pushed along by a jovial man with wavy dark hair and green eyes. A man who almost resembled. . .Mr. Gallagher?

Sophia brushed aside the locks obscuring her vision. Indeed, it was Mr. Gallagher—minus the usual scowl and layers of pomade greasing his hair into place. Kelly spoke something to her brother, which resulted in more laughter and a smile. A genuine smile from Mr. Gallagher that lifted the veil of shadow from his face to reveal a completely different man. One capable of kindness, compassion, and warmth. Quite a fine, indeed, very fine smile.

The duo caught sight of her and Mr. Gallagher halted their procession. Kelly waved in greeting while Mr. Gallagher looked as though he wished to turn around and flee.

Oh no, he'd not walk away from her again. Not just yet. Sophia closed the distance and shook her head in mock graveness. "Mr. Gallagher, for shame. You really should stop this dreadful habit of keeping secrets from me."

His Adam's apple bobbed. "Secrets?"

"Indeed. All this time I thought you incapable of a smile, only to discover you are quite proficient in the skill. You should smile more often."

Kelly crossed her arms, shooting a teasing glare at her brother. "Aye, he should, that."

Mr. Gallagher reverted to his usual countenance of stone. "Off to town, Miss Heyer?"

"I was actually on my way to fetch you. We are ready to test the carousel's engine. I thought you should be there." And now she sort of wanted him there, so she might study the curiosity that was this smiling Mr. Gallagher.

"May I come?"

Sophia lowered her gaze to Kelly, whose face could barely contain her bright-eyed eagerness. "If your brother approves."

A muscle in Mr. Gallagher's jaw twitched, but he nodded and rolled Kelly's wheelchair in the direction of Heyer Hall. Together they strolled toward the carriage house in silence. An awkward, fidgeting silence, which invited the inspection of one's fingernails or random comments about the weather. Sophia pursed her lips. Her presence seemed to have quenched the Gallaghers' aptitude for merriment. A quandary she felt compelled to remedy. "Kelly, does Wilmore suit you?"

"First it looked like a ghost had been squattin' there, but the house has come alive now that we've aired the rooms and Donovan's repaired the leaks in the ceiling. Yesterday I finished sewin' drapes for the parlor. Donovan offered to send to London for drapes, but I wanted to make them meself. As I've made linens for so many other people's homes."

Turning in her chair, Kelly swatted at Mr. Gallagher's hand. "He's spoilin' me, letting me decorate how I wish. I keep telling Donovan he should have a room done up as he likes, but he don't care about such things. Spends all his time outside, workin' the fields with the tenants."

Working the fields? Was that why he hadn't come by the carriage house or accepted her invitations? As they skirted the house and entered the rear gardens, Sophia peeked at Mr. Gallagher, whose face bore no reaction at being discussed. Odd. She'd envisioned him lounging around the manor, flaunting his newly acquired wealth and status. "I did not know Mr. Gallagher cared for agriculture."

"Aye, all he talks about. Soil and crops and harvest. In Ireland, Donovan was either workin' the field with Da or riding round the field on Thunder."

As they traversed the gardens, Mr. Gallagher still refused comment.

While Kelly's comments hardly paused for a breath. "Today we delivered cakes to our tenants, and farmer Brown said the techniques Donovan's brought about are wakin' the land. This autumn will be the first in years they can expect a big harvest. Mr. Brown nigh cried at the notion. He'd been thinkin' on packing up his family, times had got so bad."

Indeed, she had heard as much in town. The Wilmore estate had been withering away.

"But now Donovan's turned all that around. 'Tis like God knew he was needed here." Kelly patted her brother's fingers approvingly. Proudly.

The muscle in Mr. Gallagher's jaw ceased its twitching, his expression softening all the way to his green eyes. "Kelly's a mischievous lass. Tends to exaggerate." He twiddled fingers in Kelly's raven hair, mussing her braided twist.

Kelly swatted him again. "I'm not tellin' tales, rogue. Mrs. Tooley's overheard folks in her shop say you're workin' wonders at Wilmore. That you're better than they first took ya for."

Wonders, indeed. Sophia's pace slowed among the garden's warm perfume of roses. It seemed Mr. Gallagher did not require her position or influence to redeem his good name. His own talented efforts were changing minds by saving the land and livelihoods of those connected to it—the lives of good people. Brookside people. Her people. A fresh breeze seemed to sweep the roses' warmth across her cheeks. "The farmers must be grateful to you, Mr. Gallagher."

"I deserve no gratitude." Was that a blush tinting Mr. Gallagher's cheeks? Before she could discern, his voice banished it from view. "The tenants are the ones who deserve thanks. In fact. . .I've a notion about that. For the fair."

And things were going so well. "Am I permitted to know this one before it's implemented? Or is it to be another wonderful surprise?"

"He's to tell you right now." Kelly took charge of her chair and rotated to face them, blocking their path out of the garden. "I'll have ya know I scolded Donovan soundly for that surprise, Miss Heyer. Older brother or not. He'd no right to g—ah!"

Mr. Gallagher whirled Kelly's chair in a circle, turning her away from them again. A whisper of another smile nudged his mouth. "That's enough out o' you, sprite."

Rogue, indeed. "I believe the sprite was about to make a fine point, Mr. Gallagher." Sophia lifted an eyebrow in challenge.

"As was I, Miss Heyer, before the sprite interrupted." One hand firmly gripping the chair to keep Kelly at bay, he stepped toward her and leaned quite near, voice dipping low as if sharing an intimate secret meant for her ears alone. "With your approval, I'd like to involve local farmers in the fair. Set up booths in town hall to sell whatever produce is in season. Summer squash, sweet corn, berries, and the like. 'Twould bring much-needed paddin' to their pockets."

Sophia examined Mr. Gallagher for a catch, but found none. He truly did wish to help Brookside, not simply mend his reputation. Mr. Gallagher had a thoughtful tenderness she'd neither fathomed nor expected. Perhaps it was still worth trying to earn his forgiveness somehow? If she could find a new way. . .if it were even possible. "I love that notion. I'll trust you to organize the farmers' booths."

Mr. Gallagher nodded, a flash lighting his jade eyes.

She kept expecting him to look away first, continue on to the carriage house, but he did not. He held her gaze. Warmth flooded her cheeks, the aroma of roses now too distant for blame.

"Donovan, I'm off to the carousel."

Sophia broke from Mr. Gallagher's stare. Sometime during their discussion, Kelly had freed herself and wheeled in front of them where she now gave her brother a knowing look. "Feel free to join me. Whenever you're done makin' turtledove eyes at Miss Heyer."

"One word too many, sprite." Mr. Gallagher dove after Kelly, chasing her all the way to the carriage house to the tune of giggles.

Sophia gathered the hem of her dress and rushed after them. When she arrived inside the carriage house, she found Mr. Gallagher and Kelly examining the bare carousel, sanded to the raw wood grain. "Let's begin, shall we." Before she had a chance to ponder the meaning of making *turtledove* eyes.

She strode to the side of the carousel where a special on-off lever was embedded in the base to control the steam engine. Gripping the lever, she yanked it up with a clack. Seconds ticked by, dawdling.

Sophia's breathing stretched to match time's dragging pace. *Was our work for noth—*

The mechanics of the carousel groaned. Sophia's heart leapt. One of the wooden horses slowly awakened, front hooves reared as it seemed to jump, up the brass pole and down again. Another horse roused, and then another, until the entire cavalry was prancing as the carousel pedestal itself began to twirl. She exhaled through a laugh. It worked. The engine really worked. Now they could begin painting, even put in a musical element.

Perhaps God was on her side after all.

Sophia exchanged a smile with Kelly as the carousel's rotations increased in speed. Faster. And faster, and. . .a little too much faster. The horses melded into a blur, and the carousel rocked back and forth. Teetering, tottering, and swaying. Mr. Gallagher pinned her with a fierce look. Any measure of a smile slipped from her lips. *Ragwort.* Sophia slapped the lever down, shutting off the engine's power. Gradually, the cavalry screeched to a standstill.

Kelly clapped. "Amazing. May I ride now?"

"You may not." Mr. Gallagher nearly barked the words. "Too dangerous."

A migraine threatened Sophia with vague pulsating pain through her temples. "I agree it's too swift, but we have time to make alterations. It will be safe on fair day, Kelly."

"Nay." The word growled through Mr. Gallagher's clenched teeth. Kelly pursed her lips as if aware the conversation had ended. Jaw once more twitching, he seized the handles of Kelly's wheelchair. "'Tis not safe for Kelly to ride."

"It's not a bucking bronco, Mr. Gallagher. We can—"

Mr. Gallagher wheeled Kelly outside the carriage house and realm of hearing and then barreled toward her, looming a breath's distance from her face. Sophia forced herself not to retreat from the darkness he emanated. The all-consuming, brittle shadow, fissured and on the verge of shattering. "Kelly doesn't have strength to grip the wooden horse. Nor the balance needed. She could fall and—'tis too risky. I won't have my sister on that thing."

Chapter Seven

You really should stop this dreadful habit of keeping secrets from me."

Secrets. Donovan scoffed. Miss Heyer had no idea.

He trudged across the Heyer garden with its landscaped blooms and evergreens, off for another day's labor. What would Miss Heyer think if she discovered his biggest secret—the plan to reduce her life to cinders? What would Kelly think when the carousel she was so eager to ride failed on fair day?

Because of him.

Snatching a withered rose from its stem, he crushed its brittle remains with an audible *crunch*. The flames of his plan were meant solely for Miss Heyer, but what if they scorched Kelly, too? What if he couldn't control the fire made by his own hands?

"You should smile more often."

"Aye, he should, that."

Pain sliced through Donovan's heart like a shovel's blade, knocked out his breath, and stopped his feet on the outer edge of the gardens. What had he become that a smile on his face should shock his own sister? He opened his shaking palm and stared at the rose's brown ashes. Mayhap. . .he should forget his plan? He brushed the floral dust on his trousers. The new pair he'd bought, tailored with the finest everything. How far he'd come since his days as Baronet Heyer's valet.

No thanks to Miss Heyer.

"I cannot reward thievery compounded with lies. Consider yourself relieved of your post and leave immediately. Without reference."

He couldn't let himself forget what she'd done. Ever. Her presence in Brookside threatened his new life with Kelly. Therefore, she must be forced out.

No matter how fine she looked with hay in her hair.

Just a short while longer, then it will be over. Donovan collected himself with a few deep breaths and headed to the carriage house. When he entered the open doors, not a single workman or village volunteer greeted him. Instead, the smell of paint assaulted his nose, burning as it settled in his lungs. The carousel stood coated from top finial to wooden hooves to base in a brilliant white paint that shone in the sunlight. As if dusted in snow. Miss Heyer must've called off work so the paint might dry. Good. 'Twas probably best not to be near her for a while.

Donovan started for the doors, but something odd caught his attention. A blank space on the carousel's far end where an additional horse should stand. His lungs stalled. Stolen? He marched round the carousel. *No.* That woman wouldn't blame him for this—

Bench?

Somebody had replaced one of the carousel horses with a bench crafted from wooden slats, painted the same bright white and held together by a wrought iron frame. Four large spikes anchored the frame to the carousel's base. He gripped the iron and shook, hard. 'Twas sturdy. Secure. Safe.

"I commissioned that for Kelly."

Dressed in a riding habit, Miss Heyer stood beside the carriage. "It was to be a surprise." She offered a weak smile. "Mrs. Tooley is sewing lovely cushions so it's comfortable. And I also commissioned a leather belt which can be attached to the bench on either side and fastened across Kelly's waist."

Kelly? Donovan scrutinized Miss Heyer for tell of her usual society playacting. What was her game, to make him look unfair in Kelly's eyes?

"If you're still unconvinced, I will not contradict your wishes by admitting the chair was designed for Kelly specifically. I'll simply say it's to aid elderly members of the community unable to mount the horses. However, I. . .I hope the bench eliminates your concerns. I'd hate for Kelly not to be included in the fair's festivities."

Included. The word pulsed with sincerity, an unexpected compassion that lodged in his throat like a hot coal. She'd done all this to help Kelly feel included, ease his mind? "Thank you." The words slipped before he could think better. Donovan bit the inside of his cheek. Great, now he was thanking Miss Heyer. He needed out of here before his resolve vanished. Bowing a good-bye, he made to leave.

"I was about to go riding. Care to join me, Mr. Gallagher?"

The offer snagged Donovan's feet at the door. He'd not ridden in years. Not since he'd had to sell Thunder. How he'd love to feel the freedom of riding again, the land before him and cares behind. But he couldn't ride with Miss Heyer. Getting close to her was becoming a danger to his plans.

"If you're not up to such an exertion, I understand."

Not up to it? Donovan smirked, but bricked it over before facing Miss Heyer's irritatingly pleased smile. "Madam, don't bother packin' a lunch for this outing because you're about to dine on dust." And wallow there, for he'd no intention of further talk. He just wanted to ride.

When Miss Heyer and Donovan had each saddled and mounted a steed—he still couldn't believe she'd saddled her own horse—they rode from Heyer Hall at a walk, and as they set across the rolling hills of Brookside, quickened to a trot. Donovan bounced in the saddle, growing accustomed to this horse's unique rhythm, so different from Thunder. He shouldn't have boasted about his riding skills. It had been too long.

Miss Heyer indicated westward with a nod. "Race to the giant oak?"

With his lack of practice? Nay. "Is it proper to race a lady?"

"No, no. You are quite right. I shall look elsewhere for a man to accept my challenge." She winked and, with a signal to her chestnut mare, bolted toward the tree. "Take care of your petticoats, Mr. Gallagher!"

That smug faerie. Donovan nudged his horse with his boots, and the steed took up the chase, flying along the ground faster and faster till it reached full gallop. The distance between them shortened, but he couldn't overtake—nor match—Miss Heyer's pace. He'd never seen a female rider achieve such speed. And riding sidesaddle, at that. He'd no hope of winning the race. But he didn't care.

Cool air whooshed across Donovan's face. He inhaled the fresh summer air, filling his lungs till they could hold no more, and then exhaled. Completely. Sweet wildflowers bragged about the richness of the soil whilst blades of vibrant green grass nodded in agreement. Right here, in this moment, he could almost pretend. Almost imagine he was back in Ireland. Almost feel like he had a place to belong, a land to plant roots deep down.

Home.

Miss Heyer's laughter floated on the breeze. "Careful, Mr. Gallagher. You're smiling again."

Donovan chuckled. He was smiling, wasn't he? There wasn't any tension in his jaw or neck or shoulders. Not with the four-beat cadence of hooves pounding cross the land, kicking up dirt and the hefty aroma of the soil. Was this. . .peace? In Brookside, the place he thought peace could never dwell. At least not for him. Mayhap God wasn't trying to punish him after all. Mayhap. . .he was the one shoving God's blessings away?

Up ahead Miss Heyer crested the hill, reaching the oak first. Donovan brought his horse alongside the mare. "You win. No contest."

"You made a valiant effort." Miss Heyer stroked the mare's mane and stared at the view of Brookside below like a person watching a loved one near death, desperate to harvest every feature, every word, store them in memory before the bitter cold of winter. "Races are the only contest I've ever won, to my sisters' chagrin. If I were as capable in other areas, the Brookside fair would not be in dire straits."

Her *sisters'* chagrin. Were they the reason she put on airs? Donovan shifted in his saddle. *Ack, man, don't go feeling sorry for her.* "Can't be so bad."

"Oh, it can." Miss Heyer's voice cracked, shattering what was left of her porcelain doll pretenses. "I've tattered Mamma's beautiful legacy. You know it's true; you remember how magical the fair was with Mamma at the helm. In four short years, I have managed to almost completely destroy everything she worked to create. All the good she did for Brookside. If anything goes wrong this year, it. . .will be the end."

Donovan swallowed. Especially if he went through with his plan. But who would it be the end of—Miss Heyer or himself?

"I'm going to fail Mamma, again."

The pain on Miss Heyer's face plowed through Donovan's chest, overturning every-thing inside. "D–don't say that. This year will be different." What was he saying?

"Of all people, you know that is not true. You've experienced up close how apt I am at making horrendous mistakes and pitiful attempts at righting them." Wrenching herself from the view, she met his gaze, blue eyes misted with unshed tears. "My lady's maid. Fanny. She was the true thief who stole Papa's watch. When I found out, I managed to put Fanny on a train without anyone, not even the servants, learning the truth. I was such a fool. I failed to see the deception right in front of me, right by my side."

If she knew. . .

"I am sorry for accusing you, Mr. Gallagher. Sorry beyond measure for what I put you and Kelly through. Since our last encounter, I've slowly realized you were correct all along. Some things can't be undone. I know now that I can never hope to make amends or earn your forgiveness, but I will evermore be sorry."

She'd finally done it. Miss Heyer had actually admitted her wrongdoing and apologized. *Forgive*. The word rose in Donovan's throat and lodged there, cold, hard, unfamiliar. He didn't know what to do with it. With any of this.

"Please, tell me the truth behind your theft conviction, so I may at least thwart any future accusations which arise against you."

This is what he had wanted all those years ago. A chance to explain. He inhaled. "After my parents died, I. . .I brought Kelly to England to escape the famine's devastation." Left the land like he'd begged Da to do. "No one was keen to hire an unskilled Irish farmer. Finding work took longer than I'd hoped.

"We soon ran out o' the money I'd gotten for Thunder. But I refused to let that keep Kelly from eating. She'd gone hungry often enough." A phantom pain of emptiness washed over his stomach. "I stole a loaf from a bakery in a larger village. The constable was secretly part Irish and had mercy, so I spent no time in prison. Was simply ordered to leave. That's when we came to Brookside. For a new start." He'd chased after a new start so many times, it was getting old.

"I shall do all in my power to ensure this new start at Wilmore is not taken away. Your parents would be proud of what you've achieved."

Raw pain wrenched through Donovan, like the plow had caught on a boulder and ripped it from the earth. Nay. His parents would not be proud of a man like him. A thief. Deceiver. Everything Da was not. Everything Da would despise. Miss Heyer had dug too deep and found the truth he'd tried for years to plant over.

He was bad soil, through and through.

Chapter Eight

Tomorrow the course of her future would be determined.

Had she done enough to win the wager?

On a ladder propped against the wall, Sophia fixed the end of a ribbon to the far edge of the ceiling in town hall. Done. She inspected the finished product. A series of cobalt ribbons joined at the middle of the ceiling, swagged across the room in all directions, and then attached to the walls and draped to the floor, creating a sort of whimsical circus tent effect. Another one of Mr. Gallagher's ideas to turn out splendidly.

Sophia's gaze searched the bustling crowd of Brooksiders below and located Mr. Gallagher giving instruction as to the arrangement of the produce stalls. An unnatural form of severity, even for him, encased Mr. Gallagher's countenance. Any evidence he had ever smiled, gone. Bricked over stone by stone with. . .what, hate? Regret? She might never know. Her newest blunder seemed to have been the final straw, for he had avoided her ever since their ride.

Now if she could only figure out what she had done this time.

Sophia descended the ladder rung by rung. After the fair, she would attempt to speak with Mr. Gallagher. For now, however, she must focus on completing last-minute details.

She approached one of the booths and arranged cherries in a hand-woven basket. What else was left to be done? The carousel had been completed, placed on rollers, and moved by volunteers to town square this morning. Most of the artisans had finished their booths outside, and the farmers' booths were well in hand as were the interior decorations. Perhaps she ought to check the exterior decorations before the remaining daylight passed?

Sophia hastened toward the door and a hard head collided directly with her shoulder. *Ow.*

"Silly little Sophia. Clumsy as ever, I see."

Her stomach roiled. *Please, sweet Lord, let this be a nightmare.* She looked down to Gertrude's petite figure, all too real and the embodiment of annoyance.

Ragwort.

Gertrude brushed a hand over her traveling dress as if to wipe away Sophia residue. "Have not I always told you to watch where you are going?"

Burning under Gertrude's faultfinding gaze, Sophia tucked away a stray lock that had fallen from her loose bun and pocketed her dirty, gloveless hands in her apron. "What brings you to Brookside?"

"The fair, of course. I'm only sorry my attempts to convince our sisters to come fell upon deaf ears." Gertrude's lips rose in a snide smile. "They did not think it worth the journey."

No doubt because they expected her to fail. "You needn't have troubled yourself either if the journey's so tiresome."

"Nonsense. I had to see the results of your brave endeavors for myself."

Of course. She should've known Gertrude would want to be present for her downfall. Revel in winning the wager, get a head start on a lifetime of *"I told you so, silly Sophia"* while escorting her to the prison of London in shackles of humiliation. Sophia straightened her posture. Well, she had not lost yet. "The inn is filled with people who traveled from the farthest reaches of the county and beyond, all to see the carousel." All who thought it *worth the journey.*

"Then I sincerely hope the carousel does not disappoint."

And she sincerely wished Gertrude had taken the wrong train. Or, God forgive her, been thrown off the speeding caboose.

Gertrude glided through town hall. "You must show me this quaint market. I—" She seized Sophia's arm with a vise grip. "Why is that Irish pilferer here? I thought you handled the matter. Did you not press charges?"

Now would be a marvelous time for this nightmare to end. Sophia snatched her arm away but kept her voice level. "If you step outside, I am more than willing to explain the particulars. However, Mr. Gallagher is really none of your concern."

Gertrude's nostrils scrunched as if she'd caught a whiff of horse manure. "*Mr.* Gallagher? I shall see to this." Her heels clip-clopped across the room.

"Wait." Sophia rushed after her, trying to snatch Gertrude's arm or mouth, whichever came in reach first.

Gertrude staked herself in front of Mr. Gallagher and raised her voice to an unladylike volume usually reserved for scolding children and younger sisters. "This man is a thief, and I wish him to be escorted to the constabulary so I may press charges for the crime he has committed against my dear father."

Sophia winced. All activity ceased. Every eye in town hall trained stunned gazes on Gertrude, every ear held captive by her sister's boisterous accusation. A dark cloud of tension loomed over the gathering, choking her, strangling each breath into a shallow wheeze. She had to calm the situation, now. "Please, Gertrude, come—"

"I will not move a fraction until this man is escorted to the constable. Why does no one attend me? Gentlemen, take this thief into custody."

Not one man moved.

Nor did Mr. Gallagher speak a word in defense. He simply stood there, a wounded expression hardening his features and setting off the twitch in his jaw.

Sophia's heart constricted, pinching with every rapid beat. It was not fair to put him through this mortification again. She whispered in Gertrude's ear. "There are facts you are not privy to. I shall explain everything outside."

"Explain?" Gertrude recoiled from the offensively absurd word. "What is to be explained? This fiend took advantage of an elderly man." She slashed her gaze into the crowd. "If none here will bring him to justice, I shall take my charges to London and—"

"For once in your life be silent, Gertrude!" Sophia bit her tongue while Gertrude stared, mouth agape. She had not meant to yell, but it was done and she must take advantage of the effects. She could hide the truth no longer. Not if Mr. Gallagher was finally to have his fresh start.

Sophia positioned herself between Gertrude and Mr. Gallagher, placing a hand on his shoulder. "Mr. Gallagher would never take advantage of Papa. When Papa's watch was stolen, I...I made a mistake on the basis of prejudiced, partial information. I wrongly accused him, and he suffered an undeserved punishment."

Gasps and exclamations of shock fractured the crowd's silence.

She raised her voice to silence the room. "The true thief has since been found and sufficiently punished, while Mr. Gallagher has acquired Wilmore Manor by honest means and served the community as co-chairman of the fair. I readily admit his partnership has been invaluable to me." Indeed, having someone to help carry the burden had been a greater comfort than she could have known. "Mr. Gallagher is no fiend. He is a good man. An honorable man. The best man in Brookside."

Several of the townspeople clapped. Someone even cheered.

Gertrude's nostrils flared, eyes intensified to their darkest, like a stallion ready to charge. "You're a simpleton. You know nothing of the real world."

Hot tears misted Sophia's eyes. Her palm slipped from Mr. Gallagher's shoulder, but a calloused grip secured her hand before it could fall.

Mr. Gallagher squeezed her hand and nailed Gertrude with a glare. "You're the one who knows nothing, madam. Because if ya had any sense, you'd know Sophia Heyer is the life o' this town. She has you beat in every skill that counts and virtue that matters."

Warmth radiated from Mr. Gallagher's hand to hers, stilling every tremor and steadying her feet. So *this* was what it felt like to have someone be on your side? "You best leave, Gertrude. We have work to do."

Mouth pinched, Gertrude shook her head. "Before Mamma passed, she charged me to look after you. All I've ever done has been to that purpose. I derive comfort in the knowledge that Mamma cannot see the ungrateful wretch you've become." Turning on a dainty heel, she strode back through the hall.

Simpleton. Wretch.

Each word seared into Sophia's chest under the watch of Brookside's stares.

◆ ◆ ◆

Donovan had to get out of here—away from Miss Heyer—before he did something foolish. Like take her into his arms.

Releasing her hand and weaving through the crowd, he staggered outside. In Brookside's square people decorated the buildings with balloons, lanterns, and streamers. Donovan kept walking, moving. If he slowed, people might try to talk to him. And he couldn't talk right now. Right now he needed to think. Clear his head of Miss Heyer's words. Figure out what he was going to do. For that he needed solitude.

Donovan strode past the craftsmen booths, but Miss Heyer's words pursued close behind. *"I made a mistake. . . I wrongly accused him. . ."*

He quickened. The mental echo of Miss Heyer's words gave chase, nipping at his heels. *"His partnership has been invaluable to me."*

Donovan passed every single shop and then broke into a run. He didn't allow his feet to slow till he reached the bridge and collapsed on the cold stone. He panted. He'd outrun the noise. Now he could think. Now he could— *"Mr. Gallagher is no fiend. He is a good man.*

"An honorable man."

But he wasn't! His breath caught in his chest, burned.

He was bad soil that couldn't produce anything good.

"I failed to see the deception right in front of me."

Donovan cupped both hands over his face. *God, help me.* He combed fingers through the disgusting pomade that caged his hair, shook it out. Locks broke free, falling over his eyes. Over his view of Brookside and the flag waving in the distance from the top of the carousel's finial. The sun dipped in the darkening amber sky, threatening to plunge Brookside in shadow. He closed his eyes. What was he going to do tonight?

When he'd returned to Brookside, his plan to sabotage the carousel had felt right. Justified. But somehow it no longer felt like poetic justice. His plan would disappoint Kelly, the one person he couldn't bear to let down again. Hurt the townspeople, the farmers, who'd labored so hard. Harm Brookside. The town might not recover, especially with the reporter—whom he'd summoned—spreading word of the failure far and wide.

And Miss Heyer, it would destroy.

But wasn't that what he had wanted?

No. He ground his teeth. Mayhap?

He'd said he wanted justice—public vindication. Yet Miss Heyer had given him that now, sacrificed her reputation to make it happen. Then why wasn't it enough?

Propping elbows on knees, Donovan lowered his head onto fisted knuckles. He might have convinced himself he was after vindication, but way down where he'd not dared look, he'd wanted to destroy Miss Heyer. Exact revenge. In a way, he still wanted that. He wanted to punish the woman he'd known—the one who'd fired him—but he didn't want to destroy the Miss Heyer he knew now—the one who commissioned benches, saved horses, defended him.

Her, he wanted to protect. But he couldn't do that, could he? Could he change into something better than what he'd become?

"Mr. Gallagher?" Mrs. Tooley's voice cut through his jumbled thoughts.

Get it together, man. Donovan opened his eyes and stood. "Aye, Mrs. Tooley?"

The needles in Mrs. Tooley's pincushion rattled whilst she wrung her hands. "I. . . have a confession. When you returned, I lied about needing your money."

What? "The money came, then?"

"No, the parcels you promised never arrived. But I still don't need your money." From a dress pocket, Mrs. Tooley withdrew a coin purse and handed it over. "Things have been tough in the store, but I shouldn't have taken advantage."

Donovan held the purse. He understood none of this. "If my money didn't arrive—"

"Kelly's needs were supplied by. . .a person who wishes to remain anonymous."

Who would do that for him? "Who?"

Mrs. Tooley grinned. "Why I never. After the grand display she made of herself in town hall, and you still haven't guessed?"

"After you left. . .I tried to make things right."

Donovan sank onto the bridge, but his stomach seemed to fall straight through the cobbles into the brook. Sophia—Miss Heyer—had taken care of Kelly? And never once lorded that over his head or asked to be paid back?

"Why I never, you really didn't know, did you, lad?" Mrs. Tooley patted his back. "I best leave you to your thoughts."

As her footsteps faded, Donovan covered his mouth. Miss Heyer had watched over Kelly when he could not, and all the while he'd planned her ruin? The sun settled deeper into the horizon like a seed burrowing in black soil. Before it sprouted anew tomorrow, he had a choice to make. Would he be the man Miss Heyer thought him all those months ago, or would he be the man she believed him to be now? The kind of man he desperately wanted to be. The man who would make Da proud.

Could he be "the best man in Brookside"?

Chapter Nine

Alone in town hall, hand clutched over her fluttering stomach, Sophia attempted to breathe. Simply breathe. She cracked the door, peeked outside for the second time. A crowd of hundreds bustled in Brookside's square, chatting and laughing, all eyes on the carousel, waiting for its grand debut. Yet still no sight of Mr. Gallagher. Her heart bucked like a stallion, kick-kick-kicking. She had anticipated the comfort of his support today, during the vital carousel presentation that concluded the wager. Sealed her fate. After all their hard work, all they endured yesterday, was he truly not going to come?

Surely he would come. Perhaps she couldn't see him among the crowd? She must venture outside and locate him lest he miss the carousel's unveiling. Sophia dragged in a long breath. *Brave face.*

Head held high, she opened the door and marched into town square. July air warmed her skin as it played with the cobalt and gold streamers that looped across the exterior of each workshop and home. People moved in clusters, admiring the carousel or talking with artisans stationed at booths. She searched the faces, every pomade-greased head, but Mr. Gallagher was nowhere to be found. Sophia pursed her lips. Perhaps he wasn't coming after all, but why? Why would he miss the fair after he championed the farmers' produce stalls?

Something was not right.

Under a lamppost festooned with balloons, a man studied the crowd and took vigorous notes on a pad of paper. The London reporter. She angled her face away as she passed, freckles burning. One of those notes must list her name, the woman behind the steam-powered carousel—the one to blame if all went awry.

On the edge of the crowd, Kelly rolled toward her pushed by Mrs. Tooley. Something was indeed not right. Sophia hastened to meet them. "Is Mr. Gallagher ill?"

"Nay." A sigh deflated Kelly's usually jovial countenance. "But he's not coming."

Sophia's equilibrium vanished for a second and then returned, disorienting her like one preparing to sit only to have the chair snatched away. Had she blundered so badly?

"Donovan wanted me to relay a message. He said, 'After all you've done, you deserve to have the limelight alone.'"

But that was not what she wanted. Months ago that might have been her wish, but this morning the memory of Mr. Gallagher holding her hand had alleviated a smidgen of the mounting pressure, calmed her nerves. Now she must take the podium and face all those people's expectations by herself? The hubbub of the crowd buzzed in her ears, unsettled her stomach. Bowing her head, she checked her watch. Yes, she must. She could wait no longer.

Sophia thanked Kelly for relaying the message and walked to the podium in front of the carousel. As she climbed the platform, she was welcomed with mild applause. "Thank you for coming today." Her gaze traveled the crowd as she gave them a smile, but it snagged on a glowering Gertrude.

Brave face. Sophia looked away, down to where Papa sat on a chair brought out especially for him, beaming. No idea his entire life in Brookside was at stake. Her hands quaked. *Lord, forgive me.* She never should've accepted that wager. "Before we begin the festivities, I want to thank the hardworking residents of Brookside."

A round of clapping rippled through the crowd.

"I should also like to acknowledge the efforts of my co-chairman, Mr. Gallagher. We couldn't have made today possible without him." She couldn't have done it without him.

The crowd applauded once more, a few of the farmers tossing in shrill whistles.

"Now to the awaited moment, the debut of Brookside's steam-powered carousel." Sophia stepped from the platform and walked to the side of the carousel.

A hush washed over the gathering. She gripped the power lever, stomach fluttering again as she acknowledged the crowd. *For Mamma and Papa.*

In one swift movement, she flipped the lever.

Tinkling music sprinkled through the silence as the mechanisms within the carousel slowly awoke. Sophia's heart leapt. The steam engine thrummed, a base note to the building music-box melody. One by one, the carousel horses began to trot up and down. Rays of the July sun reflected off their gold-gilded saddles and realistically painted coats, the wind tossing the silk-thread manes and tails that appeared soft enough to stroke. Then the carousel's base itself moved, turned, sounding the gun for the horses to race down their circular track.

The crowd burst into uproarious applause accompanied by delighted cheers. Sophia glanced down and found the embrace of Papa's smile waiting. A part sigh, part sob ripped the pressure off her chest. She'd done it. She'd won the wager. More than that, she had actually done something right. Only God's grace could account for such a miracle. Despite her blunders, He had been on her side all along. Sophia returned to the platform. "The Brookside Summer Fair has officially commenced! Form a line to ride the carousel, and be sure to explore the artisan and produce booths." As she descended into the throng, Gertrude's distant form glided out of town. Without uttering a word. Sophia smiled. *No more nagging, forevermore.*

She made her way to Papa and kissed his cheek. "We shall have to take a turn on the carousel."

"Indeed." Papa stood, leaning on his cane. "Your mamma would be proud."

Her chest swelled to the point of aching, tears brimming in her eyes. "W–would she?"

"Your Mamma was proud of you since the womb, and neither of us could be more proud if you plucked a star from the heavens." Papa placed a kiss on her crown.

As they watched the carousel, people strolled by in a continuous stream, offering congratulations and shaking her hand. For once she felt neither silly nor inferior. Her wobbly legs had finally found their footing. Yet she could not take it all in, could not fully revel in the joy. Something felt. . .missing. Someone.

The only person, besides Papa, who had thought her capable before seeing proof. The only person who had ever stood up to Gertrude on her behalf. *"Sophia Heyer is the life o' this town. She has you beat in every skill that counts and virtue that matters."* She did not want the limelight alone. What she truly wanted was Mr. Gallagher by her side.

◆　◆　◆

He'd done the right thing, so why was he still miserable? Donovan paced the empty stables at Wilmore. Probably because he'd ruined his new start. God had blessed him with a fortune in gold, a house, being reunited with Kelly, even a chance at...love.

Doing the right thing might've saved most of those, but it could not save his friendship with Miss Heyer. Because eventually, he had to tell her the truth. Then she'd never want to see him again, and any chance at their friendship being something more would be gone. His new start again marred.

And it was all his doing.

He could no longer pass blame for his destructive bitterness. The grief that had blackened to anger and coursed through his veins like a blight, tainting everything in his reach. Donovan's feet stilled, half draped in shadow, half bathed in the light of the single ramshackle lantern. Mayhap it would've been better if he'd never found the gold.

"Mr. Gallagher?" That voice jolted through his senses.

Donovan looked up. The sun set behind Miss Heyer, silhouetting her in a pink glow. Why had she come here? "You should be at the fair." Away from him.

"As should you."

An ear-thrumming silence fell over the stable, digging a trench between them with each passing second. He kept quiet, let it work. Mayhap it would convince Miss Heyer to leave, protect her from him and the truth a little while longer.

Miss Heyer tucked a wisp of blond behind her ear, cleared her throat lightly. "Everyone loves the carousel. Your reporter said he's going to push for the story to make front page."

"I'm glad." *One less regret to plague him.* Donovan clamped his mouth shut.

The silence resumed its work, tossing aside the sands of time, deepening the void between them grain by grain. Yet Miss Heyer would not leave.

She fidgeted, wrapping both arms about herself, letting them fall. "The farmers s— sold the entirety of their produce. And the artisans all their wares. When I left, people were riding the carousel for the third or fourth time. Anyone not on the carousel was dancing in the street to the music." She chose her next words slowly, with care. "Your presence was dearly missed...by Kelly...by everyone."

She'd missed *him*?

"Certain you won't go back with me?" The question held a silent *please*.

Donovan retreated from the lantern light into shadow. He couldn't let himself enjoy what could never be. After tonight, she'd know the truth. Then she'd understand. "Nay, but you should return to the revelry."

For a moment, she still refused to stir, a heaviness seeming to weigh on her body as well as her words. "All right...but I wish to give you a present before I depart. To thank you. Let me fetch it."

"Wait." His word stopped her midstep. He couldn't let her give him a gift. A sigh shuddered through him. He hadn't wanted to spoil her big day, but it looked like he'd best tell her the truth right now. Donovan kept his gaze buried in shadow. "There's somethin' you don't know about me, Miss Heyer. Something I must confess. When I returned to Brookside, I. . .hated you and—"

"I'm aware. You were not exactly discreet." A hint of laughter seasoned her voice.

"Let me finish." Donovan swiped his pomade-free hair from his eyes, sighing. "I not only hated you; I aimed to make you pay for sacking me. That's why I nominated myself for fair chairman. I needed an excuse to be near you. . .to find something to use against you."

Miss Heyer fell into the trench of silence.

Now she was beginning to understand. "The day I came to tea, I rummaged through your private letters and learned of your wager. Ever since, I planned to sabotage the carousel on the eve o' the fair. Force you from Brookside in disgrace." His shoulders drooped and jaw tensed as he studied the floorboards. Now she knew everything. Knew he wasn't worthy of her.

Donovan waited for a burst of anger, for the betrayal to ignite sparks of fiery words from her mouth. But she said nothing. Not a word. Was she in shock? Or had he wounded her to the point of tears? He looked up to find Miss Heyer. . .smiling.

Smiling at him with a faerie sparkle illuminating her beautiful blue eyes.

"Are ya hard of hearing, Miss Heyer? I plotted to sabotage the carousel, ruin your life."

"But you didn't. You didn't go through with it, Donovan." Miss Heyer's smile did not dim. "Knowing that only makes the fair's success more precious."

Precious? "Sophia, have you had drink?"

"Let me finish." Sophia raised the dueling eyebrow that loved to challenge his every word. "You were angry and plotted to ruin the carousel, but the fact that you did not go through with your plot proves that your anger toward me has subsided. That you've forgiven my horrible mistake. Forgiven me."

"Aye." Because he'd finally realized the bitterness had only ever poisoned himself. "Mrs. Tooley told me what you did for Kelly."

"Then I shall have a discussion with her about the definition of the word *anonymous*."

"I'll pay you ba—"

"You most certainly will not. Consider it compensation for unjust dismissal, and we shall forget the whole matter." Sophia slowly retreated from the stables. "Now, I am going to give you a gift, and you, good sir, are going to refrain from being a stubborn-headed fool and accept it." With a wink, she disappeared out the door.

Moments later she returned, tether in hand, leading into his stables the black-and-white painted foal they'd delivered. The foal had its mother's strong build and fiery eyes in miniature. It'd be a gallant steed one day. She couldn't be giving him such an animal?

Sophia halted a handbreadth from him and extended the foal's tether. "Since this fellow rekindled memories of your dear Thunder, I think he belongs with you. I know you shall do a fine job raising him. Might I suggest the name Lightning?"

Donovan's gaze staggered from the rope to the foal. Could God be giving him yet another chance? A chance he did not deserve. *Forgive.* The word again thrummed into his mind. He'd thought that word was only meant for others, but might it also be for himself?

Sophia tapped the tether against his right hand. "You do not always have to pay for everything, Donovan. Some things are freely given."

Forgive. Freely given. The cold, heavy misery Donovan had worn for years slipped to the ground. This foal was his new start. A new home, new life, here in Brookside. All he had to do was depart from the shadows, reach into the lantern's glow, and accept this precious gift that showed God had not given up on him. That Sophia still thought him the best man in Brookside.

Donovan stepped forward and accepted the rope, holding on to Sophia's gloved fingers longer than necessary. "Thank you."

"You're quite welcome. Now that that is settled, are you going to propose or shall I?" Sophia squeezed his fingers and raised her dueling eyebrow, smiling in the way he'd once found infuriating.

Right now he found it irresistible. With his free hand, Donovan seized Sophia's waist and, drawing her toward his chest, planted a kiss on that marvelous smile.

When he pulled away, Sophia's freckled cheeks blushed the same pink as the sky. "While I quite approve of your unconventional proposal, Mr. Gallagher, I must insist you do things properly and take a knee."

Aye, he would, gladly.

Right after he gave the faerie one more kiss.

Novelist **Angela Bell** is a twenty-first-century lady with nineteenth-century sensibilities. Her activities consist of reading voraciously, drinking copious amounts of tea, and writing letters with a fountain pen. She currently resides in the southernmost region of Texas with pup Mr. Darcy and kitties Lizzie Bennett, and Lord Sterling. One might describe Angela's fictional scribblings as historical romance or as Victorian history and steampunk whimsy in a romantic blend. Whenever you need a respite from the twenty-first-century hustle, please visit her cyberspace parlor, www.AuthorAngelaBell.com, where she can be found waiting with a pot of English tea and some Victorian cordiality.

Civilizing Clementine

by Dianne Christner

Dedication

A big hug to my husband, Jim, who is my number one supporter.
And appreciation goes to Greg Johnson of WordServe Literary Agency, who
has provided guidance in my writing career and is a constant source of encouragement.

Part One:

Gold Rush Days—August 1849

Chapter One

Thunder shook the ground, and Clementine Cahill's slim body shivered. All alone now, she fingered her brown braid with one hand and nudged her droopy brim with the other to stare at the magical pokes Pa claimed were their golden tickets to a fair and equal opportunity. *Where is Pa?* His Louisville dream was the bedtime fairy tale she'd been raised on, far back as she could recall. One she no longer believed. She only hoped the pea-sized nuggets Pa had danced over, deeming them his "chunk of the mother lode," would buy something more appetizing than the tough biscuits growing stale by an ebbing fire.

Another band of lightning eerily illuminated her canvas home. With a frown, she stilled her hands. So far, the bulging pouches had diminished her fair and equal opportunities. Because of them, she remained at camp guarding the newly acquired stash. She tugged the waist of her baggy britches and reassuringly touched the cold steel she bore. No worries. Looters weren't fool enough to brave the storm. Nor were any bears or cougars prowling. Every instinctive creature was shoring up camp or slinking into dens.

Camp was lonely without Pa and his partners, the Soto Toro brothers, who would normally be rehashing the day's antics and weighing out their gleanings. Even the reporter, Samuel Whitburn, whom they'd taken under wing, had departed weeks earlier for San Francisco. When he'd been writing his California gold rush scoop, they'd forged a fast friendship. The loneliness would have been unbearable if not for the excitement of the storm that had blown in late that afternoon.

Clementine untied the tent flap and wind billowed inside, slamming her eighteen-year-old body with blunt force as her blue eyes peered hopefully into the menacing black-forested backdrop of the Sierra Nevada mountain range. *Where is Pa?* Bracing herself against the continuing onslaught, she placed her forefingers into her mouth and gave a manly whistle. Then listened. The only echoing sounds were a tinny pelting of rain against some mining equipment and the thrashing of trees. She couldn't even hear the lapping of the American River near camp. She sighed. *Probably holed up somewheres safe and dry. All three of 'em.* But a spooky foreboding tingled up her spine.

Pa was her mainstay, all she had in life. She detested being apart, feeling so puny and unsure about things. She caught the flap and fought the wind to fiddle with its bindings. *Stupid leather pokes. Nothin' but trouble if'n I know anythin' bout anythin'.*

◆   ◆   ◆

"Miss Clementine."

She jerked, took in the wee morning dawn. It was quiet now. Too quiet.

"Wake up, miss."

101

Bolting upright, she recognized the voice. "*Senor* Vicente?" Crossing the room and opening the flap, she acknowledged the terror in the fidgeting Chilean's eyes. Panicking, she asked, "What's wrong? Where's Pa?"

Vicente Soto Toro jerked his head to the left where his brother Flavio bent over a crude litter.

Rushing forth, she gasped, "Pa." She sank to her haunches and smoothed Pa's damp hair and met his pain-filled gaze. "Oh no. What happened?"

Senor Flavio replied in Spanish-accented English, "The river overflowed. Swept him away."

Pa finished, "A log crushed my leg." She noticed his right leg wore a bloodied tourniquet and was strapped to his litter.

She glanced nervously at Senor Flavio. "Who tended it?"

Pa explained, "The brothers took me to the camp *medico*. But we need a real doctor. I can't lose my leg."

Nodding, she asked, "But where?"

"San Francisco. Daughter, get our stuff together. Vicente went after a wagon."

Gloomy thoughts bombarded Clementine. Pa could lose his leg. She could be orphaned. San Francisco was miles away and an arduous journey even for uninjured travelers. Fretfully, she verified their Chilean friend had already departed for the wagon. She glanced at Pa, and he curled his finger, motioning her close. Leaning near, she expected him to convey something personal, loving, and reassuring, and so she met his gaze expectantly. "Pa?"

"Hide the gold. An' bring it along."

Stricken anew, she fought back tears. Her life was being swept into a fast current toward a place she didn't wish to go. But she clenched her lips and nodded. "Yup." Reluctantly, she headed into their tent and obeyed his instructions.

◆　◆　◆

Five days later, the lurching wagon, which had survived mountainous pack trails and crowded ferries, rolled into San Francisco. Clementine's gaze rose above the sideboards from her position in the back where she tended Pa. Her eyes widened. The city had changed drastically since their time tucked away in the Sierra Nevada hills panning for their golden ticket to a fair and equal opportunity. Her bottom jaw slackened as she took in the bustling surroundings.

The same wind-flattened bushes and sand hills encircled the town, but canvas tents and shanties filled every available crack and crevice between the earlier-existing one-story frame and adobe structures. Gulls swarmed over putrid garbage and animal entrails, which littered uneven, unplanked roads. People of every color and language stumbled and bustled to and fro.

Flavio drove the mules onto Montgomery Street with a whistle. "Whew-wee. Would you look at that."

When their Chilean friends picked up local phrases, Clementine usually found it endearing, if not entertaining. But this time, she could only gawk. Vicente, who rode shotgun, touched the brim of his straw *chupalla*, issuing Spanish greetings, but nobody paid him any heed.

They halted outside a slapdash building with a shingle that read PHYSICIAN. The Soto Toro brothers wasted no time placing Pa on a litter and carrying him inside. The crowded room was filled with men who turned as one to stare at them. Especially her, she realized. Curious gazes wandered along her brown braid, glanced at her men's britches, and then returned up to her face. The brothers frowned at the starstruck gazers.

"Apologies, miss," emanated an educated voice from a bearded man wearing a red flannel shirt. "Not many women here. We mean no harm."

Clementine gave a hesitant nod, feeling heat rise to her cheeks. "None taken."

But when the doctor appeared from behind a curtain to call the next patient, one of the men stood and snapped off his slouch hat, motioning her forward. "Ladies first."

"Thanks," she replied gratefully.

The Chilean brothers wasted no time getting Pa behind the curtain and then placing the litter on top of a table created out of food crates. The physician, however, paid more attention to Clementine than his patient. He smiled. "Arthur Payne. Pleased to make your acquaintance, miss."

"No need for perty talk. As ya can see, Pa needs yer care."

Dr. Payne cleared his throat. "Of course. Let's have a look." Keeping a stoic face, he removed the bandages. Pa grimaced when he poked at the wound. "Stitches held." He prodded a few more places and Pa squirmed. "But I'm afraid one of the bones needs to be reset."

Pa lifted his head. "Vicente! Take Clemmie out." She noticed that Flavio had already disappeared, probably tending the mules.

"But Pa—I wanna stay."

"No."

Dr. Payne smiled. "Let 'im keep his dignity, Miss—"

"Cahill."

"Miss Cahill," he repeated. "You'll serve him better that way."

With a reluctant nod, she turned away and ducked around the curtain Senor Vicente held for her. When she stepped into the waiting room, her gaze locked with a person of acquaintance.

"Samuel?"

The reporter hurried across the room to her. "Why, Clementine. I didn't expect to see you here. Is everything all right?"

"Nope. Pa's hurt bad. The doc's settin' his leg in there."

Samuel's brown eyes lit with concern. "I'm sorry to hear it."

Clementine was comforted to share her problem and renew their friendship.

He ran a hand through his hair. "I've missed you. And the others."

"I was jest thinkin' the same thing." His departure had left her aching over the loss. Pa had taught Samuel to pan for gold, and she'd taught him how to make flapjacks. Though he looked like a city feller, he wasn't afraid to get dirty. He didn't get offended when he was the object of a joke. Suddenly, her mind jerked to the present with concern.

"Are ya sick?"

He chuckled. "No."

"Injured?"

He shook his head. "Don't worry about me. I'm fine. Just doing a story."

"Miss Cahill." The doctor peeked around the curtain. "You can come in now."

Concern for Pa overshadowed their reacquaintance, and she broke off the conversation. "Take care, now."

"Good luck," he called.

She scurried across the room and behind the curtain, instantly taking in her pa's still form and pale face. With growing apprehension, she looked at the attending physician. "Is he—alive?"

"Yes, just resting. The laudanum's made him drowsy."

"Will he keep 'is leg?"

The physician scribbled on a piece of paper and handed it to Clementine. "I'm going to do everything I can to make that happen. Give this note to the clerk at the City Hotel. He owes me a favor. Get him in a real bed, and I'll check on him in the morning."

Such gratefulness rose in her throat, she could barely speak. "Thet's real kind, sir."

"I hate to see worry mar such a pretty face." He smiled. "Anyway, your father paid me for my services."

She'd plumb forgot all about the gold. She guessed Pa was right after all. It did provide their golden ticket to a fair and equal opportunity. She smiled with relief. "Well, I'll be seein' ya tomorra' then."

"I'm looking forward to it."

A pleasant twinge shot through her, along with the realization that she looked forward to seeing him, too. He was, after all, one of the few men with a clean-shaven face. Samuel didn't count. He was too much like a brother.

◆　◆　◆

For ten dollars a night, Clementine and Pa bought themselves one cot with a hair-stuffed mattress and a coarse blanket. Pa slept in it. She occupied a chair and slept little, given all the drunken shouts and constant footfall outside their door. But in the morning she had the luxury of combing her hair in front of a real looking glass and was amazed at the changes in her appearance over the past six months. Her cheeks had hollowed, and her skin looked rougher from the sun and elements. But if she wasn't mistaken, she'd gotten a little curvier.

A rap at the door brought an end to her vain thoughts, and she welcomed Senor Flavio into the room. With a proud grin, he placed a heaping plate of sourdough pancakes on the rough little table beside her.

"What's this?" she exclaimed with pleasure.

"A treat." Flavio grinned. "You don't have to cook."

She dug in with gusto and Flavio laughed. "Better slow down. The distinguished doctor is just down the hall. He should be at the door any moment."

Swiping her arm across her mouth, she glanced at Pa, who was chuckling.

Grinning, she asked, "How long you been awake?"

"Long enough to see you primping. Your ma used to do that."

"Ain't nothing like that. Just curious if I still look like myself."

"Do you?" Flavio inquired.

Thankfully, she didn't need to respond because of the ensuing rap at the door. Flavio glanced around the tiny compartment and told the doctor, "Guess I'll wait outside so you can come in."

"Appreciate that." The doctor entered gracefully, giving Clementine his full attention. "Hello, Miss Cahill."

She replied, "Jest Clementine," then blushed to think she'd never offered such a privilege to the Soto Toro brothers. But she was on a first-name basis with Samuel.

"Well, Clementine. How's your father this morning?"

"See fer yerself."

Pa struggled to sit up and banged his head on a rafter. The doctor chuckled. "Careful, there."

Clementine shoved her chair at the doctor. "Here."

"Good idea." He sat and drew back the blanket, examining his recent work. Finally, he said, "If you can keep it immobile, you have a good chance of walking again. Though you'll probably have a limp."

"That's great, Pa!" But his expression didn't contain any pleasure.

"I'll check on you in about a week. But you must stay off it until then. Understand?"

Pa scowled. "A whole week? I've already been off it that long. I need to get back to my work."

Dr. Payne replied, "To be truthful, you probably won't be able to resume your previous activities. It might be two months before you can really use that leg. But let's take it one step at a time."

"Wish I could," Pa grunted, unhappy with his own attempted humor.

As the doctor stood, Clementine said, "Thanks fer comin'."

"My pleasure."

Feeling disconcerted beneath the doctor's prolonged and intense gaze, she blurted, "Do we owe ya anythin'?"

"No." The doctor worried his lower lip. "But I'd consider it a good turn if you'd allow me to escort you on a picnic."

Clementine's mouth gaped. It had been the furthest thing from her mind. "A picnic?" She faltered. "But where?"

"Someplace pretty. Like you."

Pa cleared his throat, and the doctor realized his breach of etiquette. "With your approval, sir."

Frowning, Pa studied her. "I'll leave it up to Clemmie."

She shrugged, struggling to conceal the excitement marching up her spine. "Yup. That'll do, I reckon."

The handsome doctor grinned. "Good. Wear your prettiest dress."

Clementine cringed. "I don't own no dress and wouldn't wear one if'n I did."

The grin vanished. "Never?"

"Nope." She shook her head adamantly.

Studying her intently, the doctor gave a brief nod. Then he snatched his black bag. "Perhaps another time, then."

Clementine and her pa watched in astonishment and deep humiliation as the doctor quickly departed, drawing the door closed behind him.

Jerking her gaze to the bed, she demanded, "Pa? What jest happened?"

"I fear you scared him off, Clemmie."

Anger coursed through her veins. "Jest because I wouldn't wear no dress? Well, la-dee-da! I don't need ta go on no picnic with Mr. Snooty anyways." She placed her hands on her hips. "But he better not ditch you, too. Ya don't seppose?"

"Don't worry. He'll be back."

With her cheeks aglow with indignation, she turned her attention to the plate of pancakes. "Let's jest eat."

◆ ◆ ◆

Charles Cahill almost choked with Clementine shoving pancakes down his throat with a silent fury he'd only ever witnessed in her ma. He felt like strangling the snobbish physician who had raised Clementine's hopes only to immediately crush them. It was the worst sort of rejection, and his heart ached for his little girl's betrayal. Just because she was a little rough on the outside was no reason to treat her as anything less than a lady.

But after giving it further consideration, he realized he was to blame for Clementine's situation. He hadn't noticed when she'd become a woman, nor when she'd taken on the mountain-man lingo. They'd been surrounding themselves with some rough-and-tumble types over the last several years. First at the lumber camps and recently at the mining camp. What would her departed mother think if she knew he'd allowed this to happen? He hadn't been aware when Clemmie had digressed from using proper grammar. It must have happened gradually. Every time he'd uprooted her, she'd always tried to adapt and please him.

He pondered how he might set matters right again. Bribing the doctor with gold to extend another picnic invitation would be foolhardy. A faint idea niggled away at him. There was some scandalous school he'd read about in the newspaper. It was operated by English-bred women. What was it called? The Traveling Manners? Nope. That wasn't it. Given his bedridden state, after Clemmie quit force-feeding him, he had plenty of time to recollect. *The Last Resort Traveling Etiquette School.* When he'd read the advertisement, an unusual element had caught his attention. The Featherstone sisters traveled to their clients' homes. But would they travel all the way to San Francisco? He figured he had the golden tickets to Clementine's fair and equal opportunity with the snooty doctor. And it would be good practice for entering into Louisville society, too. He just needed to get somebody to haul him over to the telegraph office.

Chapter Two

"I ain't gettin' no dress!" When Clementine had chased the doctor away, the incident left her feeling humiliated, but mostly she blamed herself for disappointing Pa. It was tragic enough he had a debilitating injury, and she felt guilty adding to his misery. But good grief, it'd been so long since she'd worn a dress, she didn't even remember how it was done. She didn't wish to appear foolish. "Nope," she maintained with hands planted firmly on her hips.

"Have you noticed the ratio of men to women in this city? It's a thousand to one," he reasoned.

Relaxing her stance, she replied, "I'd be a fool not ta see, even if ya are exaggeratin'."

"I'm not exaggerating. It's probably more than that. Anyway, a dress will make you respectable. Keep the men at bay since I can't protect you like I should."

Clementine laughed. "Oh, Pa. Ya know I carry iron. Don't worry so much. I'll jest stick my hair up under my cap and pull it down so far they cain't tell I'm a girl."

Pa ran his hands through his hair. "They'll still tell. And when did you start butchering your grammar? Your ma and I didn't teach you to talk that way."

"What?" She couldn't disguise her shock. What had gotten into Pa? She talked jest fine. And why was he talking all proper like all of a sudden?

"Once, you talked like a lady."

For an instant, she froze. Her ma's gentle instructions came to mind. But that was such a long time ago, as far removed as her pa's fairy-tale dreams. They had nothing to do with the harsh realities they'd endured the last several years. She was proud of herself for adapting to a man's world, struggling to fit in as best she could. She softened her voice. "If'n I was a lady, jest what would I be doin' here in this town?"

He clenched his wheelchair armrests. "Blamed if I know."

Moving to the looking glass, she twisted her braid and shoved it under her slouch hat. Turning, she gave Pa a triumphant smile. "Now let's go find the Soto Toro brothers and git to bus'ness."

Pa was checking his gun. But she didn't miss his smug expression, as if he'd won the argument. Surely he hadn't already bought her a dress? He had gone out alone with the brothers, and they were constantly whispering about something. Well, if he had, he was wasting his gold. She could be as stubborn as anybody. But as they left the hotel room, she didn't feel so stubborn or strong. In fact, a weakness settled over her as she cast one last longing gaze. Pa claimed they wouldn't be returning. And truth be told, she'd miss that looking glass.

◆　◆　◆

Clementine tugged her hat low and tried not to sway her hips. Thankfully, nobody stared at her like the times she'd worn her hair down. Most gazes were drawn to Pa's wheelchair, and some even tossed glares when they had to concede the right-of-way. She supposed they didn't think an invalid should be taking up space in such a rough, demanding environment. Here most men were strong bodied and under the age of thirty-five.

She was grateful for the Soto Toro brothers' presence. Their strapping physiques and fierce protective air would afford Pa's security as well as her own. The brothers had caught gold fever and left prominent positions in their Chilean homeland to travel to California, where they'd met the Cahills. An affinity was instantly formed. Senor Vicente was the business-minded one, while Senor Flavio wielded charm. Together they made perfect partners for Pa's gold-digging venture. He complemented the trio by adding American know-how.

Mostly, Clementine was a boyish tagalong who did the cooking and cleaning. What little there was of it. And the crazy thing was, they'd been successful. The brothers also had a stash of gold nuggets.

"We practically stole 'em." Senor Flavio grinned, pointing toward the bay.

Stole what? Clementine's ears perked, suddenly sure there was more astir than fancy dresses. She knew they wouldn't actually steal anything, although they had hushed every time she approached. Now she looked where Flavio gestured. The morning fog was burning off so that in the distance, she could see a cove clogged with vessels all the way out to Yerba Buena Island.

"Ther' so crowded tagether. How can they sail?" she asked.

Pa chuckled. "They're abandoned."

"But why?" she gasped.

"Their crews got gold fever."

Clementine couldn't believe such costly ships could be left to rot. "But somethin' has ta be done," she insisted. It was mind-boggling to take in several hundred anchored and abandoned ships with their masts shorn of sails.

Pa replied, "There's still a few captains fighting off scavengers and hoping to get another crew. Many have gone off to the gold fields themselves."

Before she could fully digest the information, their conversation was interrupted.

"Mr. Cahill!" a panting voice hailed. "Wait up!"

Clementine whirled round to see Samuel Whitburn, the reporter, huffing as he ran uphill. When he finally reached them, he grinned at her and stooped beside Pa's chair, still trying to catch his breath.

"Samuel, lad. Good to see you again."

They clasped hands. Samuel exclaimed, "You're looking much better than the last time I saw you." Clementine realized she hadn't noticed he was still in the room when they'd whisked Pa away from the doctor's office.

"I'll mend," Pa replied. "But I won't be going back into the field anytime soon."

"I'm sorry to hear it, sir."

Samuel stood and greeted the rest of the party. He gave her an approving smile. "Nice getup. But you didn't fool me."

"Can't get her to wear a dress," Pa complained.

Clementine rolled her gaze heavenward and changed the topic. She pointed toward the harbor. "We were jest talkin' 'bout those abandoned ships. You ever see the likes?"

"I've done a couple stories on it," Samuel replied grimly. He asked Pa, "Where you staying?"

Pa eyed Clementine then replied, "We were lucky enough to find someone willing to sell us their ships."

She stuttered, "Ships? But. . .but we can't sail. Yer not thinkin'. . ." Her mind flew to possible ventures that required ships. Would they head to Louisville with their spoils? Was that why Pa wanted her to don a dress? Panicking, she fixed her attention back on the ensuing conversation.

Senor Flavio became animated. "There's a pretty clipper out there that's going to be your new home."

Confused, she tipped her head. "Pa? Are we sailin' or not?"

"Nope."

Relief flooded over her.

"We're taking up residence there while I recuperate. And we bought us a whaling ship and a brig we're going to salvage for building material. We're going into the housing business."

"That's brilliant, Mr. Cahill," Samuel exclaimed. "Which one will be your new home?"

She allowed the information to settle as the men started toward the harbor. With all the makeshift tents and overcrowded sleeping establishments, Pa was probably onto something more lucrative than panning. While she liked the idea of remaining in San Francisco, she wasn't sure about living aboard a ship.

Flavio pointed. "See that green clipper? It's tall sparred."

Ignorant of sea lingo, she was still able to pick out the chosen vessel. It appeared both majestic and forlorn with its three masts stripped of sails.

Pa grinned. "Ain't she a beauty now? Let's go check her out."

Samuel replied, "I must turn back. But I'll see you around town."

"Yep, stay out of trouble, young man."

"Of course," he replied, giving Clementine a wink.

She grinned, happy to have a friend in the area. When he'd gone, she stared at the ship. "Better than a tent. If'n I don't get seasick."

"Guess we'll soon find out," Senor Flavio teased.

"I hope we don't hafta swim to it."

"Nope. We bought us a couple fine dinghys, too."

A sudden rush of excitement swept over her. And to think she thought all the hush-hush was over a stupid dress. She should've known her pa was made of more mettle than that.

"Well, what are we waitin' fer?"

Soon Clementine found herself scrambling up a rope ladder and pulling herself over the railing of the groaning, creaking craft. She braced her feet and took a long draught of the salty air, wondering how long it would take to get used to the constant movement.

The brothers hoisted up Pa and his chair, and he started maneuvering himself about the deck. She scampered over the main deck, taking in the teak hull with brass bolts. There was tall rigging and a few barrels and coils of rope. It was a fine ship, and she found herself feeling sorry for the captain who'd lost it, even if Pa claimed the captain had been eager for the sale so he could buy his pick and shovel and head for the hills.

When Pa returned to her, he beamed. "Well, Clemmie, it ain't a castle, but it's pretty grand, isn't it?"

"Yup. Grand." And ridiculous at the same time.

"It'll probably be easier for me to take the stateroom so I don't have to go up and down that ladder. I can set up our office there, too. And I can scare off any trespassers. But right now I want to go down to the between deck."

The brothers helped pa down a ladder to an open space referred to as the passenger saloon. It had a long table and benches. Along either side were vented doors to individual cabins. The brothers had cleaned the ship. They'd moved and sold whatever they could scavenge, retaining what would be needed to make a comfortable home.

"Choose yourself a room, Clemmie."

She wasted no time, dashing in and out of cabins, discovering they were all the same, containing a bed with a mattress, a chamber pot, and little else. She wavered between one with a window toward the shore and one toward Yerba Buena Island, then opted for the latter. She bounced on the bed. Then she closed the door and lay down. Even though it was small and barren, it was more than anything she'd had for herself in a long while. A private space she could call her own.

"Clemmie! Let's check out the galley!"

Reluctantly rising, she hurried out and helped her pa to the ship's kitchen. Her gaze scanned the small area, and her lip curled with delight. "A stove," she squealed. "With plenty a room fer storin' and dicin'. We'll be livin' in grand style."

Pa's chest swelled. "Make a list of things you'll be needing. And no skimping."

Clementine smiled. "All right, Pa." She thought she'd died and gone to heaven until just a few hours later when she found herself puking over the railing. The following day, she continued to feel queasy and light-headed. Everyone had gone ashore to start the new construction business except for an old seaman called Salty, who had been hired to guard the ship from scavengers. She couldn't wait until she felt good enough to explore. Life had taken an exciting turn, and she yearned to leave her confinement and embrace it.

◆　◆　◆

One week later, Clementine remained ill. She was awakened from a long nap by the sound of a rapping on her cabin door.

"Come in," she croaked, her voice hoarse from sleep and disuse. Expecting Pa or Salty, her eyes widened to see the tall man who graced her doorway.

"I hear you're seasick."

She'd forgotten how strikingly handsome the doctor was. "Yup," she managed. "An' haven't even raised the anchor."

He smiled. "Nothing to be embarrassed about. It affects some more than others."

He knelt and withdrew a stethoscope from his bag. "Take a deep breath."

She feared she'd choke, having him so close and taking up her air space. His striking features made her aware of her own filth and tangled hair. Writhing in humiliation and remembrance of his earlier rebuff, she worried the rapid beat of her heart would reveal her anxiety. When he drew away, she managed to meet his gaze.

He smiled. "Sounds good."

"I ain't gonna die? 'Cause I feel like I'm dyin'."

He reached into his black satchel and removed a vial and spoon. "Open wide."

Feeling utterly foolish as he attempted to spoon-feed her the medicine, she shook her head. "I can do it."

"Please, it's my pleasure." She froze as he tipped the spoon then brought up a fresh cloth to dab at the corners of her mouth. "I saw your Chilean friends brought fresh water aboard. You'd feel better if you bathed."

Feeling the heat of a blush, she defended herself. "I've been too sick ta do anythin'."

"I understand. But you'll soon be feeling better." He gave her instructions for the medication and started to leave.

"Doctor. Wait!"

He turned back and lifted a brow. "Yes?"

"Can you wait fer Pa? Check on his leg?"

"I already did. I promoted him to a cane. He's healing nicely."

"I didn't know he was aboard." She faltered then wet her lips. "I guess yer happy yer work is done. That ya don't have ta come back."

"I guess you're happy you won't need to wear a dress." He cocked an eyebrow as if she might want to change her mind.

She raised her chin. "Yup."

He nodded. "It's been a pleasure."

She shrugged.

He tipped his hat and was gone.

When the door closed, she shut her eyes and tried to blot out his memory. She didn't need no shifty-eyed, highfalutin doctor smilin' his flirty smile at her and judging her either. At least this time, Pa hadn't witnessed her humiliation.

◆ ◆ ◆

Meanwhile, in a bandbox drawing room in the Philadelphia District of Northern Liberties, two sisters discussed their latest employment opportunity over afternoon tea.

Merryweather Featherstone, the youngest and most resourceful of the sisters, defended her position. "I couldn't be more delighted with the opportunity. Imagine a tropical boat ride with colorful birds and butterflies flitting about our heads. What could be more delightful? And such agreeable weather to be enjoyed when we set anchor in San Francisco."

Fiona Featherstone set down her cup and pinched her thin lips before replying, "Anchor, indeed. I daresay you forget that we will be bouncing about like a cork in the harbor. How can we teach etiquette while living aboard an old abandoned ship? I daresay there isn't any society to even be found in such a far-fetched, remote place. And I do not relish mucking through malaria-ridden jungles to get to another ungrateful woman who will hate us upon sight and rudely point out all our imperfections, making fun of our English accents."

"Indeed, Althea did have a foul mouth before we tamed it. But my dearest and vainest sister, you know full well that cholera is spreading in Philadelphia even as we speak. And surely your skin has gotten a little thicker by now? I know mine has. We would do well to focus on the end results rather than hoping for a welcoming party."

"Thick skin? Where did you pick up that crude idiom?"

Merryweather blushed. "A slip of the tongue to be sure."

Fiona's hand fluttered at her heart. "What's to become of us? Are we inheriting the traits of our charges instead of transforming them into ladies?"

When Merryweather remained quietly repentant, Fiona shook her head. "I'm sorry, dearest. You aren't my pupil any longer, are you?"

Merry smiled. She was only five years younger than Fiona, but her sister had always mothered her.

Fiona continued, "I suppose I'm just weary. How I'd wished for an idle hour or two. I'd so hoped for a delightful respite before sprinting across the country again."

Merry's blue eyes brightened as her sister's resolve weakened. "Have a scone and cheer up. You always fair well at sea. Remember the feel of air at the rail, watching the dolphins and whales play, and how luminous the sea is at night?"

Fiona grew introspective. "I do remember our voyage from the motherland with fondness."

"The journey will be restful. And I have great hope of prevailing with Miss Clementine Cahill. We haven't failed yet."

Fiona brightened. But she fingered the mauve damask armrest and sighed. "I so hoped to replace our worn drapes with new silks before we left home again. Have you noticed how shabby this room has become?"

"But dear Fiona, we are headed to the gold mines. It is our finest offer ever, and upon our return, we'll be able to replace the carpets, too."

"I will have another scone. I feel the need for fortification."

"Of course, my dear. I'll enjoy one, too. And then I'll write the letter. Surely, the best is yet to come."

Part Two:

Last Resort Traveling
Etiquette School—Autumn 1849

Chapter Three

N ow be careful, Miss Clementine."

The small boat tipped precariously as Clementine peered expectantly over the side. "I got it!"

Salty leaned and gripped the other side of the boat to counterbalance while dipping his chin to get a better view. "Easy, now."

"I know. I know." Clementine cranked the brass reel and fought against its pull. "It's a big 'un if'n I ever saw one." Over the past weeks, a routine had been established aboard the ship. Once she'd found her sea legs, taking a dinghy out fishing with Salty, her newly appointed guardian, had become Clementine's favorite pastime. While most men in San Francisco were of the young and robust sort, this seaman had sailed into the bay and gotten permanently stranded. The job Pa offered suited him because his rickety bones were begging for an easier lifestyle.

Clementine loved the feel of the brackish air and found she had a knack for fishing. For once, she was good at something—according to the praise she received at mealtime. With a giant heave, she plopped the struggling fish inside the boat. Its splat sprayed her face with seawater. The creature flopped against the floorboards. While she blindly wiped water from her eyes, it suddenly leaped, smacking her leg. Squealing, Clementine fell backward. Her eyes widened as the boat rocked precariously, and then her gaze fastened upon Salty.

"Careful now," he chuckled, remaining calm as usual. "Don't relish fishing you out of the ocean or plucking seaweed out of your hair." He clobbered the flailing fish on the head and steadied the boat.

Clementine curled up her legs, watching Salty and feeling utterly foolish. "I wasn't scared. I jest didn't 'spect that." Since they'd bought the *Dragonfish*, it had been Salty who helped her overcome her seasickness long after the doctor's medicine was gone. He taught her to work the galley stove and how to play cards. Since he was her constant companion, she strove hard to win and maintain his respect. But try as she might to get him to teach her sailor lingo, he refused. Probably one of Pa's conditions since he seemed to have taken a sudden interest in the way she talked. But she could tell it hindered Salty a bit, for he spoke slowly and often hesitated as they conversed.

Grabbing the oars, Salty replied, "No worries. A fine striped bass. Let's get it back to the ship, and we can fry it up for supper."

Half an hour later, Clementine climbed over the railing and bent back, unknowingly presenting the backside of her britches to a pair of astonished female visitors. She reeled up the stringer and manhandled it over the railing. Hoisting it over her shoulder, she turned. And stopped in her tracks.

Staring at her with mouths agape were two women so brightly arrayed in feminine apparel and style that all Clementine could do was gawk. Slowly her mouth twitched. Then she giggled at the horror she read in their expressions. She slid the fish off her shoulder and let it plop at her boots. "Didn't know we was gettin' company."

The thinner of the two collected her composure first. "I am Fiona Featherstone. And this is my sister, Merryweather."

The second woman smiled warmly. "My pleasure, Miss. . .?"

"Clementine Cahill."

There was a brief silence. As the two older women sized her up, Clementine started to feel like a fish out of water. Apprehension trekked up her spine. Although she'd thought her life couldn't take a stranger turn, something odd was definitely happening. She had a peculiar feeling it involved her. In fact, an alarming thought slammed into her mind. Surely they weren't taking her away to civilization. She did have an aunt who somewhat resembled them who resided in Louisville.

"Your father invited us aboard, my dear. And I understand he is delayed."

Her panic increased. No, Pa wouldn't send her to Louisville without him. Would he? Not after all these years dragging her with him wherever he went, from lumber camps to mining camps. She wet her lips and slung the fish back over her shoulder.

Miss Fiona shrieked. Or was it Merryweather? Guess they weren't used to a little fish slime and sea spray. With a shrug, she invited, "Foller me down to the saloon. You can wait there while I clean this fish up fer supper." The constant swish and rustle of skirts behind her made the back of Clementine's neck bristle.

She offered the sisters a seat at a long table and marveled at the way they could manipulate all their fineries. Arching a brow, she turned to head back to the galley. Behind her she heard one of the sisters whisper to the other, "My dear sister, I don't believe I will survive this one."

Whatever dire straits approached, that comment bolstered Clementine's spirits. Now if she could just keep the edge on them, maybe she'd find a way to scare them away.

At the galley, she spotted Salty. "What do ye know 'bout this?" she demanded. "What is Pa up ta?"

"Ask him yourself. He just came aboard. Before he went to his room, he asked me to have you clean up and meet him in the passenger saloon."

Clementine slapped the fish on the counter and put her hands on her hips. "I jest came from there."

"Come on, Miss Clementine. My bones are weary today. Don't trouble me so."

"Fine! Let's go."

"Not me." Salty looked sheepish. "I'll fry up the fish. You wash your hands, change your clothes, and do as your pa wishes."

Fuming now, Clementine went to the galley bucket and cleaned her face and hands. "That'll do until I find out what's goin' on."

Returning to the saloon, she seated herself across the long table from the sisters.

"It's not polite to stare, my dear."

"I'm sorry. I just never saw the likes of you before." She delighted in the cringe that marred the taller one's face. Probably older, too, given her gray hair. "Pa's cleanin' up."

"Perhaps you'd like to do the same?"

Clementine glared. "I cleaned up already." When the gray-haired one slightly wrinkled her nose, Clementine added, "It's not me ya smell. The whole place smells like this in case ya haven't noticed."

"We have noticed, my dear," the black-haired sister replied with a smile. "And we're accustomed, as we've been at sea for about six weeks now."

"Oh."

"And I hope your voyage was favorable," Pa said upon entering the room.

Clementine watched the introductions fly, furrowing her brows as she tried to piece the situation together.

"I hope you're properly settled? Flavio brought your trunks aboard?"

Nearly jerking her head off her neck, Clementine stared at her pa. "Trunks? They're stayin'?"

"Yes, Clemmie. I invited them."

Clementine saw one of the sisters nod her head as if to encourage Pa to continue his explanation. He cleared his throat. "The Featherstone sisters have a traveling etiquette school, and they've agreed to. . . well. . .er. . .school you."

"What!" Clementine shook her head. "I can read. And Salty's doin' jest fine, teachin' me ever'thin' I oughta know."

"It's not his job to teach you how to survive in society," Pa explained. "It's his job to guard the ship. But the Featherstone sisters will teach you everything you will need to know for Louisville."

Louisville again. When would he give it up? "Society?" Clementine's mouth twisted distastefully. She felt her face heat with rage and humiliation. Exasperated, she flung up her arms in surrender. "Fine. You win, Pa. Buy me a stupid dress. But send these two a packin'. Ther's nothin' I wanna learn from the likes of them."

"Of course you may wear a dress, my poor dear," Merryweather cooed. "See, sister, Miss Clementine is most amiable."

"It's none of yer bus'ness," Clementine snapped.

Merryweather flinched, straightened her shoulders, and turned her gaze on Pa.

He hardened his voice. "Clementine! Enough! You will wear a dress and do whatever else the sisters ask you to do. Now apologize this instant."

"Sorry, yer highnesses." Clementine grabbed her britches and curtsied then turned and stormed into her room, slamming the door. Her furnishings were too slack to find anything worthwhile to throw against the wall, but for once in her life she felt like having a full-fledged tantrum. Clenching her fists, she went to the window and stared out at the blue ocean and the islands beyond. Through gritted teeth, she said, "It's Pa's dream, not mine." Then she felt her anger diminish as despair descended upon her. "I don't know how to be a lady. I jest cain't do it."

◆　◆　◆

The next morning Clementine refused to come out of her room. As the morning wore on, Salty called her name and pounded on the door. The sisters tried to appeal as well, but Clementine had come up with a plan. If she didn't come out, they couldn't school her.

Hadn't one of them whispered to the other that she didn't think she'd survive this one? When they gave up, they'd leave regardless of how much Pa was paying them. And if she didn't learn how to be a lady, then Pa would have to give up his far-fetched Louisville notion, too. Then everything could return to normal. If living on a ship was normal. And once Pa healed up good, they could return to the gold fields.

But her plan gave way when she heard scratching sounds at the door and quite suddenly the entire door was removed from its hinges. Salty shrugged apologetically and scampered away in betrayal.

"How delightful!" Merryweather exclaimed. "You're awake."

Clementine pulled the bedcovers up to her chin. "Get out!"

But Merryweather perched on the side of her bed. "Your father neglected to tell you the full name of our school. It's the Last Resort Traveling Etiquette School."

Clementine cringed at the implication.

"You see, you aren't our first charge who didn't wish to be refined. And certainly not our most stubborn or our most uncivilized charge. You will discover that together, Miss Fiona and I present a formidable opposition, and we will not budge in our intentions. And this morning, our intentions are bathing you and getting you into that gown you mentioned."

"You think yer bathin' me?" Clementine clarified threateningly.

"Indeed, we are. And remember that the better you cooperate, the sooner we'll be gone."

Clementine's first glimmer of hope shone through the absurd ordeal. A secondary plan formed in her mind. Pretend to cooperate so they'd leave. "If I put on thet stupid dress, ya'll leave?"

"Leave sooner," Merryweather corrected. "We have a few other ways we hope to refine you."

Before Clementine could reevaluate her plan, Merryweather whisked back the covers and Fiona entered, chirping, "Good morning." Together they drew Clementine kicking and scratching out of bed toward a huge tub that had been placed in the adjoining cabin. "Welcome to your dressing room. Later today, Mr. Salty will be making a door between the two cabins. Every lady needs a dressing room. And we've placed an order for a few pieces of furniture to brighten the place up a bit."

Clementine stiffened, alerting her eyes for escape possibilities. But the clever sisters soon had her disrobed. She'd never even seen herself fully naked and neither should they, she reasoned. She quickly jumped into the warm tub and sank down to her neck, closing her eyes with embarrassment. When she opened them Merryweather hoisted up her own blue skirt, her eyes twinkling. "See! We wear knee pads." Merryweather arched a defiant brow and lowered her skirt again. She had to admit they came well armed and might even be dangerous. And her shooting iron was back in her cabin!

Her gaze ran along the wall, noticing a chest of feminine clothing. Then she sputtered as the sisters poured water over her head and proceeded to wash her hair. Gleefully, she took in the fact that they looked wetter than she did by the time they were finished. With their own hair sopping and disheveled, they dressed her in a clean robe and brushed her hair, debating whether she'd look better with ringlets or a chignon.

Persistent, Clementine glowered. *And strong as oxes.* Her only hope was to outsmart them, and so she would bide her time. She believed she came away with more bruises than the sisters had acquired. They wore knee pads. Ridiculous! Of course, two against one wasn't a fair fight. Her arms ached from where they'd manhandled her. But not worse than when she hauled water or carried wood. Clementine was used to physical hardships. Defiantly now, she said, "A braid will do me jest fine."

"Of course, my dear," Fiona purred. "What a lovely suggestion. In whatever areas you cooperate, we are always happy to accommodate. Braids will be most lovely."

However, she quickly discovered their idea of braiding was drastically different from her own. And when she saw herself in a looking glass, she almost didn't recognize herself. "I look jest like a lady," she breathed.

"And now let's dress you like one."

Oh! Had she said that out loud? "I s'pose yer gonna dress me, too?" Although she feigned disgust, she secretly hoped it was true because now that they'd already seen her naked body anyway, she had no idea how to go about dressing herself in such strange contraptions. And she hated feeling foolish.

She soon discovered the sisters were practiced in dressing their charges and used to explaining the purpose for all the contraptions from petticoats and corsets to shawls, bonnets, and reticules. It was somewhat comforting to know there were other *last resort* women, that she wasn't the only oddball female in the world.

Merryweather explained, "Two petticoats will suffice until you've gotten used to them."

Clementine lifted her skirts to peer at her kid slippers.

Fiona warned, "A lady only lifts one side of her skirts, and only when necessary. To lift both sides is wanton."

"You did." Clementine cast Merryweather a look of accusation.

"I was just showing you my armor," Merryweather countered. "For your own sake."

"There's usually an exception to any rule," Fiona added.

Clementine replied, "In all my born days, I've ne'r been so fettered up. If'n I don't lift my skirts, I'm gonna fall flat on my face."

"We're going to practice walking, my dear. Try smaller, slower steps. And from now on, we will replace the phrase *if'n* with *if.*"

"But if'n. . ."

Fiona cleared her throat.

"If I"—Clementine corrected—"do that, I won't git nowheres that'a way."

Merryweather sighed. "I daresay we've accomplished enough for now. Let's retreat and refresh ourselves until we meet later for tea."

Thankful to be dismissed, Clementine headed to the main deck, determined to lift both sides of her skirts as high as she pleased, walking to the rail and gazing at the other ships. Nothing could be happening aboard any of them as ridiculous as what was happening aboard the *Dragonfish.* She stood alone with her thoughts, for Salty had taken to hiding.

She placed her elbows on the rail, slightly constricted by her gown's long tight sleeves. What would become of her? Were her days of galavantin' and freedom and fishin' gone for good? And how did they expect her to cook supper in these fixin's? As she pondered her situation, she suddenly remembered how wet and frazzled the sisters had become. A smile tickled her lips. At least she'd put up a good fight. And afterward, they'd needed to rest.

At tea, she was given eating and drinking instructions. And it was then that she found out that Pa had also hired a cook so that she could devote all her hours to becoming a proper lady. What a waste of money and *fair and equal opportunities*.

Merryweather smiled, unrolling a sheet of paper. "We are proud of you, my dear. Considering today's progress, we have created a schedule for this week's lessons. In the mornings we will practice grammar, and in the afternoons walking and manners. Tomorrow, you will meet your male chaperone."

Clementine choked, spewing tea across the white tablecloth the sisters had magically provided.

"Male chaperone?"

"Indeed. A Mr. Samuel Whitburn."

"Samuel?" Clementine's heart plummeted to her feet to imagine him witnessing her humiliations. And why would he even consent, unless. . . Oh no. "Is Pa payin' him, too?"

Merryweather turned to her sister. "I'm not aware of the arrangements. Are you?"

Fiona set down her teacup. "No, I'm not privileged to that information."

Clementine shoved her tea things away and placed her head in her hands. "Ugh. I hate this." It certainly couldn't get any worse than paying her only friend in the world to turn against her.

"Take courage, Miss Cahill," Merryweather urged.

Chapter Four

The next morning Merryweather helped Clementine dress in a blue gown. It was Merryweather's favorite color—one she always clad herself in—and she claimed it complemented Clementine's eyes. The dress was high-necked with a fitted waist and bell-shaped skirt. Just as the previous day's, the skirt touched the floor, and the sleeves were fitted and long so that they hindered anything Clementine wished to do. But she found herself doing what she didn't wish, practicing grammar. As they went over the basics, she discovered that the lessons awakened her memory to areas long suppressed. Pa was right. She'd once learned the proper usage of the English language and the information remained intact, but tucked away in her mind in a place she seldom visited.

Once Ma was gone, she'd been thrust into Pa's world and done what she had needed to do to survive. Somewhere along the way, she'd found she was more accepted talking down. But now it sounded funny to say things the long way around.

"I do believe you are the smartest pupil we've ever tutored," Fiona exclaimed.

"Knowin' it ain't the same as talkin' it," Clementine replied.

"Know-*ing* and talk-*ing*. Repeat those words for me as you think about how they end," Fiona smiled.

Clementine arched her brow and accentuated, "Know-ing. Talk-ing."

"Excellent, and let's replace *ain't* with *is not*, or *am not*, shall we?"

"Did I jest say ain't?"

"You did."

She shrugged. "S'pose I can try."

"Mr. Whitburn has accepted our invitation to afternoon tea."

"Ugh! What fer? I ain't ready for thet."

"*Ain't?*"

Clementine sighed.

"In this case, you would say *I am not* ready for that."

"You know what I mean."

"You can practice your speech with Mr. Whitburn."

"An' he knows what we're doin'?"

"Do-*ing*, please."

"Do-ing! Do-ing! Do-ing!" Clementine repeated angrily, clenching her fists.

"Excellent. Yes, he understands."

"There's somethin' ya don't understand about me. I don't like feelin' foolish."

"Some-*thing*. Feel-*ing*."

Clementine took a deep, calming breath. "Some-thing. Feel-ing."

"Excellent. Now, regarding your comment. We are here so that you won't feel foolish in social situations."

"Two things. First, it's downright annoy-*ing* to get interrupted when I'm tryin'. . . try-*ing* to speak my mind. Second, I'm still gonna feel stupid when Samuel gets here."

Merryweather smiled. "Take courage, Miss Cahill. There's a scripture we'd like you to memorize. It's Philippians 4:13, 'I can do all things through Christ which strengtheneth me.'" She pressed a small book into Clementine's hand. "It's marked."

Fortunately after that, the sisters kept her busy trying to teach her to walk without grabbing her skirts—and to her credit, she only stumbled three times—so that she didn't have much time to fret about Samuel's arrival.

Tea was set up in the saloon. At five o'clock, Clementine entered the room from her adjoining cabin. To her displeasure, Samuel jumped to his feet and hurried to greet her.

"Clementine?" He whistled. "Is that really you?"

She cast Merryweather an *I told you so* glance then fixed her hands on her hips, returning her gaze to Samuel. "You'd best not be pokin' fun at me, 'cause I'm packin' iron."

Merryweather gasped.

But Samuel grinned, his eyes moving down to imagine how such a weapon might be concealed. When his gaze lifted to Clementine's steely one again, his smile vanished. "Seriously, you look beautiful."

Reading sincerity in his eyes, she allowed the compliment to stir up a pleasant feeling before she nodded and snatched up her skirts. Remembering her foible, she dropped them again and shrugged at the sisters.

Fiona clutched her hands together and tapped them to her chin. While Merryweather poured tea, Fiona explained, "There was much to be questioned in that exchange, and I realize you are friends, but let's not assume we are on a first-name basis."

"Why not?" Clementine demanded.

"Let's just look at it as playacting."

"Before we start, can I jest say somethin' to Samuel?"

Fiona sighed. "Yes, of course."

Clementine felt the heat coloring her cheeks. "I'm sorry Pa got you into this."

Samuel replied, "You took me in as family when we were on the river. I'm happy to return a favor."

"I reckon if'n I had a brother. . ." Clementine flashed a contrite look at the sisters and continued, "I mean yer like a brother to me."

After that, Clementine held her cup like the sisters had schooled and waited to see what would transpire next.

Fiona broke the silence. "Miss Cahill. Since we're having tea at your home, as our hostess, you will want to make sure everyone is included in the conversation. So it's your duty to make sure our special guest, Mr. Whitburn, feels at ease. Admirably, you've already done that. But now let's pretend he's just arrived, and this time, remember to use good grammar."

With a frustrated sigh, Clementine placed her cup on the table. Then with a trembling hand she wiped sweaty palms on her skirt. She carefully fashioned her sentence before she spoke it aloud. "Mr. Whitburn, are you working on any interesting stories?"

Well pleased, Merryweather nodded excitedly.

"As a matter of fact, I'm doing an article about the upcoming vote. 'Shall California Become a State?'"

"Well, I hardly know anythin''bout thet."

"And I just finished a piece about the city's new police department."

"Well if'n. . .*if* you should write 'bout something interesting, I'd be happy to hear 'bout it."

Samuel laughed. "I'll keep that in mind."

"That's delightful," Merryweather exclaimed. "Banter is always exciting."

Samuel offered, "I know a topic Miss Cahill might find interesting. Misses Featherstone, I understand you took the Panama voyage. How was it?"

Merryweather's eyes lit. "The voyage was unremarkable, but we did take a mule trek across the Isthmus of Panama."

"Mules?" Clementine asked, trying to imagine such a sight with all their fripperies.

"It was a muddy quagmire during a tropical downpour," Fiona added. "The other Miss Featherstone was all aflitter about colorful birds and butterflies, but it was horrid."

"Oh now, sister, you know the butterflies were blue, my favorite color and the size of my palm. And the parrots were colorful, too."

"Blue and red." Fiona smiled. "And the harpy eagle was exquisite."

"Yes," Merryweather agreed. "But the lizards were dreadful."

It hit Clementine hard to realize how much the sisters had endured on her behalf. And for the first time, she pondered what an exciting life they led. She'd been so self-occupied, she hadn't once asked them about their long trip. She leaned forward. "Why were the lizards dreadful?"

"My dear, they were everywhere. Even in the city."

"We have the red newt. It's awful lookin'," Clementine said. "And I shot a rattlesnake in our camp, didn't I, Samuel?" When all eyes fastened on her, she blushed. "I mean, Mr. Whitburn."

And from there the conversation took a dull turn. Within the hour, Samuel took his leave, using the good excuse of getting ashore before dark. Walking him to the main deck, Clementine had one private moment before he departed. "I s'pose ya won't be comin' back after thet spectacle."

He gave her a genuine smile. "Of course I'll be back. Don't look so glum. The sisters are pretty good sports, don't you think?"

Clementine's mind flashed over the events of the past couple of days, feeling guilty she hadn't examined anything from their perspective. Of course, being a reporter, Samuel would be looking at it from all angles. Well, she'd give him hers. "Ya know I don't want them here."

"So are you trying to get rid of me, too?" he teased.

She shrugged. "Jest come at yer own risk."

Laughing, he nodded. "I consider myself forewarned."

After he was gone, she retreated to her room, which now had a door that led to the adjoining dressing room. Perching on the edge of her bed, she missed not being able to lounge without wrinkling her clothing. Then her eyes lit upon the little black book the sisters had given her. She rose and leafed to the bookmarked page. Philippians 4:13, "I can do all things through Christ which strengtheneth me." What could it mean? With a shrug, she placed it back on the little table that now magically graced her cabin. On it was a looking glass, a comb set, and *Godey's Lady's Book*, which she hadn't the stomach for yet. She picked up the looking glass. "I can do all things," she muttered. "At least the girl starin' back at me might be able ta. Whoever she is. But I cain't even dress myself."

◆ ◆ ◆

That night she was in her dressing room in chemise and robe, untangling her hair, when Merryweather knocked and entered.

The sister perched on the remaining small chair. "I saw the light. Having trouble sleeping?"

"I ain't tried yet."

"I'm sure you're still reeling from all the changes."

"Fer sure. An' thanks fer not correctin' me jest now. My brain's too tired ta talk fancy."

"Maybe so, but you are doing splendidly. Here, let me do your hair while we talk."

Clementine shrugged, relinquishing the comb. "Splendid? So I'm not the worst of yer last resort bunch?"

Merryweather laughed. "Definitely not. I was wondering, Clementine. Do you have hopes for marriage?"

"Marriage!" Clementine squealed, and her sudden movement caused the comb to pull. "Ouch."

Merryweather worked to release the knot. "I'm sorry. Please remain still."

Doing as bid, Clementine emphasized her words. "I'm puttin' my foot down there. Please tell me yer not a matchmaker, too."

Merryweather began to take long strokes again, undeterred. "We do offer a marriage class, but your father didn't select it. That's why I'm asking you."

"Ha. He knows I cain't get no husband."

"Why would he know that?"

"Because I'm perty sure it's because of thet flirty doctor thet he hired ya for in the first place."

"No." Merryweather laid the comb aside and moved to the chair again. "He didn't mention any doctor."

Clementine involuntarily braided her hair as she explained. "When Pa hurt his leg, there was a doc who came to our hotel." Clementine felt her cheeks heat. "He asked me ta go on a stupid picnic."

Merryweather's eyes widened. "Did you go?"

"Nope. He told me ta put on my prettiest dress, and I refused."

"You refused to go with him?"

"Ta put on a dress. So he took back the invite."

Merryweather's eyes widened even further. "A gentleman never does such a thing."

"I figured. But it tore Pa up. Then he started harpin' 'bout wearin' a dress, and the next thing I knew, you showed up."

"Clementine. Would you like it if the doctor changed his mind about the picnic?"

"Well, I s'pose he would if'n he knew I was wearin' dresses. He seemed ta be fond of me."

Merryweather became contemplative. "We could stop in his office and pick up some of Fiona's nerve tonic." She clapped her hand to her mouth. "I was thinking out loud. It's rude of me to talk about Fiona's nerves. Please forgive me."

"Think nothin' of it. I noticed her blinks from the start."

"Oh."

Clementine raised her chin. "I wouldn't mind lettin' the doctor see me in a dress. Jest to see what he's missin'. But I wouldn't go on a picnic with him now if he came a-beggin'."

"And that's your decision to make. Just know that after one look at you, he will drop at your feet and beg."

Clementine wondered if she spoke the truth.

"May I ask one more question?"

"I s'pose."

"What about Mr. Whitburn? Would you consider him as a suitor?"

"Samuel? No, he's jest a friend. But a good friend ta put up with this whole carrying-on we're having. 'Course, Pa is payin' him."

"I'm not so sure that's the only reason he's agreed. I can tell he admires you."

"Nope." Clementine shook her head. "Yer wrong about thet."

Chapter Five

Samuel lived at the hotel and often wrote at his tiny desk under the window, but sometimes he worked outdoors. Like today. He sat on a flat rock that overlooked the bay, and the breeze rustled his papers. Seagulls dipped and squawked, and skiffs maneuvered to and fro around the docks and farther out among the ships. On the street, men hustled in and out of shops, and there was a constant line of pack mules headed toward the ferries. Usually, observation gave him inspiration for new stories. He liked to store ideas so he could go from one piece to another and keep a steady monetary income.

His deadline on the political election loomed, but Clementine was right about its dull title. He pondered what slant could spice up the title enough to spark her interest. But he couldn't focus on much except the good view he had of the *Dragonfish*, and instead of working on his piece, he found himself jotting notes about his recent experience with her and the Featherstone sisters. It wasn't the sort of thing frontier men would want to read, but people back East would eat it up. It would make good dinner conversation.

He tapped his steel-nib pen. Mostly the notes were for his personal benefit. Note-taking helped him sort out his thoughts, and he sure needed to do that where Clementine was concerned. She was such a contradiction of feminine and uncivilized. A delightful woman. Beautiful, too, with her slim curves and long brown hair. Her mouth was inviting, but the words it spewed made a man want to cringe and take cover. Overall, the eyes were what drew him. They were huge, unguarded and expressive, uncommon with women he'd known. Often they danced with a defiant wildness, and sometimes there was that hollow sadness that surfaced. It drew him like a mournful wolf's cry and gave him shivers at the same time. For he knew he shouldn't be looking into her soul and was fearful of what he might discover. He certainly didn't intend to lose himself there. Or did he?

There was an inherent danger in associating with her, for she had a way of meshing with the rugged land he loved. Like the land, she both enchanted and frightened him. It was the very reason he'd left Philadelphia to come to California. Because his soul longed for adventure. But not so much that he was willing to trade in his pen for a shovel.

Though he'd given that a try, too, he fondly mused. He'd do whatever it took to get a good story. That was his thrill. The Cahills had taken him in and foddered him with plenty of information to use in his panning story. That reminded him—he quickly made himself a note—panning wasn't the success it had been six months earlier. The easy pickings had already been gleaned, and the miners were now using sluices and other methods to extract gold. It would be his next story. The East needed to know it was changing. What had been too good to be true was becoming just that.

His thoughts returning to the Cahills, he figured he owed Charles. That was why he'd accepted the unusual proposition of helping Clementine with her etiquette training. Also, he'd needed the money. And Charles had hit the mother lode with money to spare. He wondered if Charles intended to return to the fields. He hoped not. Charles and the Soto Toro brothers seemed to be having success with their new housing project. At least while they still had material from the ships they'd purchased, he and Clementine would remain in San Francisco.

He tried to imagine what Clementine would resemble once the Featherstone sisters finished classes. He hoped the adventuresome spirit would remain. Perhaps it was the reporter's curiosity in him, but he knew he wanted to see how her story ended. He needed to know if she would become a clone of every other woman he'd known. Would her transformation be so successful that she would marry the doctor Charles Cahill had told him about? Did she want to?

Unfortunately she was blissfully unaware of his own attraction to her. He sadly recalled how she'd likened him to a brother. So the question remained, would a brother help his sister find matrimony? He didn't think so. It just didn't feel right. In fact, it made him so restless, he rose. This wasn't the place to get any work done; it only made his thoughts sink like gold in water. He jotted down the simile before he made his way toward the main street.

◆　◆　◆

Ten days into her classes, the sisters introduced Clementine's Bible lessons. She sat on the edge of her bed listening to Fiona's instructions.

"We will start with prayer. That way God can help you with your Bible lessons."

Clementine arched a brow. She wondered if her life could become any more absurd.

"I like to pray before I dress in the morning and after undressing in the evening. It's just easier to kneel without the encumbrance of formal clothing."

Merryweather added, "But prayer can happen at any time, without kneeling."

Fiona nodded. "However, kneeling shows honor and respect to the King of the universe, and it's good to make a habit of it."

King of the universe? Clementine tried to imagine their depiction of God and then realized they were addressing her.

"—and since you're the one in your chemise, why don't you kneel for all of us, and we'll do the praying."

Half frantic, half wary, she met Merryweather's gaze. "Ya mean get down on the floor like I was gonna do some pannin'?"

Fiona tapped her chin. "Why, I don't know what that resembles. Show us what you mean."

With a shrug, Clementine squatted on her haunches and went through some imitative motions.

Merryweather bit her lip, her eyes twinkling.

Clementine jumped up angrily. "Don't laugh at me. It's yer dumb idea."

Merryweather quickly sobered. Ignoring her sister's protestations, she lifted both sides of her skirt and dropped to her knees to demonstrate. "Like this. Join me?"

"If'n I have ta." Lowering herself again, she noticed Fiona open her mouth to object then close it again when Merryweather gave her a stern look.

Merryweather whispered, "Close your eyes."

Clementine obeyed. Given her embarrassment, she was thankful for the engulfing darkness.

"Lord, we thank You for keeping us safe through the night and ask for the grace to supply our needs for this day. By faith we believe we can do all things through Your strength and power. Amen."

Opening her eyes, Clementine asked, "What's grace?"

Arising, Merryweather explained, "It's the gifts of blessing God gives us. Especially salvation from a sinful life. When you pray tonight, remember three things. Begin by thanking God. Then repent of any known sins. Then petition Him for your needs."

Clementine's head spun from confusion over concepts so new to her. She had a hunch what sin was about but didn't want to dwell on it. "So in yer prayer, ya were askin' for His help for the day?"

Fiona brightened. "Yes, child. That's exactly right."

Merryweather smiled warmly. "Little by little, as we go through our lessons, you'll understand. But it helps to read the Bible I gave you."

"An' ya think He really helps ya?"

"Oh! Indeed He does!" Fiona exclaimed.

Clementine shrugged. "It's kinda silly. Kinda spooky. But I guess I'll try ta pray. If'n I don't forget."

"It's easy to forget," Fiona agreed. "The devil likes to distract us. That's why establishing a regular prayer time is wise."

Clementine widened her eyes. "Ya believe in the devil, too? Hard not ta hear of him, livin' in camp around a bunch a men. At least I don't swear. Pa never allowed it."

Fiona cleared her throat. "We are thankful for that small mercy. And to answer your question, yes, I believe in Satan. There's a lot to learn on this topic. But once you start praying, the Holy Spirit will teach you, too."

"Who's the—"

"Now let's get you dressed," Merryweather interrupted.

Curious now, Clementine watched as Merryweather squeezed her sister's hand before going to the wardrobe to lay out the day's attire. Thankfully, Clementine could do most of her own dressing now. The day's grammar lesson was combined with something new: a writing activity. The sisters had written sentences including slang like *if'n*, and it was her job to reword them into proper sentences. After that came a spelling lesson. Clementine was amazed to discover so many *ing* words. By the time her hand ached, she was start-*ing* to get the message.

Afterward, as they reviewed the lesson, Fiona explained, "Your penmanship needs some work, so we will continue working on it. Just remember, your old way of talking was mimicking the language going on around you, which was logical and acceptable for your circumstances. But now that you understand the better way, and your circumstances are changing, it is no longer acceptable. If you continue using slang, from this point forward, I can honestly say you are just being lazy. By using diligence and thinking before you speak, you can change."

"Lazy?" Clementine gently bit the inside of her mouth, considering the sting of

Fiona's statement and carefully forming her words before she replied, "It's hard to do it right, that's for sure."

Merryweather encouraged, "But you can do it. Be courageous."

It was something Merryweather often suggested. Clementine liked the idea of being courageous. And to be honest, she hadn't yet given it her all. Fear of failure kept her holding on to the old way, but she was beginning to believe she might be able to change after all. "I'll try."

Fiona rushed to her side. "Thank you, my dear girl. Thank you."

A smiled curled Clementine's lips. It was rather nice being the recipient of so much personal support and attention. And the sisters were certainly courageous themselves. In fact, she was beginning to admire them. Wanted to please them. And Pa, too.

Chapter Six

Just when Clementine thought she was getting the way of things, the Featherstone sisters introduced a new class called "The Art of Flirtation," which was quite enlightening. Seated in her dressing room with a tiny handkerchief in hand, she mimicked Fiona's motions, trying to memorize the nuances and meanings.

"Across the cheek means 'I love you.' Across the eyes—'I'm sorry.' Never draw it through your hands because that means 'I hate you.' If you draw it across the lips you are desiring an acquaintance. If you drop it, you want to be friends. Folding means you wish to speak. Resting on the left cheek is 'no' and the right is 'yes.'"

"Understand?"

Clementine touched her right cheek.

"Excellent! Now it's similar with gloves. Ready?"

Feeling dizzy from so much to memorize, Clementine nodded, telling herself, *Be courageous.*

Merryweather produced gloves and another round of orientation began. Afterward, she was congratulated for quick learning and informed that she'd get to put flirting to practice in the morning. "Mr. Whitburn is meeting us ashore and escorting us to your father's construction site."

Clementine jumped up, tossing her gloves. "Wonderful!" Of all things, she'd been hoping to get off the ship. But best of all was visiting Pa's business. She missed the Soto Toro brothers, too. For once the Featherstone sisters arrived, they'd abandoned the ship. While the sisters were nice companions, she missed her old friends. Mostly she missed Pa, because he didn't spend as much time with her now that he'd pawned her off on the sisters. She was ready to come out of seclusion.

Merryweather smiled at her enthusiasm. "It will do us all good to get off this ship. But before we quit our lessons, let's review. Tell me five things to remember when walking with a gentleman."

Clementine wet her lips, carefully thinking before she spoke. "Don't touch the gentleman. Don't walk too fast. Don't swing my arms. Don't drag my dress in the mud. Don't lift my dress too high." Then, grinning, she added, "Unless I need ta get ta my gun in a hurry."

"Mercy!" Fiona gasped. Then she slowly grinned. "You're teasing us."

"I am. But you know I'll always carry my iron."

"I would, too, if I knew how to shoot," Merryweather replied. "It would have come in handy a few times in the jungle."

"True, sister. So very true," Fiona admitted.

The next day, after the sisters' last-minute reminders—remember to always put on your gloves and tie your bonnet before leaving the ship—and their decision that San Francisco was too windy for a parasol, Salty rowed them ashore. The fog was still heavy over the bay, and Clementine was happy to be able to distinguish Samuel waiting for them at the designated pier. He reached down to help her out of the boat, and at Fiona's nod, she allowed his help. "Thank you, Mr. Whitburn. It's good to see you."

Grinning broadly, he replied, "My pleasure, Miss Cahill." After he assisted the Featherstone sisters, they began their stroll, and the sisters followed close behind. The streets bustled with men because the mail had just arrived. Long lines went from the post office on Pike and Clay all the way to the tents at Chaparral. Samuel quickly moved them away from the men, as many sought to bribe one another, which normally caused skirmishes and outbreaks of coarse language.

When they'd reached a quieter area, Clementine remembered she was supposed to practice yesterday's lessons. Quite smugly, she dropped her handkerchief. However, Samuel paid no heed, plodding on ahead.

"Mr. Whitburn. Please stop."

"Yes?"

She pointed behind her. "I dropped my handkerchief. It means I want to be friends, you know."

"You did?" He spun around but was almost too late as two young men scrambled across the street and dove for the fallen lace. One caked his chin with mud as he yelled, "Got it!" But when the unfortunate fellow opened his fingers, his hand was empty. He glared at his partner, who pointed at Samuel, who had plucked it up in the nick of time but now sat in the mud beside them.

The Featherstone sisters gasped at the comical sight, but Clementine read the male body language and felt the tension mounting between the three men. She didn't know if Samuel could defend himself, outnumbered as he was, and her hand brushed her skirt to locate her firearm. But the fellow with the muddy chin suddenly grinned, pushed himself up, and gave a hand to his partner. "Nice day for a walk, miss."

Grinning herself, she watched as Samuel rose and slowly unfisted his prize. His expression was crestfallen. "It's ruined."

"So are you," she teased.

"You almost got me killed, you know."

"I would've rescued you."

"But it's supposed to be the other way around."

"The important thing is, you got the prize," Merryweather exclaimed.

Grinning, Samuel folded it and placed it in his pocket, rubbing his muddy hands on his trousers. "Sorry, ladies."

Unsure how to proceed, Clementine admitted, "It's part of my 'Art of Flirtation' class."

Leaning close, he whispered, "And nicely done, Clem."

At the shortened use of her name, as well as the courage it took for him to use it with the sisters trailing so close, a pleasurable warmth spread through her. Unsure of his response, however, she asked, "You're not supposed to keep it, are you?"

He grinned. "I'm keeping it."

Turning around, she asked Merryweather, "Is he supposed to keep it?"

"No. But it was ruined and would soil your gloves if he returned it to you. It demonstrates his fondness for you."

Clementine felt her cheeks heat. "Oh." Samuel winked mischievously, and she shrugged. "Well, you're doing me a favor. Now I don't have to mess with it." She saw a flash of hurt cross his face and wished she'd been more tactful. "Let's just go find Pa before all this goes to your head."

They walked again, and shortly he commented, "Your speech has improved."

"Of course. I ain't lazy."

"Of course you aren't. I only meant it as a compliment."

"Thanks. I'm just a bit touchy about it."

"So I see. You're not the only one who needs to learn a few things. I've taken to heart what you said about my boring article on California becoming a state. It's an important topic but needed a catchy title."

"I'm sorry if I was rude."

"Not at all. It pushed me to do better. It's a good thing."

She discovered walking with Samuel was a pleasant endeavor, and his manner of speech soon allowed her to let down her guard. "This is sure different. Taking a stroll instead of panning with you at the river."

"Sure is," he said with a grin. "But I enjoyed both."

"Me, too."

When they reached the construction site, Pa proudly showed them around. "Come see, Clemmie. With the town's need, we're going to make a fortune."

She smiled up at him. "Do we need a fortune, Pa?"

"A man can't turn his back on this kind of opportunity."

Fair and equal opportunities, she thought. It was sad to think one needed money or dresses to possess such opportunities. But she didn't know how to change the world, so she just nodded. Seeing Pa happy lifted her own spirits.

And she wasn't the only one enjoying the outing. The Soto Toro brothers were escorting the Featherstone sisters, and she could tell that Flavio was pouring on the charm.

"See, *senoritas,* how the fog has lifted since you arrived? You must own the sun. So it warms me just to bask in your company. I miss the sunshine of my homeland."

Merryweather giggled like a schoolgirl. "You are too kind. Tell us about your country. Is it paradise?"

Of course, the Soto Toro brothers had gushed over Clementine's transformed appearance, deeming her a princess worthy of her own kingdom. And while she longed for the comfort and freedom of her old clothes and manners, she could see the benefits of becoming a lady.

Samuel also noticed the interplay happening and winked at her. Good. If the sisters were enjoying themselves, maybe Clementine would get to visit Pa's work site more often. They'd built one small home that was already occupied and were building two more.

As they prepared to take their leave, Pa told Samuel, "Take care of the ladies, won't you?"

"I'll guard them with my life."

Clementine was just ready to say she had her own means of protecting herself when Merryweather exclaimed, "He already has." The older woman explained the incident that had almost started a brawl, and from Pa's expression, Clementine couldn't tell if he wanted to laugh or cry.

"Take care, Samuel. Men have dueled over less."

Men! Well, let him deal with it, as he'd been the one to start all this tumult in the first place.

The stroll back to the docks went without further incident. But later, before Samuel handed them into the boat, he asked the Featherstone sisters, "May I call upon Miss Cahill on Saturday? I thought she might like to go riding."

Fiona seemed surprised. "What a thoughtful invitation." Yet she hesitated, whispering something to Merryweather.

Clementine was positive this was not good manners and quickly surmised the outing wasn't part of their planned lessons. She wondered what Samuel had up his sleeve. Was he offering her a reprieve?

"If Miss Cahill agrees, then we will allow it. But what of chaperones?"

"Ladies, this is San Francisco. I will be her chaperone. You witnessed my promise to Mr. Cahill."

"Mm-hm," Fiona considered.

"Now, sister," Merryweather intervened for Samuel. "Is it really necessary?"

"No. I suppose it is a bit formal for the circumstances."

"There are times for exceptions to the rule."

"And we are all friends," Clementine added hopefully.

But when Samuel helped her into the boat, he whispered, "I'm hoping for more than friendship."

As Salty rowed toward the ship, she refused to turn around and look at him. But her heart raced with the implications of what he'd suggested. The sisters' lessons worked. But she didn't know if she was ready to face the repercussions. Yet she enjoyed Samuel's companionship. And this new perspective was exciting to consider. She wished she could get advice from the Featherstone sisters but feared they'd insist on a chaperone if they knew what Samuel had whispered. For now, it would remain their secret.

◆ ◆ ◆

Clementine's next outing wasn't for pleasure. It was a trip to the physician's office, and it filled her with trepidation. Practicing her lessons in front of Samuel was starting to feel comfortable, but since it was staged, it was nothing like presenting herself before the highfalutin, discriminating doctor who'd given her such a mean set down.

As Merryweather fastened her bodice hooks and eyes, Clementine remarked, "I feel like I've lost the battle with the doctor by wearing this dress in front of him. And I don't want him to think I'm so lovesick over him that I'm chasing him. You know I don't care a hoot about him."

"But your father cares about his opinion. He represents society as a whole. He wants the world to love you as much as he does."

"Pa cares too much about what people think. Anyway, how do you know so much about Pa?"

"Perception and experience, my dear."

"It doesn't feel like he loves me when he's always off working. I'm not used to being separated from him. And I don't like it."

Merryweather finished her ministrations and moved to face her. "We came across ocean and jungle to give you lessons. Before we agreed, we gave him a list of ultimatums. We asked him to step back while we schooled you. He's only doing what he believes is best for you."

Love for her pa burgeoned up in Clementine's spirit. "Thanks for telling me. But back to the doctor, I still have the shivers about this whole ordeal. Do we have to go?"

"Be courageous," Merryweather urged. "Once he sees you, he won't care why you're in the office; he'll just be happy to see you."

"Well, I don't like to feel foolish."

"You've mentioned that a few times. Once again, I remind you humility is a great virtue. It's becoming on a lady."

Arching her eyebrow, Clementine replied, "Then let's just get it over with."

An hour later, the three women walked into the doctor's tiny waiting area, and every man in the room quickly jumped to his feet.

"Thank you, gentlemen," Fiona said, drawing Clementine along so they could accept three abandoned seats. The men settled again and Clementine cringed to see the severity of the injuries. They waited about fifteen minutes until the doctor appeared to receive his next patient. After a small disagreement in which Fiona refused to go before the polite man with a bloody bandage on his arm, another half hour passed and then they were admitted into the back room.

The doctor smiled in the manner in which Clementine had learned to despise. "What can I do for you ladies?"

Fiona stepped forward. "My bottle of Stomach Bitters is getting low, and I'd hoped you could supply me with more."

Dr. Payne's eyes suddenly widened. "Miss Cahill! Is that you? Forgive me. I didn't recognize you until this very moment. And in a dress. A beautiful dress."

Clementine raised her chin a notch. "No need to apologize."

He grinned. "I always hold to the saying that a woman has the prerogative to change her mind."

"Then you're a smart man."

"I hope you think so. The dress is becoming on you."

"Thank you. Now if you don't mind, Miss Featherstone is waiting to hear if you will supply her with another bottle of her Stomach Bitters."

"But of course." The doctor moved to a shelf and handed it to Fiona, hardly taking his eyes off of Clementine. "I'm hoping you'll take me out of my misery. I'm hoping this means you agree to go on that picnic you promised me."

Casting Merryweather a plea for help and receiving only a slight nod in return, Clementine straightened her shoulders. "As I recall, it was never promised. Best get the notion out of your head."

Surprise lit his eyes and another smile tweaked his lips. "I'm going to find that hard to do," he owned. And Clementine feared the contest was only beginning as far as he was concerned.

Thankfully, Fiona came to her rescue. "Let's run along, shall we?" And when they were outside on the street again, she clutched Clementine's arm. "You handled that perfectly. I'm so proud of you."

Clementine murmured, "Thank you." But she had mixed emotions. She felt both complimented and insulted. Again. Nothing new when it came to the good doctor. She wondered if it was his personal trademark.

Merryweather asked, "Aren't you glad we came?"

"I'm not sure. I never would have believed there was so much power in wearing a dress."

"You're learning your lessons well, my dear."

Part Three:

Clementine's Courtship

Chapter Seven

That night, Clementine mulled over all that had transpired with the doctor. Her horizons were widening beyond anything she'd ever imagined. She was beginning to trust the sisters and now felt guilty for slacking in one area—the praying. They'd been having short daily Bible lessons, and a story of sort was beginning to take form. It portrayed a God who loved her, had sent His Son like a hero to rescue her, and was waiting for her response. It was downright spooky-scary. But since the sisters seemed to know just what she needed, it was time to trust them in this area also.

Feeling silly for slipping to her knees when she was the only one in the room, she recalled the instructions Merryweather had earlier given: thank, repent, and petition. She tried to think of something for which to thank the King of the universe. *Hmm.* Sure she was thankful for some things, like not having to wear a gown and adornments to bed. She was thankful Pa was healing and had found himself a new business. She was a little thankful for the Featherstone sisters and for Samuel. But none of those things had anything to do with the King of the universe. *Hmm.* She peeked one eye open, seeking for something, when she saw it. *Dear God, I'm thankful for that Bible.* The next part was easier because she had plenty of places she fell short. *And forgive me for detesting the doctor. And for purposefully giving the sisters trouble.*

Next she considered what to ask of the King. *If You're really listening, would You help me become a lady? And let Pa forget about Louisville?* Feeling a sense of relief, she added with great relish, *Amen.* And when she climbed into her bed, she dreamed about riding with Samuel, with her hair flowing free behind her. It felt so good to be free.

◆ ◆ ◆

"Why didn't we think to bring her a riding habit?" Fiona lamented. "Are we getting forgetful to neglect such an essential? Especially in this godforsaken land."

Merryweather paced. "There might be a seamstress in town, but we don't have time to order one."

"I'll wear my britches."

"You certainly shall not!" Fiona exclaimed.

"I'm afraid we cast them to the bottom of the sea," Merryweather admitted.

Clementine grinned. "But I have another pair."

"Oh my. What shall we do?" Fiona wrung her hands. "Maybe we should send word to Mr. Whitburn that it won't suit."

"Because of a stupid costume?" Clementine demanded. "Why, Samuel camped with us. He's seen me in pants a zillion times. Don't you see, he's giving me a reprieve from all these lessons which make my head hurt."

"Ladies don't get reprieves," Fiona stated firmly.

"Ever?" Clementine gasped. "Why! I'll never marry a man who won't let me wear britches once in a while."

Merryweather stopped pacing and placed a hand on Clementine's shoulder. "Let's all calm down and see if we can come up with some sort of compromise. If we started with her trousers, we could alter one of her dresses to wear over the top."

Fiona moaned. "But her dresses are all so lovely."

"And her riding habit will be magnificent, too. But we must get started immediately. Bring us your trousers."

Clementine started toward her room and suddenly halted, turning back. "This isn't a trick, is it? You aren't going to toss my only pair of britches overboard?"

Fiona's face lit up as if it was a lovely idea. But Merryweather placed her hand on her bosom. "I swear we will use them to make you a riding costume."

"And you won't alter or ruin 'em?"

"No. We'll just find a way to cover most of them."

"All right, then." Clementine thought they were making a lot of to-do over a ride with Samuel. Her dreams flashed through her mind. In them, her hair was down and blowing in the wind. Suddenly a wonderful idea formed. "Can I wear my hair down in a braid, too?" At Fiona's look of horror, she begged, "Please?"

◆　◆　◆

She didn't know why she felt so nervous as Salty rowed her ashore. But surely it had to do with her life being turned upside down. She glanced at her friend. "I miss fishing with you."

"I miss it, too," he admitted.

"What do you make of all this?" she asked him.

"I think it's good for you. Right fitting."

She remained silent after that, but when they neared the docks and Samuel appeared, she felt her gut knot. He looked fine in his trousers, white shirt, and coat. And happy as he reached down to help her ashore.

"Thanks, Salty. Meet us back here just before sunset?" Samuel asked.

"I'll be here. You two have fun." But his look also held a warning that Samuel didn't mistake for child's play.

"She's in good care."

With a nod, Salty pushed the dinghy away, and suddenly Clementine felt nervous again. "So where's the horses?"

"At the livery. I like your getup."

Clementine shook her head. "You wouldn't believe the mess you stirred up when the sisters realized I had no riding habit. I told them britches were fine, but then they came up with this idea." She shook her head and gestured at her clothing.

"It's pretty and practical. I like it."

"I'm excited to be free from all their fussiness."

"That's what I like about you."

"That I'm plain?"

"No. That you aren't afraid to be who you want to be."

She looked at him tentatively. "You wouldn't have been disappointed if I'd showed up in my britches without all this frippery?"

"A little. But if you seemed happier, I would have been satisfied."

Soon they were at the stables, and she was given a mustang with just the right amount of spirit. As they rode out of town, Samuel opened up to her. "I love this place. I love the rugged open spaces, the mountains and streams."

"I love the freedom. Fiona calls it godforsaken. You think God's here in this place?"

"More than anywhere else. I grew up in the city, but this fits me better. I never want to leave."

"Me either. I don't know much about God. But the sisters are teaching me."

He nodded. "That's good. I come from a Christian family. I go to hear preaching every Sunday."

"I'd like to do that sometime."

"I'll remember that."

They came to an open meadow and let the horses go. Clementine reveled in the wind against her face. She yearned to undo her braid and relive her dream, but couldn't bring herself to disappoint Fiona in such a way. She was grateful they'd agreed to her simpler hairstyle. When they pulled up the horses, they stopped under a tree.

"Rest awhile?" he asked.

"Yup."

He quickly dismounted and helped her to the ground. Next he removed his coat and placed it on the ground for her. "Should've brought us a picnic."

"Oh, don't bring that up," she replied.

"Sorry." He sought her eyes. "You like the doctor?"

"Nope. He's a—" She clamped her mouth shut. "Never mind. A lady would never say what I was thinking."

"Still, I'm happy to know you feel that way. I thought all this"—he gestured—"was to bring him to offer."

"What? Never."

"Does your dad feel the same way?"

She looked down, fiddling with a strand of grass. "I don't know."

Samuel cleared his throat. "I hope he thinks good of me."

She quickly looked up. "Oh, he does. It's just he has this notion that when we're rich enough, we're moving to Louisville. And when we get there, he wants us both to fit in with society."

Samuel protested, "But I don't want to go to Louisville. I like it here."

Clementine's heart raced, but she felt the need to know more details about their circumstances. "I'm sure when Pa paid you, he didn't expect you to go to Louisville with us, too."

His shoulders slumped. "Ah, Clem. I didn't know you knew about that."

"I figured it out. I'm not stupid."

"Of course you aren't. I wouldn't be falling in love with a stupid woman."

Clementine gasped. But he covered her mouth with a kiss to show her he wasn't fooling.

When he withdrew, she gasped again. Then scolded, "Don't do that."

Sorrowful, he asked, "You don't feel the same?"

"I meant don't sneak up on me so quick I can't even get a breath first. I thought I'd die for loss of air."

Baffled, he ran a hand through his hair. "You could have pushed me away."

"I didn't want to. Just give me a warning next time."

Grinning, he replied, "Deal. Next time."

On the ride back to town, they stopped atop Goat Hill and looked down over the bay. "Think more women will ever come here?"

"Of course. I daresay another year won't pass before the miners bring their wives. The gold won't last forever, and once some of them go back where they came from, things will change. For the better. I want to be a part of it. Don't you?"

"You seem sure of what the future holds."

He shrugged. "I'm a reporter. I ask a lot of questions. But I've also got a knack for seeing the flow of things."

"I hope your dreams all come true," Clementine said wistfully.

"I hope so, too."

And the look he gave her made her wonder if she was part of his future dreams.

◆ ◆ ◆

Closing up shop for the night, Dr. Payne stepped onto the street and halted when he saw her. The woman who'd been plaguing him ever since she stepped into his office. Across the way, Clementine Cahill and Samuel Whitburn were strolling in deep conversation. A pang of jealousy shot through him. The woman was a mystery, and he was cursing himself for messing up his chance with her.

If he wanted to give it another try, he needed to move fast before Whitburn staked his claim.

He'd nose around and find out what was going on aboard the *Dragonfish* and find out more about her women companions. Probably some relatives from back East. That's probably why Miss Cahill had put on a dress. Certainly not for his benefit, like he'd hoped that day she'd stopped in with her friends.

He figured the best way to get information was to speak to the Chilean brothers who worked with her father. He knew where they were constructing houses and planned to stop by there on the morrow. He was positive he could win her back because he'd seen the attraction that first day. She was probably waiting for an apology, and she probably deserved one, too. With his new plan intact, he whistled as he made his way home.

◆ ◆ ◆

That evening, Merryweather came to Clementine, offering to comb her hair. She took pity on the older woman, figuring it must have been a boring day aboard ship. "What did you do today? Create more awful lessons for me?"

The woman's plump hands took quick strokes, taking care with the tangles the outdoors had woven into her hair. "We took a holiday. We read and rested. It was most enjoyable."

"You have been working hard."

"Thank you for noticing. But how was your ride? Was Mr. Whitburn a gentleman?"

Clementine couldn't meet Merryweather's gaze in the looking glass. "He's just Samuel," she finally replied.

"You forget I'm also a trained matchmaker. I detect more than friendship."

"I believe there could be. If Pa wasn't so set on Louisville. Samuel told me he has no plans to leave San Francisco."

"Oh, pooh!" Merryweather set aside the comb and moved to face Clementine. "If he loves you, he'll follow you to Louisville."

"But I don't want to go to Louisville either."

"Then you'd better start praying about it."

"I already did."

Merryweather's eyes lit. "I'm glad to hear it. Then wait and see what God will do."

But once she was alone, Clementine broached the subject with the King of the universe again. *I'm just reminding You, God, to please change Pa's mind about Louisville. And thanks for the Bible and for letting me meet a man who doesn't care if I wear britches. And forgive me for almost calling the doctor that horrible word and for praying out of order. Amen.*

Then she reached for the Bible and turned to the place Merryweather had marked. She read and read and fell asleep with a hunger to know the King.

Chapter Eight

lementine sat in the saloon with pen in hand as the Featherstone sisters had left her to finish her latest assignment. She was supposed to transpose a letter to Samuel thanking him for acting as her chaperone in their recent lessons and telling him that his services were no longer required as she was moving into the final polishing stages of her etiquette training.

She believed their riding excursion was the reason he was being released. Clementine knew the sisters would critique her penmanship, so she couldn't make the letter personal. But it was hard to keep it professional when she kept remembering the kiss they had shared. Her only ever kiss. She wished she'd responded differently to it, but she hadn't been schooled in the art of kissing. Poor Samuel. If he pursued her after his obligation was released, he would know exactly what he was getting with her—an unpolished gold nugget, for sure.

Reservations plagued her as she composed the letter that might bring an end to their association. For she couldn't be sure he was interested in her beyond the assignment Pa had paid him to fulfill. She was more than aware that the interest he'd recently shown her could be extra-special playacting on his part. That being the case, after the sisters proofed her letter, she quickly added a post note before she placed it in an envelope and gave it to Salty to hand deliver.

> *Samuel,*
>
> *I enjoyed our ride together and cannot forget our kiss. I'm sure it's not ladylike to admit it, but you know the truth about me, so that's that. Still, I can't help wondering if you were just playacting the part that Pa paid you to fulfill. On my part, I have feelings beyond friendship. Hoping this isn't good-bye.*
>
> *Clementine*

◆　◆　◆

A male visitor called on Clementine at the ship, but it wasn't Samuel as she'd hoped. She'd envisioned him hurrying to her side to reassure her that his feelings were genuine. Instead, it was the highfalutin doctor. And she couldn't have been more startled when Merryweather told her that he was waiting for her in the ship's saloon.

He stood waiting, hat in hand. "Hello, Miss Cahill. Thank you for seeing me."

"Is Pa all right?"

"Oh yes. I didn't mean to frighten you. I hoped we could talk."

Clementine's heart sank with relief, then dread. She glanced at Fiona, who sat at the far end of the table acting as chaperone while pretending not to listen. Clementine hoped he wasn't going to ask her about that blasted picnic again. But remembering her lessons on being a proper hostess, she replied, "Please. Have a seat."

"Thank you. I've acted badly, and I've come to apologize for my behavior. Now that I realize you are a multifaceted woman, I also realize how wrong I was to judge you on your clothing preference."

Her emotions wrestled with how to respond. She wanted to lash out at him while they were on the topic of his past behavior; however, she knew that wasn't the ladylike thing to do. "I see. Pa always says the important thing is to learn from your mistakes."

"And it was a mistake because now it feels as though I've ruined our friendship. And I'd really like to restore it and come calling on you. I hope you'll forgive me and give me another chance."

She'd expected as much. Hadn't Merryweather told her he'd be on his knees begging for forgiveness? But she didn't want him to come calling and needed to set him straight about it. "I respect you for coming here today. And I forgive you, too. But you'd be wasting your time if—

"Wait," he interrupted, "before you make up your mind, I want you to know I talked to your father. I apologized to him, too, and asked if I could call on you. I wouldn't be here without his permission."

Thanks a lot, Pa, she thought. She wished Pa had told her so that she knew what he was thinking about the matter. Was Pa set on the doctor courting her? Or would the apology be enough? Would it make a difference if Pa knew about her feelings for Samuel? She wrung her hands, looking for the right words. "Then I best talk to Pa and the King before I give you my final word on this."

She noted the smile that flicked across Fiona's face and was pleased she'd said the right thing.

"The king?"

She nodded. "You know. God."

"Oh. Of course." A grin creased his face. "Thank you for giving me your consideration and taking it to such a high power. I'll come back next week for your answer. I hope it's yes."

She didn't like the way he teased about God. While all condescension was gone and he seemed genuinely contrite, he still made her uneasy. "You're welcome."

Fiona cleared her throat. "I'll see you to the rail, Doctor."

Looking startled, as if he'd forgotten about their chaperone, he quickly agreed. "All right. Until next week, Miss Cahill."

Clementine stood as they started away, and she overheard him tell Fiona, "You're looking especially radiant today, Miss Featherstone. The tonic must be working for you." She sank back into her seat, already regretting having opened the door to him again.

◆　◆　◆

That evening, Clementine went to her pa's room to discuss the doctor's request. Once she was seated, he said, "I'm glad you came to see me. I have a delicate situation to discuss."

"I suppose it's about the doctor. He came to see me today."

"Oh, good. We were wrong about him, weren't we? He's a good man after all."

"Maybe. But even though he apologized, I still have a feeling he's shallow on the inside. Pretty on the outside, but—" She broke off. "I have to know, Pa. Are you set on me seeing him?"

"Not if you don't care for him. It's your decision. And we don't even know if he's willing to move to Louisville. I don't want you getting your heart broken."

"But what if I don't want to go to Louisville? What if I want Samuel Whitburn to come calling?"

Pa's face expressed shock, and then it hardened. "Then I'm afraid you're going to be hurt again."

Clementine's heart sank. "I know you paid him to call on me before, but I think he really cares about me."

Pa shook his head. "We were wrong about him, too. He's doing a story on your etiquette lessons."

"What?" Clementine shook her head in denial. "I don't believe it."

"It's true. Dr. Payne warned me about him, and I sent Flavio to talk to him. While Flavio was there, he saw his notes."

Clementine clenched her fists. "You mean he was just seeing me to get a story?"

"I'm afraid so. And I mean to confront him about it. I'm giving myself some time to cool off so I don't break his neck."

Placing her head in her hands, she groaned, "This is so humiliating. Right now I don't want any man to come calling on me. Can you tell them all to stay away?"

Pa put his hand on her shoulder. "I'm sorry, Clemmie. Don't make any hasty decisions. But however this all turns out, just remember that when we go to Louisville, you'll be getting a fresh start. Take a few days and we'll talk about it again. And if you want, we can sell out to the Soto Toro brothers and leave for Louisville sooner."

She stood and fell into his comforting embrace. It was the only place that felt normal and safe.

Later in her cabin, she remembered the message she'd added to Samuel's letter and felt the shame of her humiliation wash over her anew. He must think she was a foolish woman. She imagined how he must have laughed at her each time they'd been together. In desperation, she sank to her knees.

Oh King. You are the only One who can mend my heart. I feel so betrayed.

Suddenly the story the sisters had taught her about Christ's own betrayal came to mind, and how He'd gone to the cross to save mankind. Tears streamed down her face as the Holy Spirit worked a miracle inside her soul.

Now I understand. Oh, thank You, Lord, for loving me. Come into my heart and heal it. I don't know what to do anymore. You know I don't want to go to Louisville, but I don't want the doctor's attentions either. I'm sorry I took so long to let You in. Please forgive me and help me, too.

Chapter Nine

After sleeping in late, Clementine absentmindedly pushed her eggs around with a fork.

"My dear, are you feeling poorly?"

Nodding, she glanced at Merryweather. She knew she should warn her about the article but felt too drained.

"While it's not polite to mention it, your eyes are puffy. Why have you been crying?"

The words spilled out of Clementine in angry accusations against Samuel Whitburn. She concluded, "He's played us all for fools."

Merryweather's hand flew to her bosom in a gesture of disbelief. "I can't believe it."

"Senor Flavio saw his notes. I'm the one who feels like the biggest fool of all. He kissed me, and I told him I liked it."

"Oh no! That rapscallion!" Her cheeks flamed in anger. "You get some rest. I'm telling Fiona, and we're going to have a few words with Mr. Whitburn." She left the saloon, shouting in a very unladylike manner, "Mr. Salty! Get the dinghy ready immediately!"

Feeling partly vindicated already, she squelched the desire to go with them and give their traitor her own set down. But, unfortunately, unless they packed their bags for Louisville, she'd run into him at some point. Better to let the sisters do the initial confrontation. And Pa. Meanwhile, she could just sink further into her shame or hold a little longer on to the fantasy that it was all a misunderstanding. That there was a happily-ever-after waiting for her that didn't include Louisville.

She bit her lip. Or was Pa right? Was Louisville the place that would make all their dreams come true?

◆ ◆ ◆

When the Featherstone sisters were of a mind, anything could be accomplished. And now, with Mr. Whitburn's address in hand, they headed staunchly to his place of abode. Sweat trickled down their necks as they leaned against a support post and waited for more than an hour. Finally, a neighbor happened out of the room next door to Mr. Whitburn's. He tipped his hat and started down the street, seeming in a hurry.

Fiona quickly started after him. "Excuse me, sir. Could you tell us if you know Mr. Whitburn?"

The stranger halted and smiled. "Samuel? Yeah, he's a good chap. Why?"

"We need to get a message to him."

"It won't do you any good to wait. He's gone to Sacramento to do a story about a new theater. Don't know when he'll be back."

Fiona exchanged a glance of utter disappointment with her sister.

Merryweather asked, "Will you give him a message next time you see him?"

"Sure."

"Tell him the Featherstone sisters are very upset to discover he was writing a story about Miss Cahill. That we demand a meeting with him. He can send a message to the ship upon his return."

"I heard there were some women living on one of those ships. Thought it was hearsay. I don't know what you're talking about, but I'll give him the message."

◆ ◆ ◆

A week passed. Given Clementine's dismal mood, the sisters decided to cease lessons. In fact, they gave Clementine a paper certificate of completion along with many verbal affirmations about her accomplishments. It was understood now that they would soon be departing. This only added to Clementine's gloominess. At first, they said they'd stay until the situation was settled with Mr. Whitburn, but after several days, Pa claimed the scoundrel had probably skipped town for good.

"It's just as well," Clementine bemoaned. "I don't think I could ever face him again. I only hope he changes my name when he writes the article."

"Of course he will, my dear," Merryweather commiserated.

But their conversation was interrupted when Salty stepped into the saloon with the same sheepish expression he sported the day he cut the door into her cabin.

"What is it?" Clementine inquired.

"Samuel Whitburn's requesting permission to come aboard. I didn't give it to him."

Without a word, Clementine jumped to her feet and snatched up her skirts using both hands as she ran out of the saloon. She climbed the ladder and ran to the rail. She'd already hitched up her skirt and had her shooting iron in hand when the breathless sisters caught up. Pointing it down at Samuel, she said, "You've got a lot of nerve showing up here. I'd as soon shoot you as hear anything you've got to say. Now get outta here before I lose control."

"I see you weren't kidding about your gun, but I'd rather you not aim it at my head, Clem. It might go off, you know."

Using both hands now to keep it steady and perfectly aimed, she replied, "Don't call me that."

"I never intended to write a story about you. I don't know where you heard such a thing."

"Senor Flavio saw your notes."

He shook his head regrettably. "Oh, those. It's true I jotted down some notes, but that's just how I do my thinking. And I've been doing plenty of thinking about you, Clem. You're even in my dreams. Now please put the gun down, and let me come aboard."

Wavering a bit, Clementine lowered the gun. "There's no way of knowing if you're telling the truth, but in case you are, I probably shouldn't shoot you. How about I'll just shoot a hole in your boat and let you swim ashore?" She raised her gun again and pointed at his dinghy.

"Wait! If you do that, you'll never hear the truth. Or the words you long to hear."

Her gun hand growing weary, she rested it on the railing. "I'd be a fool to trust you, and I'm real tired of feeling foolish."

"I should've come right away when I got your letter. But I had an opportunity in Sacramento, and I had no idea what you were thinking about me until I got home and talked to my neighbor. You're more important to me than any story, and I never would have gone if I'd known the lie you were believing. It hurts you'd even think I'd do such a thing. Didn't our kiss mean anything to you?"

"You know it did."

"I meant it when I said I'm falling in love with you. I just hope I live to be able to say it again."

Clementine tossed her gun and Merryweather caught it with a gasp. Then she wadded up her skirts and started over the rail. When Samuel saw what she was attempting, he maneuvered close and went up the rope ladder to assist.

"Oh, Clem," he said as he helped her into the boat. "Darling."

She turned and faced him. "Tell me again."

"I love you. Will you marry me?"

She flung her arms around his neck. "I love"—but she wasn't able to finish her sentence, for the boat rocked and tipped, dumping them both into the murky waters. Clementine sank beneath the water, and when she came to her senses of being capsized, she kicked to the surface. Samuel grasped her hand and pulled her to the boat, where he clung with his other hand.

He grinned at her. Water dripped from his hair and his eyelashes. "You do?"

"I'm coming!" Salty shouted.

With one arm, Samuel pulled her into his embrace. "I've got you now."

"Yes, you do. I hope you'll never regret it."

"Never, though I have a feeling life with you could be perilous. I love you so."

"I love you, too."

"And you'll marry me?"

"Yes." She swiped wet hair from her face. "I just hope Pa's not too disappointed about Louisville."

Salty had reached them now and was tossing a rope. Clementine caught it.

"Let's just get you safe; then we'll make plans. But if Louisville is where you want to go, then we will."

Clementine's heart overflowed with love just as she had her second ever kiss. This time she was completely ready, and the only thing that hampered it was Salty's constant beckoning.

◆　◆　◆

The Featherstone sisters' farewell dinner was a bittersweet affair. All family and friends were there, except the good doctor who'd taken his rejection bitterly.

Salty had caught a mess of fish, and the cook, knowing it was a special occasion, had cooked it to perfection. Though they'd not made specific arrangements yet, everyone was aware of Clementine and Samuel's marriage plans.

"Delicious." Clementine smacked her lips. "The only thing that would make this better is if'n I would've caught it myself. You will allow me to wear pants and go fishin' with Salty, won't ya, honey?"

Across the table Fiona arched a disapproving brow. But Merryweather just smiled, aware that Clementine was teasing them.

When Clementine patted her skirt, Samuel choked and cleared his throat. "I'll let you if you quit threatening me with your firearm. I don't find it amusing, Clem. Deal?"

"Deal," she giggled. Then she grew serious. "I could've searched the world over and never found anyone who suited me more than you."

"Speaking of travel," Pa began, keeping a straight face. "I know you've got your heart set on Louisville, but I'm starting to like it here in San Francisco. I hope you don't care too much if we just stay."

"And business is lucrative," Senor Vicente added.

"And the company is pleasant." Flavio winked at the sisters.

Clementine's heart raced. "You mean it, Pa?" She knew if she married, she wouldn't have to follow him to Louisville, but the decision of letting him go alone had been so hard that she'd been putting their marriage plans off, hoping something like this would happen. It suddenly hit her. Fighting back tears, she said, "God's answered my prayers. *He* is our golden ticket to a fair and equal opportunity, Pa."

"Yeah, He's been speaking to me, too."

She nodded, turning her gaze to Merryweather. "Now if we could just get you and Fiona to stay."

"Oh, Fiona wants to go home and get new draperies and rest awhile before we go on our next adventure."

"Assignment," Fiona corrected.

"You sure you want to travel through Panama again?" Clementine asked. "This could be your home base."

"It's tempting. But we love the adventure. And thanks to Mr. Whitburn's article, we'll get plenty of work. Maybe we can come see you again someday."

Flavio raised a disapproving brow at Samuel. "What article is this?"

"Not the one you imagined. I'm doing a story on the Featherstone sisters' Last Resort Traveling Etiquette School."

With a grin, Clementine said, "No use wasting good notes. It's a tribute that will put their school in a good light. And he's promised to give me a pseudo name. And if he doesn't keep his promise. . ." She patted her skirt.

"You gotta quit doing that," he warned.

"I don't know if you can stop Clemmie from doing anything," Pa said with a chuckle.

"Wanna bet?" Samuel grazed her lips with a kiss.

It melted Clementine on the spot. Her hand fell away. "You win."

Pa cleared his throat, and they both had the good sense to look embarrassed.

"Maybe we should stay a bit longer. Seems the couple could use instructions on what is and isn't done in public," Fiona warned.

Merryweather replied, "Sometimes, sister, rules are broken."

Dianne Christner lives in New River, Arizona, where life sizzles in the summer when temperatures soar above 100 degrees as she writes from her air-conditioned home office. She enjoys the desert life, where her home is nestled in the mountains and she can watch quail and the occasional deer, bobcat, or roadrunner.

Dianne was raised Mennonite and works hard to bring authenticity to Mennonite fiction. She now worships at a community church. She's written over a dozen novels, most of which are historical fiction. She gets caught up in research, having to set her alarm to remember to switch the laundry or start dinner. But her husband of forty-plus years is a good sport. They have two married children, Mike and Rachel, and five grandchildren: Makaila, Elijah, Vanson, Ethan, and Chloe.

She welcomes you to visit her website at www.diannechristner.net.

The Marriage Broker and the Mortician

by Anne Greene

Dedication

I dedicate this novella to all my readers who have fallen in love. Enjoy!

Chapter One

I said hands up, lady!"

"Who are you? What do you want?" Eve Molloy grabbed one of the four posts of her bed and glared at two masked men who'd forced their way through the door into her rented room. Downstairs, clatters, clangs, and voices rose and fell as the other boarders ate dinner at the long dining table. They were too noisy to hear if she screamed.

The taller intruder towered above her. He jerked her hands from the post, backed her against the room's striped wallpaper, and slapped her face. Her head banged against the wall.

She gasped. The sting took her breath away.

He kicked the door shut behind him with a dusty, booted foot. "Shut up."

The dinner racket from below faded. The invader who slapped her pressed a long six-shooter to her temple. Cold gray eyes skewered her. The red bandanna covering the lower part of his face quivered. "Don't scream, and you won't get hurt."

Her stomach churned into knots. His dead eyes promised he *would* kill her. She needed her money to return to her job at the San Francisco Hibernia Orphanage, but she wouldn't risk her life. Six other precious girls at the orphanage depended on her return, and she would rescue them as she had the six prospective brides this trip. She shook her head and whispered, "I won't scream."

The shorter, heavier invader, wearing a dark mask, jerked drawers from the dresser and spilled her personal items on the floor. "Where's that money?" He discovered her gun, held the revolver up for his cohort to see, unbuttoned his long duster, and stuck her weapon into the wide belt holding his double holsters.

The stench of liquor and unwashed bodies nauseated her. Her stomach roiled. She clenched her fists. She would not retch. She must focus. Was there anything distinctive about the men besides their height? Icy gray eyes above a red bandanna, and searching brown eyes above a dark bandanna. Both wore Stetsons pulled low over their foreheads, black gloves, and long dusters buttoned tight. Black clothes. At another time, seeing them dressed in identical outfits would have made her chuckle. Not today. The aura of menace surrounding them caused goose bumps to prickle on her arms. She yearned to scream, but if she did, they would kill her. And no one could hear her. She clamped her lips.

The thug ransacking her room scuffed his alligator boots through her clothes on the floor. He upended her mattress, stripped her bed, and then pivoted toward her.

Glacial fear iced her heart. The room darkened. She would *not* faint. Irish lasses did not faint.

The reek of whiskey closed in as Alligator Boots grabbed her arm and pawed at her dress. "Where's that money?"

"Stop! I'll give it to you." She turned away.

The giant ruffian grabbed her arm in a viselike grip. "Don't move."

"I but sought a bit of privacy."

"Forget that!"

She pulled in a deep breath and unbuttoned the top three buttons of her green-checked cotton dress, slipped her hand down inside to the bust line of her corset, and tugged out the small bag of coins. "Now leave, both of you. This is everything I have." She dropped the bag in the oversized, outstretched hand.

"Not everything." His steely gaze leered.

Footsteps on the stairs and laughter grew closer as diners from downstairs made their way up.

"We don't have time for that," the searcher's gruff voice grunted. His alligator boots scraped the wooden floor as he strode for the door. "We got what we came for."

The towering bandit brushed the six-shooter's cold barrel down her cheek and grabbed her hands. "No rings." Gloved fingers shoved back her hair. "No earrings." He glanced at the shambles of her room. His red bandanna swayed. "Nothing else worth taking." He shoved the weapon against her chest over her rapidly beating heart. "Don't raise an alarm until an hour has passed. Or I'll come back and hurt you. You won't like what I will do."

◆　◆　◆

Rafe Riley's button boots clicked on the wooden floor of the boardinghouse. He stopped and swerved into the dining room. What was causing the hubbub?

Another shooting? A murder? A robbery? Happened every day in Eureka.

A large group of men and women surrounded a slender lass with masses of disheveled red hair and wide green eyes enthroned on one of the wooden dining chairs. An Irish miss not far removed from County Cork or he'd be far off target.

From the raised voices talking with her, he gathered she'd been robbed of everything she owned. He strode over, gazed over the heads of the crowd, and then elbowed his way to her side. He barely recognized the beauty, she was in such a fluster. By the look of her simple dress and flat shoes, the thieves hadn't gotten much. Why pick on her?

"Look at the state o' you." Rafe took both her tightly clasped hands in his.

"Humph, you wouldn't look so elegant yourself if you'd just had all your belongings stolen." Her emerald eyes sparkled like jewels in the sun. She jerked her hands out of his grasp and made a futile attempt at smoothing her flyaway tresses.

"'Tis sorry I am that you had that experience. Can I be of service?"

"The two thieves ran out not fifteen minutes ago. If you haste, you can catch them." She pointed toward the door. Heads in the crowd swiveled toward the front door of the boardinghouse. Not one of the troop of men circling her moved to follow the criminals.

"Long gone by now," a skinny boarder in a bowler hat muttered. "Most of us here are salesmen passing through. We're not lawmen."

"Right. Who knows where the robbers are by now." Rafe gazed out the window at the empty expanse of landscape spread from the boardinghouse to the Feather River and beyond. Not even dust rose from the street. "Robbers, bushwhackers, and murderers hide in caves in those hills. Once they escape town without capture, even the sheriff with a large posse hesitates to follow them. Too many places to be ambushed."

The crowd muttered agreement and melted away, leaving her sitting alone with her back to the trestle dining table.

"Anything I can do to help?" Once again Rafe gazed into her eyes. His world tilted. His heart stopped beating, hiccupped, and then drummed like an Irish bodhran. Those huge sea-green eyes with unbelievably long auburn lashes etched his heart like an unforgettable daguerreotype. He tore his gaze from those bewitching eyes to the rest of her face. The faint imprint of a hand marred one cheek of her creamy complexion. "Are you hurt?"

"Not physically. It takes more than a robbery to frighten me."

Lady had spunk. He smiled. But how had that clog gotten into his gullet? He cleared his throat. "Name's Rafe Riley. I mine gold here in Eureka. I also own the mortuary."

"Unfortunately the two thieves aren't dead, so I don't know how you can help."

She was a feisty one. "I offer my sympathy. And my money if you have need of it."

"I don't take charity." Her shoulders slumped. "Is there no sheriff in Eureka?" Those magnificent eyes, green as the greenest valley in Tipperary, gazed into his.

He swallowed the huge lump jamming his throat. "Sheriff Talbot and his posse are scouring the countryside, tracking a gang of outlaws that robbed the assay office." He handed her a nearby glass of water. "Might I ask your name?" As if he didn't already know her name. As if her unforgettable face hadn't kept him from sleep all this week.

"I'm Eve Molloy."

"May I offer you dinner, Miss Molloy? I'm too late to chase the thieves, but perhaps I can be of help in some other way."

"Thank you, I would appreciate dinner." She held up her small embroidered purse by its drawstrings; he'd heard women call such an item a *reticule*. The flat green tapestry looked empty. "As you can see, I can't pay."

He helped her up and settled her dark shawl around her shoulders.

Some pink tinted her pale cheeks. She smoothed her long, riotous curls. "I seem to have lost my hair combs as well. Please overlook the disorder."

"Your hair is the most glorious I've ever laid eyes on. Don't let the slight disarray bother you. The view is quite charming."

Her cheeks turned scarlet. "Please don't use flattery, Mr. Riley. If I'm to dine with you, I'd appreciate honest words."

"Forgive me, Miss Molloy, but I speak *only* honest words."

She drew white gloves on and up over her elbows and then lifted her long green and white skirt and breezed toward the boardinghouse door.

He put a hand to the small of her back, and a slight tremor vibrated his fingers. Did she feel the same attraction to him that he did to her? A sliver of anticipation tiptoed up his spine.

Gold and red leaves fell from the few trees scattered along the boardwalk as he escorted her across the street to Eureka's only hotel. After summer's heat, he raised his face to the cool wind that blew in the promise of an early winter.

Would they serve steak today or only fish? The Italians who controlled the restaurants in both the lodging house and the hotel didn't advertise a menu. They served whatever fish or meat they could secure at the best price and biggest profit. Dinner offered only one or the other.

She lifted her long skirts and her small shoes made no sound as they crossed the wide dirt street and entered the new wooden structure.

Settled at a table by the window of the restaurant, he leaned forward in his seat across from her, his elbows on the table. "So, Miss Molloy, tell me your tale. You're new in Eureka, are you not?"

"Yes. I rode in on the stage a week ago last Wednesday. I brought six brides-to-be with me." She smiled, placed her reticule on the white tablecloth, and removed her gloves.

Was he dreaming? She lit the entire restaurant with her smile. Once again he cleared his throat. "Oh yes. I've heard of you. You're the marriage broker from San Francisco." He'd not only heard of Eve; he couldn't dislodge her from his mind.

She nodded, folded her gloves, and laid them beside the tapestry purse.

She didn't seem nervous or upset now. She looked calm and totally in control. Poised. A slight smile turned up the corners of her mouth.

A man might do anything to see another real smile on those lovely pink lips.

"Every one of my young ladies paired herself with a groom of her choice. I attended the last wedding this morning." She frowned. "Before I was robbed." Her long, slender fingers held no rings.

She was single. He'd noticed that earlier.

He directed his gaze to her swanlike neck. Her beauty made his heart ache. He cleared his throat. She would think he had a cold. He gulped a drink from his water glass.

Their dinner arrived, and the dark-haired waiter arranged the filled plates before them, giving Rafe a respite to attempt to take his thoughts off Eve's beauty and ground himself. *Hide your feelings, man. Watch yourself.*

Blamed if he wasn't as nervous as a youth on his first buggy ride with his sweetheart. "Appears you and your young ladies are the talk of Eureka." He cut into his steak as if he weren't vitally interested in her, in what she did, and in what she would do now. "You're not from around here?" Why was he babbling? He knew where she hailed from.

She took a sip of water. "No, we traveled here by a wagon and oxen I purchased in San Francisco."

"Couldn't your brides find husbands there?"

"Alas, they are all orphans from the Hibernia Orphanage. At age eighteen all children raised in the orphanage are given a suit of clothes and twenty dollars, and they're sent out to live on their own." A frown marred her rounded brow. "The boys do all right. But what type of work are girls of eighteen going to find? And where will they live with no family to help them?" Color tinted her cheeks pink. "Girls have little choice except to become scullery maids or enter a life of crime, or even become prostitutes."

Eve didn't mince words. Nor blush at the harsh reality of life. The few women he knew would say something coy or drop their heads and refuse to speak. This girl had gumption. He liked that.

"And how did you gain acquaintance with these young ladies?"

"I was also raised in Hibernia Orphanage. Last year when I became of age, the orphanage had an opening for an Irish dancing teacher." She glanced up from her plate. "I took immediate advantage of the opportunity."

"So you know firsthand the lack of options your young ladies face." She was younger than she looked. Perhaps her air of confidence and self-assurance made her appear older.

"Quite so. I understand the depth of despair when a lady is thrust out on her own to face a cruel and unwelcoming world." She bit her lip as if she'd said more than she had planned to reveal.

"So the grooms pay you for the ladies?"

She briefly ducked her head, then straightened and turned the gaze of her incredible Irish green eyes on him. "The grooms pay for the ladies' passage to Eureka, plus a small amount for my time, my effort, and to compensate me for being absent from my job for several weeks."

"And the robbers took everything you earned."

Her eyes grew moist. "Yes. As well as the money for my passage back to San Francisco."

"So that leaves you in a pickle." He couldn't let the most adorable woman he'd ever met walk out of his life. Somehow he must keep her in Eureka. "Do eat. Your dinner's getting cold." He cut a bite of steak and took his time chewing.

"You're very kind." She delicately forked some mashed potatoes into her attractive mouth.

He forced himself to look away from her lips. "Tell me more about this marriage broker business. How did you get started?"

Dimples played around her mouth. "I do have one living relative. My grand-uncle, Michael O'Shaughnessy, who resides here in Eureka."

Rafe suppressed a start and schooled his expression. He'd have to tell her. But later. Let her enjoy her dinner first.

"I wrote to Uncle Michael of my plan to bring six ladies from the orphanage to find suitable husbands in Eureka. I know it's a gold rush boomtown with few women living among the many, many male prospectors."

"And so it is." Her first bite appeared to have whetted her appetite. She concentrated on the mound of food on her plate.

Watching her delicately but quickly devour her food caused his heart to lurch. When had she eaten last?

"Uncle Michael arranged for six Christian men of upright character who had expressed a need for wives to meet my six ladies from Hibernia." She spoke matter-of-factly, her attention on her dinner.

"And did your uncle Michael O'Shaughnessy keep his part of the bargain?"

A smile lit her face like gold shining among the rocks of the rushing Feather River. "Oh yes. Each one of my ladies was more than pleased with the man Uncle arranged for her." She frowned and gazed into Rafe's eyes. "Uncle brought double the six men we needed, so each girl had an option. But I noticed one man lurking on the edge of the group." She gazed at him under those incredible auburn lashes. "He wore a black Prince Albert suit with silk-faced lapels, light gray waistcoat, and black derby hat. . .much like the clothes you have on."

The coffee he'd lifted to his lips tipped and joggled into the saucer before he gained control and took a gulp. "You've found me out!"

"Aren't your garments a bit formal for a mining town?"

"They are somewhat confining, but the clothes act as a signboard of my mortuary profession." He sipped his coffee and cleared his throat. "So you noticed me looking over the brides."

"You *are* quite tall and distinctive."

"I confess. Your uncle advertised, and I answered."

"But none of my girls suited what you look for in a wife?"

"They were all fresh, young, pretty, and appeared to be capable of making fine wives."

"But not for you?"

Her smile exposed straight white teeth. Dimples played games around her lips. A twinkle sparked her eyes to the darkest green. He ran a finger beneath his cravat, which had suddenly grown too tight. He clinked his cup on the saucer, and the awkward movement mussed the white tablecloth. "Um, yes. One lass caught my eye."

"But she chose someone else? I'm so sorry. I plan to bring six more girls in a few weeks. I just need to find a way home and back again. I must talk with my uncle."

"Um, about your uncle. . ."

"You've seen Uncle Michael?"

"Yes. I know him slightly. I met him a week ago when we twelve men met your wagonload of girls." How could he console her? "I met him again today in the course of my business."

"He's a lovely man, don't you think?"

"He seemed so last week. I'm sorry, but today I never spoke with him."

"But you said—"

"I'm so sorry to be the one to convey the bad news. I met your uncle today in the course of my undertaking business."

Her face paled, and she blinked rapidly.

"Friends of his brought his body to the Feather River Mortuary, my place of business. I just left there before I went to your boardinghouse. I came to tell you of his demise. His friends told me where you were staying." He laid his hand on where hers were clasped together on the tabletop.

"But. . ."

"Those men who robbed you must be the same two who shot your uncle to death. We prospective grooms also gave him money. Probably you both should have taken care of the marriage arrangements in a more private setting where strange eyes couldn't witness the exchange of money. For the most part, this is a lawless town."

Tears, like the morning dew on the grass in Limerick, sparkled in her green eyes.

He tilted her chin up with his index finger. Again his world shifted. The lass needed him.

He couldn't let Miss Malloy return to San Francisco.

No matter what it took, he would keep her in Eureka. He'd fallen in love with the spunky Irish lass.

But she must never discover the secret that had driven him here.

Chapter Two

"Thank you for dinner, Mr. Riley." Eve gave him her best smile.

"My pleasure, Miss Molloy."

Despite his fancy clothes, her dinner partner seemed a nice man. Clean-shaven, with a face that verged on handsome, he looked much younger than his Prince Albert formal attire suggested. He couldn't be more than five years older than she.

However, since that awful day when she turned five years old, she'd disliked being around mortuaries and dead bodies. Though she'd been so young, she'd never forget tears streaming down her face and her heart breaking as she stood between her parents' caskets. Why had God allowed that awful carriage accident? Peace hadn't come until she acted as go-between for her first young lady orphan with a wonderful marriageable husband. But she still hated mortuaries.

So, though he was an appealing, charming, and kind man, she hoped never to see Mr. Riley again. Surely Uncle must have closer relatives than she to take care of his funeral and burial arrangements. She must immediately seek a way to pay her lodging bills and return home.

How wretched to lose Uncle Michael before she'd even had an opportunity to get acquainted with him. How unfortunate her dear uncle had been murdered. To whom could she now go to ask for funds to return to her job at the orphanage? How could she bring the other orphans here who depended on her for husbands?

What a quandary You've landed me in, Lord.

"Might I ask what you plan to do in order to return to San Francisco?" Though his dinner was only half-eaten, Mr. Riley laid his napkin on the table.

"I shall find a position here in Eureka until I earn my passage home."

"And after that, will you return to Eureka now that your uncle has passed to his reward?"

"There were six men"—she gave him a saucy smile—"including yourself, who failed to appropriate a bride. After I return to my job at Hibernia and save enough money, there are six more young girls who will soon turn eighteen. I am like a mother to these young ladies, and they depend on me to keep my promise to obtain suitable Christian husbands for each of them. So, yes, I shall return." She frowned and wrung her gloves in her fingers. "However, I have no idea how long I shall be away." She gathered her reticule and shawl.

"Please stay a moment longer." He laid warm fingers on her hand.

A tingle traveled up her arm. The tall gentleman was certainly attractive. She loved how his dark, wavy hair spilled over his forehead as if he'd not taken much thought to his appearance. Made him seem even younger. She smiled and settled back in her chair.

He left his fingers resting on her hand. What a lovely new sensation. She should move her fingers away, but how pleasant to have his wide, masculine hand cupping hers. Who would have thought such a dandy would have such a work-hardened, strong hand?

"When you return, perhaps you should only fetch five young ladies back with you."

"Whatever for?"

"Do you recall that I said I had the greatest interest in one of your young ladies?"

"You did mention one lass caught your eye."

"You are the one who caught my fancy." He rose, skirted the table, and knelt on one knee of his cashmere striped trousers. "Miss Marriage Broker, would you do me the great honor of becoming my wife?"

Her hand flew to her throat, where her heartbeat pulsed double time. Air seemed to have evaporated from the room. She dragged in a deep breath. The dark brown eyes gazing up at her looked solemn with promise. He shoved his hand through his dark mahogany hair, raking the thatch back from a high forehead. A scar cut across the tan of his brow and dipped into his eyebrow, giving him a slightly mysterious expression. His full lips, with which he'd expressed his out-of-nowhere proposal, had firmed and looked serious.

She blinked rapidly. Other diners gaped in their direction. What possessed the man? Certainly he was quite good-looking and well set up, but she'd just made his acquaintance. Certainly he was Irish and perhaps a Christian since he'd passed Uncle's judgment. Certainly he'd offered to help. But she'd not imagined taking a husband for herself. She had a position at the orphanage and the responsibility of the other six girls waiting there for her return. And more soon-to-be homeless girls grew closer to eighteen each year.

Thoughts of the two bandits who'd threatened her sprang to her visual memory. How tempting to have a protector. She shook her head. But she was Eve Malloy, and Eve Malloy stood on her own two feet.

"Um, sir. . ." She cleared her raspy throat. "I barely know you. Please rise, you're making a spectacle of yourself."

He squeezed her hand. "You brought six lasses to wed six men whom they'd never met, and by your own words said each one found someone to wed. I'm a Christian and seeking a wife. Why not choose me? Why are you so different?"

"*I* am not desperate. I can find employment until I save enough money to return to San Francisco. I have experience. I have a talent." She shrugged. "And I have no wish to wed."

Still the stubborn man didn't rise.

"I'm afraid I didn't make myself clear. I own a lovely mansion that begs for a wife's delicate touch. I run a business that sorely needs a woman's sympathies to console mourners of those who have passed to their heavenly home. I have money, influence, and high standing in this community. . .and I need a wife."

His low voice had risen, until with his last words, every head in the restaurant pivoted in their direction.

Her thoughts grew clearer. "You have blindsided me, sir, with your kind offer, but I must decline." She plucked her hands from his and motioned for him to rise. "If I marry, I shall wed for love alone. Not because I must, or because a man has a need in his life he wants to fill, but because I desire to share my life with another." Her heartbeat slowed. She was right. She knew it. "I shall only marry when I meet a man I love with all my heart." *And he shall feel the same way about me.*

"But Eve, that *is* exactly how *I* feel about you. You are light, you are life, you are everything a man could ever want."

Of course, now that she'd revealed what she wanted, he would declare he felt that way. How transparent he was!

"Please rise, sir, and let us never speak of this again."

Chapter Three

Rafe tossed on his feather mattress. Perhaps he should have courted Eve before he asked for her hand. But he'd never felt this way, and she expected to leave Eureka soon. Perhaps never to return.

A knock on his front door reverberated up the stairs to his bedroom.

"Give off!" he yelled.

The knocking grew louder and faster.

"Okay, okay. I'm coming!" He yanked up his pants, shrugged into his shirt, and rushed down the stairs and through the entry.

The thunks on the door grew louder.

He jerked open the polished mahogany door.

A small, red-faced man wearing prospector's garb stared up at him. "Me partner's just died in a cave-in. Can you come right now?" The man bent over and vomited in the bush beside the front door.

The odor rose to engulf Rafe's air space. He held his breath

"Me partner were as close to me as me brother. I can't stand to see him lying there all crushed with rocks and bleeding."

"I was up at all hours working the last two nights. I'm beat." Rafe shifted on his bare feet. "Would it be possible for this to wait until morning?" Rafe buttoned his shirt.

"Nay, man! I. . .I lost my claim gambling, and I'm afeared the new owner's not very patient. He wants to prospect my claim at first light." The agitated man waved his hands like a rooster learning to fly. "Me partner and me was trying to hack out a few more gold pieces before the new owner took over." The bald-headed man's mouth opened and shut as if he couldn't spew out any more words.

The first streaks of light glowed on the horizon. Rafe knuckled his sleepy eyes. He wouldn't be able to sleep again anyway. What was another sleepless night in the scheme of things? Best take care of this matter so he could make time to see Eve.

"Follow me. Fill me in on all the details while I arrange things." He strode to the barn. His new client followed him.

"What's your name?"

"Name's Peterson. Claim's halfway up the mountain or I'd a been here sooner."

"What's your partner's name?"

"Jim Davis."

Rafe shoved open the barn door and groped in the darkness for the harness to hitch the horses to the wagon. His teams seemed as sleepy as he and stood docile, heads and tails dragging the hay while he harnessed them to the wagon. He hefted the necessary embalming materials for on-site into the wagon. "You have a hut on your claim?"

"Yep. Good-sized one."

"Fine. We'll carry Jim's body inside your shanty, and I'll embalm him right there." Rafe fumbled through the assembled caskets. "You want one with a silk lining?"

"You got one with a *silk* lining?"

"Yes. I buy the silk by the roll and tack the lining inside the casket myself."

"High priced?"

"Higher than a cloth lining."

"You put cloth around a wood casket, don't you?"

"Of course. That's the normal way."

"I'll take the cloth lining then. Jim wouldn't mind."

"As you like." Rafe rummaged through the line of caskets until he selected one lined with white broadcloth. "Do you have friends who will dig the grave? Or do you need my services?" Watching for splinters, he heaved the oblong wooden box into the back of his wagon.

"I'll find some. It's a trek from my claim to the churchyard. Reckon you'll have to use that big horse-drawn hearse with the fancy glass lamps and black drapes. I can afford that much for poor Jim."

"I'll drive back for the hearse while you and your friends dig Jim's grave." Rafe loaded the toxic chemicals beside the empty coffin. Even in containers they smelled noxious. He snugged his crated and securely wrapped camera under the wagon seat where his prized possession would be less jostled.

The heavy wagon didn't even tilt when he vaulted onto the driver's seat. "Hop on up and show me where Jim died."

The sun had risen halfway to the center of the sky before Rafe pulled the horses to a standstill outside an opening in the side of the mountain. "How far inside?"

"Not far. Cave-in is just a few feet."

He bent and followed Peterson into the dank area.

"Hey, Riley, I always wondered how you drop that casket down into that hole. What's your secret?"

Rafe grunted. Always the same questions. "I recruit you and a couple of your friends, and we lower the casket into the grave with leather straps. Pretty simple, really."

"How much you charge for all this?"

"Standard rate is $100. But embalming fluid's gone sky high. High rate of bodies, so price of fluid goes up. I'll have to charge you $110."

"Seems stiff." The aging man scratched his scraggly beard. "Tell you what. I'll pay $110.00 if you speak the words over Jim's body."

Rafe nodded. "Done."

He looked forward to speaking over a dead man's grave. Only good thing about the whole mortuary business. Everything else he disliked. Each time he planted a body, his aversion grew.

But the miners expected a eulogy. He didn't deliver one. Too many dead prospectors gambled, drank, and stole when given the opportunity. He'd not fumble around for good words to give the deceased a celebration of praise. Instead he delivered a short sermon about the hardships of a miner's life. Then he gave an invitation to whoever attended the funeral to become a follower of Jesus. Sometimes he got carried away. At times men at the gravesite drifted away before he finished, so he'd learned to keep his sermon short. He liked to include the fact that for a believer, to be absent from the body meant to be present with the Lord. So he started with that before the prospectors had a chance to disappear.

Without the opportunity to utter a sermon, he would have given up his grisly occupation long ago. But the money kept pouring in. He detested the whole process from gathering up the often bloody, broken body to the wearing of the Prince Albert suit. Except for one other thing.

"You want a picture of the deceased inside the casket?"

"Yep. I'll send it to his folks back home. Jim and me was good buddies. Grew up in the same town. His folks would like that final picture."

"The picture won't cost you a penny more. It's a gift of Feather River Mortuary."

"That's mighty fine of you, sir."

Rafe would have taken the daguerreotype with or without Peterson's permission. When Rafe finished embalming the dead man, no matter how battered his appearance had been, the deceased appeared to be sleeping peacefully. Rafe rotated his tired shoulders. He was good at what he did. And a dead man didn't move the several minutes often necessary to expose the picture.

But was the gruesome work he performed worth the wealth he'd accumulated? Was the job worth his chance to share his faith?

Had it not been for the photographs and the preaching, he would have sold his business long ago.

He bent and grasped Jim's limp shoulders, and Peterson grabbed the bloody ankles. They lugged the body fifty feet to the hut, went inside, and unloaded Jim on the crude wooden table.

Rafe set to work. He raised his scalpel. He made a small incision.

When he finished, he needed something more pleasant to occupy his thoughts and to cleanse his mind. He gathered his tools, did the preliminary wash from the bucket of fresh water Peterson supplied, and stowed everything back inside his wagon.

Then he turned his teams toward his own claim. The peace of his place by the rushing waters of Feather River always brought him closer to God. He could pray there. And hear God's voice more clearly in the quiet beneath his big oak with its roots sunk deep in the banks of the river.

His teams knew the spot and stopped without command, lowered their heads, and nibbled grass. He vaulted down from the driver's seat, peeled his Prince Albert coat off, tossed it on the seat, and stretched his arms, his shirtsleeves so much more comfortable. His polished short boots sank into the carpet of grass. He lounged down, eased his back against the tree trunk, and drew in a deep breath of the fresh outdoor scent of his own space. A breeze over the rushing water carried pine fragrance mingled with autumn's musky odor to his senses. The canopy of bright blue sky brought peace.

First he prayed and then he dreamed.

He smiled. He would give his left hand to photograph Miss Eve Molloy seated on the side of this green hill with her red hair glistening in the sunshine. Of course no daguerreotype captured color, but *he'd* never forget the sight. He'd say something droll to bring out that lovely smile with the dimples playing around her sweet mouth. When the whispering breeze tousled her hair, he'd reach down to touch the silky curls with the excuse of smoothing her runaway hair.

He'd invite her to a picnic this afternoon. Perhaps show her his claim. Certainly invite her to have dinner inside his mansion tonight. Ma was anxious to meet Eve.

But he'd never let Eve see the family pictures he stowed in the secret chamber hidden inside his library wall.

Chapter Four

Eve dragged her feet into the boardinghouse, moved to the parlor, arched her back, and gave the tired muscles a good rub. Settling onto the horsehair settee, she kicked off her shoes and wriggled her toes. September dryness encompassed Eureka, though as she kneaded her toes, her long black stockings felt damp.

Clara Swingler, the boardinghouse owner, gazed at her, sewing draped in her lap, needle raised in her hand. "So how did your job hunt go?"

"Looking for a job has never been such a despairing task." Eve leaned back against the hard cushions and closed her eyes.

"I would hire you here as a cook, but our Italians won't stand for having an Irish girl invade their kitchen. Nor the dining room either. Antonio hires only his own countrymen. Says he can't trust outsiders." She shook her gray head and pursed her wrinkled lips.

"I knew that, so I didn't apply here. Antonio even hires the housekeepers." Eve opened her eyes and brushed back her drooping hair.

"Surely someplace in Eureka is hiring."

"I applied at the Carter House Inn."

"Certainly that combination inn, restaurant, and general store has an opening. I know they are short of help inside the general store. I had to wait fifteen minutes this morning for the overworked clerk there to total up my purchases."

"Did you know the Germans control hiring at the Carter House Inn? The rude German woman tore my application in two and laughed. 'We not hire Irish. We trust only Germans to work for us. Try someplace else.'" Eve wrinkled her nose. "Mrs. Krautmeyer was quite direct."

Clara nodded and picked up her sewing. German herself, she understood the woman's direct ways. She began stitching a hem in a navy flannel skirt for her growing daughter. "I'm sorry, my dear. I shall extend you credit here for your board. For a few more days at least." The plump, gray-haired landlady gazed over her spectacles. "I'll not throw you out onto the street." She clucked her tongue. "But I do understand the Germans' point of view. Every immigrant group here in California tends to stick together with the people and cultures they know."

"True. I even tried to find work at the laundry."

"Of course you wouldn't find work there. The Chinese keep tight hold of the laundry business. That's the bottom of the pay scale, and they reserve the boiling clothes business for themselves." Clare threaded her needle then stuck the slender sliver into the material and began hemming once again. "Although I have heard of a few Chinese hiring onto some mining camps as cooks." She shook her head. "Don't ask me how that turns out. I can't imagine eating Chinese food myself."

"The Germans advised me to ask for work at the gold assay office."

"And?"

"The nice man at the office simply said he doesn't hire women. Period." Eve rested her head on the back of the settee, folded her hands across her lap, and heaved a sigh.

Clara looked up, her face bright. "Perhaps you could apply with the rancheros who drive the beef herds in."

Eve sighed again, deep and long. "Even they refuse to hire an Irish cook. They prefer their Spanish cuisine."

Clara kept her gray curls bent over her sewing. "Actually, I might know where you could find employment."

"I will try anything. I'm desperate."

"Certainly the job will pay enough for your room and board here, plus a little more to put aside for your passage back to San Francisco. And if they like you, I'm sure the owner will raise your pay."

Eve jumped to her feet and perched on the footstool beside Clara's old-fashioned high-laced boots. "Tell me, please. I really must have work. I have not a cent to my name!"

A devilish glint lit Clara's gray eyes. "The Grand Hotel has an opening for an entertainer."

Eve's shoulders slumped. "I'm no entertainer."

"You told me you hold a position at the Hibernia Orphanage as an Irish dancer." Clara's thick fingers stroked Eve's curls. "I'd call that entertainment."

"But I teach. I don't perform."

◆　◆　◆

The tiny hotel stage opened an intimidating void in front of Eve. The dining tables a few feet below the small platform overflowed with customers. The rattle of silverware, din of voices, and clomp of feet of the German waiters would surely overpower her music. She coughed. Cigarette smoke swirled like a fog onto the stage. The stench permeated even the heavy stage curtain.

She tried to smooth down the costume the hotel provided, but the short tartan skirt landed well above her knees. The outfit wasn't authentic. She'd thought the tight-fitting blouse had been the incorrect size until Blaze, the designer, informed her otherwise. She'd been happy earlier that at the last moment in San Francisco she'd packed her dancing slippers. They had tucked nicely into a free space in her luggage.

Yet how could she perform? The piano player, Whitacre, whom she'd practiced with earlier that morning, fell dismally short of the music she was used to back home. With the skimpy costume and the awful music, how could she force herself to prance out on that stage in front of all those people?

Her stomach rumbled. Two nights past, she'd eaten dinner with Mr. Riley. Since then, she'd had only water. If she wanted to eat, she must force herself to parade out on that stage.

She gazed to the opposite side of the small platform where Whitacre drummed his hands on the piano keys, and shook her head. He frowned, pounded harder on the ivories, and used his head to nod encouragement. His expression indicated she had an obligation to step out and perform.

Were her feet rooted to this shadowy place behind the curtain?

Whitacre twisted his face into a grimace, attacked the keys harder, swiveled his head, motioning to her to come out, and replayed her intro.

She could not.

Her stomach rumbled.

Dear Father God, please help me do this.

Both Clara and Whitacre had declared she would quickly become accustomed to performing and would even learn to enjoy her time in the limelight. Beneath the crazy green tam atop her curls, she shook her head. At least she didn't have to sing.

The house lights went out.

A hush fell over the diners.

Gas lights at the edge of the stage spotlighted the entire wooden stage surface, creating an oasis of light in the dark room. Whitacre stopped playing.

She pulled in a deep, relieved breath.

After a short interval, the pianist banged out a loud entrance to her song.

Her stomach growled so loud she barely heard the melody bars she needed. If she wanted to eat, she must dance.

She pirouetted out onto the stage.

A roar and loud hand-clapping buffeted her ears, overwhelming the music. She improvised until faint notes from the piano tinkled through the audience uproar. She caught the beat and then lost herself in executing the complex steps.

Soon she would finish. For the first time she allowed herself to glance down at the seated audience. And almost swooned. She faltered and lost her rhythm.

There, hunkered down at the front table, close enough the gas lights revealed day-old bristles shadowing his cheeks, presided Mr. Riley. A scowl darkened his face.

Heat radiated through her body and settled on her face. Barely perceiving the piano notes, she managed not to stumble as she executed the last steps to her dance. She curtsied.

The crowd erupted with cheers, whistles, and loud applause.

Again she curtsied and then twirled across the stage and finally off to the safety of the shadowy area behind the curtain.

The crowd pounded the tables, whistled, and shouted lewd names. Men stood and stomped their feet. "Eve, Eve, Eve," they chanted.

She cringed behind the curtain, clinging to the dusty material. Her face burned. The audience hadn't been appreciating her dancing. They hadn't paid high-ticket money to see Eve, the Authentic Irish Dancer; they'd handed over their wad of cash to see her wearing her scanty costume. Why hadn't she realized the almost entirely male audience only craved to see more of her body? She could have turned somersaults or sung off-key or simply stood onstage, and they would have begged for more.

Dear God, what have I done?

Chapter Five

Rafe leaned against the rough, wooden exterior of the Grand Hotel. He melted into the deep shadows the night cast over the unlit street. A lone horse and wagon rumbled down the alley. That back door would open any second, and Eve would emerge. After tonight's performance, a lady like Eve would not show her face boldly walking through the hotel's crowded dining room, out through the lobby, and then out the front door into the crisp evening.

No, she would steal out this back door and hurry to her boardinghouse. Eve couldn't have known how her performance would affect tonight's audience. She couldn't have known the Italians expected every lonely prospector in Eureka to shell out high dollars for her show. The innocent girl brought out every protective nerve in his body. She needed someone to look after her. She needed him.

The door slid open, and the overhead gas light revealed a mass of red hair above a pair of emerald eyes peeking out.

"Miss Molloy, may I escort you home?"

Her eyes widened, and she ducked back inside. Then the door squeaked open again and she emerged, her bewitching face looking sheepish. "Mr. Riley."

"May your thoughts be as glad as the shamrocks. May your heart be as light as a song. May each day bring you bright, happy hours that stay with you all year long."

"Ah, Mr. Riley, you do have a silver tongue."

"I thought you might be in need of this." He unfurled the cape he'd bought and fastened the navy broadcloth around her shoulders, covering her deficient costume.

"Thank you, Mr. Riley. How very thoughtful of you." She blinked those unforgettable eyes. "How did you guess I would be in need of this?"

"The Irish have a grapevine bearing all manner of fruit."

"So you knew I would appear onstage tonight?"

How could he answer? Of course he knew. The whole town knew. And every male in Eureka had paid a week's earnings to gape at Miss Molloy on stage. And she'd seen him stageside.

"Let's just say, Miss Molloy, that you are in need of a good dinner and a friend. I'm afraid the Grand Hotel is already filled with rowdy diners, and your lodging house is well past dinnertime. So might I invite you to my home to dine?"

"Oh no, sir. I've never dined alone with a gentleman in his home."

"Ah, but Miss Molloy, we shall not be alone. I have a full staff of servants, and my mother lives with me as well. Please accept my invitation."

Eve clutched the long cape closer and tucked her hand into his offered arm. "Thank you, Mr. Riley. I shall be happy to dine with you." A low growl from her stomach area accompanied her words. "But I must change clothes first. Do you mind?"

◆ ◆ ◆

Rafe led Eve past the long row of mansions that had mushroomed overnight in Eureka. When he arrived, gold nuggets had been so plentiful a man need only dip his pan in the river and bring out wealth beyond imagination. Not so much these days. Gold was here but had to be wrested from the land and the water.

So the avenue just off Main Street, as yet unnamed, traveled through a double line of stately mansions that rivaled any built in San Francisco. Proud owners planted trees and landscaped yards to showcase their new homes. Gas lamps lighted their way.

"This federal-style mansion, built after mine, belongs to a longtime friend, Danny Duggan. Duggan's running for mayor this year." He chuckled. "Danny likes my style. Copies me when he can."

"I see." Eve gazed wide-eyed at the long row of mansions bordering each side of the dirt street.

He led her up the walk to his own federal-style mansion and ushered her inside.

"Mam, where are you?" Rafe called up the beautiful curved staircase.

"Right here, son. I'll be down presently. Please don't wait on me." A melodious voice drifted down from above.

"Okay, Mam, come when you are able." Rafe smiled up. "Mam wants to dress for this occasion. You're the first lady I've invited to dine. She's rather excited."

He walked her through an impressive hall to a beautifully appointed dining room. The lines were elegant but simple. Would she like the modern white fireplace?

Seated at the massive dining table he'd imported from San Francisco, Rafe at the end and she at his right hand, he lifted his water glass in a toast. "*Slainte!*" He lightly clicked her lifted glass with his. "If you're lucky enough to be Irish, then you're lucky enough."

"Erin go bragh!" she breathed. "I love to celebrate Ireland."

"As do I. But I find America an exciting country, full of opportunity."

"Yes, if one is a male." The dimples played around her mouth.

He longed to reach out and trace those dimples with his index finger. Instead he clasped his hands, bowed his head, and asked Jesus to bless their dinner. Then he nodded to Stewart.

The butler moved quietly behind them, serving steak, potatoes, and steaming bowls of vegetables.

Delightful odors filled the room.

Delicate as an elf, Eve spooned out small portions of each offered plate. "I love this china pattern. What is it?"

"That's Ma's choice. I think she calls it Rose Floral Burgundy."

"It's lovely." She turned a dessert plate over. "*Staffordshire China.* The burgundy borders are charming. Not too masculine. Not too feminine." She tilted her head and smiled at him. "Perfect."

His face heated. "I'm so glad you like them."

"Every piece of furniture, every picture, and every decoration in your home is also perfect."

"Ma's taste. She had nothing until I moved her to Eureka. She had a fine time going through San Francisco selecting items to fill this house."

He turned to the butler. "Thank you, Stewart. Just leave the serving bowls on the table and you may retire to the next room."

Stewart nodded and moved quietly out of the room to stand just outside the door.

Eve immediately began eating.

"A silent mouth is sweet to hear, but I'd hoped to take this opportunity to tell you about myself. With your permission?"

She nodded, her mouth chewing ever so ladylike.

Would he be so mannerly if he were as hungry? Probably not. He straightened and lowered his voice to what he hoped was his most agreeable tone. "I hail from New York. My brother and I arrived penniless when we disembarked the ship from Ireland." She nodded, her attention on the steak she cut into tiny pieces and placed into her mouth.

"We lived in one of the dirty, overcrowded slum houses where ship captains direct newly arrived Irish." Usually he didn't let his mind dwell on those nasty days, but she must know him if she were to like him. "My brother and I worked at any odd job we could get—unloading cargo from ships, boxing in the ring for money, driving wagons to collect garbage, that sort of thing."

"Hmmm." She nodded and continued forking a bite of mashed potatoes into her mouth.

"Then we heard news of California gold. Heard gold lay in the streets for the gathering. Heard every man who made his way to the golden territory struck it rich. But we had no funds to travel.

"Then one lucky night my brother and I won a horse in a game of Faro. One horse, two brothers."

Now she watched him, her lips slightly ajar, a forgotten bite of asparagus tilting on the fork in her hand.

He reached across the table and moved her hand so her fork lay across her plate. "So Braden and I drew straws. He got the short end." Rafe took a sip of water to wet his raspy throat. Harder to tell than he'd expected.

"So the horse belonged to you?"

He nodded. "Named her Gold Rush for luck."

"Did any of your other family members journey to New York from Ireland with you?"

"We'll talk of that at another time, if you don't mind." He wouldn't share that. A man was allowed *some* secrets. "So Gold Rush and I joined a wagon train and set out for the gold coast. I paid our way by hunting. Took us almost three months to arrive in Eureka, where my money ran out."

"But, being a man, you had no problem securing a paying job."

"True enough. With the little money I earned, I staked a claim. Turned out God blessed me, and my claim has a rich vein of gold running through the hill as well as clustering in the rocks and gravel of my share of the Feather River bottom."

"And so, being the upstanding man you are, you sent money to New York to your brother, of course."

His heart lurched. But he nodded and plowed on with his story. "Too much money went to New York. Gang members there robbed Braden and killed him." He rushed on to get over the painful memories. "I wrote a friend in New York and sent money. He took care of Braden's burial and sent me his possessions." He fingered the worn gold cross hanging from a chain around his neck. "I kept this and hired a couple bodyguards for myself. They sleep in the house and stay close but remain discreet."

"Oh." A frown marred her smooth round forehead. "Are you expecting more trouble?"

He'd said too much about his past. He took another sip of water. "I sent money for Ma to leave New York, and she came with the stagecoach." The best investment he'd ever made, bringing Ma here. She was happy for the first time in her life. And he hadn't even known he'd needed a wife—until Ma paid O'Shaughnessy to fetch one for him. Then he still hadn't wanted a woman to love until he laid eyes on Eve. She changed his world.

"My claim struck a rich pocket of gold and paid off so well, I invested in a new business."

"The mortuary." She wrinkled her pert little nose.

"Right. And the business pays even better than the claim. Hundreds of men arrive here from all over the world to mine gold." He shrugged. "But many die from mine accidents, sickness, murder, and various other causes. Our local doctor couldn't handle the influx of dead bodies. So I bought property and set up my mortuary business. Then I opened the graveyard close to the new church."

"Why a mortuary?" A frown puckered her auburn brows.

"The town needed one." He cleared his throat. "At first I worked the business alone, doing everything. There was so much business, I purchased a hearse. I thought the dead deserved a proper send-off."

"I've seen that hearse. It is quite spectacular."

"Yes, overdone for Eureka, but the miners like the thing. The town is bound to continue growing. And that horse-drawn monstrosity is another signboard for my business."

"Like your clothes."

He nodded. "My two endeavors grew so lucrative that Ma talked me into building this showy home." He gazed around the dining room. "Seems huge and cold, even with her living here." He placed his hand over Eve's. The heat from her soft hand sent his heart racing. "Mansion needs a wife's touch. Needs a welcoming face for a man to come home to." He swallowed. "Needs you."

She ripped her hand away as if he'd burned her fingers. "We agreed not to discuss that topic."

You did. "My mansion shows the people of Eureka that I plan to remain here permanently. This gold coast has been good to me, and I aim to return whatever I can to the people here."

"That's very gracious of you." Her eyes wouldn't meet his.

"Eve, would you give me permission to court you?"

She scooted back her chair and rose. "I'm sorry, Mr. Riley. As I told you before, I am not seeking a husband."

He vaulted to his feet and touched a hand to her arm. At least *this time* she hadn't said she didn't want to discuss the matter. Perhaps she'd begun to like him. "Please sit down. I have some business matters I need to discuss with you."

"I will remain, Mr. Riley, if you promise not to mention marriage again."

"These other matters are of vital importance to you, so please stay."

She let him seat her again but tapped her fingers on the tablecloth and tweaked her practical navy shawl around her shoulders as if she planned to depart at the first opportune moment.

Why was she so opposed to marrying him?

Chapter Six

Eve glanced around the well-appointed dining room. Wealth screamed at her from every corner. The polished mahogany dining set, chairs with ivory padded seats, a china cabinet stuffed with sparkling glasses, and a sideboard set with a large silver tea set. Expensive-looking pictures hung tastefully on the brocade walls. She'd expected no less when he'd driven her inside the double iron gates enclosing lush green grass that led to the three-story brick Federal-style building.

What did such an affluent man want with her?

And what else could the stubborn Irishman have to say to her? He'd seen her at her worst on the stage but hadn't mentioned that debacle. He *was* a gentleman! And actually quite attractive with his broad shoulders and pleasant tenor voice. If she gave him half a chance, he'd probably sing a lilting Irish love song.

Not that that would be so very unpleasant.

She tapped her fingers on the damask tablecloth. "You said we had business to discuss?" Perhaps he knew of a job. If she starved, at least she would never have to appear on the Carter House Inn's stage again. But if he knew of a job—

A small, delicate-boned lady bustled into the room. "Sorry 'tis I'm late, son, but I supped long ago."

Mr. Riley rose.

She glanced, with birdlike movements, at Eve. "'Tis not often I'm pressed into service to chaperone upon a lady friend." Her warm, cordial smile wrinkled the smooth skin of her face. "There not being that many women in Eureka that please me, son." She laid an affectionate hand on Mr. Riley's shoulder and stood on tiptoes to kiss his cheek.

"Thank you, Mam. Please meet Miss Molloy. Miss Molloy, my mother."

The diminutive lady, an older portrait of her son, extended a small hand. "'Tis so very happy I am to meet you, Miss Molloy. My son tells me lovely things about you."

"And I'm quite happy to meet you, Mrs. Riley." Eve held on to the hand shaking hers so warmly, and a glow filled her heart. Mr. Riley's mother was exquisite and appeared to be quite a loving person.

"Please sit down with us, Mam." Mr. Riley pulled out a chair for her next to Eve.

"Thank you, son." The lady shook her white cap of curls, walked to the far end of the table, and seated herself. "I shall have a glass of tea, Stewart." She nodded at the servant and then turned back to Mr. Riley. "I'll just be sitting here listening and quiet as a church mouse."

Mr. Riley nodded, returned to his chair, and then cleared his throat. "Miss Molloy, my position as the mortician of Eureka also holds other responsibilities. As yet, we have no lawyer here in town. When pressed to the job, I act in that capacity."

"As if your job as mortician were not awful enough," she murmured under her breath. What on earth could the handsome fellow be blustering about? "And how could your position possibly affect me?"

He seemed loath to continue. Was he trying to prolong their time together? She reached for her reticule. She'd love to spend time with Mr. Riley's mother, but she must rise early tomorrow and set about finding a job. Either that or starve.

"Your uncle O'Shaughnessy left a will of sorts. A friend of his handed me the hand-written document to carry out his last wishes."

A trill of hope fluttered in her chest. "A will?" Uncle's stake had paid out well enough to finance her trip here and her return trip to San Francisco. But she'd noticed Uncle's miner's clothes and worn-out boots. He hadn't appeared to be endowed with cash. When Uncle met her at the stable, he'd sent her directly to Clara's modest boardinghouse rather than the more exclusive Carter House Inn or Grand Hotel. Clara's one-story wooden house, square on Main Street with its false front to make the dwelling look larger, was comfortable enough but sparse. Not a place an up-and-coming man lodged his relatives. She hadn't thought to wonder where Uncle lived. She'd been too occupied with getting her six wards happily married. She smothered a shudder. And then the robbery and Uncle's murder. Whatever means he had or who his relatives might be hadn't entered her mind.

"Yes. Seems you are your uncle's only living relative."

Rafe's smile strengthened her trembling insides. "Oh?"

"Michael O'Shaughnessy had many friends. Seemed a garrulous person. But no other relatives. And no wife or children."

"How very sad." Tears pricked her eyes.

"At fifty, he probably felt he was too old for the young ladies you brought as prospective wives."

A tear leaked out and Eve swiped the wetness with a finger.

"And the will?"

"Yes, son, do get to the will." Mrs. Riley leaned on the table, her chin in her hand, her brown eyes bright with interest.

Rafe stiffened his shoulders. "Oh yes, the will." He reached inside his breast pocket and slipped out a white wood-pulp sheet.

Where had Uncle gotten the expensive paper? She'd found paper scarce in Eureka.

Rafe cleared his throat. "I leave all my earthly goods to my niece, Eve Molloy. My goods consist of my gold claim, my shanty, and all my prospecting tools, as well as all moneys earned from said mine. All property inside the shanty shall go to my niece as well."

Eve's back stiffened ramrod rigid. Her heart stuttered. "Uncle left me his shanty and gold stake! That's wonderful news. I shall have enough money to return to San Francisco!"

Chapter Seven

Rafe's heart dropped to his stomach like he'd swallowed the pieces of lead he used to hold the casket in place inside the hearse.

Bad news for him, but he loved the way Eve's eyes brightened as if she'd experienced an unexpected Christmas. Had God ever created a more beautiful woman since he formed the original Eve and set her in the Garden of Eden?

"Where is Uncle's money? I need to return to San Francisco as soon as I possibly can."

When had she fitted her gloves back on? With her so anxious to leave his home, how could he win her heart as she had conquered his?

He hated to see the beautiful expression of joy on her face fall, but he had to tell her the worst. Best to get it over with. He stiffened his shoulders and made his voice businesslike. "The two thugs stole any money your uncle had. They ransacked his shanty. I'm afraid there is no money." He couldn't force a real smile, so he gave her the one he used on the newly bereaved. "There's only the basic shack, your uncle's prospecting tools, and his claim." He yearned to hold her in his arms and protect her from this bad news and any future bad news she'd have to endure. Instead, he shoved his hands into his pockets.

"Oh." The luminous light in her eyes dimmed but then brightened again. "I'm angry at those thieves, but God knew this would happen. Nothing takes Him by surprise."

"Yes, and I'm certain He will provide for your needs." What an awful position for her. And yet, without her uncle's money, she couldn't migrate back to San Francisco. With her here, perhaps she would relent, and he could court her and win her love. Was God working things out for them? Yet he'd be a beast if he didn't help her. "If you would allow me, I'd be happy to provide money for you."

She straightened the high-collared neck of her dress that reminded him of the fallen rust-colored leaves, and gave him the brilliant smile that lit his world. Was that the same dress she'd worn a few days ago? He didn't pay much attention to women's attire, but the fitted frock looked extremely fetching on her. He cleared his throat. She would have captivated him wearing a gunnysack. His cheeks heated. She'd looked beguiling in that costume she'd worn onstage. But he'd wanted to jump up on that platform and shield her from all those male eyes ogling her.

"Thank you for your offer, but I must decline." Dimples played around her mouth. "Would you escort me to Uncle's claim? I shall move into his shanty and not owe Clara any more money for my room and board."

He flapped his lips, trying to find words. "What? A lady like you can't live in squalor like that shack. What will you do there?"

"Why, search for gold, of course."

He jolted from his seat and paced the room. Thoughts churned like a mill wheel inside his brain. He faced her lighted face and swallowed. "That shanty and that claim are no fit place for a female." He clenched the back of a dining chair. "You have no idea what back-breaking, icy-cold labor mining requires. It's man's work scraping out a living panning for gold."

She rose and put a soft hand on his arm. "Oh, but I do know how to work hard. I'm quite frugal. I will wrest gold from that claim and soon be on my way back to the orphanage." Her bright face tilted up. "You shall see."

"There is no way you can work a claim. The job's mind-boggling and laborious for a man. A woman isn't built for that sort of work. There must be some other way." He raked a hand through his hair. "It's dangerous for you out there alone in the wilderness. You'd be easy prey for both man and beast."

"Nevertheless, I shall search for gold until I save enough money to return to San Francisco."

"You are an unreasonable woman."

◆ ◆ ◆

Perhaps Mr. Riley had been right. Eve had squatted by the icy water almost a week and her pan had yielded barely an ounce of gold. Perhaps Uncle's claim was a dud, and he'd neither found any gold nor had any money. Perhaps that was why the two murderers had come for her money after leaving him.

She plopped down on the grassy slope of the rushing river and lay on her back, gazing at the cloudless blue canopy of sky. The musky scent of autumn rose around her. Soft green grass turning rusty and hard prickled the back of her neck.

Her stomach rumbled. She'd used her first gold nugget to purchase food at the general store. The exorbitant prices made her hair stand up on her head like a porcupine's quills. Already her food supply dwindled. Where would she get more? She'd not eaten all day. Would she ever be able to save enough money to make her way back home?

To save on feed bills, she'd sold her oxen and wagon. Perhaps she should have charged a higher price. Costs in Eureka were sky-high, and she probably hadn't asked for enough. She closed her eyes. She was so tired.

Rustling in the bushes near the shanty roused her. How long had she slept splayed out on this grassy slope in the sunshine? She jerked to a sitting position and reached for the gun she'd purchased with the money she received for her oxen and wagon. She had only a few bullets, so she must make them count.

Nothing stirred around her. The river rushed a sparkling course over boulders and smaller rocks and pebbles. The wind whistled through the surrounding pine trees, wafting pine scent through the air. Faint voices drifted from the next claim a mile downriver. Nothing unusual.

Except. . .

What in the world? Three huge baskets crowded the doorstep of her shanty.

She jumped to her feet and rushed over. The containers bulged with flour, yeast, milk, fruit, slabs of meat, and other wonderful foods she hadn't tasted since her dinner with Mr. Riley. Who could have left these wonderful edibles on her doorstep?

She lifted her skirts and ran to the edge of the piney woods, so thick the sun barely penetrated. Rustling far away told her whoever had visited was too long out of sight for her to even catch a glimpse.

"Thank you, Father, for whoever was kind enough to leave these provisions for me!"

She spent all afternoon roasting moose or elk meat, she wasn't sure which, on a spit near her front door, its succulent odor wafting through her claim, making her stomach knot. When she kneaded bread with its lingering yeasty scent, her mouth watered. She stored the rest of the food in the empty food press inside the shanty.

"And a lantern and candles! Oh, thank You, Father God!" She whirled in happy circles around the tiny living area that housed a makeshift kitchen and bedroom area. She'd spent the last two nights sitting in the dark before retiring because she'd run out of candles. Whoever left the food understood her problem with the darkness.

She shivered. But they must have been watching her shanty and noticed she had no light. Goose bumps rose on her arms. She was not as alone as she'd thought out here on this isolated claim. Someone had an eye on her.

She shivered and hugged her arms around herself. "I'm just a little frightened. Yet You are with me, Lord, protecting me." And that same someone had left only life-sustaining items. Surely the eyes watching her were benevolent rather than scary.

She spent all afternoon singing praises to God for His wonderful provision. Then she ate, lit the kerosene lantern, and fell asleep with her head cradled in her arms across the splintery wooden table.

One week later, on the precise same day, more baskets of food arrived. This time she caught sight of long Prince Albert suit tails disappearing into the brush.

Mr. Riley? Why would he provide for her in such a lovely manner? And he had not forced his presence on her. Nor had he mentioned marriage.

Despite the lack of obvious love in his proposal, perhaps the man had a heart.

Chapter Eight

Miss Molloy, you are working yourself to death on this played-out claim. I'd be pleased if you'd allow me to court you."

Eve wiped her dirty hands on the back of her oversized coveralls. "Why, sir, it might be prudent if you introduced yourself first." The rugged-looking man, dressed in denim trousers and red-checked flannel shirt, looked robust enough to fell large trees. Perhaps he was a lumberjack. She'd seen him numerous times in church, so his unexpected arrival didn't scare her. Nevertheless she dropped her hand into her dungaree pocket and clasped her revolver.

"I'm Danny Duggan. I'm campaigning for mayor of Eureka. But I caught sight of you working this lonely claim all by yourself and figured you might need a man to help you out."

Eve gazed up at the brawny, auburn-haired giant, the picture of Irish joviality. "Thank you for your kind offer, Mr. Duggan, but I prefer to work my own claim." She shoved her red hair out of her face and wiped her still-dingy hand on the apron wrapped around her waist. "As to your offer to court me, I'm not interested. But I can make us a cup of tea while you tell me a bit about yourself. I am of voting age. I would vote were I allowed. And I would vote for the best man to be mayor of our town. Someone very much needs to bring civilization and law to Eureka." She sat on the riverbank and slipped on her shoes. "I'll encourage several of the brides I brought to start a suffrage movement here."

He grinned. "And I'm sure you would be the one to do just that. I'm a progressive man. I'd encourage the right for women to vote." He whistled and a prancing bay stallion emerged from the thick grove of pine trees that surrounded her shanty. "I didn't come empty-handed." He moved to the horse and lifted the flap of one bulging saddlebag, and his big hands lifted out a bundle of printed sheets. "I'm not easily dismissed. I came prepared to plead my case. You see, I noticed you several weeks past when you arrived with that wagonload of lovely lasses from San Francisco. I was much chagrined when you did not offer yourself as a bride since I am in the market for a lovely wife such as yourself."

"You appear to be a responsible man, Mr. Duggan, and I shall be more than happy to bring a girl from the orphanage for you on my next return trip from San Francisco. I charge fifty dollars for the girl's transportation from there to here." She smiled. "Of course, each girl will make her own choice when she arrives, but I'm certain one of my girls will take an instant liking to you."

"Thanks so very much, Miss Molloy, but it's you yourself I have a great interest in making my wife. There's no need for you to ruin your hands and break your back working this claim." His deep gray eyes searched the area. "This secluded spot is not safe for a woman."

"From all appearances, Mr. Duggan, you'd make some lady a fine husband. But I assure you, I am perfectly capable of mining my own gold and caring for myself. I'm quite happy out here." She smiled. "Please wait out here while I fetch us a nice cup of tea."

She went inside, stirred up the fire in the fireplace, placed the kettle on the iron arm, and swung the kettle over the heat. Soon the shrill whistle alerted her that the water was boiling, so she brewed the tea. With a cup in each hand, she kicked aside the leather curtain that served as a door and handed Mr. Duggan his tea.

They sat together on the flat rock that worked as a stoop to her shanty.

He handed her one of the printed sheets and told her his story about why he ran for mayor. He mentioned some changes he'd like to bring to Eureka. The foremost of which was to send for another lawman to help the overworked sheriff.

"Perhaps two lawmen might be more appreciated, Mr. Duggan. Had there been a lawman in town when Uncle was murdered and I was robbed, perhaps neither tragedy would have occurred." She bit her lip. "Invite at least two more lawmen to Eureka, and I shall at least campaign for you, since I cannot vote."

"I will do that for you, Miss Molloy. Perhaps when I am mayor you will reconsider your feelings and allow me to court you."

"No, Mr. Duggan. I have no plans to remain in Eureka. I have a passion to fetch six additional orphan girls here to obtain suitable, loving husbands." She sipped the last of her tea. "If I marry you or any other man, I would be tied down and no longer available to assist the girls I've helped care for from their teens. They need my aid. They have no one else to provide for them."

"But—"

"I cannot abide thinking any of my girls will have to face life outside the orphanage alone, with no money and no means to make a living." She set her teacup down on the grass beside the stoop. "No, Mr. Duggan, but you would be exactly the right husband for Katie Mae."

His lips turned down at the corners. "And what would this Katie Mae be looking like?"

"Ah. She's a beauty. She's a dainty, dark-haired artist who would look just right on your arm, Mr. Duggan. She would bring life and joy into your bachelor existence."

His broad face lightened with a grin. "I do fancy a lass with dark hair. And I have a room in my house where she can paint pictures to her heart's content. Windows all around." His gray eyes twinkled. He handed her his teacup. "You bring that lass back, and I'll wed her in a wink."

"But, Mr. Duggan, you must know each girl has a choice. She must approve the man she weds."

"Tell her of me, and when she sees me, she'll want to wed me all right." He stood, raised his hands, and revolved slowly for Eve to view. "Who wouldn't want to wed me?" He whistled for his horse. "I'm rich, I'll be mayor, and I'm handsome. What's not to like?"

She smiled at his sunny temperament and joking promotion of himself. He did seem a good man. She simply must get back to Hibernia to bring Katie Mae and the other five girls here. "I can take nothing more than this printed sheet of your attributes from you, Mr. Duggan. I shall pass it on to Katie Mae. Once you meet my beautiful Katie Mae, you'll have no more thoughts to spare for me. Katie Mae, with her perfect rosy complexion, her perfect figure, and her perfect personality, will be just the right lady for a mayor's wife."

◆　◆　◆

Eve glanced up from her sluicing pan.

Clara Swingler, her former landlady, and a man so tall he swayed back and forth like a drunken sailor walked toward her.

"Eve, I'd like to introduce you to Sam Murphy. He's out of work and would like a job helping you work your claim." Clara waved a hand at the tall, dark-haired man clad in prospector's denims and toting a heavy backpack who had trudged to the claim with her. "He won't charge you much."

"Ma'am, I'd be pleased to work for you. I'm strong, and I know how to pan gold and use a sluice box as well as a dredge. If you pay me with a bit of bread and some of that cake I smell, I can sleep in the tent I got in my backpack." The shy-looking giant gave her a timid smile.

"How fortunate. Yes, I'd love to hire you, Mr. Murphy." She shook her curls back from her face and arched her aching back. "But Clara, how did you know I needed to hire a worker?"

Clara's gray eyes twinkled. "Don't look a gift horse in the mouth."

Eve turned to Sam Murphy. "Why are you willing to work for almost nothing?"

"Well, ma'am, it's like this. A fella from town sent me here. He's paying me good, but he swore me into keeping his name out of this. He bought me a new gun and some bullets so's I could protect you from wild animals and wild men, he said. But I cain't tell you his name. He made me swear I wouldn't on a stack of Bibles."

Eve winked at Clara. "Oh, I wouldn't dream of asking you to break your oath." Eve smiled. "But perhaps you could describe your boss a bit."

"Well, ma'am, he didn't say nothing about not telling you what he looked like." He scratched his dark hair. "The man's tall, over six feet by several inches. Almost as tall as me."

"Yes?"

"He's got a pleasant enough face."

"Pleasant enough?"

"Well, I did hear some of the ladies from the church call him more handsome than a man has a right to be."

Would those church ladies be speaking of Mr. Riley. . .or perhaps Mr. Duggan? The prospective mayor wanted Katie Mae in the worst way. He didn't want Eve killed and unable to bring the orphan to Eureka. "And what else?"

"And he pays me right smart."

Who did she owe for this unexpected gift of a hardworking man to help her make Uncle's claim pay? She must know. Already her heart warmed to both men. "Well, is the man a churchgoer?"

"Oh yes, ma'am. And he goes every time the doors open."

Hmm. She'd never missed a service since she'd come. But both Mr. Riley and Mr.

Duggan had been in attendance as well. Though Mr. Duggan seemed to make a big show of singing and glad-handing people. But perhaps he was simply a more outgoing personality than Mr. Riley. She shoved her hands to her hips. "Certainly you can describe something about the man who is paying you."

Sam Murphy scratched his head, his muscles bulging beneath the short sleeves of his shirt.

"Tell me this, then. Is the man who pays you running for mayor of Eureka?"

Mr. Murphy grinned so wide a gap in his back teeth showed. "Oh no, ma'am. The man who sent me is too busy gathering dead bodies to run for mayor."

A flutter sent delicious spasms through Eve until her toes tingled. "Oh, well, thank you very much, Mr. Murphy. Now since you already know how to prospect, I shall leave that portion of the work up to you. Would you like roast elk for supper?"

Sam's face lit like candles decorating a Christmas tree. "Oh yes, ma'am, I surely would."

"I'll leave the two of you then." Clara waved her fingers and turned to leave.

"Thanks so much for coming, and please give Mr. Riley my thanks."

Clara shook her gray head, laughed, and scampered back through the pines as if she were a lady of thirty rather than an older woman.

Though Eve had no intention of letting either man court her, knowing Mr. Riley was so very thoughtful of her well-being brightened her world. God used all kinds of people to do His will, and God loved taking care of widows and orphans. "Which one of the girls would make Mr. Riley a suitable wife?"

"What's that, ma'am?"

"Just talking to myself, Mr. Murphy. It's a habit I've acquired living out here alone."

"Yes, ma'am."

She pulled her long hair off her neck and stretched. Somehow, none of the girls she planned to bring on her return trip to Eureka seemed to fit with Mr. Riley at all.

What type of woman would make a good match for the handsome, thoughtful, elusive, and distinguished mortician? If only he didn't own such a dreary business. She shivered. "His beautiful hands touch all those dead bodies."

"What's that, ma'am?"

"Just talking with myself again. I'm sorry, Mr. Murphy. Might I call you Sam?"

Mr. Riley really was a lovely man.

Chapter Nine

Rafe clapped a hand on Danny's back. "So you're mayor now. Good for you. I expect you'll clean up this boomtown." He propped a foot on the end of his parked hearse. Busy street sounds played background music to their conversation. Wagons with horses' hooves muffled by the rutted dirt road, footsteps on the wooden boardwalk, muted conversations, and a dog barking in the distance proclaimed normal life in Eureka. No gunshots this early in the morning.

"No doubt I will. The first item on my agenda is to wed that lass you're protecting out on the O'Shaughnessy claim. She'll be a great boon for entertaining in my mansion, don't you agree?" Danny jutted his chin in the air and smirked.

Rafe's foot hit the dirt road. He leapt up on the boardwalk and grabbed Duggan by his open shirt collar. "You stay away from Eve Molloy. Every man in town knows I'm courting that lady."

Danny broke Rafe's chokehold on his collar and stuck his face close to Rafe's. "The lady in question doesn't know you're courting her, else she wouldn't have enjoyed our cozy, private talk on the banks of the Feather River." He spit in the dirt. "Far as I can see, Miss Molloy is up for snogging. And I intend to kiss her and make her my wife." He stepped back and grinned. "Seems to me you're too late, with too little."

Rafe gritted his teeth and hooked his thumbs in his waistband to keep from punching Danny. "We've been friends as long as we've both been in California. Don't push your luck."

"So what if we both like the same lady."

"Today that friendship ends. I said keep away from Eve. Hands off! Do not go near her. She's off-limits." His face heated. He planted his button boots on the boardwalk and his hands on his hips.

"And if I do?" Danny reached over and flipped Rafe's tie.

"You up for the donnybrook of the year?" Rafe glared, unfastened his hidden gun belt, and lowered his gun and holster to the dirt.

"You that serious, Riley?" Danny backed away, held his hands up and away from his gun belt.

"I'm that serious." He raised his bare knuckles in a fighter's stance and moved toward his best friend.

"Then I reckon I should tell you I asked Miss Molloy to be my wife." Danny backed toward the edge of the boardwalk.

Rafe's head exploded. He leapt on Danny, knocking him off the boardwalk, and they both rolled in the dirt of Eureka's single street. He landed on top and punched his old friend in the mouth. Blood spurted.

"Hold on!" Danny parried his fists.

"I said stay away."

"Listen to me. I was slagging you. Eve said stay away, too. She said she wasn't interested in being my wife even though I could give her everything she needs." He grunted. "Get off my chest, you big lummox."

Rafe halted another punch to Danny's face. His knees straddled Danny's chest, and he held the new mayor's hands flat in the dust. "Talk fast or you'll be spitting teeth."

"Eve heard from those church ladies earwigging that I'd been telling around town that she was going to be my wife."

"Did you?"

"Did I what?" Danny squirmed in the dirt, trying to get away.

"Tell everyone in Eureka Eve said yes to becoming your wife."

Danny twisted his head and spit dirt. "Well, I reckon I did. But when Eve heard of my plan, she squelched the rumors."

Rafe slid off Danny's chest. "What did Eve say to you?"

"Said she had just the right lady back home who would make me an excellent wife."

"Did you tell Eve you'd take that orphan girl as your wife?"

"Yes." Danny struggled to his knees and wiped his bloody mouth. "And I'll head right out there this minute and reaffirm the news to her. The more I think about that Katie Mae, the better she sounds to me."

Rafe jumped to his feet and brushed dust off his suit. "You do that." He frowned. "Guess this outfit's ruined." He gazed at the crowd that had gathered. "That's all for today, folks; you can go along about your business."

"Too bad. We had bets going," the owner of the Emporium said.

"Yeah, we had three to one for Duggan to win. He's got thirty pounds on you, Riley." Antonio turned and strolled back toward his kitchen.

The crowd melted.

Danny unfolded from the dirt, still wiping blood from his lips. He held out his hand. "Friends again? It's better to be a coward for a minute than sorry for the rest of my life." Danny winked. "If I'd meant business, you'd be the one lickin' dirt from your missing teeth."

Rafe thrust out his hand and shook Danny's dirty paw. "As long as you stay away from Eve, we're friends. Only a stepmother to a hated stepchild would blame you for falling for my lady."

"Your lady, huh? By the way, did you know Eve hates that mortuary job of yours?"

◆ ◆ ◆

"Hey, Rafe! We got those three bodies down at the Devil's Neck Mine to pick up." The tall, skinny miner who often helped with retrieval of clients gazed down from his prancing horse.

Rafe rubbed January's nose. The horse pushed his long head into Rafe's hands for more. "Yeah, I know, Harry. I'll crack on over with the hearse and meet you at the mine."

"Don't forget to bring that bag of Irish soil the men like to be buried with. All three of those poor fellas were Irish."

"I'll take care of the dirt." Rafe climbed through the rear doors of the hearse to the inside, pushed back the black, fringed curtains, and gazed around. Did he have the straps necessary to lower the caskets into the graves? Yes, there were four of them stacked neatly on the small shelf under the right window. Two to use and two spares. He counted the caskets he kept inside. One extra. Probably wouldn't need the additional one, but at funerals one never knew if the deceased had angry friends or if there would be a shoot-out over the dead man's gold nuggets and claim. He checked his six-shooter then shoved the weapon back into the waistband of his black trousers, now smudged with dirt. He buttoned his formal coat, hiding the weapon and the tear along his thigh. No telling when he would need his gun or what might happen in this explosive town.

He checked the lashings around his camera and made certain the precious box was secure under the window. Then he shut the curtains, climbed out the double rear doors, and clapped on his derby. He unhitched the horses from the rail and sprang up into the driver's seat. "Gadup!"

The hearse lurched ahead, and he directed his team toward the mines. "What do you think, girls?" he yelled to the horses. "Time I sold this business. Yes?"

◆ ◆ ◆

Rafe gazed over his new purchase. The Concord Carriage looked splendid. Surely Eve would be impressed. The padded leather seat was the best to be had, and the high-raised back with top folded down for the sunny day looked splendid. He'd traded the hearse for the only fancy carriage for miles around. He'd kept his two favorite mares, matching bays, but he'd sold his Prince Albert suits. Never wanted to wear those stifling outfits again. If God gave him the woman he loved, he'd wear tails at his wedding. Sure, he'd taken a lickin' on the trade, but picking up those three mangled bodies yesterday had pounded the last nail in the coffin. He'd made his decision. Eve hated his business. So did he. He'd sold at a loss, but he didn't need the money. He had enough.

He needed one thing. He needed to win the hand of the woman who cluttered his thoughts every moment and refused to leave. She'd taken residence in his brain, and he couldn't get her out. He hopped into his carriage and leaned back on the padded seat cushion. Good to get into comfortable clothes again. He'd neglected his claim lately and was half-tempted to sell the stake, except the land had so much gold just waiting to be mined. And gold nuggets still lay on his share of the bottom of Feather River. Too bad Eve's stake hadn't panned out. Except if hers had, she'd be back in San Francisco by now carting back another load of homeless girls. One of whom she'd try to foist off onto him. As if he could look at another woman after having met Eve. What a spunky lady. How could she not realize that he loved her?

God had a boatload of work to do to change that stubborn lady's mind. If God hadn't given him peace in his heart, he'd have given up on Eve and nursed a broken heart the rest of his life. She was such a fine lady. He'd never meet her like again. He'd do this one last thing. He was crazy, but he'd try one more time. If God didn't soften her heart toward him, he'd admit defeat. But he'd keep right on protecting her until she was able to make her own way in this rough boomtown. A man could do no less.

Faint heart never won fair maid.

He turned Lily and January's heads toward Eve's claim.

How would he change her mind?

The drive wasn't long, and he reached her place just as the sun reached its golden hour for picture taking, the hour before sunset. He'd brought his camera. Would he be able to get a candid photograph of Eve before she noticed him and ordered him to stop?

He halted the team and tied them to a tree far enough away from her shanty that the rushing river would cover his footsteps and she would be unable to hear him approach. Then with gentle hands, he unloaded the huge camera. He hauled the precious box, the silver-plated copper treated with the toxic fumes, and the glass plate to place over the exposed picture to protect the image, in his arms. He stole on tiptoes, his boots making no sound in the brown grass, to where she would be kneeling by the river with her prospecting pan.

He lifted a hand to Samuel Murphy and then made a shushing motion to his lips. Good to see the man earned his salary keeping both eyes open for any trouble Eve might face.

Samuel waved, patted the six-shooter hanging from his hip, and then returned to his work panning for gold farther downriver from Eve.

Good to know she never worked her claim alone. Faithful old Sam kept a close eye on her and did most of the backbreaking work on her played-out stake. Rafe grinned. He paid Sam well; the man had better be on the job.

And there Eve was with the sun reflecting rays from her radiant red hair, tousled by her work and the slight wind ruffling through the pine trees. How glorious she looked, hair falling over her eyes, slight body bent over the sparkling water, and an intense expression on her delicate face.

Tiptoeing, he set the camera on his collapsible tripod and adjusted the viewfinder. He centered her one-third way down the picture and to the right with pine trees embracing her from both sides. An awesome frame. He wrapped his hand around the button holder. He was lowering his finger on the trigger when she turned. He pushed the trigger, taking the picture, capturing her upturned face with an enticing smile and look of welcome.

Perfect. He removed the copper plate and carefully lowered the glass panel over the captured shot. Some daguerreotypes took minutes to expose. Some did not. This one hit all the right targets and took the shortest possible time to expose. His heart lifted and he grinned.

He had a winner.

◆　◆　◆

Could that really be Mr. Riley? The tall man wore fitted denim jeans that did wonderful things to show his muscular legs. His dark brown western-style shirt matched his dancing eyes and fit his chest like a glove, highlighting broad shoulders that tapered to a slim waist.

Her heart fluttered.

But, unlike every other man she'd met in Eureka, he wore no guns.

Why?

Oh yes. He had bodyguards. Where were they? He said they were discreet. Perhaps they hid in the pine woods.

What did Mr. Riley carry in his outstretched hand?

"Good evening, Miss Molloy. I took the liberty of catching your image in a picture. I hope you don't mind." His cheeks flamed. "Of course, if you do, I shall hand the plate over immediately and you can do with the daguerreotype as you like."

"Mr. Riley. I'm flattered you thought me worthy of taking a daguerreotype. It's so kind of you. May I see the picture?"

He placed the plate in her hand, his mahogany eyes shining.

Her mouth dropped. "Why, this is lovely. I'm so impressed." No one had ever in her life thought her worthy to sit for a portrait. A few of the other orphans she'd grown up with had pictures of themselves, but she had none. In fact, no one had ever taken a special interest in her at all. And Mr. Riley had employed such pains to capture her with a candid frame. Why, the man was exceptional. Who would have thought that elegant undertaker or even the rugged man she saw today would be a photographer?

He bowed. "I'm pleased you like it." He smiled. "Would you join me for a carriage ride and a picnic?" He took the picture and held the exposed plate carefully in both hands.

She gazed down at her coveralls and frowned. "I'm a mess."

His chocolate eyes melted into admiration. "You could never be a mess."

How had she not noticed he was so handsome? Or did he look better in more casual clothes? She'd never expected to find a man extremely attractive, extremely kind, and extremely rich. Not that she cared about the rich part. She wrinkled her forehead. And for some reason he had an interest in her. Her cheeks heated. Even though he'd seen her at her worst onstage.

She dried her hands on the towel lying beside her on the ground. "In that case, I shall be more than happy to join you for a picnic supper."

"I have a special place I'd like you to see."

Would he drive her in that awful hearse? Somehow she didn't care. He'd caught her in an enchanting photograph, and she'd not breathed properly since. If the man still wanted to court her, she'd agree. Even despite his awful job. If he were poor as a church pastor, she'd let him court her. This vibrant man who captured her in a photograph had captured her heart.

She blinked. And shook her head. But she really, really didn't want a husband. She didn't want to lose her independence. And couldn't lose her ability to travel back to San Francisco to gather her dear orphans. The man was impossibly attractive, but she didn't want a husband. And, obviously, Rafe Riley was a man accustomed to being in charge. He didn't take no for an answer. Yet he charmed her enough to make her knees tremble when he came near. He made her heart beat fast and caused delightful shivers to spider over her body whenever he came close. The man's nearness scrambled her brains.

Why had she agreed to this picnic? She bit her lip. A momentary weakness. She must remain strong for the girls.

No, she could not let Mr. Riley, though he stole her breath with his every look, sweep her off her feet. No, she definitely would not let him court her. Nor would she marry him.

Chapter Ten

How should he start? Rafe clicked to Lily and January, "Gadup, girls!" He turned their matching bay heads toward his claim, just five miles up the furrowed dirt road. Not nearly time enough for him to calm his racing heart. Even in coveralls, Eve looked appealing enough to marry on the spot. He restrained himself from reaching across the seat and touching her hand.

"Where is this special place?" Her smile lit her face and his world. "I do wish you'd let me change clothes."

"It's but a picnic, lass. On my claim. I think my stake a particularly beautiful spot just upriver from your place."

For a few long moments they rode in silence. Where was his speech when he needed his silver tongue? She overcame him with her presence. He'd never met a woman like her. The wind from the buggy's movement tousled her hair as if air fairies played with the bright tresses.

"So you are not working today?" She gave a blithe toss of her head.

"Ah, no." He directed the team to the cutoff that led to his claim. He wanted just the right place and the right moment to tell her.

He hitched the girls to a tree close to the water's edge so they could drink and nibble on the last of the green grass. Then he tugged the lunch basket from the rear of the buggy beneath the lowered top.

"This is a lovely spot." She made a complete revolution, her arms spread, her eyes wide. "So nice the way the wind sings through the pines, and so beautiful how the meadow meanders down to the river. You didn't build a shanty here?"

"No, I had but a tent, a horse, a pick, a shovel, and a sluice pan when I arrived." He frowned, the images speeding through his memory. "'Bout froze that first winter." He gazed at the few oaks towering among the pine trees. Gold, bronze, and brown leaves fluttered to the ground with each wisp of wind. "Going to turn cool soon. Last year the temperature dropped to twenty degrees, and rain flooded us three times a week or more. But for now, this is the finest weather California has." He inhaled a deep breath of fresh air tasting slightly of pine and sunshine.

He spread the quilt over his favorite spot under the big oak whose roots plunged deep into the grassy bank. Large gold and red leaves softened the ground under the quilt.

"But now you are rich?" She settled on the edge of the quilt and helped him unload the food basket.

"Didn't happen overnight." He handed her a napkin and a perfectly browned chicken leg. Stewart had done a masterful job with the picnic. The cook turned butler had proven himself a fine employee. He would give Stewart a raise with his next cash payment.

"Tell me about your gold strike." For once her bright eyes settled on him rather than the food.

"I about starved that first year until I learned how to use a wooden sluice. Before that I dug down into wet clay beds where I'd heard gold lay in big nuggets."

"A sluice?"

"Yes. A water channel controlled by a gate. Like a flume."

"So with a sluice, you found a lot of gold?"

"Enough to realize the money in Eureka didn't lie in gold nuggets." He dipped a cup into the Feather River and passed her a drink of clear, sparkling water. "I smartened up the first time I walked into town to buy grub. Sky-high food prices ate up all the gold I'd spent two laborious months digging up."

"So you did what?" She bit into her chicken leg.

"I bought a gun and went hunting. Killed all my food."

"And saved all your money?"

"Yep." He spread preserves on a biscuit and offered the flaky scone to her. "Eureka suffered from a good deal of wickedness, with stealing, drinking, gambling, and murdering. Plenty more than there is now. But I roved around town some, trying to decide how best to invest what money I had."

"And?"

"Men seemed to die a lot—sickness, accidents, and gunfights. The need to bury the bodies overwhelmed the pastors at the two churches. They needed help. So I pitched in when I could." He chuckled. "Then one bright day with the broad canopy of blue sky overhead, this black hearse and four-horse team rolled into town."

"The one you own?"

"That's the one. Created quite a stir. I decided on the spot to invest in that hearse and really help those pastors out." He snugged his back against his oak, stretched his legs flat on the quilt, and smiled. "Worked into a profitable profession."

"Yes, but such a dreary one."

"I worked hard, long hours, day and night. Was always available. Went wherever I was needed. But I hated the whole procedure." He moved his hand so his fingers lay next to hers on the quilt. "I enjoyed 'speaking the words over the graves' as the miners say. Gave me opportunity to tell folks of my faith and invite them to join with Jesus if they hadn't."

Her lips rounded in an O. Her green eyes turned into sparkling gems. Pink tinted her cheeks.

"But the task grew dreadful. I've gotten to know many of the prospectors and liked most of them. Hard to gather up their bodies when they died so young." He inched his hand so his touched hers, small finger to small finger. "So I sold my business today."

She jerked to attention. "Really! That's lovely."

Her smile put the sun to shame.

She lowered her eyes. "I mean lovely since you really didn't enjoy the business." She moved her hand away to reach for a napkin. "But this claim doesn't look as if you've worked it recently. How will you make a living?" She dabbed her lips and placed her hand down again so her little finger touched his.

"Right. I have been too busy with the mortuary job." He winked. "Between you and me, I think my stake's about petered out."

"But what will you do?"

"I have enough money. And I own the mansion. Ma's independent and strong, so she doesn't require much care and she's no expense to speak of. I'm in a position now to do the type of work I've always hankered to do."

"Oh, what is that?"

"I take pictures." He gazed around the lovely spot. "Landscapes, boomtowns, and one beautiful young lady, if she'll allow me."

◆　◆　◆

Eve sighed. He'd brought her to this lovely spot and told her more of his life story. His every word tugged at her heart. Now, with heart wide open, she gazed at his finely chiseled face, dark chocolate eyes, straight Irish nose, and beautiful lips. His dark hair fell over his forehead in such a way she wanted to run her fingers through and push the strands back to watch them fall again.

She shivered with delight each time she allowed her eyes to land on his broad shoulders and strong hands. And she knew of his kind heart. Had it not been for his generosity, she would have starved like he had his first winter in Eureka. She'd never met a finer man. Fortunately he was persistent to the point of stubbornness.

She moved her fingers closer to that strong, warm hand, letting her pinky fold over his. If only he would kiss her.

He lifted her broken-fingernailed hand in his warm, strong fingers. "Eve." He cradled her hand while he deftly shifted on the quilt to kneel on one knee. "I love you more with every beat of my heart. Would you do me the great honor of becoming my wife? I know this is short—."

"No such thing." She planted a finger on his lips, squirmed to her knees, and faced him. "I've known you long enough, Rafe Riley." She thrust both arms around his neck, leaned forward, and kissed him.

Oh, the kiss was sweet. His compelling lips answered her every imagination of what a kiss might taste like. Fiercely delicious. . .and warm. . .and lingering.

She gently moved away so she could see his reaction. "Yes, Rafe Riley, photographer, I shall be most happy to become your wife."

Rafe wore that *I've been run over by a horse* smitten expression that she loved to witness on all the prospective husbands for all the Hibernia brides she brought to Eureka. Yes, he loved her.

He cleared his throat. "I've plenty of money to send away for those other girls from the orphanage that you're so concerned about. As your husband, I'll be happy to make that long trek to San Francisco with you. Can't have my wife traveling unprotected." He grinned. "We'll be certain to bring back that bride for Danny."

"Oh, Rafe, I love you. God is so wonderful. So almighty. So gracious. He has given me everything I've ever wanted. I've never dreamed of getting married myself, but I do have a yearning for children of my own."

"Those you shall have, my dear bride." He heaved a great sigh. "But there's something I need to confess. If you change your mind with the telling, then so be it. I can no longer keep my sin a secret."

Chills flitted up and down her spine. What secret could possibly be so horrible she would not marry him? He was more than Prince Charming to her Cinderella. She settled cross-legged on the quilt, her oversized coveralls draping her legs.

"Have you ever heard of Rattlesnake Rick?"

"Yes, of course. He robbed the overland stage. What—"

"He's my first cousin, my aunt Colleen's son."

"Oh?" Goose bumps pimpled her arms.

"He heads a gang with Big Dolph, Bill and Rome Baxter, and Cyrus and George Skyler. They stole eighty thousand dollars of gold bullion."

"Really? They did? That's a fortune."

"The sheriff captured the gang, but Rick escaped with the bullion."

"How is that *your* sin?" How symmetrical his face, even with his forehead furrowed and his dark brows lowered. How could she have resisted him for so long? And why? "It must have been difficult for you."

◆　◆　◆

Rafe hugged his legs, shoulders slumped. "Rick and I were close growing up. We were the same age." Rafe fought the memories flooding his brain. He raked his hand through his hair. But he must confess. He could keep no secrets from the woman he loved. "We lived next door to one another and were inseparable. When Braden and I emigrated here from Ireland, Rick tagged along. He sailed to Canada, and Braden and I came to America." Rafe settled back against his oak for support in the telling of his nightmare, curled an arm around Eve, and tugged her against his chest. Her hair smelled like summer flowers. Should he really share his sin with her? Would she still love him after she heard?

"I wasn't happy Rick chose Canada, but even then he'd started banding together with a crowd I wanted no part of. I tried to reason with him, but Rick was hardheaded and bent on his own way."

"But he moved to California, didn't he?"

"Yes. When he got news of the gold rush, he followed me here to Eureka."

He kissed the top of her head. She fit perfectly in his arms. He could be so happy with her. "Rick didn't like the grinding work prospecting required. He'd disappear for days then return and bunk with me while I built the mansion. He always had money to burn."

"When I asked where he got all his money, Rick invited me to join his gang."

"You didn't?" She shook her head. "Of course you didn't."

"No. I didn't. I tried to share my faith with him, but Rick turned a deaf ear and went his own way."

"You did your best." She stroked his arm.

"Not sure about that. But I tried." He hugged her closer. "Are you warm enough?"

"I'm fine. Just anxious to hear about *your* sin."

"Rick was on the run. The law stuck to his heels and had captured his gang. Rick worried they would corral him, too, so he told me where he hid the gold."

"And you told the sheriff?"

"And I told the sheriff."

"Of course you did. You're a Christian man. That was the right thing to do."

"Was it?" He traced a finger over her soft cheek. Could he tell her the rest? His chest ached with his secret. "I have a family photograph hidden in my library. There is a secret chamber behind one section of my books." He rested his chin in the softness of her hair and inhaled the fragrant flower scent. "Rick and I were always together as kids. In the photo we're standing next to one another."

"Was Rick angry you told the sheriff where he hid the bullion?"

"No. He never knew." Rafe blew out a big sigh. "I told the sheriff where Rick holed up. The sheriff formed a posse, rode out with them, and shot and killed my cousin."

"Oh, I'm so very sorry, Rafe. But you didn't know they would kill your cousin."

"Yes, I did. Sheriff was known for administering his own style of justice. He'd seen too many judges paid off and murderers go free."

"Oh!" She pulled away from him and crouched to face him. "Why?"

"I betrayed him." He gazed down at his hands. "Rick had changed from the lad I grew up with. Lawmen didn't nickname him Rattlesnake Rick for no reason. My cousin had grown mean. And dangerous. Women and children weren't safe around him. He'd murdered two men."

"Then you did what you had to do."

"Did I?" He frowned and reached for her. She was so delicate, so cherished, in his arms. "Then why do memories haunt me of the great lad he was growing up?"

"People change. Your poverty spurred you to strive and to live a better life. His poverty goaded him to take what didn't belong to him and to hurt people. And Rick never became a Christian, did he?"

"No, he refused to darken the steps of a church. He wouldn't listen when I tried to tell him of Jesus and His love and forgiveness."

"So knowing Jesus made all the difference in your life."

"Yes."

She squirmed around in his arms to look up at him. "I know your secret, Rafe. And knowing only makes me love you more."

"You're a precious gift." He bent to kiss her lips.

She tasted so very sweet.

She bounded to her feet. "God has given us the gift of His Son and the gift of each other." In her ridiculous overalls, she spread her arms wide and twirled on the grass beneath his tree. "Let's have an outdoor wedding. Right here in this lovely spot. Where we can breathe in fresh air and gaze up at towering mountains."

"That sounds grand."

"We can invite the Germans, the Chinese, the Italians, and the Irish. We'll all mix together and maybe stop distrusting one another."

A cool wind rustled vibrant-colored leaves from the oak that showered down over them both.

Eve laughed and turned her face to the falling leaves.

He hopped to his feet and began gathering the picnic leftovers. "Or our wedding dinner may create a brouhaha!" He laughed.

"Why should it? We are all Americans. We all uphold the Constitution and obey the laws of America. I see no reason why we can't all trust one another." A mischievous expression flitted across her sweet face. "Eureka will never forget our wedding reception dinner."

He nodded. He'd do anything for his angel. "Will next week be too soon for you?"

"Perfect!"

She gazed up at him, her hands clasped as if in prayer. "Do you think after we wed that you and I could take your wagon and honeymoon in San Francisco?"

"Sounds like an excellent plan." He grinned. Ah, his beautiful wife-to-be had such a nurturing streak. How had she not been snatched up by some man long ago? God must have kept her just for him. "You could visit Hibernia Orphanage and quit your job."

"Oh yes. One of the other girls can step up and become the Irish dancing teacher. And we could bring six of the girls back with us to become Christmas brides."

"My dear wife-to-be, your plan is exactly what I had in mind as well."

She stood on tiptoes and kissed him on the tip of his nose. "After we are married, I would really prefer not to give up my position as marriage broker, if you don't mind."

"Nor would I have you give up your love task." He kissed her hand. "You are a mother to the motherless."

"And soon-to-be wife to the most fabulous man alive." Eve twined her arms around his neck and kissed him thoroughly. When she finished, she gazed at him with an impish smile. "That's so you will never forget just how much I love you."

"As if I could." He caught a falling red leaf in his hand. "Thank You, almighty God," Rafe breathed. "You've given me the desire of my heart."

Anne Greene delights in writing about gutsy heroines and alpha heroes who aren't afraid to fall on their knees in prayer. She and her hero husband, Army Special Forces Colonel Larry Greene, live in McKinney, Texas. Two of her four children live nearby. Tim La-Haye led her to the Lord when she was twenty-one, and Chuck Swindoll is her pastor. Anne's highest hope is that her stories transport the reader to an awesome new world and touch hearts to seek a deeper spiritual relationship with the Lord Jesus. To learn more about Anne, visit her at www.AnneGreeneAuthor.com. She teaches a novel writing class on her blog www.anneswritingupdates.blogspot.com. She contributes monthly to www.heroesheroinesandhistory.blogspot.com. Anne loves to visit with her fans. Tweet with her at @TheAnneGreene, and discover her on Pinterest (TheAnneGreene).

The Lye Water Bride

by Linda Farmer Harris

Dedication

To my husband, Jerry, for being my first and foremost
editor/critique partner, my motivation, inspiration,
and forever love. Thank you for helping my dreams come true!

To our daughter, Amanda, whose love of historical fiction also ignited
and fueled my passion for it. Your insights and advice have been invaluable.

Appreciation to Rhonda Gibson for encouragement and mentoring;
Farmington New Mexico Cafewriters, Southwest Christian Writers
Association-Durango, and the Wolf Creek Christian Writers-
Pagosa Springs, Colorado for critiques and fellowship.

All for the honor and glory of my Lord and Savior Jesus Christ.

Chapter One

Jo Bass slid her hand along the shelf under the countertop until her fingers touched her .31 caliber pocket revolver. "I've offered you a fair price for your nuggets, Mr. Carmady."

The grizzled miner shifted his backpack until the handle of his pickax lay within easy reach. His eyes roamed around the area behind the bank teller until they focused on the steel safe in a wooden frame midway up the back wall.

"You can take them to Sacramento." She unlocked her knees and steadied her stance. "Janson's supply wagon leaves at noon." She pushed the nuggets into the shallow well under the filigreed grill of her teller's cage. "He'd welcome the company." She sucked in her stomach to quell the surge of adrenaline coursing through her body.

"Aw, Miss Jo, I don't mean to be contrary." Carmady twisted his leather poke, but didn't open it to retrieve his nuggets. "I jest worked so hard and what yor' offerin' is a piddlin' amount."

She brought her gun hand from under the counter and studied him before she pulled her pocket scales to the center of the counter. She opened the case, wiped the two weighing surfaces with a woolen cloth, then pushed the scales and counterweights beneath the grill.

"You should weigh them yourself. These handy scales read the same as that monster over there." She pointed at the stationary beam balance scale on a desk behind her. "Let's recalculate their worth."

The man behind Carmady let out a loud sigh and changed his position.

She peered around the miner at the man, a head taller than herself, and as slim. Hair black as an abandoned coal mine, but longer than a city businessman's, full side-whiskers, but beard about five days old. His thin mustache didn't cover his lip. Dusty, wrinkled clothes. New western hat.

Frustration permeated the man's six-foot frame. He flexed his jaw but didn't move again.

Carmady scooped up his nuggets and lined them up in a row.

She took a sheet of paper and pencil stub from her cash drawer. "I used the lye water to verify the gold content in the nuggets. You weigh each nugget, and I'll write down what you say. The nuggets are numbered one through eight from your left to your right. Please pick them up in the same order."

He weighed each nugget.

She wrote down the numbers he called out. "I'm going to use this vial of water to figure out how much to pay you for each nugget."

She swirled the fresh water, dumped it, and refilled it half full. "The water level is marked in milliliters. Gently drop nugget number one in the vial. Don't let the water splash."

Eight times she tweezered out the nugget and wrote out the density equals mass divided by volume formula for each one.

"What's that fancy figurin' you're doing?" Carmady leaned forward with his face close to the iron grill. "Why'd you circle them numbers?"

"They indicate how close each nugget is to pure gold. I use this chart to make the payouts." She slid a rate sheet under the grid.

Carmady held it up and turned it in different directions. He looked down at the eight nuggets lined up on the counter.

The man behind Carmady stepped around him and assessed the rate sheet. "Her calculations are correct. Same as before. She's giving you top dollar."

Jo thanked the man with her eyes but kept her lips in a thin, tight line.

Carmady passed the sheet back to her. He picked up his nuggets and rolled them around in his hand. One by one placed the nuggets in the well.

"Credit these to my account, Miss Jo. Doubt Sacramento could do any better."

Jo put the nuggets in a metal lockbox. She entered the transaction in her logbook and wrote out a receipt. "Mr. Carmady, your confidence in Dry Diggins Branch Bank is appreciated." She reached under the grid and patted his hand. "I'm sure your next deposit will be the richest we've ever seen."

Carmady chuckled and walked out the door.

She straightened the wooden plaque with her initials—M. J. B.—carved in an elaborate script. She preferred Mildred Josephine Bass, but it would take up the whole counter. "Sir, what can I do for you?"

"I understand a Mr. Bass owns this establishment. I'd like to do my business with him."

Jo's cordial smile froze under narrowed eyes. "Mr. Bass isn't available today. As equal partner, I can help you with whatever banking, assaying, or claim business you want to conduct."

"With all due respect, ma'am, I prefer to do my business man-to-man. No offense intended."

She opened her mouth then closed it to keep the caustic reply swelling up in her throat from reaching her tongue. She swallowed and rubbed her tongue against the roof of her mouth.

"Sir..."

"Keller. Zeke Keller." He put his large hands flat on his side of the transaction counter. "When will Mr. Bass be available?"

"I'm not sure." She leaned forward and mimicked his action. "He..." From the corner of her eye, she saw the door curtain a few paces beside her open.

Thaddeus Bass stumbled against the door frame. "Jo, time to close." His breath wheezed in short gasps. "Tell gentleman...first tomorrow." He swayed, and the flush on his cheeks deepened.

"You shouldn't be out of bed." She hurried to him. "I'll assist"—she looked back at Zeke and frowned—"Mr. Keller; then I'll close." She put her arm around Thad's waist and tried to push him back behind the curtain.

"Jo, lock the door—" Thad's knees gave way, and his full weight collapsed against her.

She staggered, fell. Before she could wiggle her way from under Thad's body, she felt him being lifted up.

"Where do you want him, Mrs. Bass?" Keller held Thad like a sleeping child.

Jo scrambled to her feet and held back the curtain. "The second room on the right." She skirted around them and ran to the open door. "Put him here." She flipped back the sweat-soaked blanket and moved aside for Keller to lower Thad's limp body onto the bed. If Thad fell again, she'd need to rig a hoist to do her own lifting. Twice was once too many.

"Does Dry Diggins have a doctor?" Zeke stepped back to the doorway.

"Dr. Goldman comes once a week from Sacramento. He left this morning." She snugged the blanket around Thad. "He prepared a ginger and herb tea for me to give him for wracking dysentery."

"My mother put her faith in chicken broth."

"Mrs. Sims brought a covered crock of broth over after the doctor left."

"Nice to have caring neighbors." Keller leaned against the door frame. His fingers crimped a careless crease in his hat brim.

"You need to go, cowboy." She rushed at Keller, took his forearm, and ushered him to the front door. "I appreciate your help and your concern. Come back tomorrow. We open at ten." She didn't wait for any comment before she flipped the outside OPEN sign to CLOSED and bolted the door.

As Thad slept, his restless legs made the blanket jump like frogs in a covered basket. She shut the window but didn't put in the wooden security peg.

Pounding on the front door became louder, more insistent.

Satisfied Thad still slept, she sped to her teller window, grabbed her gun, and went to the door. She lifted a corner of the black window curtain and saw Zeke Keller's hand raised for another strike.

She unbolted the door and opened it enough for him to see her and the revolver. "Mr. Keller, I would appreciate a little courtesy. Especially since you are aware of the need for peace and quiet."

"I do apologize, madam, but it is paramount, if not imperative, that I secure my funds today." He held up his poke. "With your capabilities, I'm sure it won't require much of your time, and I'll be on my way."

She tried not to be taken in by the smile that brightened his face, the western hat in hand, or the brown eyes that reminded her of a curious speckled fawn.

"I'd hope my corroboration of your assessment for Mr. Carmady would put me in a good light."

She glanced at the railroad clock on the wall beside the door. "I'll give you fifteen minutes. Whatever is left you must bring back tomorrow." She met his straightforward gaze with equal strength. "Agreed?"

"Agreed."

Jo opened the door, let him step inside, and bolted it behind him.

He emptied his leather poke into the metal bowl reserved for flakes and nuggets. He dumped two canvas sacks full of coins in the teller's well.

She placed the gun within easy reach on the shelf under her counter, then pointed to the clock. "It's four fifteen. I'll put the nuggets in the lye water first. I'll count your money while they bathe."

She took the bowl of gold to her work counter and started the process. She put the foreign coins and American eagles in small piles. From the drawer, she took a booklet, wrote his name on the front of it, and entered one thousand dollars on the first line.

"Please initial the deposit amount. We issue bank drafts, gold dollars, and exchange treasury notes during regular banking hours."

The lye water, poured into glass jars, was ready for the tests. After each bath, she strained the water through a dense cotton swatch and presented the cloth as proof no gold stayed in her possession. She cleaned and rinsed the nuggets, strained the water, collected the flakes, and weighed everything with a precision gained from experience and her father's tutelage. Clean vials and fresh water made the calculations go faster.

Jo spoke each calculation aloud as she wrote it on her sheet. She passed the sheet to him.

"I'm impressed with your work. I accept your calculations, Mrs. Bass."

"It's not M—"

"Yes, yes, I realize I owe you an apology for my bluntness earlier. Mr. Bass trained you very well. You are to be commended for your acumen and skills."

She pulled the sheet back to her side of the counter and completed the transaction without further eye contact. "Your account is established, gold evaluated, and money deposited. It's all recorded in your bankbook and my ledger with four minutes to spare. The gold will be sent to the San Francisco Gold Exchange in two days. Anything else I can do for you, cowboy?"

She looked up at his soft chortle. "I thank you for your time. Please have a pleasurable evening, Mrs. Bass." He used his western hat to give a farewell salute.

She'd be switched before she tried to tell him again she was Miss Bass.

He let himself out the door. She bolted it behind him.

Arrogant beast. Maybe he should deal totally with Thad.

Hundreds of men poured into Dry Diggins daily. Why did she want to keep cowboy in front of her teller's cage? His beard? Beards on some men were attractive. Her aggravation at his arrogance didn't suppress her heart flutters, or her interest in Zeke Keller.

She tidied her area and readied everything for the next day's business. She took everything from the lobby wall safe to the large safe in the cellar. No one but Jo and Thad knew the safe existed, hidden behind a rolling wardrobe. They transferred all contents from the upstairs wall safe and metal lockbox to the cellar safe each night.

A late lunch of a small, cold ash-baked potato, a slice of beef jerky, and tepid water made her stomach queasy. *Please, Lord, I can't get sick, too. Mr. Hawkins is late returning from Sacramento. I can't run this bank by myself.*

A yawn warned her to sleep while Thad didn't need her attention. She went to her bedroom and changed into a housedress before she hung her banking dress inside out on the dressmaker form to air out and refresh before the morrow.

Jo made a pallet outside her brother's door and soon napped. Wisps of dreams swirled around like smoke from a miner's campfire, but the man she chased stayed a step ahead. He always rounded dark corners and vanished, his identity hidden by the dream smoke.

◆　◆　◆

Zeke stood on the bank's roofed porch and looked north at the crooked road the locals called Main Street. The buildings and tents rose helter-skelter along the street, not like the uniform streets of his New York hometown. Here, shanties sprang up wherever the owners conceived the idea for a dwelling.

The same phenomenon that fascinated him a week ago on his first day in Dry Diggins played out again at four o'clock every afternoon. *Siesta.* The constant and loud commerce slowed like a clogged rocker box. From four to six, man and animal luxuriated in sleep or a quiet, idle pastime.

How could these men be frantic about gold one minute and slumbering without care the next? He yawned and yearned to hurry to his own bed, but the reality of his situation kept him awake.

He folded the deposit receipt and put it inside his vest pocket. He looked at his watch and chortled again. *"Four minutes to spare."* The bank's CLOSED sign added to the fortress feel of the building. Why would a man bring a beautiful wife to this tent town? He felt a strong urge to rap on the door and caution the fiery redhead to be vigilant until her husband could be her escort again.

Instead, he stepped into the street. Each step forced him to marshal his defenses against the desire that grew stronger as the woman's shiny green eyes seared his memory.

His pulse buzzed in his ears. Not again. Why must he be attracted to another man's woman? Well, not this time. The stable opened at six o'clock. Enough time to ready his valise and bid adieu to Dry Diggins.

Chapter Two

J o, I need you. . ." A thud drowned out Thad's raspy voice. "Jo. . ."

"I'm here, Thad." She leaped to her feet and kicked the pallet to the wall. She turned the doorknob and pushed, but the door didn't budge. A low moan sounded each time she leaned her weight against the door.

"Thad, the door won't open. Pull from your side."

She heard a long, guttural moan. She yanked and pushed, but the door didn't move. The window.

She raced outside to Thad's window. The sill rose two feet above her head. She looked around for something to stand on. The ladder. Their traveling trunks barricaded the six-rail ladder against the rear of the shed and proved as unmovable as the bedroom door. She ran inside the bank for her stepladder.

Stretched as high as her tiptoes would allow, Jo peered through the grimy pane. She needed to be a head taller to see the floor and what prevented the door from opening.

"Woman, what are you doing?" Frazier Hawkins ran toward her. "Get down before you fall."

Jo tottered on the stepladder. "Mr. Hawkins." She clutched the ledge with both hands. "Thank heavens you're back." She climbed down and smoothed her dress.

"Oh. Miss Bass. I didn't recognize you. Please forgive my outburst."

"You're tall enough to see the whole room. Is Thaddeus all right?"

Hawkins climbed up and cleaned a peephole with his coat sleeve. "Mr. Bass is lying against the door." Hawkins lifted the window.

He stuck his head in, his shoulders too broad for more than that. "Mr. Bass, can you hear me?" Hawkins twisted to push more of his neck and shoulders through the window. "Mr. Bass, look at me."

Hawkins backed out. "He's breathing, but not moving." He jumped down and faced Jo. "Someone small must climb through the window and pull him away from the door."

Jo measured the space with her eyes. "Watch him. I'll be right back." She dashed to the outside entrance of their living quarters.

She returned dressed in her brother's trousers cinched around her waist and the sleeves of his shirt rolled to her elbows.

She climbed through the window. Crouched beside her brother, she rocked his shoulder. "Thad, wake up. You must move away from the door."

She pulled him by his feet until she could open the door without hitting Thad. Her voice carried into the yard. "Mr. Hawkins, please come help me get Thad back in bed."

She knelt beside her brother and felt his forehead. His cold, dry skin alarmed her.

Spittle oozed from the corner of his mouth as he turned his head, groaned, and drew up into a fetal position.

Hawkins picked up Thad and laid him on the bed.

Thad's shallow breathing continued at a steady pace, but his awareness stayed submerged, too deep for Jo to rouse.

She beckoned Hawkins to follow her out of the room before she propped the door open with the writing desk chair.

"Thank you for your help. I couldn't have done this alone."

"My pleasure, Miss Bass." He appraised her up and down. "Trousers for women. That's a far-fetched idea."

"Well, it served its purpose for modesty today. I must alter an old pair of Thad's to keep on hand for future window climbing." She broke into a gale of laughter.

He didn't share her mirth.

Her gaiety transformed into a somber request. "Can you handle the banking alone today? There are things I need to do."

"Certainly, lovely lady. If my services are no longer needed until the bank opens, I'll have enough time to eat breakfast at the boardinghouse."

Jo's breath stuttered at his glistening eyes and courtly bow. The slow grin that played across his lips spiked her discomfort to a confusing level.

She snapped the door lock, pulled up a corner of the window curtain, and watched Hawkins until he disappeared. Father would salivate over this specimen of the perfect son-in-law: sophisticated, with banking experience, and trustworthy. Did she have to love him before he became a husband?

◆　◆　◆

Zeke Keller closed Mrs. Sims's boardinghouse door and set his valise on the deck.

He'd decided to go north into Oregon Territory, then into British America. Quick jobs along the way would keep body and soul together until he could clear his name.

The shout of the stagecoach driver and the drum of horse hooves reached him before the coach came into view.

When it pulled up in front of the boardinghouse, he saw the man he held responsible for his fugitive status open the coach door. *What's Frazier Hawkins doing in Dry Diggins?*

Zeke ducked behind a stack of crates and shoved his bag into a crevice.

Hawkins spoke to the driver before he walked toward the bank.

Zeke followed from a safe distance. *Odd. No luggage. No companion. No disguise.*

About to round the corner of the bank building, he heard Hawkins shout, "Woman, what are you doing?"

Zeke pulled back and flattened himself against the building wall. He heard a soft female voice reply.

Hawkins's voice changed to a gentleman's tone. "Oh. Miss Bass. I didn't recognize you. Please forgive my outburst." *Miss Bass? His heart lurched with hope. Not Mrs. Bass?*

He peeked around the corner and saw Jo dash to an outside entrance of the bank. Hawkins stood atop a stepladder, his face against a windowpane.

Keen on confrontation, Zeke stepped toward Hawkins. The door burst open, and Jo ran out wearing baggy trousers and a man's shirt.

He froze, a startled outcry glued to his tongue. Even dressed in men's clothing, her loveliness struck a favorable chord in his heart.

Hawkins jumped off. She mounted the stepladder and threw a leg over the sill. Zeke crossed the street to wait for Hawkins.

Jo. He raked his hand through his hair. *Miss Jo.* No matter what the miners called her, she had to be Mrs. Bass.

A torrent of memories rose to mock him. *Betsy never loved you. She used you to obtain information about the new security system.* He shook his head hard to knock loose the memories' grip, but failed to alter the reality of his life as a fugitive.

He couldn't close his eyes at night without seeing the smug look on her face as the New York police led him away, accusing him of embezzling from his own bank.

Chapter Three

Adeep sigh started the litany of things she wanted to do before Thad woke again.

In her room, she undid the trousers and let them drop to the floor. She stared at the pile of Thad's old bulky trousers. *Cut to my size, hemmed to the middle of my leg, no one would see them under my skirt.* She put the pants on again and pulled her housedress over them. A lightweight shirt wool would be more comfortable.

She wrote her measurements in her sewing journal. The trip from New York, and the bare bones living Thad demanded, reduced her figure by two dress sizes. Her mirror reflected more of a secondary schoolgirl than a twenty-two-year-old young woman.

A soft hum hovered in the back of her throat as she searched through her trunk for the wool yardage she'd brought from home. Fabric, notions, selected patterns, and her sewing machine were the personal luxuries her brother allowed. If she failed at banking, she could set up a tailor shop.

"Forward thinking, dear sister," had been Thad's reasoning. Their father agreed. Her hurt cut deep. They expected her to fail.

Jo laid her sewing back in the trunk and tiptoed to Thad's room. She scooted the side chair close to his bedside and, head pillowed on her arms, let sleep soothe her weary body.

A touch on her head jarred her awake.

"Didn't mean to startle you, sis." Thad sat propped up in bed. Pale and gaunt, but eyes alert.

She flung herself across his chest. "You're awake. I was so worried. Are you hungry?"

"Something warm for my throat." He pulled the coverlet higher on his chest.

She made prompt work of his request and joined him with her own bowl of vegetable broth.

He gave her his empty bowl. "Have you reconciled last week's books?"

"Yes, the records are ready to send to Father with this week's gold shipment. Would you like for me to get your file box and complete your sheets?"

"No. I. . .uh. . .need to do that myself. It can wait until I feel better."

"Let me help. It would ease the burden on—"

"No. Leave it alone, Jo. It's not your concern." Thad sat up straighter and swung his legs out to get off the bed.

"Stay in bed." She patted his leg. "I won't mention it again."

Jo collected the dirty dishes and carried them to the kitchen before she went to their shared office. The room's earth tones and leather furniture exuded corporate high finance. Father's portrait lent the right air of elegance for private consultations.

Thad's file box sat on the edge of his desk. Their back-to-back flat-top desks made a large working surface. Maps and plats could be spread over the surface without a wrinkle. Glass-front shelves lined the wall behind them.

She walked to the file box and ran her fingers over the latches. Thad had been so secretive with his new transaction logs. He sealed them in the bag to their father without showing them to her.

A quick snap and answers wouldn't depend on Thad. She rocked the case back and forth with one hand. This report was important. It needed to be sent, but Thad wasn't in any condition to do it.

Pros and cons lined up, assembled like equally matched armies on a battle line. The tiebreaker—trust should be stronger than a file box latch.

She went back to Thad's room and sat down in her chair.

His eyes opened and blinked to focus. "Did Hawkins make it back?"

"Yes, he came in on the early-morning stage. He's doing the banking for us today. I'll tell you about our adventure when you feel like laughing. . .a lot. I did conceive a sewing project from it."

"Perfect. Keep up your skills." Thad scooted down on the bed and let her reposition his pillow and draw up the covers. "Is the building across the street still available? It would be a good storefront for you."

◆ ◆ ◆

Jo tied her bonnet straps a little tighter than usual to compensate for the wind she saw gusting on Main Street. She opened the bank door and stepped outside.

Zeke Keller leaned against the wall beside the door.

"Well, cowboy, did you sleep on the bank's doorstep? The bank won't open for another two hours." She locked the door.

"I want to discuss a sensitive matter with you."

"I see. You'll have to talk while we walk." She lengthened her stride as she moved down the makeshift boardwalk.

He fell into step with her. "How are you acquainted with Frazier Hawkins?"

"I hardly think that's any of your concern." She stepped off the boardwalk and crossed the street.

Zeke stepped in front of her. "What do you know about him? This man can't be trusted."

"At the risk of being rude, I reiterate, it's none of your business. I hired Mr. Hawkins as a teller and courier. His credentials and letters of reference are impeccable."

"Do you have copies of his portfolio? Are you sure they're legitimate, duly notarized?"

She stepped around him. "I know he worked for a New York bank that closed because the owner embezzled ten thousand dollars and stole eighty thousand in silver and gold coins, land deeds, and jewelry. The owner escaped police custody and hadn't been recaptured when Mr. Hawkins came to Dry Diggins two weeks ago."

"Who told you those lies?"

Jo stopped midstride. "Mr. Bass does not lie, nor does he take to idle gossip."

"Bass?" Zeke stepped back. He caught his wide-brimmed hat before it blew off his head. "Is your bank part of Bass International House of Finance?" He held up his hand. "Wait, was that Thaddeus I carried to his bed for you? You didn't call him by his first name before. He was so gaunt and thin. His face so fevered I didn't recognize him."

He stroked his chin. "I saw the announcement in *Bankers' Magazine* that Bass Senior intended to send his son to California to open a branch bank. It didn't say Thaddeus had married or his wife was also a banker."

"Thad's not. . .he doesn't—"

A commotion at the end of the street robbed her of her full confession.

Seven miners raced pell-mell toward them, Carmady among them. "Open the bank. We've got gold the size of your fist."

"Whoa, fellas. The bank won't open for"—she flipped up her shoulder brooch and opened the case—"an hour and fifty minutes. Be there when the bank—"

"There's more coming. We jest ran faster. They'll storm the bank."

Jo sized up the seven sweaty, panting men and the runners behind them. "Okay. Carmady, go get Mr. Hawkins at Mrs. Sims's."

Carmady looked down the street toward the boardinghouse then back at Jo. He squinted and tightened his face in disagreement.

"Go on. You'll be first in line for your efforts." Jo clapped her hands like a starter's gun.

Carmady took off like he'd dislodged a methane fissure.

The other men ran to the bank door, leaving room for Carmady at the head of the line.

Jo turned to excuse herself from Zeke's company, but he was gone.

When she reached the bank, the line curved down the street, the end out of sight.

The din swelled to mob volume when she admitted Carmady.

Hawkins entered behind him, then closed and locked the door. He moved behind the counter and readied his space.

"Thank you for coming on such short notice, Mr. Hawkins." She felt an unexpected shyness flit across her face.

"How do you want to handle this?" Hawkins tilted his head, his smile shrewd but not mischievous, almost like they shared an intimate secret.

Jo snatched up a beaker to hide her confusion. "I'll measure and test the gold. You do the log work. Some of the men don't have accounts yet. In the hubbub, some may not have brought their papers."

She worked with the lye water and the nuggets then passed them to Hawkins.

Jo had a bell in her hand when she went to the door for the next miner.

The cacophony in the street ceased. Men bent forward but didn't leave their places in line.

"I know you want to register your gold and go back to your claims." She waited until the rousing affirmations changed to head nods. "It takes time for me to come to the door."

She held up the bell and gave it a rapid shake. "I will leave the door unlocked. When I ring this bell, the next man in line comes in. If anyone comes in without the bell, I will lock the door again."

The men murmured amongst themselves until one man addressed her. "We'll give it a go, ma'am."

"Pass the word so no one ignores the bell and gets the door locked." Guffaws from the men nearest her made her laugh. "Mr. Partrich, are you ready?"

He jiggled his poke and stepped lively through the door.

The rest of the morning reminded Jo of a game of show and tell. She smiled, laughed, and rejoiced with the men as they brought their shows and she told them their worth. She grew more anxious each time she excused herself to check on Thad. He'd never slept this long. *Lord, please don't let Thad die while I'm doing bank business.*

She asked the next miner to send his wife to sit by Thad's open door. Mrs. Russell came with her market basket and knitting. She took charge of Thad and the kitchen. Soon, the bank smelled like bone marrow broth and fresh bread.

At noon, Jo stepped outside to ask for a brief break so she and Hawkins could eat.

A man the others called Troubadour held up a basket. "We figured you'd be tired and be needing a bite to eat 'bout now." He gave Jo the basket. "Mrs. Sims made the chicken and fixin's. Mrs. Wakefield made the pie. The milk isn't cool, but it's fresh."

"Thank you." Jo took the basket. "We'll eat while we work."

The miners shouted loud enough to reach Coloma eight miles away.

Carmady held up a pail. "Mrs. Sims and Mrs. Wakefield fixed up grub for us, too. We all dropped a nugget in this bucket for them to divide. Imagine they'll be in tomorry, if you ain't too tired to open."

"We'll be open at ten." She saluted the men and carried the basket inside.

Hawkins lit the lamps inside at nightfall, and the miners lit torches outside.

Nibbles of chicken, biscuits, and dried apple pie throughout the afternoon saved Jo. Her strength and buoyancy never languished, and her mental acuity never failed.

The last miner vowed to name his first girl after her. "Mildred Josephine, you say. Best you write that down so's I spell it right. She'll be called Jo for short, 'xactly like you."

"I'm honored, Mr. Linzy." She tucked in a wayward curl from the spiral knot at the nape of her neck. "If she's a redhead like you and me, you'll have your hands full."

Jo closed the front door on the miner, locked it, and leaned back against it. Exhaustion tempted her to sink down and sleep.

"Miss Bass. Miss Bass?"

Jo opened her eyes. A young girl she didn't recognize stood in front of her. "Who are you?"

"I'm Charmalea Russell. Momma says I'm to stay the night in that chair outside Mr. Bass's room so's you could sleep. She left a pot of broth simmering for you." Charmalea took Jo's hand and led her to the kitchen. "Mr. Hawkins had his fill and went on to the boardin'house. He said to say he'd see ya tomorry."

Jo ate the broth Charmalea ladled into a bowl. She dunked a cold biscuit without saying a word.

"I know about caring for sick folks, so you don't have to worry none about Mr. Bass." Charmalea pushed a small portion of pie to Jo. "If he turns for the worst, I'll come get you straightaway."

Jo rubbed her eyes. "Yes, right away, Charmalea."

"Momma'll bring breakfast for you. My sister, Vernice, will sit with Mr. Bass."

The drone of Charmalea's chatter followed Jo to her bed. Still shod, she stretched atop the coverlet.

Chapter Four

The miners' stampede provided the chance Zeke needed to fall back a small distance behind Jo.

The men ran to the bank door and formed a line with dozens more filing in behind them.

She looked around, shrugged, and went back to the bank.

Zeke started toward the bank but dived back into his hiding spot when he saw Hawkins and Carmady in a race toward the men.

Zeke leaned against the wagon and bided his time. He must convince her Hawkins couldn't be trusted.

Jo appeared once, rang a bell, laughed with the men, and went back inside.

Mrs. Sims and Mrs. Wakefield, who seldom served food outside their homes, rallied the wives and daughters and a few boys to help. Even Zeke became tangled in the eating frenzy.

"Your fistful of gold in the bank already, sir?"

Zeke turned toward the youthful voice. "No, ma'am, missed this bonanza."

Her so-sorry frown changed into an introduction. "I'm Lucy Wakefield. I don't believe we've met."

"Pleased to make your acquaintance. I'm Zeke Keller."

Lucy pointed to a triple-decker wooden tray filled with dried apple pie slices. She signaled for him to follow her down the line of waiting miners. She gave each man a slice.

Mrs. Sims worked ahead of them. "Wish it could be more than jam and bread. I gave the chicken to Miss Bass and Mr. Hawkins. Next time, you folks give me a heads-up when yor' gonna find this much gold."

Again—Miss Bass. Mrs. Sims's choice of words was a tad earthy, but she said *miss*. Before he could ask her or Mrs. Wakefield, Carmady came along swinging a water pail.

"Drop in a donation for the grub and milk." Carmady rattled the pail.

Zeke heard the bank door but didn't turn in time to see who opened or closed it.

Siesta came and went, but Jo never came out again.

After the last miner left near midnight, Zeke sidled up to the front door. Female voices murmured inside, but he couldn't understand the conversation.

He turned to leave when a firm hand seized his upper arm.

Frazier Hawkins wheeled Zeke around to face him. "I thought that was you. Handing out pies like you don't have a care in the world. What are you doing in Dry Diggins, Meade?"

Zeke flinched at Hawkins's use of his real last name. "Searching for you and your girlfriend." Zeke jerked his arm out of Hawkins's grip. "You framed me. I didn't rob the bank or those people. You did."

"That's an intriguing tale, Meade, but you can't prove it. The safe was open. The bank bag and some valuables were found in your room. The guard saw you before you nearly killed him with that blow to the head. He'll recover and testify at your trial."

Zeke stepped closer to Hawkins. "How did you open the safe? Was the guard in on it?"

"Chew on that while you rot in jail."

"You snake in the grass. I'll find a way to vindicate myself. So help me."

"You'd better hurry. There's a fugitive recovery agent on your trail." Hawkins stepped within biting range of Zeke's nose. "I saw you talking to Miss Bass this morning. Do that again, and she may not be as lucky as the guard."

Zeke jabbed a right cross into Hawkins's stomach, forcing him backward. Then snapped the banker's head back with an uppercut.

Hawkins reeled back against the building. "That's going to cost you, Meade. She won't see it coming either." He touched the side of his face but stayed crouched down. "You'd better start running."

Zeke reached for Hawkins's shirtfront. Clamor from the saloon three doors down made him draw back and slip to the side of the bank building.

"This isn't over, Meade. Run while you can."

Zeke did run—to the shack where he'd stored his gear after the first time he saw Hawkins.

◆ ◆ ◆

"Lucy, come in. I was hoping I'd see you today." Jo hugged her friend.

"The pie business was lucrative yesterday."

"Your pies and Mrs. Sims's chicken and bread got us through a long day." Cowboy stepped through the door, but Jo didn't acknowledge him.

"Jo, Mr. Hawkins is a delightful man, and a handsome catch. You should smile like that more often when you talk about a man."

Jo ignored her teasing. "Do you have your bankbook?"

"Uh, I want to open a new account. I. . .uh. . .will be the sole signature on it." Lucy held her deposit sack close to her chest, her shoulders heaving with deep breaths.

"Not a problem. I can open one with this deposit. And. . .uh. . .Mr. Wakefield can come by later and. . . add his name to the account." She pushed the ledger toward Lucy. Thad would enforce bank rules—no accounts for women without a man's signature. No harm in a preapproval. Mr. Wakefield could come in at his leisure.

Lucy pronounced each name as she wrote it. "Lucy Stoddard Wakefield."

Jo took the ledger, blotted the signature dry, and held it out to Lucy.

Lucy shook her head. "Would you keep this ledger in your safe? I'll bring John in when I'm ready for him to sign."

"Certainly. Let me know when you want to put Dr. Wakefield on the account." Jo wiped the excess ink from the blotter. "Have you thought about buying the log cabin across the street? Prime location for a pie shop with the post office and bank nearby. The Coleman brothers are asking a nominal price for it."

"As a matter of fact, I'm thinking about it. The older Mr. Coleman will shave down the price if I throw in a perpetual weekly tin of dried apple pie."

"He's a savvy businessman." Jo took Lucy's paperwork to the wall safe. She turned back and Zeke Keller stood at the counter. They were alone.

"Why am I not surprised, cowboy?" She came to the counter and clenched her hands together on top of it. "I suppose you want to warn me against Mr. Hawkins. . .again."

"No, I can see that's futile. Women find his charm irresistible. I didn't realize he appealed to married women with sick husbands."

Jo pulled her gun from under the counter and leaned close to the iron grill. "Be very glad we have a cage between us." She leveled her gun. "Get out of my bank. Your gold went in today's shipment. Do your banking in Sacramento or San Francisco."

Zeke backed his way to the exterior door. The .31 caliber pocket revolver pointed at his heart—inducement enough.

The moment the door closed behind him, she laid her revolver on the countertop before her shaking hand flung it. She hurried to lock the door.

She sat on the stool she used at the counter, took a deep breath, and closed her eyes. Maybe she'd overreacted, but that man brought out emotions she couldn't control. Zeke's face reflected off the back of her eyelids. She rubbed her eyes, but his stricken gaze became sharper.

Chapter Five

Jo sat in *her* pew, second row, right, third seat in. Thad had rallied enough to be left alone for the two-hour service, but was too weak to travel the three blocks.

The makeshift pews under the largest tent in town served as the local church where Reverend Noland welcomed the faithful once a week.

She dressed up on Tent Sunday. The scent of cedar chips permeated her heavy fabric skirt. The sachet's perfume lingered lightly on the bodice. She hand-pressed a wrinkle on her sleeve.

"Folks, if you're ready, we'll begin." Reverend Noland stood at the front of the tent with his Bible in his left hand, held against his chest, and his right hand raised for attention.

"Normally, we'd open with 'Amazing Grace.' Today I want to tell you about another song. Robert Robinson wrote the words in 1757."

"Hey, preacher, that's older than any of us here. Got any new songs?"

The laughter and foot stomping took a minute to die down.

"I do indeed, but first I want to comment on this one." Reverend Noland pointed to two youths on either side of the tent. "These young men will hand out a paper with the lyrics."

Reverend Noland motioned to an older man seated in front of him who strummed his guitar. While the lyrics were passed around, Reverend Noland sang, "Come thou Fount of every blessing, tune my heart to sing thy grace."

Soon, others joined in singing.

Jo read the words but didn't sing. She beamed with polite surprise when Frazier Hawkins took the seat beside her.

He rustled his copy of the lyrics and sang on the third verse. His efforts fit the verse "call for songs of loudest praise."

She read the phrase, "Jesus sought me when a stranger, wandering from the fold of God." *I haven't gone anywhere, God, but You haven't been seeking me.* The rest of the verse tightened around her heart. "He, to rescue me from danger, bought me with His precious blood." She laid the paper in her lap.

The wind flapped the tent roof like a sheet on wash day. The two tent poles behind Reverend Noland swayed and bowed in toward her as if to confirm God's presence.

A clap of thunder sent a ripple of groans throughout the congregation. Men scurried to let down the tent's four grungy gray side panels. More rain could make it the wettest month in Dry Diggins' history, and the worst for above-ground digging.

She turned to the crowd in the rows behind her. Her smile was fixed but sincere.

A streak of lightning ushered Zeke into the tent and to the back row of logs. He flicked his hat and shivered off raindrops.

Jo didn't look away until he glanced around the room and met her glare.

Disgraceful. How could he show his face in church after his accusations against her and Mr. Hawkins? She looked back. His seat was empty. *As it should be, Mr. Keller; this isn't the place for you.*

◆　◆　◆

So much for running between the raindrops. Zeke laughed at the quip he'd given his mother about not wearing his waxed jacket when it rained. He sat down on the nearest backseat log. He shivered from the sudden change in temperature.

A youth handed him a paper. The familiar song replaced the chill. The organ wheezed more than it played a note, but joyful noise rose to the tent top.

He tapped his foot in time to the music as he read the words. For a few moments, he was back in New York, sitting in church with his mother. Mellow with the memory, he looked around the crowd and into Jo Bass's searing eyes of condemnation. Frazier Hawkins sat next to her.

Zeke stuffed the lyrics page into his jacket pocket, pulled his coat collar up, and pulled his hat down for his escape into the pelting rain.

◆　◆　◆

Jo's body and her heart's bitterness stayed as rigid as the tent poles. She didn't open her pocket Bible to 1 Samuel 7:12, the text for Reverend Noland's sermon.

The preacher passed his hand across the audience. "I heard about the rich strike. . ."

A roar of affirmation and clapping filled the tent.

He let the tumult diminish. "Some of our congregation cashed in their gold and went back to family and loved ones."

Murmurs and grunts dribbled through the group.

"Their treasure was more than the gold in their pockets. What is your greatest treasure?"

Jo didn't hesitate. *Family.* A thought sprang unbidden: *But am I their treasure? Father sees me as a potential bride price. Thad's jealous, wants me to fail. Mother never saw me at all.* She pressed her fingers against her lips. *I have no value or worth to anyone. I'm no one's treasure.*

Reverend Noland raised his lyrics sheet above his head. "You're God's treasure." His piercing gaze left no one untouched. "He wants you to bind your heart to Him with a fetter so strong it can't be removed. Will you say this very hour—'Here's my heart, O take and seal it; seal it for Thy courts above'?"

Jo refused to yield to his pleas. Even when the lyrics paper floated to the floor, she didn't retrieve it. She left during the final prayer. Her bitterness included more than God.

Chapter Six

Jo compared her duplicate copy of the gold transfer ledger against the sheet brought back from Sacramento. "This can't be right," she whispered. "I copied it verbatim."

The discrepancies started before Thad became ill. Small amounts. Transposed numbers. All from Jo's station.

She went to the cellar, rolled aside the wardrobe, and opened the large safe. The top ledger in the stack contained the figures she needed. She took the one below it, too.

Back upstairs at the kitchen table, she opened the ledger to the last transfer, then to the one before it. She spread her copied sheets in the order of the transfers.

"Why didn't I see this before?" She pushed back from the table and put her hands over her face. *Father's right. I'm not cut out for finance.*

She flipped open her timepiece brooch—two hours before opening. She verified the last four shipments against her duplicate ledger. The last three didn't match. The incorrect figures on each sheet showed up in odd places. A nine on her duplicate sheet became a two on the transfer sheet. A seven became a smudgy one. On the last duplicate in question, the five became a three.

Fifteen thousand gold dollars missing. Thad had accompanied each shipment until he became sick. Hawkins was honest. Where was the money? Who forged the records? She must tell Thad when his thinking wasn't fevered.

She took the ledgers back to the cellar safe and locked them away.

A new ledger, no mistakes. Each entry checked twice, each ounce of gold logged and initialed in the ledger, each coin deposit placed in a separate cone of paper, much to the chagrin of waiting customers.

Day after day, she tried new ways to protect her ciphering, signature, and record keeping. By the end of the week, all she knew for sure was that her handwriting improved. No more curlicues, decorative strokes, or ending swirls. Numbers were the hardest to protect against forgeries. But now she needed to find out what happened to the money.

◆ ◆ ◆

Zeke scratched his eight-day-old beard. He hadn't seen Hawkins since the threats, but the constant vigilance was wearing thin. He took his meals in his room, entered and exited the boardinghouse from the kitchen.

He reclined against the door frame of the empty Coleman building. It gave him a view of the boardinghouse front door, and Hawkins, if he came out.

He looked down Main Street at the new businesses. Mr. Coffee's tavern, Elstner's hay yard, and Vasquez's stable had sprung up overnight. The rumor about the horseback relay mail service hadn't materialized yet. This town would need another bank before year's end.

"Mr. Keller?" Lucy Wakefield stood in the muddy street.

He doffed his hat. "Good morning, Mrs. Wakefield." He crossed the porch to assist her up the steps.

"Nice beard. Jo likes beards. Much better than mustaches alone."

"Jo?"

"Miss Bass. Across the street. Bank." Lucy wagged her head. "I saw the way she looked at you when I opened my account." Lucy winked at him. "She's smitten with you."

"*Miss* Bass? She's not married? Thad isn't her husband?"

"Our dear Miss Bass is quite eligible." She opened her purse and dug inside. "She's a formidable whist player as well. Do you play cards?"

"No, ma'am. Horse races are more my style."

"Pity. I host rousing games on Thursday evenings." She held up a key. "Would you mind?"

"Not at all." He pushed open the door and stepped back to let Lucy enter.

"Thankfully, you were lounging about."

"Lounging about? I'm waiting for the bank to open."

Lucy didn't comment, but her low chuckle echoed as she walked into the building.

◆　◆　◆

Jo saw Zeke and Lucy across the street on the porch of Coleman's empty building. She watched until she heard her back door open and close. *That door needs a bell, too.*

She turned to see Hawkins standing by his teller window.

"Mr. Hawkins, good morning. I hope your time off proved profitable."

"Indeed it was, Miss Bass." He slanted his head at a coy angle. "Business in San Francisco kept me occupied with a series of most lucrative transactions."

Jo brought out a stack of papers and lined them up along their contiguous counters. "I've changed the way we enter calculations in the ledger and on the transfer sheets."

She tutored Hawkins in her new method for the next hour. They tried it out on the first depositor. By the end of the day, it proved its worth. She put the last of the day's receipts in the safe behind her, bid Hawkins a good night, and opened the front door to flip the OPEN sign.

The floorboards behind her squeaked.

Jo spun around. "Mr. Hawkins." She walked with stiff, measured steps into the teller area. "I thought you left."

"Miss Bass, I've given this a great deal of consideration and felt I should mention my concerns." He took off his fawn-colored bowler hat and held it at his side. "Yes, well, I thought this matter of utmost importance." He gestured with his hat toward the inner door. "Could we sit in your kitchen?"

She led the way and put the water kettle on the stove. "What is your concern, Mr. Hawkins?"

He rubbed a spot on the tablecloth. "On the day of the big strike, I saw you talking to a man who's a criminal. E. K. Meade's a dangerous fugitive." He looked up from the spot. "I've sent a wire about him to the New York Police Department."

She set a cup of tea in front of him then brought her own cup to the table. His missing right index finger sent a chill up her spine. "I spoke to many men that day. Meade doesn't sound familiar."

Hawkins stirred in a teaspoon of sugar before sipping his tea. "I saw the two of you together from Mrs. Sims's parlor window. I lost sight of him when the chap came to fetch me the morning of the stampede. Do you remember him now?"

She sipped her tea. "No recollection. I guess the frenzy of the day wiped it away."

"You'd best stay away from Meade until the recovery agent captures him."

"I shall be on my guard, Mr. Hawkins. However, I don't make a habit of consorting with criminals."

"I didn't mean to imply any such thing. I'm simply concerned with your safety." He rose and set his chair back in its place at the table. "Until Dry Diggins has a sheriff or at least a federal marshal, I'm sure your father would take grave offense should I not be concerned with your well-being." He moved to the edge of the table.

She stood and repositioned her own chair against the table. "I will convey your care and consideration to Father."

Hawkins reached her side in one swift move. He took her hand and enclosed it in both of his. "My dear, nothing would please me more." He raised her hand and kissed her knuckles.

She pulled her hand from his grasp.

"Until the morrow." He closed the back door behind him.

She ran to the door and locked it. She needed another bell. Over the next hour she became a woman on a mission.

Simon Walters, ten-year-old son of the Empire Mercantile owner, scampered around the store but found no bell or suitable noisemaker. "Miss Bass, I can ask Pa to order a dinner bell for you like Mrs. Sims uses."

"Ask your pa if you can come to the bank with me. I won't keep you long."

Simon came back in a heartbeat with permission and a level of enthusiasm only a ten-year-old could exhibit.

Jo showed him her improvised front door alarm and told him her desire to put one on the back door. Together they redesigned the front doorbell and rigged a cluster of horseshoe nails for the back door.

"Gotta run, Miss Bass. Pa could use doorbells at the store." Simon sped out the door. He left behind the new and improved tinkle of the front doorbell.

◆   ◆   ◆

Lucy came in at noon with her deposit. Jo leaned enough to the right to make Lucy turn around. "Looking for someone?"

"Uh...no...one doorbell ring could mean two people." Jo brought her body to its full height. "How can I help you today, Lucy?"

"He likes you, you know."

"He who?"

"Don't be modest with me, Jo. You were looking for Mr. Keller."

"Preposterous. He's rude and unconscionable." Jo held out her hand for Lucy's money bag. Why should she care if he liked her? She never wanted to see him again.

219

"He was particularly pleased to learn you're single." Lucy peeled off her morning gloves and went to the end of the counter. "May I brew us some tea? I took a pound of Chinese tea in trade yesterday. I want to try it."

"Go ahead. You know where everything is."

Jo served four customers before she had time for tea with Lucy in the kitchen. "What did you mean he's glad I'm single?"

"Merely that. I understand if you're not interested." Lucy opened Jo's dry goods cabinet door. "Any sweet biscuits?"

"No. Thad's appetite is returning."

"Oh, pardon my manners. I should have asked about him first thing."

"He's on the mend."

"Splendid." Lucy poured them both another cup. "I want to explain about asking you to put my deposit in the safe." She lifted her cup, but put it back on the saucer. "I plan to divorce Mr. Wakefield as soon as I have enough money to live independently."

Jo bit her lip. She leaned forward, uncertain how to react to Lucy's decision.

Lucy took her cup to the sink. "When Thad's healthy again, Mr. Hawkins will be out of a job. Does that make you sad?"

Jo followed with her own cup and saucer. *Hmm. Does it?*

Chapter Seven

Hawkins was all smiles and his debonair best when he returned from lunch. "I filled out the slips for tomorrow's shipment. They're ready for your approval."

"How thoughtful." She took the forms and put them in the safe. "I have a telegram for my father. After it's sent, the rest of the day is yours."

She handed him the paper. "I'm asking Father to send an auditor. We can't afford any more mistakes. I don't know how deep my errors run."

"You're too hard on yourself, Miss Bass. Your new system is mistake-proof and a real credit to your business sense."

She clenched her teeth to stop the flush of joy racing up her neck. A lifetime with someone of her choosing who valued her. The idea resonated with her and took root.

◆　◆　◆

Jo woke from her nightmare with a dread stronger than any she had ever felt. The dream didn't vary, but the words "keep it safe" chased after her.

The next morning she set out the statement books as usual. One of the ready-slips dropped out of her hand and drifted across the floor. Butterfingered and incompetent. She picked it up and swished it in the air. The light from the overhead lamp brought the paper under scrutiny.

She closed the bank at her usual Saturday noon. She knew what she had to do. She pulled on her under-trousers, her warmest wool day dress, long socks, walking boots, and traveling coat.

She headed to the stable. It had been a year since she had been astride a saddle, and the prospect of a fast day's ride scared her.

"Mr. Vasquez, I need to ride to Sacramento today. Do you have a horse that will carry me there and back? I want to return this evening."

"*Senorita* Bass, *no es posible*. Sacramento is *un día viajes*. . .uh. . .one day travel. You and horse must rest and eat."

Jo nibbled her bottom lip and frowned. "I must go to Sacramento today."

"Senorita, *lo qué es tan importante*."

"Importante? Oh, important." She stepped in closer. "I must send the bank's deposits to my father. I can't wait for two days for the stage."

"*Mi hijo*. . .my son. . .rides to Sacramento today. He is *honesto*. He can take your deposits with him, no?"

"Secrecy is critical. Will he follow my instructions?"

"His English is good. He will keep your *secreto*."

"I'll return within the half hour. Can he go then?"

"Sí, Senorita. Xavier will be ready."

Jo gave her saddlebag and instructions to Xavier at the appointed time. He and his horse ambled away from the stables. Perhaps on their way to siesta.

Excellent. No one would suspect he carried a week's worth of receipts and gold. Why sending it early and secretly was so important, she didn't know. The dream. It had to be the dream.

◆ ◆ ◆

Reverend Noland stood in front of the congregation, hands interlocked in repose. His announcement of this last meeting with them cast a gloomy mood among the people. The songs, his standard ones, and the whooping and hollering from two weeks ago were gone.

"My, but we're a quiet bunch this morning. There's a place in worship for silence and reverent contemplation. As long as there's no snoring."

The ripple of laughter from the full pews held no mirth. The side flaps were rolled up, and folks crowded around the outside.

"I want to leave you with the reminder that Jehovah God is ever present. He is Jehovah-Rapha, the God who heals our afflictions. He is El Roi, the God who sees us in every circumstance of our lives. Nothing escapes His awareness or care. God knows us and our troubles."

Jo sat beside Thad on the back pew, his first outing since the onset of his illness. The smell of damp wood and sawdust vexed her nostrils and triggered a series of small sneezes.

Thad shook a few hands of the steady stream of well-wishers. His weak smile thinned with each pat on his shoulders.

"Are you tired, Thad? Is the dampness aggravating your breathing? Do we need to go home?"

"No. Sitting up and moving around helps." He smiled up at another bank customer.

She hoped to see Hawkins, but instead she saw Zeke Keller. He stood at the edge of a group outside. His eyes burrowed into her soul. Her heart fluttered. A sense of being unconditionally cherished and treasured settled around her like a fine wool blanket on a subzero midnight. Why should he of all people make her feel that way?

Jo closed her eyes to break the connection, to exchange it for the feel of Hawkins's lips on her hand. Nothing. Hawkins didn't make her heart flutter like Zeke did. Movement stirred the air, and she opened her eyes.

Thad leaned forward, elbows on knees. He clasped his hands together and bowed his head on his hands.

Jo started to touch his shoulder but drew back. She'd never seen Thad pray before.

Reverend Noland caught her attention. "...God's forgiveness will give you everlasting peace. You can do nothing to earn it." The preacher knelt in the fresh-spread coarse sawdust.

Thad got up, went to the front, and knelt beside the pastor.

Jo pressed a hand to her heart and with the other swiped at a tear. What troubled Thad?

She glanced around for Zeke. He was in his place, but close behind him stood Frazier

Hawkins with what looked like a gun pressed in his back. She patted her dress pocket for her gun.

Zeke's slow nod at something Hawkins said in his ear didn't match the glint in his eyes.

Was Zeke the man Frazier had warned her about last week? Surely not. Well, one way to find out. She slipped out of her seat and headed around the corner to the back of the tent. She marched up to the two men.

"Miss Bass, this is a private matter." Frazier gripped Zeke's shoulder. "Please go back to your seat."

She put her hands on her hips. "Is this the man you warned me against?"

"Yes," the two men said in unison.

She looked from one man to the other. "What's going on?"

"Nothing that concerns you, my dear." Frazier softened his voice and smiled the term of endearment.

"Why are you holding a gun on Mr. Keller?"

Frazier tensed and scanned the crowd behind her. "Keep your voice down." Frazier put his gun inside his jacket. "Who's Keller?"

"Yes, Miss Bass." Zeke maneuvered out of Frazier's grip, spun around beside Jo, and slid his arm around her waist. "Keep your voice down."

Jo pitched to the side to escape his grip. "Let me go."

Simon Walters ran toward the tent, his arms flailing like a broken windmill blade. "Help. Cave-in at Diamondback Mine."

People jumped to their feet. Women and children moved back, and the men charged into the street.

"My dad's gone for the doc. He said bring digging tools and whatever you have to help the hurtin'." Simon ran to the head of the crowd.

Zeke held Jo close to his side, but Frazier disappeared into the sea of running men.

Jo didn't struggle against his arm. "Is it true what Frazier said? Are you a fugitive?"

Zeke kept hold of her. "I am. I promise to tell you all about it when this is over. They need everyone's help." He turned her to face him. "Please trust me."

"Jo, I need to go home." Thad held on to a tent post, doubled over at the waist.

She ran to her brother. Zeke ran to catch up with the men.

Chapter Eight

Jo arranged Thad's pillows and laid a light blanket over his feet.

The pristine room with its spick-and-span accessories assuaged her guilt at leaving him alone. He'd decided to keep on his trousers, shirt, and socks.

"I must go help. If nothing else, I can corral the children."

"I'm fine, sis. I wish I could go help." He scooted back against the headboard to sit more upright. "Bring me *Bankers' Magazine*. I can at least do some reading."

Jo moved the small bedside table within his reach and brought the magazine, a meat sandwich, and a glass of water. "If I'm useless at the mine, I'll come back straightaway."

Thad nodded, but the magazine already held his attention.

She hurried down the street toward the mining district. The screams and wails reached her before she saw the chaos.

Her expectation of being a children's nanny was squelched within minutes. Bodies lined the road. One side—the dead; the other—the dying. The injured gathered in an open space where men erected a tent.

Shouts and the scrape of metal on rock sounded like a swarm of hornets chasing an intruder.

She sucked in a breath. Blood, missing limbs, ravaged bodies on her left, and men gasping and moaning to stay alive on her right. She'd seen death once—her mother's.

Reverend Noland ran to her. "Take this." He shoved paper and a pencil stub into her hands. "Get names and next of kin." He pointed to the gravely injured. "Start with those without folks attending them."

Jo felt rooted to the spot. *Run. Run home. This isn't your problem.* She tried to move.

"Hurry. Some of them don't have much time." Noland headed for the line of deceased miners.

She looked at the nearest man. Mr. Carmady? She knelt beside him before she realized she'd taken a step. "Doc is on his way. Do you have family here?"

Carmady raised his head enough to see her. "No family." He tried to sit up. "Troubadour's in the mine."

"Lay still. I'll find him for you." She looked around. Plumes of dirt billowed from the mine opening.

"Who are you looking for, Miss Bass?" Zeke took her elbow and steered her to one side.

She lifted her head and stared at Zeke. "I'm looking for Mr. Troubadour."

Zeke put his hand on her arm. "Troubadour didn't make it. He's been identified."

Jo tottered and reached out for Zeke.

"Whoa." He caught her before she sank to her knees.

"He's dead?" She tugged on his shirtsleeve. "How can I tell Mr. Carmady?"

"I'll go tell him."

"No. It's my job." She held on to Zeke's arm for support. "I promised."

A deep breath and deeper sigh fortified her against the nausea churning in her stomach. She knelt beside Carmady and took his hand. "Our friend Mr. Troubadour is. . .he is. . ." She squeezed her eyes closed to keep the tears from splashing on Carmady.

"He's dead, ain't he, Miss Jo?"

She nodded but didn't open her eyes. She felt Carmady's hand touch hers. For an instant, she wanted it to be Zeke comforting her.

"Sir, where are you hurt?"

Jo opened her eyes to see a young man kneeling on the opposite side of Carmady.

He took Carmady's other hand and felt his pulse. "Is this your daughter?"

"Naw, she's my banker." He winked at Jo. "Though I'd 'dopt Miss Jo, if'n I could."

Jo stood. "Are you a doctor?"

"Paul Goldman Jr., at your service." He smiled up at her. "I was visiting an expectant mother when word came about the cave-in. Father's on his way."

Jo bent and patted Carmady's arm. "I'll move on down the line while you take care of *Pa*." Perhaps the dying side wasn't all dying after all.

She saw Zeke and Reverend Noland move along the row of dead men. Zeke didn't act like a fugitive. He wasn't trying to hide and seemed more concerned about the injured than himself.

Jo recorded the men and two women in her row. A few were moved under the surgery tent. She took her list to the reverend.

He tucked the papers in his pocket. "Mr. Keller said he needed to go back to town. I asked him to bring back whiskey and bread."

Jo surveyed the disaster site. The entire town must be here. Whiskey, easy enough, but the bread was a different matter. She scanned each pocket of activity. Where to find bread? She closed her eyes and tilted her nose heavenward to rise above the odors clustered around her. The Russells smelled like wild yeast bread.

"Reverend Noland, Mrs. Russell bakes bread. Cowboy—I mean, Mr. Keller won't know that. I'll get the bread."

She run-walked to town trying with each step to remember where the Russells lived. She stopped and imagined looking north from the bank porch. Her father's depositors were represented on his New York map by numbered short nails. She didn't have the luxury of a printed map, so she had made a mental one.

She smiled and lifted her skirt hem enough to let her run the short distance to the Russell home.

Charmalea answered the door. Moments later she brought out two loaves of day-old bread. "It's all we have, but Mama says you're welcome to it." She looked back into the room behind her. "They brought Dad home a bit ago with a broken leg and arm."

Jo gave her a hug. "Family first, Charmalea. Always." She left and headed toward the cave-in.

Family first. Always. Thad had been alone longer than she'd anticipated. She'd check on him then go to the mine.

She went to the bank's back door. It was partially open. She stepped inside. "Thad?" She dropped the bread and ran to her brother.

He was unconscious in the hallway. Blood seeped from a corner of his mouth and from a cut above his left eyebrow.

"Thad, wake up." She used the hem of her skirt to blot away the blood on his forehead and chin.

He cried out and moved his head away but didn't wake up. She saw no other visible injuries. Good.

She pulled her gun from its double-sewed pouch in her dress pocket and left him to inspect the other rooms.

The gaping hole where the safe had been stopped her in her tracks. A digging bar lay in the rubble of the splintered wooden frame. Drag marks scored the wooden floor from the teller area to the back door. The cellar door lock was too high to break off even with a long pinch point bar. The cellar safe was secure. No more complaints about her stepladder.

The back door had been pried open without breaking the lock.

Jo went back to the unconscious Thad.

Chapter Nine

The front door rattled like someone testing the lock. A couple of light taps followed by louder knocks.

Jo picked up the bread and put it on the kitchen table. Her gun still in her hand, she walked to the front door. "Who is it?"

"Beatrice French. I'm the bank auditor from your father."

Jo put her gun in her pocket and opened the door. "I'm Jo Bass. Please come in, Miss French."

"Call me Bea. I hope this isn't inconvenient. I don't usually arrive on a Sunday, but your father thought it best I get here as soon as possible."

That *was* fast. The telegram was sent five days ago. Why would Father send a woman when Mr. Young was his best auditor?

"I should have waited until tomorrow, but no one was at the boardinghouse." She set her valise inside the door. "Everyone I saw was in some sort of a panic. I thought I'd try finding you or Mr. Bass."

"Oh my goodness. Thad." Jo wheeled and ran back to her brother.

He sat against the wall, legs straight out. His hands cradled the sides of his head. His groans filled the narrow space.

"I'm here, Thad. Who did this to you?"

"Don't know. Heard back door." He touched the corner of his mouth. "Saw no one." He bent his knees to roll over and stand.

"Sit for a few more minutes. That cut on your head may make you dizzy."

He didn't argue. He rested against the wall.

Bea cleared her throat. "What happened? Who is this man on the floor?"

Jo guided Bea to the kitchen. "That's my brother, Thaddeus. We were robbed less than an hour ago. I was at the mine cave-in and he was here."

"Did they break into the safe? Are your funds and ledgers gone?"

"They took the safe. Pried it out of its framed shelf and dragged it out the back door."

She tucked a stray strand from the braid she had looped and knotted on the back of her head. Her side curls were not as long, spiraled, or thick as Bea's mahogany brown hair, but they were as stylish.

Bea sat down at the table. "I must admit you're unusually calm about having been robbed."

"I'm more concerned about Thad. The safe and its contents can be replaced."

"A noble sentiment. But I doubt your depositors will be as understanding."

Jo heard the springs squeak on Thad's bed. "Excuse me a moment." She found Thad stretched out on his bed fully clothed.

He motioned with a feeble hand toward the end of the bed. "Blanket. Head hurts. Can't think."

"You rest. I must take bread to the mine. It's long overdue." She went back to the kitchen, explained the bread to Bea, and together they hurried to the cave-in.

They found Reverend Noland in the surgery tent. He doused a chunk of bread in whiskey and laid it against a man's leg. A woman Jo didn't know tied a strip of cloth around the leg. He and the woman repeated the process on several of the injured.

"It's like the loaves and fishes in the Bible." Noland held up the last whiskey bottle and soggy crumbs from the last chunk of bread. "Exactly enough to go around."

Bea wrinkled her nose and rubbed its tip. "Why did you put wet bread on those people?"

"Some of the men were too close to the exploding wooden beams. A poultice of bread draws out splinters embedded deep enough that removing them by knife could be dangerous in this unclean surgery."

"Are you a doctor, Reverend Noland?" Jo rubbed at a spot of blood on her skirt.

He smiled and wiped his hand on a strip of cloth the woman handed him. "This is my wife, Helen. Yes, I was once Dr. Noland before God called me to heal men's souls instead of their bodies."

"Would you come examine Thad? He has a cut on his head. I couldn't tell how deep, but the bleeding's stopped. The Goldmans need to stay in case more folks are found in the mine."

"How did it happen?" Noland picked up a doctor's bag and held out his hand to his wife.

Jo leaned forward and lowered her voice. "The bank was robbed. Thad was attacked."

"Bank robbed?" A bystander lunged at Jo and took hold of her forearm. "Is my money gone?"

Jo pulled him into a confidential embrace and shushed his outcry. "Your money is secure. If you tell no one, and I mean no one, about what you heard, I'll buy you a whole pie from Mrs. Wakefield."

"A whole pie?" He cut his eyes to look around without moving his head.

"Come to the bank first thing tomorrow morning. Tell no one."

He scuttled off like a horned toad getting to shade.

"Interesting bribe. Not worth a lot in the scheme of things. Do you think he'll keep his word?" Bea plumped her lace collar and adjusted her matching bonnet strap.

Jo raised one shoulder and pursed her lips. "Hope so."

Their services no longer needed, Reverend and Mrs. Noland accompanied Jo and Bea to town. Along the way, Mrs. Sims caught up with them and Jo introduced her to Bea.

Mrs. Sims took Bea's arm like a jolly friend. "You come on along with me and refresh yourself. I'll send someone for your grip."

Chapter Ten

Jo turned her attention to the Nolands. "Any chance you'd consider staying here as the permanent doctor during the week and the reverend on Sundays?"

Reverend Noland linked his arm with Helen's. "We'll take that up with the Lord tonight. Maybe our ministry is being healers of both soul and body."

Thad's snores, once an irritant, were now music to Jo's ears.

Reverend Dr. Noland examined Thad and brought Jo the news. "A few more days of rest are all he needs to recover from his ailment. I cleansed his cut, and it will heal naturally. It may scar."

"Thad'll love that. A testament to his bravery in the Wild West."

Noland accepted the teacup Jo handed him and sat by his wife at the table. "How are you holding up?"

"Fair to middling." She stirred a chip of sugar into her tea. "As soon as Thad is back to work, I'll be fine."

"I saw the debris from the robbery when we came in. Let me help you clean it up." He followed Jo into the banking room.

"Any chance you have carpentry skills, too, Reverend Doctor?"

"What do you have in mind?"

"Put a hinged panel over the hole. We'll purchase another safe and keep the door."

"Clever." He picked up the usable pieces of the frame. "We'll need more wood strips and a door panel."

"Follow me." Jo paused at the kitchen door. "Mrs. Noland, I have some preserves and jams I'd like to share with you."

"When do you have time to put up preserves?" Helen fell in behind Jo and the stepladder she carried.

"They're gifts from families departing Dry Diggins." Jo stood on the ladder and unlocked the cellar door. She lit the two lamps, gave one to the reverend, and went down the cellar stairs.

"Hammer, nails, handsaw, wood, even a spare door." Jo pointed to the tools near the woodpile.

"Ah, it's a split door. Separate the two pieces and you have a finished panel perfect for your project." He wrestled the door upright. "Helen, hand me a hammer and screwdriver."

Helen sorted through the mishmash of tools. Like a nurse assisting a surgeon, she presented the requested tools.

Carpenter Noland struck the door frame and it fell into two equal panels. He put the extra panel back in its place and selected a couple of boards from the woodpile. "Let's go make a safe cover."

Helen lit the way to the stairs.

Jo grinned at the boyish way Carpenter Noland bounded up the stairs. She extinguished the lamps and closed the cellar door. She and Helen gathered the pieces of destroyed frame scattered on the lobby floor and put them in the kitchen firebox.

Helen, as handy with hammer and nail as the reverend, soon had a new frame ready for him to attach the half-door panel.

Jo swept up the sawdust.

The reverend wiped his hands with his handkerchief. "There. At least the robbery isn't obvious." He picked up the tools. "Do you want these back in the cellar?"

"Yes." Jo picked up the reusable wood and carried it to the cellar door.

Light knocks on the windowless back door next to her made her reach for her gun, still snug in its pouch. Yes, she could pull the trigger on an intruder.

"Who is it?"

"Zeke Keller. I need to talk to you. Please let me in."

"Go away. I have no intentions of opening this door."

"It's urgent, Miss Bass."

"Everything is urgent with you, cowboy. Whatever it is can wait until tomorrow."

"That may be too late. It's a matter of life and death."

Reverend Noland stepped up beside Jo. "Life and death? Who's out there, Miss Bass?"

"Zeke Keller. He wants to come in."

"Then by all means let him in. He's not a fickle fellow. This must be serious." Noland put the tools by the cellar door.

She snorted her disapproval but unlocked the back door. "This better be good. I'm letting you in because the reverend vouched for you."

Zeke slipped into the hallway and put his back against the solid wall. "Thanks, Reverend." He turned to Jo. "Can we go somewhere away from the door?"

Jo locked the door and led the way to the kitchen.

Helen poured a fourth cup of tea, and for a few minutes, only the rattle of cup against saucer broke the silence.

Jo sat across from Zeke, Helen on her left, and the reverend on her right.

Zeke pushed his teacup to Helen for a refill. "Thank you for letting me in, Miss Bass. Please let me have my whole say before you put me out." He took a swallow of tea.

Jo rolled her eyes heavenward and back down to stare at him. "This isn't a party, Mr. Keller. Speak your piece then leave."

He took the last gulp and set the cup on its saucer. "First, it's not Mr. Keller. It's Meade. Ezekiel Keller Meade. Sister nicknamed me Zeke when I was little. Mother's maiden name is Keller."

Jo's chair scraped the floor as she jumped to her feet. "Frazier was right. You are a criminal." She pulled her gun and leveled it at him. "Get out of our bank. Now."

Zeke flattened his palms on the table. "Jo, please listen. I'm innocent. I was framed. I'm trying to clear my name."

"Miss Bass, don't be hasty." Reverend Noland mirrored Zeke's posture. "Zeke is not a threat to you. At least hear him out."

"Why are you siding with him? He may be the one who robbed our bank. How do you know you can trust him?"

"I'm a superb judge of character. His and yours. Helen can tell you I'm right."

Helen nodded. "Walt has the gift of rightly judging people. Let Mr. Meade tell his side; then decide what to do."

Jo lowered her gun. "Talk fast. My tolerance is worn thin." She pulled her chair away from the table and sat down. Her gun lay on her lap. How could she have been so foolish to think Zeke was the man who would cherish and treasure her?

"You know the basics. Someone embezzled cash and stole valuables from my New York bank. Evidence was found in my room. The night guard identified me as his attacker."

Helen poured him a fresh cup of tea, and he threw it back like a stiff drink.

"The safe was new, put in the day before. Everything was transferred to it. I had the one key."

"Don't new safes come with two keys?" Jo held out her cup for a refresh.

"Yes, but the company sent one. The representative said the second one would be hand-delivered in two days. The robbery happened that night." He waved off Helen's attempt to refill his cup.

Jo didn't move or break eye contact with Zeke. "What business did you have in town this afternoon that took you away from the mine?" She straightened in her chair.

"I saw the man who I believe framed me leaving the mine. I've been watching him for nineteen days hoping he'd lead me to the proof I need to clear my name. The good reverend here asked for whiskey and bread. I found the whiskey." He grinned at her. "Heard you found the bread."

She didn't return his grin. "And who is this mystery man you've been trailing for over two weeks?"

"That's not important right now. I. . ."

"What's not important right now?" Thad stood propped in the doorway. He glanced around the table. "Meade? E.K., is that you? What are you doing here?"

Jo put her gun in its pouch and sprang to her feet. She led Thad to her chair and knelt beside her brother. "Do you know this man?"

"Yes, we were on the merchants' exchange board together. He's the man I wanted you to meet two Christmases ago."

A vague memory wafted in her brain of Thad extolling the virtues of his fellow board member. A stuffy, stodgy board member from the way Thad described him. Zeke couldn't be that man.

"Thad, he's wanted for embezzlement, fraud, theft, attempted murder, and whatever else. He admits he's a fugitive."

"I read the account in *Bankers' Magazine*, and I don't believe it for a minute." Thad spoke with renewed vigor. "Who do you think did it, E.K.?"

"E.K.? Ezekiel? Zeke? Keller? Meade? My head's spinning. Pick a name and stick with it." Jo darted into the hall quicker than a hummingbird, brought back her counter stool, and set it next to Thad.

Laughter broke the smothering tension.

"Zeke Keller is the best one for now." He leaned toward Thad. "I was framed, but have no proof, and all the evidence is against me." He sat back and locked his hands behind his head.

"Jo, did you tell him about our robbery?"

"No." She craned her neck at him. Her brows scrunched in disbelief. "I didn't think telling a fugitive we'd been robbed was a good idea. He may be here to discover if we suspect him."

Zeke stood, toppling his chair backward. "I didn't rob your bank, or mine." He picked up his chair. "Please believe me."

A grumble from Thad's stomach sent another chorus of laughter around the room.

Jo sighed at the absurdity of the whole thing. "I have a whole baked chicken and hard-crust bread. Let's eat." She pointed Helen to the dish cupboard, the reverend to the water pail, and Zeke to the firewood box, and Thad she ordered to sit still.

Jo introduced Helen to Thad and told him about the safe cabinet repair. "I'm surprised we didn't wake you with all the activity."

"Dead to the world pretty much described my day."

Each time she looked at Zeke, she squirmed at the zing that coursed through her heart. She wanted to believe Zeke, but it would mean he was right about Hawkins.

Thad balanced his chair on its back legs. "Heard a crash. Saw the open back door, got hit."

Thad's chair came back down with a thud. "Jo, how much did they get?"

"Nothing." She speared a pickle and bit off the end.

"Nothing?" Reverend Noland wiped his mouth with his handkerchief. "We fixed the hole."

She finished her pickle. "We were robbed of one heavy, empty safe." She considered the last pickle in the jar. "I sent a special courier to Sacramento yesterday with all transferrable receipts. Ledgers and other assets are secure. Nothing stolen in the robbery."

Thad put his elbows on the table and his head between his hands. "Has Hawkins gotten back? Was the delivery successful?"

"I didn't send Hawkins."

"What?" Thad sat upright. "We agreed he would be our exclusive courier." He reached toward Jo. "You may have jeopardized the deposit."

"I may have saved our bank." She picked up her plate, fork, and knife. "There have been some irregularities in the return receipts. Thad, I didn't tell you right away because you were so sick. At first I blamed myself." She put the dishes in the sink.

"Numbers were transposed. I thought I wrote a seven, but it came back a one. My sheet always went with the deposit and returned to me with the corresponding receipts. They would match, but I remembered the totals differently. I dismissed it because you got sick and I had to run the bank by myself. I'd asked Father for an auditor. Beatrice French arrived late today."

She smiled at her brother. "You suggested I hire Frazier Hawkins to help out as I needed him."

Thad returned her smile. "I met Hawkins on the stage after one of my deposit runs.

His credentials were flawless, and Father confirmed he wasn't involved in any scandals or wrongdoings."

Zeke pounded the table. "Provable wrongdoing." He unballed his fist. "He was my New York bank partner. I believe he framed me, and I think he had a confederate."

Thad half rose from his chair. "He wasn't mentioned by name in the newspaper. He used his Washington job in his references. I didn't make the connection." Thad settled again in his chair. "Jo, Hawkins must not be allowed back in the bank. I'll see to that tomorrow."

Jo hugged her arms tight across her waist.

Zeke sprang to her side. "Jo? What happened? Did he hurt you?" He knelt by her chair. "He said he'd hurt you if I talked to you again. Did he?"

His eyes said he cared for her, but how could he? She'd disdained him.

Jo shook her head, slow and deliberate. The better question was, when had she started to care for Zeke? Her hand didn't shake when she stroked the side of his face. "Call it intuition, but I felt unsettled, confused around him." Her hand rested on his cheek. "It defies logic, but I do trust you."

Thad clapped his hands in snappy bursts. "I knew the two of you should meet. Peas in a pod."

Jo ignored her brother. "What can I do to help vindicate you?"

Zeke accepted a chair from Thad and scooted close to Jo. "I must leave Dry Diggins." He took her hand and flattened it against his heart. "You won't be safe with me here. Hawkins said he sent a telegram to the New York police. It's a matter of time before a recovery agent arrives."

Jo bit her taut lip and willed the tears to stop.

Zeke rubbed his thumb along her cheek. "Will you wait for me while I clear my name?"

She nodded and buried her face in his shoulder.

Chapter Eleven

Jo met Xavier Vasquez on her way back to the bank from Lucy's. He put the saddle-bag over his shoulder. "I have the receipts. Let me carry the pie box for you."

"Did you have any problems?"

"No. It was easy to find the building and Mr. Stapp. He was pleased with your letter of introduction and offered his *hospitalidad*."

"Would you consider becoming a bank courier for me? You may have to travel as far as San Francisco." She unlocked the bank door and pulled the receipts from the saddle-bag before hanging it on its peg.

He put the pie on the counter. "*Sí*, if I can ride my own horse."

"Absolutely. It's twenty dollars a trip, plus your expenses."

"Expenses?"

"Food for you and your horse, a hotel room and stabling, if you stay overnight, and a stagecoach ticket when needed."

"Sí, Senorita Bass. I will be your courier."

"Wonderful. Here's your pay for Saturday's trip. I'll let you know when I need you again."

"Sometimes will you send your friend to give me instructions?"

"My friend?"

"Sí, Senor Hawkins, the man who works here with you."

"No. Your instructions will come from me. Why do you ask?"

"*Papá* says the *senor* asked questions about your visit to the stables. Papá tells him you asked about a horse to ride for pleasure, perhaps to visit a friend in Coloma. Papá was sad he didn't have such a horse for you."

"Your papá is a wise man. Thank him for me."

Xavier gave a slight bow and left.

Thad came into the lobby dressed for outside. "I must deal with Hawkins first thing. Besides, I feel like a walk today. I've been confined too long. The morning air will do me good."

"Let's close the bank, and I'll go with you. You shouldn't have to face him alone. I'm the one he worked with."

"No. Keep the bank open. I'll be fine." He put on his hat and was out the door before she could argue.

A few minutes after ten, the doorbell tinkled. It was the man from the cave-in.

"I come to get my pie. I told nary a word to nobody about the you-know-what."

"You're a true gentleman, sir." She set the pie box on the countertop and opened the

234

lid. "Confident of your trust, I asked Mrs. Wakefield to bake a special pastry for you. She calls it a turnover. You're the first to try her new small pie."

She took out a palm-sized folded pastry and put it in his outstretched hand. "Inside is blackberry jam."

"Never saw anything like this before. All for me, you say?" He sniffed the pastry long and deep.

"Yes." She closed the lid on the pie box and pushed it toward him. "And a whole dried apple pie, too."

The miner bit into the turnover and wiped his mouth with the back of his hand. "There was this one fella who told a startlin' thing this morning at Mrs. Sims's breakfast table. Considering no one knowed about *it*."

She almost laughed at the way he hunched his shoulders and lowered his voice.

"He says if'n the bank is ever robbed, he knows who done it. Sounded like one of those clairvoyants I saw once in a traveling circus."

Jo tapped the top of the counter and nodded.

He licked his fingers after the last bite and swiped his hand down his pant leg. "He says there's a bank robber already in town jest itching to carry off the bank's money."

The miner lifted the box lid and poked his finger into the piecrust. He licked his fingertip.

"Who was talking?" She tried to put a careless tone in her voice.

"He's sort of a dandy." He closed the box lid. "Slicked-down hair with a bushy mustache, but no whiskers."

"What's his name?" Her voice trembled.

"Mrs. Sims called him Frazier. Don't know if'n that's first or last."

She stepped around the counter and walked toward the door. "Save some pie for your morning coffee. If you hear anything about *it*, come to me straightaway."

It took a few minutes to compare Xavier's returned paperwork with the extra duplicate she'd made but hadn't sent. She held it up to the morning sunlight. No changes. No alterations. She had her answer.

◆　◆　◆

Loving the chime of the doorbell, Jo set her teacup on the kitchen table and quick-stepped to the lobby. Bea French stood at her window.

"Good morning, Jo." She walked behind the counter and scanned the room. "No mess?"

Jo pointed to the wooden panel. "Good as new—without the safe. Father can send a replacement."

"That will take months. What will you do in the meantime? You can't leave assets unprotected."

Something in Bea's demeanor didn't sit right with Jo. Bea didn't have an auditor's compulsive attitude.

"Your father said you hired a Mr. Hawkins for busy days until your brother recovers his health. I want to meet him."

"It is true. We've worked together." Jo busied herself with dusting the counter.

"I understand he's quite handsome."

She stopped dusting. "Yes, and quite charming."

"I'm guessing he's more than socially charming."

"He's a gentleman." For an instant, Jo wanted to tell Bea of her suspicions, but something about Bea's interest in Hawkins stopped her. "He loves banking, and with his credentials he would make a good partner."

"Partner?" Bea dipped her head at a suggestive angle. "Banking or otherwise?"

"Banking, naturally."

"Your father asked me to look into this potential investment property." Bea opened her crocheted linen bag and pulled out a piece of paper. "Do you know where this is?"

Jo read the specifications and used her mental map to remember the property's location. "This is the Amerson homestead. They had a run of bad luck and left before Christmas. The property is about a mile out."

"When can we look at it?" Bea rustled the skirt of her forest-green walking dress.

The elegance of Bea's color-coordinated outfit wasn't lost on Jo. She planned to sketch the simple lines and note the rich color and expensive fabric in her sewing journal. "I can go in the morning."

"Tomorrow it is then." Bea retied the strings on her bag. "We'll go to the property before we look at your concerns with the accounts." She pulled her skirt up enough to reveal her delicate but mud-soiled slippers. "I suppose these won't do for traipsing into the wilderness."

Jo's sensible shoes felt rough and heavy on her small feet. "Did you bring stouter footwear?"

"No, I thought the property would be in town. The mercantile should have shoes."

"Don't forget wool stockings." Jo lifted her own skirt. "They make wearing boots much easier, plus they keep your feet dry and warm." For an instant, she thought about mentioning her trousers. But she didn't need that getting back to Father.

"I suppose this attire isn't appropriate either."

"It's warm and substantial. You'll need to hold your skirt a little higher when you walk."

"Jo, how do you stand this forsaken place? You're a woman of culture and breeding. You should be wearing silks, lace, and satins, not. . ." Her assessing gaze said it all.

"I want to own my own bank. This is my proving ground."

"Couldn't you prove yourself in New York or Philadelphia at the best banks in the land?"

"Not when my father owns two of them."

"Point taken." Bea draped her shawl snug around her shoulders. "Until tomorrow." She glanced up at the overhead doorbell. "Hmm."

Jo sat down on her counter stool. *Curious* was the word for this whole thing. If Bea thought the ledgers were taken in the robbery, wouldn't immediate reconstruction be the wisest course of action? What did a bank auditor do in a case like this?

The doorbell pulled her away from more speculation.

A burly man, taller than any she had ever seen, filled the doorway. She expected the floor to give way and drop him into the basement.

"I'm here to consult the owner. Can you get him for me?"

Jo let out a short breath and slid off the stool. "I'm Jo Bass, co-owner of this establishment."

He pulled off his hat and stuffed it inside his coat. "Beggin' your pardon, ma'am. Don't often meet a lady banker in my line of work."

"What line of work is that, sir?"

"Fugitive recovery agent, ma'am. I'm Reeves Danforth. Commissioned by the state of New York." He opened the leather pouch hanging from his shoulder. The wad of paper he withdrew exploded like wedding confetti. Sheets sailed to the floor in all directions.

More agile than she expected, he recovered the papers with alacrity uncommon in huge men. He whisked one of them in front of her.

"I'm looking for this man."

"You look like you've traveled a long ways, Mr. Danforth. I don't have coffee or anything stronger, but I'd be pleased if you'd join me for a bold cup of tea."

"As long as it's hot, I'd drink straight water."

Jo went to the front door, flipped the sign to Closed, and led him to the kitchen.

"May I offer you fresh bread and preserves while we wait for the water to boil?"

He let his leather satchel slide to the floor beside his chair. He peeled off his thick coat to reveal a shoulder holster and badge. "Hope you don't have misgivings about me wearing a gun to the table."

She pulled her revolver out far enough for him to see it. "Don't mind at all." She sat across from him. The face on the flyer was unmistakable. She closed her eyes and willed this moment to pass. It didn't.

"Do you know this man? Has he come in the bank?"

"Yes, and I know where you can find him."

They discussed Danforth's plans and what would happen to the fugitive.

She reopened the bank after Danforth left, but no one came in.

Chapter Twelve

The next morning, Jo looked like she'd taken on a pugilist and lost. A cool compress did little to restore her complexion. The mile walk to the Amerson homestead loomed heavy before her. She dressed for the trip and went to the kitchen to fix breakfast.

How could she face this day knowing what Reeves Danforth had to do?

"You're quiet this morning, and you look like you fought demons all night." Thad chopped up his egg. "You should go for an outing."

"I'm taking Miss French to the Amerson homestead. Father wants to acquire some investment property. Did you know about this?"

"No." Thad frowned. "Did she bring a letter from him?"

"Only the property specification." She handed him a slice of buttered bread. "It's rather odd, isn't it?" She buttered bread for herself.

"By the way, Hawkins isn't in town. The bartender said he saw him ride out day before yesterday." Thad sprinkled pepper on his egg. "When am I to meet Miss French?"

"I'm meeting her at Mrs. Sims's. We'll come back to the bank and go over our ledgers. At first I thought we'd reconcile the ledgers before we left, but she wants to see the property first. And the recovery agent came by yesterday afternoon when you were out." She gave him the highlights of their meeting. "I got busy and forgot to tell you."

The breakfast table chat ended with Thad's offer to clean the dishes and ready the lobby for the day's business.

◆ ◆ ◆

Bea kicked at a rock. "I haven't hiked a mile in my whole life." In her wilderness ensemble, she looked like an Eskimo princess in the Sahara Desert.

"You've danced more miles than that at a spring ball."

Bea waved her booted foot in front of her. "How can you stand to wear these ten-pound weights?"

Jo looked down at her own leather miner boots. "It takes awhile." The double layers of wool socks kept her feet comfortable. "My brother's anxious to meet you. Something about not being sprawled on the floor this time." She quickened her pace. "Let's hustle and we can return before lunch. I'll treat you to a slice of Lucy's apple pie."

"Tell me about Mr. Hawkins. Is he a potential suitor?"

"Mr. Hawkins, a suitor? Oh my." Jo looped her scarf one more time around her neck. "I doubt that could happen." She put her hand on her cheek.

"Has he kissed you?"

"My hand. Etiquette, nothing more."

"That's how it begins. First etiquette then intimacy." Bea's dainty steps took on a military stride. "Would you favor that?"

Jo quickened her pace to match Bea's instead of answering. "Mr. Walters at Empire Mercantile now owns the five-acre homestead, three-room cabin, and mine. The Amersons exchanged it all for a grubstake back to Kentucky."

"Can we go in the mine?"

Jo indicated a cave midway up a small hillside. "See the pile of rubbish next to it? That must be clean-out from a recent cave-in. Can't see much without a lantern."

Bea walked up to the opening. Jo followed close behind.

"How do you know about mining?" Bea took several steps into the cave. "Don't you stay in the bank all the time?"

Jo followed her in. "I listen."

More light streamed from the hole in the ceiling.

Bea moved aside and let Jo move a few feet deeper. "Then listen to this." She picked up an iron rod. "Hawkins will never love you." She swung the rod in front of her like a blind man's cane. "He's mine and so is the money."

Jo stepped back. "He doesn't love me." She kept her eyes on the moving rod. She wore the one dress she hadn't put a gun pocket in yet. "What money?"

"Don't patronize me. I know how Frazier Hawkins works. He told me about this property. Oh, don't look so shocked." Bea hit the ground with the tool. "He'll manipulate your father into purchasing properties, marry you to keep it in the family, and if you or your father don't cooperate, he's prepared for that, too."

Jo backed up again. Her heels hit an outcropping. "Bea...I have no interest in Frazier. I...uh...favor Zeke." She moved one foot along the rock wall until it slipped back.

"You're the first mark Frazier really likes." She raised the rod. "But a grieving father is easy picking, too."

The blow grazed the side of Jo's temple. She fell back against a weak support beam and cratered into an alcove. The wood and part of the roof fell in front of her.

Chapter Thirteen

Zeke replayed the events of Sunday and Monday from every angle. Jo's soft hand on his cheek and her willingness to wait for him dominated his thoughts.

Everything else blurred and jumbled together when he tried to reconstruct the sequence of events. First, Hawkins left with two men Zeke didn't know. They went into the boardinghouse. Zeke purchased four whiskey bottles at the saloon and paid Simon Walters a quarter to deliver them to Reverend Noland. Next, the three men traded the boardinghouse for the saloon and stayed there the rest of the afternoon. How could Hawkins be involved in Jo's bank robbery?

It was time to get out of Dry Diggins. Zeke rubbed his temples. He couldn't risk staying at the boardinghouse or the shack. He'd dodged Hawkins and Danforth, but soon someone would make the connection between him and the wanted poster.

The Monday stages served as hospital wagons for the ambulatory wounded, so he waited for the Tuesday morning stage.

He needed to talk to Jo before he left. Bag in hand, he went down the back stairs to the kitchen door. As he stepped off the stair's last step, he heard Jo hail someone. He crept forward to see who. From the back, the woman looked like a catalog advertisement for a clothier.

He thrust his bag behind the upholstered settee and went out the back door. The woman with Jo was too tall to be Mrs. Sims or Mrs. Wakefield. Not being able to take his meals at the table proved a disadvantage. Was she a lodger?

The women went down the rutted path to the creek. He couldn't follow without being seen, so he lingered at the last possible hiding place—the Vasquez stable.

"Can I help you, Senor?"

Zeke turned. "Xavier, right?"

"Sí, Senor. I remember you from the cave-in. You helped the reverend."

"Yes, and now I need your help." Zeke pointed to the path Jo had taken. "Where does that road lead?"

"To Senor Amerson's mine. It goes no farther."

"How far?"

"Maybe a mile. Do you want a horse to take you there?"

"No. Why would Miss Bass and her friend go there?"

"I wondered that, *también*. Miss French wears boots too big for her feet. The walk back will not be pleasant."

"Did you meet Miss French when the stage arrived?"

"No. I carried her bag from the bank to Mrs. Sims's. Senorita Bass called her an auditor."

"Why would she take an auditor for a walk?"

Xavier turned his palms toward heaven. *"No lo sé."*

Zeke settled in behind a bale of hay overlooking the path. Shielded from the crisp January morning breeze, he drifted into a dreamless sleep.

"Senor, wake up. Senorita French has returned."

Zeke leaped to his feet and looked at the path.

"Not there, Senor. She went to Mrs. Sims's."

"Where did Miss Bass go?"

"She did not return with Senorita French."

"Saddle a horse for me." Zeke took off in a dead run to the boardinghouse. As he rounded the corner onto Main Street, the afternoon stage to Sacramento rocked to a start. He saw a window passenger before she pulled back. No. It couldn't be. He couldn't halt the stagecoach.

Xavier had a horse ready for him when he returned.

Go after the stage. Go see if Jo is at the bank. Go to the Amersons'. Lord, where do I go? Zeke mounted and reined his horse in a tight circle. *Foolish to ride to the mine if she's at the bank. Waste of time if she's on the stage.* Maybe Xavier had missed her. *Lord, a little help here.*

The horse decided for him, trotting down the rutted path.

Chapter Fourteen

Zeke held the reins in one hand, gripped the saddle horn in the other, and pressed his knees tight against the horse's ribs. He bounced and groaned his way to the Amerson homestead.

The horse trotted to the empty hay trough in the makeshift corral.

Zeke dismounted and jogged to the cabin. No footprints marred the dust on the floor. He headed to the outbuilding. Nothing. That left the mine on the hillside.

"Jo Bass," Zeke called in all four directions. He waited then called again. Nothing.

Slide marks scratched up the ground cover alongside the path.

He walked to the mine. Rock and chunks of timber covered all but a foot at the top of the opening.

"Jo Bass." His throat ached, but he continued to yell. "Jo, are you here?" He clawed at the debris in front of him. "Honey, are you in there?" His anguish echoed back at him. He wiped the dirt off his hands. "Jo, where are you?"

Zeke decided to return to town, praying she'd be at the bank. Midway down the hill, pebbles bounced past him and piled at the bottom.

He scrambled back to the mine. "Jo Bass, are you in there?"

A hand popped up in the narrow opening at the top. "Help me."

"I'm here, my darling." He climbed a few steps toward the top of the debris. The sound of earth moving inside made him yell again. "Move back."

A shovel. A scoop. Anything to dig with. Nothing.

He sat down and let his soul center on the single hope of help he had. A hope that hadn't materialized for him in the recent past. *Is this one of those crisis prayers, Lord? Scripture says to rely on You. Why did You let me be charged with a crime I didn't commit? I need You now more than ever. Please help me rescue Jo.*

He rolled to his knees and pushed to stand. A wad of beige whizzed past his head and swung back to hit him in the shoulder before it bounced against the cave-in debris.

Strips of cloth knotted together hung through the narrow opening. A rock dangled from its end.

He cupped his hands around his mouth. "I have it." He braced his left foot against the debris wall, wrapped the "rope" end around one hand, and pulled. Hand over hand he pulled. The rope changed from beige muslin to white linen before he saw Jo's head in the opening.

"Keep climbing, Jo." He kept the rope taut until her waist passed through the hole.

She let go of the rope and slid down the mound on her stomach.

He lifted her to her feet and against his chest. "You're hurt." He eased her back enough to look at the side of her head. "You need a doctor."

She laid her head against his chest again. "Thank God you found me."

He gathered up the rope and led her to the horse. "Wait. What did you use for rope?"

She lifted her skirt enough to put her foot in the stirrup. *Enough* exposed the hem of her trousers. She mounted the horse and laid the improvised rope across her lap. "Wool petticoats make good ropes. Glad I wore my girl-trousers."

He swung up behind her. She nestled against him, and he kissed the scraggly bun semifastened to the nape of her neck. He reached around her to control the reins.

Halfway to town, he felt her body sag and sway in the saddle.

"Jo, stay awake. A little farther, then you can rest." He tied a knot in the reins and hooked them around the saddle horn.

She shifted her weight back to the middle of the saddle. "I talked to God today."

"What?"

"I asked God to help me and He did. He saved me from Bea. He sent you." She rose up in the stirrups and stretched her back. "He's not just for Sundays, you know. He's here all the time."

Zeke waited for her to sit again. "I talked to God today, too. I've been angry because He didn't rescue me from the robbery accusations. But He brought me to you. I must leave, but I know God will take care of us, even if He doesn't vindicate me."

She turned enough to look back at him. "Frazier Hawkins and Bea are scheming to defraud my father and gain control of this bank."

"Betsy. Her name's Betsy."

"Bea is Betsy? How do you know her?"

"I'm convinced she helped Hawkins frame me. I just can't prove it."

"I should've listened to you. It would have saved me a lot of pain." She raised scuffed-up hands.

Chapter Fifteen

Zeke reined the horse away from the stables and headed for the bank.

Dusk gave them enough light to see the throng of men gathered in front of Mrs. Sims's boardinghouse. Zeke stopped the horse and slid off. "Wait here."

He came back a few minutes later. "Do you feel up to listening?"

"I'm a mess, but I can listen."

He held out his hands to help her dismount. "Don't react. Play dumb."

"That's hard for a redhead to do." She dusted off the front of her dress and pushed in a few hairpins. "Any smudges on my face?"

"Adds character."

"Ugh. Men." She used her sleeves to wipe her face. She forgot about her appearance as Zeke led her to the nearest group of men.

"I say we hang 'em." Murmurs of agreement grew louder. "We can use that oak tree in front of Elstner's. It's strong enough."

A man to Jo's right stepped into the center of the group. "What about that Hawkins guy? He masterminded the mercantile robbery. His neck oughta stretch with theirs."

Zeke squeezed her arm. "Shhh."

"Didn't you hear? That New York recovery agent took him into custody."

"He doesn't have authority out here."

Another man stepped up. "I witnessed Hawkins's confession. He robbed a bank in New York and framed his partner, Meade. Convinced the deliveryman to give him the second key and paid for his silence." He spit on the street. "That low-down skunk beat up the guard then threatened him into lying about who attacked him. He wrote it all out and signed it. Said he'd take his chances in court."

The "hang 'em" man added the next layer. "Now the interesting thing is, a woman gave out the alert about Hawkins, his whereabouts, and his appearance. The agent knew about Hawkins's missing index finger."

"That agent better be on his toes. Hawkins is a wily one, that's all I got to say."

"Did he name his New York accomplice?"

"Yes. I took the agent to the telegrapher. Didn't see the message, but the operator said it was a woman."

Zeke tugged Jo away from the rabble-rousers. He took her home. Their quick good-bye left a lot unsaid.

◆　◆　◆

Thad handed a plate of scrambled eggs and bacon to Jo. "You're amazing. After your ordeal with Miss French, you should be resting."

"I must find our bank's missing money. I told Mr. Danforth about our shortages. He said Hawkins claimed to know something about our empty safe and who took it, but denied being part of the robbery. He also said he had nothing to do with our deposit shortages."

Thad set his plate opposite Jo and sat down. He pushed his eggs around, sighed, and let his fork clatter against the plate. "I hate banking. You should be Father's successor, not me."

He speared a clump of eggs but didn't eat it, then pushed back his chair and left the room. He returned with a bulging bank bag and a ledger.

"I took the money, Jo." He put the bag in the middle of the table. "I changed the slips and made it appear you did it."

"Why would you frame me?" Tears muddled her vision as she touched the bag.

"Because Father would forgive you. He would send me to jail." He reached across the table and took her hand. "Sunday I realized that I couldn't let you take the blame. The money's all there. Please forgive me, Jo."

"Of course I forgive you. I love you." She held both of his hands in hers. "How long have you been changing the return receipts?"

"Since the first time I took a shipment to Sacramento. It was so easy, like a game. It didn't feel like stealing. I was relieved not to be behind the counter. When I got sick, I figured you'd be too busy to notice the shortages."

"What did you plan to do?" Jo put her hands in her lap.

"Take the money and be a mountain man, I guess." He drummed his fingers on his chin. "Anything but banking."

Twice she tried to comment on his revelation. Twice she failed.

"I made the correction entry in the ledger yesterday. I'll tell Father what I've done before I leave."

"You made full restitution." She slapped the bag. "This will go on the next shipment." She took her plate to the sink sideboard. "We'll persuade Father to let you quit."

Thad opened the ledger. "This telegram came while you and Miss French were at the Amersons'." He handed her the telegram. "They discovered the overnight robbery at the mercantile shortly after you left."

She read it and laughed.

Auditor Young ill. *Stop.* Arrive 3 weeks. Confirm.

"Father will accept a bookkeeping error from me. I'll send a reply saying error found, hope Mr. Young gets well soon."

Thad brought his plate to the sideboard. "I'm truly sorry, Jo." He hugged her and cried.

"I should have realized you were unhappy. I thought you were jealous and wanted me to fail."

"You love banking. Why would I want you to fail?" He hugged her again.

"You talked about sewing instead of banking. You always urged me to set up shop."

"Father said sewing is your heart's desire. I tried to be supportive."

"I don't want to sew for the public." She lifted her skirt enough to expose her girl-trousers. "Let me tell you how these originated."

They laughed, swapped stories, and planned their day. Thad put the money in the cellar safe, sent the telegram to their father, and came back to report that the mercantile robbers had been hanged.

◆ ◆ ◆

"Mr. Partrich, welcome. Do you have gold for me today?" Jo smiled.

"No, Miss Bass. I need to withdraw a small sum." He handed her a note with the amount scribbled on it.

"Are you traveling?" She opened the daily cash box.

"No. I want to make a china cabinet as a wedding gift for young Dr. Goldman. He will marry in the spring."

The doorbell jingled as she counted out the money.

"They will be so blessed by your gift." She gave him the money. "Anything else, Mr. Partrich?"

"When will you marry, Miss Bass? There are plenty of young men around here for the choosing."

"Oh, not for a while. I still have a lot of lye water to use. Besides, he'd have to love banking as much as I do."

"Don't put it off too long." He pocketed his money and left.

She set the cash box back on its shelf.

"Yes, Miss Bass. When will you be choosing?" Zeke stepped up to the counter.

Jo cocked her head to one side and pasted on a rueful grin. "One must have choices before one can choose." She twitched her lips into a pout.

"Well, I have a candidate for you." He walked around the end of the counter. "I want to be first in line. I'm tired of waiting behind the one at the counter." He held out his hands.

She gazed at his outstretched hands then into his eyes. "It's true, you've never walked straight in before. Always second in line."

"Let's change that. As soon as Agent Danforth sends word that the judge accepts Hawkins's confession, I'll receive a letter of vindication."

She put her hands in his.

Zeke danced her around. "I'm free, Jo. I don't have to run anymore."

The doorbell rang. She stopped their dance and pulled back her hands. "Yes, you do."

She let him gnaw on that while she helped a customer. Two more people came in before she could answer the question etched on his face.

She held out her hands to him. "You must run straight into my arms."

He obliged.

Author's Note

Lucy Stoddard Wakefield, known historically for her two dollar dried-apple pies, lived in Dry Diggins in January 1849 and sold pies out of her home until she purchased a store front on Main Street. Her weekly Whist parties were popular and well attended. Strong women entrepreneurs, Lucy Wakefield and "Josephine Bass" remind us that their successes carved out a path still followed today. Two men were hanged at the end of January, 1849, for robbery of a miner not a bank. In the fall of 1849, Dry Diggins was renamed Hangtown and in 1854 became Placerville, California.

Linda (Lin) **Farmer Harris** and her husband live on a cattle ranch at Chimney Rock in Southwest Colorado's San Juan National Forest. She was the first editor of American Christian Romance Writers' (now ACFW—American Christian Fiction Writers) Write to the Heart Newsletter. Her travels in Mexico, passion for the Harvey Girls and the Indian Detour Couriers, plus her skills as a nationally certified interpreter for the deaf are included in her historical fiction for adult and middle graders. Readers are welcomed to connect with Lin at www.lindafarmerharris.com.

A Sketch of Gold

by Cynthia Hickey

Chapter One

California, 1851

Rose McIlroy blinked away tears as she made the last cut to her hair. Her papa's latest get-rich scheme was the wildest yet, and as usual, it was Rose who would make the most sacrifices. Nineteen years old and she was being shorn to look like a young boy.

After selling their home in Boston, they'd traveled forever on the train to San Francisco, sold every remnant of femininity Rose owned, bought two mules and supplies, and now camped on a bluff overlooking a patch of thick forest. Tomorrow they'd reach Rich Bar, a mining town guaranteed to make them wealthy, or so Papa said.

"It can't be helped, dearest," Papa said, lifting the strands of hair the color of mahogany shot with gold so the wind would catch them. Hair the same shade as her dear mama's had been. "Women are scarce where we're going. I won't have you in harm's way. It's best you look like a lad."

She turned and stared at him for a moment. While she loved him dearly, sometimes she wondered whether he'd taken a knock to the head as a child. His absentmindedness had driven Mama to distraction at times, God rest her soul.

"Very well. Lead the way." She put a foot into the stirrup of her mule named Bob and swung into the saddle. She'd no sooner planted her rump before finding herself lying flat on her back, staring at the mule's belly, with dust gritting her teeth.

"Need to tighten your cinch a bit more, dearest." Papa held down his hand. "That could have been a bad accident."

Rose spit dirt and swiped her arm across her eyes to dislodge dirt caked there. Bad accident indeed. It also did nothing for her sour mood. "I think it best you stop calling me dearest. You wouldn't call your son by such an endearment." She tightened the cinch on her saddle and climbed back on. This time she stayed put.

"Very well. Boy, or Rory, it is." Papa grinned and marched to Fred, his mule. "Onward." He thrust a fist into the air.

Despite her poor attitude, Rose couldn't help but smile at his enthusiasm. Hopefully that, along with God's favor, would see them through the next few months.

With a click of her tongue and a kick of her heels, Rose followed her papa down a steep path to flatter land. As pebbles rolled before them, she gave thanks for the sure-footedness of Bob and glanced to her left where she could catch a small peek at the ocean every few minutes. The ocean was the one resounding positive to her papa's latest so-called adventure.

"Your mama loved the water," Papa called over his shoulder. "You share that love. She'd be right pleased about this latest venture."

Rose doubted that very much, although Mama would have gone along, as always, biting her tongue and praying they didn't lose everything. Rose sighed and shifted to a more comfortable position in the hard saddle.

She didn't know a thing about mining. Neither did Papa. Living in tents and hoping to find gold in freezing water. *Lord, help us.* Her feather bed, parties, and meals cooked by a chef seemed ages ago. Already her hands sported blisters, her nails were chipped, and if she scrunched her nose, the pain of a sunburn warned her it was past time to put on her hat.

"No fretting, dear. . .uh, boy. We'll make a go of this and be rich by Christmas. I guarantee it."

She grimaced. She would hate her new endearment by morning. "All right, Papa."

"Have I ever steered you wrong?"

"No, Papa." *Oh, so many times.*

By late afternoon, a niggling feeling told Rose something was wrong. "Papa? Shouldn't we have reached Rich Bar by now?"

"It's right around the bend. I guarantee it."

"The sun will be setting soon. Aren't there bears in this country?" She thought she'd read about them in the guidebook Papa had given her. "It's growing chilly. Maybe we should set up camp."

"In a bit."

She sighed and continued to follow as she had always done. By nightfall, Papa admitted they were lost and would find their way in the morning. Rather than pitch tents, they rolled up in bedrolls by a fire. Rose tried to block out the rustling of nearby small animals and what seriously sounded like a growl. The fire kept wild things away, right?

"Dear. . .uh, boy?"

"Yes, Papa?"

"It will be all right. I guarantee it."

She smiled despite her reservations. "I know." She did love him so.

"You won't regret leaving Boston. Soon you'll have all the fancy gowns a young woman could want. Wealthy men will seek your hand in marriage. Why, I'll have to beat them off with a stick! We'll be rich, and you'll leave me all alone."

"I'll never leave you, Papa." How would he survive without her?

Marriage wasn't something she thought on anymore. Not since Mama's death of influenza or since leaving Boston with few coins jingling in their pockets. God had abandoned the McIlroys. Her one-line prayers of "Lord, help us" were whispered more out of habit than a desire to converse with God. If the McIlroys were to prosper, or survive until the next day, it would be because of Rose's efforts, not divine intervention.

Papa's snores carried from the opposite side of the fire and mingled with the other night sounds. Rose sat up and put another log on the fire, then poked halfheartedly at the embers with a stick. What if they didn't reach their destination in the morning? What if they wandered the forest until their remaining supplies ran out?

She wrapped her blanket around her shoulders. "Lord, help us."

◆　◆　◆

Jackson Westin checked his saddlebags to make sure his sketching supplies were secure then directed his mule to head down a five-mile hill so steep, there were times he wondered whether the mule's hind legs were in front. When he reached the bottom, he removed his hat to let the breeze cool his perspiration. How did men do that on a regular basis without their heart giving out?

"Whoo-ee, mister. I ain't never seen anyone fool enough to ride down that hill. Most folks lead their mules." A grizzled old man spit a wad of tobacco at Jack's feet.

"Well, that explains it." It probably wouldn't be his last greenhorn mistake. "Where can a man lay his head here in Rich Bar?"

"The Empire is a good place, I reckon. You can't miss it. Has the name painted on the outside wall." The man's watery gaze studied him. "You don't look like a miner."

"I'm not. I'm here to sketch the mining and send the pictures to a newspaper back East. Once I can, I plan on finding a little slice of heaven and building my own newspaper office."

"Them fancy folks interested in us? Well, I'll be hanged." He shook his head and shuffled away.

"Lord, we made it." He slid from his mule and led the animal down a street Jack couldn't wait to sketch. Rich Bar's main road cut through buildings made of canvas, scraps of wood, and a combination of the two. He spotted three doctors' offices, a lawyer's office, a mercantile, and at least ten saloons. From the cursing that issued from the doors, God was needed in Rich Bar. Perhaps Jack could play a hand in bringing Him there and pass his hat come Sundays.

He continued on and stopped in front of a two-story building with a canvas front. Painted in big black letters were the words The Empire. So this was his new home. He shrugged, tied his mule to a hitching post, and stepped inside.

Every wall of the cavernous front room was covered in scarlet fabric. An elegant mirror hung from one wall. Tables covered with green fabric dotted the space. Up four steps, he spotted a straw floor of a room consisting of glass sconces, a large sofa, and carved chairs.

"Need a room?" A bird of a woman approached, wiping her hands on a red calico apron.

"Yes, ma'am."

She nodded, pointed to a book on the bar, and instructed him to sign his name. "You've got the third room on the left, upper floor. Enjoy your stay."

Jack signed the guest log with his full name, retrieved his things from the back of his mule, which a young boy promised to take care of, then climbed the stairs to a hall lined with purple and blue fabric. Colorful but not repulsive. He opened a wood door hanging by leather straps.

In his room sat a bed so large and heavy it had to have been built on the spot. A simple chair sat next to a washstand. Hooks were placed along one wall to hold a guest's things. Not an uncomfortable room, especially after weeks of riding on the back of a mule.

He went to an actual glass window and parted a set of red calico curtains. On the street outside, a group of men greeted a middle-aged man and one much younger. Good-natured ribbing and slaps on the back echoed to where Jack watched. He pushed open the window.

"What do ya mean you were lost?" someone yelled.

"Rich Bar ain't hard to find. Follow the water."

"Or the smells of unwashed miners!"

The boy removed his hat, revealing a head of auburn curls and a sunburned face. A pretty lad. Jack guessed him to be around the age of fourteen. While he looked embarrassed, the older man seemed to think it all great fun.

"We're heading upriver," he said. "Don't want to be crowded when I strike gold. We'll replenish our supplies and head north a few miles. Come on, boy."

The young man's legs wobbled as he hit the ground. Once he had his land legs back, he followed the other man toward the canvas-built mercantile. Jack grinned. He may have just found the people he would use as his models for his sketches. What a better interest story than a frail young man and an enthusiastic father?

Why would such a delicate-looking boy want to come west searching for gold? Both the young and the old looked to be of fine stock. What could have possessed them to give up the finer life for the grueling one of miners? These were the questions those back East wanted answers to. Answers Jack was more than happy to give.

He left the window open and headed downstairs to make sure the boy made good on his promise to care for his mule. If the two Jack wanted to sketch and write articles about were headed north, then Jack needed a reliable means of transportation to get back and forth.

He spotted the mule being led into a corral at the same time he spotted the newcomers heading into the mercantile. He increased his pace to enter feet behind them.

The range of goods available surprised him. Along with bolts of red calico, there were tins of biscuits, flasks of brandy, and boxes of crackers. Not to mention several barrels of pickles and tons of mining equipment.

The two he shadowed approached the counter and filled their saddlebags with dry food items, flour, sugar, coffee, and jerked meat. While the older man carried on a conversation about the amount of gold taken or not taken out of the mines, the boy turned, leaning his elbows on the counter.

He fixed eyes the color of a summer sky on Jack. His breath catching in his throat, Jack nodded at the prettiest "boy" he'd ever laid eyes upon.

"Is there a problem, sir?" The boy raised his eyebrows.

"No, just making your acquaintance. I'm Jackson Westin. Most folks call me Jack."

The older man thrust out his hand. "I'm Roy McIlroy and this is my son, Rory. Pleased to meet you."

Jack explained his mission in Rich Bar. "I'd like to follow the two of you around and send reports to the papers back East."

"Why us?" Rory asked.

"You are the two most unlikely miners I've ever run across." Especially since Jack knew the boy was really a girl, and she was quite lovely indeed. Oh yes, the newspapers would eat her story up.

Chapter Two

"This is it," Papa declared, sliding from the back of his mule. "Feather River. Our home."

Rose glanced at the river rushing past, then searched for a high spot of land on which to pitch their tent. At least they were only a few miles from Rich Bar. If she needed a taste of civilization, such as it were, a short mule ride would accomplish any need she might have for other people. If she were completely honest with herself, she wouldn't mind catching another glimpse of that handsome newspaper man again, either. Hair the color of a field of ripe wheat and eyes as green as a meadow, he ought to sketch self-portraits rather than a skinny pretend-to-be boy with shorn hair. A man as fine as Jack Westin wouldn't take a second look at her.

A flat area about fifty yards from the river provided the perfect place to pitch their new home. Nearby rocks would give them a fire pit.

Already, Papa hunched over at the river's edge, a pan in his hand. He took off his hat and waved it at Rose. "I'll be up in a bit."

She shrugged and unrolled their tent. It didn't matter to her if she unpacked their things. She'd be the one doing the cooking and whatever cleanup needed to be done. It was best she knew where everything was.

By the time she'd finished, Papa had moved upriver a ways. She shaded her eyes and looked for landmarks. She didn't want him getting shot for inadvertently infringing on someone else's claim.

"Howdy." Two men, muddy to mid-thigh, full bearded, with looks in their eyes that sent ants scurrying up her spine, approached where she stood. "You mining alone?"

"My papa's right there." She motioned her head in that direction and took a step closer to the tent where she'd stashed their rifle. She needed to make it a point to keep it close at hand.

Could they see through her disguise? She wet her lips with her tongue and took another step toward the tent.

"It ain't often we see someone as young as you out here," the taller man said. "We've got the claim one over. You need us, you give a holler."

Perhaps she'd misjudged them. Maybe it was nothing more than curiosity about the newcomers that had them staring so intently at her. "I'll do that. Much obliged." She watched them stroll away, then turned to look for Papa. The bank where he'd crouched was empty.

"Papa?" She put her hands around her mouth and yelled.

When he didn't answer, she approached the water's edge. He sat on a rock, pan dangling from one hand, and stared at the water.

"Come sit a spell, dearest." He patted the rock next to him.

"We had company, Papa." Rose sat. "It won't be wise for me to leave our things for long."

"Miner's code. No one will bother our site."

"Not everyone can be trusted." She watched as the sun glittered over the water. "It's a pretty place."

"Full of gold. I guarantee it."

"Looks rocky to me." Rose dug the toe of her boot into the mud at the water's edge. What did she know? She'd never mined a day in her life. Any information she might have came from another book Papa had given her on how to become rich by mining for gold.

"Gold hides in the rocks. Everyone knows that." He stood and stepped onto another rock that jutted over the water. "See that sand right there? There's gold. I know it."

"I'm sure you're right, Papa." Rose stood.

Papa jumped from the rock to stand on another. His foot slipped. He went down hard and rolled into the water.

"Papa!" *Lord, help us.* Rose rushed to the bank in time to see him floating downstream. "Grab on to something." She dashed down the bank, leaping over rocks and debris. "Papa, say something." He did nothing more than bob like a log on the water.

There! A bit of land stretched into the water. She increased her speed, hoping to reach the sand bar before Papa did.

Her booted feet pounded across the dirt. At the end of the bar, she jumped into the water and snagged her father's arm before he was swept past. She linked her other arm around a small tree that leaned over the water, its branches trailing in the water like a man's fingers.

"Help!" Her feet slipped. She tightened her hold on Papa and did her best to keep his head above water. "Please, wake up."

"Take my hand." Jack Westin leaned over, his hand extended.

Rose reached out.

He clamped his hand around her forearm and pulled. She kicked against the water, dragging Papa by the neck of his shirt.

When she reached dry land, she flopped onto her back and gasped for breath like a fish. "See. . .to my. . .Papa."

Jack's gaze searched her for a momen; then he nodded. "Looks like he hit his head. He's got a good-sized knot. Through a rip in his shirt, I can see there is a scrape across his ribs. There might be a crack or two."

"Take him to. . .the doctor, please." She pushed to her feet. "I'll follow."

"Are you all right?" Again he fixed his gaze on hers.

She nodded. "Yes, thanks to you."

"I won't leave you here alone. How long until you're ready to go?"

"As soon as I can saddle the mule."

"Tend to your father. I'll take care of the mule."

❖　❖　❖

Jack thanked God he'd had the thought of checking on the McIlroys to make sure they found their claim all right. If he hadn't shown up when he did, he wasn't sure Rory would have had the strength to pull his father from the water. "His" father. He shook his head at the poor disguise. Anyone who laid eyes on her knew Rory couldn't be anything more than a girl, especially with wet clothes clinging to dangerous curves.

He ducked into their tent to grab her some dry clothing. Spotting the rifle, he grabbed the gun, along with a blue flannel shirt, and rushed to the mule. By the time he had the animal saddled, Rory and her father were stumbling toward him. Good. The man was conscious.

"I'll ride with your father so he doesn't fall off the mule." Jack tossed the dry shirt to Rory. "You might want to put that on."

She buttoned the shirt over the wet one and took the reins he held out to her. "Thank you. Again."

"No problem. Let's get your father to the doctor." Jack helped the older man onto his mule and then climbed on behind him while Rory mounted her mule.

Soon the mules were picking their way along the river toward Rich Bar and one of the town's three doctors. "Good thing I came by," Jack said, admiring the way Rory sat in the saddle. Back strong and straight.

"What brought you by?" She glanced over her shoulder.

"Just wanted to make sure you found your claim, and to find it myself. If I'm going to fashion my articles after you and your father, I need to know where you live."

"About that. . ."

"Please don't say no. The people back East will be very interested."

She sighed. "I don't see how it's any of their business. I suppose you'll be paid?"

"Handsomely. See that hill across the river? I've put a deposit down on that piece of land. Once I have enough, I hope to open my own paper."

She narrowed her eyes. "Is there a need for a paper out here?"

"Maybe not now, but someday, when more and more people flock to the area."

She shook her head. "It'll dry up like every other mining town has." She turned back to the front.

"Don't mind. . .him," Roy said. "No faith, that one. Lost it when my wife died."

"Faith in God or people in general?" Jack hoped it was the latter. He'd almost lost his faith himself once, when his parents died in a fire. But he refused to give in, and instead spent more time in God's Word than before. "I'll be having church on Sunday. I'd like the two of you to come."

"I doubt my boy will come, and I have a feeling I'm going to be set up for a while. Rory, you'll have to work the claim," he called out.

Rory's shoulders slumped, but she didn't turn around. It was almost as if she'd known the course of her future without anyone saying a word. It occurred to him that he'd seen her twice now, and not once had a semblance of a smile teased her lips. Well, third time was the charm, or so it was said. Jack would make it a point to get her to smile and tell him her real name. He doubted it was Rory.

"Don't mind my son. He's a bright lad. If there's gold to be found, he'll dig it out."

"Hush, Papa. Rest yourself. No more foolishness." Rory spurred her mule faster as the buildings of Rich Bar loomed ahead. She stopped at the first doctor's office they came to and parted the curtains that made up the door. Tacked to the canvas wall was a hand-printed sign that read DOCTOR ROBBINS. Seconds later, she peered back outside.

"The doc's here." She hurried out to help Jack get Roy inside.

"Hit your head, did you?" A tall, thin man in a white coat motioned for Roy to lie down on a cot. "That's quite the goose egg you've got."

"Head isn't what worries me," Roy said. "Think I busted some ribs. Hurts to breathe."

"Let's make sure you didn't puncture anything." The doctor bent over the cot and pushed and prodded Roy's midsection until the motions almost caused Jack to feel pain, too. Why couldn't the doctor be a bit gentler? From the paleness of Rory's face, she thought the same.

Roy gritted his teeth and endured.

"Yep, a couple of cracked ribs," the doctor said, straightening. "I'll wrap them up. Give them a week's rest before going swimming again."

Jack followed the doctor to the back of the tent. "I don't think they have money yet. Would you be willing to take a few coins now, and I'll pay you when I come across some funds?"

"*We'll* pay when we come across some funds." Rory stepped next to them and crossed her arms. "We're in a tent, gentlemen. I can hear you."

"That's fine. I'm used to it." The doctor carried some bandages to Roy's cot. "At least you aren't trying to pay with whiskey." The doctor thrust out his hand. "Something is better than nothing."

"I hope to see you at church on Sunday." Jack returned his shake. "I'm holding service down by the river at nine."

"You're a preacher?" Rory's eyes widened. "I should have known." She marched from the tent, leaving Jack with a strong desire to know what she meant by her statement. He'd pray nightly to see her at the service.

Chapter Three

"Take a day of rest," Papa said. "I'd like you to attend that young man's Sunday service and relate back to me what he teaches." He scooted against the wall of the tent, grimacing against the pain in his ribs.

"Someone needs to work the claim." Rose shook her head and handed him a plate of flapjacks.

"The Lord says to rest on the Sabbath. The gold isn't going anywhere. I guarantee it." He poured maple syrup over his breakfast. "You can exchange the bits we found this week into coin while you're in town."

Rose sighed. It looked as if she would be going to church. Well, she didn't have to let the preacher man know she was there. She'd hide in a tree and listen just enough to relay the message back to Papa.

"I heard tell Jackson gave some money to a miner in need so the poor man could head back East." Papa talked around a mouthful of food. "There aren't many people as kind as Jackson in this world."

No, the man seemed too good to be true. Rose pushed her food around on her tin plate.

"I also heard he helped that doctor get rid of that extra liquor and only took a fourth!" Papa shook his head. "After being promised a third. Yep, the world needs more men like Jackson Westin." He pointed his fork at Rose. "You should set your cap for that man."

Rose set her plate aside and grabbed her hat, sure she'd hear more tales of the good Jackson when she arrived in town. There wasn't anyone exploiting Rose's good deeds. She'd given a gold nugget to a saloon girl the other day so she could receive a doctor's care after a drunk miner beat her up. Mama would say not to clash your cymbals on a street corner. That God rewarded the good. Maybe so, but it was nice to receive accolades once in a while.

She leaned over and kissed Papa's cheek. "I hate leaving you here alone. What if you need me?"

"You'll only be gone a short time. I'll sleep until you return."

With one more assessing look, she ducked out of the tent and marched to climb onto Bob's back. She nodded to other miners as she traveled along the riverbank. Many waved their hats in greeting; others shouted in triumph and held up handfuls of gold dust. She nodded and continued, relieved more than she could say that the other men left her and Papa to their own devices.

On the outskirts of Rich Bar a group of Indian women, bright blankets spread underneath them, ground nuts and seeds into something the consistency of flour. The women were entirely naked, except for grass skirts tied loosely around their waists. Rather than be embarrassed, Rose watched them work and bought a loaf of the bread as soon as one came off the fire. Who was she to judge how the savages lived? They were a kind people, nicer than some of the more "civilized" folks she'd met.

Happily munching the tasty treat, she continued into Rich Bar. From the small crowd gathered under a large oak tree, she surmised she'd found the outdoor church service. She continued past, tying Bob to a post outside the bank, then approached a smaller tree to the right of the gathering. Grabbing hold of the lowest branch, she swung herself up and pulled the branches around her to give her protection from Jackson's sight.

"Today, I read to you from the book of Matthew." Jackson's voice rang clear to where Rose hid. "Chapter six, verses nineteen through twenty-one. 'Lay not up for yourselves treasures upon earth, where moth and rust doth corrupt, and where thieves break through and steal: But lay up for yourselves treasures in heaven, where neither moth nor rust doth corrupt, and where thieves do not break through nor steal: For where your treasure is, there will your heart be also.'"

"We need our treasures," someone called out. "How else are we going to eat?"

Another said, "Is that why you give your coins to the poor? Are you trying to buy your way into heaven?"

Jackson held up his hands. "Not at all. This verse tells us not to focus too much on our possessions, but to keep our eyes on God. The Bible also says a worker is worthy of his hire. You can't buy your way into heaven. Salvation is a gift."

"Good," the mercantile owner shouted. "I was starting to think you were one of them *loco* preachers."

Rose smiled. The good Jackson's grin never faded. Instead, he answered questions in a calm voice. The man had to be hiding a secret. No one was this good all the time. She made a vow to find out what fueled his masquerade. Perhaps he was in Rich Bar to swindle the hardworking miners out of their gold. She gasped. What if he'd chosen to supposedly draw sketches of her and Papa in order to take their claim?

Her foot slipped on the branch, and she scrambled to keep her seat. If she were to fall into the middle of the service, she'd never live it down from the miners. They already made jokes about the slight lad trying to do the work of a grown man.

Branches rustled as she grappled for a firmer hold, skinning the palms of her hands in the process. No matter. She'd left uncalloused hands in Boston. Here, hers were as rough as a man's. She straddled a branch, linking her ankles around the limb.

Leaves fluttered around the man preaching the Word of God. He glanced up, his wide-eyed gaze clashing with Rose's. Criminy, she'd been caught.

◆ ◆ ◆

What was that crazy girl doing now? How was Jackson supposed to protect her if she put herself in harm's way on a regular basis? He already spent most of his days perched on a rock, one eye on his sketch pad and the other trained on her as she mined at the river's edge.

Quick as a wink, Rory jumped from the tree, landing on the other side, and dashed away from the church service. Jackson shook his head and passed his hat, grateful for any bit of funds to put toward his new house and to help others. Service complete, and a hundred handshakes later, he headed for the mercantile, disappointed to find out Rory had moved on. He really needed to find out her real name.

There she was. He spotted her coming out of the tent serving as a bank. She tucked a small bag into the front of her shirt and swung onto the back of her mule. As she trotted out of town, Jackson made a dash for the livery.

He'd barely crossed the town limits when Rory popped out of the bushes. "Why are you always following me?"

"You said I could."

"I said you could sketch me and my father. I've changed my mind." She pointed toward town. "Give us one day without feeling like a bug under a magnifying glass."

He needed a different tactic. "Would you like to see what I've sketched so far? I'll be putting some in the post tomorrow."

Her eyes narrowed.

He grinned. The curiosity of a woman was something he could always count on.

"I suppose Papa will want to give his approval." She turned her mule toward her camp.

"This is one of the most beautiful stretches of land I've had the privilege to travel each day," he said. "Trees kiss the sky. The sun casts diamonds across the water. Yes, it's one of God's best creations."

She humphed.

"You don't agree?" He pulled his mule alongside her.

She cut him a sideways glance. "I don't believe silence must always be broken by mindless conversation. But yes, the view is lovely."

He laughed, startling birds from the trees. Getting to know her better was going to be fun. "Why did you hide in the tree during the church service?"

"I only attended because Papa wanted to hear what you had to say."

Not exactly an answer to his question, but he could work with her answer. "What did you think?"

She sighed and glanced his way. "A timely point, considering the drive of the miners."

He wanted to ask about her loss of faith but decided to hold his tongue until she trusted him. Not that she had come right out and said she didn't trust him, but the look in her eyes spoke volumes. What had he done for her to feel that way?

Roy sat outside the tent when they arrived and raised a hand in greeting as Jackson slid from his mule. "How are you feeling?" he asked, approaching the other man.

"Fair to middling. Nice to see you. Sit while Rory fixes us the noon meal." He waved toward a three-legged stool.

"He has sketches for our approval," Rory said, opening a crate outside the tent.

Jackson dug his pad from his saddlebag and pulled the stool closer to Roy. "I think several of my sketches portray life in town and in the camps quite nicely."

Roy flipped through the pages, stopping when he reached one of Rory. Jackson had caught her profile as she watched the sun set over the water. He'd wished for pastels to capture her likeness in color, but it was still a pretty picture. One he intended to keep for himself.

"Oh." Rory peered over her father's shoulder then straightened and met Jackson's gaze with a stern one of her own. "How long have you known?"

"That you're a woman? From the moment I set eyes on you in the mercantile. No worries," he said. "I won't send that sketch to the papers."

Roy closed the sketch pad and handed it to Jackson. "I want my girl's secret kept."

"My lips are sealed." He slid the pad back into his saddlebags. Any fool could see the softness in the curve of her cheek, the graceful lines of her neck. He shook his head. That was the main reason he kept so close to the McIlroys. He couldn't risk anything happening to Rory. He turned. "What is your real name?"

She squared her shoulders. "It's Rose."

It suited her. She was beautiful, with sharp thorns if anyone got too close. "I won't say a word." He rubbed his hands together. "What's for lunch?"

"Biscuits and jerky." She handed him a plate. "I've beans on for tomorrow. You're welcome to them if you fancy breaking a tooth."

"Does she ever smile?" he asked Roy.

"Used to all the time. But my girl's happiness fled with the death of her mother and thinking she's responsible for the decisions of an old man. I think she smiles in private now in order to keep her stiff upper lip."

"Someone has to take care of you." She patted his head. "I don't mind. It isn't a hardship caring for someone you love."

Roy took her hand and kissed the back of it. "My dearest."

The love between father and daughter tugged at Jackson's heart. After the death of his parents, he'd been raised by a fun-loving aunt, but she, too, was gone now. He'd give all the gold he had in the bank to find a love like the one between Rose and her father.

Someday God would give him a woman Jackson could give his heart to. He only needed to be patient. He studied the lovely features of the woman in front of him. If those lips were ever to part in a smile, Jackson would be a lost man for sure.

Chapter Four

R ose!" Jackson pounded up the riverbank to where she mined. "We need you in town."

She straightened, wiping her hands on her brown wool pants. "What for?"

"There's a woman having trouble birthing, and the only doctor not out helping someone else is drunk as a skunk." He grabbed her mining gear and headed for the tent.

Her blood ran cold as she dashed after him. "I don't know anything about birthing babies. Besides, she won't let a young boy help her."

"You'll have to let her in on your secret." He cast her a solemn look. "She's going to die if you don't help."

"But..." She sighed. Even not knowing anything about helping a woman have a baby, she couldn't turn down a cry for help. "Saddle Bob. I'll let Papa know."

"I heard and I'm coming with you." Papa carried a black bag in his hand. "I studied a bit of medicine during one of my ventures. Rose and I are better than nothing."

Lord, help us. Papa's adventures rarely turned out well. Still, a woman had instinct, right? An intuition to tell her when something was wrong? Rose would have to rely on that. "But...your ribs."

"Are healing every day. Stop squawking and let's go." Papa gave her a stern look that brooked no argument.

Soon, Bob and Fred were saddled and the McIlroys thundered toward town behind Jackson. The closer they got to their destination, the more Rose's apprehension grew until her shaking hands could barely hold the reins.

They pulled up in front of a ramshackle cabin so poorly built that light shone through the cracks in the wall. A thin, grizzled man met them on the porch.

"You a doctor?" He eyed Papa.

"I am today." Papa slid from the mule and motioned for Rose to follow. Rose swallowed against the mountain in her throat and squeezed through the narrow door. A girl around the age of five played with a doll on the dirt floor. She never looked up as the others marched toward the one bed in the house.

The woman on the bed was massive. She rolled in agony, clutching her stomach. Her triple chins quivered with each wail from a mouth thrown wide. Rank sweat poured from the folds of her skin.

Rose shrank back.

"There now, Mrs. . . .uh, find out her name, dearest. Let's see what's going on here." Papa pulled aside a threadbare blanket. "Just in time. I see the baby's crown."

The woman mouthed obscenities and screamed.

"Her name is Mrs. Woodburn," Jackson called, before ducking back outside.

The coward. Rose glanced around to see what she could do. They'd need hot water and rags. A blackened stove in the corner would provide one; the second was nowhere to be found in the hovel. "Clean rags, Jackson!"

She lit the stove under a pot already filled with water and accepted the knife Papa handed her.

"Sterilize that."

She nodded and held the knife deep in the flames. When the tip glowed red, she handed it back, keeping her gaze averted to give the woman a bit of modesty.

Mrs. Woodburn grasped her hand. "Get it out." She squeezed, grinding Rose's bones together.

"My papa is doing his best. Nature must take its course." She dabbed at the woman's forehead with a corner of the blanket.

"Here." The formerly silent child handed Rose what looked like Jackson's blue flannel shirt. She grinned, then skipped back to her doll and copied the actions of her mother.

Rose's eyes widened. Mercy. A child pretending to give birth. She'd seen it all. She met her father's amused glance.

Papa shrugged. "She's an odd child, I've heard."

The wail of a newborn filled the tiny cabin. The baby's father gave a whoop from outside. The mother's eyes closed.

"It's a boy," Papa said. "Take the child, dearest. Mother isn't doing well."

Rose's eyes widened as blood spread under the woman. She cradled the newborn to her chest and made her way to the rickety kitchen table. Cleaning the infant was a job she could do. By then, the mother would be ready to nurse. She had to be. Rose had nothing else to give the poor baby.

The newborn son wailed in protest as Rose wiped him down, proving there was nothing wrong with his lungs. He had to be the largest newborn she'd ever laid eyes on.

"Leave the child. I need you." Papa waved her over.

Rose's legs trembled as she knelt next to him. "What do I do?"

"Hold these rags here. We've got to stop the blood." He dug in his bag, pulling out a needle and catgut. "That big boy tore her up good."

Rose glanced at the woman's pale face. "Is she going to die?"

"She might. It isn't looking good. The boy?"

"He seems healthy." What would the poor thing do without his mother?

The little girl peered over Rose's shoulder. "Mama dead?"

"No, honey." Rose shook her head, pressing the cloths against the woman as hard as she could. "Go play."

The child shrugged and went to stare at her new brother. "He's loud."

Mrs. Woodburn took a shuddering breath, then no more. Tears pricked Rose's eyes as she pushed to her feet, bloodstained hands held out in front of her.

"Fetch the husband," Papa ordered.

Hands shaking, Rose stumbled outside. She stared through her tears at Jackson and Mr. Woodburn. She shook her head.

"My wife!" The man shoved into the cabin.

"Rose?" Jackson caught her as she fell and lowered her to the top step. "Tell me what to do."

"I don't. . .know. My hands. . ." She held them out to him.

"Come." He took her by the elbow and led her to the river. "I'll clean them for you."

He ripped off a sleeve of his undershirt and, as tenderly as she'd wiped the newborn, cleaned her hands. "I'm sorry, Rose. I had no idea you would have to go through something as horrible as this."

◆　◆　◆

Her tears were almost his undoing. When he'd heard of Mrs. Woodburn's troubles, he hadn't thought twice about fetching Rose. There weren't many women in Rich Bar, and the innkeeper had refused to come help the woman she'd rivaled with since arriving more than a year ago. He'd thought of one of the saloon girls, but thought perhaps Rose might know a bit more about nursing than they.

Once her hands were clean, he drew her close and rocked her like a small child. A little girl approached them and sat in the dirt next to him. She stared out at the water without speaking. A good thing. With Rose in his arms, Jackson's thoughts had taken a dangerous turn.

What would Mr. Woodburn do without a wife and with two children? The three sat and watched the water, Jackson resting his chin on Rose's curls until Roy joined them. He squatted in front of his daughter.

"There was nothing we could do." He cupped her cheek. "At least the babe is fine."

Rose nodded and sniffed. "A big, healthy boy."

"Mr. Woodburn will take the children to San Francisco where his wife has family. He wants us to watch his claim for him."

"One more thing to do," Rose murmured. Then, seeming to notice for the first time that she sat on Jackson's lap, she scampered to her feet, her cheeks pink.

He sighed, missing the feel of her immediately. "I'll escort you home."

He reached over and ruffled the little girl's hair before standing. She giggled and raced for the house. A strange child, indeed. Perhaps she didn't understand her mother would no longer be around to care for her.

"Come for supper, Jackson. We've earned it," Roy said.

"Let me buy the two of you dinner at the Empire," he offered. "Rose shouldn't have to cook after an afternoon like this one. Wait for me." He rushed into the house and pulled some coins from his pocket. "Mr. Woodburn, something to help you get the young ones settled." He dropped the money into the grieving man's hands.

"Much obliged. I need a wet nurse, though."

"I think one of the saloon girls is nursing a babe. I can check for you."

The man frowned. "No help for it, I suppose. Much obliged."

Jackson nodded and hurried outside. "I need to stop at the saloon."

"A drink after a day like today is mighty tempting," Roy said. "But it's a bad habit to get into."

Jackson laughed. "One of the girls gave birth a while back. I'm hoping she'll care for the new babe."

Rose shot him a quick look. "You're unbelievable, Jackson Westin. Does nothing rattle you? Do you ever have an unkind thought or do a bad deed?"

"I had some impure thoughts when you were sitting on my lap." He winked and rode ahead of them as she gasped.

By the time he joined the McIlroys at the Empire, he was a few dollars poorer as the saloon girl wanted payment to do a good deed. Money well spent in Jackson's mind. The poor child needed to eat. Maybe, in God's wisdom, Mr. Woodburn would take a new wife, saving not only his children but an embittered woman from a sad life. It could happen, and did, all the time.

They were seated at a table for four and informed the only thing on the menu for that day was rabbit stew. Jackson shrugged. It still kept Rose from cooking. Since she still looked a bit peaked from the afternoon, he figured they'd eat anything palatable.

"Don't say such things," she hissed as he sat next to her. "If someone heard or saw, my disguise would be no good."

"It's hard for me to look at you as a boy when you're a beautiful young woman," he replied with a grin.

Her face flushed. "Papa, make him stop."

Roy laughed. "Maybe it's time for you to put aside the pants. If Jackson is interested—"

"*I'm* not interested!" She glared at them. "If my true identity becomes common knowledge, there will be no end of eager suitors. No, thank you." She slapped the table.

"No need to get defensive," Roy said. "Just putting the idea out there."

Jackson stared at a burned spot in the wood of the table. Was it the idea of court-ing itself that was disagreeable to her or the fact it was Jackson who was mentioned? It shouldn't bother him, not with her views on his faith, but it still pained him to think she might find him undesirable. It was time to lighten things up.

"The first time you smile at me, Rose McIlroy, pants or not, you'll find me asking Roy for permission to court you."

"Are we here to eat or torment me?" She narrowed her eyes.

He grinned. "Maybe a little of both."

She huffed and straightened as plates brimming with meat, vegetables, and a thick broth were set in front of them. "Let me eat in peace. This is a rarity."

"As you wish." Jackson dug into his meal, suddenly ravenous. Teasing Rose sure worked up an appetite.

He nudged her foot under the table, chuckling as she snatched it back. Oh yes. Jack-son was going to court Rose whether she liked it or not, and he was going to show her just how much God loved her. When he accomplished that. . .he'd be on bended knee in front of her with a ring in his pocket. He couldn't imagine any other woman sharing his dream of a home on the hill overlooking the river.

"Stop staring at me as if I'm a choice side of beef." She kicked him.

"Oh, my dear, but you are simply delicious." If she were to put on a dress, he'd lose his mind.

Roy leaned back in his chair. "I don't know what's going on between the two of you, but I'm going to enjoy my seat at the show."

No more so than Jackson.

Chapter Five

Several weeks had passed since the day of Mrs. Woodburn's death. Since the grieving widower had grabbed at the chance to make the wet nurse of a saloon girl his wife, Rose hadn't had to watch the man's claim after all. Now, with Papa healed, she had more idle time on her hands than she liked. Time she spent thinking way too much of Jackson.

She cast a sideways glance to where he perched on a rock with his infernal sketch pad. If he could make a sketch out of gold, the man could build his house and find a wife, leaving Rose alone.

She stuck her finger in a hole in her pants. She needed new clothes, but the thought of purchasing more pants and men's shirts made her shudder.

What would she do if Jackson moved on? After accompanying Papa to several church services, Rose felt God tapping on her shoulder, slowly healing her from the pain of Mama's death. Perhaps. . .there was a reason they were mining this section of Feather River. If Jackson had his say, he'd tell her it was all part of God's mighty plan. Maybe it was. She'd be patient and see how it played out.

Picking up the pan next to her, she moved to the water's edge, ignoring Papa's protests that he was able to mine and there was no need for her to put her hands in the icy waters. If she didn't do something productive, she'd lose her mind and head to Rich Bar to buy a dress. She was quickly growing to hate the itchy wool pants. Not to mention, she wanted to see Jackson's reaction when she actually looked like a woman.

She ducked her head to hide a smile and dug the pan into the sand on the river bottom. The sight of her in a dress might actually make him speechless. She swirled, dumped, and repeated, almost missing a chunk of gold the size of the nail on her pinky finger. She clutched it between two fingers and held it to the sunlight before dropping it into her breast pocket. Slowly but surely, their funds at the bank grew. She feared it only fueled Papa to keep mining. How much would be enough for him? She'd seen the way greed and the quest for more ate at a man, leaving but a former shadow of his past self.

Two hours later, and more gold in one morning than they'd mined in weeks, she straightened and popped her back. As she turned, she noticed Jackson staring at her with no pretense of sketching.

"Arching your back doesn't do much good for your disguise," he said, grinning. "But it does improve the view."

She groaned and marched to where Papa mined upriver. The man played havoc with her emotions. "A good day for me." She dumped what was in her pocket into the tin can Papa used to collect the day's work.

"We'll be rich before winter. I guarantee it!" He bounded to his feet and grabbed her in a hug. "You have the Midas touch, my dear. We're equal partners. I'll let the bank know to put half in your name."

"You don't have to," she said, her words muffled by his chest. "We're family."

"Someday you'll find a man to marry, and I'll be alone."

She shook her head. "We stay together." If she married, and it was a mighty big *if*, then Papa would come with her. What would he do without her?

"I've worked up a hunger," Papa said, releasing her. "Ask Jackson to stay for supper."

"Like he does every night?"

"He contributes to the meal. This morning he brought a tin of biscuits and some of that stew his landlady made."

True. Jackson did help. She peered around Papa to where the other man had returned to sketching. They should have put a time limit on how long they would be his models. If she were honest, she wanted him to come around because he enjoyed their company, not because he could make money off their story.

"Perhaps we should put down roots here," Papa suggested as they strolled arm in arm to the tent. "It's a beautiful place, and I guarantee it will grow."

"Most mining towns don't. They wither and blow away like dust."

"Jackson seems to think it will stay. That's why he's purchased the land across the river. Wouldn't you like to give up our wandering ways?"

"I would. Where would we build our house?" She glanced up and down the river to where dozens of others mined.

"There's a pretty little piece of land behind Jackson's property that shares a creek with his. It's got a lovely stand of cottonwood trees." Papa perched on a stool. "I'm getting old, dearest. I want to settle down. Maybe find another wife."

She stared at him as if he'd grown another head. "Where do you intend to find that wife?"

"I could marry one of the saloon gals."

She clapped a hand over her mouth. "You wouldn't!"

He shrugged. "Most likely not. Perhaps I'll put a notice in the paper."

She knelt in front of him. "Aren't I enough, Papa?" Her heart sank to her knees.

"I miss your mama." He raised sad eyes to hers.

"You can't replace her."

"No, but I can ease my loneliness. There's a need in a man that a daughter can't fill."

She stood. "The day you bring home a wife is the day I start wearing a dress." She ducked into the tent to retrieve dishes for their meal.

Plopping onto her cot, she covered her face with her hands. Instead of her leaving Papa, he was going to leave her. What would she do then?

Jackson's deep voice rumbled through the opening in the tent. It might be a good time for her to rethink her opinion on being courted.

◆　◆　◆

Jackson stirred the pot of stew in front of him and waited for Rose to emerge from the tent. How would she react to just the two of them at the meal?

"Where's Papa?" She handed him a plate.

"Went to town to send a telegram."

She paled. "He's really going to do it."

"Do what?"

"Send for a bride." Her shoulders sagged.

"I know of a widow woman in San Francisco who would be perfect for Roy." Jackson glanced in the direction the man had gone. "I could write to her. The thought of him getting hitched doesn't seem a favorable one to you. Perhaps knowing the woman is a good one will ease your mind."

"Stop trying to help!" She tossed her plate to the ground. "You don't always have to help." She covered her face with her hands and raced for the water.

She hadn't gone far before she tripped and fell. Jackson was immediately on his feet and at her side. "May I help you up?" He raised his eyebrows. He'd be danged if he'd help her without asking first. Not after her little outburst.

"Shut up." She slapped his hands away and sat where she'd fallen. "I'm sorry. I'm a bit cross. I tend to get this way when the future is uncertain." She wrapped her arms around bent knees.

"You're bleeding." He pointed to where she'd skinned her knees through a hole in her pants. "Let me." He reached for her.

"Stop. Please." She raised tear-filled eyes to his. "What is it about you that makes me insane? No one is as good as you all the time. Tell me your secret."

He sat next to her, taking one of her hands in his. "God, mostly, and a desire to be the man He wants me to be. You're a good woman, Rose. Folks are always telling of how you help the saloon girls and the natives."

"It's the right thing to do." She rested her head against his shoulder, sending his heart soaring. "I don't care if anyone sees us. I need you to just sit here with me."

That was something he was more than happy to do. He put an arm around her shoulder and pulled her closer. They sat and watched the sun descend past the trees. Jackson wanted to do that very thing with her every night for the rest of his life but wisely held his tongue. Now was not the time to tell her of his feelings. He grinned. Not until he coaxed a smile out of her.

"The front of my house is going to face the water," he said, keeping his voice low as he might speak to an easily spooked horse. "It'll have a big window in the front and another in the back to watch the sunset. A fireplace will take up an entire wall in the parlor. I'll order roses to plant around the necessary to help hide the smell, and I'll build a breezeway to the kitchen to keep the heat out of the main house. I'll build five bedrooms and fill them with children."

"Alone?"

He chuckled. "I'll need a wife to help with that part."

"You have grand plans, Jackson. It'll be a beautiful place." She took a deep breath. "I suppose it's time for me to make some of my own."

"What are your dreams?" He turned her to face him, her features in shadow.

She shrugged. "I've never made any. When Mama died, Papa was my future. Now he may not need me much longer. I've some thinking to do. Perhaps Papa is right and Rich Bar will grow. They'll need a schoolteacher. I could teach."

"I'm going to continue my work as pastor here." He stood and pulled her to her feet. "I'll need a wife for that, too."

"Maybe you should put a notice in the paper like Papa." She pulled her hand free and headed for the tent. "I'm afraid supper is a bit overcooked."

He'd eat burnt leather if it meant more time holding her in his arms. He started to ask her what she had against him as a suitor but held his tongue. Time would bring all things to light.

They ate in silence, only lifting their heads when they heard Roy's whistling as he rode up the trail. He unsaddled the mule before joining them. "Notice is sent. Now we wait." He rubbed his hands together.

"Jackson knows of a wife for you." Rose set her plate down and ducked into the tent.

"You do?" Roy took his daughter's seat and added more stew to her uneaten portion. "Why didn't you say so?"

"You didn't tell me you were interested in finding a wife." He pulled his gaze away from the tent. "Mrs. Miller is a godly woman, thirty years of age, with two children ages twelve and fourteen. Her husband died in a boating accident. I'm sure she'd be more than willing to correspond with you. I'll send her a telegram in the morning."

Roy grinned. "Well, things are moving mighty fast. My Rose would love siblings."

"Who says?" she shouted from the tent.

Jackson laughed. "She's a bit put out."

"I know." Roy sighed. "She's put her efforts into caring for me; now she has no dreams of her own. I need to find her a husband, Jackson."

"I'll find my own husband!" Rose slapped the tent wall.

"Wonderful," Roy said. "That's decided. I saw you started building on your house last week."

"Yes, sir." Jackson wrenched his gaze away from the tent, wanting nothing more than to head inside, drag Rose out, and find someone to marry them. "I hired some down-and-out miners. Want me to find you some?"

"I reckon that's a good idea. If I've got a family coming soon, I need to be prepared." His smile faded. "My Rose Marie, that's my dearly departed, would be pleased to know I won't spend my older years alone. I've waited too long to fulfill the promise I made her as she died. But a man's heart needs time to heal."

Jackson knew that for a fact. He also knew that if Rose chose someone else, he might never get over the heartache.

Chapter Six

R ose."

She turned from the cook fire as Jackson rushed toward her.

"The first paper I'm published in." He thrust it at her. "They want many more."

She snatched it before it fell into the fire and sat on a stool. The sketch of Rich Bar was exquisite in detail. Those who looked upon the drawing would feel as if they strolled the dirt streets. On one edge, Jackson had drawn her and Papa standing under the oak tree where Sunday services were held. She'd recognize the ratty hat she wore anywhere. Her eyes scanned the article.

"Folks really are interested in me and Papa. How strange." She read of how subscribers wrote to the paper wanting to know more about the young man and his father who seemed so out of place in the mines. She huffed and handed the paper back to Jackson. "You did well."

"Yep, not a soul can tell you're a woman from that sketch." He folded the paper and stuck it in the back of his pants.

A commotion on the trail pulled Rose to her feet. A trail of mules, ridden by Papa, a thin woman, and two equally skinny kids, plodded toward them. "They're here." Rose took a deep breath and clutched the top button of her shirt. "That means there will be a wedding tomorrow."

Jackson slipped his arm around her waist. "I'm here to help. You don't have to adjust alone."

"Thank you." She still didn't know how anyone could be as kind as him, but she thanked God for bringing the handsome artist-preacher to Rich Bar. She took another deep breath and, on trembling legs, stepped forward to meet her future stepmother and siblings.

"Dearest!" Papa slid to the ground. "Come meet Ethel. This is Daniel and Sophie." He pointed at the children.

Ethel smiled, the action erasing the tired look on her face. "I'm pleased to meet you."

"Likewise." Rose peered around her at her silent offspring. Papa had chosen to build a house cut into the side of a hill rather than take the time to build one from wood. She counted five mules loaded with supplies. They were going to be crowded.

"I'm going to take them to the house," Papa said. "We'll return shortly. You and I can sleep in the tent until things are official."

Rose nodded, slipping her hand into Jackson's. Just the touch of him grounded her, reassured her that things would be fine. "I'll fix some stew."

"Just this time," Ethel said. "Then the cooking will fall to me."

What would Rose do with her time then? All that was left was mining, and with winter approaching, the water was icier than ever. She squared her shoulders. Now was not the time for self-pity. The grin on Papa's face was worth any sacrifice Rose might make.

She glanced up at Jackson. "I don't know how to do anything but cook and mine."

"What have you always wanted to do?"

It was hard to think with the warm look in his eyes settled on her. She pulled her gaze away. "Sew fancy dresses, I think." She shrugged. "Not much use for that out here. Funny, isn't it? That I desire nice things when I wear rags? I told you I've never had time to dream."

"There's no time like the present to begin." He headed for his mule and pulled a sketch pad from his saddlebag. "Here's a blank pad and a charcoal. Start designing."

Was it possible? With someone else to care for Papa, could Rose actually indulge in herself? "I don't know where to start."

He took her hand and led her to the stool. "Just put charcoal to paper. The image will come."

"What if I'm no good?"

"You won't know if you don't try." He planted a kiss on her forehead so tender, tears sprang to her eyes. "Roy told me you would put on a dress when he got married. Draw the one you plan to make."

She scoffed. She'd bought yards of blue calico just last week and purchased a fairly new petticoat from one of the saloon girls. She'd been sewing on the dress in private. She already had something to wear to the wedding in the morning. But. . .perhaps if she were to dream. . .she could design her own wedding gown for that far-off, maybe, day.

The day passed and Rose completely forgot about supper until Papa and his new family tromped to the fire. She gasped and clapped the pad closed. It would be leftover beans and chunks of tinned meat. She'd never let her chores slip before.

She ducked into the tent and grinned. Perhaps dreaming wasn't something forbidden for Rose after all. Arms full of supplies, she headed back outside, relieved to see Jackson had started the fire.

"I'm so sorry," she said, setting things on a board stretched across rocks. "I lost myself in the day."

"No worries." Ethel smiled. "It will give us time to get acquainted while I help you."

Rose wasn't much for small talk, but if it made Papa happy, she'd do her best. She twisted the top off the canned meat and dumped it into yesterday's beans. A sprinkle of precious salt and a dash of pepper and. . .were those carrots and an onion? Her mouth watered as Ethel opened a pouch she'd brought along.

"Straight from my garden." She made quick work of cutting up the vegetables and adding them to the beans. "I've brought seeds with me. We'll plant them together come spring."

Rose smiled.

◆　◆　◆

Jackson's heart almost pounded out of his chest. All it took to make Rose smile was a handful of vegetables? If he'd known that, he would have traveled days to bring her every variety known to man. Her wide smile showed even, white teeth and lit up an already beautiful face.

Her smile didn't fade as the meal progressed. In fact, it spread every time she lifted the lid on the pot and took a sniff.

"What?" She glanced his way.

"I. . .uh. . .nothing." He turned and headed for the water.

He stared at the setting sun casting glimmers of color across the ripples and tried to find a way to untie his tongue so he could do the very thing he'd promised himself he would do. Ask for permission to court Rose. He knew Roy would grant him permission, so why the hesitancy? He acted like a boy in short pants!

He picked up a flat rock and skipped it across the water. Tomorrow would be the time to ask Rose if she would accept his courtship. Times weren't as rigid as they used to be, but when it came to matters of the heart, Jackson preferred the old-fashioned rituals.

Spotting Roy taking some garbage to the heap behind the tent, Jackson hurried toward him. "Roy? A word?"

"Anything, my boy." Roy dumped the onion skins and carrot tops.

"I'd like to court Rose."

"I thought you were already doing that." He cocked his head. "I've seen the two of you wrapped in each other's arms by the river. If she hasn't slapped you already, she'll be open to something more meaningful. I guarantee it. I have no objections."

"Thank you, sir." Jackson shook Roy's hand and walked with him back to the supper fire.

Rose handed him a plate. "It's delicious. I have no idea why I was so worried about not cooking. Ethel is a marvel."

"You'd be just as good with more supplies." He grinned and found a place to sit, motioning for her to sit on the log next to him. "Another day and we can sit around a table."

"Maybe in your house. Ours is barely big enough for the five of us."

"Are you saying I'm too big?"

She flashed that amazing wide smile again. "At over six feet tall, I'd say you are."

"What changed with you today?" He studied her face. One half was in shadow, the other lit by the fire's glow. "You're grinning like you'll never stop."

"I owe it all to you." She put a hand over his, sending heat rushing up his arm and straight to his heart. "Spending hours hunched over a sketch pad dreaming erased years of weight off my shoulders. Then, to have Ethel arrive with vegetables. . . Why, the day can't have gotten any better. Thank you for encouraging me to stop work long enough to dream."

"My pleasure." He lifted her hand and kissed her palm. "What did you dream of?" He hoped it was him.

"That, Mr. Westin, is a secret." She spooned a mouthful of beans into her mouth. "Delicious. I still need to find something meaningful with which to fill my days, when I'm not mining, that is, but there will always be time to dream from now on."

"Well, I reckon I wondered about you." A man stepped from the shadows. "I thought it suspicious that a grown man was spending so much time with a lad. Now"—he flicked one of Rose's curls—"I see the lad ain't a lad but a comely lass."

Jackson stood and planted himself in front of Rose. Roy left Ethel's side and joined him.

"You can't fault a man for caring about the welfare of his daughter," Roy said, holding up his hands.

"I can if it keeps me from seeing a pretty woman every day." He sneered, missing one of his front teeth.

Jackson felt Rose put a hand on the small of his back. "She's spoken for, mister."

"By who?"

"Me."

Rose gasped.

"What kind of man lets his woman dress like a boy?" He shook his head. "No, I reckon you're telling a lie. I aim to spend time with that lass. If not her, then the old woman or that younger gal."

"I never in all my born days"—Ethel marched up, a frying pan in her hands—"heard a man call me old. Now git, before I bash in your head."

Rose stepped next to her. In her hand was a sizable rock that could dent a man's skull. "And if that doesn't convince you, this rock will. Do you still think harassing a couple of women and a child is worth the pain?"

"Maybe not right now, but there will come a time when you're alone, missy." He spit at their feet and melted back into the shadows.

"Papa, get the gun. I'll be carrying it with me from now on." Rose resumed her seat on the log.

Jackson scratched his head. What had just happened? Instead of the men chasing off the threat, a couple of steel-spined women had handled the situation with no guessing as to their intentions. Who was taking care of whom here?

Feeling a bit emasculated, he plopped next to her and pushed his supper around on his plate. Rose didn't need him. He couldn't ask her to marry him unless he made her love him first. Well, he could do that. It would just take a little more time than he'd thought.

It was better this way. He didn't want her to accept his proposal out of a need for a home anyway.

"What, exactly, did you mean by the statement that I'm taken?" Her eyes flashed.

"Roy gave me permission to court you. I intend to do just that." His tone should have left no room for argument. He was sadly mistaken.

"Really?" Her eyebrows rose. "Shouldn't I have a say in the matter?"

"Are you opposed?"

"I don't know. A girl does like to be asked. She doesn't like matters of the heart decided for her." She tapped his head with her spoon. "It behooves you to remember that."

"Are you going to give me an answer?"

"Not today." She took her plate to a stool on the other side of the fire.

Jackson followed and dragged her behind the tent, not caring what the others thought of his heavy-handed ways. "Why not? I thought we got along fine."

"Oh, Jackson, I'm not good enough for you." She lifted the canvas wall of the tent and left him alone.

Chapter Seven

Rose should have worn pants. The minute she stepped from the Empire, a horde of dirty miners hooted and hollered and fell into step behind her. Not only did she feel uncomfortable, but Ethel and Sophie did, too, if the stiffening of their spines was any indication. She'd made good on her promise to carry a gun and now had a pretty pearl-handled revolver, courtesy of a gold nugget, strapped to her thigh. Wait. Sophie wasn't uncomfortable. Instead, she preened and sashayed as if she strolled the streets of a large city.

Heads high, the youngest with a simpering smile, the three females made their way to the patch of lawn where church was held. Waiting for them were Papa, Jackson, and Daniel.

Jackson's eyes widened with approval as his gaze settled on Rose. Her face flushed. She hadn't cut her hair since that one time, so her curls bounced on her shoulders, tied away from her face with a ribbon that matched the blue in her dress. She'd never felt prettier, despite the clunky boots on her feet.

Averting her gaze from the leering grin of their visitor from the night before, she took her place next to Ethel and faced the circuit preacher who planned to train Jackson a bit more in the art of pastoring throughout the winter months.

"Dearly beloved. . ." The preacher's words flowed around her as she kept her gaze locked on Jackson's.

Of course she wanted him to court her, very much. But a man like him needed a woman just as kind. A woman whose hands weren't roughened from hard work or her skin freckled from working hours in the sun. No, Rose wasn't good enough for such a man, and the thought almost ripped her heart out.

She pulled her thoughts back to Papa's special day. While she missed Mama more than ever, seeing the happiness on her father's face relieved some of the pain. Mama would have liked Ethel.

"You may kiss the bride."

Again, Rose glanced at Jackson as Papa kissed his new bride. Jackson winked and grinned.

Rose ducked her head. She couldn't let him see how she felt. Over time, he'd realize she wasn't the woman for him and find someone more fitting. She linked her arm with Sophie. "You and Daniel will share the tent with me tonight. Tomorrow, we'll all be under one roof."

The girl nodded and pulled away. "I'm getting married as soon as possible." She lifted her pert little chin. "At fourteen, I'm old enough. There are plenty of men to choose from, and I can have a home of my own." With a swish of her pink skirt, she sashayed away, heading straight toward a group of young miners.

Rose motioned her head for Jackson to follow the silly girl. He nodded and hurried after her.

"Howdy." The visitor from last night blocked her path. "Name's Hank. Thought I should introduce myself."

"Not necessary." She tried to push past him.

"Join me for the potluck."

What potluck? The only contributors had been Ethel and the innkeeper's wife. "I'll eat with my family, thank you."

"I insist." He grabbed her arm hard enough to leave bruises and tugged her along with him.

From across the way, Jackson looked torn as to whom he should protect. Rose shook her head. She could handle Hank. After all, what could the man do with hundreds of onlookers? Most of the miners would step forward with no more than a yelp from her.

She sighed and allowed Hank to prod her toward the food table. Maybe if she humored him. . .

"Once you've filled my plate, join me under that tree." Hank headed toward a cottonwood.

Rose narrowed her eyes. Oh, she'd fill a plate for him. She filled it with a bit of everything and a heaping dose of precious salt someone had donated.

After handing him his full plate, she sat back, her own food untouched, and watched him grimace as he shoveled in mouthful after mouthful. She turned her head to hide a grin, only to find herself once again staring at Jackson.

"What's that fancy pants got that I ain't?" Hank tossed his empty plate in the dirt. "I've got a pile of gold in the bank, I'm strong, and I aim to head to San Francisco come spring."

Manners. Cleanliness. The list was long. Instead, Rose shrugged. "He's a family friend."

Hank leaned back on his hands. "I hope you use salt sparingly when we get hitched. It's precious out here and can ruin a good meal."

Hitched? She shot him a stern look. "I'm not planning on getting married, Hank. If that is the notion floating around in your thick skull, you can think again."

"But. . .you shared a meal with me." He glowered. "You ain't one of them teasing kind of women, are you?"

"No, just an independent one."

"Well, that won't do at all. Where did your pa find his woman?"

"On the recommendation of a friend. You could always try the paper." She pushed to her feet and gathered their dishes. "No offense?"

He sighed. "Nope. I had to try, though. Especially after seeing you all gussied up."

Rose laughed. The man was all bluster and no bite. "Good luck on your quest." She strolled back to the table and set their dishes on one end. Grabbing a fried chicken leg, she watched as Jackson unsuccessfully kept Sophie from being surrounded by eager young men. The girl wasn't pretty by most standards, but she was a step above plain, and that was enough out here.

◆　◆　◆

Keeping an eye on Rose and another on Sophie had to be the hardest job Jackson had ever undertaken. What was Rose thinking having lunch with the very man who threatened her the night before? If something were to happen, there was no way Jackson could reach her in time. Somehow, he had to convince her that he was the man for her and get married so he could keep her safe at his side.

When she left Hank and the man didn't follow, Jackson relaxed. Perhaps the gruff miner wasn't as dangerous as he'd seemed.

Sophie's giggle dragged him back to the crowd surrounding her. The foolish child. She batted her lashes and swished her skirts like one of the saloon girls. Roy and Ethel had their hands full with this one for sure. When a man got too close, Jackson stepped between them.

"Call off your guard dog, Sophie," the man said. "I only want to get a feel of your golden locks."

She pushed past Jackson. "Feel all you want."

"That's enough." Rose parted the crowd like Moses parting the Red Sea. "Get back to your mother."

"You ain't the boss of me." Sophie stomped her foot.

Rose planted fists on her hips. "I am until tomorrow. Now go!" She pointed.

With another stomp and a pout, Sophie whirled and stormed away.

Rose turned to the men. "All of you get out of here. She's nothing but a child, and a foolish one at that. And you—" She poked Jackson in the chest. "Can't you handle one little girl?"

"I haven't had much experience."

She groaned and turned away. "Help me get Ethel's offspring back to camp."

"That, I can do." Boy howdy, she was gorgeous when riled. "You look wonderful today."

"Save the compliments. I've heard enough for a year. I should go back to wearing pants."

"Please don't." He grabbed her hand, holding tight when she tried to pull free. "The men will get used to you as a female, and most of them will be respectful. What did Hank want?"

"To marry me."

Jackson's heart fell. "What did you say?"

"No, of course." She glanced up at him. "Who do you think I am?"

"A lovely woman who feels as if she's being crowded out of her home."

Her face fell. "You would be correct. What am I going to do?"

"Marry me." He held his breath. His heart threatened to pound free.

"Gosh. Two marriage proposals in one day." Pain flickered across her eyes. "I must also give my second no. We discussed this last night."

"We discussed nothing. You spouted off some harebrained excuse—"

"Harebrained? You poke fun at my feelings now?" Her eyes shimmered.

"No, but I at least deserve an explanation." He pulled her onto a bench in front of the mercantile. Sophie and her brother sucked on peppermint sticks from a bench a few feet away.

"What more can I say?" She finally managed to get her hand free and folded her hands in her lap. "You're too kind to marry someone like me. You see a woman in need and want to meet that need. That isn't enough, Jackson."

Oh, how wrong she was. Dare he tell her of his love for her? How she was the sun rising and setting for him each day?

"You want to be a preacher. I've just rediscovered my faith. How can we be suited for each other?"

"Darling." He put his hand over hers. "Can't you see yourself through God's eyes or the eyes of the town? Your list of kind deeds is as large as mine. Still, God doesn't love us for what we do but because we're His children."

"Maybe." She shook her head. "Until I figure out what it is I want out of life, I'm no good for anyone. Jackson, I've just learned how to dream."

He wanted her dreams to include him. He sighed and pulled back, placing his arms along the back of the bench. Time was what she needed. Fine. He'd give her until spring, then ask again right before the circuit preacher left. Somehow, during that time, he would help her see her worth. "Let's get those two rascals home before Sophie gets into more trouble."

"Thank you for understanding." She stood and smiled down at him.

"I don't understand anything, Rose, but I've never been one to force my attentions on a woman, and I won't start now."

"I've hurt your feelings."

Stabbed him in the heart was more like it. "I'm fine."

"Perhaps you should send away for a bride." Her voice caught. "Someone more fitting a preacher's wife."

"I'm finished with this conversation, Rose McIlroy." He motioned for Ethel's children to follow and headed for the livery.

"I'll marry you, Mr. Westin." Sophie slipped her arm in his. "Right now, if you want."

Spare me! He unhooked her talons. "Thank you, but no."

She shrugged. "Your loss." She mounted one of the mules and grinned. "I'll be married within the month. Wait and see."

Good grief. He climbed onto his own ride and led the group toward Rose's camp. Like it or not, Rose needed him around. He grinned. His next article would be all about the young lad coming clean about being a woman and how the father remarried. Rose would be so beset upon with suitors, she'd come running to Jackson to save her. He prayed his plan wouldn't backfire and Rose wouldn't find something she preferred more.

Still, he was willing to take that chance if it opened her eyes. To use Roy's words, he'd be married to Rose by spring, he guaranteed it.

Chapter Eight

Rose stepped from her crowded home and into a frigid wind blowing across the river. Mining would be an icy venture that day. Still, she preferred it over the stuffiness of their cramped cabin. She shaded her eyes with one hand and searched for Sophie.

Where was that girl now? It had become a full-time job keeping her from marrying the first dirty miner who asked. It had gotten to the point where Rose felt like saying let the girl go and reap the consequences.

Jackson still came by on a regular basis to sketch the family, but not every day. Rose sometimes didn't see him for a week, and his absence left a hole nothing else could fill. She kept her ears open for news of him sending for a wife. Now that winter had set in, even a milder California one, she didn't think he'd find a bride before spring. The selfish satisfaction she felt kept her up at nights.

Her love for him should mean she wanted what was best for him. But if he were to wed, her heart would shatter. She doubted she would ever recover from the loss.

There she was. Rose pulled her oversized coat tighter around her and marched to where Sophie and Hank snuggled next to a large boulder. She stopped a few feet away and cleared her throat.

"She's a bit young for you, Hank." The man had to be thirty, if he was a day.

"Hush, Rose." Sophie kissed the man's cheek. "We're getting married come Sunday."

"Does your mother know?"

"I'm going to inform her this instant." She swished her skirts and raced for the house.

Rose shook her head and glared at the older man. "For shame, Hank."

"She's of childbearing years." He brushed off his pants. "I don't reckon it's any business of yours."

He was right. She sighed and headed downriver, pleased to see Jackson approaching in her direction. His grin chased away the winter temperatures.

"Good morning, Rose." He slid from his saddle. "Would you like to see the latest newspaper?"

"Yes, please." She took it from him and scanned his drawing of Papa's wedding to Ethel. Her eyes widened as she read the article. "My secret is out."

"Folks are loving it." He handed her a stack of letters. "Mail."

Gracious. There were so many. She clutched them to her chest. "Your articles will bring people to Rich Bar. Perhaps my days as a teacher are getting closer."

He frowned. "I thought your dream was to open a dress shop."

279

She shrugged. "Teaching is a more responsible, profitable occupation. Women won't need fancy clothes out here."

"They will as we grow more civilized." A look of sadness clouded his features. "Follow your dream, Rose. I haven't stepped aside for you to choose second best."

"What do you mean?" She clutched the letters tighter.

He ran a hand through his hair. "There are probably at least ten marriage proposals in that stack you hold. Since you don't want me, I'll stand back while you make your decision."

"I've said I don't plan to marry." Oh, why wouldn't he listen? If she couldn't have Jackson, she didn't want anyone else. Knowing he needed someone better than her was like a sore on her heart that never healed.

"Go read your letters." He turned and climbed back on his mule and then rode away.

It was for the best. If only she could convince her heart.

She sat where Hank and Sophie had vacated and opened the first of the envelopes. One after another were proposals of marriage, just as Jackson had predicted. But one... one was from a woman in Boston who said she recognized the look of sadness portrayed on Rose's face as she'd gazed at Jackson on the day of the wedding. Leave it up to Jackson to sketch Rose's true feelings.

The woman went on to say not to let her heart's desire fade. That she'd loved a man once and let him go. She regretted it to that day.

Rose sighed. The woman probably hadn't been unworthy of the man she loved. Yes, Rose was kind. She'd given gold to a saloon girl and sent her back East to her family. She gave food to the hungry. She'd made her peace with God. Still. . .her unselfish thoughts about loving Jackson rather than shoving him away showed her true colors. For his sake, she ought to forbid him to visit.

She glanced at the almost complete house on the hill. A grand place. A home that needed a family. Yes, she needed to tell Jackson there was no hope in his waiting.

Tears stung the backs of her eyes. She knew what needed doing but didn't have the strength to do it. She shoved to her feet.

One booted heel caught on a root protruding from the bottom of the boulder. With her hands full of letters, she was unable to stop her fall. She crashed like a felled tree, striking her head. As she lay there, the letters fluttering and falling into the river like white leaves, darkness slowly engulfed her. She could hear the birds, the rush of the water, but opening her eyes took too much effort. She heaved a sigh and gave in.

"Dearest." Someone shook her shoulder, and not very gently. "Rose."

She pried open one eye. Ah, she was in the house in the side of the hill. "Papa?"

"Girl, you scared ten years off my life. I have no idea how long you lay there before I found you. It was around supper time. I've sent Daniel for the doctor."

A million miners pounded in her skull. She tried to sit up, only to have nausea assail her. "Ugh."

"Lie still." Ethel placed a cool rag on her forehead. "You've a knot the size of Jackson's house on your head."

"You're lucky to be alive," Papa said, patting her hand. "I guarantee it. Why, if we hadn't missed you at supper, you could have lain there all night and died of exposure."

She doubted that. Not a grave chance of that in California. But there was the danger of wild animals. "I'm glad you missed me, then." She closed her eyes and went back to sleep.

◆   ◆   ◆

Jackson sat next to Rose's bed. A fist clenched his heart every time she mumbled his name. Why wouldn't she admit her love for him? He bowed his head and prayed for God to show her not only how God viewed the beautiful woman in front of him, but how Jackson felt every time he saw her.

"Wake her up." Dr. Robbins, the same doctor who had cared for Roy's broken ribs, rushed into the cabin. "She shouldn't sleep long with a knock to the head."

Jackson shook her. Fear slithered up his spine when she didn't waken. "Rose!" He shook her harder.

"Stop." She lifted a feeble hand. "Let me be."

"The doctor is here." Jackson stepped out of the man's way, but his gaze remained glued to Rose's pale face.

"Let's see what we have here, young lady." The doctor smiled. "Nice to see you dressed like your true self. You didn't fool many people, you know."

"Had. . .to try."

Jackson chuckled. As feisty as always.

"Fetch me a lantern so I can see better, would you?" the doctor asked as he parted Rose's hair. "Nice bump."

"Thank. . .you." She struggled to a sitting position. "I went to great pains to get it."

Jackson floundered, torn between following the doctor's request and helping Rose. Finally, he grabbed the lantern and hurried back to her side.

"I need the stepmother, please, and a bit of privacy." Dr. Robbins spared Jackson a glance. "Unless you married this gal without my knowing, you need to step outside."

Right. Jackson nodded and went to fetch Ethel. After sending Ethel inside, he paced, ears straining to hear the doc's words. He couldn't hear a darned thing through the sod walls. What if Rose called for him?

"She'll be fine." Roy clapped him on the shoulder. "I guarantee it."

"Do you ever lose your optimism?" Jackson plopped on a chair left outside for lack of room inside.

"Oh sure, but my faith keeps me going. God isn't going to take my girl. Not yet." Roy sat next to him. "It'll take more than a knock to the head to kill a McIlroy." He folded his hands across his middle and leaned back on the chair's two hind legs. "When are you going to marry her?"

"When she says yes."

"She's a stubborn one. You might have to wait awhile."

He was getting tired of waiting.

They sat in silence, occasionally taking turns glancing at the doorway, both breathing a loud sigh when Ethel appeared. The doctor followed close behind.

281

"She'll be fine," Dr. Robbins said. "Another day in bed, then a few days of no work and taking the powder I left, and that gal will be up and about again. Wake her every hour throughout today."

"Thank you." Jackson pumped his hand then dashed back to Rose's side.

He smoothed a curl away from her forehead. "You scared me half to death."

She gave him a weak smile. "Clumsiness."

Jackson took the stool the doctor had sat on. "How many marriage proposals?"

"Quite a few."

"Any interesting ones?"

"No." She closed her eyes. "Don't bring up this subject again, Jackson, please."

He groaned inwardly. They'd have to bring it up again, and soon. The moment she was back to her healthy self, he'd ask her one final time and take her answer as the last word. He couldn't torture himself forever. He'd rattle around in that huge house of his, alone, until the day he died. Maybe he'd sell and move away from Rich Bar where he wouldn't see Rose on a regular basis. He wouldn't be able to bear the pain.

"What would you like to talk about?"

She shrugged. "Any gossip in town?"

He laughed. "You've only been in bed a day."

"Sophie married yet?" She smiled.

"Not yet, but she's hand in hand with Hank down by the river. Don't worry, he'll care for her. He might be a bit bossy, but his eyes shine when he looks at her." Was she regretting turning down the man's offer for herself?

"That's all that matters."

Unfortunately, the light in Jackson's eyes when he looked at Rose was in danger of dimming. He prayed that wouldn't happen. "I should let you rest."

She started to say something then reached for his hand instead. "Thank you for coming."

Thank you for coming? He shook his head as frustration welled. "Rose McIlroy, you're driving me crazy. I see the way you look at me." He knew he should stop talking, but it was as if someone had lit a fire inside him that wouldn't stop burning. "One way or another, I'm going to get it through your head that you are going to marry me. Everyone else sees it. Why can't you? Your father wants to know why we haven't gotten hitched yet. I'm sure the rest of the town feels the same. I had hoped that hit on the head would have knocked some sense into you." He bolted to his feet. "Look at me."

"I am."

"No. Really look at me. What do you see?"

"A good man. One without a selfish thought in his head, and I'm full of selfish thoughts."

"Hogwash." He grabbed a Bible off the kitchen table. "You've plenty of time to read. Look up verses on how God sees you. No one regards you higher than He does. But I'd come close. Come see me when you're ready to be truthful about yourself." He stormed out of the cabin and to his mule, disregarding the curious looks on Roy's and Ethel's faces.

He stopped and rested his forehead on the mule's saddle, already regretting storming away from Rose. Still, she needed to hear the truth. Until then, he would stay away. He didn't need the money from the newspapers back East anymore. He'd stop his sketches.

The one he'd drawn of Rose in the beginning already hung above his fireplace. Someday he'd show it to her. In the meantime, he'd work on getting his own newspaper office up and running. He lied to himself that business would heal the ache in his gut.

Chapter Nine

Sunday afternoon, Rose sat on a makeshift seat and watched as Jackson performed the wedding ceremony for Sophie and Hank. Rose hadn't seen hide nor hair of Jackson since her fall, and tears had soaked her pillow every night. Still, she had no one but herself to blame. This was what she wanted, right? She shivered as a brisk spring breeze cooled things off and clouds gathered overhead.

Sophie and Hank were heading to San Francisco the moment they said their vows. Mules packed with supplies waited next to the mercantile. Ethel sniffled into an embroidered handkerchief as she sat next to Rose. She reached over and patted the older woman's hand.

"You're a good girl, Rose." Ethel wiped her eyes. "A comfort to me as my firstborn leaves the nest. At least I've got Daniel, not that I see much of him. He's taken to hanging out with a group of miners upriver."

Rose nodded, not sure what to say. The boy came home for half the meals and crawled into bed long after dark. If she were his mother, she'd put a stop to his shenanigans. Not that Rose would likely have children of her own.

Ceremony concluded, Rose stood back as Ethel said good-bye to her daughter. Across the way, Jackson also watched, keeping his gaze averted from Rose. He'd held true to his promise then. He was staying away.

She read Papa's Bible every night before bed and was no closer to accepting Jackson's proposal than she'd been a week ago. Not that she doubted God's love for her. Not for a second. But the thought of a man such as Jackson loving a woman such as she took some getting used to.

She glanced around at the crowd. Other than married women, and her, there was no one for a healthy man to marry other than saloon girls. How long until Jackson put a notice in one of those papers he wrote for?

The object of her thoughts veered away from the others and strode to a newly erected canvas tent. Staked in front was a sign that read Rich Bar News. When had he accomplished that? Rose really needed to make it to town more often than just on Sunday.

Right before her eyes, the citizens of Rich Bar were accomplishing their dreams while she sat back and watched hers walk away. Tears welled in her eyes. She fisted her hands so tightly, her fingernails dug into the palms of her hands. Why couldn't she take the steps needed to go to him? Why was she so afraid?

No more. God's Word said He did not give her a spirit of fear. She whirled and dashed to Ethel's side. There was something she needed to do before it was too late, and she needed her stepmother's help.

◆ ◆ ◆

Another week passed as Rose worked feverishly on her project, staying up late into the night hours to finish. When she had completed it, she stood back and smiled at the result. Perfection. Just like her sketch. The fact her creation held a bit of Mama made it all the more special.

She marched outside and headed for the newspaper office. It was time to give Jackson her answer.

Heart racing and palms sweating, Rose parted the flap on the newspaper office tent and peered inside. Jackson and a woman in a red dress leaned against a printing press. The woman giggled, running painted nails down Jackson's arm. He grinned like a fool as he peered down at her.

Rose withdrew, letting the flap fall back into place. She'd waited too long. He'd chosen a girl Rose had given money to so the woman could leave behind her sordid life and start anew. It looked like she'd bought a new dress instead. Blinded by her tears, she lifted her skirts and raced for the livery and Bob.

Back in the saddle, she did her best to get the beast to hurry home. Instead, the stubborn mule planted his hooves in the dirt and refused to move. "Come on, please. I've got to get out of here." She slid to the ground and yanked on the bridle. "Now is not the time to be stubborn."

"Perhaps he's taken a page from your book." Jackson leaned against a stall. "What's the hurry, Rose? Did you want something?"

"Not a thing," she forced through a throat clogged with tears.

"I've a stack of mail waiting at the office."

"Burn every one of them." She dropped the reins and collapsed onto a bale of hay. "Leave me be. Go back to your lady friend."

"Daisy? She's finished her business."

"That was easy enough to see." She kicked at a clump of dirt on the ground.

"What are you talking about?" He sat next to her. "Do you have a problem with her putting in an advertisement for a husband? She's tired of waiting and tired of the life she's living. She's decided to take matters into her own hands."

Just as Rose had decided. Was it possible she'd been confused about what she'd seen? "You aren't courting her?"

"Heavens, no. Setting up the paper has kept me too busy." A grin spread across his face. "You thought she was making advances?"

"No." She pushed to her feet and moved back to Bob.

"Rose McIlroy, you're a terrible liar." He stood too close. The crisp scent of his aftershave sent her senses reeling. "Tell me."

"Tell you what?" She put a foot in the stirrup.

"You know." His breath tickled the fine hairs on the back of her neck. She really needed to leave.

He reached around her, taking the reins from her hands. She was boxed in. A smelly mule in front of her and a solid, very nice-feeling Jackson behind her. He placed his hands on her shoulders and turned her to face him. "Tell me," he said in a husky whisper.

"No." Her voice broke. "It's too late."

"It's never too late." He'd eaten a peppermint, the aroma washing over her. "Tell me."

She squared her shoulders and stared up into his face. "I love you, Jackson Westin. Whether I'm good enough for you or not, the idea of you leaving or taking someone else kills me."

He ran his thumb down her cheek. She leaned into his touch. "I could never choose anyone else." He lowered his head.

◆　◆　◆

She tasted as sweet as he'd imagined. A small moan escaped her, fueling the fire inside him, and he deepened the kiss before pulling back. "Marry me. Tonight. Before I do something we might both regret."

She gave a sweet smile. "I doubt I'd regret it, but it certainly wouldn't be proper. Tonight, by the river." She cupped his face. "Meet me at sunset, right as the sun kisses the water."

"I'll be there." He lifted her into the saddle, not able to believe his good fortune.

She bent down and kissed him again, then clicked to the mule and rode away.

Jackson needed a shave and a bath. He hurried to hang a CLOSED sign on his office and headed to the Empire. While he'd been living in his new house for weeks now, he knew the innkeeper sold shaves and a bath. It would beat a chilly dunk in the river.

"I'm getting married today!" he shouted as soon as he entered the building. "Everyone is invited to the river at sundown. I need a shave and a soak."

The innkeeper grinned. "On the house, Mr. Westin. Let me heat some water."

While Jackson waited, he bought a sarsaparilla and relished his good fortune. Good things came to those who waited, and he thanked God he'd had the patience to wait. Now the fulfillment of his dreams was mere hours away. Soon Rose would be his wife. The day was going to be long until sunset.

He finished his drink and sat in the barber chair in the corner of the main room while an older woman filled his bath in a private room upstairs. He closed his eyes, still thinking on the night to come as the barber gave him a smooth shave. After that, he lowered himself into a tub of hot water and leaned his head back.

He'd caught sight of Rose peering into his office and knew from the shocked look on her face what she'd come to say. He'd hurried after her as fast as possible, relieved to see her mule acting stubborn. He grinned at the memory and stayed in the tub until the water grew chilly.

Then he mounted his own mule and rode home to get dressed. He eyed the storm clouds rolling in. *Please go away.* Rain would ruin everything.

His house was in sight when the clouds opened up and dumped more rain on the town than he'd seen in the months he'd lived there. Already the river was rising. If he dressed quickly, he might have a chance of crossing back over before it was impassable.

He rolled his suit and stuffed it into his saddlebags. "Come on, boy," he told the mule. He probably should have given the animal a name other than Mule. Heart in his throat, he rode to the edge of the river. Water slapped the boards of the bridge he'd had built. Mule refused to put one hoof on the boards.

Groaning, Jackson slipped from the saddle and grabbed the reins. "There's a sugar lump for you if you get me across."

The animal snorted and jerked its head.

"Come on!" Jackson pulled harder. Water sloshed his feet. "You ungrateful beast." He unhooked his saddlebags and slung them over his shoulder. He'd go on foot.

By now, water ran over the bridge ankle deep. Jackson gripped the railing and trudged ahead. Nothing was going to keep him from getting married today.

He slipped, wrapping his arm around the rail. His legs kicked for a footing. *God, help me.* The opposite shore seemed so far away. Still, he fought the rushing water, moving hand over hand across the bridge. The smart mule had already run for the barn. No matter. Jackson was determined, and sheer will would get him across.

Rose appeared on the opposite shore, her cloak billowing in the wind. She opened her mouth to shout, but the wind ripped her words away.

Jackson focused on her and continued his fight. His feet slipped on the wet wood. This time, he fell to his knees. Water rushed to his waist, stealing his saddlebags. His new suit. No matter. He'd marry Rose in coveralls if that was what it took.

A roaring filled his ears as a wall of water raced toward him. He wrapped both arms around the bridge railing and held on as an icy wave washed over him. He was prone on the bridge now. The only thing saving him was his death grip on a thin rail of oak. He prayed the hired men had built the structure sturdy.

Water filled his mouth. He coughed, swallowing more of the river. Then, a lull. He struggled to his feet, sliding them across the boards, keeping his gaze on the woman waiting for him.

Roy, a lasso in his hand, had joined her. He twirled the rope around his head, then let it loose. It fell several feet too short.

Was there nothing that man hadn't dabbled in, or was it simply that Roy looked at things in life as possible rather than impossible? He let loose the rope again. This time it landed a foot from Jackson.

With a prayer, he let go of the railing and lunged. Success! He grabbed the lasso and struggled to get it around him as another wave washed him into the river.

Rose screamed his name.

The rope cut into Jackson's rib cage as he was pulled through the water. After what seemed an eternity, he lay on the shore and gazed into Rose's precious face. "I made it."

Tears, or rain, fell down her face. "You foolish man." She leaned down and kissed him. All was right with his world.

Chapter Ten

Inside the cabin, Rose donned the wedding gown she'd made from ordered silk and lace and from her mama's own gown. She and Papa might have moved around the country like gypsies, but the one thing Rose had always refused to leave behind was Mama's wedding dress.

"A vision, you are." Ethel clasped her hands under her chin. "That man warming himself by the fire outside is a lucky one."

"I'm the lucky one." Rose stood still as Ethel placed a paper flower in her hair. "I still can't believe he chose a woman like me."

"And why shouldn't he? You're a fine girl, Rose. Don't you ever forget that." Ethel stood back and tilted her head. "No one other than our good Lord is perfect, and no one ever will be. The thing to do is ask forgiveness and move on."

Rose nodded. She'd dwell no more on silly notions of unworthiness. She would view herself through the eyes of God and the man who loved her.

"I wish you'd wait until tomorrow, though." Ethel shook her head. "No party afterward? I've never seen a couple more in a hurry than the two of you."

"We've waited so long already."

"It's raining."

"We'll wait for a lull." After watching Jackson's determined trek across the bridge, nothing would hold Rose back. "Papa said he was going to put up a tarp."

"He did. Over the fire. Your groom needed somewhere to get warm, and we all know he can't see you in your dress."

Rose took a deep breath and ran her hands down the silk skirt. Mama would be proud of her.

"Come, dearest." Papa stuck his head into the cabin. "We're ready for you."

Rain thudded on the sod roof. Rose shrugged, lifted her skirt, and followed.

Tears sprang to her eyes as she slipped her arm through Papa's elbow. The miners stood in two rows and held tarps over their heads, providing a dry passageway to where she had promised to meet her beloved a few feet from the river's rushing waters. They whooped and hollered when Rose made her appearance. The kindhearted men had formed the walkway with a slight curve so she couldn't see Jackson immediately.

When she did, her heart stopped then pounded over the sound of the rain against the tarps overhead. Another tarp, tied to stakes, kept Jackson dry. He wore a dark suit and a shiny gray vest. She giggled. Courtesy of the saloon owner, she guessed. No one else in town had such fancy duds.

His eyes darkened when he spotted her. He held out his hand, taking her from Papa.

"You're the most beautiful thing I've ever seen."

Her face flushed. "You're mighty pretty yourself. Borrowed?"

He nodded and grinned. "Lost my suit in the river."

"Don't remind me." She shuddered and turned to face the circuit preacher. It wasn't until that moment that she realized she was going to be a preacher's wife. Fingers of dread started to skitter up her spine. Instead of giving in, she squared her shoulders. She would not be afraid. Not with Jackson at her side. With him, she could be anything she needed to be.

"Dearly beloved, we are gathered here. . ."

The crowd of men behind them quieted as the preacher began to speak. He read from the book of First Corinthians, and peace enveloped them all as the rain stopped. One by one, tarps fluttered to the ground like the rush of mighty wings. Rose couldn't envision a more perfect wedding day.

Over the mountain, the sun descended as clouds parted. The sun's rays kissed the waves of the river with shades of gold and pumpkin. She squeezed Jackson's hand.

Moments later, he slipped a simple band of gold on her left ring finger and pledged to love her forever. She gazed into his face and said, "I do."

The paper flower in her hair, bedraggled from the damp, was plucked by Jackson's hand and tossed into the water as he lowered his head to kiss her. The kiss, simple and sweet, heated her blood more than the passionate one at the livery. This kiss held the promise of more to come. Of years of passion, laughter, tears, and dreams.

"I now pronounce you man and wife," the preacher said.

The miners resumed their loud whooping as Jackson and Rose turned to face them.

Tears streamed down Papa's face as he clasped the hand of his wife. He smiled and nodded, giving his blessing to the married couple.

Rose released her husband's hand and went to her father. She placed a kiss on his weathered cheek. "Thank you for bringing me here."

"It was a tough haul, but we made it. That man will make you happy, I guarantee it." He pulled her into a rough hug.

Rose laughed. "He already has, Papa."

Since the river was still too dangerous to cross, the miners escorted the wedding couple to the Empire, where a spread of beef, potatoes, and early spring vegetables were set out as a wedding feast.

"I don't care if this mining town does dry up," Rose said, glancing into Jackson's face. "I don't want to live anywhere else."

He chuckled. "That's good, because that house on the hill cost me a fortune. Do you mind if I write and sketch one more for the papers back East? I think they'd love to know how our story turned out."

"I don't mind at all." She pulled him down for a kiss.

◆   ◆   ◆

Jackson rolled over in their rented bed and stared into the face of his bride. For three days they'd lived at the Empire. Today was the day he took her home. Finally, the river had dropped enough for them to cross over the bridge.

"Are you ready?"

She smiled and stretched. "More than ready. It's been a long few days."

"From the ruckus outside, I'm guessing we'll have a crowd escorting us over the river."

"I don't mind." Her eyes twinkled. "As long as they leave immediately upon reaching the other side."

"I'll insist." He kissed her and threw aside the quilt covering them.

Sure enough, they stepped into a bright spring day to the sight of a line of miners on the backs of mules. Several more animals were loaded with supplies.

"Wedding gifts," Papa said, waving his arm with a flourish. "The town wants to do right by their new preacher."

Warmth filled Jackson as he reached for Rose's hand. They were blessed indeed. A newspaper and a chance to spread the Gospel. Not to mention the most beautiful woman in California stood next to him with tears shimmering in her eyes.

He helped her onto Bob and then climbed on behind her. They led the miners through town and across the bridge to home.

There was no need to tell the men to leave. They dropped off the supplies, shouted well wishes, and left.

Jackson took a deep breath and pulled Rose to the house, eager to show her the inside. He opened the door with a flourish, scooped her into his arms, and stepped across the threshold. "Welcome home, darling."

"Oh, it's beautiful." She craned her neck to stare at the tall ceilings. "The fireplace takes up one whole wall." She took a step toward it, but he held her back. "I'll show you that last. Come."

He tugged her through the dining room and through a breezeway into the kitchen. "To keep the heat from the cooking fire out of the main house."

"You've thought of everything." She ran her hand across the stove. "Did you strike it rich?"

"I made a fair amount. You'll want for nothing."

"You're all I want."

He showed her upstairs next. "I had the bed built here. There's no moving the monstrous thing." After sleeping on the giant of a bed at the Empire, he'd wanted the same for his house. The man he'd hired had carved an ornate pattern on the bedposts and headboard. "There's no other quite like it."

"I don't imagine. How many bedrooms?"

"Four, not counting this one. How do you feel about a large family?"

"I'd love one." She wrapped her arms around his neck. "Forget the fireplace. Let's spend the rest of our life in this room."

He claimed her lips. "That, my love, sounds wonderful, but I have a gift for you downstairs."

"You spoil me, Jackson."

"I've only just begun." He pulled her after him, stopping in the doorway of the parlor. "Close your eyes."

She did as instructed, a smile stretching her lips. "What fun. A surprise."

He led her to the fireplace. "Open your eyes."

"Oh, it's gold." She removed the sketch he'd made of her a year ago. Her short curls framed her face.

"I drew a second one in ink to match the first charcoal sketch and sprinkled gold dust while the ink was wet. Other than you, it's my most treasured possession."

"A sketch of gold. Of me, no less." She drew her finger across the drawing. "What if I wouldn't have married you?"

"Then I would have tucked it away and stared at it each night before falling asleep." He took the sketch and replaced it on the mantel. "I never had any intentions of marrying anyone but you. If you would have said no again, I would have lived my life as a bachelor."

She snuggled under his arm. "I'm glad I said yes. You're the fulfillment of my dream."

He pulled her close. "And you've always been mine."

Cynthia Hickey grew up in a family of storytellers and moved around the country a lot as an army brat. Her desire is to write about real but flawed characters in a wholesome way that her seven children and five grandchildren can all be proud of. She and her husband live in Arizona where Cynthia is a full-time writer.

Love Is a Puzzle

by Pam Hillman

Chapter One

The pack mule brayed, jerked against the rope, and shied away, almost pulling the tall, broad-shouldered man off his feet.

Instinctively, Shanyn Duvall ran and grabbed the end of the rope, hauling back.

The man tossed a frantic glance at her and shouted, "Get out of the way, ma'am!"

The mule squealed and lunged again. The rope slid through Shanyn's hands, burning. With a mighty heave, the animal jerked loose and, bucking and braying, attempted to dislodge the pack on its back.

Three men raced out of the mercantile and dived for the rope. Wild with fright, the mule twisted, turned, and headed straight toward Shanyn.

The tall man grabbed Shanyn and lifted her onto the mercantile's small stoop as the crazed mule bucked past. Breathing heavily, she pushed her hair back with shaking hands. "Goodness, that was close."

"A mite too close, if you ask me, ma'am." The stranger slapped his hat against his buckskin-covered thigh. Dust flew. Dark eyebrows drawn together, he pinned her with a pair of stormy blue-green eyes. "That was a fool thing to do."

"I agree." Shanyn eyed the mule, caught but still fighting the other men. "Definitely not the smartest thing I've ever done, butting in where I didn't belong."

Surprise lightened his scowl, and he chuckled, a smile curving up one corner of his mouth. "Well, at least you realize the error of your ways, ma'am."

"That I do." She nodded, offering an answering smile in return. "I'm looking for Thom Branson, the leader of the survey team. Is he here?"

"No, ma'am. Sorry. Mr. Branson is down at the wharf checking on a shipment of supplies. I'm Nick Johnston, guide for the party heading into the mountains."

The crazy mule lunged against the ropes, two men attempting to keep him still long enough for a third to unbuckle the pack. Mr. Johnston straightened when it looked like the mule was going to get the best of them, but as the animal finally stopped bucking and stood quivering, Mr. Johnston stopped, one boot on the porch step. Narrow and assessing, his gaze never left the struggle still playing out before him.

Shanyn took a step forward. "Mr. Johnston, I don't suppose you know where I can find my father, Obadiah Duvall, by chance?"

He glanced at her, his clear blue-green gaze raking her face. His brow puckered, and he shook his head. "No, ma'am, don't reckon I know Mr. Duvall."

"But surely you know my father. He's a cartographer. He's been with Mr. Branson for years."

"My partner and I've just hired on to lead the next expedition into the Sierra Nevadas. I haven't met anyone by the name of Duvall."

From the looks of the orderly piles of supplies, heavy wooden boxes lashed tightly with leather straps, a stack of sturdy tripods, and crates with the words "Sierra Nevada Typographical Surveyors" stamped on the side, the party was about to head into the mountains. She was just in time to see her father for a few days before he was off again. "When does the party leave?"

"Tomorrow. Daybreak."

Daybreak?

Disappointment cut through Shanyn. After traveling eight months, seven on board a clipper sailing around the tip of South America, she and Aunt Skeet had landed in Sacramento just this morning. She'd left her aunt to settle in at her father's boardinghouse while she found his place of employment. Shanyn sighed.

"Something wrong, ma'am?"

She shook her head. "It's nothing, Mr. Johnston. It's only that my aunt and I just arrived this morning and—"

"Alone?"

Shanyn frowned. "Pardon?"

"You and your aunt. You traveled to Sacramento alone?"

"There was no one else." She shrugged. "I'd hoped to spend some time with Papa before he left on another expedition, but it can't be helped."

"How long since you've seen him?" Sympathy colored his words.

"Two years. He wasn't sure how long this job would last or if he'd head back East. He sent for us last fall, saying he thought he'd finally found what he was looking for."

"And what was that? Gold?"

Shanyn shook her head. "My father isn't interested in panning for gold."

"Everybody's interested in the gold, ma'am."

"Including you, Mr. Johnston?" He didn't look the type to pan for gold with his fringed leather buckskins, but she'd been surprised before.

He shrugged. "I've done my share of prospecting, and I'll probably do so again."

"But. . . ?"

"I promised to guide Mr. Branson and his party through the mountains." He arched a brow at her. "So if your pa isn't looking for gold, what is he looking for?"

"A place to put down roots." Her gaze lifted, took in the mountain range in the distance. "He wrote long, glowing letters describing those mountains, even sent drawings. Said they were the most beautiful he's ever seen."

"He's right. It is beautiful country, Miss Duvall." An odd look crossed his face, pained. Just as quickly, it was gone, and he looked over at her, a half smile on his rugged face. "But it can be dangerous. Even more so with folks from all walks of life crawling all over."

A movement toward the street drew her gaze, and she spotted Mr. Branson hurrying her way, his form thinner than she remembered, his horn-rimmed glasses making him just as distinguished as ever.

She stepped off the porch and waved. "Mr. Branson."

His gaze lifted, his eyes grew round behind his spectacles, and his mouth opened, but no greeting escaped his lips. His steps slowed even as a pucker of concern drew his eyebrows together.

He stopped in front of her, hands held out. "Shanyn? Shanyn Duvall?"

Shanyn clasped his hands, smiling up at the first familiar face she'd seen since she left Virginia. "We're here. My aunt and I arrived just this morning."

His eyebrows lifted. "Skeet's here?"

"Yes, sir. We traveled around the Horn."

"Let me look at you." He stepped back and shook his head. "My, my, you've grown up. How long has it been? Six, seven years?"

She laughed. "Ten, Mr. Branson. The Appalachia Expedition, in the Appalachian foothills."

"Ah, yes, I remember." He smiled, his eyes twinkling. "You were just a kid, but you were so anxious to prove your worth as a mapmaker. Obadiah was so proud of you."

Shanyn frowned. Why was Mr. Branson speaking of her father in the past tense? Was it just a slip of the tongue?

She placed a hand on his arm. "Mr. Branson, where's Papa?"

He frowned. "Didn't you receive my letter?"

Dread pooled in the pit of her stomach. "What letter?"

He clasped her arms and suddenly she didn't want to hear what he had to say. "Shanyn, I'm sorry, but your father is. . .he's dead."

◆　◆　◆

The color leeched out of Miss Duvall's face. Nick braced himself in case the girl fainted dead away.

"Dead?" She shook her head, a pucker of disbelief between her arched brows. "No, he can't be."

Branson held her at arms' length. "I'm sorry, Shanyn."

"What—what happened?"

"I don't know. After we mapped the area all the way to Dry Diggins—well, most folks call it Hangtown—back in the springtime, we ran out of funds from Washington and had to come back to Sacramento to wait for supplies. Obadiah decided to stay in the area. You know how he was about painting and carving those puzzles of his. He hasn't been seen since."

"Then he might not be dead."

"Shanyn, no one's heard from him in months."

Her frantic gaze shifted to Nick. "But Mr. Johnston—"

"Just Nick, ma'am."

"Nick, couldn't my father be alive?"

Nick searched her face, the hope she so desperately sought stamped across her features. He shrugged. "It's possible, but—"

"See, Mr. Branson. He could be alive. We can search for him on this trip."

Branson shook his head. "Shanyn, it's useless. You can go miles and miles without ever seeing another human being in those mountains. I'm sorry you came all this way for nothing."

Shanyn clenched her fists and blinked back tears. "Mr. Branson, take me with you.

I'll look for Papa. He can't be dead."

Nick glanced between the two of them. "Sir, I don't think—"

His boss held up one hand. "Under any other circumstances, I wouldn't even consider it—"

"Because I'm a woman?"

"Partly, but not because of the reason you think. This is rough country, Shanyn. It's not like it is back East."

"Mr. Branson." Shanyn stood tall, which wasn't much more than shoulder-height to Nick. "My father taught me everything he knew. And I can read his maps blindfolded."

"I don't doubt that." Branson took off his spectacles and cleaned them with his handkerchief, eyeing her. He glanced at Nick. "I am shorthanded. I've had three of my party just up and abandon us for the gold fields in the last week."

Nick shook his head. He could count on one hand the number of women he'd guided into the mountains in the five years he'd been a mule skinner. "Mr. Branson? You can't be serious. A *woman*?"

"Two." Shanyn crossed her arms and glared at him. "My aunt will be traveling with us as well."

Chapter Two

S hanyn grabbed the map off the table, rolled it, and stuffed it into one of her father's sturdy canvas packs.

"Shanyn, are you sure about this?"

"Aunt Skeet, that survey expedition leaves at daybreak, and I intend to be on it."

"But what good will it do?" Her aunt tossed her hat onto the bed.

"What if Papa's alive? What if he's hurt and needs us?"

"We've been over this already." Aunt Skeet plopped her hands on her hips and stared at Shanyn, a perplexed look on her lined face. "Looking for Obadiah in this rugged country will be like looking for a drop of ink in the ocean. We've both been on enough of these expeditions to know how futile this is. It's likely he'll never be found."

Shanyn jerked her head up. "Aunt Skeet, don't say that. He's your brother."

"I don't mean to be harsh." Her aunt's features softened, and she took Shanyn by the shoulders and turned her to face her. "But if Obadiah hasn't showed up in all this time, it's unlikely that he will. You know that, don't you?"

"We have to try." Shanyn bit her lip. "I'd never forgive myself if we didn't look for him."

"Very well, then." Her aunt turned away and began separating her father's personal belongings from the maps. She held up a small wooden box about a foot square. "Oh, look, one of Obadiah's jigsaw puzzles. Beautiful, isn't it?"

Pausing in her packing, Shanyn took the box from her aunt. A cartographer by trade, her father's true passion lay in painting sweeping landscapes, but canvas, oils, and brushes cost money, and very few people could afford oil paintings. When Shanyn was a child, he'd turned his artistic skills to carving puzzles to keep her occupied and as a way to bring in extra cash between expeditions.

Shanyn's eyes misted as she ran the tips of her fingers over the scene he'd painted on the top of the box. Majestic mountains, with a clear mountain stream tumbling over rocks, and a miner's shack nestled among the trees. A miner knelt at the edge of the stream, panning for gold.

She eased the lid off the wooden box and riffled through the colorful pieces inside. Her fingers itched to spread the pieces on the table and get to work. As she'd grown older, her father's puzzles had become more and more difficult to assemble. Unable to resist, she picked up an irregular piece, not much bigger than a nickel. Flipping it over, she groaned.

"Ugh. Double-sided."

Her aunt laughed. "Obadiah sure liked to make things difficult, didn't he?"

"Don't talk about him in the past tense, Aunt Skeet. Please."

"I'm sorry, sweetheart. I'll do better." Her aunt turned away. "Here are some more puzzles. A dozen or more."

Shanyn eyed the piece. Tiny markings against a green background revealed that the back of this puzzle was a map. "Well, this one shouldn't be too hard. The back's a map."

"Let me see." Her aunt peered at the small piece of wood, shook her head, and handed it back. "I'll need better lighting than this to make heads or tails of it."

Shanyn rubbed the smooth edges of the cool wood between her fingers, thinking. Suddenly, she grabbed the puzzles and added them to the pile of maps.

"What are you doing?"

"I'm taking them with us." She tapped the puzzle boxes. "If Papa drew maps on the back of this puzzle, then it stands to reason he did it on the others. They might lead us to him."

◆　◆　◆

Nick scowled at the darkening sky. They'd been on the trail less than a day and were already getting wet.

He eyed the long train of pack mules strung out in front of him, Shanyn Duvall and her aunt sandwiched in the middle of the pack. The two women had shown up long before daylight, loaded with bulky canvas packs. He'd assigned one of the young drivers to help them, but the way the two had set in to lashing their belongings to the mules showed they clearly knew what they were doing.

Bailey rode down the line, turned his horse, and fell into step beside him. "Wal, is Branson ready to make camp? My bum knee's acting up somethin' fierce."

"He's worried about their survey equipment getting wet, but he doesn't want to camp near the river. Went into this long spiel about watershed, how we're surrounded by mountains, and based on his calculations, how quickly we could be washed away in a flash flood from this rain."

"Wal, a body cain't argue with that."

"Yeah, but I didn't need a fancy degree to know not to camp here."

Bailey grinned and swept a hand over the group spread out in front of them. "Fancy degrees bring in fat bankrolls. Just look at that. Ain't that a sight for sore eyes?"

Nick grunted. "If you say so."

Bailey's bushy brows pulled together in a frown. "Now what's that supposed to mean? You afraid Branson'll get gold fever and sneak off in the middle of the night?"

"Nah, he wouldn't do that." Nick shook his head. "Besides, they've got way too much equipment to get far."

"And some of it cost a pretty penny." He gestured toward Shanyn and her aunt. "Take that Miss Skeet, there. I thought she was going to have a conniption fit when I almost dropped one of those packs. Something about a perambulator and a circum-something-or-other. I never heard of such gewgaws."

"It takes a lot of stuff to survey the land." Truth be told, Nick was looking forward to watching the surveyors work. But he wasn't looking forward to carting two women around.

Bailey squinted at him. "So if that's not what's got a burr under your saddle, what does?"

Nick sighed. Bailey wouldn't let it go, so he might as well spit it out. "I just don't think it's a good idea to pack two women into the gold fields."

Bailey grew quiet, scrubbed a hand through his beard, then sighed. "Now, Nick, just because your ma—"

"This isn't about my mother, Bailey. This is about taking two women where the men outnumber women a hundred to one." Nick scowled at Shanyn's back. "Mark my words, Bailey, there's going to be trouble."

◆　◆　◆

Rain fell in heavy sheets.

Mr. Branson had decided to push on, and Shanyn couldn't blame him. They needed a good campsite away from the river. Nobody could dispute that.

The trail became more treacherous, sloping upward, twisting and turning, as they moved away from the river. She followed behind the string of pack mules, her eye on the man—hardly more than a boy—leading the mules that carried her father's maps and puzzles. She itched to make sure the oilcloth was tied down securely, to ensure that none of her father's precious work got wet.

Suddenly, one of the mules slipped. Braying, the animal scrambled to keep its footing before slamming into the mule behind him. One of the packs burst open, spilling its contents on the ground beside the trail. Wooden puzzle pieces scattered across the ground, their bright colors dotting the wet leaves like flowers drooping in the rain.

The young teamster kept going, urging the mules to the top of the incline where he finally stopped. Shanyn jumped to the ground, intent on rescuing her father's work.

Nick rode into view, pointed at the gaping pack, and growled, "Secure that flap before anything else gets wet."

Dismounting, he headed toward Shanyn, boots splashing through puddles.

"Stop!" Shanyn splayed her hands in front of her. "You'll trample the pieces into the mud."

He stopped, hands on hips, the rain sluicing off the floppy brim of his hat. "Let me help."

Before she could protest, he hunkered down and picked up the puzzle box farthest away and scooped some of the pieces back inside. Shanyn bit back the urge to cry as she carefully and methodically picked up each piece. They were wet, muddy, and some of the pieces of the puzzles had even mixed together. How on earth would she ever get them all clean and separated? She motioned to the area where the pieces had comingled.

"Don't put those in your box. I'll have to sort through them and figure out which pieces go with which puzzle."

Thankfully, he didn't argue but did as she asked. As they knelt beside the trail, the rest of the pack train passed by and continued on. The rain continued to fall, and the hem of Shanyn's skirt grew heavy as she knelt on the leaf-strewn ground searching for tiny pieces of painted wood. She glanced at Nick. "I suppose you think I should leave the puzzles here."

"Not at all, ma'am." He shrugged, shifting to his left and deftly plucking three small pieces off a rock and tossing them in the box. "I reckon these little doodads mean a great deal to you now that your pa's gone."

Shanyn stiffened. "He's not gone."

He glanced at her, his eyes full of pity. "Yes, ma'am."

Shanyn looked away and scanned the ground, looking for more puzzle pieces, but the ground was empty.

Empty, just like his words of agreement had sounded.

Chapter Three

The rain shower moved out just as quickly as it had come, and by the time they made camp uphill from a small stream, the sun was shining again. Nick led a string of mules down to the water. As they drank their fill, he spotted Shanyn rinsing the puzzle pieces along the water's edge upstream. Seemed like a lot of work for a few pieces of a child's toy.

But women were sentimental about family heirlooms.

He remembered when his ma and pa had traveled overland to California. Pa was more concerned with his guns and his horses, but Ma was determined to hold on to the china that had been passed down to her from her great-grandmother. If those hand-carved puzzles and maps were all Shanyn had left of her father, who was he to judge?

He picketed the mules and gathered more wood on the way back to camp. By the time he made it back and tossed an armload of logs beside the fire, Shanyn had spread out the puzzle pieces on a piece of canvas to dry.

Miss Skeet helped the cooks prepare supper for the men. Nick poured himself a cup of coffee and hunkered down beside Shanyn. "How's it coming? Did you lose any pieces?"

She shook her head, lips pursed. The sun, bright and piercing after the rain, landed on a smattering of freckles on her cheeks, touching her skin with a soft glow. "I'm not sure yet. If I did, I can probably re-create them."

He glanced at her in surprise. "You can do that? I thought your pa made all the puzzles."

"He did. But if I had to, I could repair a piece here or there."

"Don't let her fool you, Nick," Miss Skeet called out. "She's got the knack for painting and making puzzles just like my brother."

A hint of a blush stole over Shanyn's cheeks. "I'm not nearly as good as Papa."

"I'm sure you do just fine."

She smiled. "Thank you."

Branson and his assistant, Austin Whitman, walked over. Branson frowned at the map in his hands. "Johnston, can you tell where we are?" He spread the map out, pointing. "There's Sacramento. I think we should be somewhere in this vicinity, but with the rain today, it was hard to pinpoint landmarks. And there's no trail anywhere in this area."

Nick studied the map. The landmarks, such as they were, looked to be fairly accurate, with several of the main trails marked, but the rest had been left bare. If he gauged the distance they'd traveled against the distance to Hangtown and how far they were from the river, he could make a pretty good guess.

Before he could make up his mind, Shanyn tapped a spot on the map and made a circle with her finger. "Here."

She'd stuck her finger on the exact spot he would have chosen, given the rough estimates of the map drawn in the field. How'd she do that? She'd never even been in this area. He glanced up and their eyes met. She arched a brow. "What?"

His lips twisted in amusement. "Nothing."

"And where would you say we are, Mr. Johnston?" she challenged.

"Oh, about here." He tapped his finger maybe a quarter-mile to the left of where she'd pointed, the difference not enough to quibble about. Her hazel eyes narrowed, and he winked at her. Crimson bloomed across her cheeks.

Whitman wedged himself between Nick and Shanyn. "Well, Miss Shanyn, that was mighty impressive, given you've never been in the area before."

"It's one of Papa's maps. I've been reading his maps since before I could barely walk." She shrugged, as if that explained everything.

Nick's gaze flickered between Whitman and Shanyn. The pasty-faced clerk stared at her with obvious fascination, but she didn't notice, her attention so focused on her father's map.

Branson bent over the map, squinting through his spectacles, then pointed at a jagged peak in the distance. "Johnston, you've led expeditions all over these mountains. How far away is that peak?"

"'Bout a mile."

"And those over there?"

Nick squinted, thinking. "Two, maybe three miles."

Shanyn studied the peaks, pointing toward the landmarks. "If what Nick says is correct, this is way off. It wasn't surveyed?"

"We came into this area right before winter set in, heading toward Hangtown. A storm was rolling in, and the fog was so thick we could barely see three feet in front of us. We decided not to survey but head straight through. Obadiah sketched it as best he could." Branson shrugged. "And our guide took off in the middle of the night. Gold fever. Just up and left us to fend for ourselves."

He tapped the map, considering. "Whitman?"

"Yes, sir?" Whitman straightened to attention.

"Tell the men we're going to camp here for a couple of days. We'll survey a five-mile radius along each side of this trail and draw up new maps. Assign crews to each quadrant."

"Yes, sir."

Whitman hurried off to talk to the men, and Branson turned back to Nick and Shanyn. "Johnston, I'll need you and a couple of your men to guide each crew."

"Yes, sir."

"Good. Shanyn, with your skill at reading Obadiah's maps, I'd like you to assist Whitman with familiarizing himself with the maps."

Shanyn smiled, her eyes lit with excitement. "Yes, sir. I'd be glad to."

Nick turned away, his gaze landing on Whitman as he talked to the men on the other side of the clearing. Was Shanyn excited over getting to spend more time with her father's maps, or did it have more to do with the citified mapmaker she'd been assigned to work with?

◆　　◆　　◆

Shanyn frowned at the puzzle in front of her. She'd been on the trail for a few days, and this was the first chance she'd had to work at putting the puzzles together again.

Aunt Skeet glanced at her. "What's the matter?"

"Several of the pieces are missing."

"Is that one of the puzzles that fell out on the trail?" Her aunt stepped closer, stirring up a batch of dodgers. "Do you think some of them got lost on the trail?"

"I don't know. Nick and I searched the ground pretty thoroughly. I can't believe we'd miss this many."

"Maybe Obadiah never finished this puzzle."

Shanyn shook her head. "It can't be that. You know he always carved out all the pieces, then assembled the pieces and painted the picture on the finished product. No, this puzzle was completed, but several of the pieces are gone now. It doesn't make sense."

She stared at the scene, the white water crashing down a steep slope, a rough-hewn shack that looked to be in danger of falling into the water. A man in a red-checked shirt panned for gold alongside the stream, with dark storm clouds roiling overhead. A lone eagle soared high in the sky.

Shanyn studied the puzzle, trying to fit the extra pieces in, but there were big gaping holes in the puzzle, and the pieces she had couldn't be connected to the parts she'd already assembled. She stood, found a sturdy flat crate, sandwiched the puzzle between it, and flipped it over so she could look at the back.

The clear lines of a map stared back at her, big chunks missing where the puzzle pieces were missing. Did the map on the back have anything to do with the picture on the front? Who was the man panning for gold? Did it matter? Was he just a gold miner her father had sketched during his travels?

And why were some of the pieces missing?

She glanced at the rest of the puzzles packed in her father's packs. Were there more missing pieces? Was her father trying to send her some kind of message?

"I think I'll go for a walk." Maybe getting away from camp would clear her head. "Do you need any help with supper?"

"Nope. The stew needs to simmer a couple of hours."

"I'll be back by then."

"Why don't you ask Austin to go with you?"

Shanyn winced. She longed for peace and quiet and a chance to sit and sketch without distractions. She'd barely been able to move ten feet from camp without Austin. She liked the man well enough, but four days in his company was beginning to wear on her nerves. He didn't understand that she needed to concentrate when sketching.

"Somebody's coming."

Shanyn turned, her heart thudding against her rib cage. Was it Nick's crew? As the surveyors drew closer, she spotted Bailey in the lead. As the old guide rode by, he doffed his hat. "Howdy, Miz Skeet. Hope you got some good vittles in that there pot. I'm near starved to death."

Aunt Skeet laughed. "I imagine we can rustle you up something soon as you get washed up."

Shanyn turned away, wondering at the disappointment that it wasn't Nick's crew that had ridden in.

Chapter Four

Nick scowled as he went in search of Shanyn. He'd been gone for four days—guiding one of the survey groups over rough terrain, taking care of his mules, and helping the men with their precious equipment—only to return to find Shanyn gone.

Her aunt had pointed in the direction of a high bluff leading away from the creek. He climbed higher into the mountains, growing more worried by the minute. Why had Branson and Whitman let her wander off alone? One wrong turn and she'd be lost forever in these mountains.

Finally he spotted her, high on a rocky outcropping, sketch pad in hand, her attention on the sun setting in the distance. Her fingers flew over the canvas, so intently focused on the red, gold, and purple sunset that she never noticed him. He moved closer, his ire rising with each step. He didn't bother to hide his approach, but she never moved.

A mountain lion, a bear, or a crazed miner too long in the woods could attack her, and she wouldn't be aware until it was too late.

He moved into her line of sight, and finally her gaze lifted and met his. Her lips parted, and she smiled. As he climbed to her side, her gaze shifted back to the panoramic view in front of her. "Isn't it the most beautiful sight you've ever seen?"

Nick eyed the sunset, one of a thousand he'd seen. Then he glanced back at Shanyn's face, shining with joy more brilliantly than the colors along the horizon. He nodded. "Yep, I reckon it's pretty enough."

"Pretty enough?" She arched a dark brow and kept sketching. "Nick Johnston, where's your sense of adventure, your joy in the beauty surrounding you?"

Nick let his gaze roam across her face and wanted to admit that she'd added a lot of beauty to the area. But his tongue couldn't wrap itself around the words. He didn't know her well enough to tell her how beautiful she was.

As the sun dipped below the horizon, the light began to fade. He could feel the night around him come to life, hear the night creatures calling to one another, the frogs croaking, night birds singing. He glanced around, saw the jagged rocks, the shifting shale, the scraggly brush clinging to the side of the cliff, the dips and sways that hid the nocturnal creatures who fed at nightfall. Yes, he saw the beauty—but he'd lived in the wilds long enough to notice so much more.

"I see danger lurking behind each rock: slippery slopes to walk over to get back to camp, a mountain lion or bear stalking its prey, or a porcupine or badger to run afoul of. That's what I see."

Frown lines marred her smooth forehead as she tucked her sketch pad into her satchel, jumped down from the rock, and brushed past him. "Did you come out here just to ruin a perfectly beautiful sunset?"

"I came to make sure you didn't get lost—or killed."

"I know the way back."

Nick fell into step beside her. "That's not the point. It's dangerous out here. Mountain lions and bears are all over these mountains. And if that's not enough to worry about, there are men who haven't seen a white woman in months."

"I'm not that far from camp, Nick. It's just over the ridge." She turned to face him. "Have you ever been in these mountains alone?"

"Yes, but that's different."

She skirted around an outcropping of rock, and he followed. "How so?"

"Well, because I know the area. I know my way around. And I'm a—" Nick stopped midsentence. Shanyn and her aunt had traveled around the Horn to meet up with her father. She could read a map better than most men he knew. And when she'd stepped off that rock, she'd made a beeline toward camp. She didn't need his assistance to make it back, but she did need his protection. "You didn't bring a gun. If you're going to wander off from camp, you need to be armed."

Her lips twitched, and he got the feeling she knew exactly what he'd been about to say. Finally, she nodded. "Point taken. I'll make sure to bring a rifle with me the next time I venture out."

Nick clenched his teeth and stair-stepped down a rocky hillside before reaching out a hand to help her down. How could he make her understand it wasn't safe to venture away from camp alone even if she was armed? "Shanyn—"

Her foot slipped, and eyes wide, she screeched in alarm. Nick tugged on her hand, pulling her toward him, straight into his arms. The impact knocked him off his feet and he fell backward, the hard rocky earth jabbing into his back. He gritted his teeth and absorbed the impact even as Shanyn's bulky pack slammed into his face.

◆ ◆ ◆

Shanyn pushed against Nick's chest, mortified. He wasn't moving, just staring at the sky.

"Nick? Are you all right?"

"I'm fine."

She scrambled to her knees beside him. "Are you sure?"

His gaze shifted, dipped, and focused on her face. The shadows deepened the blue-green of his eyes, and his jaw clenched tight. "I'm sure."

He rolled over, groaning with the effort.

"You are hurt."

His chest rose and fell as he took one long, shuddering breath. "I'm fine. It's just—"

"Lie still." Shanyn pushed against his chest, both hands flat against the warmth of his rough cotton shirt.

"Shanyn, stop." Nick captured her hands in one of his. As surely as his strong hold captured her fluttering fingers, his blue-green eyes caught and held her gaze. The tension around his mouth softened, and his lips twisted into a slight smile. When his gaze dipped, swooped across her face, toward her lips, and then captured her gaze again with the speed of an eagle in flight, she gasped.

Heat surged into her face, and she jerked her hands away. She looked away, face burning. Her gaze landed on his strong hand splayed on the ground, pushing himself up to a sitting position, then toward her pack, sketch pad, and pencils scattered on the ground.

"If you're sure."

"I'm sure."

She jumped up, started gathering her pencils, paints. She stuffed her supplies into her satchel, all the time every nerve-ending focused on Nick. The slap of his hat as he brushed the dirt off his clothes, the rustle of his clothes as he stepped nearer, reached down and picked up her sketch pad, and handed it to her.

She stuffed it into her bag then risked a glance in his direction. "We'd better get back."

His gazed searched her face. "Reckon so."

Chapter Five

By the end of the week, Nick wanted to throttle somebody, or at the very least, grab a string of pack mules and head back into the wilderness.

At least once a day Shanyn disappeared, and he felt obligated to search for her. It didn't take long to figure out that she'd climb up to the highest peak she could find to sketch. Mostly, he kept his distance, letting her sketch.

The surveyors all had a language of their own, and Shanyn was right in the middle of it. They had journals full of numbers, distance, charting, elevations, sketchings of the mountain ranges, streams, animals, and vegetation. Whitman was somewhat of a botanist, and he spent his days scouring the area for undocumented species of shrubbery, trees, and animals.

At night, everyone gathered around the makeshift tables and discussed the day's work. Lively discussions about the names of the plants and animals ensued. Nick didn't know the proper names of any of them, but he and Bailey set them straight on some of the common names, and especially what the locals called a plant or animal.

Shanyn amazed him most of all. With the information brought back by the crews and a few fluid strokes, she could take one of the original maps that left so much to interpretation and set it to scale. Even though she wasn't officially part of the survey team, the cartographers had started coming to her when they ran into questions regarding one of her father's maps of the area.

Late afternoon on the sixth day, Shanyn sat at the makeshift table, painting.

Austin leaned over her shoulder. "Shanyn, you do have your father's talent."

"Thank you, Austin." She smiled, the look on her face saying she didn't want to be interrupted. Nick had learned over the last few days that she preferred to be left alone when she was painting. He could understand that. Some things required concentration, and he figured painting was one of them.

Swede, Whitman, Bailey, and two of his teamsters huddled around her. Johnnie, a bit of a rough teamster who hadn't had enough of a stake to head into the hills, leaned over her shoulder. "Now don't that beat all." He spit a wad of tobacco, then grinned at her. "That's about the purtiest thing I've ever seen."

After a few more strokes, she gathered up her brushes and started cleaning them while the men talked about her painting. She never said anything, just kept a polite smile on her face, but he could tell she was distracted.

"I saw a mama bear and two cubs yesterday."

"Really?" Shanyn's gaze flickered in Austin's direction. "I'd love to see the cubs, but—"

"I could show you where they are if you're of a mind to paint them."

Nick shook his head. "I don't think that's a good idea, searching out a bear and her cubs."

Austin threw him a challenging glance. "If Shanyn wants to see the bear, what can it hurt?"

"Plenty." Nick sipped his coffee. "A bear's nothing to mess with, and one with cubs is even worse."

"Nick's right." Shanyn's gaze waffled between the two of them. "It's a bad idea."

"It's definitely a bad idea." Nick plopped his hat on his head. "Besides, I heard Branson say we were breaking camp soon."

◆   ◆   ◆

Hangtown was like a bed of ants stirred with a stick.

Silently, the party of surveyors rode through town. Men spilled out of tents, pushing and shoving. Some were laden with packs, shovels, and pans, while others haggled over the price of a blanket or a bag of flour.

As they passed an open-sided tent, one man held up an oilcloth poncho, shaking it and shouting at the merchant. Next thing Shanyn knew, he charged the other man, and they went down in the street, rolling.

Nick ignored the chaos around them and kept going, leading them to a knoll outside of town. Soon they'd set up camp, the nights on the trail making the task go quickly and efficiently.

Shanyn helped her aunt start supper, all the while itching to get out her sketch pad. The hodgepodge of tents, cobbled-together cabins, and lean-tos and the roil of humanity drew her. Mr. Branson had already asked for copies of several of her sketches. He planned to publish his papers someday, and her work would be included alongside her father's.

Nick wouldn't like it. If he thought there was danger in the woods, he'd have a fit if he knew she wanted to explore Hangtown. But if she didn't go into town, how else was she going to find her father or record what she saw?

She'd ask him to take her. That would solve her problems. And Nick wasn't like the rest of the men. He let her be while she sketched. A couple of times she'd spotted him watching her while she worked. She'd known he only meant to keep an eye on her. At first it was a little unnerving, but after a while, she got used to the idea and was actually relieved that he'd be close by if something ever happened.

"Aunt Skeet, I'll be right back."

She went in search of Nick and found him repairing some packs. "Nick, since we're going to be here several days, I'd like to go into Hangtown to see if anyone's seen my father."

"Hangtown has a reputation of being rough, and it's only gotten worse the last few months. I don't want you to go by yourself."

"I've been in rough towns before, Nick. That's the nature of surveyors. They're always needed where the newest mining boom is. And Mr. Branson wants me to sketch the town for him. I'll—"

"Tomorrow. First thing."

"All right." Shanyn smiled. "But I could go by myself—"

"Shanyn—"

"Johnston!" Mr. Branson and Swede hurried toward them.

Nick tossed his repairs to the side. "What's wrong?"

"One of my men is gone." Mr. Branson jerked off his spectacles and rubbed his eyes.

"Maybe he's just taking in the sights of Hangtown."

"No. He's gone." He started pacing. "If it was just that, I'd let him go, but he took some of our equipment, some picks and shovels, and one of your mules."

Nick jumped to his feet. "What?"

Shanyn gasped. That changed everything. "What are you going to do?"

"I'm going after him." Nick settled his hat on his head.

"Swede, grab two of your best men and go with him." Mr. Branson eyed the men.

As the men left, Shanyn placed a hand on Nick's arm. "Be careful."

He smiled at her, then reached out and tucked a lock of hair behind her ear. "I will."

Shanyn shivered at his touch, then gave him a tiny smile and turned away. He pulled her back, his gaze intense.

"I meant what I said. Don't go to Hangtown alone."

Chapter Six

D on't go to Hangtown alone."
Nick's words rang in Shanyn's ears as she wove her way through the streets, a small portrait of her father in her hand. Nick had been gone two days. She couldn't—wouldn't—wait any longer.

Men, some in rags, stared at her, but when she showed them the likeness, they just shook their heads and kept walking. After an hour of fruitless searching, she stopped walking and took a deep breath.

A couple of rough-looking characters stepped off the steps of a nearby saloon and headed her way. Apprehension skittered up her spine, and she darted toward the nearest shop. As she ducked under the awning, an elderly man glanced up. Her gaze met his before glancing back to the men crossing the street. Thankfully, they kept walking.

"You in trouble, missy?"

"No. I just. . ." Shanyn paused. Nick had been right. Maybe she shouldn't have come to Hangtown alone. Most of the men were respectable, law-abiding citizens, but some weren't. Gold, liquor, and frayed tempers could make a man do the unthinkable. "No, I'm fine. Just made a foolish decision to come to town by myself."

He grunted. "Yep. Hangtown ain't no place for a lady, that's for sure."

She held out the painting. A daguerreotype would have been better, but this was all she had. "Have you seen this man? He's my papa. He's a cartographer."

The old-timer squinted at her. "A carto-what?"

"A cartographer. A mapmaker."

"Ah." He nodded and peered at the painting. "Did you paint this?"

"Yes, sir." Shanyn brought his attention back to her father. "So have you seen him?"

"Can't say as I have." He handed the cameo back. "Sorry, missy."

Shanyn sighed. With the thousands who'd descended on Hangtown recently and their scramble to get to the gold fields, she wasn't likely to find anyone who'd known her father.

The old-timer tapped her father's portrait. "If you're looking for your pa, you should set up shop right here and paint portraits of all these miners. They'd pay in gold to get their likeness made. And it'd give you a chance to ask about your Pa."

"I'll think about it."

He waved at a man crossing the street. "Hey, Charlie, get over here. This little lady is looking for her pa. Show him the picture, missy. Charlie's been running Charlie's Sundries and Supplies well over a year now. If anybody's seen your pa, it'd be him."

The middle-aged man stopped, nodded, and took the picture. He nodded. "I seen him."

Shanyn's heart jumped. "You have? When? Where?"

"Well, here in Hangtown, of course."

"How long ago?"

Charlie scratched his head. "Oh, a couple months or so. Maybe longer. Time sort of slips by out here if you know what I mean."

"Did he say where he was staying? Or anything?"

"Nope. But he was a strange one, that. Didn't want a pick or a shovel or anything much to do with panning for gold. Kept wanting to know if I could get him some paints." He scratched his head. "Oil paints."

"That's him. That's my papa!" Shanyn's heart danced a little jig, and she wanted to hug Charlie.

"Well, I got that paint for him, if you want it. All kinds of little tubes and jars and paintbrushes." He motioned to the small portrait in her hand. "Tiny little things that you'd use for that kind of thing."

"You still have the paints?"

"Yep. Your pa paid for them up front, and I ordered 'em, just like he said. But then he never picked 'em up."

The old miner stepped up and tapped the picture. "Like I said, if'n you want these miners to take time to talk to ya, offer to paint their likeness. Only way ya gonna get 'em to sit still long enough."

◆　◆　◆

Nick fought his way through the crowded streets, looking for Shanyn. He'd told her to stay close to camp, but she'd ignored him. Didn't she know that Hangtown was no place for a lady?

They'd lost the trail of the thief yesterday, only to return to camp and find her gone.

Raucous laughter spilled from one tent after another. Drunks reeled in the streets and lay passed out in the alleys, while other men went about their business, gathering supplies to head into the mountains to pan for gold.

All the time, miners were trekking into Hangtown with their earnings, some to spend it all in a den of iniquity, only to turn around and head back out as soon as they were broke.

Where was Shanyn? He scoured the crowded streets, looking for women, who were few and far between. Periodically, the squeal of feminine laughter, a feather bobbing through the crowd, or the swirl of a skirt caught his attention. But no Shanyn.

There!

Down the street, surrounded by men. His heart raced. Just as he'd expected.

A woman as pretty as Shanyn Duvall didn't parade down the streets of Hangtown without attracting a lot of attention.

He stalked forward, intent on pulling her away from all her admirers and getting her safely back to camp.

"Well, would you look at that?"

Nick pushed through the crowd and spotted Shanyn, a piece of charcoal clutched in her fingers as she quickly sketched a likeness of the street. The crowd stood silently behind her, watching her every move.

"Shanyn, what are you doing?"

She smiled up at him. "Drawing."

He reached for her arm. "I think you need to get back to camp. Now."

"It's fine, Nick. No one's going to hurt me."

"Leave her alone."

"Miss Shanyn, is this man bothering you?"

The mood of the friendly faces turned as quickly as some of their fortunes had. They didn't like that he was about to break up their fun.

"No, no, gentlemen. It's all right. Nick is a friend, and he's come to escort me back to camp."

"Will you be here tomorrow?"

"Can I have that drawing? I'll pay you for it."

"No, I saw it first. I want it."

"I want one of them there puzzles you told us about."

Nick waited until Shanyn had assured the men she'd be back soon.

"Nick Johnston?" Charlie stepped out of the mercantile and pulled Nick into a bear hug, slapping him on the back. "When did you get into town?"

"This morning."

"Did you catch that scalawag who stole your mule?"

"Nope. He gave us the slip."

Charlie scowled. "If he keeps up that kind of life, he's not likely to survive out here. I reckon you're here to check on Shanyn."

"I came to escort her back to camp." Nick eyed her. "She seems to think it's all right to wander around Hangtown unescorted."

Shanyn lifted her chin. "I can take care of myself."

Nick exchanged a glance with Charlie, and the older man sighed. "Miss Shanyn, he's right, you know. I think you're safe enough here with me or back in camp with Nick, but it really is too dangerous to wander around alone. Maybe Nick could bring you back tomorrow if you'd like to sketch some more."

A grubby miner walked up to Shanyn. "You the lady looking for your pa?"

"Yes. Have you seen him?" Shanyn dug in her pocket for the picture of her father.

"Nope, can't say as I have, but I saw some of them puzzle boxes at Martha's Kitchen. Some gent left some pictures and boxes with little painted pieces inside. I never could make heads or tails out of them little pieces, but the pictures on some of those boxes was right purty."

Shanyn clasped the man's arm. "Who's Martha? Where does she live?"

"Martha Hogue. She keeps the miners fed up in Hogueville." He thumbed over his shoulder. "Two, maybe three days' ride up the trail."

Shanyn's gaze met his, and Nick knew she was determined to make the trip.

Chapter Seven

Nick, I've got to find this Martha." Shanyn hurried to keep up with him as they left the middle of town and headed back toward camp. "She's got Papa's puzzles, and they might lead me to him."

He stopped and looked at her, concern knitting his brows together. Compassion filled his blue-green eyes. "Shanyn, are you sure you want to do this?"

"Do what?"

"Keep searching for your father. I'm afraid you're just going to be in for more heartache."

Shanyn put a hand on his arm. "Can't you see? I have to do this. I have to know if Papa is dead or alive."

His gaze searched hers. "Is that all there is to it?"

"What do you mean?"

"You keep working on his puzzles, looking at his maps as if those two things are somehow going to lead you to him, but the puzzles are just scenes he's painted, the maps just show the places he's mapped out for Mr. Branson. What makes you think there's anything in either of them that will help you find your father?"

Shanyn shook her head. "Papa's been hiding clues in his puzzles all my life. At first they were just simple things, like two puzzle pieces cut the same size." She smiled. "I remember once he painted a beautiful picture of the creek close to our house. A huge oak tree stood next to the creek, and it had a big knothole. Papa included two pieces in the puzzle, one that showed the hole where the hollow was, and another that had a tin can nestled in the spot. For the longest time, I couldn't figure out what the tin can was for or why it was included with the puzzle. But Papa just kept smiling. Once I figured out that the extra piece fit in the hollow tree, I knew he'd hidden something there. And sure enough, I found a small can full of brushes and paints in the tree."

Nick turned her to face him, both hands on her upper arms. Shanyn shivered at his touch. His eyes searched hers. "I won't deny that there might be clues hidden in the puzzles, but I don't think they're going to lead you to your father. No one's seen him for months. That means he's de—"

Shanyn stopped him with two fingers pressed against his lips. "Please, Nick. Just take me to Martha. Maybe he's been there since he left Hangtown."

"All right." He sighed. "We'll leave at first light."

◆ ◆ ◆

Branson decided to send a survey team on ahead to Hogueville with Nick and Shanyn. It made sense. Instead of using all his resources around Hangtown, he'd spread his crews along the established trail and map out the well-traveled areas. Then they'd branch out, adding to the maps as they could.

Nick led the smaller party through a pass, a day out from Hangtown. Shanyn and her aunt rode along with him, along with Swede, Whitman, and a half dozen others.

He would've been just as happy to leave Whitman behind, but the man was Branson's right-hand man, and if they were going to be a forward crew, working ahead, it made sense to have the man along.

As much as he grated on Nick's nerves.

Whitman urged his mount up beside Nick. "Johnston, I think this is a good place to camp tonight."

Nick nodded. "We'll continue on for about a mile. There's a ridge up ahead. It's well protected from the elements and attack and will offer a good backdrop for protection."

"Attack? From what?" Whitman motioned around him. "In the absence of Mr. Branson, I'm in charge, and I insist we stop here. It's a good spot. The elevation is high enough."

Nick reined in. "Whitman, Branson hired me to guide his group and to give my opinion of the best route to take, as well as the best campsites. I'm telling you that we'll be better served at the site just over the ridge."

Whitman laughed. "Johnston, take a look around you. The men under my charge are West Point graduates, engineers, cartographers, and botanists from the finest schools back East. I myself spent two years in the employ of the U.S. Bureau of Topographical Engineers. I think we all know a good campsite when we see one."

Nick stared at the man, then rested his hand on the pommel of his saddle. "Suit yourself."

Smirking, Whitman turned in his saddle and addressed the rest of the party like some kind of general. "All right, men, we're going to camp here tonight."

Nick reined off the trail to search out a cranny that butted up against a hillside. The rocky outcropping gave his back a measure of protection. Shanyn approached, a worried frown on her face. "What was that all about?"

"What?" Nick swung the saddle off his horse, then started rubbing down the mare.

"Austin. You looked like you were arguing with him."

Nick laughed. "We weren't arguing. Just a difference in opinion."

"What opinion?"

"I advised going on down the trail to camp, and he insisted on camping here."

She looked around. "You don't think this is a good spot?"

"It's good enough, but only if you don't know that there's a better spot up ahead, one with more protection for a party of this size, a steep horseshoe-shaped cliff where we could picket the horses and keep them safe against attack, a position we could defend, if necessary."

Shanyn frowned. "You think all that's necessary."

He shrugged. "Maybe, maybe not. But it's my job to guide the party along the best route and find the safest place to camp. If he insists he knows best, there's not much I can do to change his mind, is there?"

◆ ◆ ◆

When it grew dark, they brought the horses in closer, ran a picket line, and settled in around the campfire. Shanyn and Aunt Skeet ladled out beans and sourdough biscuits to go with the two rabbits Nick had caught in snares.

Shanyn gathered the dishes and headed to the creek to rinse them. She wasn't surprised when Nick got up and followed her. He didn't like for her or her aunt to be away from camp, especially after dark.

"You don't have to come with me."

Without saying a word, he fell into step beside her. She shook her head. He was determined to protect her. At the creek, she handed him a stack of dishes. "As long as you're here, you might as well make yourself useful."

He laughed. "Yes, ma'am."

As they rinsed, Shanyn glanced over at him. "Nick, why are you overprotective of me and Aunt Skeet?"

"Wasn't your father protective of you?"

Shanyn thought, then shook her head. "No, not like you. I grew up in the woods, reading the stars, then compasses. Papa never seemed to worry about me that much. Not that he didn't love me. He just didn't worry because he knew I could take care of myself."

The only sound was the rippling water and the scrubbing of tin plates. Behind them, she could hear the murmur of the men and the snort of one of the horses.

"Maybe I am a bit overprotective," Nick finally admitted. "Especially when it comes to women and children. On the way overland, my youngest sister was out gathering wood for the fire and got bit by a rattler. She died later that night. My little brother died on the trail. Cholera. After we arrived in California, Pa staked a claim high up in the Sierra Nevada. Ma got caught in a blizzard and never made it back to our cabin."

Shanyn's heart ached for Nick's loss. "I'm sorry. And your pa? Is he still alive?"

Nick shook his head. "Nope. Claim jumpers killed him, thinking he'd hit the mother lode. There wasn't enough gold on that claim to buy a pound of coffee."

"Is that why you're against mining?"

He shrugged. "Mostly. Gold—and greed—make people do crazy things."

They gathered up the scoured pans and headed back to camp. Halfway there, Nick reached out a hand and grabbed her wrist. "Stop."

She froze at the note of warning in his voice. The men around the campfire kept talking. Laughter rang out. The horses whinnied, hooves shuffling, acting restless. Shanyn shivered when Nick's thumb rubbed across the inside of her wrist.

"Nick?" she whispered. "What is it?"

"I'm not sure. Come on." He led her into the circle of light, then dropped the tin plates into her hands. "Stay close to the fire."

He slipped away into the darkness. One minute he was there; the next he was gone. Shanyn edged closer to the fire. The horses grew more restless.

Swede sat up. "Shh. What's that?"

The others fell silent, listening as the horses shifted nervously, snorting and stomping the ground. Swede and another man calmed the horses, and an uneasy silence fell over the camp.

"Where's Johnston?" Austin stood, searching the group of men.

"He heard something. Or felt it. I'm not sure."

A wild screech that sounded like a woman in pain made Shanyn's hair stand on end. "What was that?"

Suddenly, the horse on the far end of the picket line squealed and reared in fright. The horses and pack mules were jerking free from the line, bucking and screaming in fright. The men all scrambled toward them, attempting to capture them before they escaped.

Another screech overrode the other sounds. A gunshot pierced through the wild frenzy of screaming horses and shouting men. In the silence that ensued, the horses calmed. Then Nick strode into camp, carrying his gun.

"What was that?" Austin asked. "A mountain lion?"

"Yes."

"What was a mountain lion doing so close to camp?"

Nick hunkered down next to the fire and poured himself a cup of coffee. "He was after the horses. Like I said earlier, there isn't enough protection in this campsite."

"We can't lose the horses. What are you going to do about it?"

"Already done."

"Done?" Austin scowled at him. "What's that supposed to mean?"

"Lion's dead." Nick shrugged and took a sip of coffee. "He won't bother the horses anymore."

Chapter Eight

Nick sat in the shadows, gun resting easy in the crook of his arm. All was quiet, and everyone had settled in for the night. But he couldn't sleep. Not after the scare with the lion.

He'd told Whitman that the lion was after the horses, which was very likely, but he couldn't shake the thought that the smell of roasted rabbit had enticed the animal to draw closer to camp. Just thinking about what might have happened if Shanyn had gone to the creek alone to rinse the dishes tied his stomach up in knots.

The odds of having something else happen tonight were slim, but he wouldn't take the chance. He tuned out the snores coming from Swede and listened to the night. Crickets chirped and night birds called to one another. A slight breeze stirred the trees, and the sound of water cascading over the rocks below them was soothing. Even the horses had settled down and were dozing.

There wasn't anything to worry about. For now.

He heard a rustling in the dark, knew someone was awake even before Shanyn's soft scent reached him. Even out on the trail, Shanyn and Miss Skeet managed to keep fresh with some kind of sweet-scented soap that smelled of rose petals and lavender. How he knew it was Shanyn and not Miss Skeet, he couldn't guess. He just did.

Her scent surrounded him as she sat on the log next to him. He swallowed as her shoulder brushed against his. "Can't sleep?"

"No."

"There's nothing to worry about."

She laughed, a throaty chuckle low in her throat. "Then why are you still awake?"

"Somebody's got to stand guard. I got elected."

"No, you volunteered, as always. How did you know?"

"Know what?"

"That it was a lion."

"I didn't know, but from the way the horses were acting, I knew it was something big and something they were afraid of. Bears don't tend to wander around this time of night." Nick shrugged, the rustle of his sleeve against hers making him keenly aware of her presence. "A lion was the logical choice."

The quiet peace of the night had shattered into a million tiny pinpoints of awareness when she joined him, but he couldn't think of anything *except* Shanyn with her so near. Her silky hair, the color of dark molasses, rippled down her back. She pulled it over her shoulder and, dividing it into three thick ropes, began to plait. "I see. I never would have thought of that."

He stood, grabbed the coffeepot, and poured a cup. Taking a sip of the hot liquid, thick enough to clog his throat, took his breath away. Grimacing, he tossed the bitter brew into the underbrush.

"Would you like some coffee?" she asked.

He turned and eyed her where she sat on the log, her shawl wrapped around her against the slight chill in the air, her hair now neatly plaited and hanging over her shoulder. "No, no need to on my account, but thank you for offering."

Nick walked to the edge of camp, wishing she'd go back to bed. She had no clue how her presence affected him.

◆　◆　◆

Shanyn studied Nick, frowning. He stood at the edge of camp, brooding. That was the only word she could think of to describe his silence.

She moved to stand beside him, speaking quietly. "Nick, have I done something to upset you?"

He froze, one eyebrow quirked upward. "Why would you say that?"

She sighed. "You've been acting strange all evening, especially since the lion showed up. If there was something I could have done differently, something to help protect the camp, then I'd want to do it. I don't want to put anyone in danger."

He chuckled, and she wondered what she'd said that was so funny.

He reached out, grabbed her braid, and ran his fingers along the strands. Shanyn could feel the slight tug on her hair where he held her captive.

Capturing her gaze, he stepped closer, and when she went to step back, he held her fast by her braid. "Shanyn, you didn't do anything—"

He broke off midsentence as Swede stopped snoring. Shanyn couldn't move, just kept her gaze glued to Nick's lips, pressed together. They were as still as a couple of statues in a garden.

Swede grunted, tossed around, plumped up the coat he'd rolled into a pillow, and settled in again. A soft snore escaped him.

Nick tugged on her braid, bringing Shanyn's attention back to him.

"You'd better get back to sleep. Sunrise will be here before you know it."

Then he was gone, melting into the shadows, leaving her standing at the edge of the campsite.

Alone.

◆　◆　◆

They arrived at Hogueville the next day, and Austin didn't argue when Nick picked out a campsite on the outskirts of town. After the incident with the mountain lion, he seemed more than happy to let Nick decide where they'd camp.

After an uneventful night, Austin and his crew set about surveying the quadrant along the trail that led from Hogueville to Hangtown. Branson and the rest of the men would map from Hangtown toward them, and the two teams would meet in the middle.

Nick's job done for the time being, he saddled two horses and went in search of Shanyn. The whole purpose of coming to Hogueville had been to find Martha Hogue, and if he didn't escort Shanyn into town, she'd go alone. She'd proven that back in Hangtown. When she saw him, she blushed but quickly masked her pink cheeks by grabbing her hat.

"Are we heading to Hogueville?"

"I reckon." Nick glanced around. "Where's your aunt?"

"She's not feeling well." Her face pinched. "I think she's worried that I'm going to be disappointed again."

"You know there's a strong chance she's right?"

She nodded, the hope in her eyes dimming. "I know."

He searched her face. How could he tell her that he agreed with her aunt? That this Martha might be another dead end, and there would be no evidence of anyone having seen her father for months? He sighed. Time enough to mop up her tears if his worries proved true.

He reached out a hand to tuck a strand of hair behind her ear. "Well, I suppose as long as there's hope, that's all that matters."

She turned her face into his palm for the space of a heartbeat. His breath hitched, and he moved closer, his hand cupping her jaw, his gaze drawn to her mouth. He'd walked away last night, but wild horses couldn't drag him away from her right this minute. He dipped his head and tasted the sweet nectar of her lips.

Her lips softened under his, and he bit back a groan of pure pleasure.

He drew back, his gaze studying her face. Dark, sweeping lashes rested against her high cheekbones, and her lips were plump and moist where he'd just kissed her. Even as he feasted his gaze on her face, her lashes swept upward, revealing wide hazel eyes that tempted him to sweep her into his arms and claim her lips again.

"Nick?"

His name was barely a whisper on her lips.

What was he doing? She was on a quest to find her father, a man whom Nick, and everyone around them, believed to be dead. Her world had been turned upside down in the last week, and here he was, throwing her into another tailspin by offering her—

Offering her what?

He blew out an unsteady breath and stepped back, unable to think with her so near. There'd be time enough after they found Martha for him to analyze his feelings and what they meant.

"You wanted to know what was wrong last night." His voice came out low and husky, almost a growl. "Now you know."

Chapter Nine

S hanyn rode beside Nick, her thoughts whirling so fast, she wasn't sure if she was coming or going. What had happened back there? One minute she'd been focused on finding her father; the next she'd been in Nick's arms, his lips pressed against hers, his arms pulling her closer.

And if he hadn't pulled away, she'd have let him kiss her again.

She sneaked a peek at him, but he rode slightly ahead and to her left, jaw clenched and attention focused straight ahead. Her heart pounded. Did he already regret kissing her? He'd acted like it was the last thing he wanted to do. Goodness, he'd sounded plain mad about the whole thing.

She looked away, focused on the trail leading toward Hogueville, fighting the urge to say something—anything—to bring things back to an even keel between them.

But what could she say? That she was sorry he'd wanted to kiss her and even sorrier that he regretted it?

Instead, she kept silent.

They rounded a bend and Hogueville came into view, nestled alongside a stream, tents and hastily constructed cabins dotting the hillsides like an overturned bucket of coal scattered across the floor. There was no rhyme or reason to the chaos, except wherever someone found a spot to set up camp along the meandering streambed peppered with mining claims. Much smaller than Hangtown, this settlement looked like a way station to gather a few supplies and move on.

Nick reined in, overlooking the town, and Shanyn pulled to a stop beside him. She kept her attention on the mining camp.

"Shanyn?"

She looked at him, saw the worry in his eyes. His mouth worked to form the words, even while her heart thundered in her chest. He was going to tell her the kiss had been a mistake and that it would never happen again. She steeled her heart against his rejection.

"I'm sorry. I shouldn't have taken liberties back there."

Relief swooshed through Shanyn. Nick didn't regret kissing her because he hadn't wanted to, he was afraid he'd offended her. "You don't have to apologize—"

He chuckled. "I think I just did."

"Well. . .well, then, I'll apologize, too."

"For what?"

"For"—her face flamed—"for kissing you back, that's what."

With that, she kicked her horse in the flank and headed down the trail into Hogueville.

Nick's laughter rang out behind her, embarrassing her more than ever.

◆ ◆ ◆

The placer miners along the creek bed stopped, each of them staring as Shanyn and Nick drew closer. Nick caught up with her and gave her a warning glance. Shanyn let him take the lead, glad to have him with her even if she wasn't sure how she felt about him anymore.

A brawny man stepped forward, blocking the trail. "There ain't no claims left on this stretch of river. You'd best be moving on."

Nick reined in. "I'm not prospecting. We're looking for someone."

"Ain't we all?" someone called out as more men gathered, all gawking at Shanyn. The man's gaze shifted from Nick to Shanyn. "This your woman?"

Nick ignored the question. "We're looking for a woman named Martha. Could you tell us where to find her?"

The big man with the ruddy complexion stared at them. "Aye. Up the hill there. You can't miss it. Martha's Kitchen is the cabin with the big pot of stew always bubbling over the fire. Just follow your nose."

"Thanks." Nick reined away, and Shanyn followed.

They found the cabin just as the man had said, and Nick helped Shanyn down. A stout woman with a head full of frizzy red hair greeted them, her eyes lighting up when she saw Shanyn. "Landsakes, ain't you a sight for sore eyes."

"Excuse me, ma'am?" Did Martha recognize her? Maybe from some of her father's paintings?

Martha wiped her hands on her apron, then grabbed Shanyn's hands in both of hers. She spread her arms wide. "It's been a month of Sundays since I saw another woman. Oh, just let me look at you."

Disappointment swept over her. Martha didn't recognize her. She was just glad to see another woman. *Any* woman.

Martha pulled her inside the two-room cabin. "Now come in and tell me all about what's happening in Sacramento. What the ladies are wearing, the latest in hats. Is the bustle in or out this year?"

"Have some coffee, you and your young man." Martha reached for the coffeepot, then whirled back around, coffeepot in one hand, a tin cup in the other. "Landsakes! I was so excited, I forgot to ask your name. I'm Martha Hogue, by the way."

"Shanyn, ma'am. Shanyn Duvall."

"Duvall, you say?" Martha froze. "Obadiah's girl?"

"Yes, ma'am."

Martha's sigh was so dejected that Shanyn knew instinctively what the woman had to tell her wasn't good. She swallowed. "I heard he'd been seen in these parts and you might know where he is."

"I haven't seen him in months." Martha turned away and rummaged in a trunk in the corner. "But he left something for you."

Martha placed a bundle on the table. "Obadiah left these things with me months ago for safekeeping. He said to give them to Mr. Branson or you, whoever showed up first."

Shanyn fingered the bundle but didn't open it. "But where is he? Where did he go?"

Martha shook her head. "He didn't say, but he talked about the treasure he'd been looking for all his life. Treasure that would make his little Shanyn happy." She shrugged. "I figured he'd found gold, even though he hadn't done any prospecting that I know of."

"Maybe he'll come back." Shanyn's heart pounded against her chest. Somehow she'd hoped to arrive in Hogueville to find her father or, at the very least, to learn that he'd been spotted in the last few weeks and was expected back anytime. But Martha's words stripped away her last hope of finding him alive.

Martha's gaze met hers, pity lacing the crow's feet around her eyes. "I don't see how, dearie. No one's heard from him for months, and he would have come down for supplies or to get his gold weighed at the very least."

"But Papa wasn't searching for gold." Shanyn shook her head.

"He might've been. Who knows?"

"But wouldn't he have told you? Told someone?"

Martha shook her head. "It's not healthy to ask questions around these parts. If someone wants you to know something, they'll tell you. Otherwise, they keep it to themselves."

Shanyn glanced from Martha to Nick, stricken with the realization that what Mr. Branson, Swede, Nick, and the rest of them had been trying to tell her all along was true: her father was dead, and she'd been chasing a dream trying to find him. Her gaze flickered, dropped to the bundle her father had left for her.

"What will you do now? Will you go back to Sacramento?"

She blinked back tears. "I—I don't know."

Martha patted her hand. "You're welcome to stay with me as long as you need to, but Hogueville is no place for a woman alone."

"But you're here."

Martha smiled. "That's different. I'm old and wizened and worn slap out. You, on the other hand, have your whole life ahead of you."

◆　◆　◆

The clomp of boots sounded outside. Nick glanced out the door just in time to see a weatherbeaten miner plop down on one of the benches in front of Martha's Kitchen. He tossed his hat on the table and called out, "Martha, you got any stew, cornbread, biscuits? Anything at all? I'm about tuckered out."

"Be right there, Zeke." Martha patted Shanyn's hand. "You two stay here. Take all the time you need."

Martha bustled outside, leaving Nick and Shanyn inside her shanty. Shanyn picked at the bundle in front of her, and Nick leaned against the table, watching her. He'd wanted to spare her from this, but she'd insisted. And maybe it was for the best. If she hadn't come all the way to Hogueville and met Martha, not knowing might have haunted her for the rest of her life.

"Are you going to open it?"

Her hazel eyes, awash with tears, lifted to meet his. "I'm afraid. This is the last thing I'll ever have of Papa's." Her words were barely a whisper. A single tear spilled over and tracked down her cheek. "I know I should've accepted that he was dead that very first day when—when Mr. Branson said he hadn't seen him, but I couldn't. Nick, I just couldn't. I'd waited so long to see him again."

Tears spilled over and ran down her cheeks. Nick closed the distance between them and pulled her into his arms. She wrapped her arms around his waist and pressed her check against his shirtfront. His heart broke over the tears she shed for her father.

When her sobs quieted, she pulled away. He loosened his hold but still held her, unwilling to let her go.

"It hurts to think he's"—she paused, hiccupping—"he's out there somewhere. . .

"Shh. Don't think about it. He was doing what he loved, exploring new lands, seeing beautiful waterfalls and grand vistas, and carving puzzles. He would want you to remember him doing the things he loved."

She sniffed. "And how did you get to be so smart, Nick Johnston?"

He shrugged. "By living out my dreams."

"And what are those?" she whispered, her words barely audible.

Nick wondered if she could hear the thunderous beat of his heart.

"My dreams? Nothing too fancy. Some land. Horses." She lifted her head, her gaze searching his. Tears spiked her eyelashes, and her cheeks were splotchy and her eyes swollen from crying, but she was still the most beautiful woman he'd ever seen. He cupped her face and wiped the tears from her cheeks with his thumbs.

"Is that all?"

His gaze swept over her face. "A home. A family."

Her lips parted, and to his amazement, a blush swept over her cheeks. She pulled out of his arms, smoothed the package with both hands, and reached for the string.

Nick stuffed his hands in his pockets, feeling like a first-class heel. What was he thinking? Shanyn had just lost her father, and she needed time to grieve, to make decisions. She didn't need him to confuse her with his half-baked ideas of a place to settle down, a home, and a family.

A home with her right smack-dab at the center of it.

"I've got to see to the horses."

And with that profound announcement, he bolted.

Chapter Ten

A home. A family.

That was what Nick wanted. What she wanted. And what Papa had been trying to find for them as long as she could remember. Shanyn stared at the empty doorway without really seeing the open space that led to Martha's yard. Instead, her mind filled with pictures of Nick—the way his blue-green eyes looked when he was listening to her talk about her paintings, and the way he soothed a cantankerous mule or a frightened horse.

He didn't lose his temper with the men, with the animals, or with her. He just went about his business, making sure things got done and somehow taking care of her in the process.

Papa had always talked of finding a place to settle down, that was true, but sometimes she wondered if he'd be happy tied to one place. Maybe the idea of a home was more for her and Aunt Skeet than for himself.

Truth be told, Papa had been on the move ever since her ma had died when she was seven.

She fingered the bundle on the table, numbness setting in. She'd fought the truth from the moment Mr. Branson had said her father was dead, but she couldn't fight it any longer. She'd have to accept that she and Aunt Skeet were alone in the world, and they'd have to make decisions about a future that didn't include her father.

But will that future include Nick?

Her heart stuttered in her chest. It was true. She wanted him in her life, but did he feel the same? Yes, he liked her, and—her cheeks heated at the reminder—he'd kissed her, and he was adept at protecting her and watching out for her, but that didn't mean that his feelings went any deeper.

Even as her thoughts roiled in confusion, she untied the string and peeled the oilcloth back. Inside she found one of her father's boxes of puzzles, but with no picture painted on the front.

Which meant he hadn't finished this puzzle.

No matter. She could assemble the pieces inside and paint the picture on the front. Maybe the activity would keep her mind off of Nick. Maybe she could even start carving and painting puzzles of her own, painting portraits for miners. If the response in Hangtown was any indication, she might be able to make a living for herself and Aunt Skeet with the artistic skills she'd inherited from her father.

She opened the box, dumped the pieces on the table, her smile bittersweet. More than likely this was her father's last puzzle, a piece of him she could treasure always. Flashes of green, blue, white, along with rippling water and clouds, peeked at her. Looked like it was another breathtaking scene of the mountains.

After sorting the pieces and rearranging them, she frowned.

Had Papa intended to turn these pieces into a completed puzzle? It didn't make sense, though. None of them matched. The colors were all wrong—nothing fit. She fingered two pieces with distinctive cuts, locking them together and then pulling them apart as she pondered the odd assortment spread out on the table.

She pushed the two together once again, running her fingers over the perfectly smooth fit. Frowning, she sorted through the pieces, found another that interlocked with the ones in her hand.

One after the other, she connected the pieces together, ignoring the painted picture, concentrating only on shapes and sizes, cuts and compatibility. Every piece fit together like a hand in a glove. Oddly enough, the landscape even made a bit of sense in a strange, distorted way.

If she squinted.

But the shading was all wrong, just enough to throw the picture off.

Was this one of her father's games? Something new he'd come up with to make her think? But for what purpose? It was obvious he'd placed all these puzzle pieces in this box for a reason.

Turning one of the puzzle pieces over and over between her fingers, she gazed out Martha's open door, thinking. The sound of laughter from Martha's customers rolled over her. Then Nick strolled into view, one of the canvas packs over his shoulder, a pack like the one her father's puzzles were in. Shanyn straightened, looked at the puzzle that fit together, but somehow didn't.

"That's it," she whispered, remembering the puzzles back in camp, the pieces that were missing. Some were the same odd shapes, the same colors. Surely—

"What is it?" Nick stopped in the doorway, his gaze sweeping over the puzzle.

Shanyn tapped the puzzle. "These are the missing pieces to the other puzzles."

Nick stared at the puzzle. "Are you sure? That looks like a complete puzzle to me. You've already put it together."

"Yes, but—come look." Shanyn grabbed his arm, pulled him closer to the table, and waved a hand over the puzzle. "The pieces fit, but the scene—the colors—are all wrong. It looks okay from a distance, but not if you look at it up close."

Nick stared at the landscape, then nodded. "I see. It sort of looks like each piece was painted separately, not all together like the other ones you showed me. Did your father ever paint anything like this before?"

"Never. He was too much of a perfectionist to paint something this. . .disjointed." Shanyn placed the puzzles back in the box. "We've got to get back to camp."

Martha stepped inside. "Oh, you're leaving? Why don't you and your aunt stay here? There's a thunderstorm brewing, and you'd be a lot more comfortable here than in a soggy tent in a camp full of men."

"Are you sure? I don't want to impose."

"I insist."

"Thank you, Martha. We appreciate the invitation."

"Go on with you now." Martha shooed them out the door. "You'll want to pack up your things and be back before that storm blows in."

Back at camp, Shanyn went in search of her aunt while Nick went to get pack mules to carry their belongings back to town.

"Aunt Skeet?"

"Did you find the woman, Martha?"

"We found her. She's really nice."

Aunt Skeet searched her face. "From the look on your face, I can tell the news wasn't good."

Shanyn shook her head. "She hasn't heard from him in months."

Her aunt wiped her hands on her apron and folded Shanyn in her arms, then held her at arms' length, her gaze stern. "You've got to accept that he's gone, Shanyn. If Obadiah was alive, he would have gotten word to us somehow."

"I know." Shanyn took a deep breath. "But it hurts."

"There, there. I know it does."

"Martha wants us to stay with her while we're in Hogueville. I told her we would."

"Oh, I don't know about that." Her aunt glanced around. "Austin needs me here to cook for the crew."

"Swede can handle meals for this bunch. And I have some more news for you. About Papa's puzzles."

◆　◆　◆

The first drops of rain had started to fall by the time they returned to Martha's. Shanyn grabbed one of the packs and hurried inside, while Nick and Aunt Skeet followed with the remaining packs.

Martha dished up big bowls of stew and set them on the table inside. "Nick, there's plenty of stew if you'd like some."

"Thank you, ma'am, but I'd better get back to camp."

"Nonsense." Martha motioned to a chair. "Sit. Eat. You might as well wait until it stops raining. No need to go out in this."

Throughout the meal, Skeet and Martha chatted like long-lost friends, Martha peppering Skeet with questions about life back East. Skeet and Shanyn asked questions about Martha's life before Hogueville.

"Horace wanted to seek his fortune in California, and there was nothing to keep me in Tennessee. So we came West. He died in his sleep well over a year ago. Just laid down one night and didn't wake up the next morning."

"I'm sorry."

"Thank you, Skeet." Martha's smile was tinged with sadness. "I still miss him, but the years we had were good ones. I can't complain."

As soon as the table was cleared, Martha headed outside to serve another customer, and Shanyn dumped the contents of one of the puzzles on the table. "You won't believe what I found when I got here."

"What?"

Shanyn started turning pieces right side up, explaining about the mismatched pieces her father had left with Martha and how they might fit with the puzzles they'd brought with them.

"Well, this will be interesting." Skeet stared at the puzzles. "So you're going to put them all together?"

"It won't take long."

"It'll take long enough." Aunt Skeet poured another cup of coffee, eyeing her. "Shanyn, why are you doing this? Putting all these puzzles together isn't going to bring your father back."

Shanyn glanced at Nick. "I know, but he separated those pieces for a reason, and you know Papa didn't do that on a whim."

"You're right about that. Obadiah wasn't one to do something like that without a good reason." She moved to the table and pulled out a chair. "Well, if you're determined, I might as well help. This is going to take a long time. There's no way to fit all the puzzles on top of this table."

"What if you put a piece of oilcloth or canvas under each one? Then you can move them out of the way or layer them on top of each other if you need to?"

"That's a good idea." Shanyn grinned at Nick. "Want to help?"

His gaze met hers, and she had the feeling he did want to stay. Maybe just to be with her, or perhaps because the idea of putting the puzzles together intrigued him.

"Sorry, it's stopped raining, and I need to check on the horses."

"Of course. I wasn't thinking."

As he left, Martha called out, "Be sure and stop by for supper, Nick. Zeke brought a haunch of venison, so there'll be a fresh pot of venison stew on the fire."

Shanyn dipped her head and concentrated on the puzzle. Would he come back? She sure hoped so.

Chapter Eleven

Nick glanced at ick "I A
ing about he the on a wh
and right over that

Nick stayed busy the next couple of days, taking care of the pack mules and the horses, making sure they were fed and watered. With so many claims along the river, he ended up moving their camp farther away just for grazing.

In the evenings, he'd even tried his hand at carving some soft wood into small interlocking pieces. He couldn't draw worth a flip, but he was a fair hand at carving, and after he got the knack of it, his little pieces of wood fit together almost as well as the ones Shanyn's father had made. He remembered Shanyn talking about how her father carved the pieces first, then painted them.

He didn't have time to visit Shanyn, which might be for the best. On the third day, Mr. Branson's party rode in. He'd had more men desert their duties, so he decided to combine crews and equipment, hoping to make up for lost time.

Branson and Whitman mapped out a new schedule, and the remaining men left early the next day to survey the area to the west.

Nick was working on a broken bridle when Bailey rode into camp. "Nick, Mr. Branson's been looking for you. He's over in Hogueville talking business with a couple of miners. I think they're looking for someone to make a trip to Sacramento."

Nick frowned. "We've already got a job. Working for Mr. Branson."

"I think Branson is the one who suggested it."

"All right." Nick downed the last of his coffee and grabbed Bailey's horse. "I'll see what he wants. Where are they?"

"Just down the street from Martha's. A brand-spanking new store just going up. You can't miss it."

He found the place easily.

"Nick. There you are." Mr. Branson motioned to two men standing in front of the new building. "These two gentlemen are looking for someone to bring supplies in from Sacramento to stock their store, and I could use more supplies myself since we're going to be working this area for the next few months. Would you and Bailey be willing to make the trip?"

"I don't see why not," Nick agreed. "I'm working for you, Mr. Branson."

One of the men reached out and shook Nick's hand. "Jonathan Stark, at your service. It was a stroke of fortune that Mr. Branson showed up when he did, and that he'd engaged such a trustworthy guide as yourself, Mr. Johnston. My partner and I were at our wits' end on how to supply our new store without leaving Hogueville. You are an answer to prayer, sir."

In spite of his tattered and worn clothes, the man's speech identified him as a shrewd businessman.

"If you don't mind my asking, why go all the way to Sacramento? Why not stock your store out of Hangtown?"

"Prices too high there. We've already got a shipment of goods coming around the Horn. Should be in Sacramento by the time you get there. But if they're not, I'll give you a list of things to purchase and a letter of recommendation for my business partner there."

Nick nodded. "When do you want me to leave?"

"Give us a few days to put together another order. And I imagine there are others who'd like to tag along with you and send letters and such. Speaking of letters"—his eyes twinkled—"that Miss Skeet has gained quite a following from the miners."

"You mean her niece, Miss Shanyn?"

"Well, Miss Shanyn's been quite busy herself the last few days, what with her paintings and sketches. But her aunt's writing letters for miners who can't write for themselves. And on top of that, they've been helping in Martha's Kitchen. Just a fine setup if you ask me. Three women in Hogueville. Before long, we'll have a thriving little town here."

The two men went on their way, and Branson walked with Nick toward camp. "There's something else I'd like you to do, Nick."

"Yes, sir."

"I feel responsible for Shanyn and her aunt, and I'd like you to take them back to Sacramento." Branson took off his glasses and rubbed the lenses with his handkerchief. He squinted, looking a bit out of sorts. "I've known the family for years, and I don't know what they're going to do now, but I don't think Hogueville is the place for them to settle."

Nick's heart pounded. Shanyn and her aunt were here on suffrage from Mr. Branson. He'd allowed them to travel with him, and as he said, he was partly responsible for them. If he wanted them to return to Sacramento, they might not have much choice. "Have you asked them what they want to do?"

"Not yet."

"What about Shanyn's painting, and her father's puzzles? Could she make a better living here or in Sacramento?" He didn't even mention Hangtown as an option.

"Maybe, but it would be difficult. If they return to Sacramento, however, they can stay at the quarters I've rented and then accompany me back to Virginia when I return. Surely they have family back East." Branson patted him on the back. "See what you can do, my boy. Shanyn seems to trust your advice, and Skeet always follows her niece's lead."

"Yes, sir."

Nick turned, looking toward Martha's. More tables were out front with several miners enjoying an evening meal. Skeet and Martha were serving stew again, but Shanyn was nowhere to be seen.

He fingered the small pieces of wood in his pocket. Could he convince Shanyn to return to Sacramento? And if Mr. Branson's plan was to take them all the way back to Virginia, did he want to?

◆　◆　◆

Shanyn stared at the sixteen puzzles she and her aunt had assembled over the last few days in between helping Martha cook and clean and continuing to paint and write letters for the miners. They'd even taken in some laundry. Good, honest work that brought in some money for Martha and allowed Shanyn and her aunt to pay their way.

Martha had even asked them about staying on and helping her run Martha's Kitchen. Aunt Skeet thought it was a fine idea, but Shanyn didn't want to commit. Every time the discussion turned to whether they'd stay on and help Martha, all Shanyn could think of was Nick.

Martha and Aunt Skeet had long since gone to bed, but Shanyn stayed up to finish the last puzzle. When she finished, she spread all of them out on the floor to study them.

She squinted, frustrated by the dim light. What was it about the puzzles that she was supposed to see? Somehow if she could just unlock that riddle, maybe she could move on with her life.

She started at a rap against the door. "Who is it?"

"It's Nick."

Her heart did a little jig when she heard his voice.

She let him in, and he sidestepped the puzzles. "I saw your light was on and thought I'd stop in. Looks like you got them all done."

"Yes." She nodded.

"You don't sound too happy about it. Did all the extra pieces fit into the other puzzles like you thought?"

"Perfectly." She sighed, something niggling at her.

"What's bothering you, then?"

"If Papa went to so much trouble to carve all these pieces that fit together, but that also fit into sixteen larger puzzles, there had to be a reason."

Something more than just a game for her to unravel.

"A map to a rich claim maybe?"

Could it be a gold mine as Nick and Martha suspected? Papa had never been one to seek quick riches. She shook her head. "When did Papa have time to pan for gold?"

Nick shrugged. "He could have stumbled on it by accident. Besides, there's nothing wrong with panning for gold. Hundreds of thousands are doing it."

"Have you?"

"Here and there. I just haven't found it to be as lucrative as some have." He shrugged, grim. "And seems like folks are less likely to kill you over a string of mules than a claim."

Shanyn's heart twisted. Nick had good reasons to steer clear of mining.

"Does there have to be a reason?" He hunkered down, studying the puzzles that covered most of the floor. "Couldn't he have just been looking forward to stumping you?"

"I can't see him going to that much trouble just for fun." Shanyn froze. "Wait a minute."

"What?"

"Look." She pointed out three of the puzzles. "The terrain on these are flatter and the grass is greener as if they're at a lower elevation, maybe closer to Sacramento. The mountains are in the distance in that one. Closer on this one." She waved her hands. "I think those three go on the left."

Nick nodded. "I see it. Let's rearrange them."

"Okay." Shanyn grabbed the corners of the oilcloth one of the puzzles was on. Nick took the other side. "This one goes in the top right corner."

They rearranged the puzzles, then stood back. The panoramic scene swept left to right, from ships in the harbor to snow-covered mountain peaks.

"What do you think?" she asked.

Nick pointed. "While there's a lot left to the imagination, put in order like that, that would be Sacramento, Hangtown, the American River with the North, Middle, and South Forks as you go farther inland, and the Sierra Nevada along the top."

Shanyn nodded, a sense of euphoria sweeping over her that she'd figured it out. Her gaze met Nick's, and he winked. A warm, fuzzy feeling engulfed her, and she couldn't help but grin.

They'd figured it out. *Together.*

She faced the puzzles on the floor, standing shoulder to shoulder with Nick. "That's what Papa was trying to tell me. Those smaller pieces he pulled out made a puzzle, but like you said the other day, they fit into the larger puzzles, then those puzzles made a bigger picture."

She cocked her head, studying the arrangement in the dim light. "Do you notice anything odd though?"

He frowned. "Like what?"

"Well, each individual puzzle is a scene from a mining town, or a miner panning for gold, with the white water rushing toward the ocean. Except—"

"Except the one in the top right corner."

"Exactly." Shanyn peered closer. "It's a cabin with a man standing beside the stream with an easel and paints, his gaze on the valley spread before him. It has nothing to do with gold." Shanyn knelt, ran her fingers over the image of the artist with his canvas. "Can you take me there, Nick? Can you find this place that Papa painted?"

Chapter Twelve

Nick wanted to say yes. Staring into her beautiful hazel eyes filled with tears, he wanted to give her everything she asked for, but he couldn't. He reached up and cupped her face. "I'm sorry, Shanyn, but there's no way to find your father's claim based on this. It would be like looking for a piece of gold dust in the ocean."

"But this means something. I know it does."

"I believe you, but there's just not enough here to find him."

She sighed, closed her eyes, and he could see that she'd accepted defeat. "You're right. I let my excitement get the best of me." She smiled and moved to pick up the nearest puzzle. "Too many years of putting together Papa's puzzles and following his maps made me forget how vast this country is. I'll put these away so we can get some rest. It's been a long day for both of us."

Nick's heart skipped a beat, then resumed beating, fast and furious. He snapped his fingers. "Wait."

Her gaze met his, a question in her eyes.

"Didn't your father paint maps on the back of the puzzles?"

"Yes. Why—"

"Let's flip these over and see what the other side looks like." Nick shrugged. "It's worth a try."

They turned the puzzles over, carefully flipping the entire group, keeping them in order. Nothing was labeled, but with all sixteen puzzles together, it was easy to spot the major towns, the tributaries, the streams, the mountain ranges, and all of the known camps.

Shanyn traced the route all the way from Sacramento to Hangtown on up to Hogueville. From there, the trail led due east. "Can you find it? Can you take me there?"

"Nothing's changed."

She turned, her hazel eyes pleading. "What if you're right? What if he found gold? What if someone followed him and—"

Her voice broke, and Nick took her in his arms, tucking her head against his chest. He kissed her forehead, then held her away from him. "If I take you to see this valley, then do you promise to return to Sacramento?"

Her gaze searched his, and she nodded. "Yes. I promise."

Nick turned away, the puzzle pieces in his pocket weighing heavily on his mind. He'd done as Mr. Branson asked, made her promise to return to Sacramento where she'd be safe.

But for some reason, the thought didn't make him feel any better.

◆ ◆ ◆

Mr. Branson and Austin decided to ride along. They wanted to get a visual of the area, and it was as good a time as any. Shanyn wanted to go faster, but Nick wouldn't be hurried. He estimated it was about a day's ride from Hogueville to the high mountain valley, but he'd brought along a pack mule with plenty of supplies in case they had to make camp.

The mules picked their way up and over a steep hill, wound around another outcropping of rock, then found a narrow path that climbed upward at a dizzying rate. They rode single-file for over an hour.

When the ground leveled out, Shanyn rode closer to Nick. "How do you know we're going in the right direction?"

"We're going east."

"But what if we miss it?"

Nick shifted in the saddle. "People and animals follow the easiest route, and we've been following a faint trail. As long as we don't run into several canyons veering off into different directions, I think we'll be fine."

Branson pulled out his compass, sighted, and headed forward. "We're veering away from the river. I haven't seen a miner in over two hours. Are you sure this is the right way?"

"Papa wasn't looking for gold. I'm sure of it. So it would make sense that he'd want to get away from the hordes of miners."

Austin spoke up. "We're getting above the timber line. Maybe Obadiah never even came this way. What if he just painted that puzzle for the fun of it?"

Shanyn tamped down her annoyance. Austin didn't know Papa at all if he believed that. "Papa wouldn't have painted the map on the back if it didn't relate to the landscapes somehow."

"It makes no sense. The painting you described was of a beautiful mountain meadow with grass and trees, and a mountain stream flowing through it." He waved his hand before him. "There's nothing here but dirt and rock."

"She's right." Mr. Branson urged his mule forward. "Obadiah was very methodical, even when creating whimsical pieces such as his puzzles. We'll continue on to the next ridge. Hopefully, we'll see something there."

They had to ride through several switchbacks to make it to the ridge Mr. Branson had indicated. They dipped low, then rode higher again. Sometimes they found a faint trail. If not, Nick let the mules have their heads.

Nick was in the lead, and when he topped the ridge, he stopped, sat back in the saddle, and rested his hands on the pommel. Shanyn urged her mount faster, then came to a complete stop as she stared at the high mountain valley spread out before them.

At least a mile below where they sat on the ridge, a placid lake, as blue as the sky above, winked at them through the evergreens, and a stream studded with rocks meandered through the valley toward the lowlands. Shanyn sucked in a breath of pure mountain air, hardly able to take in the beauty of the valley in front of her.

Mr. Branson and Austin joined them, both as mesmerized by the view as Nick and Shanyn were.

"That's it," she whispered. "That's the valley he painted."

Almost afraid to look, she scanned the entire valley, looking for the cabin her father had painted. Was the cabin a figment of his imagination, or was it real?

Her heart lurched. Nestled among the trees sat a small cabin with a long front porch. Smoke curled from the chimney.

Even as she watched, a man stepped off the porch, a crutch under one arm.

"Papa?" Shanyn breathed his name, then shouted it a second time. "Papa!"

The words echoed against the mountains and came back to her.

Papa. Papa. Papa.

He turned, stood stock still, then waved. "Shanyn!"

Chapter Thirteen

Shanyn's father slapped Mr. Branson on the back. "Thom, I knew you'd come."

Mr. Branson looked sheepish. "If it hadn't been for Shanyn and Nick here, I'm afraid I might not have. We'd given you up for dead. What happened?"

"Last spring I was exploring and found this valley. I knew it was what I'd been looking for my whole life." Shanyn's father pulled her close and kissed her forehead. She wrapped her arms around his waist and gazed up at him, eyes shining.

"I went back to Hogueville and hired a couple of men to come up here and help me build a cabin. They came willingly, but I didn't find out until later that they thought I'd struck it rich." His gaze shifted between Nick and Austin as if he thought the two of them would run out and start panning for gold any minute. "If there's any here, I haven't found it, and neither did they."

"They kept talking about moving on, and about that time a band of Indians passed through, headed toward their summer hunting grounds. They were a peaceful tribe, but those two didn't know that." Mr. Duvall laughed. "I might have spun a tale or two about how savage they were. Scared those two so bad they didn't dare leave for another month. Thankfully, they helped finish the cabin, but I woke up one morning and they were gone. Took my horse and my pack mule, too."

"I started hiking out but fell before I got to the ridge up there. Broke my leg, and I've been here ever since." He grew serious. "I'm glad you showed up when you did. My leg's almost healed, but I don't know that I could walk out of here anytime soon."

"Oh, Papa, if you hadn't left those puzzles for me with the maps on the back, we wouldn't have found you." Shanyn glanced at Nick, her eyes shining with moisture. "And it was Nick's idea to look on the back after we figured out they all fit together."

Nick gave a short nod. Shanyn was solely responsible for saving her father's life. She'd been the one to insist that they keep searching. She'd never given up hope, not really.

Branson cleared his throat. "Speaking of supplies, Nick had the foresight to bring a pack mule with us. Let's see if we can rustle up some supper. This calls for a celebration."

◆　◆　◆

Nick hunkered down, a blade of grass in his hands, as he watched the horses nibbling on the lush summer grass, the peaceful valley just the kind he'd been looking for his whole life.

Mr. Duvall had built his cabin in a spot that overlooked the entire valley, with water close by, but with no danger of flooding. He'd chosen well, but then he would. He was a cartographer, an engineer by trade.

He stood when he spotted Shanyn's father hobbling toward him, his hand-carved crutch under his arm. "Evening, sir."

"Evening, Nick." The older man turned, breathed in deep, and let his gaze roam over the valley. "This is my favorite time of day, just before the sun dips below the tops of the mountains, when the shadows are long and the valley is bathed in a soft, pure light."

"I can see where Shanyn gets her love of sunrises and sunsets."

Mr. Duvall chuckled. "The first few weeks after my accident, I sat on that porch and painted from noon to night. I couldn't do much else."

"From what I've seen of your work, I imagine you enjoyed it."

"I did. Until I ran out of paints. Shanyn is convinced she never would have found this place without your help."

"I didn't do anything, Mr. Duvall—"

"Obadiah will do, son. I never was one to stand on ceremony. Thom also tells me that you and your partner, Mr. Bailey, have a nice string of pack animals. He speaks highly of you."

"Yes, sir." Nick ran the blade of grass through his fingers, eyeing Mr. Duvall. What was he getting at?

"See that saddleback in the mountains?" He pointed to the opposite end of the valley where the setting sun reflected off the reservoir of sky-blue water fed by the mountain stream. "That's where those Indians came through. From what I gathered, and the bit of exploring I was able to do before my accident, I'm convinced there's a route through those mountains to Eagle Valley. This area will see more guides, more pack mules, even a stage route someday, probably a lot sooner than you'd think."

Nick nodded, trying to keep his surprise from showing. Growing his string of horses and mules and someday owning a stagecoach would be a dream come true. Routes would need to be surveyed, roads built, way stations picked. It could take years, but it was a future he embraced.

"Nick, you're just the kind of man this country needs, so I'll get straight to the point. In the space of three hours since you've arrived, I've seen the way my daughter looks at you, and I feel obliged to say my piece. You and Shanyn have gotten to know each other quite well over the last few weeks and—" Mr. Duvall paused, shifted his weight on the crutch.

"Mr. Duvall, I respect Shanyn. I'd never do anything to hurt her. I'd protect her with my life."

"I know that. And that's what I'm trying to say, although I'm doing a poor job of it." His gaze bored into Nick. "My daughter cares a great deal for you. Did you know that?"

Nick waited, heart pounding. Well, she'd seemed to welcome his kisses, but that wasn't something Nick planned to share with her father. "Well, I'd like to hope that she does."

"Good. I'm glad you feel that way. In light of that, I'd like to know your intentions, because this valley won't be big enough for both of us if you break my daughter's heart."

Nick stared into the distance, unsure what to say. Did Shanyn care for him enough to marry him? Her father seemed to think so. "So I have your blessing to ask your daughter to marry me? That is, if she'll have me."

"You do." Mr. Duvall nodded. "Now, if you don't mind, I'd better get off this leg. Shanyn will have my hide if I injure it again."

"Mr. Duvall?" Nick followed him toward the cabin. "I mean—Obadiah, sir. Could I borrow a small paintbrush and some paint?"

Chapter Fourteen

When Nick woke the next morning, Shanyn was nowhere to be found. Which didn't surprise him in the least. She was probably hanging off a cliff somewhere, painting the sunrise.

He stepped to the edge of the porch and scanned the mountains surrounding the valley. "I wonder where she got off to," he muttered. "The view from here wouldn't do?"

"I guess not. You're going to have your hands full keeping up with that one, Johnston." A chuckle from the other end of the porch drew his attention. Whitman, chair tipped back against the wall, boots propped up against a post, grinned at him. He lifted his coffee cup in salute. "I defer to the better tracker."

Nick scowled, stepped off the porch, and followed his instincts. If he knew Shanyn, she'd head for the highest peak she could find. When he found her, she was seated on an outcropping of rock, a blanket wrapped around her shoulders, her paints and brushes spread out beside her. The sun, well on its way to greeting the morning, bathed the valley in gold and green, the sky in varying shades of blue. The horses grazed peacefully in the meadow, and smoke curled from her father's cabin.

But Nick had eyes only for Shanyn. He inched closer, using every bit of the tracking skills he'd learned over the years. He leaned against a tree within twenty feet of her, close enough that she could see him if she wasn't so focused on the scene below.

In her haste to beat the sunrise, she'd plaited her dark brown hair, and the resulting braid hung down her back. Strands escaped to wave in the early morning breeze. She tipped her head to the side and studied her painting, comparing it to the panoramic view below. Nick drank in the sight of her even as she focused on the valley coming to life.

He waited, absolutely still, knowing she'd spot him eventually. He knew the exact moment she became aware of his presence. Her lips twitched, then relaxed, and she tipped her chin up as if she was going to pretend he wasn't there.

He fingered the wooden pieces in his pocket. He hadn't had time to carve enough for a twelve-inch square puzzle, but the pieces he had finished were just big enough for the task he had in mind.

She managed to ignore him for another ten minutes, a record. Then her lips twitched, and her hazel eyes flickered in his direction. "I see you, Nick Johnston. You can come on out now."

Nick grinned, straightened away from the tree, and headed toward her.

◆ ◆ ◆

Shanyn's breath caught, and all thoughts of capturing the perfect sunrise on canvas fled as Nick lowered himself to the rock a few feet away, rested his weight on his elbows,

341

and looked out over the valley, giving her the quiet she needed to concentrate on her painting.

Her fingers shook as she touched her brush to the palette in her hand. But instead of painting the sunrise, she found herself mixing paints on her palette, trying to capture the exact shade of his wind-tossed dark hair, the pale blue-green of his eyes. Nick's nearness took her breath in a way the sunrise never could.

He glanced over his shoulder, his brow furrowed. "You're not painting."

"I—" Her face flushed as she looked at the dabs of color on the wooden board in her hand. "I'm finished for now."

"I didn't mean to interrupt. I just wanted to make sure you were all right."

She smiled. "Always my protector."

"I'll leave." His green-eyed gaze probed hers, the intense look on his face making her squirm. "If that's what you want."

She got the feeling he was talking about more than just leaving this rock and letting her get back to painting. Her heart pounded. She didn't want him to leave. Not now. Not ever.

"No," she whispered. "I don't want you to leave."

His gaze still holding hers, he reached out a hand, and she took it. Her insides turned to mush and her heart started pounding, but instead of kissing her, he pulled her to his side, his arm wrapped around her waist. Then he pointed toward the mountains on the other side of the valley.

"Your father thinks there's a route through the mountains and that we could build roads, start a stage line." He glanced at her. "What do you think? Would you be happy living here?"

She searched his gaze, knowing her answer would seal her future. "Yes." Unable to stop the tears from springing to her eyes, she blinked and whispered, "Very."

He reached out a hand and tucked a strand of hair behind her ear, his fingers lingering there, making her shiver.

"Cold?"

"No." She shook her head.

A smile played over his lips even as his gaze swept across her face, over her lips, and back up to capture her gaze again. He wanted to kiss her. She could see it in his eyes, feel it in the way he held her anchored against his side.

Disappointment as wide as the valley stretched out below them slammed into her when he pulled away. He reached into his pocket and pulled out a neckerchief-wrapped bundle and handed it to her.

"I made you something."

"What is it?"

He leaned back and watched her, the serious look on his face belying the feelings swirling between them. "Open it and see."

With shaking fingers, she untied two corners of the kerchief, then the opposite corners. She grinned. "It's a puzzle."

He didn't return her smile, didn't comment, just watched her with those mesmerizing blue-green eyes that she could drown in. She bit her lip and spread out the puzzle pieces.

There weren't many, and instead of forming a picture, the pieces looked like they held words.

Heart pounding, fingers shaking, she started putting the pieces together until the small, hand-lettered message was displayed. She blinked back tears, lifted her gaze to his, and nodded. "Yes. Oh yes, Nick Johnston, I'll marry you."

He smiled.

And *then* he kissed her.

CBA bestselling author **Pam Hillman** was born and raised on a dairy farm in Mississippi and spent her teenage years perched on the seat of a tractor raking hay. In those days, her daddy couldn't afford two cab tractors with air-conditioning and a radio, so Pam drove an Allis Chalmers 110. Even when her daddy asked her if she wanted to bale hay, she told him she didn't mind raking. Raking hay doesn't take much thought, so Pam spent her time working on her tan and making up stories in her head. Now that's the kind of life every girl should dream of. Visit her website at www.pamhillman.com.

The Golden Cross

by Jennifer Rogers Spinola

Chapter One

Canton Province, China
March, 1849

S*uk-suk? Uncle?"* called Ming in her native Cantonese, peering through the door as she heard his tired feet plod across the wet, muddy ground toward the little bamboo frame house. "How is the rice?"

Uncle Wang didn't answer. A grim look shadowed his face, lining the corners of his eyes and mouth with wrinkles, with an expression as dark and grievous as the rain that poured outside.

"Do not ask me, *qiānjīn*, my good daughter," he sighed, borrowing the word from Mandarin. He slipped off his muddy, broken sandals and stepped onto the packed dirt floor. His long, thin braid, threaded with gray, hung over his shoulder—the braid he'd grown out since childhood, required of all Han Chinese men by the Qing dynasty under penalty of death. "Pray to the Lord instead. He knows our need."

Ming bit her lips to keep back a cry of despair, latching the rickety door behind her uncle and hurrying to fetch him a dry cloth. Her stomach knotted with hunger, and she tried not to notice the hollows in her uncle's cheeks as he sponged wet strands of hair back from his face. His bony fingers, with their earth-blackened nails, wore blisters. Scars from the metal farm scythes mingled with the slashes from leaves and stalks crisscrossed the backs of his hands.

It had been a hard three years—and her uncle had nearly exhausted himself fighting the land and losing. The succulent *choy sum* greens, the purple sweet potatoes, even the beautiful lychee trees had all surrendered one by one to heat, weevils, and a one-two-punch of drought and blight.

Only a few scattered farm animals and the precious rice paddy remained. Thanks to a broken dam and torrential rains, roiling brown floodwaters had crept into the tender rice plants and broken down the stalks, uprooting the plants.

For the first time, Ming had nothing to feed the chickens. No melon peels or sweet potato scraps. No leftover rice.

Uncle Wang slaughtered their single pig last year, determined not to let it suffer and starve.

"It's that bad?" Ming whispered.

Uncle Wang met her eyes above the cloth, their dark teardrop shapes sparkling dully in the dim lantern light. "We will ask God again."

"Qiānjīn," Ming's uncle had called her in Mandarin. "Dear daughter" or "a thousand pieces of gold." A rare term of endearment in Canton Province of southeastern China, where parents more commonly called their children harsher names in Cantonese like "no-nothing" or "lazy worm"—sometimes tongue-in-cheek, sometimes not.

And here she stood, not even his daughter but his niece who had no place else to go when her parents died—first her father in a farming accident and then her mother from disease.

Ming turned back to the little clay fire pit, trying to hide her expression. If only she had a thousand pieces of gold! She would buy her uncle a new pair of sandals and serve him the best lobster with ginger and noodles, thousand-year eggs, and rich broth of pork and mushrooms. He would hire servants to work the fields and rest his tired old bones by the fire instead of slaving for hours in a muddy bog that seemed unwilling to cooperate.

Ming pressed her eyes closed and busied herself with the little serving of rice and water spinach, spooning it into a round clay bowl.

The beam where dried tea leaves once hung in fragrant clumps now lay empty, so she poured plain, steaming hot water into a rounded teacup, one edge cracked. If she imagined hard enough, she could still smell the rich, warm flavors of tea leaves instead of briny water, and the sweet fragrance of jasmine blossoms instead of cheap clay.

"It's your turn, Uncle," she said out loud, setting the bowl and teacup on a plain tray with simple wooden chopsticks. "I have already eaten." She placed the bowl on a low table and knelt across from Uncle Wang, pushing the tray closer. "We will pray to God to save our harvest. The Maker of heaven and earth can stop the floodwaters, can He not?"

Uncle Wang knelt at the table, but his eyes pierced hers with an intensity that made her look away.

"You are not telling me the truth," he said softly.

"About God?" Ming raised her head.

"You have not eaten already." He pushed the tray toward her with a sort of sternness. "Our God does not approve of falsehoods, Ming."

Ming looked out at the sheets of rain splattering past the cracks in the bamboo and thatch door. "Maybe He would approve so that a hardworking uncle could eat a meal," she finally said, pushing the tray back toward him. "I am young, Suk-suk. You must eat."

"Ach." Uncle Wang made a groaning sound and stood to his feet, his trouser knee ripped. He looked bonier than Ming had ever seen him, and his thin old tunic flapped around his scrawny chest like an empty bean pod. "There are two of us here, qiānjīn. How can I sleep with a clear heart if you lie awake hungry?"

He shuffled to the kitchen partition and found a cracked bowl and chopsticks on the shelf. "If anyone should go hungry, it is me. I promised to care for you, and I have failed."

Uncle Wang eased himself back down to the table and silently scraped half his rice from his bowl into hers.

"No, my uncle." Ming's eyes filled with tears. "It is my duty to care for *you*. That's what any good daughter would do." She looked away, smoothed the folds of her rough, homespun *hanfu* robe, which spilled across her unbound feet. "Dingxiang's messenger came again today," she said softly.

Uncle Wang's gaze hardened. "I have said no to him already. Do you want to marry this worshipper of pagan gods?" His voice blazed. "He chases after women like a fox after chickens, and he loves opium like I used to. He will ruin you!"

"I am nothing but a burden to you." She swallowed nervously. "I do not want to marry him, but I want you to live. I have no dowry. It is not fair that you starve on my account, especially when Dingxiang is so determined. He will pay you handsomely; his messenger said so." Ming closed her eyes, imagining her uncle clothed in the luminous, brightly colored silk robes of the courts in place of his coarse garments.

Uncle Wang's fist banged the table lightly. "No! I will not allow it." His eyebrows knit together in anger. "I will not give you to a man who prostrates himself before the idol poles and offers incense to evil spirits—no matter how much he pays."

Ming closed her eyes. "What if I have no choice?"

"There is always a choice."

"But if he comes for me? I cannot stand up against a wealthy man like Dingxiang. What will I do?"

"*A bird does not sing because it has an answer,*" quoted her uncle in low, familiar tones—and Ming knew the rest of the proverb before he finished.

"*It sings because it has a song,*" she said.

"Yes. You have a song. It is God's song. And He will provide for us. He will provide a way out."

Ming looked at the grains of rice in her bowl, and the bits of dark green water seaweed shimmered as tears gathered in her eyes. "Why, Uncle? Why do you care for me?"

"The Bible says children are a blessing, my daughter," he said quietly, straightening his tray on the table. "And it is right. God's Word is good." He smiled, the tired folds around his eyes relaxing. "He will take care of us no matter what. Even if—" He broke off, looking into a distance Ming couldn't see.

"Even if what?"

"If we die, we die." His eyelids trembled as he blinked. "There are worse things than death, Ming. I have lived it. I have felt it there in the streets, blinded by opium—filthy, a beggar covered with flies and lice and fleas. Wanting nothing more than more, *more* of the drug! I'd nearly sold my soul for a taste of the stuff until the Lord cured me."

And He had—at a Christian hospital in Guangzhao, through the tireless care of foreign missionary doctors and nurses. Ming had heard her uncle's testimony hundreds of times, and she listened in hushed reverence—unlike the neighboring villagers, who laughed and even spat at his worn face. "*Blasphemer of the gods!*" they called him, hurling small stones or clods of dirt. "*May your ancestors curse your crazy old gray head!*"

"But my life is different now." Uncle Wang looked up at her. "Now I know where my soul will go when I leave my body. I am not afraid."

Ming's eyes glanced quickly up to the empty shelf where the household gods used to sit. Swept clean, and a rough wooden cross nailed in their place.

"I believe, too," she whispered. "But I am so hungry."

"The Lord Jesus knew hunger." He folded his hands for prayer. "Let us ask Him to fill us with His patience and His love."

◆　◆　◆

Uncle Wang plodded out into the murky mist to work again after Ming cleaned the table, his pants torn at the knees and his cone-shaped straw hat on his head. Looking through the window as she wiped the rice bowls, she saw him sway a moment, like a scarecrow in the wind, and then crumple, paper-like, into a heap.

"Suk-suk! Uncle!" she screamed, dropping the rice bowl and chopsticks so that they clattered to the earthen floor.

He did not move, his arms splayed out from his sides like broken birds' wings. His glazed eyes fluttered in his pale face, half open, and his chest heaved, up and down, up and down, as if struggling to fill with air.

"Speak to me! Are you all right?" Ming rushed to him and gathered his head in her lap, patting his cheeks. "Are you hurt?"

He moved his lips as if to speak, but no words came out—just a weak garble, a thin moan like wind around the eaves. He seemed weak, shrunken, as if his frail heart might stop beating any second.

The long, graying *queue* braid and shaved forehead looked dull and lifeless against the rough earth and sparse grasses.

"No, Suk-suk—you will be all right." Ming's tears splashed onto his lined forehead. "Wait here! I will get help. You'll see."

She half dragged him out of the boggy edge of the rice paddy, dirtying the hem of her robe, muddying her legs and feet up to her shins. She sloshed and pulled, gripping him under his arms, until she found a patch of dry ground for him to lie on, his ashen face slumped to one side.

"Wait for me, Uncle," she pleaded, smoothing back the graying hair that lay plastered against his forehead. "I will get Ayi Chyou."

Ming tucked up her robe and ran barefoot across the wet grass, down the soggy dirt path, to her closest neighbor. Surely Ayi Chyou would be at home, pounding rice or mending shirts. Several of her pigs had managed to survive the long, hungry days of the summer, and Ming traded eggs and spring onions with wrinkle-faced Chyou until poverty and hunger forced them to butcher their chickens. Their vegetable patch had scorched brown from disease, and then Ming had nothing to trade.

"*Ayi!* Grandmother!" Ming called in the respectful vernacular for elders as she approached the little earthen cottage. "Help! Please come help my uncle!"

She paused to rest her gasping lungs outside the door, waiting for Chyou's short, stout figure to appear in the doorway.

"Your uncle?" Chyou poked her face through the doorway, her messy gray hair tied back in a knot. "What's wrong with him?"

Ming bent over, arms crossed across her middle as she tried to catch her breath. "I don't know," she said. "He's ill, and he's fallen. Please, won't you come, Grandmother? He needs help!"

"Grandmother?" muttered Chyou through thin lips. "I'm not your grandmother. Your parents died early, you know. You are bad luck!" Her brow tightened into a hard line. "I cannot risk bad luck resting on my house, too."

"I respect you like a grandmother, Ayi Chyou, though I do not deserve to call you by such a name," Ming begged meekly. "And if you come, you will be helping my uncle, not me. No bad luck will come to you. I am merely the messenger!"

"Your uncle brought this on his own head!" Chyou's eyes burned with sudden angry fire, and she pointed a stubby finger at Ming. "He forsook the gods, and now he bears their wrath! You have shamed your ancestors and the sacred spirits—both of you!" She shook her finger. "He deserves to die. It is your fault these droughts and floods have come to Guangzhou! Stay away from my house, you omen of bad luck!"

Ayi Chyou put both hands on her hips. "I hear that Dingxiang is coming again to fetch you this week," she mocked in a singsong voice. "But not as a wife, of course—for you do not deserve rights in his court! Not after disgracing the gods and our entire community. You should serve in the kitchen with Dingxiang's slaves, you good-for-nothing. Mark my words: He will shame you and discard you like an old piece of kindling, and you will be back here begging at my door."

Ming's pulse beat faster at the thought of being bought and sold like a kitten in the market, expected to bear a stranger's children without any voice or recourse whatsoever. Besides the shame of living with a man without the vow of marriage, Chinese concubines could be buried alive with their owner upon his death.

That is, if his wife didn't poison her first.

"And when you come knocking on my door then, I will give you the same answer—no! Call on your own god, since you have disgraced your ancestors." Chyou tried to close the bamboo door, but Ming stopped her.

"Grandmother, please! I beg you." She threw herself on her hands and knees in a formal, prostrate bow of humility and desperation, forehead to the ground. "I will do anything! I will work for you however long you say—and you may have anything in our home you find of worth. Just help my uncle. Please."

"There is nothing you can give me." Chyou's eyes became angry black gashes in her sullen face. "You are bad luck, and that will never change! Leave my house at once."

The next house far over the fields belonged to the merry Kwan family, but after Ayi Kwan blamed Ming and Uncle Wang's forsaking of the gods for their daughter's sickness, she found only silent loathing in their cold stares. Now when Ming passed their house on her way to the market, they turned their backs or slammed their door, whispering, leaving the sweet, aching fragrances of rhododendron and magnolia blooms along their lane to remind her of what she'd lost.

A single dog barked at her from the Kwan house, hackles raised, until she trudged the hills to the next farm, a little ramshackle house where the Wongs and their three children raised pigs and sweet potatoes and gingerroot. She could smell the pigs already; their stench hung in the air over the distant green rice paddies.

But before she could even mount the hill to the Wongs' house, she heard the elder Wong shouting from the field.

"*Gun kai!*" he hollered, furiously waving her away. "Get out of here!" The harsh and vulgar form of the phrase, without a hint of politeness. The same angry words he'd hurl at an aggressive street beggar. "You are bad luck!"

From the next house, the woman who sold chestnuts slammed her window shutters closed.

Ming had nowhere else to go. She stood in the dirt path, wind blowing the grasses against her legs and dust into her eyes, and turned back toward home.

Chapter Two

As rain drummed on the brittle thatch roof, Ming tossed and turned on her hard pallet, willing herself to rest. The screaming emptiness of her stomach stole all her thoughts, along with the swollen rice fields and ruined stalks. The memory of those beautiful, ruined lychee trees, their leaves now brown and withered.

And her uncle lying crumpled on the ground, the lines in his neck wobbling with his shallow breaths.

He was alive, yes, but he was dying. Ming knew it. She pressed her eyes together, thanking God for the clump of wood ear mushrooms she'd found on a dead lychee tree near his limp form. She'd walked that way a dozen times to fetch water from the spring; why had she never seen them before?

And yet there they appeared, crinkled like clumps of brown-black paper against the smooth dullness of the tree bark.

Ming had filled her cupped hands with the mushrooms and plucked some cattail stalks from the edge of the river, then rushed to the house, boiling it all in a pan of water. "Drink, Uncle," she murmured, gently spooning the broth into Uncle Wang's mouth. After some time, his eyes flickered open, and he raised himself up on one arm.

Arm around him, she had helped him hobble back to the house and finish the rest of the broth.

Now he slept, his strength somewhat revived.

What will we do, God? she prayed silently, listening to her uncle's shallow, exhausted breathing on the other side of the thin woven grass partition. *How will we live?*

The misty drizzle brought a chill that crept through the chinks in the bamboo, and Ming shivered under her thin blanket. All around seemed damp, dark, hopeless. Without food or income, their only option would be to beg in Guangzhou: a miserable, humiliating life that would probably end in starvation anyway.

And if Ayi Chyou spoke the truth, and Dingxiang really ordered her to his court, refusal meant certain death. For herself and possibly her uncle. How could she do it? How could she go with him, and conversely, how could she refuse?

There seemed to be no way out.

She forced her eyes closed and tried to rest, her mind closing around the few verses of Chinese scripture she had memorized, the way the pale-faced missionary had taught her: "I can do all things through Christ who strengthens me," she whispered.

Over and over, until the quiet darkness of the room and the steady dripping of the leaky roof caused her eyelids to sink closed, closed, in a shallow, desperate sleep.

◆ ◆ ◆

The shadowy stillness of the dark hut seemed to swirl and shimmer, like stones under rippling river water, and Ming felt a brightness that made her wince. Light, shards of transparent light mingled and danced, glowing with such brilliance that she covered her eyes with her hands.

She thought of sitting up but could not—she could only squint against the dazzling golden radiance that shimmered and sparkled, blinding her at first until, slowly, she distinguished a strange shape: the glowing outline of an odd rectangular form with bumps and points.

The image hovered closer and closer, and Ming watched in awe as map-like lines appeared marking roads, and then rivers, and then the sharp contours of mountain ridges rose up as if to meet her.

It's a place, thought Ming in a sudden burst of clarity. Two brush-painted characters appeared, stroke by stroke, one for "beautiful" and one for "country," and as she watched, a corner on the left side of the map began to dazzle in tones of gold. Gold, and more gold, piles of it—sparkling, glinting, more gold than Ming had ever seen or ever imagined. Without meaning to, she reached out both hands toward the gold, longing to fill them.

But before she had time to catalog her thoughts, she heard a voice speak. Or rather, she *felt* it speak—because afterward she could not recall the sound of the voice, its pitch or its timbre.

"*Go*," said the voice. "*And take the Good News there.*"

Go where? What news?

The light abruptly faded, and Ming opened her eyes in the darkened room. The drip of rain off the eaves echoed in her ear, and its familiar damp chill soaked through her thin blanket.

Ming ran her fingers across her cheek and touched fine grooves in her skin where her face had pressed against her pillow.

Had she been sleeping, then? Dreaming, perhaps?

She crept to her feet and slipped over to the window, looking out at the night-black field. Clouds still hung heavy over the hillsides, and the only point of lantern light she saw came from the direction of the Wongs' farm.

The Chinese characters she had seen suddenly appeared in her mind, and she traced them on the palm of her hand: One for "beautiful," *mei*, a vertical fork cross-stroked with lines, and another squared one for "country," *guo*.

"Mei" for the sound of the second syllable in *America*.

The United States of America, known by some as "the beautiful country." Or *Meiguo* phonetically.

The same map she'd seen.

Ming tiptoed over to her uncle's half of the partition, straining her eyes to see in the blackness of the room. There he lay gently breathing, in the exact same position she'd left him in hours ago: arm under chin, thin legs curled up. He had not moved.

She fixed the blanket gently over his shoulders and then settled back down on her pallet, shivering under her blanket and pondering the strange memory of gold and light—and when she opened her eyes again, the skies were tinted blue with morning.

◆　◆　◆

"I think we should leave," Uncle Wang said as he shuffled to the little wooden table. "We will die if we stay here."

"I agree, Uncle." Ming toyed with the long hem of her robe as she heated water for a simple birch tea, not sure if she should mention the glowing map and piles of gold. The dream still lay clear upon her sleep-fogged mind, if it had been a dream at all. "But we don't have relatives anywhere else to welcome us. Where would we go?"

"America," said her uncle, looking up from the table. "Meiguo."

And Ming dropped her clay teacup with a clatter.

"America?" she gasped. "Why would you suggest such a thing?" She bent to pick up the cracked teacup with trembling hands.

"There is gold there." Uncle Wang coughed, his chest shuddering. "Everyone's talking about it, and this week at the market, several of the stalls were empty. The families had all gone to America to pan for gold. To the north of us, they say hundreds have gone."

Ming's pulse shuddered in her throat. "Gold? You mean like real gold?" She felt dizzy, remembering the golden sparkles along the map of the United States.

"Nuggets from the rivers in California. 'Gold Mountain,' they call it—*Gam Saan* in our Cantonese—the city of San Francisco. They say the ground is full of gold, and a man can pull up a handful of gold nuggets the size of eggs just as easily as pebbles." He ran his hand over his face and stared out the window, his eyes looking large and luminous. "We could leave this place, Ming, and start over again in America. You would be free of Dingxiang, too."

She stood silently, coaxing the few pieces of dry kindling into a sputtering fire. "When did you learn of this gold, Uncle?"

"I've known for a while, and I've kept it in earnest prayer with the Lord." He cleared his throat. "But it's not a safe place for a young woman. I couldn't keep my promise to God to raise you if I left you here alone."

"That's why you didn't go?" Ming felt her cheeks flush with something akin to anger. "Because of me?"

"Yes." He ran his finger along a scratch in the table. "But I can't stay here and starve to death, either, or beg in the city. Who will take care of you then?"

"Uncle." Ming spun around from the fire and turned to face him, lowering her eyes to his. "We must go. I will go with you."

"You?" Uncle Wang's eyebrows lifted over his wrinkled forehead.

"Yes, me." She sat down across the table, for the first time not minding the painful rumble of her empty stomach. "Is there food in California?"

"Lots of it." His eyes glistened with either longing or tears; Ming couldn't tell which. "Beautiful weather and sunshine. Almonds and wheat and oranges. Fish this big brought right out of the rivers." He widened bony hands to demonstrate. "No drought. No flooding. And people eat like kings."

Ming glanced out of the window at the chilly rain dripping off the corner of the roof, and a puff of smoke from the recalcitrant kitchen fire made her eyes burn.

"The Lord spoke to me last night in a dream," she said softly, meeting her uncle's gaze. "He told me to go to America and take the Good News there."

For a second, Uncle Wang's jaw hung slack, as if he couldn't believe his ears, and then he began to blink faster. "Well, if He has spoken, we must go." He clasped her small hands in his large rough ones. "He will provide for us, little Ming. I will find a place for you—a place where I can send money while I work, until I am able to bring you myself."

"No." Ming spoke sharply. "I will work with you. I am young, Uncle! I can work hard. I promise I will do my best to make you proud." Her hands began to tremble with excitement. "If we stay here, we will die. You know that as well as I do."

"But it's not safe for you! It's a man's work. The place is crawling with dirty men."

"If God is sending me, He will keep me safe. Besides, if I stay, I will be taken by Dingxiang within the week," she added softly.

Uncle Wang leaned back and rubbed his forehead. "But I have no money for a ticket, my daughter! And nothing to sell except this poor old farm." He thought for a moment, resting his head in his wrinkled hand. "Unless I indenture myself to a land-owner in California to pay for the fare first, and then go to the gold fields. I hear that's what some others have done." He seemed to slip deep in thought as his line of vision trailed off into the distance. "But I am old, and no one will want me for a worker or a servant."

"Oh, is that possible?" Ming clapped her hands in excitement. "Then I will indenture myself, Uncle—and you can go straight to the gold fields. Don't you see? I can pay for our tickets while you begin to work straightaway."

He blinked again, faster, and suddenly turned to face her. "You are serious, Ming? Do you think it could work?" He pursed his lips together. "I hear the landowners are kind, and they will pay you well. They are not like the landowners in Guangzhou. They do not use whips or sticks to beat their workers, and they have something we commoners don't have: courts. Why, if someone mistreats you, you can take it to a judge! Can you imagine such a thing?"

His face fell for a moment, shadows along the creases and folds. "But it's no good. We don't speak the language. Not a word! How will we manage?"

"Oh, no! I can learn the English language, Suk-suk—I've always been good at languages. You'll see!" Ming leaned across the table and grasped his hand.

"I can't read even in my own language."

"But I can." Her eyes sparkled. "I used to eavesdrop outside the school for wealthy landowners and do my lessons on clay tablets and sheets of tree bark. I did it for years until they moved the school closer to Guangzhou."

"Bless you, Ming." He took a shuddering breath. "Do you know what the characters for your name mean?"

"Shining," she replied without pause. She traced the characters on the palm of her hand with her finger.

"It is a God-given name, because your soul shines. You are a daughter to make anyone proud." His eyes curved slightly into a smile as he studied her silently for a moment. "Even so, aren't you afraid, child?" He pushed his thin, ropelike braid over his shoulder and leaned back. "America is a faraway place, farther away than anywhere you've ever been—across an ocean so big, you will not believe your eyes. You will know no one. You will be surrounded by strangers, in a language you've never heard. How can you not be afraid?"

"*Be not afraid of growing slowly,*" Ming said, beginning the proverb softly.

"*But be only afraid of standing still,*" he finished, his voice nearly a whisper.

"That is my answer." She sat up straight. "God has spoken, and we must do what He commands."

Chapter Three

The greenish waves and swells pitched around the little steamship, making the deck rise abruptly and then fall, and Ming felt her stomach lurch with nausea. It had been two months since the steamer took off from the coast of China in a rainy mist, and at first Ming had thought it heavenly when the sun glimmered down on the rippling sea in turquoise sheets of sparkles, flashing into a distant blue horizon.

The steamship had been christened the *Berea*, which Ming recognized from the book of Acts—and took as another sign of God's favor. Uncle Wang had sold the farm and farming tools for a few *wén*, along with the groves of dying lychee trees, and packed nothing in their trunk except some modest clothing and the portions of Chinese scripture the missionaries had given him years before.

But soon after they set off from the port came the roiling stomach. The place became misery: the cramped cabin with hard, narrow bed and endless billowing of the waves, and the stench of too many passengers (mostly men, who smoked opium and played *mah jongg* by lamplight), everyone crammed in too little space, with hardly light to see. Rats crawled and roaches skittered. The stale cabin air reeked of filth and body odor. Noise—constant noise!—of goats bleating, engines clanking, children crying, men laughing and chatting, roosters crowing, sailors crying out their orders up on deck. Fights broke out over the use of the tiny little cook stove and ship rations, and Ming started to think that hell must be like being trapped in the belly of a ship forever: ink-dark, loud, foul-smelling, and utterly wretched.

The cabin crawled with farmworkers and laborers from all over southeast China, telling coarse stories in language unfit for women and children. She plugged her ears to forget the bawdy tales and rats scampering under the bunks and sounds of retching. She tried to block out the stench of urine from overturned chamber pots.

For the first time, Ming began to wonder if she'd made a mistake and the dream of America's gleaming golden shore had tricked her. Perhaps she and Uncle Wang would have fared better back in Guangzhou, waiting out the summer and winter to give spring and planting another try.

Early one afternoon, as Uncle Wang lay sleeping on the rough bunk, Ming could take it no longer. She watched the light through one of the dim windows, a beautiful shimmering sun after days of rain, and wrapped her cloak around her. When the sailors finished washing the deck and some of the men went up on deck to smoke, she slipped up the rickety stairs after them for a breath of fresh air. As one of the few women on board, Ming usually stayed close to Uncle Wang or some of the other women on the ship, most of them mothers or farmwives, but today she could not wait.

The deck made her seasick, with its lurching and tilting, but the smell of vomit and garlic in the cabin caused her little meal of hard biscuits and dried fruit to slither toward her throat. Maybe a bit of salt air and sunshine would help settle her stomach.

And then, on a corner of the deck, as she glanced over from clutching the rail with shaking fingers, she saw a young man laughing. At *her*.

All Ming's gentle Christian goodness seemed to smolder and wilt as she caught a glimpse of his smooth face and black eyebrows, his blue Mandarin-style jacket and white stockings, and the tilt of his lips turned up in mirth. She'd grown accustomed to the whispers and nudges of wealthy landowners in Guangzhou as she, a common peasant girl, passed them in her homespun robes, but she and Uncle Wang had paid for their ship ticket in wén like every other Chinese passenger. Who did he think he was?

"You, too?" the fellow asked in Mandarin. He bowed politely, the warm sun shining on his dark hair and long queue braid, the same Manchu-imposed hairstyle as Uncle Wang's, but thicker and black as a raven's wing. Ming didn't answer, so he tried again in Cantonese. The rich, warm, familiar tone startled her, and she jerked her head up.

"Excuse me?" she asked, keeping her voice low and reserved as custom dictated of an unmarried woman. Men didn't often speak directly to girls they did not know, but he seemed young, and the steamer overflowed with men—so all the etiquette practices faded a bit when away from home. She bowed politely, if not a bit coolly.

"You're seasick, too," he continued in perfect Cantonese. The young man's face shone bright with merriment. "It happens to everyone, you know. I just thought after two months it would fade a little, but it hasn't."

"How did you know I spoke Cantonese?" Her robe and cloak didn't stand out as distinctively Cantonese, nor her long black hair, tied back in a thick knot.

"Just a guess from. . .I don't know. Something about you. I'm from Nanjing, but my mother is Cantonese." His mirth subsided into a pleasant cheerfulness, more casual than the way unfamiliar men usually addressed Ming. "And I wasn't laughing at you. I mean, not exactly. It's just funny how things happen out on the sea."

Ming tried not to look down at the ocean, rippling with endless waves, as another swell lightly tipped the deck. Rigging creaked, and she felt glad, for at least a moment, to have something—someone—distract her from the nausea.

"So you're going to America, too?" she tried again. Polite conversation helped; words kept the telltale saliva from forming in her mouth.

"Oh yes. To *Jinshan*—San Francisco, or Gam Saan in our lovely Cantonese—to dig for gold. I'm going to be rich. I'll make thousands—no, millions! And I'll open my own shop, put all the other shops out of business, and open more shops. Then I'll buy hotels and property and make a fortune. When I go back to China, I'll be welcomed into nobility." His dark eyes shone like polished chestnuts as he leaned forward toward the sea, gripping the deck. "I've wanted an opportunity like this all my life, and at last it's come." He closed his eyes and breathed in the sea air with a long, delicious sigh. "I'll buy land, maybe a palace, and see the world! That's what I'll do."

The ocean wind had pulled strands of hair out of Ming's bun. She brushed them out of her eyes and back into place with delicate fingers, turning to hear him over the crash of waves against the ship.

He seemed to break from his cheery reverie and looked out toward the horizon, flexing his long fingers on the deck rail. "What about you?" he asked as if an afterthought. "Why are you going to America?"

"To stay alive," Ming quietly replied.

"Oh." He glanced over at her. "That's. . .well, a worthy goal. Certainly."

She said nothing else. He opened his mouth to say something else, perhaps good-bye (as her answer seemed to take the wind out of his sails, judging by the slight slump of his shoulders). "What's your name?" he finally asked, shielding his eyes from the sun to look at her curiously.

"Ming. Of the Wang family. I'm here with my uncle," she added, to make sure he knew she was properly accompanied.

The young man nodded, careful to keep a polite space between them. "Wang Ming. A solid Cantonese name."

Ming swallowed, feeling sick again. "You?"

He took what seemed an eternity to answer, and with each second his face seemed to fall more. Darkening like a smudge of clouds on the horizon, until a sort of despair and a hint of anger pooled in the once-bright eyes.

"Call me Jonah," he said—in tones so low and sagging Ming had to lean closer to hear.

"Jonah?" she replied sharply. "You mean, like from the Bible?"

"You've read the Bible?" His head jerked up suddenly.

"Yes." Ming's fingers trembled. "My uncle and I are believers! How did you hear about the Bible? The Word of God?" She tingled from excitement, like the prickles of cold rainfall that sometimes swept over the deck.

He opened his mouth and closed it and kept his head down, not meeting her gaze. "My father is a Christian minister," he mumbled.

"A minister?" Ming clapped a hand over her mouth in surprise, covering her teeth in accordance with the Chinese custom for graceful women. Chinese Christians were rare; Protestant missionaries had given their lives in China to teach the Bible through hospitals, schools, and small missions, but a free-flowing, reproducing Christian faith had not yet fully taken root among the Chinese people.

Ming herself had never met another Chinese Christian in her part of Canton Province.

"How did your father come to know the God of the Bible?" she asked, breathless.

"He was raised from the dead."

"What?" Ming turned to him with a gasp.

"Yes. That's what he and my mother and about twenty eyewitnesses say." He shrugged. "And I'm glad, because I love my father. He'd been run over by an ox cart, and a Chinese convert to Christianity prayed for him. He recovered, and the doctors say he'd been dead—fully and completely dead—for several hours. There's no explanation for how he survived and even went back to work in two days."

"That's amazing." She breathed out slowly. "God really does perform miracles, even in our day. I've heard stories like that, but. . .your own father? Imagine."

"He's the best man I know." He gave a slight smile, his gaze at once faraway and misty. "And that's his life now. He preaches the Good News to anyone who will listen."

"Go," the voice had said in Ming's dream. *"And take the Good News with you."*

"And you?" she asked, hoping she didn't sound too direct or forward, which was unbecoming for a polite young Chinese woman. "Are you a believer as well?"

"Yes, but. . ." He let out a long breath, and his eyes darkened. "It's complicated." He turned his head away.

Jonah, he had called himself.

Ming hesitated, pressing her lips together, then gathered her courage to ask again—hoping he wouldn't think she was prying. "Why do you call yourself Jonah? It's not your real name, is it?"

"No. I'm Bao. My family name is Zheng."

"Bao means gemstone," Ming said aloud without thinking, and the old proverb leaped into her head: *The gem cannot be polished without friction, nor man perfected without trials.*

Instead she replied, "An appropriate name for a man seeking treasure."

"Yes, but that's the thing." He let his face fall into his hands for a moment. "My treasure and my father's aren't the same thing. He wants me to be a teacher of the Bible like he is, a pastor or a missionary, and it's not me. It's not my calling." He shrugged. "Or if it is, I don't want it. I have bigger plans for my life."

Ming looked out over the sea a long time, not sure if she should speak or not. "What do you think God's plan is for you?" she asked gently.

"I don't know!" He threw up his hands. "I really don't. That's why I call myself Jonah—because deep down, my father is probably right about what I should do. But it's not what I want for my life." He set his jaw. "I have my own plans, and they don't include eking out a living teaching the Bible to unwilling people like my father does. He's been stoned once and beaten unconscious by a mob, and we've had to flee to several different cities to keep our home from being torched. No offense, but what kind of life is that? God gave me a good education, and what for? To teach in a church like my father who can barely read? To have rocks and cattle filth thrown at me by fools who are afraid of offending the old gods? And my father still won't give it up."

Ming's eyes sparkled. "Your father's one of God's faithful messengers! Is there any higher calling than that?"

Bao sighed. "I mean no disrespect—I love my father. But my family raised me in fine schools where I learned reading and writing, math, science, and the history of the world." He closed his eyes and breathed in as if reliving the books, the scrolls, the ink and brushes. "I worship the true God instead of our ancestors and idols—why can't that be enough?"

"So that's why you call yourself Jonah."

"Because I'm running away from Him. Yes. Sort of." He sighed again, and then his eyes sparkled with sudden mirth. "And if I am Jonah, well, God hasn't sunk the ship yet or tried to swallow me with a whale, so I figure He must be okay with me digging gold in California."

Ming's eyebrows shot up, but she said nothing.

"Although we still have a couple of days left," Bao said almost as an afterthought, rubbing his chin. "So maybe I shouldn't be too hasty."

"Please don't," she replied smartly. "I don't feel like being thrown overboard in a storm anytime soon."

"It wouldn't be you. It'd be me." He shrugged. "That's how the Jonah story goes, anyway."

"Sure. While the rest of us pitch and moan and get thrown around the cabin. Not a pretty picture any way you look at it." Ming tried not to think of seasickness, of nausea, feeling that cold fried rice slipping up her throat again.

Bao laughed, and when he looked at her again, his eyes seemed focused and black, with a warm intensity that she hadn't noticed before. "You're clever," he said softly. "I've never met anyone quite like you, who speaks her mind so boldly."

"Do I?" She felt her face heat with embarrassment. "I'm sorry."

"You shouldn't be."

Before she could retreat, Bao, lowering his head closer to hers, said, "Look." He drew something from his pocket. "I've never shown this to anyone."

He dropped something from his cupped hand into her palm, and his fingers touched hers ever so slightly. She stepped back with flaming cheeks, grateful they were standing in full view of a deck packed with passengers so that no one would question her virtue.

"It's a cross," Ming said, almost afraid to look at him. She kept her eyes turned down, stirring the leather cord with her finger. "A golden cross."

"My father made it." Wind from across the sea stirred long strands of Bao's hair. "After he became a Christian, he melted down one of the household gods and hammered it into a cross."

"So why don't you wear it? It's a necklace, isn't it?"

"Yes." Bao shrugged, and his stiff shoulders looked like he felt uncomfortable. "I don't feel ready to wear it yet."

"Why not?"

He shifted his feet on the deck and looked away, squinting at the sun as the ship turned slightly. "I feel like if I put it on I should follow my father in his service as a minister or a missionary, like he wants me to. And I can't."

Ming didn't know what to say, so she kept her lips pressed tightly together. The cross glinted in her upturned palm, the color of golden afternoon sun sparkling on the water.

"It's beautiful," she finally said.

"Yes," he replied. "Very beautiful."

But he wasn't looking at the necklace. He'd focused his eyes on her, his gaze tipped down and intense. So still that she could see his black eyelashes.

She felt heat crawl up her neck and started to bow and excuse herself, fleeing for the dark coolness of the cabin, when someone shouted: "Land! We've sighted land!"

"Land?" Ming whirled around.

"Have we arrived early?" Bao leaned out to see better.

All around came a rush of shouts, and a crush of people crowded along the ship railing so thickly that Ming could hardly move—everyone straining for a glimpse, standing on tiptoe, craning their necks to watch the sea for some sign of distant earth. Some wept openly; others shouted to each other in noisy exuberance. Children jumped up and down, unable to contain their excitement.

The muddle of people forced Ming away from the railing, small as she was, and she felt herself pushed and trampled in the fray—until she could no longer see anything but the corner of Bao's black hair.

In her cupped hand she still held the necklace. "Sir!" she cried to Bao, trying to push her way through the crowd to return his golden cross. "Mr. Zheng?" She tried to reach out her arm and pass the necklace back, but when someone nearly ripped the cord out of her fingers, she snatched back her hand and held it tightly to her chest.

Of course. Gold. What was she thinking? Many of these passengers were impoverished laborers, and she'd been warned of pickpocketing while on the ship.

There stood Bao—just across the deck. He had turned toward her as if trying to make his way in her direction, his mouth still partly open like he wanted to speak. And then the crowd covered him completely.

When she'd made her way meekly through the masses of passengers, Bao had vanished.

◆　◆　◆

It would be four and a half months before Ming could leave the plantation in southern California, and she'd never seen Bao again—neither when crowds filed off the ship nor on land. Worse, she had no idea how to reach him. Unsure of what to do, Ming kept his precious cross necklace with her belongings, hidden inside an empty glass medicine vial in case someone rifled through her things.

Uncle Wang signed on with a group of Chinese miners in a newly opened section of San Francisco, and he visited Ming twice a month with earth-stained fingernails and bags of tea, salt pork, and rice from one of the big general stores in San Francisco.

"Look for a young man named Bao from Nanjing," she pleaded with Uncle Wang each time before he departed. "Bao of the Zheng family. I have something valuable that belongs to him."

At the farm, Ming began to regain her strength and recover from both the long season of malnutrition in China and exhaustion from the sea voyage. Like the other laborers, she ate from the crops: spinach and greens, tomatoes, beans, onions, lettuce, peppers. She worked from sunup to sundown watering and weeding the immense plantation with other workers, then hoeing up new beds from soft, loamy soil. Unlike the floods and droughts that had plagued Canton Province the past few years, the vines and plants of California produced plump, glossy vegetables with a sweeter flavor than the Cantonese varieties: the result of perfect weather and always just enough warm, gentle rain.

In snatches between harvesting beans and tomatoes Ming would stop, wiping the sweat from her forehead and thinking inexplicably of Bao and his laughing black eyes.

Summer hung hot and mild like a silk shawl, with immense stars that twinkled over the soft, humid countryside like brilliant fireflies—so different from the initial image she'd had of San Francisco when the *Berea* finally steamed into the ship-clogged harbor.

It had all been so jarring: a jumble of merchant ships and masts so thick Ming couldn't imagine how a steamer the size of the *Berea* could fit through. Sails were visible from one end of the harbor to the other, and the horizon bristled with boat rigging. The shore had been built up to the beach with brick shops, dusty roads, storefronts, and noisy horse carts. The salty, stinky smell of the harbor and port, the screams of seagulls, and the clatter and shouts of the city permeated everything.

English and more English, the strange chatter of unintelligible words, and the pink, sunburned faces of burly, hairy, American prospectors. Their long, thick beards, their strange boots and trousers and flat hats, and their oddly light-colored eyes. Ming had never seen blue eyes, never seen hair the color of pine wood or straw. The men talked loudly, smelled like sweat, and towered over both her and Uncle Wang.

Ming fared better than she expected at life as an indentured servant on the farm, once the homesickness for rural Guangzhou and Uncle Wang settled a bit. Nestled in a quiet valley rimmed with orange and pomegranate trees, the plantation stretched across undulating hills and through cool morning mists, and Ming might have thought it beautiful if she wasn't constantly working. She toiled in the fields with other poor women from China, Asia, and South America, and bunked with them at night in exhaustion. All the while she struggled to pick up any words of English she could and find some sense or meaning in its bizarre sounds and cadences. On holidays or rare days off, with nowhere else to go, Ming spent quiet evenings along the beach, listening to waves crash against the rocky shore.

On the other side of that ocean lay her homeland, the place of her birth, and Ming felt small there against the smooth sand and low, shrubby saltbushes. China seemed as far away as a sad and beautiful dream, just out of her reach—a bittersweet love drowned in painful memories of starvation and want.

In September, California officially requested statehood, and American women arrived in San Francisco from all over the country, hoping to find wealthy husbands. Ming just prayed she could find one anywhere who loved her and loved the Lord.

As summer drew to a close, Ming penned a letter to Uncle Wang, informing him of her upcoming release. The debt for their two tickets had nearly been paid; Ming would be free to go by the end of October.

While she waited for Uncle Wang's response, she prayed for favor on Uncle Wang's earnings, and for a place to work and serve among the Chinese laborers looking for gold. She prayed for Bao, too, wherever he had gone, those black and shining eyes mingled with promise and yet guilt.

Uncle Wang's response to Ming's letter came slowly, and with a bit of hesitation and wariness (Ming thought) as she read down the lines of his ornately stroked characters. He would come for her, he said, but he didn't know what she might think of it:

My dear qiānjīn,

I will come for you as I promised—I give you my word—but I have started to ask the Lord if the gold fields might not be the right place for you and if there might not be a better place for you to stay. I fear for you here. The stories we heard in China weren't quite true; it is a hard life for a man, so imagine a young woman like yourself and all the dangers you might face here. Seek the Lord and ask Him if He might have another, safer place for you, little Ming.

My earnings have not been what I had hoped for just yet—still struggling most days to break even. Most of the gold in this area has been mined already, but I will not give up. Tomorrow we move for a new stretch of river that the Americans abandoned months ago; our group leader has reason to think there is a valuable gold vein they missed. We will find it.

I believe the best is yet to come. Rest in the peace of our Lord.

Uncle Wang

Ming blinked at the letter again by the flickering candlelight of the sparse women's quarters, strangely troubled by her uncle's words. *"Dangers,"* he had written, and her heart quivered a little.

She had never considered living apart from Uncle Wang—and how could she? She missed him terribly. He was her second father and the only father she truly remembered. In the whole state of California, there wasn't a single face she recognized like his, with its kind, familiar wrinkles and gentle smile lines. The thought of living far away from him among pale American people she neither knew nor understood frightened her.

Worse, it had been four months, and Uncle Wang's report meant he and his crew still had not unearthed the gold they'd expected. It had been on again, off again—little pannings in one stream that netted a few gold flakes, and absolutely nothing in others. Not anything like the images they'd had of gold lying in fat, chicken-egg-sized nuggets in a streambed, just waiting to be snatched up.

Cold foreboding filled Ming.

Over half a year had passed since she sailed from China, two months at sea and four and a half months at the farm. She and her uncle still had hardly a wén more than they had when they left Guangzhou. (Or penny, as she learned to call the peculiar little American coin in English.)

But at least they'd cheated death, ate enough, and lived close enough to visit. That would have to suffice.

"No, dear Suk-suk," she penned back hastily, trying to mask the panic in her words. *"Do not send me away! No matter what happens, I will stay with you. I will work with you, alongside you. I am strong—the Lord will help me."*

Then, *"Have you heard any news about Zheng Bao?"*

She sealed the letter before she could hesitate.

Uncle Wang's reply came within the week: *"I have asked many men, and none of them have heard of the young Zheng man you describe. Perhaps he is no longer in San Francisco?"*

Ming's heart fell. But she read on:

"*As for me, I will not abandon you in this cold city, my good daughter. I would sooner abandon my own right hand. Rest assured, I will be there in October to get you,*" wrote Uncle Wang. "*Let us count the days together.*"

Chapter Four

The Chinese prospecting camp could not have been more different than Ming had imagined, even in her most pessimistic dreams. Populated by rough, loud-speaking Chinese men who rarely bathed, the encampment sprawled like a giant migrant village along the muddy banks of one of the steams. Men smoked around campfires, sang bawdy songs until late at night, and wasted their meager earnings on card games or American beer from the saloons.

Horror rose in Ming's throat when Uncle Wang's rented horse and cart clattered up to the dirty campsite with so many ragged, dusty, tent-like structures, they reminded her of beggars' slums in Guangzhou.

"I told you it would be hard for you, my dear," said Uncle Wang soberly, gazing at her from across the cart. "If I could do anything to change it, I would. I will work from sunup to sundown to find enough gold to send you away from here."

"No. I will stay with you always." Ming tried to make her voice sound confident. She fixed her gaze on Uncle Wang's loving face, grateful for the color that ruddied his cheeks since leaving Guangzhou. He was still thin, but the gaunt hollowness had left his eyes, and his arms and shoulders looked strong.

Ming wanted to hug his arm and never let him go, so dear were those smile lines around his kind eyes, curved like a crescent moon, and the gentle set of his wrinkled lips. She had missed him every day at the farm; now they stood side by side, and she would not let him send her away again.

"I'm afraid, though, that you will suffer here." Uncle Wang reached out and patted her arm with his free hand. "It is the best I can do, my daughter, my jewel. I give you my word: We will leave this place behind for better things."

Ming ducked her head as she noticed men coming out of their tents to stare at her, smoking in silence.

"You know what they say about jewels and gemstones, Uncle," she said softly, keeping her gaze down and hoping no one would notice the flush of humiliation in her cheeks. "They cannot be polished without friction."

She suddenly remembered standing on the sunny deck of the *Berea* next to Bao, when that same proverb had threaded its way through her mind. She thought of his golden cross, packed tightly in her little trunk of clothing, and his long strands of hair as the sea breeze stirred them—black and glossy as the lacquered curve of a rice bowl.

"Ah. And man is not perfected without trials." Uncle Wang knew the rest of the proverb, too, and he looked over at her. "The Word of God says that, too, Ming—only His perfection is lasting, eternal. You make me proud," he said, clucking to the horses and pulling the cart to a stop. "You will see. We will do well in this land, and our Chinese partners here will help us. Just give us more time."

Uncle Wang got down from his seat and came around to help Ming down from the wagon. She pulled up her long robes and stepped shyly onto the graveled ground, suddenly mindful that she, a woman, was an extreme rarity in these parts. On the farm she had bunked and picked lettuce with plenty of women, young and old; here in the gold fields, she had entered men's territory.

"I have warned the other men not to bother you," said Uncle Wang quietly, striding protectively by her side with her bags under his arm. "They are a good bunch, for the most part."

"For the most part?" Ming repeated, not meaning for her voice to sound so questioning. Her heart pounded under her robe.

"Yes. It has been months since they have seen a woman, though, except for the few that live with the camp."

Ming meekly followed Uncle Wang, pretending not to notice what seemed like hundreds of eyes watching her as she walked through the mass of tents and campfires. Men glanced up as they polished boots and frying pans, cleaned gold pans and pickaxes, mended their trousers, and shook out blankets and bedrolls—most of them frozen in midmovement as she passed. Heads began to congregate over the tops of the tents, whispering together, their long queue braids falling over their shoulders.

Most of the men looked as if they'd spotted an apparition, or an angel—so transparent came the looks of wonder and interest in their haggard, work-hardened faces, straining for a glimpse. And she saw shame, too, if they looked too long, ducking their heads back down to finish their work.

A few workers, though, stared unabashed and brazen, their dark eyes and faces following her over the tops of the tents. Several of them even slipped along the path behind her, shadow-like, until Uncle Wang snapped a warning in Mandarin that made them chuckle and turn back.

"Where are the other women?" Ming whispered. Her heart beat so loudly she was sure everyone could hear it; her face flamed at the humiliation of so many stares.

"There aren't many, but you'll meet them. Some of them do laundry to bring in some extra money, and others keep the children."

"There are children here?"

"A few, with nowhere else to go while their fathers look for gold."

"Can I do laundry, too, with the other women?" Her heart picked up a hopeful beat.

"Maybe, but I prefer to keep my eye on you myself, if I can." The lines in his face hardened slightly.

"Why?"

"I said the men here are *mostly* good," Uncle Wang said in low tones. "Not *all*. That's enough for you to know."

Ming swallowed hard and said nothing for a long time.

"I thought you said we had the courts in this country," she said finally. "That they could settle our differences and keep law in a civilized manner."

"You are not working for Americans anymore," he replied. "We are an alliance, a company. We share everything—our resources, our gold, and together we prosper. But unless our own violence gets out of hand or we have enough money to hire a lawyer, the American courts don't really care what we Chinese do among ourselves. The West is new, Ming, and people make their own justice more often than not. And that is where you need to be careful."

They turned across a dusty path, and Uncle Wang shifted Ming's bags to his other arm. "This is our home for now," he said, pointing to a small tent on a smooth plain of earth near some flowering gum trees. "It's not much, my daughter, but at least we can eat here. We can live and survive here." He smiled, showing well-preserved teeth. "And there's always the hope of gold tomorrow."

"I pray so." Ming made herself smile. "We will be happy here, Suk-suk. You'll see."

Uncle Wang lifted the flap of the tent and showed her the two partitions, just small enough for her to bend and duck inside. On her side, which had been swept so clean she could see the lines of the rough straw broom, he had placed the best new blankets, the cleanest linens, a soft little pillow, and a tiny table with a pretty lamp.

"There is embroidery on the pillow," Ming murmured in disbelief, touching the ruffled edge with her fingers—exotic American goods in strange shapes and textures, far more ornamental than the common Chinese homespuns she remembered. "And rosebuds on the quilt." A simple but beautiful quilt, in pale blues and pinks of spring flowers. In all her life, Ming had never owned anything so beautiful.

"You are a young woman," said Uncle Wang, setting her bags down at the entrance of the tent. "Not a dirty prospector. This is what the salesman recommended for a lovely young girl."

Ming closed her eyes, trying to hold in the beauty of the moment, the gesture, and the unexpected tenderness that flooded her heart. Next to the lamp Uncle Wang had left a little bouquet of mountain yarrow, its tiny, creamy white petals and yellow centers smiling up like a cluster of lace.

He'd placed a portion of the Chinese scriptures on the table for her to read, and a rough-carved wooden cross of wild cherrywood hung on the wall of the tent.

On Uncle Wang's side, through a tiny crack in the tent partition, Ming saw just three things: a rough wool blanket, a Chinese Bible, and an old work shirt rolled into a pillow.

"Oh, Uncle," said Ming, horrified, running her hand over her smooth blankets and quilt. She got down on her knees and bowed low to the ground. "You shouldn't have done this! It must have cost you all your earnings. I'm only your fatherless niece, Uncle—how could you?"

Uncle Wang brushed it away with a wave of his wrinkled hand. "Nonsense, little Ming. It's the best I can do under the circumstances." He raised her up from the ground and patted her head like a child. "Now get some rest, because we've got a long day tomorrow."

"I'll pan gold?"

"With the rest of us. You will be safe with me."

Ming's heart leaped up as she brushed the dusty soil from her knees, tears burning in her eyes. At last she would experience what she had come all the way from China to do, and maybe she could even help repay Uncle Wang for everything he had bought for her—the blankets, pillow, lamp. He was a good uncle, better than any girl could ask for.

And she would bring him the gold he deserved.

◆ ◆ ◆

"Quick, Ming, a bigger pan." Uncle glanced at her over his shoulder, raising his voice slightly over the roar of the river water. In his hand he and Po Huiqing held a long, rectangular wooden cradle or rocker down on the stream bed, alternately pouring water into the screen on top and letting it trickle down to the slatted bottom. Huiqing and Uncle Wang sifted through the finer gravel and sediment on top, searching for golden flakes.

"Did you find something?" Ming's heart picked up a beat.

"Not yet. But the color of the gravel and soil is changing. That often means gold is near."

It had been several weeks since Ming had come to the camp, and now fading golds and russets of November tinged the bare, scrub landscape. The wild asters had faded, and nights unrolled crisp and frosty, with huge stars that hung over the streams and hillsides like strings of paper lanterns.

Exhaustion colored every single day of panning gravel in ice-cold streams, backbreaking squatting and sifting and standing, cold-numb hands and fingers. Sunlight on the water dazzled Ming's eyes until she could barely see, and sun burned her cheeks and the bridge of her flat nose pink.

Gold nuggets were heavy, and Ming learned how to sort through the pebbles and sediment until denser particles fell to the bottom. From these small pieces often came a glimmer of something shiny, a fleck of light, and everyone held their breath to see if the weight and heft of the flakes or nuggets warranted a celebration.

"I'll get the pan for you, Uncle Wang. The deep or the shallow one?"

"The shallow one."

"I thought so." Ming blinked, seeing sun-stars from the water and what seemed hundreds of different colored stones and shapes. She rubbed her eyes on her sleeve and dropped her dripping, gravel-filled pan, stretching out her aching back, and hurried up the bank to the old wheelbarrow Uncle Wang shared with several of the men in the camp.

She knew many of the men now, and they treated her with mutual respect—affection, even. Especially since she rose at the same early hour they did, marching off to the river at dawn with Uncle Wang to pan for gold, and stopping only when night fell too dark to see.

Back at camp, Ming patiently mended their trousers and socks, listening to their stories of home, and gave them the feminine touch they so badly missed. Ming, the only sister some of the men would have until their return to China, baked bean cakes over the hot coals and shared them with Uncle Wang's friends, wrote letters to relatives, pounded herbs in a mortar to cure a fever, wrapped bandages around smashed thumbs, trimmed hair.

Some of the men still stared a little too long, their eyes hungry with longing for a woman, but no one touched her. No one even bothered her, really, except for Liu Pong. His manner chilled her, made her uncomfortable.

And there he sat near Uncle Wang's wheelbarrow, smoking on a stone at the edge of the river. He looked up at her approach, that smug smile of his showing at the corner of his lips.

Ming ignored him, quickly sorting through the mining equipment—gold pans, pick-axes, old kitchen bowls.

"What do you need?" Pong bowed and let out a puff of smoke from his rolled tobacco cigar. He stood and came to her side a little too eagerly, Ming thought, his gaze bold and unflinching.

"I'm just getting a pan for my uncle." Ming bowed crisply. "But thank you."

Pong had come recently, stout and ruddy with an ugly scar over his right eye and an intense, penetrating manner. His pigtail hung long and greasy, and she'd seen Uncle Wang sizing him up with narrowed eyes when he asked to join their smaller partnership within the alliance.

Uncle Wang had shaken his head no, and Ming felt relief. For some reason she distrusted Pong. He stood closer than Ming liked, always quiet, always watching with what seemed unusual craftiness.

"What is it, my flower? I can help." Pong spoke Cantonese with a heavy Mandarin accent, dropping his voice so low that Ming could barely hear him. Which meant that neither could Uncle Wang, over the rush of river rapids.

Ming ignored him, lifting a stack of heavy pans and shovels out of the wheelbarrow to reach the bottom.

Pong moved closer and breathed out smoke again, studying her in silence. "I see why that young man was looking for you."

"Why? What young man?" She jerked her head up, her words spilling out before she could stop them.

"Ah. So you are interested." Pong smiled an oily smile, dropping his cigar and crushing it with his foot. "I thought so."

Pong was bluffing. Ming turned coolly back to the stack of pans and shovels, taking a purposeful step around the wheelbarrow away from him.

"The young man from Nanjing," he whispered, flickering his gaze over her in a way that made color rise to her face.

Ming tried not to react to his words, but she failed. She flinched, knocking a tin cup from the wheelbarrow onto the grass as she fumbled for the pan.

Smooth as a slippery lizard, Pong appeared on her side of the wheelbarrow and fetched the cup, drawing himself up so close to Ming that she had to lean backward to see him. He smiled, showing yellow teeth.

"Forget him. Marry me." Pong breathed out the smoky remains of his cigar.

Ming found her voice and spoke boldly, stepping back. "I am not marrying anyone now. I will stay and work with my uncle."

He nodded, not changing his expression.

"You know, though," Pong said softly, touching her cheek with one rough finger, "you could make more money if you wanted to. Some other fine women have already taken me up on my offer. It's a booming business." He nodded toward Uncle Wang with a sly smirk. "Nobody has to know. Just you and me."

His breath smelled of onions and strong tea, and she flinched at the odor and at the unexpected touch.

She grabbed the pan and backed away from him, indignant. "Make money doing what, laundry?" she asked coldly.

Pong's sudden laughter startled her—coming out in a disbelieving snort and then turning into a shuddering roar. Doubling him over so that his ruddy face turned ugly scarlet. He laughed so loudly that even Uncle Wang and Huiqing looked up from the stream.

Ming fled, not sure what had just happened, and climbed back down the riverbank. She passed the pan to Uncle Wang with shaking fingers, grateful for the wind off the water that cooled her hot face.

"What happened, Ming?" Uncle Wang stood up straight, glaring fiercely over in Pong's direction. She could barely see him now, still bent in what looked like laughter as he disappeared over the hillside.

"I don't know, Uncle." The river currents ran fast, and Ming had to raise her voice to be heard over the rapids. She stepped back across the stones, holding her robes up out of the water until she found a smooth spot to kneel and dip her pan. "Pong just asked me if I wanted to make more money, so I asked him if he meant doing laundry. I don't know what's so funny about that."

As soon as she said the words, Ming realized her blunder.

More money. Other women. Booming business. All at once she remembered hearing talk around the campfires about men and saloons, and Pong disappearing late at night, and how he sometimes smelled of cheap perfume in the mornings.

And that's what he'd offered her.

In this land of pickaxes and dust, boots and beards, Chinese women found few roles beyond merchants' wives, small business owners, and the occasional mother and house-wife—and not so many virtuous jobs in between.

Of course Ming had seen the women coming in and out of saloons in San Francisco with painted faces and low-cut dresses. Guangzhou, too, had its own seedy district that the few "honorable" Cantonese men and Confucian priests avoided. But no one had ever suggested she might become one of those women herself.

The idea horrified, humiliated her. Even as a poor farm girl who had no real value in Chinese society, she felt shaken, sullied. God had created her, and the Bible taught that He valued and cared for women.

Uncle Wang stalked over to her through the water in his rubber boots, cupping his hand around his ear to hear over the water's roar. "What did he say? Something about doing laundry? What?"

Ming reddened, not sure how much she should tell him. There was a chance she could be wrong, but at the way Pong had laughed, she didn't think so.

No wonder Uncle Wang had ordered her to stay with him, right by his side, so he could ensure her safety.

Huiqing—heavyset, placid Huiqing, with the round face and gentle demeanor—shook his head in disgust and muttered something in Uighur that Ming couldn't under-stand. "That man's no good," he finally said, switching to Cantonese. "I don't know what he's up to, but he's trouble. I'm telling you."

"Did he hurt you?" Uncle Wang put his hands on his hips.

"Well, no."

"He'd better stay far away from you," growled Uncle Wang, still glaring in Pong's direction. "Ming, I forbid you to go near him again, or even speak to him."

"Don't worry. I won't. In fact. . ." The glint of something brilliant caught her eye in the dull gravel of her pan. "Uncle," she gasped, jerking up her pan and digging her fingers through it. "Uncle, is this gold?"

Uncle Wang's eyes bounced between Ming and the pan, as if still registering the change in topic, when Huiqing cried out in his native Uighur.

"It's gold!" Huiqing finally managed. "Ming, you've found gold!"

She sifted through the stones and sediment in her pan, stopping on a flat, oddly shaped nugget the size of her thumb. And another smaller, oblong rough piece, shining like a large kernel of metallic popcorn. They lay there on the dirt of her palm, gleaming in the sun.

"My little Ming, you've found gold!" Uncle Wang cried, gripping her arm in excitement. "Where did you scoop up this pan?"

"Right here!" She shifted the pan and pointed.

"There's more!" shouted Huiqing, pawing the wet rocks. "Look at this one!" He held up a piece the size of a small robin's egg. "Gold, real gold!"

Ming covered a cry with her hand. So far they'd only found flakes, or smaller pieces the size of corn kernels. Nothing so big, so lustrous—nothing that could possibly be worth so much. She knelt, pan of stones in one hand, and picked up the pieces of gold in the other.

"Are we going to be rich, Uncle Wang?" she exclaimed, cleaning the glowing nuggets in the clear river water with trembling hands.

"I don't know, Daughter. I don't know." He dug a pan into the rocky riverbed, his whole face a furrowed grin. "But it will help us eat. That is all I wish for right now."

◆　◆　◆

The gold brought in less money than Ming had imagined, after they divided it evenly with Huiqing and the rest of the Chinese alliance, but it still left enough for Uncle Wang and Ming to buy some badly needed clothing and gold panning equipment and some better candles and lanterns, as well as stock up on extra rice and meal, vegetables, and a side of more expensive salted beef instead of pork. Uncle Wang bought a bigger tent just in time for winter, and he and Huiqing went in halves with two other men to buy a larger cradle with a better mesh screen for sifting finer sediment.

Ming avoided Lui Pong completely, regretting only that she could not hear more about Bao. The curiosity needled at her: Had Bao really been asking about her? If so, where was he? And how did an unscrupulous man like Pong know about Zheng Bao?

The new cradle netted another double handful of fat gold nuggets, nearly as large as the last ones, and Ming started to think that perhaps she had been wrong about the gold fields—and their time would be easier than she expected. Uncle Wang opened a bank account at one of the gleaming new banks, with the hopes of one day renting a house in town or, if their luck continued, perhaps even buying one.

So far, San Francisco had turned out well for the two of them, like an unexpected friend. She'd heard of violence between Chinese and American miners, but for now, the two groups kept a respectful distance, working together at certain mining camps in relative peace. The Chinese traded with the Native Americans and the Spanish, and Ming had been able to pick up a little Spanish at the market—and learned how to roast flavorful green chilies and pound buttery avocados with salt and lime.

Even the California winter unfurled mild and beautiful, with delicate frost hanging on the wild grasses. Moonlight shimmered through the bare leaves of the gum tree, leaving swirls of black and silver shadow across the dried grass as Ming knelt by the small cook fire, frying straw mushrooms, carrots, and cabbage, serving it all on steaming rice. She kneaded dumpling skins from strange, white American flour, filled them with ginger and finely chopped beef, and steamed them under a kettle—making Huiqing weep in homesickness for the hilly plains of northwestern China.

After serving the last bits of the meal to a few other down-on-their-luck prospectors, scraping out the pan, Ming got down on her knees in the new tent and thanked God for bringing them to Gam Saan, Gold Mountain, and for more than enough rice to fill their bowls.

The next day, news came that boatload after boatload of three hundred South Americans had docked in the San Francisco harbor, urged on by the lure of gold. A few days later, seven hundred new Chinese would-be prospectors crowded the narrow city streets, causing havoc in understocked general stores and clothing shops. Immigrants overran the sleepy harbor town of Yerba Buena, and land became so scarce that entrepreneurs started renting out boats for a night's sleep in lieu of a hotel room.

Organized crime rings sprouted up among the Chinese and the Mexicans, importing women for the brothels, staffing the saloons and gambling halls, and cutting throats in dark alleys when things got ugly.

The price of eggs and single slices of bread shot up to a dollar apiece—more than triple what they had been before—and a barrel of flour went from eight dollars to eighty-five dollars the minute miners discovered gold nearby. California couldn't import enough fruits and vegetables across rough Western terrain to feed the crowds, and many of the miners began to suffer from scurvy with symptoms of bleeding gums, tooth loss, and fever.

Almost overnight, people could barely afford to eat.

A week later, steamers and clipper ships carrying a stunning two thousand Chinese and South Asians landed in the port, with immigration lines that blocked roads and intersections for hours. Fights broke out, a cart overturned in the melee, and police herded many of the newcomers into local jails to sort out the mess.

Everything in San Francisco began to change.

Chapter Five

Ming could recall the exact day her hope of prosperity in California came to both an end and a beginning: a cold, dreary January day after the New Year of 1850, a cold snap chilling the air. A sullen afternoon when everything they'd exhausted themselves for seemed to disappear, like clouds of dust on San Francisco's dirty, crowded streets.

Close to a month had passed since anyone in the alliance had panned any gold at all—and with the dropping temperatures, Ming could hardly bear the water's ice-cold chill. Ming panned alongside the others until her fingers turned numb, losing feeling for so long that finally Uncle Wang ordered her to take a rest.

The river crawled with prospectors, many of them squabbling over territory, so she and Uncle Wang and Huiqing had walked almost six miles to pan an abandoned stretch of river far from the gum trees, in a flat hillside plain gusting with cold winds. Normally Ming loved the river, flashing and brilliant and full of light and energy, but ever since winter it flowed dark and sluggish, like a bad omen of things to come. Trees hung skeletal and bare over the river, birdless and silent, and sullen clouds reflected in the shallows at the river's edge.

Twice the river had failed her; once in Guangzhou, when its swollen banks stole their rice crop and lychee trees for three successive years, and again now as it refused to give up its gold.

Already Ming worried about far more than finding gold; rumors swirled that American miners wanted the California legislature to levy a foreigner's tax on the Chinese and anyone else nonnative who had come to seek gold. The tax was hefty, too—one that would leave them with little to nothing left after they'd paid the tax and bought the barest necessities on which to live. If the tax passed, Ming and Uncle Wang might be forced to return to China—or worse, live hand to mouth in the city of San Francisco. The city that, just in the past few weeks, had exploded in new streets and sections, each seedier than the next to suit the crowds of men: saloon after saloon, brothel after brothel.

In the early fall, Ming had often accompanied Uncle Wang to the market, but after so much harassment and catcalls in the streets, he forbade her to even venture out of the camp.

Camp had changed, too—their alliance had swollen to unmanageable numbers, and now three more rival alliances, two Chinese and one Mexican, had nosed their way into the same strip of land. Men came to blows, fighting, always fighting: threats of murder and violence rose up between the rival alliances as they argued over boundaries, and sharp disputes sounded among the Chinese in her own alliance as they scuffled over equipment and rations and responsibilities.

Night after night Ming lay awake listening to drunken men sing and shout, swear and argue. The washerwomen whispered about public hangings, and coarser men went to view them. Theft crept into the camp, and hard-earned tools and food suddenly vanished.

She shook Bao's golden cross necklace out of the medicine vial and wore it around her neck for safekeeping, and just in time, too—for only two days later someone pilfered rice, cooking pots, and some of Uncle Wang's clothing right from their tent.

Boatloads of Chinese women began to trickle into San Francisco, and rumors spread that they came exclusively to staff the brothels. *"It's a booming business,"* Liu Pong had said. The thought chilled her, disgusted her—but apparently, from the excitement among the camp, he unfortunately spoke the truth.

For not long after that, a crowd of drunken men had surrounded her tent, shouting in slurred Mandarin for her to let them in. After all, why pay their hard-earned dollars for what they assumed they could take for free?

Uncle Wang, Huiqing, and several other Chinese men had threatened them with clubs until they backed off, but Ming changed after that. She never slept well, never rested, never let her guard down.

Just panning, always panning, always sifting sediment with freezing fingers, always scanning the gravel until her eyes felt like they saw double. Always kneeling, bending, shivering, back aching, neck smarting, legs throbbing from hiking rough, rocky terrain. Diphtheria came through the overcrowded camp, killing two men and putting about thirty others on bed rest, and cough and influenza followed.

Men left gold panning and became low-wage-earning construction workers, miners, fishermen, or migrant workers for American companies. Some headed east to try their luck in other American towns like Boston or New York, perhaps plying their trades in a fresh venue. Others became drifters or beggars in San Francisco, and many went hungry.

Uncle Wang sold the large tent and bought a smaller drafty one, in a reversal of fortune, and took most of their money out of the bank in San Francisco so they could afford rice and eggs and winter cabbage.

And when days with no gold trickled into weeks, Huiqing and some of the men sold their meager, weather-worn equipment and purchased tickets back to China.

Ming started to wonder if she and Uncle Wang might be forced to follow them.

◆ ◆ ◆

Ming couldn't imagine going back to Guangzhou so soon; Uncle Wang, however, like most Han Chinese men, kept his long braid in case they became desperate. Without the government-imposed hairstyle, men wouldn't be admitted back into China so long as the Qing dynasty remained in power.

Ming felt caught between two worlds: a land of starvation and flooding back home, and a Wild West slowly slipping out of civilized control.

It was on this gray day in January that Ming first mentioned the possibility of going back home. The dream of shimmering gold she'd had back in rural Guangzhou seemed faded and impossible now, silly even. Nothing around her glittered; the gold had disappeared.

Maybe she'd been mistaken about the dream all along.

"You know Huiqing will allow us to stay with him in Xinjiang," Ming said as she trekked along the river's edge, the long grasses clinging to her dusty robes. "Maybe we should accept."

"And return to China?" Uncle Wang looked at her solemnly, then sighed and sat down on a large river rock, the water clogged with brown fallen leaves behind him.

"Yes, Uncle." Ming drew up her robe and sat down meekly next to him. Her throat burned with infection, and she longed for rest, rest—anything but the beastly hunger and exhaustion of this place, the sound of men's laughter, and the smell of horse manure and dust and cook-fire smoke. At least in Guangzhou they'd had a roof over their heads, even though it leaked, and the fragile hope of harvest after the winter rains.

Uncle Wang didn't speak, and Ming heard nothing but the gurgle of water behind him. Winter birds soared overhead with throaty cries, and her eyes followed them against the barren gray sky.

When she looked again, Uncle Wang was fingering the worn blade of his pocket knife. Silently, he lifted it to the back of his head and—with one liquid movement—sliced off his long braid.

"Uncle!" gasped Ming, clapping a hand over her mouth. "What have you done?"

"I'm staying, Ming," he replied weakly, sheathing the knife with shaking hands. "We're staying here in America."

She stared, unable to comprehend what she'd just seen.

"Your hair," she whispered. "You've been growing it for years."

"All my life." Uncle Wang put the knife in his pocket. The long braid lay across the rock, a lifeless gray snake.

"They won't let you back into China without the Manchu braid and haircut!"

"Exactly."

Ming stared at her uncle's head, bare of its braid, smooth like one of the young American men fresh from the barber shop. Then the truth dawned on her: Uncle Wang had cut off all temptation to go back home.

"But why? We're failing here. Lots of people are."

"God has called us. We're staying."

"If He's called us, Uncle, then why aren't we finding gold?"

Uncle Wang sighed. "Staying is hard, my daughter. I know that." He leaned back and crossed his arms. "But I believe God sent us here. With all my heart, I believe that this place called 'Gold Mountain' is where He wants us. He's shown it to me in His Word, and every time I pray, He tells me to stay here and never go back." He paused, and light played in the clouds for a moment. "If we return to China, what is your future? You are a young woman without any rights, without any dowry, and you will be taken or bought by the wealthiest man who offers. Who knows that in a moment of hunger or desperation we may not relent and ruin your future, ruin your hope? There are not many Christians in China, little Ming—and strong young Christian men are perhaps fewest of all."

Heat rose to her face suddenly as she thought of Bao, of the sudden rush of affection she had seen in his eyes on the windy ship deck. *I've never met anyone quite like you,* he'd said, in that beautiful Cantonese of his. She could feel the gold of his cross necklace against her skin even now, warm from her flesh, and wondered again where Bao had gone—and if he ever thought of her. Surely by now he had forgotten her, if he even lived in California.

Perhaps he had given up by now and gone home to China like the others, lost in a sea of a thousand other faces.

"Well, what possibility do I have here, Uncle?" Ming was too ashamed to lift her eyes.

"Here you have hope, my little Ming, if you can survive." Uncle Wang's voice sounded solemn. "Here a woman may hold a job—even run her own business! It is not that way in China, my dear."

"But what about the foreign miner's tax, if it's true? How can the Americans pass a tax like that? We will have nothing left!"

Uncle Wang tipped his head to hear her better over the sound of water on rocks. "They have every right," he replied quietly. "It is their land, Ming, not ours. We are guests here. We are not citizens. Do not forget that."

The field stretched quiet around them for a moment, and then Uncle Wang started to stand to his feet. He swayed weakly and then sat again, groping for a handhold on the rock. His eyes scrunched closed, and he wiped his forehead with a shaking hand.

"Uncle? What's wrong?" Ming fell to her knees beside him. Leaves fell from a tree, flitting toward barren earth, and for a moment she felt like she were back on the farm, willing him to stay alive, to breathe, to live. Hope fleeting and brittle, like dry winter grasses.

Uncle Wang didn't answer, and she touched her hand to his forehead. His skin burned hot like a coal oven.

"Uncle! You're sick!" Ming gasped.

The land spun as she passed him the remains of water in her small jug and then tugged him to his feet. "You've got to get back to the tent! I'll find you a doctor."

"We don't have money for a doctor." His voice rasped a bit as he staggered forward, leaning on her arm.

"I'll find money. I can't lose you now."

Ming half-pulled, half-carried Uncle Wang back to camp, begging the help of two young Chinese men whom she assumed, from their conical straw hats and rough tool belts, must have been hired as construction workers.

Another wave of men had left the alliance and camp for China or other work in San Francisco, and the area looked deserted, dusty, with many of the tent lots vacant and cook fires cold and black. Yuanjun, the man they called upon to diagnose illness and mix Chinese herbs and medicines, seemed to have left, too; the spot where his tent used to stand lay bare.

She helped Uncle Wang into the tent and rapidly sorted through their cooking pots and gold panning tools to see what they might have of value to sell. They owned so few belongings worth much.

Then her eyes lit on the beautiful patterned quilt Uncle Wang had bought her, and the embroidered pillow; she wrapped it over her arm and rushed down the sandy path toward the market.

◆   ◆   ◆

"Miss. Miss. Excuse me?" A ragged man approached Ming in Mandarin as she stood over her little cook fire in bare feet, shivering while she stirred a small pot of chicken and broth for Uncle Wang. A fragrant swirl of steam curled up, pungent with ginseng, garlic, wood ear mushrooms, and medicinal herbs bartered from one of the Asian vendors in the burgeoning section of Chinese markets in San Francisco. At least the pillow and quilt, along with her shoes and winter shawl, had bought enough ingredients for a pot of soup that she prayed would heal him; after that, it was anyone's guess where their next meal would come from.

Guangzhou had appeared all over again: the emptiness and poverty. Only now she was surrounded by thousands of dirty men in the same predicament.

Where is the gold, God? her heart cried out. *You said I'd find it here!*

"Miss?" the man said again, switching to Cantonese.

Ming looked up at an elderly man with graying hair, in tattered clothes. "Can I help you?" She paused from her stirring to wipe strands of hair back from her face with her wrist.

"Do I smell ginseng?" The man eased closer, his mouth a hungry line. He set down his knapsack and peered into the pot, rubbing his chin with calloused fingers.

"Yes, from the market. They said they are from northern China, brought on a boat just this week." She added in a handful of chopped celery leaves, which herbalists claimed had healing properties for the lungs and blood pressure.

The man's eyes brightened, a glittering black mixed with something like longing, and he shifted his weight from one foot to the other. "How much?"

"How much ginseng?"

"No, how much for a bowl?"

"Of my soup?" Ming glanced across the pot at him, startled.

"Yes."

She stirred a ladleful of broth over the chicken legs. "I've never sold my cooking before," she said, stirring the celery leaves into green bits over the bubbling surface of the soup. "Normally I'd give it to you without cost, but it's for my uncle. He's not well." She glanced back toward the tent.

"I'll give you five dollars." The man drew a folded bank note from his pocket.

"For the pot?" Ming gasped. Five dollars was a lot of money; more than she'd earned selling her pillow and quilt.

"No, for a bowl." He reached into his knapsack and produced a rough dish. "I'd do almost anything for a taste of home. It's what I remember. They don't eat like we do, the Americans," he said with a sigh. "I was a fool to leave Shanghai for this place. I've got more money than I did back home digging roads and ditches as an old man, but what's the use if I long for home with every breath?"

Ming hesitated, speechless at the thought of five whole dollars for a single bowl of soup. Her mind jumped to the biblical story of Esau selling his birthright for a bowl of red stew; she wondered if it were right to take the man's money.

"Ten. I'll make it ten." The man reached into his pocket for another bill. "My final offer. Will you do it, miss? I'm awfully hungry."

Ming's mouth fell open. And before she fully comprehended, she had taken the man's bowl and filled it to the brim with steaming soup.

"Take it, sir, and may the Lord bless you," she said. He passed her the money, ten whole dollars, and Ming just stood there in disbelief as the man pulled chopsticks from his knapsack and began to eat, blowing on the broth and slurping up bits of chicken and ginseng with gusto.

The image of the money in her hand didn't make sense; the whole scenario seemed like something out of a bizarre dream. Even stranger, the man's eyes glistened as if they held tears.

"Is it too hot?" she finally asked as he wiped his eyes with work-calloused fingers—half afraid he might snatch the ten dollars back.

"Oh no. It's just right. It soaks up my longing," said the man with a fragile smile that nearly broke her heart. "There's just nothing like our home cooking anywhere in this country, even where we Chinese work in town. Saloon food is so terrible, no wonder they serve so much beer! And the boardinghouses are so expensive I'd have to hock my horse just to eat."

Ming knew he spoke the truth; meals in town consisted of little more than a day-old loaf of sourdough bread, if a person could scrape enough dollars together to buy one.

"The problem is, you see, there aren't enough ladies here to make food the way it ought to be made," the man was saying.

"What way is that?"

"Why, with care," he replied indignantly, as if stating the obvious. "Men, if they stop working long enough to eat at all, don't know how to cook—they just throw things in the pan, burn most of it, and hope it turns out right. Women, you see, trim the carrots first, and cook them until they're tender." His eyes reddened again. "That's the difference."

Ming bowed, not sure what to say in the face of such deep emotion. She'd never thought of how she cut her carrots or anything else—she just did it. "People are the root of the country," she finally quoted the old proverbs, "and food is the first necessity of people."

"But food is more than for filling the belly. It fills our hearts, too."

His words rang in her head like a temple gong: *"It soaks up my longing."*

Ming had been hungry for so long, it seemed, that she had forgotten the inner yearning of tastes and memories, of dumplings and steamed buns and spices. But as a young girl, hadn't she thrilled to watch her mother press the shrimp wontons together with rice-floured hands, or blanch green stalks of bok choy in boiling water to serve with fragrant oyster sauce? The sweet, cherry-like fragrance of a soft white lychee broken open in her hands—didn't the image call to her, haunt her, even now?

Those flavors had been more than a meal; they knit together memories, faces, happiness—invisible bonds that held her together.

She recalled Huiqing's tears as he'd eaten her steamed dumplings, cooked on a skillet over a cook fire, and how he laughed and cried as he ate, tasting and remembering.

"Thank you, miss—thank you." The man shouldered his knapsack, bowl in hand. "I'll tell everybody about you. I know a lot of people who'd pay for a meal like this, you know?"

He bowed and headed on down the dirt path, still cradling the steaming bowl with both hands like it contained something precious.

Ming watched him go, feeling slightly dizzy at the rush of astonishment and confusion. The pot bubbled, and she stirred it with shaking fingers. Her senses trickled back, and she stuffed the money inside the pocket of her robe before someone filched it from her.

Ten American dollars! And what had he said about not enough ladies here to make the food taste right? Or more specifically, to make the food taste like home, to make food with love and tenderness, and to fill the longing of the heart.

Ming blinked, the blanks in her mind starting to fill with ideas and questions. Could it be possible, she wondered, that a woman in this wild region full of rough, hardened men could mean more than a smile in a saloon? What if God used her feminine touch to soothe and nourish, to heal the tired body through simple, home-cooked meals and flavors that reminded them of home?

California overflowed with men—larger crowds of dirty, lonely, homesick men than ever before. Farmers, carpenters, bankers, well diggers, and everyone in between had flooded San Francisco, with more and more boats arriving daily. Discouraged prospectors gave up gold mining and worked the farms, the mines, and the newly constructed city streets, with more Chinese and foreign immigrants constantly coming to pan the rivers everyone else had abandoned.

Her bare feet ached with cold, scratched and bleeding from the long walk home from the market. Their clothes hung threadbare, and their bag of rice had just emptied.

Worse, Uncle Wang's aged body was wearing out, and she needed him.

"Oh, God," she whispered, pressing her eyes closed in a prayer. "Show me the way!"

And when she opened them, two men stood in front of her, holding out soup bowls.

Chapter Six

It didn't take long for the Golden Fortune restaurant to take shape, moving from the front of Uncle Wang's tent and rough cook fire to a makeshift food stall on a busier street, and finally, a little rented shop on the outskirts of San Francisco's expanding Chinatown. Uncle Wang recovered, although still weak, and sold all of his mining equipment. Instead, he washed dishes and handled imported Chinese ingredients like lotus root and snow mushrooms for Ming, who hired Aihong and Ang, two of the washerwomen from the now defunct Chinese prospecting alliance, to cook alongside her.

Ming hung silk flags outside the shop to show Chinese ethnicity, then draped the windows with curtains of traditional Chinese red and gold. She decorated the glass windows with feminine paper flowers and graced the tables with tablecloths and wildflower bouquets—a sure sign that women staffed the kitchen. Her efforts worked to draw in crowds of hungry Chinese men: hungry for a meal with echoes of home and hungry for a woman's pure and gentle presence.

Together Ming and her crew served up bowl after bowl of Chinese and Cantonese specialties: sweet and sour stir-fried pork, fried dumplings and steamed pork-filled buns, fried rice, *congee* rice and chicken stew, and stewed beef brisket.

Lines formed outside the door until the neighboring laundry owners squabbled with Uncle Wang, and the Golden Fortune bought more tables and extended its hours to breakfast and dinner as well. Three times in two months the owner of the building raised the rent, and three times Ming and Uncle Wang got down on their knees and begged God to supply enough customers to pay both the exorbitant new rent and their workers as they'd promised.

"It's not right!" Ming cried as they counted out their dollars at the end of the day. "The owner doesn't have the right to raise the rent like that, Uncle, and you know it! He knows it. We have a contract."

"Maybe not, but it is our livelihood," Uncle Wang replied quietly. "We cannot read all the fine print in his legal contract, and he's aware of that, too, I'm sure. But who is bigger, Ming—a landlord or our God?"

And all three days God sent the right amount, so specifically that Uncle Wang wept one evening as he tallied up the month's earnings and expenditures, circling the final total in bold, inked strokes: just enough to pay Aihong and Ang, plus the rent, down to the penny. He pegged it on the wall as a sign of God's favor, and there it stayed for weeks and months, a testimony to God's faithfulness.

Any income Ming and Uncle Wang made went straight back to the restaurant, and after several months they'd earned enough to rent the tiny apartment overhead for their living quarters.

Americans, too, began to trickle into the Golden Fortune, intrigued by its exotic ingredients and flavors, and Ming quickly learned how to bake sourdough bread for them: the tangy, chewy loaves made famous in San Francisco. She'd serve a thick slice alongside a bowl of stir-fried beef with common American vegetables: carrots, sweet broccoli, cabbage, all swirled in a thick, sweet, Cantonese-style brown sauce.

When the Foreign Miner's Tax passed the California legislature in April, forcing nonnative miners to pay twenty dollars a month to continue mining, scores of Chinese men left mining for good. But the restaurant continued to grow, and Ming studied advertising and business until she fell asleep at the dining-room table, lamp still on.

It was at this time that Ming, as she tried to sleep in her hard bedroll over the restaurant, closed her eyes and dreamed again of gold.

◆　◆　◆

Ming struggled to sleep over the clatter of wagon wheels on cobblestone and the echo of voices, which rang up from the streets even at night. But as the noise of the city faded into the darkness of sleep, Ming saw again the glowing outline of Gam Saan or Gold Mountain—the United States of America.

Only this time, to her amazement, the shape of the country shifted and morphed into the shape of a human heart, a man's heart. She watched as he moved in liquid motions, first bowing his head in prayer and then lifting chopsticks to his mouth to swallow a mouthful of rice—*her* rice.

After he had eaten, his heart began to sparkle and glow with the glitter of gold that had dazzled Ming's eyes over a year ago, pulsing and glistening in brilliant light. He then put down his chopsticks and offered the rest of his rice to a crowd of people, and as they ate, their hearts began to sparkle, coming alive, beating, and the people raised their hands in praise to God.

Ming listened as they cried out in prayer to Him in Cantonese and Mandarin, mingled with minority languages from all over China: *"Worthy is the Lamb who was slain!"* they sang together, from the book of Revelation.

Then came the voice that Ming had heard once before, in clear Cantonese: "Do not work for food that spoils," it began, quoting John 6:27, "but for food that endures to eternal life, which the Son of Man will give you."

And that was all Ming remembered before she opened her eyes in the darkened room.

◆　◆　◆

The room lay still, her quick breath the only sound. Uncle Wang had already risen, she assumed, and was working down in the restaurant, for his bedroll lay empty. The clatter and laughter had receded from the streets below, and a single dog barked in the distance, the sharp sound echoing against the bricks of the nearby shops.

The dream was real, she thought, looking out the window to a sky full of stars, unusually bright through San Francisco's veil of salty fog. It had actually happened, and she wasn't imagining it. She recognized the elements this time: the pulsing gold, the voice without describable sound, the borders and edges of America that fluidly changed shape.

She had heard the prayers, heard the verses—and with a heavy, sinking feeling, Ming knew she had fallen short. She had "worked for food that spoils" and nearly forgotten the command to *"go, and take the Good News there."*

That had been her calling in Guangzhou: to take the Good News to America and share the Gospel with those who didn't yet know the Lord.

When was the last time she'd offered the Good News to anyone or even mentioned the name of Christ? Sure, she and Uncle Wang prayed together and read the scriptures, even attended some of the small churches in the area. They'd gone for a while to an American church closer to Chinatown, where congregants had shaken their hands and made them feel welcome, but Uncle Wang couldn't understand much of the English-language sermon. Ming had struggled to translate spiritual words with deeper nuances into Cantonese for him: words like *sanctify*, or *justification*, or even *glory*. They didn't know the songs, didn't read music, and just stood there like toads on a log (Ming thought) with their mouths open, trying to remember when to sit or stand.

Some Chinese Christians had formed a church on the other side of town, she heard, but they couldn't travel so far with all the restaurant preparations that constantly consumed their time—even if they could afford a rented cart to get there each week.

And that's where they remained stalemated, working to pay the bills and stay one step ahead of financial ruin.

But as Ming looked out over the city, its horizon ribboned in the blue of dawn, she wondered for the first time about the people who lived along these streets, worked here, honeycombed in apartments and tents and boardinghouses. Smoke from furnaces and chimneys billowed up into the darkened sky, like the smoke from the city of Sodom after the Lord destroyed it. How many of these thousands and thousands of men, Chinese and otherwise, would find their lives hidden with Christ in heaven if San Francisco fell this very day? How many men had already sold their souls for liquor and brothels and sin, and how many would do it today, as soon as the sun rose?

That was one of the reasons Ming had come: to continue the good work the missionaries had started in China—even offering up their lives—and share the Gospel with those who had never heard.

But how could she? Ming's breath frosted against the glass. She was just one girl, and her uncle was frail and elderly. What did they possibly have that could take the Gospel to so many people?

A wooden pushcart squeaked faintly in the street below, a sign that dawn would soon break. A lamp flickered on in the next building over, all its windows dark except for that single burning light.

One light. One small light in the middle of the darkness.

"You do have something to help you take the Gospel to your city," came the whisper from inside Ming.

"You have a restaurant."

But a restaurant offers food!

"Offer Me, the Bread of Life, and your customers will never go hungry."

Ming dressed quickly, ideas and thoughts rushing through her head as she brushed out her long, black hair and pinned it up. Of course—a restaurant! What better way to meet people of the city than through food that nourished their bodies with warm vegetables and healing broth?

How God wanted her to share the Gospel while serving food, Ming didn't know—but the thought intrigued her, made her hands tingle with excitement as she pinned a pretty flowered pin along the side of her bun.

She fingered her simple Chinese-style robes, so different from the American gowns with their puffed sleeves and light, floral fabrics, the ruffled collars and bustled skirts, and she wondered what life as a Christian woman would hold in a place like San Francisco. Would she grow old alongside Uncle Wang, working tirelessly to serve her customers and teach them about the Word of God? Or would she somehow find love, even here?

Wait a minute. Ming put down the brush and tried to remember.

A man. There had been a man in her dream, and it was his heart that had sparkled like gold after he ate her rice.

Who was he? Where had he come from, and how did God expect Ming to meet him? Was he a Christian leader who would partner with her and Uncle Wang to reach Chinese immigrants with the good news of Christ, or someone else entirely?

The golden cross she wore around her neck glinted in the lamplight as she turned toward the simple mirror on her dressing table, and suddenly something made sense.

She pulled on her robe and shoes and rushed down the narrow stairs into the restaurant. Ang already bustled about the kitchen, lighting the cook stove and putting carrots and rice on to boil, and Aihong would arrive shortly to start chopping chicken and onions. Ming bowed to Ang and hurried past her into the dark dining room, curtains still drawn, where she found Uncle Wang hunched over his work at one of the tables. A single lamp burned, flickering shadows on the wall.

"Uncle Wang," she said, sinking into one of the chairs to catch her breath. "The Golden Cross."

"What's that?" He looked up from something he was carving out of wood. Curls of wood shavings covered the tablecloth, like little curls of blond hair.

"We should rename our restaurant the Golden Cross. After all, didn't God send us here to share the Good News?"

Uncle Wing's face smiled in astonished increments: first his eyes, crinkling at the corners, then his narrow cheeks, and finally his merry mouth, showing his teeth. He laughed out loud, shaking his gray head.

"You see, qiānjīn, God and I talked last night, and I thought the same thing," he said, lifting up his carving.

A cross—a large one—with hand-lettered Chinese characters running down the vertical post: *Jīnsè de Shízìjià,* or in Mandarin, "golden cross."

◆ ◆ ◆

It was a balmy late summer day when Ang whispered to Ming that Uncle Wang had been talking to a customer for several hours. Uncle Wang had propped the restaurant doors open, letting in pleasant evening light, a beautiful pale blue hue, and Ming could smell the salt from the ocean.

"Who is he?" Ming whispered back, spooning rice and mushrooms into a bowl.

"I don't know. A young man, he seems to be, and it looks like they are praying."

"Praying?" Ming's heart leaped up. "Perhaps he is one of the missionaries' converts, then."

"I don't know. But they've been talking for a long time. I wondered if you knew him."

"I don't know. I'll take a look."

Since spring the Golden Cross restaurant had taken a very different turn. Uncle Wang had gone in search of American missionaries he'd seen preaching in Chinatown in broken Mandarin, and he invited them to use the restaurant to preach. They closed the restaurant on Sundays, and the Golden Cross became a church of sorts, where missionaries and Chinese Christians gathered to preach, listen, and sing in Mandarin and Cantonese, the doors always open and service times posted outside the restaurant.

Against her better financial judgment, Ming and Uncle Wang opened a pantry project, making some extra bread and rice dishes to hand out to the homeless and beggars with the missionaries' help. Uncle Wang gave his testimony of being saved and cured of opium addiction to them and to the church, and eventually on the street corners with the missionaries, standing on an empty apple crate.

Ming found a woman named Jia who had beautiful lettering skills and paid her to write out some scripture verses in beautiful Chinese script, which she then pasted on the walls, and Uncle Wang agreed to always serve plates with a blessing from the book of Numbers: "May the Lord bless you and keep you."

Aihong quit, angered by the religious environment that clashed with her traditional ancestor worship, but Ang coaxed Jia into staying on to cook.

And it was Jia, amazingly, who became the first person in their little group to answer the missionaries' invitation to salvation in Jesus Christ one Sunday, standing up from her dining room chair and walking boldly to the front of the room, stepping around the beggars and drifters and men in tattered clothes who had slipped in to hear the message.

"Mercenaries kidnapped me to serve in the brothels of San Francisco," she said in her clear voice. "But near the harbor, a wave swept me overboard—and the shipmates left me for dead. A small boat of fishermen rescued me, still unconscious, and brought me to shore. They gave me medical care and American clothing, and not knowing my name, they called me 'Mary' and let me go. Since my captors thought I had perished, they stopped looking for me—and I found work washing laundry. I got my life back." She clapped a hand over her mouth to choke back a sob. "But the other women didn't. They were afraid, so afraid. Most of them so young."

The missionaries and women in the room surrounded her, tears streaming unabashed.

"I am free today from the hell those men intended me to live, and I want to be free from eternal hell, too," she said. "I believe, and I want to be baptized."

After Ming's initial shock and joy had given her breath back, she placed a hand on Jia's arm. "Are there many of them?" she asked, feeling the ache in her heart deepen until she could hardly bear it. "Many women brought to America like you against their will?" Images of Liu Pong and his cold smile made her want to double over, vomit.

"Many." Jia met her eyes. "You cannot imagine how many. Or how they live. Americans say there are no virtuous Chinese women in this country, but they don't understand that most of us don't choose that life. It is forced upon us. We are bought, sold, kidnapped, coerced, lied to. The *tongs*, the Chinese crime network, are unspeakably cruel to those who might try to escape."

Ming hid her face, finding no words to speak.

Fortunately Abigail, one of the missionaries, spoke for her. "The Presbyterian Rescue Mission has been making plans to reach out to those women," she said gently. "They want to prepare a safe house for women to run to and find ways to reach out to them and eventually rescue as many as they can. Will you help us?"

"I will do anything." Jia did not flinch.

"Do you not fear the tongs?" Ming asked, feeling weak in her legs.

"Do not fear those who can kill the body but cannot kill the soul," said Uncle Wang softly.

"Matthew 10:28," Ming murmured. "You are right, Uncle." She took Jia's hand. "We will fight back against this darkness together. After all, whom should we fear but our Lord? Jia, our apartment is yours if you need a place to stay."

Since then, she and Jia had worked together side by side, studying the Bible together by lamplight after work and riding across town to the rescue mission. Ang became pregnant with her family's second child, and when she could no longer work, the Presbyterian mission sent them a young Yao girl who had run to them for help. Nuying, as they called her, needed work until the mission could help her buy a ticket back to her home in southern China. And so Nuying joined the women upstairs in Ming's little bedroom, with Uncle Wang sleeping on a pallet in the main room.

Nuying spoke little but worked hard with sad eyes, and Ming prayed for her often as their paths crossed—pleading with God to keep her safe, to heal her heart, and to restore her joy.

Unfortunately, Nuying's forte wasn't cooking, which felt at first like a setback compared to Ang's skill in the kitchen. Nuying burned the dumplings and put too much salt in the broth, no matter how hard she focused on her tasks, and Ming saw tears in her eyes as Jia gently corrected her sloppy chopping and not-quite-baked bread, still jelly-like in the middle.

"I don't think she's cut out to be a cook," Jia whispered. "She's got a good heart, but good hearts don't necessarily know how to steam a dumpling."

Ming's hands fluttered to her forehead as she tried to think of what to do. "God sent her, Jia," she reminded her. "We've got to trust Him."

"Or pray for Him to send someone else," said Jia with a slight bob of her eyebrows.

On that balmy summer night, soft with breeze, Jia pulled Ming aside and motioned to the little table where Uncle Wang sat, deep in conversation with a young Chinese man. Ming could see nothing more than the back of his long queue braid, but she couldn't make out the words over the clatter of dishes and laughter of customers.

"Who do you think he is?" Jia whispered.

"I don't know. You don't think it's someone looking for Nuying or for you, do you?" Ming felt her heart beat faster in her throat.

Jia frowned and shook her head. "I don't think so. Your uncle was patting his shoulder and smiling at him like a son."

Ming drew back in surprise. "I have no idea. I can't imagine who it could be."

She put down the plate of noodles she'd been rolling from flour and wiped her sweaty, greasy face with a damp cloth, smoothing her hair back into place. Picking up a serving tray, she piled it high with plates of dumplings, sautéed spring onions, and glistening chicken congee, then headed into the dining room and served the plates one by one, smiling and bowing as she gave the Christian blessing.

Her customers bowed back, chopsticks in hand, and Ming headed back to the kitchen for the teapot to refill cups. Quick service, without being asked—that was what she thought God wanted her to offer at the Golden Cross. Extending His loving hand to the roughest of customers, serving them as Christ would.

She had just stepped between two tables, steaming teapot in hand, when the man at the table with Uncle Wang suddenly pushed back his chair and stood.

And Ming nearly walked right into none other than Zheng Bao, the same young man she'd met on the deck of the *Berea*.

Chapter Seven

Ming stood there, teapot dripping, until she came to her senses and bowed. "Excuse me," she said, hoping she hadn't burned him with the hot teapot. "I'm very sorry."

"Oh no, I'm the clumsy one," said Bao in the same fluid Cantonese he had used on the ship.

Neither of them spoke for a moment, and Bao tipped his head slightly, as if trying to see her better. She saw his dark eyelashes under black brows blink rapidly twice, three times. "Don't I know you?" he asked. "Didn't I meet you on the ship?"

"Yes, I think you did."

"Wang Ming." He breathed out her name in soft tones. "I remember."

"You are Zheng Bao. Or Jonah, as you said you preferred to be called. I remember, too."

Ming became suddenly aware of heat flooding her cheeks as Bao bowed, not taking his eyes off her. He looked leaner than she remembered, stronger and tanned by the sun. His braid still hung glossy black under his dark blue cap, and his clothing looked new—the typical Mandarin jacket and pants in shades of beautiful red and blue. The Gold Rush must have been good to him; he looked robust and healthy.

"Are you still Jonah?" Ming finally asked, not sure what to say.

"Not exactly." The corners of his lips curved up in a slight smile. "I have a lot to tell. But first," he asked, his gaze bouncing between Ming and Uncle Wang, "how do you know each other?"

"He's my uncle," said Ming.

"The one you traveled with from Guangzhou?" He glanced at Uncle Wang in surprise.

"The same." Ming's forehead wrinkled. "But how do you know my uncle?"

"I didn't until tonight."

Uncle Wang laughed and clapped Bao on the shoulder. "I hope to get to know you a lot better, my good son."

Ming's eyes widened. *My son,* he had called him.

She wanted to ask more, say more, but something caught her attention: the smell of smoke from the kitchen. Diners shifted in their seats, and someone commented—in an annoyed voice—about the long wait.

"Oh no—Nuying must have burned the dumplings again," Ming said, backing away from the table. "I'm sorry, but I've got to go see to the damage. We are desperate for more help back there." She bowed again, glancing over at the line of hungry men coming through the doorway, mostly Chinese with a few pale faces. "Excuse me, Mr. Zheng."

He didn't sit. "What kind of help do you need?"

"Sorry?"

"Help in the back. You said you needed help."

"Oh." Ming shifted her teapot to the other hand and started to turn. "Just kitchen help. One of our cooks is new, and it's hard work." She nodded to the men at the door. "I'll be right with you!" she called out in Mandarin and then in English.

Uncle Wang got up quickly from the table and greeted them, pulling out chairs right under the carved wooden cross.

Bao took a step toward Ming. "I can cook. May I?"

Ming had imagined Bao's face a hundred times in the past year; now here he stood in front of her, about half a head taller than she remembered. "May you what?"

"May I help cook?" Bao started to roll up his long sleeves.

"You?" Ming gasped.

"Sure. I owe you and your uncle a great debt. Please allow me."

"What debt?" Nothing he said made any sense. Then—in disbelief, "Can you really cook?"

"I can. Well, a little." His cheeks flushed a bit, and he grinned. "I'll try, anyway. Please, Miss Wang—Ming—I must talk to you. I'll explain. Can you show me the kitchen?"

The burnt smell grew stronger, and Ming, speechless, rushed toward the kitchen over the scrape of chairs and hiss of cooking pots in the back—Bao following behind her.

Bao quickly washed his hands in a basin of water, and Ming watched, lips open in disbelief, as he looked around the kitchen and grabbed an apron off a peg on the wall. The apron was an old one that had belonged to Aihong, a tiny and slight woman—far too small for a tall young man. Bao wrapped it around his waist anyway, tying it in the back.

This can't be happening. Ming pressed a hand to her forehead, wondering if she'd been in San Francisco too long and lost her mind.

"You can't be serious, Mr. Zheng." Ming jerked her attention to the smoking pot on the little cookstove, where Jia fanned furiously. She overturned the dumplings into a trash bin, then filled the scorched pot with cool water and scrubbed with a rough cloth.

Tears ran down Nuying's cheeks; Ming watched out of the corner of her eye as Jia patted her on the shoulder, speaking to her in low, encouraging tones.

"I am serious." Bao spoke again. "Here. Give me the pot."

Ming, at a loss for words at his confident tone, meekly handed it over, and he began to scrub. Brisk, harsh strokes with strong hands that scoured out the burned particles in a matter of seconds—much faster than her slim fingers could have accomplished. He rinsed the pot out and handed it back. "Good as new. What else can I do?"

When Ming didn't answer, he grabbed a freshly washed bunch of carrots and bok choy and began chopping, his knife rattling across the wooden cutting board in rapid-fire strokes. Neat piles of finely chopped vegetables appeared on the cutting board like green and orange haystacks.

"Who is he?"

Ming jumped as Jia suddenly appeared at her ear, whispering. "Why is he back here?"

"I have no idea." Ming rested her hand on her forehead. "I met him on a ship, and he knows my uncle. Only, actually he doesn't. They just met tonight."

Jia's eyebrows quirked in an expression of astonishment, and Ming shrugged. "It's a long story."

"It must be."

"How do you cook so well?" Ming asked him hesitantly, chopping ginger and garlic on a wooden board for dumplings.

"My mother was sick a lot, and my father was always working in the fields and at his business, and later preaching, so I picked up the slack." Bao bowed an "excuse me" and passed around to her other side, taking over the pot of noodles Jia had left to rush plates into the dining room. "Besides, I love cooking, spices. The idea of creating something completely new from an array of completely different and separate ingredients. It's fascinating."

Ming felt herself staring, and she dropped her head in embarrassment. Never once had she heard a man speak like that about a mundane chore like preparing food.

Then she remembered: the golden cross.

"Oh!" she gasped. "You must have come for your cross." Ming reached around her neck and pulled off the cord, light glancing off the gold as she cupped it in her hands.

"My what?" He looked up from the pot of noodles he'd started frying, deftly tossing in a handful of chopped spring onions.

"Your cross necklace. The one your father made." She held it out to him, still warm from her skin.

"Oh, you still have it!" Bao's face lit in a flash of joy. He wiped his hands on the towel over his shoulder and reached for it. He touched the cross to his lips, then lifted the cord over his head and around his neck, tucking it under the front of his shirt.

The movement startled Ming. "You're wearing it?" she said. "I thought you weren't ready to wear it. To assume the responsibilities your father expected."

"I think I am now." His eyes held something sober, something deep. "Thank you for saving it for me."

It took a moment for Ming to process what he'd just said, so she busied herself folding dough for dumplings, pleating them with her fingers around the ground pork and ginger.

"You know, you don't have to work back here in the kitchen to get your necklace back," she finally said meekly. "It's yours. I didn't mean to keep it."

"I'm thankful for the necklace, but that's not why I came."

"It's not?" She looked up, startled.

"No." His dark eyes met hers. "I've been praying to find you for a long time, if you'll excuse me for being so forward. I've never forgotten you."

Her heart pounded in her throat. "Someone...told me you were looking for me," she said, too embarrassed to meet his eyes. "Do you know a man named Liu Pong?"

Bao scrunched up his face as he stirred the noodles, as if trying to remember. "No. I don't think so. Why?"

"Because he mentioned you."

"I just asked around." Bao shrugged. "Hoping that somehow I'd find you."

Blood rushed to her face. "Why, exactly, did you want to find me?" She kept her eyes on the dumplings, pressing the pleats together with flour-dusted fingers.

"To tell you that God has been working in me," said Bao, turning his head to face her. "At first I did well in the gold fields, and I left them to start a business—a hotel business. But I'm a bad manager and poorly trained for such a job. I failed and lost everything I'd invested. In total humiliation, I worked as a common laborer on the streets, driving carts, delivering goods. But somehow God began to find me."

He turned the hot pot of noodles onto a large platter with a sizzling sound, and the smell of onions, celery, and beef made her empty stomach murmur. It had been hours since she'd eaten; with so many hungry people, she couldn't spare even a minute to eat.

"How did God find you?" she asked, finishing the last dumpling and carrying the plate to the stove.

"Through street preachers, missionaries." Bao scraped out the noodle pot. "Once I was delivering some bags of nails to a general store on the other side of town and heard singing. It was a church—a Chinese church—meeting together in the rain, under a temporary tarp, and I couldn't move, couldn't do anything. It was the most beautiful sound I'd ever heard. I stopped to listen, just for a moment, and out of the blue a man approached me on the street and asked how to find peace with God."

He shook his head. "I wasn't expecting it and hadn't lived wisely, but he still asked me—me! I told him the best I could in my clumsy, embarrassed way, figuring it was the worst evangelistic speech anyone had ever given, but do you know what happened?"

Ming looked up.

"He said he believed, and he got down on his knees on that dirty, rainy sidewalk and prayed to receive Christ, just like that. Weeping and confessing his sins and asking God to forgive him." Bao's eyes reddened slightly, and he turned back to the plate of noodles, adjusting them slightly with his chopsticks and sprinkling green onions and toasted black sesame seeds on top. "I couldn't believe God would use someone like me to teach a man like him. I met the same man on the other side of town, weeks later, and he'd already led two other men to Christ. All he had was a shred of Chinese scripture he'd found in an abandoned mining camp, ready to be used as kindling by some homeless men, and he asked me to teach them—to help them grow in the Lord."

Bao handed the plate of noodles to Nuying with a slight bow, and she received it with eyes as round as rice balls.

"I began to pray for the men, and for others, and I saw miracles happen. I saw people saved, just by the little teaching I gave them. I saw men leave the saloons and the brothels and stop gambling their money away, and become honest workers, workers with a future. Some of them started businesses; others became respected in the community and returned to their families in China with changed hearts." He picked up an order sheet and studied the items, then reached for another pan. "I started to think that maybe God had other plans for me here, and that the gold I run after should be eternal gold—riches that money on earth cannot buy. My father said it many times, but it never made sense to me until now."

Ming pressed her lips together, taking it all in. "So why did you talk to my uncle?" she asked gently. "And why did you say you owed us a debt?"

Bao smiled, showing white teeth. "God answered my prayer through you," he said.

"You and your uncle. You see, I started doing well in my delivery job, and I'd started setting aside money to start my own delivery business when a man approached me to go halves and start together. I didn't know the man well and didn't have a settled feeling about him, so I did something new: I prayed and asked God's wisdom."

"What did He say?"

"Well, I'd just been wrestling with God about joining this man, when I suddenly felt maybe I should give it up altogether and pursue my father's path instead—the lonely, beautiful way of preaching the Gospel. I was walking along the street outside, asking him for a sign. And then I saw your restaurant."

"Our restaurant?" Ming heated oil in the skillet, looking confused.

"I saw the name Golden Cross as soon as I lifted my eyes from praying. And when I looked again, I saw it on the wall: the wooden cross in the dining room, just visible through the window in a gap in the curtains. So I came in and ordered some tea and rice, and when your uncle brought it to me, he said, 'The Lord is calling you, my son. Don't be afraid to answer.'"

The dream about the man eating my rice. Ming closed her eyes, the clear memory rushing back.

"How did my uncle know?"

"I have no idea. He said it's just what God told him to say, and so he said it. And then he sat with me for hours, reassuring me of God's plan for my life, His calling, and that He would provide for my future." Bao reached for a box of mushrooms and rinsed them in a basin of water, then dried his hands on a towel. "Your uncle knows so many scriptures, Ming—I am ashamed to sit at the same table as a man like that. I should have been memorizing them all along, but I haven't. I'll start now, though—and let God use me as He wishes. All I ask is for His wisdom to guide me."

A rush of tenderness filled Ming's heart at the thought of dear Uncle Wang, his work-hardened hands and the smile lines at the corners of his eyes.

"Bao," she said softly, dropping dumplings into the sizzling oil, "you don't need to be ashamed. You're answering the Lord now, and that's enough for Him. He will use you in ways you can't imagine to reach people who so badly need to hear the Gospel of Jesus. Your father, if I may say so, will be proud when he hears the news."

She smiled. "You aren't Jonah anymore—you're Abraham, carrying the precious faith into a new land by God's design. He will lead you, guide you, and tell you where to go and what to do."

"Then you are Sarah," said Bao, turning to face her, his eyes blazing with dark and glorious warmth, a mixture of fascination and delight. The same way he'd looked at her on the deck of the ship, sea winds blowing strands of his long, dark hair.

"Sarah?" Heat flooded Ming's cheeks. She tipped her gaze down, afraid to look up at him, and reached for another plate for dumplings.

"The one Abraham loved," said Bao softly, tipping her chin up with one finger. "The one with whom he spent his life and raised a family that blessed the nations of the earth. I want to be a blessing, Ming, for greater things than gold, for spiritual, eternal things— and I'm asking you to join me."

The plate tipped in Ming's hand, and she spilled dumplings all over the counter.

"There's no Hagar in the picture, is there?" she finally asked, trying to pick them up with trembling hands.

Bao threw back his head and laughed. "See? That's what I love about you. You're so clever. You're. . .amazing. Of course there's no Hagar." He put his hand on her shoulder and gently turned her toward him. "Only you, Ming—shining one, brighter than all the gold I could find in California."

The intensity in his eyes made her look away, caused her stomach to burst like butterflies.

"I mean it—I haven't been able to forget you ever since I met you that day on the ship. I've looked for you for months, and now that I've found you, I don't want to let you go again." Bao picked up the spilled dumplings without missing a beat, dropping them into the hot pan. "You love the Lord, and you've served your uncle better than any woman I know. You're different from anyone I've ever met—you're strong, and smart, and. . .and so very beautiful." His voice shook just a little, either from emotion or from nerves.

The sight of Bao saying those words in Cantonese, standing in her restaurant kitchen with Ang's too-small apron wrapped ridiculously around his middle, made stars swirl across Ming's vision.

Bao meant "gemstone." The pearl of great price she might give up everything to hold, to own, to stay with for the rest of her life.

"The tea's finishing!" Jia rushed in with a stack of dirty plates.

Ming jumped at the abrupt change in tone of the kitchen, vaguely aware that the dumplings might be burning again—and this time it would be her fault.

Bao took the teakettle from Jia, his bright eyes still on Ming, and rinsed it out in a basin. Then he filled it with boiling water from the stove and looked through the rows of bins and bottles—oyster sauce, dried hot peppers, sesame oil—until he found the large tin of oolong tea.

"You remember what I said, don't you, Ming?" he asked, taking off the metal top and lifting fragrant tea leaves with cupped hands. The pungent smell of roasted, dried tea filled the kitchen, sweet and richly spicy, and for an instant Ming recalled the emerald hills of tea plantations in the mountains of Guangzhou, their leaves sending out waves of fragrance.

"You said a lot," she said, her voice unsteady as she stirred the dumplings in the pan and put on the lid. "Which part do you mean?"

"About cooking. About how you can create something completely new from different ingredients." He sifted the tea leaves into the teapot. "Two items, water and dried leaves, become one beautiful thing they could never be otherwise: tea. And it holds together our whole civilization. China would fall without it." He grinned. "And so would I."

Two become one. Ming's head filled with the dizzying scent of tea.

"Will you?" He set down the teapot and faced her, bold and brilliant. "Will you say yes to me, shining one?"

And she realized she hadn't answered him.

"Yes," she said with a laugh, covering her mouth with her hand. "I will."

Jia brushed past her with another towering stack of soiled dishes, then dumped them by the washbasin. She stopped short, hands on her hips. "Don't ask me, but it looks like something's going on here," she said, her eyes bouncing back and forth between Ming and Bao.

"Does it?" Bao smiled, not taking his gaze off Ming. *"Lovers' hearts are linked together,"* he began the proverb.

"But always beat as one," finished Ming with a pounding heart, feeling the blood rush red in her cheeks in one beautiful, joyous thrum.

Epilogue

Bao and Ming married in August 1850, and Bao joined the restaurant as cook and co-manager for two more years. During those two years, the Golden Cross continued to open its doors for Sunday services, missionary and Bible training, and Christian ministry throughout the southern San Francisco area.

Bao and Ming worked closely with the Presbyterian Mission House to rescue girls from Canton and Hong Kong (sometimes as young as eleven) from brothels and sweatshops, eventually adopting three of the youngest orphans.

In 1851 the Chinese *tong* partially burned the restaurant in retaliation, but the Golden Cross rebuilt. The restaurant became successful enough that in 1852 Bao and Ming left the restaurant under Uncle Wang's oversight, and Bao became a full-time pastor.

The Zhengs soon started a mission church with a direct ministry to miners and other immigrants, with a message that would change the fabric of San Francisco forever.

Jennifer Rogers Spinola, a Virginia/South Carolina native and graduate of Gardner-Webb University in North Carolina, lives in the U.S. with her Brazilian husband, Athos, and wild children. Jennifer lived in Brazil for nearly eight years after meeting her husband in Sapporo, Japan, where she worked as a missionary. During college, she served as a National Park Service volunteer at Yellowstone and Grand Teton National Parks. In between homeschooling high-energy kids, Jennifer loves things like adoption, gardening, snow, hiking, and camping.

Gold Haven Heiress

by Jaime Jo Wright

Dedication

Dedicated to
Andy Kamla
You have taught me there is a God-given
golden lining to every circumstance,
and faith is always greater than our reality.

And to Joanne—my second mom.
For teaching me that surviving is a walk of faith
and in it one finds joy.
I treasure you.

Acknowledgments

My Cap'n Hook, for giving me freedom and loving me. Dad and Mom, for helping Peter Pan
play in Neverland and CJ sprinkle fairy dust like Tinkerbelle.

To Abby Breuklander and Nancy Stevens,
for researching the crazies out of ca. 1850 California,
and to Keli Gwyn for her virtual tour of gold country.
Thanks to Bonnie Roof and to my "Clutch" friends for your prayers and support!

To my sisters, Kara, Laurie, Halee, and Sarah,
for keeping me sane and surviving my tsunamis.
And to Anne, the sister of my heart, the one God knew I needed.

Chapter One

Gold Haven, 1951

If he were any other man, Jack Taylor would have rained down oaths and curses the minute the deluge of filthy water drenched his face. Not only his face, but his hair and his new white shirt, tailored jacket, and leather shoes. But Jack Taylor wasn't any other man. He bit back his oath and muffled his curse, choosing instead to dive into brown eyes that reminded him of rich, earthy soil. He would drown in them happily. He knew somehow, in this very moment, his life had changed for eternity.

The woman, who couldn't be much older than her early twenties, dropped the wooden bucket on the parched earth at her feet. Jack looked beyond her and took in the sad little vegetable garden with three wilted potato plants, and. . .yep. . .three wilted potato plants looked to be about it.

"Where did you come from?" He tempered his tone as he wiped water from his face and rubbed his hand on a dry patch of his trousers.

She retreated a step, curling her arms around her torso and lifting her chin. That one small movement of stubbornness contradicted the fear reflected in her eyes. Jack could tell she wanted to exude confidence. But the bucket of water she'd launched at him proved she was really scared out of her wits.

"Miss?" He tipped his head and waited, trying not to gape at the jagged and scabbed wound running from her right temple to the edge of her jaw. It was thick, and puckered.

"I live here." Her first words, and they were musical. There was something magical about her, and she had put a spell on him. But then, Elias had warned Jack he was susceptible to being too empathetic. Jack cleared his throat in an effort to distance his emotions and take a more pragmatic view of the situation.

"You live here." It wasn't really a question, more of a statement. One didn't *live* in a ghost town. He glanced at the rickety miner's shanty. One of maybe nine dilapidated and abandoned structures.

Her arms tightened around herself. "Yes." There was brittleness in her tone. Not bitter, but a shake that threatened to shatter if someone pushed too hard. "This is my home."

"Your home?" Hardly. It couldn't be true. Gold Haven had been deserted for months now. Just like everywhere else, it seemed gold fever was drying up, along with the gold. Not to mention, she was a woman, and precious little in this land was friendly to a lone woman.

A breeze blew and lifted her reddish-brown hair across her face. She reached up and brushed it aside, revealing the pure side of her face. It seemed she was content to leave the other cheek covered by her hair, like a shield over her wound. She stared at him, her lips forming a tight, straight line, all color gone from her face. No answer for his redundant question was forthcoming.

Jack cleared his throat and ran his palms over his damp hair. "Perhaps I should start over." Although his confidence had wavered a bit now that he resembled a sopping wet fop instead of a wealthy businessman with a mission to save the newly christened state of California. He extended his hand in a friendly gesture, although in normal social circumstances, she would have presented hers and he would place a kiss on her fingertips.

She eyed his hand. Blinked. Her thin eyebrows wavered between a frown and confusion.

"Jack Taylor." At her lack of response, he curled his fingers into a loose fist, then withdrew his hand.

No answer. Her lips quivered. She blinked. Instead of offering her name, or at best an apology for her dousing, the woman sniffed and lifted her delicate nose with false bravado.

Jack waited, and then her voice broke the stillness of the abandoned gold mining town.

"Get off my property." Her words quivered with emotion. "Now."

◆　◆　◆

A bit of remorse tangled with her defense. She despised being cornered like prey by a predator. Thalia Simmons willed the man away. Her tenacity would not last long—it never did. Even her instinctive reaction to throw the dirty bucket of water in Mr. Taylor's face surprised her, but he had trespassed into the remnants of her potato garden—or rather the leftover plot with plants the previous owner had failed to dig up. It was food, and she was sore in need of it, even if the few potatoes she'd found were half-rotted in the red clay earth.

She met the stranger's gaze. His stare was not unlike those she'd become accustomed to in the past four years of her pathetic life. Open admiration, suspicion, desire. . . Thalia paused. No. Desire was missing from his eyes. Perhaps it was a welcome relief for now, but that would eventually change. All men were the same.

He was muttering under his breath. Thalia braced herself for a show of temper as she observed the frustration in his sky-colored eyes. The breeze blew. A vibrant blue stellar jay swooped overhead, squawking its scratchy call. The empty shanty she'd found refuge in echoed the tense pause between them. Mr. Taylor's eyes narrowed. He toed a clump of bunch grass.

"I don't understand how this is your property. Is this your claim?" Doubt reflected in his eyes. The place was as deserted as a graveyard.

"Yes. It's mine." Thalia knew her argument rested on quicksand. But all her life she'd had to fight for what belonged to her, and all her life she had lost that fight. Her resolve had dwindled to miniscule proportions, and she could already feel it running out.

He mirrored her crossed arms, and she noted how his shirtsleeves stretched over muscular biceps. He wasn't soft like some of the other well-dressed dandies she'd experienced.

"I beg to differ, miss. I hold it on good authority the claims round these parts have long given up the ghost. The land around Gold Haven is worth pittance for gold."

He was right, of course. But maybe, if she begged, he'd respect at least a ten-by-ten patch of land?

"Who else lives here?" Mr. Taylor's firm voice yanked Thalia's attention from her wishful thinking. The longer he stood there, the more insecure she became. She wasn't plucky, or brassy like the other girls she'd spent the last several years with. She was broken. A broken person could do little against someone fully whole. Thalia refused the impulse to touch the wound scarring her face.

"Are you alone?" he pressed with more assertiveness.

She had no intention, through hell or high water, of admitting to him she was alone. Enough bad had happened in her life. She had no desire to be at the mercy of a rich dandy.

Maybe retreat *was* the best option. Thalia turned her back to him and hurried toward her potato plants, reaching for a rusty hoe she'd pilfered from another shanty closer to the river. The man followed her. She could feel him behind her, his imposing presence, and the element of strong persistence rivaling her need to hide.

"Miss—" He stumbled over her name.

Thalia hooked the dirt with the hoe, hoping her lack of response communicated she was finished giving her name, her smiles, or herself to any man.

"Do you intend to ever speak to me beyond a snippet of a phrase? Or will it just be silence?"

Thalia gripped the garden tool, her knuckles white. Turning, she saw his look drop to the wound slicing broadside down her right cheek. He averted his eyes from it. For the hundredth time, she wrestled with being thankful that drunken sot of a miner slashed her with a broken bottle and hating the marring deformity for its ugliness.

"Very well." Mr. Taylor smashed his damp hat on his head, squashing dark curls springing up from the water she'd tossed on him. His chiseled features drew into a perplexed frown. "Is there someone else I might speak with? Your husband perhaps?"

Husband? That would never be her blessing or curse. One would simply never exist. Tears welled in Thalia's eyes, but she blinked rapidly, refusing to admit defeat yet again. When the gold began to run dry over a year ago, the mass exodus of miners, Chinese laborers, entrepreneurs, and prostitutes was a small version of the biblical Israelites hurrying toward some new promised land. Gold had been her personal Egypt, and slavery her personal horror.

Thalia couldn't resist touching her scar. Her freedom came in a different way, and she had no intention of losing it, even if she starved to death first.

"Leave me alone," she whispered.

"She speaks!" Mr. Taylor's eyes brightened, which deepened the creases at the corners of his eyes. But she didn't see any humor in the situation.

"Please leave," Thalia tried again.

"Are you all right, miss?"

For all that was good and holy, the man was worried about her! Why wouldn't he just take instruction?

"Miss?" Mr. Taylor urged her to answer.

"I'm fine." Thalia couldn't help the snap to her voice. Guarded would be the best posture to take against the concern in his eyes. "I want you to leave my garden and my home. There's no need of you here, Mr. Taylor."

"Jack," he corrected.

Well, that was awfully familiar and completely disconnected with anything gentlemanly, regardless of his posture, speech, and clothes. But Thalia was never one to act on pretense. Most of the time, she'd never made first *or* last name acquaintance with the men she met.

"I'm inquiring as to what your status is here. Your name, perhaps, would be a fine beginning."

She debated on giving him a new name, one she hadn't borne since birth. It might be a relief to start fresh. To not be the popular Thalia, the beauty of a soiled dove who had made more money than any of the girls in Madame Agatha's brothel. The tent shanties of the red light districts had been her home for the last four years, and she was lucky to be alive. Many of her friends had died from sickness or abuse. One had killed herself, and Thalia had found her body, pasty white after she'd poisoned herself.

She stared up at the man who bested her by a good six inches, and whose dark hair made his blue eyes brighter. The kindness in them would dissipate once he found out her past. The pity for her facial deformity would be replaced with repulsion. There was no reason to hide who she had been only a month prior. She was Thalia. Thalia Simmons. A whore.

So she told him so.

Chapter Two

Jack hoisted his trunk over the side of the wagon. His friend Elias reached up and took it from him, his black arms bulging with a strength Jack knew he'd never possess. Their eyes met in mutual satisfaction. Gold Haven. A new start. For all of them. Elias hauled the trunk into the tent he'd constructed earlier. It would do for Elias and his wife, Celeste, until they could shore up one of the vacant shanties. Jack nodded to himself. Yes. This would be good. He wondered briefly if what he sensed was a tiny bit of what the Lord felt when He looked over His creation and breathed a deep breath of pleasure. Of course, Jack shoved away any remnant of self-pride. This beginning, in Gold Haven, was all because of God.

He stood in the wagon and rested his hands at his waist, ignoring the sweat soaking his shirt between his shoulder blades. It was dry, hot, and the land needed rain, but he could see the American River not far from the skeleton of a town. Its waters rushed over rocks and tripped around boulders, making riffles and patches of white water. How many men had given their last bits of energy to pan and dredge the river for gold? He turned and looked at the ramshackle buildings, tilted sideways, ripped canvas blowing in glassless windows. Gold Haven was a failure of a town, and this sad place hid another broken life.

Thalia. She'd tried to sound defiant when she blatantly admitted her occupation, yet a deep pain was embedded in her brown eyes. The kind of pain that would need surgical efforts to be removed.

She was just the sort of person Jack was revitalizing Gold Haven for. His dream to take a wasteland of man's attempts and turn it into a place of redemption was never far from his thoughts. Jack swung himself from the back of the wagon. He was glad to be rid of the rich man's clothes he'd worn day after day, instead exchanging them for workman's duds. He preferred to till the land, grow barley, and give Gold Haven and its occupants a new future. Jack was ready. When the world told him his calling had failed before it began, he could think of only one thing: faith was so much stronger than man's designs.

◆ ◆ ◆

Thalia peeked around the corner of her shanty, her hand splayed against the rickety plank wood pretending to be the siding of the building. She watched a big Negro man and Jack Taylor hoisting barrels from the bed of the wagon. What were they intending to do? Pan for gold? Her stomach curdled at the thought. There were two ways that scenario would end. Either she would have to tolerate their presence in Gold Haven until the gold-blinded men realized the place was tapped of all its riches, or they would find the elusive golden treasure, yell "eureka," and it would be Sutter's Mill all over again. She'd lived through it once, suffered through it for years, and now was willing to die before she went back.

"Miss?"

Thalia yelped and spun on her heel, her hand scraping the siding. A sliver penetrated her palm, but she ignored it to face the lilting voice that disturbed her spying. She met deep brown eyes reflecting wisdom uncommon to a young woman her own age. Her burnished skin was like the milky brown of coffee laced with heavy cream. Black hair spiraled and frizzed around the woman's face, but kindness, not unlike Jack's, embodied the woman.

"Jack told me I might find you here." She smiled. Thalia swallowed. A woman was a rare thing in these parts, unless of course they were like Thalia. Even Negro women weren't prevalent. Especially without their owners.

The woman reached for Thalia's splinter-pierced hand. "You jumped pretty high. I didn't mean to scare you."

Thalia tucked her hand in the folds of her threadbare gray calico. She'd stolen it off a clothing line when she'd wandered through Coloma, a gold mining capital.

"I'm Celeste." White teeth flashed in a beautiful smile. Celeste's Southern accent was tinged with another tone Thalia couldn't place.

"Are you free?" The words escaped Thalia before she could hold them back.

A shadow flickered in Celeste's eyes. She ducked her head then breathed deep, releasing a sigh. "For now."

The feeling was mutual, though their circumstances were far different. Thalia's shoulders relaxed. She knew instinctively she could like this woman, but inviting people into her world, into her life, was a dangerous trail to walk. She noticed Celeste's eyes travel to the wound on her face.

"That looks like it's healing well, but it'll be a ragged scar." Celeste lifted her hand as if to reach out and touch the injury. Thalia jerked away and understanding marked Celeste's face.

"I know. Isn't nothing worse than the mark of a man. I have my own, you just can't see them."

Thalia had heard the stories, of the white owners whipping their slaves. Of the black women being taken from their families and used as mistresses. She could see in Celeste's eyes and hear in her words that Celeste's scars weren't very different from Thalia's.

"And the man who did that wasn't never punished, was he?" Celeste's sad smile reflected Thalia's soul.

"I wanted to kill him," Thalia admitted. "Later I wanted to thank him."

Celeste's laugh trilled the tones of a songbird. "Now I sure never would thank my master. When I run free of him, I didn't look back."

How could she explain, to a runaway slave, that being marked by the man who had purchased her for the night had been the only gift God had ever given to her? It had bought her freedom.

Chapter Three

The wool blanket did little to ward off the chill in the night air. Thalia readjusted her body on the hard-packed dirt floor and stared at the ceiling of her shanty. Clanging sounded from the two canvas tents the visitors had erected earlier in the day. Only God knew what on earth they were doing in the growing dark that required the pounding of hammer and metal. Thalia rolled onto her side. Celeste was kind, but their appearance in Gold Haven was fast infringing on Thalia's freedom. She had traversed many miles by foot to stumble into the deserted town a few weeks prior. The late summer showed yield to a few stingy gardens planted and left behind. But, better than that, the appeal was the complete and utter lack of humanity. Survival would be difficult here, if not impossible, but Thalia was willing to try. She had no money for commerce in any nearby towns. Not when one egg was equivalent to three dollars and—she pulled the worthless blanket up to her chin—a new blanket would put her out five whole dollars. She didn't even make that in one night under Madame Agatha. A measly twenty-five cents to sell her body and her soul…all of the coins going to Madame. Her value was less than that of one chicken egg.

A scratching sound captured Thalia's attention. She opened her eyes and squinted into the darkness. The tiny rustling noise warmed her, and she waited until two miniature black eyes peeked out from the darkness a mere three inches from her nose. The mouse's nose twitched and long whiskers tickled the floor.

"Hello, Ounce," Thalia whispered. The mouse had appeared her first night here in Gold Haven. After three weeks, they had built a foundation of trust. She'd never entertained the idea of befriending a mouse, but Ounce was pleasant company.

Ounce edged closer. Close enough for his whiskers to brush Thalia's nose. She smiled. "Hungry, little fellow?"

Thalia was certain the mouse nodded.

"Me, too," she whispered.

Ounce sniffed and scampered a foot away, nosing at something on the floor. He gave up interest when it turned out to be an inedible spot of something.

"I'm sorry, Ounce." Thalia imagined having a thick slice of cheese she could share with her uncommon friend. But if eggs were expensive, cheese was even worse.

A heavy knock on the shanty door rattled the building. Ounce scurried away into the darkness and Thalia thrashed into a sitting position, startled by the interruption of her nighttime conversation with the mouse.

Thalia scrambled to her feet, discarding the blanket. A heavy square of tattered canvas hung in the window to the right of the rickety door. It was almost humorous someone bothered to knock instead of just poking their head inside. She tugged the door open, its rusty hinges prohibiting smooth movement.

Jack Taylor's tall frame was silhouetted in the doorway. His broad shoulders almost touched the frame on both sides, and Thalia's heart sank to the depths. She knew why he was here, and in that moment, she wrestled with hopes and unrealistic dreams versus the stark reality of her circumstances. Money would help her survive, but then she would return to who she had been.

"I'm not taking men." Her voice filled the emptiness of the shack.

Jack jerked, stunned realization registering on his face as he raised a lantern to better see her. "No!" His voice was gritty with tired wear. "No, no. I just brought you some dinner."

Thalia eyed the basket he held out toward her. Celeste must be behind it, as the cloth-wrapped meal was accompanied by a sprig of wildflowers. It was too feminine of a touch to be attributed to a man. Her eyes flew up to meet Jack's. Food. Her stomach rumbled. The rotting potato she'd dug up earlier in the day had been rancid. Probably a leftover from last fall.

"And I brought a blanket." Jack handed her the basket of food, then drew a wool blanket from where it hung over his shoulder. "Nights can get a tad chilly, and I figured. . ." His voice trailed off as Thalia continued to stare at him.

Awkward silence passed between them and finally he muttered, "Well, say something."

She cleared her throat. He made her nervous in a way no other man had. "Th–thank you." There. She said something. He should be happy now because it was about all she could muster.

Reaching out, Thalia took the dark brown blanket. The warmth of its weight instantly warmed her heart as well. She set the basket down on the floor. "Y–you can come in, if you'd like."

He looked over her shoulder at the barren room; then his gaze returned to her. Discomfort flooded his face. Thalia read his mind.

"Just to visit while I eat," she added. She wasn't propositioning him, if that was what he thought.

Jack shrugged. "I'd best get back."

She mustered a hesitant smile.

He returned it. "I just want you to know, miss, I don't mean to upset you by coming to Gold Haven."

Thalia averted her eyes and made pretense of unfolding the blanket to wrap it around herself.

Jack continued as if he owed her an explanation. "I came here because I want to rebuild this town. I want to turn it into farming resources. Barley will grow well in this area, and maybe even grapes."

Thalia tightened the blanket around her, considered throwing it at him, but was unwilling to part with its warmth. Of course, he was here to make more money. He already had money, that much was obvious, but apparently he wanted more.

"I hope you'll find a place here." Jack finished whatever he'd been saying as Thalia ventured off into panicked thought.

Find a place here? How did she begin to interpret his words? To find a place in a new town meant she returned to her past lifestyle. Silk dresses, bodices dipped low to entice, money, men, greed, and lust. It disgusted her. But he wasn't offering anything else, and it was impossible for Thalia to interpret his words any other way. She had glimpsed what appeared might be an actual gentleman, but that hope vanished like the moon hiding behind a cloud.

Chapter Four

Jack kicked at a stone, and it bounced and rolled across the ground. He approached the campfire circle, Elias and Celeste sitting on a makeshift bench of two rocks and a board stretched over them. Celeste's modest dinner, scooped onto tin plates, balanced on their laps. Beans, some jerky, and bread. It wasn't fancy, but Celeste was a godsend. Jack was pleased Celeste had met up with Elias a few months ago, marrying him out of necessity and subtle attraction. He figured in time, the two would find love, but it was none of his business. They'd formed a friendship, including him in the mix, and Jack was thankful for their presence.

"How'd it go?" Elias's deep voice met with Jack's grunt as he sank cross-legged to the ground.

"The woman is as scared as a mouse." Jack reached for some bread. "But she took your food, Celeste."

"That's good. She so tiny, she'll blow away in a stiff breeze." Celeste smiled and cast a shy glance at her new husband. Jack squelched some jealousy. Finding a good wife in these parts would be like finding gold in a manzanita bush. Impossible.

"Wonder where she's really from," Elias mumbled around a mouthful of beans.

Jack ripped off the crust of his bread. "My guess? She's traveled to where the business is." He didn't bother to soften his words for Celeste's sake. She was a lady in his mind, but she'd seen everything and worse in her life.

"I wonder how she got free of it." Empathy washed across Celeste's face. Jack knew little about Celeste, except she'd come from New Orleans and had some French blood.

"Hate to say it, but that slice on her face probably made her undesirable." Jack rethought his words and added, "*If* she was part of a real brothel. Thing is, in a lot of these towns, it really wouldn't matter."

Elias nodded in agreement and Jack chewed a bite of bread, speaking around it. "Things are going to change by next week. If she thinks our coming to Gold Haven is an intrusion, just wait until the rest of us get here. Life in these parts is hard enough as a man. It isn't going to be friendly to a woman like Thalia, not without a man to look after her."

"And what man will take her?" Celeste murmured.

The three of them sat silent in their thoughts. Elias's spoon clinked against his plate. Celeste busied herself with wiping the rest of her beans up with a slice of bread. Jack was no longer hungry. He toyed with his bread as Celeste's question echoed in his mind. What man indeed?

◆ ◆ ◆

Thalia crouched by the water's edge, dragging the bucket through the river. She wasn't looking for gold, but rather liquid to assist the paltry gardens into growing more. Summer was harsh. It hadn't rained in these parts since late May, and even the river was down. At least her stomach was full. The bread Celeste had sent with Jack tasted like manna from heaven. It settled with warmth in Thalia's stomach, and she made sure to leave a crust for Ounce. The mouse was nibbling it in the corner of the shanty when Thalia exited earlier in the morning.

She rose to her feet, stones crunching under her worn shoes. She started as a hand reached around hers and took the bucket. Jack.

"Let me help with that."

"It's not heavy." Thalia reached for the bucket, but Jack pulled it away. He looked more rugged this morning. His shirt was plain cotton, with suspenders stretched over his shoulders. Worn brown trousers and sensible shoes. His chin was covered in whiskers, evidence he might be giving up shaving altogether.

"No matter." Jack's fingers tightened around the handle. He looked over the river to the hills beyond, the groves of cedar trees, and patches of grass. "Hard to believe this place was filled with rockers and sluice boxes."

Thalia had seen her share of those. Men sifting through earth from the water beds, water racing down the sluice to uncover nuggets—it was all so. . .vain.

"Where did you strike it rich?" The words filtered through her gritted teeth. Thalia didn't want to know, but yet she did.

Jack sniffed and kept his eyes focused on a deer across the river that was tiptoeing over the rocky shoreline. "Not far from Coloma in forty-nine. After that? My mercantile."

Oh. Thalia grimaced. Almost worse than a miner, he was one of those thieving businessmen who created lofty prices for goods and bankrupted the world around them.

"Poor miners. You probably made more at that than mining." She hid her embarrassment for speaking her thoughts aloud by bending over to pick up a stone and toss it into the river.

"I did." Jack nodded. "A lot of it."

Well, he wasn't humble.

"I've lived the last six months of my life quite ashamed of that. Greed can eat a man alive, whether panning or selling goods."

Or maybe he was humble. The only thing Thalia was certain of was that Jack Taylor was a conundrum.

She reached for the bucket. "May I have it?"

He smiled. It reached the corners of his eyes and revealed a long dimple in his right cheek. "Certainly. After I've carried it where you'd like it."

Pretending to be a gentleman would not ease his way into her bed any more than plunking down a few coins would. Thalia narrowed her eyes, trying to read Jack's face for sincerity. His desire to help looked authentic. Thalia wanted to believe, to trust, but life had taught her far differently.

"The little garden over there." Thalia pointed toward the shanties. She'd found a tomato plant. A wiry, yellowed plant with four green tomatoes sporting black scabs on them. Water might revive them enough to make them turn red. A meal. Or four maybe.

Jack crossed the land in long strides, and Thalia hurried behind him, hoisting her skirt in her hand. She'd never felt as ugly as when he stopped suddenly and turned, his eyes grazing her body. "I meant to tell you, I have a few dresses."

"Excuse me?"

He cleared his throat nervously. "Some of the goods from my store before I closed shop. There's a yellow one with little flowers all over it. It's probably about your size."

Calico. A far cry from the silks she'd worn for Madame Agatha. Thalia remembered her favorite. Emerald green, with a neckline dipping deep in the front and lace crossing her bare shoulders. It'd quickly become the worst dress in her memory. Stained with her own blood the night the drunk had slashed her face.

"I like yellow," Thalia admitted, though taking a handout from Jack might indebt her to him. A debt he might return to claim?

"There's no need to repay me." He answered the doubt that must have flickered in her eyes. "I don't want you to think I'm. . .asking for favors."

"You wouldn't get anything." Thalia's words were blunt, and then she softened them as she saw a wounded expression in Jack's clear blue eyes. "I have nothing to give."

The admission pained her. It was more than true. She had nothing. No money, no belongings, not even herself. She was used up and unworthy of any Christian kindness. Yet here stood Jack Taylor. Rich off gold and economy, an interloper in her ghost town, a *man*. And yet he seemed kind. Genuine. Thalia lost herself in the blue of his eyes as their gazes locked for a long moment. Oh, how she wished she could believe he was good. But he wasn't. He was here to make more money off the abused, the broken, the greedy, and the dead of heart. It was unforgivable really. She would do well to remember that.

Chapter Five

"Mind if I knit while you garden?" Celeste's voice broke the stillness. Thalia looked up from her tomato plant that she'd watered and was now tending by picking off dead leaves. Jack had left a mere minute ago. It was as if they were taking shifts to befriend her, or dupe her into trusting them. Thalia wasn't sure which, and she really hoped the large black man with Jack didn't take the next shift. His face was kindly enough, but he was intimidating in frame.

"Go ahead." Thalia nodded as Celeste seated herself anyway, as if she hadn't intended to wait for permission.

Celeste's needles clacked as she knitted a dark green sock. "Is that a tomato plant?"

Thalia broke off a yellow, shriveled leaf. "Yes." Small talk was going to be the death of her.

Celeste sighed and dropped her needles and sock in her lap. "I have to be honest. . . and it's only right you should know."

Thalia froze, her finger poised over another dead leaf. *Please. Just leave me alone.* She wanted to beg aloud, but she couldn't even find her voice. Celeste carried on, unaware.

"Jack Taylor, he be a good man."

Thalia drew her hand away from the tomato plant leaf. Celeste fingered her knitting needle, the concern in her eyes fitting the fervency in her voice. "He's a godly man," Celeste continued. She looked down at the sock she was knitting and then held it up for Thalia. "This is for my husband, Elias. We married a few months ago. Jack put us together."

Thalia resumed picking off the dying leaves, but her ears were perked now. Jack Taylor. The miner, the merchant, the matchmaker. The man was an enigma.

"I run from my master." Celeste's admission resonated with Thalia. "He wasn't a good man. Most white men weren't. They thought I'm some belonging they can pass around to work for them, *slave* for them." Her brown eyes burrowed deep into Thalia's. "We aren't so different, you and me."

Thalia looked away. So Jack had told Celeste what she was. Part of her was relieved she didn't have to. They were similar, her and Celeste, but yet Thalia had received payment for the wounds she bore, where Celeste's had just been inflicted without asking.

Celeste undid a row and then began to knit again, her needles clacking. "Twas a miracle I made it to California without dying. I pretty much was near half dead when I wound up on the doorstep of Jack's store. But he took me in, no matter people think bad of him. He knew Elias, and we was of the same color, so he figured Elias could help me

411

find someplace to live. I don't know as Jack figured we'd wind up getting married, but sometimes, you do what's needed to survive."

Yes. Yes, one did. The dull ache Thalia fought against in her heart every day increased to a persistent throb, awakened by the camaraderie she found in the other woman. Thalia pushed back her straight hair that hid her cheek wound. If Celeste was going to share her story, then she could share a small part of hers.

"A man gave me this. About a month ago."

"Did it get infected?" Celeste paused knitting, her eyes caressing the jagged stripe on Thalia's face.

"No." Thalia shook her head. At least she didn't think so. Just an angry scab, thick and ugly. "But it will always be there, and because of it my madame tossed me out. She wanted beautiful girls, and I'm no good anymore."

Celeste was quiet, and Thalia appreciated that. She didn't want empathy or pity. Understanding meant more, and Celeste communicated it by her silence.

"It bought me my freedom—from her anyway." Thalia heard her voice quiver. The mere memories were enough.

"Yet you're still running, aren't you?" Celeste's question made Thalia's eyes burn with tears.

"I have to." The admission tore from her throat. "Madame Agatha may not want me, but others still would. I don't want to be that person anymore—I can't."

"I know," Celeste whispered.

Thalia swiped at a tear rolling down her cheek and clung to the hand Celeste extended. "I thought I'd found a place to try to make some sort of home here. To live off the land, somehow, and hope I didn't die."

"And then we come."

Thalia's shuddering breath was her acknowledgment to Celeste. "You came. Jack came. A man with big dreams, like all the other men. Running over whoever gets in their way, just to see the shimmer of that blasted gold."

"Jack isn't like that, Thalia."

"Maybe not." Thalia released Celeste's hand. Images of Jack, his smile, his dimple, his handsome frame, and the offer of a yellow dress, built a case against her doubts. "But I can't afford to take a chance. What's here for me if he rebuilds this town?"

Celeste's eyes darkened and Thalia nodded.

"You know. You understand. I need to go somewhere I can be alone. No man is going to leave me be in a town where it gets around I have services they may want. I'm used up, Celeste, and my only hope is me."

The woman with as many scars as Thalia drew her brows together in an earnest plea. "I know that's what you feel, and I know that's how life has made you. But there be hope. I'm happy now, Thalia. I have me a good man in Elias, and I believe my master isn't coming for me here. The good Lord gave me my freedom, He'll give you yours."

Thalia raised an eyebrow. The *good Lord* hadn't seen fit to give her freedom since the day she was born to a daddy who beat her like she was nothing but a dispensable rag doll. What would change God's mind now?

Celeste lifted her knitting needles and began to work on the sock. "I didn't have no faith before the Lord brought me to Jack. But He's using that man, He is. You're going to be amazed at what Gold Haven becomes and how you fit in."

Amazed? The deep, aching sorrow didn't leave Thalia's chest. Amazement wasn't something she longed for. She didn't want miracles and signs and wonders. She just wanted to be left alone, and all of it was being threatened because of one man. Jack Taylor.

Chapter Six

The next several evenings, Thalia stationed herself by the open window, pleased that Ounce scampered up to sit by her on the sill. Together, they observed the happenings down by the tents Jack and Elias had put up. Another tent sprang up with the arrival of a wagon driven by a Chinese man bearing an odd assortment of supplies. The nightly clanging of metal proved to be a small forge, and Elias hammered faithfully, repairing a broken-down moldboard plow and a harrow that was delivered by two more men. It was horrible. Ominous. Even three more additions to Gold Haven were like the final signature on a deed.

Soon it became apparent they were planning on even more company. During the day, Thalia tended her pitiful garden plots, and Jack and Elias set to work shoring up the shanties on the verge of falling down. It was generous that they were fixing them in advance of the arrival of more people, instead of leaving them to be fixed by their new owners, but she tried to ignore that. Tried to ignore Jack. He left her alone, for the most part, but as he passed her, she sensed his searching contemplation on her back, or saw him lift his hand in a small wave.

It was all she could do to ignore them as she attempted to plot out the next course in her ever-evolving life. Gardening was her one reprieve, her time alone without outside influences muddling her mind.

Now she knelt in the dirt by her plants that were as destitute as she. Thalia thumbed a leaf from one of the potato plants when pounding on the front of her shanty snatched her attention. She dropped her hand and pushed off the ground. Curious and a bit concerned, she rounded the small building to spot Jack yanking her door off its hinges.

"What are you doing?" Panic laced her voice. She would lose her privacy! He had no right! She hurried to the doorway, not sure if she would snatch the crowbar from his hand or choose to do nothing.

Undeterred, Jack leaned the door against the side of the shanty and brushed his hands together. "I asked Elias to make new hinges."

Well then. Thalia wasn't certain how to respond as her panic eased and misgiving settled in.

Jack waggled a hinge in the air for her to see. "We need to sturdy up this place if you're going to live here all winter."

"I can't pay you." She'd told him that before about other kindnesses, but never had kindness been given to her without a mark of debt. Thalia avoided looking straight into his eyes. They pierced into her soul, like a preacher she'd once met when she was twelve. Only he'd told her quite directly she was headed for hell. At least that was one wrong Jack had yet to commit, even if it was the truth.

Jack chuckled at the irony of her statement. "Goodness knows, I'm not looking to make more money." He tossed the new hinge into the air and caught it in his palm. It was heavy, basic, and stronger than the shanty door itself. "Someone's got to look after you."

The six words traveled to her heart and set her skin to little bumps. No one in her entire lifetime had ever said such a thing to her. Least of all a man.

He didn't seem to notice how his words affected her. Jack braced the crowbar against the jamb and levered the old rusted hinges from the door frame. It didn't take much strength. "I'll be fixing the door, too." He pulled out the bottom hinge. "This place is about ready to fall over."

Thalia swallowed. Was he real? She had the vague memory of an old aunt telling her a story about a man who rescued a damsel in distress. The hero image had implanted in Thalia's mind, but the years tarnished it into a distant, laughable tale.

"Thank you." She spoke under her breath, and the moment she offered her gratitude, she wished she hadn't. She was vulnerable to kindness because she craved it.

Jack grinned.

She could get accustomed to watching him smile. It was so warm, so gentle...

"Oh, and Celeste found that yellow dress I promised you." He bent and picked up a yellow calico bundle balled up and resting on top of his wooden toolbox. Shaking it out and holding it by the shoulders, he looked quite silly with the pretty gown held in front of his broad chest. It was simple, and nothing at all like the silks she'd worn in the brothel. No. It was prettier. It was ladylike. It wasn't stolen like the faded gray one she wore every day.

Jack pushed the dress toward her. "It's yours."

"I—can't." Thalia played with her hair, tugging it over the right side of her face and over her scar.

His eyes shadowed. "It's not going to do me any good, Thalia."

They stared at each other for a long, silent moment. Finally, Thalia reached out and took the dress. As she did so, Jack held on to one of the shoulders. His eyes narrowed with feeling.

"We're going to take care of you, Thalia."

She couldn't answer. She didn't even know what he meant.

"You're not alone anymore." His husky voice burrowed into her soul. Jack released the dress, but Thalia feared he retained a tiny piece of her trust, and maybe her heart.

Chapter Seven

She never left his mind, and it was going to drive him mad. Jack pounded the last nail into the new board on her shanty's door and edged around the corner to watch her frame as she knelt over a hole she'd dug in the clay earth. Thalia dropped in a few seeds she'd pilfered off some plant she'd discovered and pushed dirt over them. Should he tell her they probably wouldn't grow to produce anything? When Thalia wasn't aware of his presence, Jack had traversed some of the paltry remains of the vegetable gardens. Her time spent tending plants that were either near dead or dying was both noble and pitiful. Thalia was fighting to survive, and alone, she would never make it.

Jack turned away from her and returned to the front of the shanty. He lifted the door to hang it on the hinges he'd installed. The sun beat onto his shoulders, and he focused on his work. She would fit right in with Gold Haven. She just didn't know it, or trust it.

"Need help?" Elias's rich baritone broke into Jack's thoughts. He stepped away from the door.

"Just a few things left here and I'll be done."

Elias ran his hand over his head, wiping away sweat as he surveyed Thalia's shelter. "Looks like the whole thing be needin' remade."

"I know." Jack nodded. He had every intention of doing so, too.

"Can't save everyone, you know." Elias's words brought Jack to a halt. He faced the man he called partner and comrade.

"I don't know what you're trying to say." Jack set his shoulders. He rarely came to issue with Elias, but the man was bluntly honest. Something Jack appreciated, but also something that he could sometimes do without.

"Her." Elias tipped his head at the back of the shanty and Thalia's garden. "She ain't wantin' to be saved."

"She does." Jack ignored his friend and slammed the hammer against a loose nail on a piece of siding.

"Celeste says she wants to be left alone."

"Didn't we all at one point?" Jack's irritation was growing. Elias, of all people, should understand what it meant to have someone give him a roof over his head and help him start a new life.

"I'm just sayin'." Elias grabbed the hammer from Jack's hand. "You ain't the Lord. You ain't never gonna be. An' she'll move on an' pro'ly die or start up in her old ways. It's what we do, we slaves."

"She isn't a slave." Jack slammed his hand against the shanty wall.

"Naw, she ain't like me or Celeste, but she slavin' to what she knows. But I knows that breakin' free is somethin' the Lord's gotta do. Not you."

"I know that." Jack ground his teeth. What was Elias getting at? Was he insinuating Thalia was a worthless cause? It took a lot of brawn to say something like that when they'd all been washed-up failures, misfits, or broken down at some point.

"Just makin' sure you knows it."

"What are you getting at, Elias?"

The bigger man blinked thoughtfully. "I gettin' at you best watch yourself. Gold Haven is what you're doin' to make things right after gettin' rich while everyone else gots ruined. But some of these people that's goin' to come here? They ain't all goin' to be saved, an' it ain't your fault when it happens."

So that was it. Jack released a breath and with it some of his temper against Elias. The man was watching out for him, making sure he realized that while Gold Haven was going to be turned into a place of hope for all the people who needed a new beginning, it wasn't Jack's role to save them all.

Maybe he wasn't capable of being a healer, but he sure could use his wealth for something other than himself. Jack clapped his hand against Elias's shoulder. "Thank you, friend. I hear you. But I'm also not going to stop trying to help. So let's get this place sturdier and then get to work clearing our first field for winter barley."

Elias's teeth shone white in his smile. He chuckled deep in his throat and shook his head. "You say you hear me, but where *she's* concerned?" A twinkle settled in Elias's eyes. "I think your wishin' to save that one might be a tad stronger than anyone you've ever met before."

Jack ignored the man's observation as he took the hammer Elias handed to him. It wasn't worth responding to.

Chapter Eight

Thalia rounded the corner of her shanty when the men's voices stopped her. Yin, the Chinese man who had come to town, was in deep conversation with Jack and Elias. A fourth voice added to the mix, and she thought she recognized it as George, one of the older men.

"…get ground plowed and we can get the barley planted. A good winter's crop will set us up good come spring."

Thalia leaned against her shanty. Someone, probably Jack, pounded a nail, then stopped.

"The plow's ready to go," Jack said.

"An' I gots the harrow ready, too." Elias's baritone was followed by Yin's broken English.

"I open shop soon as supplies come."

Thalia's chest constricted. It was as she feared. Preparing the soil to grow barley? Opening a shop for newcomers? Jack was planning to make more wealth in the partnership of these men and with a whole new type of gold. Farming.

"I know of three more joining us at the end of the week. I'll get more tents set up," George said.

"Good." Jack's authoritative voice was definitely the lead here. "I want to take one of the wagons and head to the city. It'll be a bit of a trek, but there'll be folks there needing a fresh start."

Of course there would. Washed-up miners, failures, men looking for anything to make money on. Times were desperate now that gold was scarce. Thalia could see Gold Haven in a few short weeks, turning into another shantytown. Soon after there would come a brothel, a makeshift saloon…she'd seen it all before. Claustrophobia clawed at her throat, panic threatening to stir whatever nightmares the claustrophobia didn't.

Thalia whirled and her elbow cracked against the side of the shanty. She cried out, but it didn't stop her. She needed to run. Anywhere. The memories overtook her like demons clawing at her soul. She would never escape, she would never get out, and she would never make it on her own.

Her feet stumbled over the uneven earth as she raced for the river's edge. A momentary respite, but maybe she could gather her wits and come up with some sort of plan. She pushed through some brush and swiped at a leafy branch that grabbed at her waist. Past the manzanita bushes, dodging brush grass.

"Thalia!" Jack's shout jerked against her hearing. She ignored him. He'd earned no rights to her, no reason for her to stop at his command.

A stone in her path caught Thalia's toe as she shot a glance at him over her shoulder. The ground rushed toward her, and she landed with a cry in a patch of leafy bushes.

"Thalia, stop!" Jack's yell bounced off her ears and dissipated in the strength of her sudden loathing. He was a horrid, greedy man. Everything Celeste had said was untrue. There was nothing amazing happening in Gold Haven, only the recurrence of a nightmare.

She crawled across the ground, through the small bushes, struggling to regain her footing. Jack's leather-gloved hand brought her up short as he grabbed her arm and yanked her upward.

"What are you doing?" Jack's urgent words gave Thalia the energy to turn on him. Her hand cracked against his face.

Stunned, he blinked several times, but his grip never released. She pulled against his grasp, her free hand prying at his fingers to free her forearm.

Jack hauled her out from the bushes and pushed her away from him once they were cleared. He ran his palm over his reddened cheek, staring at her in disbelief, and then behind her at the bushes.

"Have you completely lost your senses, woman? You just crawled through the thickest patch of poison oak."

As Thalia's fury waned, Jack's words set in. She glanced at the leaves. At the ground. Back at her shanty, and then into Jack's eyes. They were filled with irritation mixed with concern. He shook his head.

"What got into you? You're going to be miserable if you break out from poison oak."

Thalia blinked and crossed her arms over her chest, lifting her chin. He was probably right. She probably would be. But she'd been through so much worse, what was a little poison oak when her entire future was threatened once again?

◆　◆　◆

It was worse than she'd imagined. Much worse. Thalia lay her head on the floor, using her old gray dress as a pillow. Her eyes were slits, swollen and irritated from poison oak. Her arms and hands were inflamed, blistering, and she had the irrational thought that cutting them off would be preferable to the deep, burning itch.

Ounce's paws tickled her leg as he scurried up onto her chest to perch on his hind quarters and peer into her face. The mouse tipped its head to the side, nose twitching, as if to say she looked horrible. The discomfort had begun during the night, and it was apparent her body was more hostile to poison oak than others who'd scuffled with the plant. Thalia had no desire to spiral into the depths of self-pity, but with the ruination of her hope for privacy in a deserted gold mining town, poison oak was close to pushing her into that abyss.

A firm knock on the door snagged her attention. Most likely Celeste with some sort of breakfast food she passed off as leftovers, but Thalia knew she'd made just for her. She crawled to her feet, her eyes squinting against the daylight as she opened the door. A surprised oath met her ears, and she could make out Jack's appalled expression. He muttered again, under his breath this time. He reached for her hand and pulled her out of her shanty into the sun. It burned against her skin.

"Blast, it's worse than I imagined."

"I'll be fine." Her words flowed thick over swollen lips, even as she reached up to scratch a blistered section on her bare forearm. She would never admit how miserable last night had been or that Jack had been right.

Thalia wished she could strip to her camisole. In the not-so-distant past, she would have. But it was a moment like this, under the surveying eye of the handsome intruder, that she craved to be seen as decent, even though, in the deepest shadows of her heart, Thalia knew she never would be.

Jack brushed past her into her dwelling. He started to curse again but this time bit his tongue, as if God's higher power stopped him. "You have no bed." His incredulous observation insinuated he was frustrated it had never dawned on him before. "Come."

He didn't give her the option. The pull on her hand irritated her skin. Thalia stumbled after him until they made it down the street to the miniature tent city. She counted, her vision blurred, and could make out two more tents.

Jack pushed aside a tent flap and led Thalia in. A makeshift mattress was thrown on the ground, and the scent of bay rum permeated the air. It was his tent. Thalia wasn't appalled by entering a man's tent unchaperoned, but it certainly wasn't going to help Jack's stellar reputation to have a prostitute in his personal quarters.

"Lay down," he commanded.

On his bed no less.

Jack motioned toward the bed, still holding her hand. The insurgence of old memories cascaded down on Thalia with force. Men. Beds. Alone.

She pulled away, her skin on fire for more reasons than the poison oak. "No. I'm fine."

"You're not fine. You need caring." Jack tugged her hand again. "Please, Thalia, trust me. I mean you no harm. I'll get Celeste. You're going to be miserable for a few days."

Thalia swallowed, and even that was difficult with the swelling.

Jack bent near. The deep pools of his blue eyes fixed on hers.. "I want to take care of you, Thalia. Please. Let me."

His hand cupped her arm. She jerked away. While her upper arms were free from outbreak, his touch chafed like poison oak. He was poison. He had to be.

She backed away and stumbled for the tent's door. "I don't need you to take care of me." And she didn't. She never had. She'd always cared for herself, even if it cost her soul and her freedom. Anyone who'd made promises to watch over her before had ruined her in some way. Her father, her uncle, the man who'd first introduced her to Madame Agatha, and every greedy, success-seeking, filthy-pig-of-a-man since. She could close her eyes and imagine them away, but she could never successfully imagine away the despair of a broken promise.

Thalia could not bear another one. Especially from Jack, whose sky-colored eyes seared her soul with the tenacity of a traveling preacher carrying a message meant to save her, but spoken in a language she could not understand.

Chapter Nine

Celeste helped Thalia slip the buttons through the holes on the bodice of her dress. Her lithe, dark fingers made quick work, and she slipped the yellow calico over Thalia's shoulders.

"I'm sorry," Thalia breathed as warm California air hugged her skin.

Celeste smiled as she laid the garment on Jack's mattress. "No mind. I've had plenty of practice helping my mistress."

The reality of her words ate at Thalia's conscience. Celeste had been enslaved and served her own time in the confines of life's prison. "Were you a maid then?"

Shadows passed over Celeste's face and her high cheekbones blushed. "I be many things."

"How did you escape?" Thalia knew she probably shouldn't ask, but she couldn't help herself. Their eyes met in mutual understanding of being shackled in different ways, but bearing the scars nonetheless.

Celeste moved behind Thalia and lifted her heavy tresses off her shoulders to tie them in a tail. "It's a long story, and I don't know if I'll ever feel free. Some days"—her fingers brushed Thalia's neck as she tied the leather strap around the low ponytail—"some days, I'm sure my master will have chased me all the way from N'awlins and he'll take me back." Celeste moved around Thalia to her front. "But I'm gonna believe different. My life be the Lord's. He be my way of escape."

Maybe slavery was worse than prostitution. Or maybe it was the same? They'd both been owned, bought, paid for. . .

"Now, into the tub with you."

The water in the round, metal tub sloshed. "I don't see how a bath will help." Thalia dipped her toe into the water.

"Yin said it'll ease the inflammation," Celeste explained. The Chinaman. Thalia could see through her swollen eyelids that the water was black.

"What is it?"

"Yin boiled the manzanita branch. Washing in it's s'posed to make that itching go away and make you less swollen."

Thalia eased her body into the water with a shiver. "I can't submerge my face."

"Slosh that water on it. Hopefully it will help. Yin said some natives teach him this, and he knows herbal medicines well. It's a good thing Yin be in Gold Haven. Our future looks good here."

Thalia closed her eyes and bit her bottom lip. The water was cold from the river and hadn't been warmed, yet it instantly soothed the fiery burn of her poison oak.

"Gold Haven is a dead town." She spoke the words through teeth clenched from the chill in the water and the dread in her heart. Celeste soaked a rag and laid it over Thalia's inflamed face.

"Not for long. Jack be dreamin' for all of us here in Gold Haven. Elias, Yin, me, and some of the older miners were surely hard up. We need to be safe, and Gold Haven will be just that. I'm glad we found you here, waiting."

When Celeste spoke, her words threatened to soothe Thalia, but soothing wasn't something Thalia had ever learned to trust. It was the deceptive lull that came before another wound was inflicted by circumstance or person.

◆ ◆ ◆

Jack poked at the fire with a stick as he took a long draw of coffee from the tin cup Yin handed him. The Chinaman smiled and bowed, his conical skull cap covering his head. He spoke broken English, but Jack was learning fast that Yin would be a valuable asset to Gold Haven. Not just in providing laundry services, but in assisting in the supply store Jack intended to set up when the time was right. The man was a genius with numbers and reasoning. He would be a good business partner.

Jack wrapped his hands around the hot tin cup, his calluses providing the needed barrier from getting burned. Chinamen were the lowest of California society. Blacks, natives, and Chinamen had almost no place but in servitude or slavery. It was appalling, this man-made caste system that crept unspoken into the culture. Jack hoped he could change that in Gold Haven. A community, pooled resources, faith. It might be an unrealistic dream, but it could happen. Now that George, the old washed-up miner, was here, Jack could see it all coming together. Much hinged on the old man who'd given up his farming background to get rich. Filthy rich. Instead, he'd turned to liquor when he'd spent more surviving in this expensive California gold mining region.

Celeste flipped open Jack's tent flap and approached him, her simple dress brushing the ground with a soft rustle. She glanced up at the stars before bringing her focus back on Jack. A soft smile curved her lips, and Jack understood why, as every day passed, Elias grew more devoted to this woman he had married.

"She's sleeping. I do say Yin's manzanita water soothed the poison oak." She included Yin by casting an appreciative nod in his direction. His hand stilled over the Chinese characters he etched in his journal. He nodded.

"I'll keep an eye on her through the night." Jack sipped his coffee.

A frown touched Celeste's eyes. The brown of them stared at him with a tiny flicker of censure. "It ain't proper."

Jack tipped his head to the side and raised an eyebrow at Celeste. He understood convention and all, but with Celeste as the only woman, and the rest being men, he couldn't imagine there would be much recompense to their reputation. "Who am I trying to impress?"

"Well"—Celeste shrugged—"I'm just saying, even if we live here in wasteland it don't mean we throw away what's right. And you wouldn't want Thalia to think. . .well, she's been—"

Jack raised his hand to cease Celeste's stumbling. "I understand. I'll treat her respectful-like. It's my hope she gets a good rest and the rash clears up significantly overnight."

"My hopes as well." Celeste cast a glance in the direction of her and Elias's tent. "I'll be off then. If you need anything, please call for us."

"We'll be fine. I have Yin here, too. He'll be up most of the night anyway, writing in that journal of his."

Celeste moved toward the tent, hesitated, and then faced Jack for one last moment. "I know you'll take good care of her, Jack. Same as you did for me."

His swig of coffee choked his airway at her words. Jack watched her retreating form, her dress more than likely hiding the physical scars of slavery much like her heart bore the emotional scars. Elias, by the grace of God, was helping her to heal. It wasn't anything Jack had done. Not really. His eyes skimmed over Yin as the man sat engrossed in his journaling, then glanced toward his tent. The woman who lay inside was hollow. He saw the same fear and exhaustion reflected in Thalia as he'd first seen in Celeste. Strip away the poison oak inflammation, the timid persona, and the determination to claim Gold Haven as her own, and all that was left was a wounded soul needing saving and love. Saving could be done, but love? That was something entirely different. Whether familial, friendship, or romantic, it had to be born from God's love. Not a love that demanded something in return.

Jack swiveled his gaze onto Elias and Celeste's tent. The soft murmuring of their voices met his ear as they conversed over their day. Maybe love *was* possible here. Jack set his coffee cup on the ground and drew a deep breath. He had another woman to help save, something he hadn't bargained on when he'd begun implementing his vision of Gold Haven. This time, there was no Elias to pair her to. He slowly rose to his feet, the weight of his consideration settling heavy on his soul. There was only him.

Chapter Ten

Thalia stirred, the brush of a hand on her forehead pressing a cool cloth against her swollen skin. She opened her eyes and blinked several times, realizing the swelling had decreased and her eyesight had improved. The tent was dimly lit, crickets chirruping outside. She caught a whiff of coffee just as her vision focused and locked with Jack's.

"The cloth is soaked in manzanita water. It seems to be helping," Jack explained softly and rapidly as if to assure her she was safe and his intentions were pure.

"Where's Celeste?" Thalia's puffy lips muffled her words.

"She went to bed."

Silence. The dripping of water into the bowl as Jack re-wet the cloth and squeezed out the excess. He held the cloth against her cheek, its cool moisture soothing the burn.

"You needn't bother yourself with me." Thalia really didn't want his ministrations. It was difficult to trust that Jack, as a man, could be anyone more than someone out for his own best welfare.

"I'll bother," he said, shifting the cloth to the other side of her face.

More silence. She heard someone outside cough and a fire crackling.

"Why?" she whispered.

His hand paused, holding the cloth over her neck. Their eyes locked, and then he looked away, lowering the cloth onto her neck. "Why what?"

He was feigning ignorance, Thalia could tell. She might be timid, but she was also honest. "Why would you help me? You know what I am."

"Do I?" Jack countered.

"I told you."

"So you did." He removed the cloth and dunked it into the basin.

"Well?" She couldn't let it rest. He was skirting the questions and the root of her inquiry.

Jack wrung out the cloth. His fingers slid under her hand, his touch burning almost as much as the poison oak. Lifting her hand, he pressed the wet cloth against her skin and the backs of her fingers.

"I don't believe I know Thalia Simmons." His words sliced through the peaceful stillness of the tent. "I don't know who she *really* is. Her dreams, her hopes, even her prayers."

She swallowed and turned her head away, the pillow soft beneath her head. A tear rolled down her cheek. Why did he have to look into her soul, as if faith could drag her from the pit into which she'd sunk?

"I don't have dreams." And she didn't.

"Of course you do. You're here, aren't you? In Gold Haven? If a claim could be town-sized, you would have demanded it, and I'd be a claim jumper." Jack's fingers shifted beneath her hand, innocent enough, but wakening her senses more than the touch of any man before him.

If he could see that, then why did he stay? If he cared, why did he keep bringing in more strangers?

"I know you don't trust me." Jack's dark hair fell over his forehead in a wave as he bent over her hand, examining the rash in the dim light. His voice was a gentle murmur. "That's understandable."

He drew the cloth away from her hand and resoaked it in the manzanita water, wringing it out and draping it over the edge of the basin. Drawing a deep breath, Jack rested his hands on his knees. "So?"

Thalia searched his face. His kind eyes, his rugged jawline, and the confident set to his mouth.

"What is Thalia Simmons's biggest dream?"

Had anyone ever asked her what she wanted? Her throat closed as Jack's gaze burned into hers. He waited for an answer. No. He *expected* an answer. Her chest constricted with emotion, as if someone had piled bricks of gold on her chest and asked her to breathe deeply.

"To be free." Thalia's whisper cracked the thick silence.

As if Jack wasn't prepared for her to speak, his eyes narrowed and he leaned his head to the right. "Pardon?"

Her voice strengthened with the purpose behind her dream. "I want to be free." When she finally admitted it aloud, conviction followed on the heels of her honesty. Thalia fought the subtle pull to drown in Jack's tender, concerned expression. It was obvious to her now. Freedom was no longer in Gold Haven, and it wasn't Jack who needed to leave Gold Haven. It was her.

Chapter Eleven

Jack had been gone for several days now. Thalia ran her hand over her bare forearm as she studied Yin boiling water for tea over the open fire. Her poison oak had disappeared thanks to this man's watery medicine, but she had yet to disappear from Gold Haven.

Thalia turned her back on the Chinaman and hiked toward her empty shanty, miserable garden, and healthy patch of poison oak beyond it. All three confirmed Thalia's conviction to leave Gold Haven. Yet here she was, days later. Was it because Jack had left to travel to a thriving gold town miles away? Was it his absence that made her content to stay on a while, as if with Jack's departure, peace rose in his absence?

But the ache in her just seemed greater, and Thalia was loath to admit, even to herself, that she watched for him.

Dust rose in the distance. A wagon. No. Two or three? Jack. And others.

Thalia hurried into her shanty and slammed the door Jack had built. The walls were stronger, too, and the roof sealed against the absent, late-summer rain. While she'd rested in his tent, Jack had taken the time to shore up her dwelling before he left. It was further confirmation Celeste was right about him, and Thalia was desperately, horribly wrong.

Ounce skittered along the far wall, paused, and sat on his haunches. His little paws poised in front of him, and his nose scrunched.

"I'm not staying." Thalia's confirmation to the mouse did not make her feel any better. Ounce's whiskers twitched.

"I'm not," she reconfirmed and turned her back on the rodent to peek out her window.

Jack's wagon rolled past. She ducked behind the wall as his head turned and his gaze swept her shelter. He didn't need to be given the impression she was waiting for him.

Thalia waited a few minutes. The inside of the shanty was stuffy, and Ounce had scampered away, leaving her alone with her thoughts. Well, there wasn't any reason to keep hiding here. She reached up to button the top three buttons of the yellow calico Jack had given her.

She tugged open the door and steered herself toward the tents. Celeste would be there. Elias, helping Jack unload his supplies. There would be newcomers, and maybe Thalia could gather information to help her plan a quiet, subtle exit from Gold Haven.

Gravel crunched beneath her shoes as she approached the wagons. Men bustled around them, some unloading personal supplies, others drawing out tools for barley farming. Scythes, rakes, flails. Jack was very serious about farming and his newest venture. Thalia watched him as he hoisted a pack from the wagon bed and dropped it on the ground next to Yin.

The Chinaman smiled, his almond-shaped eyes twinkling. He flipped open the canvas flap on the top of the bag, then wiped his hands on his draping coat as if his palms were sweaty with anticipation. Bending over, Yin reached into the pack and pulled out bluing to preserve the whiteness of laundered clothes, a large coil of line rope for hanging laundry, and other laundry supplies. So Yin was to be a laundryman, too, in addition to running a store?

Celeste exited her tent, her regal back straight. Thalia paused a moment and took in the radiance of her creamy-brown skin. She was beautiful. She had found peace.

Celeste noticed Thalia and waved her over. At her movement, Jack looked up. His eyes softened at the corners, and Thalia focused on Celeste as she approached. There was no way she could understand how to read or interpret the sensitivity that always seemed to cross Jack's face when she was present.

"Isn't this exciting?" Celeste practically beamed joy. Her black curls spiraled around her face, the rest tugged up under a flowered turban. Thalia managed a smile. Exciting wasn't the word she would have chosen. What was happening only confirmed she needed to leave Gold Haven.

A wiry man, new to the town, edged past her with a pack tent rolled under his arm. He gave her a sideways glance.

Yes. Leave. Sooner rather than later.

"Here." Jack's gravelly voice interrupted the lift of her nose and the glare she leveled on the stranger who'd now paused to look at her over his shoulder. Did she have *prostitute* tattooed on her face somewhere? Why couldn't she escape the looks?

"Thalia?"

She jerked her attention to Jack who waited for her to respond. In his hand was a newspaper, rolled and tied with a string.

She eyed it as if he coddled a rattlesnake.

"Take it." Jack gave it a little shake in her direction.

"Why would I want a newspaper?" She honestly had no idea why Jack would bring her one, but disappointment flickered in his eyes, so she reached for it.

"I be wishing I could read!" Celeste smiled and tapped the paper with a finger. "Full of news and life and ideas!"

Ideas. Yes. It was what Thalia had hoped to find coming over to this crowd in the first place. She raised her eyes and met Jack's. "Thank you."

He gave her a short nod, but a smile tipped his lips, surrounded by days' worth of beard. "Just thought of you for some reason," he said.

His gesture warmed her insides, and Thalia unrolled the paper. Better to turn her attention away from the usurper who had moved in and transformed her sanctuary from a solitary escape to a town newly breathing life.

Celeste and Jack moved to a crate filled with canned goods. Thalia took the opportunity to rest on a wooden stump someone had set near the fire circle. As the men moved around her, shouts and exuberant chatter emphasizing the excitement of new potential and hopes beyond just gold, Thalia opened the paper to the middle. A headline in bold in the bottom left corner snagged her attention:

427

WIFE NEEDED
Thirty-year-old man, respectable bachelor, sober, God-fearing, and intelligent seeks a woman in pursuit of creating a new life in gold country. None seeking to be rich need apply, as the advertiser entertains an unconquerable aversion to wealth-seeking females. Prefer a woman who wishes to start anew.
Address: William Forgraves, Union Grove Post Office, California

Thalia's heart beat so hard she thought if Celeste looked her way, she might see it thudding through her dress. Man in need of a wife who wanted to start anew? She jerked her head up and swept her gaze over her surroundings. Celeste and Elias carried crates of canned goods into an abandoned shanty. Yin was busy preparing dinner for the newcomers over an open range across the way. Jack was unhitching the horses from his wagon, and the newest members to Gold Haven were busy pitching heavy canvas tents. She could be free—of all of this. Of the expectations any new town placed on her.

But would she be entering a different sort of bondage? What if this William Forgraves wasn't as God-fearing as he implied? What if he was like her father, the type who wielded a fist when one didn't respond as he wished? Thalia smoothed her hands over the paper, the ink leaving a black dust over her palm. But even if he were, she could run away, the same as she was planning to flee from Gold Haven anyway. Only with this marriage, perhaps she would have the means to survive and a platonic relationship could be formed. She was fine with being a hardworking wife, caring for any children who may be born of her wifely duties, but if Mr. Forgraves would give her the freedom she desired to live a peaceful life? It would be worth it.

She lifted her eyes and they locked with Jack's as he raised his head and looked her way. It would be worth it, she convinced herself as she lost her way in his eyes.

◆　◆　◆

"What's this?" Jack eyed the envelope Thalia handed him, much like she'd been wary of the newspaper when he'd given it to her last week. His fingertips grazed hers as he took it. They both hesitated; then he withdrew, taking the envelope with him.

Thalia watched him study the address on the envelope. She already knew it by heart, the name a familiar echo in her mind. *William Forgraves.* It had taken a week to summon up the courage to write it, a deep breath to ask for stationery from Celeste, and nerves refusing to cower beneath the look of question Celeste had given her.

But Jack was heading out again, intent to recruit more townsfolk. So far he had brought with him three more Chinese men with an assortment of skill sets, a Negro farmer, and about four washed-up men whose efforts to pan for gold turned as mucky and worthless as the river-bottom silt. Celeste and Thalia remained the only women. So far. It would only be a matter of time before a madame arrived, her girls in tow, then a saloon, or three, and the town would come alive with debauchery. But she wouldn't be here.

Jack stuffed the letter into his chest shirt pocket.

"You'll see it's delivered?" Thalia had to be certain he wasn't going to forget. It was her best chance of escape and survival.

A shadow crossed his eyes, but he patted his chest pocket. "Of course."

She could tell he was curious, so she looked toward the horses he'd hitched to the wagon. "You're lucky to have them," she murmured aimlessly. He was, too. Many men couldn't boast a mule or an ox, let alone a matched pair. Just another bit of evidence of the wealth Jack had accrued hiking prices as a merchant and pilfering any newfound gold straight out of the hands of equally greedy gold panners.

"God has blessed." Jack tightened a cinch on the one bay mare. Her haunch twitched as a fly landed on it, and he swiped it away with a leather-gloved hand. "I bought this pair a year ago. They've served me well."

He stroked the mare's neck. The horse twisted her head, nudged his arm, and Jack ran his hand up the white blaze on her nose. He was kind, even to a workhorse. The veins on Jack's forearms bulged where his muscle defined his strength. He worked hard. There was nothing lazy about him—not like a wealthy man who preferred to be served.

Maybe this farming venture would be very successful, and he would build a big house. He would need help—servants—to keep up the persona of the town founder.

"Will you be hiring anyone?" It was an honest question. The worst scenario. If the proposition from William Forgraves fell through, perhaps she might find employment from Jack. Decent employment.

His head jerked up and he searched her face. His brows drew together and he cocked his head to the right as if he couldn't quite comprehend the intention behind her question.

Oh good heavens!

"A maid? A cook?" Thalia sputtered out her explanation.

"No!" Jack blustered. He swiped his hat from his hand and ran his gloved fingers over his hair in a nervous gesture, then smashed his hat onto the dark, thick mass. "Why would I hire help?"

Thalia drew back and wrapped her arms around her chest. The wagon against her shoulder reminded her she could steady herself against it as her anxiety rose and timidity returned. She didn't reply. Jack rubbed his hand down his face and across his mouth. He glanced over his shoulder. Elias approached, his bag slung over his shoulder, ready to accompany Jack.

Leaning toward her, Jack's voice dropped lower. "Why would you think I would hire servants?" His tone was incredulous she would have such an impression of him.

"I just thought. . .with Gold Haven. . .it's your future. The inheritance you'll pass on to your children. You'll want to make good on your station, your wealth." Thalia kept rambling her explanation, but the more she stumbled, the darker his eyes became.

Jack reached out and gripped her upper arms, his hold as firm as his words. His hat tipped back on his head, and his breath warmed her face. "Thalia, I am not, nor will I ever be some glorified town ruler. Gold Haven is for everyone."

Maybe doubt flickered in her eyes, she wasn't certain, but it most definitely boiled in her heart. Thalia felt the tiny little shake of fervency he gave her shoulders before he released her and stepped away as Elias reached them. Thalia glanced at the big man whom Celeste was learning to love and then back at Jack.

So he didn't want to live wealthy and pompous? That was well and good, but it didn't change the fact he had money, and lots of it. Jack would never, *never* understand what it meant to be alone and scraping to live.

"Have a safe trip." Thalia's words pushed past the lump in her throat.

Jack's hand rose in an absent gesture to his shirt pocket and the letter stored inside. It was as if he knew what it held when he captured Thalia's gaze. "I'll return, Thalia. I told you I would take care of you."

It didn't matter. She had told him not to bother himself, and still he did. Thalia hoped her letter found William Forgraves willing to take her as a wife. The sooner she left here the better, before Jack claimed some strange sense of ownership over her.

Elias cleared his throat, and Jack broke the tension between them to pull himself up onto the wagon seat. He took the reins from Elias and slapped the horses' backs. The wagon rolled forward, and with it, Thalia's letter. The letter might very well form the next part of her life, and would most certainly take her away from the paradox that was Jack Taylor.

Chapter Twelve

He did return, just as he'd promised. After he'd taken care of the letter Thalia had given him, Jack and Elias had driven their wagon through the ramshackle buildings of the city and parked it in front of a tent with a wooden cross dangling in the doorway. They retrieved Reverend Green there, and the middle-aged, pastoral influence was a welcome reprieve to Jack's chaotic insides. The letter, the haunted look in Thalia's eyes, and his promise to always care for her burned him like a hot iron from the blacksmith's forge. How could he best fulfill that promise when she wanted little to do with him and yet everything in her eyes begged him never to leave?

After a few days, they packed the last of the supplies in the wagon, and Elias, Reverend Green, and Jack returned to Gold Haven. Another letter burned in Jack's chest pocket. It was a reply to Miss Thalia Simmons.

George, with his crotchety limp, met the wagon as they rolled into Gold Haven. The old gold panner swiped his floppy hat from his head and wiped sweat from his brow. Late August was unfriendly, with both heat and lack of rain. He gripped the wagon side and peered into the bed, completely ignoring the preacher-man who perched on the bags George eyed.

"Seed?" the man rasped.

"Yep." Jack hopped from the wagon seat. He clapped his hand on George's shoulder. "We'll be ready to plant the winter crop when it's time."

George leveled a look on him, the furrows in his brow matching the ones that must have been in his mind. "Gotta get to clearin' the land. Barley needs a place to take root, ya know."

"I know." Jack tossed a lopsided grin at Elias who rounded the wagon.

Elias's smile stretched clear off his face. "I be off to see my woman for a kiss an' some coffee. Can start clearin' tomorrow an' I'm plannin' on gettin' the harrow proper set, too."

"You do that, but be quick about it," George groused with little empathy. "I'm gettin' plumb tired of waitin' to do something." He limped off next to Elias, muttering a mile a minute about the barley planting.

Reverend Green slid from the back of the wagon, but his eyes were fixed on something beyond Jack. Jack turned and followed his look to a splash of yellow calico, a heavy blanket of hair glistening copper in the sunlight, and a face that never really left Jack's mind. He transferred his scrutiny to the reverend.

Well, shucks. Maybe bringing the preacher-man here wasn't such a good idea after all. It might be good for Jack's soul, but by the look on the reverend's face, he might have more interests than just feeding a man's spirit. It took only a split second for Jack

431

to confirm it wasn't an idea he was fond of. He'd already shouldered the responsibility of caring for Thalia, and it grated on his nerves to think of handing it over to anyone. Even a preacher.

Thalia's eyes weren't planted on the reverend, however, and for a brief moment of satisfaction, Jack realized she had homed in on him. Until she neared them and asked in her hasty, breathy voice, "Did you happen to bring a letter in return?"

The letter. Yes. This had nothing to do with him and everything to do with William Forgraves. Neither he nor the reverend seemed to have any long-term future with Thalia.

Jack reached into his pocket and pulled the letter forth, ignoring the light flickering in Thalia's eyes. It wasn't anticipation and it certainly wasn't love; it was full-blown hope reflected there. He could read it etched into every tiny crease around her eyes, in the set of her lips, and in the used-up way her shoulders sagged. She would gravitate to one more man. Only this one might be her way to freedom, to a new life. He knew what Thalia wished for, and he knew what the letter held. Hope wasn't something she had seen much of in her life, and now he extended it to her in a missive.

Thalia took it from his hand. Jack held on to the other end long enough for her eyes to lift to his.

"I'll take care of you." His words were definitive. This wasn't her only option. His promise still stood, although Jack was very aware he hadn't outlined *how* he'd take care of her. It was guesswork trying to determine what he could say to her face that wouldn't send her running.

The reverend cleared his throat with a nervous cough. Jack released the letter and shifted his weight to his other foot.

"Uh—Thalia, this is our new preacher."

Thalia blanched. What a dolt he was, Jack mentally chided himself. Of course she wasn't going to be like most womenfolk and embrace the idea of a Christian influence in Gold Haven. Her experience with preachers was probably far less inspiring.

She tipped her head in a nod.

Jack had to continue since Reverend Green waited for a proper introduction. He gave the reverend Thalia's name, and Reverend Green gave her a warm, platonic greeting. But Jack could tell Thalia noticed the admiration glimmering in the preacher's eyes. She mumbled something about needing to read her letter and with a swift spin on her heel, she hurried away, head down and shoulders bent as if a monster chased her.

"She's shy?" Reverend Green eyed Jack with curious inquiry.

"No." Jack decided to state his claim then and there. "She's wounded, and she's mine."

Reverend Green's eyes rivaled the size of large nuggets. He pressed his mouth together and gave a swift nod. "Very well then. I hear you." Reaching for his bag from the bed of the wagon, he took his leave.

Jack's conscience stung him, but he'd make it up to the preacher later. He couldn't leave Thalia alone with the letter before he'd said his piece. Breaking into a jog, Jack shadowed her footsteps down the empty street.

"Thalia!"

She didn't stop. She probably felt he was always chasing after her. Jack couldn't deny he wasn't. The woman was about as spooked as a deer trying to dodge its hunter.

"Hey." Jack reached out and gripped her arm, stopping her agitated walk. She glanced at his hand. He released her. "Thalia, before you read whatever is in that letter, you need to know. . ." His words trailed. Jack drew in a deep breath, confidence oozing into him with the faith of a man who had long learned his lesson. "Faith is far stronger than reality, Thalia."

She blinked. "I don't know what you mean."

Jack had been there, too, and not very long ago. He'd been consumed with his own quest to be successful, much in the same way Thalia sought her freedom. He had succeeded, and now that his pockets were lined so thick he could spit gold in his sleep, he found his quest empty—in fact, it trapped him. But that was before he realized faith was his way to a far more meaningful life, and never once had his faith in the good Lord led him astray.

He skimmed Thalia's face, memorizing the plea in her eyes and the shaking quiver in her chin. Her freedom wouldn't be found in a letter; it would be found in faith. But often, one needed to be steered toward faith, and now. . . Jack reached out and trailed his fingers down her cheek and over her scar. Her skin was soft beneath his calluses, her body stiffening beneath his touch. Now he was certain his step of faith was the right thing—the best thing to do.

"I'll take care of you, Thalia," Jack repeated.

"I don't need you to." Even her stubborn murmur teaming up with tears in her eyes didn't defeat him. She was strong, she was an independent woman waiting to break free, but he would show her that the best way to care for her was to teach her faith. Even if it meant watching her walk away.

Chapter Thirteen

"What do you got there?"

Thalia jumped at Celeste's voice in her ear. She crumpled the letter in her hand and hid it in the folds of her skirt like a child caught reading a forbidden novel.

"It's nothing." Which wasn't true. It was everything.

The look Celeste cast her was doubtful. She brushed past Thalia and started to take down the dry, laundered shirts Yin had hung on the line earlier in the morning. As she slipped the pins from a shirt, Celeste spoke over her shoulder.

"Jack told me he brung a letter with him. Addressed to you. From a *man*." The emphasis wasn't lost on Thalia, but she could tell by Celeste's tone it wasn't judgmental or suspicious of Thalia's intentions. Nor was it teasing and hopeful of a hidden romance. It was more stern—protective. The kind of a tone an older sister would use when wary about safety.

Thalia shifted on her seat. She pulled the letter out and smoothed it across her lap.

"Well?" Celeste's back was to Thalia, and she folded a pair of Elias's trousers. Thalia could tell by the straightness of Celeste's body that she was listening with intent.

There wasn't any reason to hide the contents. Not really. Thalia traced the first sentence with a fingertip. Her life was about to change. Either for the good or potentially for the worse.

"Dear Miss Simmons. . ."

"Miss Simmons?" Celeste turned, a clothespin in the corner of her mouth. "You don't know him for real?"

Thalia ducked her head. No. She didn't. But she certainly wasn't going to tell Celeste that with her background, strangers weren't as intimidating as they might be to some. Although—Thalia reached up and touched her scarred wound—she had also learned when influenced by evil they could be quite dangerous. She fingered the letter once again, doubts invading her decision.

"Go on," Celeste prodded.

Thalia drew a deep breath and continued reading. "I would be honored to take you as my wife—"

"Your wife!" Celeste spit the clothespin into her basket and rammed her hands on her hips. "No. No, you ain't gonna be no mail-order bride."

Thalia threw the letter on the ground, equally offended. Celeste had no claim over her. Just like Jack. Promising they'd care for her, but Thalia knew the truth. In time, when Gold Haven bustled and grew, she would be forgotten.

"We're not family, Celeste," Thalia argued in return. "You've no rights to me."

"No?" Celeste pursed her lips and her dark eyes snapped. "But yet you'll hand off your rights to a strange man?"

"It's nothing new for me." The words escaped her mouth before she could stop them. Celeste's eyes widened. Thalia sniffed, anger biting at her heart. "At least this way, if he holds to his promises"—she bent and retrieved the letter from the dusty ground, waving it at Celeste—"at least I'll have a place to call my own. I'll be free."

"Free?" Celeste's brows winged up to hide beneath spiraling black curls. "Sounds like you'll be slavin' to another man."

"Like you?" Thalia crumpled William Forgraves's letter into a ball. "Didn't you wed up with Elias? What choice do we have out here in this wasteland? Men and their gold? We inherit nothing but abuse. Unless we safely attach ourselves to a man who'll at least let us live in peace. It's all I can ask for, Celeste."

Celeste's hands fell from her hips. She closed her eyes tight then opened them. "When I married Elias, it was Jack who gave me his word of honor that Elias be a kind man. And I'm growing to love him. But this man?" Celeste pointed at the paper Thalia clenched in her fist. "How do you know he won't do *that*?" She raised her index finger at the scar on Thalia's cheek. "And what's worse, you'll bear his name! His children, too."

Thalia didn't answer. She couldn't. Celeste spoke her worst fears. But a woman only had so many options, and though Jack had saved Celeste, he had ruined Thalia's by moving his dreams right into her abandoned town. Gold Haven was his now.

"Let Jack take care of you," Celeste begged, rounding the cold fire pit to rest her hands on Thalia's shoulders. "He's good at taking care of people."

Thalia shrugged away from her friend's touch. She swallowed the lump in her throat and pushed hair away from her face as she shook her head. "Taking care of people? No. He's out to make his mark and found his own kingdom here in Gold Haven."

Celeste frowned. "What are you talking about? You think Jack wants to be some high and mighty master over all us nobodies who've followed him here?"

"Seems to make sense to me." Thalia wrapped her arms around her middle. It made sense, and yet it didn't. None of it fit Jack's outward actions, but nothing else could explain his intentions here.

Celeste gave a small laugh of disbelief and blew a sigh through her beautifully carved lips. She turned back to the clothesline, and Thalia could tell her friend was vexed by the way she snatched the pins from the clothes, throwing them at the basket. Celeste balled up one of her dresses, then spun on her heel and stalked toward Thalia.

"I'm going to tell you something, and you're going to listen."

Thalia pulled back. Celeste was on fire, her eyes spearing her. Yet Thalia was sure there wasn't anything that could change her mind.

"Jack Taylor has handpicked each one of us for this town." Celeste waved her arm toward the tent shanties. "Yin? He be working a gold mine and abused by all the white men who thought he be no better than worthless rock. Elias? He made nothing black-smithing compared to other white men. Me? You know my story."

"So he's a saint?" Thalia heard the sarcasm in her voice, but she couldn't disguise it any other way. These people worshipped Jack Taylor.

"No." Celeste's hands found their familiar spot at her hips. "Not at all. A few years ago when the rush was at its height? He struck gold. One of the first. Then he opened his own business and took every miner for all their pennies. He done get richer than a king. But—"

"But he found God." It was everyone's excuse toward redemption. Thalia's chin shook, and she bit the inside of her cheek. But where was God night after night when she wept into her pillow after men would leave her behind like they deserted their garbage? Where was God when the man sliced her face? Where was God when Jack marched into Gold Haven and ruined her respite?

"Jack did find God." Celeste wagged her finger. "And don't you mock it. He lives his faith. He gives and never be proud of his generosity." Celeste looked up at the blue sky, the white clouds like an umbrella from the searing sun. She tipped her head to catch Thalia's eyes. "Jack's paid for every one of us."

Thalia frowned. Paid for them? In her world that carried an entirely different meaning.

"He pays George a wage for heading up the barley planting. He pays Yin for the services he provides us. He bought all them supplies, the tent Elias and I sleep in, my dress, *your* dress. This whole town be paid for by Jack *for us*! To make Gold Haven into a place of redemption for those of us the gold rush ruined. Gold Haven is for you. It's Jack's mission."

Thalia retreated a step, but Celeste reached for her and wrapped her hand around Thalia's fingers clenching the letter. Celeste gave her hand a little shake.

"Don't leave Gold Haven and Jack for a man who ain't proved his worth. Have faith in what God be doing in your life, Thalia. Ain't no accident you're here, that you were left behind because of your wound, and that Jack came along."

Thalia twisted her hand free. She wanted—no, she *ached*—to listen to Celeste, to believe her. But if she did, then she would have to accept Jack Taylor, and all his kindness, his care, and whatever else he wanted to offer her. And if she accepted Jack, then she ran a far greater risk, a risk she'd never taken. Loving. She might learn to love, and never, in her entire life, had love rewarded her. It was a risk Thalia could not, and would not, take. Ever.

Chapter Fourteen

She left a crust of bread in the corner of her shanty. Ounce wiggled his nose, smelling the delectable farewell offering.

"Good-bye, friend." Thalia crouched, reaching out her index finger. Ounce stretched his fuzzy neck forward until his whiskers tickled her skin. "Be careful of owls and snakes."

Standing, her movement caused Ounce to scurry away, and with him he took the last remaining possibility Thalia might change her mind. It would be difficult to explain she'd stayed in Gold Haven for a mouse, and the probability of that happening was very slim. Still, she would miss Ounce. He had been her first friend in Gold Haven.

Celeste's shadow splayed across the dirt floor as she entered the doorway. Thalia turned and she was certain regret showed on her face.

"So you're really leaving?" The lilt in Celeste's voice was replaced with sadness. Loss. Something both women were experienced in, only this time, Thalia realized, she was causing her own grief. Every other circumstance, she either had been forced against her will or had chosen it as a means to survive. This one, she'd thought mirrored the need to survive, but if she believed Celeste, Thalia was choosing to run, not save herself.

"I need a new beginning."

Celeste pushed a spiral curl behind her ear. "I was hopin' you realized you could find that here."

Thalia still found it difficult to believe. Gold Haven couldn't be a true haven, could it? The last few years of the gold rush warred with that concept, and she had suffered for it.

She reached out for Celeste and they joined hands. "One day"—and Thalia meant it from the depths of her heart—"I pray I can have the faith you have and that you believe Jack has."

Celeste squeezed her hand in return. "So do I, Thalia. I will pray it be so."

They embraced, and Thalia almost changed her mind, almost convinced herself Jack *would* take care of her, and Celeste's claim that Gold Haven would be a community of redemption *was* possible. But life had taught her differently. Jack believed faith was stronger than reality, but Thalia knew different. Reality always shouted louder, and the tiny glimpses into God's heart were in these small snippets of time, when one friend held another in a bittersweet farewell.

◆　◆　◆

The wagon jostled her until her jaw hurt. Or maybe her clenched teeth caused the pain. The silence between her and Jack was palpable, and the bump of his shoulder against hers unnerved her even more. The reins rested with a nonchalant ease in his gloved hands, his eyes set firm on the horizon and peace etched into his face. She rubbed her hand over the sleeve of the yellow calico dress he'd given her. Almost daily she'd worn it, and now it was already wearing thin. She would meet her future husband in a dress given to her by another man. The irony of her life and the subtle repetitions weren't lost on her.

"Thank you," she ventured as the town grew in the distance. Its contrast to Gold Haven was stark. Gold had succeeded here, and here lived the many who thrived in its shining shadows.

Jack gave the reins a small slap on the horses' backs. He nodded in acknowledgment but didn't say anything, which was almost worse. Thalia wondered if Celeste had told him why she was accompanying him to the city and why she wouldn't be coming home with him. But he'd been the letter carrier. He probably had already figured it out.

"Thank you for my dress."

He tossed her a sideways glance. "Yep."

"And for fixing my shanty."

"Yep."

Gracious. Thalia picked at a thread coming loose on the cuff of her sleeve. "And staying with me when I had poison oak."

"Of course." He flicked the reins again. Was he anxious to get to the city and be done with her?

Thalia cleared her throat with a small cough, then decided to be silent.

Jack sniffed.

One of the horses snorted.

They rolled down the main street, and Thalia had the strong desire to close her eyes and shut it all out. It was so familiar. She forced herself to look at the predominantly male population, and this time she saw something different. Altogether different. Eyes of appreciation rested on her face, took in her scar, and then swept over her only to stop when they saw the man on the seat beside her. She turned to look at Jack, a confident set to his jaw and his expression strong. Was this what it felt like to be safe? To be beside someone to whom not only she belonged but she had *chosen* to belong?

Her thoughts scraped to a halt as Jack pulled the wagon up next to a boardwalk. A mercantile sign met her, with pyramids of canned goods in the window. Nothing pretty, nothing feminine. This was a mining town. Jack swung himself off the wagon, and before Thalia was ready, he was on the ground reaching up to help her down from her seat. His hands settled on Thalia's waist, and he steadied her as she found her footing.

The crowd around them faded to a distant murmur. She stared into his blue eyes, gasping for emotional air as she realized this was the last time she would see him. He made her feel far safer than she ever realized until now, when she was ready to walk away from him. She'd fought against his kindness, and now it seemed like an awful mistake. She'd doubted his intentions, but she could still change her mind. She could climb back onto the wagon and return to Gold Haven. He'd said he'd take care of her. What if she let him make good on his promise? Celeste would take her in, and if Jack could find reputable work for her, maybe she could—

"All the best, Thalia." Jack's rough voice interrupted her frantic grasp at decision making.

She nodded. Mute. He released her waist and stepped away. His smile touched only his mouth. "God go with you."

For the first time she could almost believe God would. But then Jack was gone, disappearing into the crowd, and she was once again alone. William Forgraves was her future, not Jack Taylor. She must leave him behind. Like she always had to do with everything else she had come to love.

Chapter Fifteen

She pulled the letter from her ratty, green velvet purse.

Miss Simmons,

I would be honored to make you my wife. Please meet me on the twentieth of August at the Bingham Boardinghouse to make arrangements.

To our future.

Sincerely,
William Forgraves

He used his full name. Formal. Distant. Thalia sucked in a deep, calming breath, held it, and then let it out. She had procrastinated for the better part of an hour. It was time.

The boardinghouse door loomed in front of her like a cavernous pit. She'd had this same feeling in her stomach before. Sick, cold, and detached. Celeste was right. How was entering marriage with a strange man any sort of newfound freedom? But *she* was right also, Thalia reminded herself. Experience had taught her that in spite of best intentions, and no matter how much determination beat in her heart, survival would require her to sell herself. She was loath to ever repeat that again. Better to bind herself to one man, stranger or not, than to be used by many. Thalia lifted her hand and touched her deformity with her fingertips. She had physical evidence of its horrors on her face, on her body, and deep in her heart.

She moved her fingers to the top button of her dress, then smoothed her hands down the bodice. Certain she appeared proper, Thalia determined three things: She would not tell Mr. Forgraves of her past until after they had married so he wouldn't be tempted to abandon her before they were pledged. She would leave him at the first sign that he would raise his hand to her. If he truly was a man of faith, she would seek to understand it herself, and pray Celeste and Jack's influence on her might take root into something deeper.

Thalia pushed on the door to the boardinghouse. A *whoosh* of cinnamon, oranges, and nutmeg met her nose in a mixture of scent blended to welcome boarders. Not that the scruffy, filthy men of this region would recognize it, but Thalia took comfort in it. A woman lived here, that much was certain. The foyer had dark wood floors, a beautiful chandelier, and a winding staircase leading up to the rooms. To the right was a closed parlor, to the left a short hall winding toward a dining area, and in front of her, a wide, walnut reception desk. Empty. The entire place was void of life.

440

She walked toward the desk, her shoes echoing on the floor as she did so. A tiny bronze bell sat on the desk, so she reached for it and gave it a timid ring. The ledger lay closed on the desk. An inkwell, a pen, and a pair of spectacles lay beside it. Footsteps sounded on the stairwell, and Thalia looked up as an older woman descended in black widow weeds.

"Oh darling." She clapped her hands together, her wiry gray hair springing. "My apologies, dear. I'm Widow Harris. I was just readying a room for a new tenant."

Thalia could imagine the beauty of a room she could never afford. It surprised her that instead of being enticed, she longed for her shanty, for Ounce, for the dust and heat, for Gold Haven, and if she were honest. . .for Jack.

"Can I help you?"

This was the moment. Thalia could not retreat. She had no other option now. "I'm to meet a Mr. Forgraves."

"Ahhh!" The widow slipped the spectacles on, but her eyes sparkled. "He's waiting for you."

The ache in her stomach grew. Thalia ran her finger around her collar. "He is?"

"Yes." Widow Harris pointed toward the parlor. "In there."

Thalia turned and twisted the ribbons on her purse. This was it. Her future. Maybe her freedom.

Her feet echoed on the wood floor. A clock ticked. The parlor door was shut. Thalia's hand hovered over the doorknob. She prayed. For the first time. *God, give me strength.* And for the first time, she believed He would. She twisted the doorknob and pushed open the door.

William Forgraves stood framed by the window at the far end of the room. His back was to her, his hands at his waist, coattails pushed out. A tailored coat, tailored trousers. Oh heavens, he was rich.

Thalia took the moment to sweep her gaze over him, to understand him by his stance alone. She'd done it many times before. Were his shoulders straight? Confident. Thrown back? Arrogant. Sagging? Defeated. This set of shoulders was held straight and oddly familiar. Dark hair curled over a starched white collar.

Thalia sucked in a gasp as he turned.

Blue eyes blazed with an icy fire, smoldering with determination and claiming her with their intensity.

She breathed the name the moment she gathered her breath. "Jack!"

Chapter Sixteen

It was mortifying, humiliating, and almost worse than the moment they'd first met. Jack was here, in the parlor where she was to meet her betrothed. Why?

"Why are you here?" Her question was breathy, and she further mangled her already mauled purse.

"Why are *you* here?" he countered, daring her to admit it.

She knew that he knew why, but it was obvious he wanted to hear it from her. To explain herself. Yet he was at fault, too.

"Did you read my letter?" Thalia couldn't imagine Jack would be the sort to tamper with private messages. "And where is Mr. Forgraves?"

Jack surveyed the room with his eyes as if looking for Mr. Forgraves, and finally rested his gaze on Thalia. His nonchalant shrug revealed the truth she already suspected.

"You?" Thalia put her hand out to steady herself. Finding the edge of a chair, her fingers curled around it. Nothing made sense. *William Forgraves* had advertised in the paper. *William Forgraves* had sent her a letter of acceptance. *William Forgraves* was by no means Jack Taylor, and she believed that Jack Taylor may be a lot of things, but he wasn't a liar.

There was no apology on Jack's face, just the same quiet confidence she'd witnessed on the wagon ride to the city.

"William is my legal first name. Forgraves is my mother's maiden name, which she gave me as a second middle name. Might I formally introduce myself? William Jack Forgraves Taylor, ma'am."

The explanation didn't assuage Thalia's shock or her consternation, nor did it satisfy the leap in her stomach at the thought he had known all along she was offering herself up as a mail-order bride.

"Why?" she whispered. It was all she could ask. "Why would you do this to me?"

Jack stepped toward her but stopped with a few feet remaining between them. "I would ask you the same thing. Why would you do this to *me*?"

She clenched her fingers around the wood frame of the chair. "I—I . . ." What could she say? No explanation would be anything new to Jack.

He ran his fingers through his hair, and the dark strands flopped over his forehead. It hinted at his more rugged side. The side she knew far better than this *William Forgraves*.

"I promised I'd take care of you."

"And this is how you do it?" Thalia dropped her purse onto the chair. Incredulous, she rubbed her hand at the nape of her neck. What did this mean to her plans now? Her future?

Jack shrugged out of his jacket as if it were too warm for him. He frowned. "Would you have let me take care of you any other way?"

"You purposefully put the advertisement in the paper for me? You deliberately placed the paper in my hands so I would be tempted to reply?" As the realization sank in, Thalia couldn't decide if it was horribly deceptive or incredibly gallant.

No regret accompanied his firm nod. "Yes. I did." Jack's step swallowed the remaining distance between them. His hands cupped her upper arms and a whiff of his bay rum cologne met her with a warm invitation.

"Thalia." Jack's thumbs stroked her arms. "You were willing to come to a man you didn't know, to *marry* a complete stranger, on your own accord. I needed to set you free to run away so you weren't forced into accepting my care. But I wanted to be sure when you ran away, you would run away to me."

"Why do you care so much?" Comprehending his reasoning was as difficult as reconciling the tenderness in his eyes.

Jack's hands slid up her arms to hold her neck with a gentle touch. He tipped his head forward, claiming her gaze with his. "You wanted to be free. It was your dream. In your freedom, you chose William Forgraves. So in the end, you chose me."

His words rooted in her soul, and Thalia could almost feel a tiny bud blossom. "But you know who I am."

"I know who you *were*."

"I don't have your faith."

"But you want it."

"Yes, but—"

"And you are willing to enter into a promise with a man you don't know?"

"Yes." She swallowed. Embarrassed. Ashamed.

Jack's thumb stroked her cheek. "Then promise me this, Thalia Simmons. Promise me you will step back and see the hand of God in our lives. He redeemed me from my greed, He's guiding your steps into freedom from your past, and He brought us both to Gold Haven."

His words resonated with Celeste's story of Jack's generosity, his sponsorship of every misfit and miscreant he'd invited to Gold Haven. It hardly seemed possible that a new beginning was within her grasp, and freedom had been offered to her from Jack. Not to mention, thinking was difficult at best with Jack's calloused thumb smoothing over her scar.

Thalia scrambled for words. "So what does this mean? What do *you* mean? Do you have a job for me?"

Jack's chuckle told her she should read his mind, maybe even his heart. And she did, but she was afraid to say it out loud.

"The advertisement was real, Thalia. I was looking for you. I just needed you to find me."

He trailed his fingers down her scar, healed but forever with her, and also the catalyst for finding this man who valued her need to determine her own path.

Jack moved slow, giving her every opportunity to pull away. What he didn't understand, and might never fully realize, was that she was drawn *toward* him, when in her past, she had always wished to retreat. Thalia closed the gap between them, his breath warm on her lips right before they met. They merged together in a subtle kiss, softly transferring from her lead to his. His hands found her waist and eased her closer, yet his kiss remained nonthreatening, promising guardianship as well as freedom.

She leaned away, and Jack let her. His hands dropped to her shoulders.

"Please come home, Thalia. Where you belong."

"And the future?" She had to ask. Faith was a tentative and shaky step requiring more courage than Thalia thought she might have.

Jack reached up and pushed the hair away from the side of her face, revealing her scar. He shrugged. It wasn't the answer she expected.

"I don't know. We see where we are led, but we walk together. You become my wife, which you came here to do. We follow Elias and Celeste's example and we learn to love. And you, dear Thalia, become an heiress to the best God has to offer. A new life. Freedom. Let Him set you free."

She closed her eyes as Jack drew her into his embrace. She rested her forehead on his shoulder, breathing deep of him and the promise he offered. So this was the Jack Taylor Celeste had insisted she recognize. Thalia met Jack's soft look. She reached up and touched his mouth, his jaw, and finally brushed his lips with a kiss she freely offered. His faith had brought him here, stepping out, praying she would follow. And she had. And she would.

Professional coffee drinker **Jaime Jo Wright** resides in the hills of Wisconsin. She loves to write spirited turn-of-the-century romance, stained with suspense. Her day job finds her as a director of sales and development. She's wife to a rock-climbing, bow-hunting Pre-K teacher, mom to a coffee-drinking little girl and a little boy she fondly refers to as her mischievous "Peter Pan." Jaime completes her persona by being an admitted social media junkie and coffee snob. She is a member of ACFW and has the best writing sisters *ever*!